Peter Robinson grew up in Yorkshire, but now lives in Toronto.

Not Safe After Dark and *Other Works* is Peter's first collection of short stories to be published in the UK. It includes 'Innocence', winner of the Crime Writers of Canada's Best Short Story Award.

His Inspector Banks series has won numerous awards in Britain, Europe, the United States and Canada. There are now sixteen novels in the series.

Not Safe After Dark ✓

PETER ROBINSON

NOT SAFE AFTER DARK

&

A NECESSARY END

PAN BOOKS

Not Safe After Dark first published 2004 by Macmillan.
First published in paperback 2005 by Pan Books.
A Necessary End first published 1989 in Viking by Penguin Books Canada.
First published in Great Britain 1989 in Viking by Penguin Books.
First published in paperback 1990 by Penguin.
First published by Pan Books 2002.

This omnibus first published 2007 by Pan Books
an imprint of Pan Macmillan Ltd
Pan Macmillan, 20 New Wharf Road, London N1 9RR
Basingstoke and Oxford
Associated companies throughout the world
www.panmacmillan.com

ISBN 978-0-330-45232-8

1 3 5 7 9 8 6 4 2

A CIP catalogue record for this book is available from
the British Library.

Printed and bound in Great Britain by
Mackays of Chatham plc, Chatham, Kent

NOT SAFE AFTER DARK

For Sheila

CONTENTS

INTRODUCTION

I remember once talking to a famous crime writer about getting a short story out of my home being burgled, and she replied, 'I get a short story out of everything.' That certainly put me in my place. It also serves as a useful opening to this introduction because some writers I know find that short stories come easily, whereas I don't.

I think this is partly because I have become so used to thinking in terms of the novel, with the broad canvas it offers, that it's hard to work in miniature. I carry a novel around in my head for a long time – at least a year, waking and sleeping – and this gives me time to get under the skin of the characters *and* the story. Also, plotting is probably the most difficult part of writing for me, and being asked to write a short story, which so often depends on a plot twist, a clever diversion or a surprising revelation, guarantees that I'll get the laundry done and probably the ironing, too.

That said, there is nevertheless a great deal of satisfaction to be had from writing short stories. Partly, of course, it's the quick pay-off. A short story is, by definition, *short*. Consequently, you get that wonderful rush of having *finished* something far more quickly than you do with a novel.

But it isn't only the instant gratification that makes short stories so attractive to me, it's also the new possibilities they offer. When you work primarily as a series writer, as I do, most of your time goes into the creation of that series. That, of course, is as it should be: I wouldn't be writing the Inspector Banks books if I didn't want to. But there's always the temptation to try something different, and to risk a week or so doing this is a lot easier than to risk a year or more on a project that might easily meet with rejection.

Short stories also offer a wonderful opportunity for the series writer to spread his or her wings and fly to new, exotic places, to meet different people and to try out different techniques. The Inspector Banks series is set, for the most part, in Yorkshire, but these stories range from Toronto to Paris, from Florida to California. The Banks books are third-person narratives, while many of the stories are first-person. Banks is a policeman, but you'll find very few policemen between these covers. A number of the stories, such as 'Murder in Utopia' and 'Missing in Action', are set in different periods of history.

While short stories come from the same seeds as novels, usually they come as ideas that can *only* be developed into short stories. 'Innocence' was one exception to this rule. After writing the story, I couldn't let go and went on to write an entire novel from Reed's point of view, expanding the events of the story, but my publishers turned it down. I put it aside for a while, then thought that perhaps if Banks was there it might work better. Thus, Reed became Owen and 'Innocence' (1990) became *Innocent Graves* (1996). Both the short story and the novel won Arthur Ellis awards in Canada.

A sense of place has always been important in my work and is no less so here. In Florida one December I witnessed a Christmas singalong around the swimming pool, Santa in his usual outfit leading the crowd on electric piano. Only this took place in twenty-seven-degree heat and they were singing 'White Christmas', something I think they don't usually have down there. Needless to say, the absurdity of the scene was not lost on me, and in 'Some Land in Florida' Santa ends up in the pool with his electric piano thrown after him – still plugged in!

The first historical story I wrote, 'The Two Ladies of Rose Cottage', was inspired by both a place and by my interest in Thomas Hardy. I once paid a visit to the house where he was born in Bockhampton, Dorset, and stood in the room where he was cast aside as dead by the doctor who delivered him, only to be revived by a quick-thinking nurse. As I looked out of his upstairs window on much the same view he often enjoyed as he wrote his early books, this short story of murder and deceit ranging over more than a hundred years began to form in my mind, and Hardy himself even makes a brief appearance in it.

Other stories have their origins in such diverse sources as an unusual piece of information ('Carrion'), fragments of dreams ('Fan Mail'), stories recounted by others ('The Wrong Hands' and 'Memory Lane') and research for other works. I doubt that I would ever have written 'In Flanders Fields' or 'Missing in Action', for example, if I hadn't spent so much time researching the Second World War for *In a Dry Season*.

Sometimes, as in 'Gone to the Dawgs' and 'The Duke's Wife', I was asked for a story on a specific topic – in these cases, American football and Shakespeare respectively. But no matter how much or how little is given, or demanded, there is always a lot to change and more to add, all subjected to the constant 'What if?' of the writer's imagination.

While I did mention earlier that most of the stories here represent a break from Inspector Banks, there are three Banks short stories in the collection. In a way, they were the hardest for me to write because I'm so used to giving Banks plenty of space. There's little room for significant character or plot development in a short story, or for the creation of multiple points of view. Still, it was impossible to resist the temptation to try, especially to have Banks attempt to solve the mystery of a man who claims to have been murdered in a previous lifetime, as happens in 'Summer Rain'. You'll have to judge the results for yourself.

Finally, the Inspector Banks novella 'Going Back' is a special case and has never been published before. I wrote it early in 1999, so it came between *In a Dry Season* and *Cold Is the Grave*. At that point I didn't know that I was going to send Banks home to deal with his old school friend's disappearance in *The Summer that Never Was* (2003) and I wanted to show him interacting with his family and responding to the place where he grew up. In manuscript, it reached 106 pages, too long for any of the magazines or anthologies that regularly published my stories, and too short for separate book publication. And so it sat there gathering dust until I came to write *The Summer that Never Was,* when I incorporated parts of the novella into the novel – mostly details about the street Banks grew up on, his relationship with his parents, the music he listened to and the books he read as an adolescent.

When I came to revise 'Going Back' for this collection, I had to shift it chronologically, so that it now falls between *The Summer that Never Was* and *Playing with Fire*. I also had to try to avoid too much repetition of details I had cannibalized for the novel without spoiling the original conception. It was a difficult balancing act, but I hope you enjoy the final result, along with the rest of the stories in this collection.

PETER ROBINSON
FEBRUARY 2004

ACKNOWLEDGEMENTS

Individual stories first published in different form as: 'Summer Rain' © *Ellery Queen's Mystery Magazine*, New York, December 1994. An Inspector Banks story; 'Fan Mail' © *Cold Blood II*, ed. Peter Sellers (Mosaic Press: Oakville, Canada, 1989); 'Innocence' © *Cold Blood III*, ed. Peter Sellers (Mosaic Press: Oakville, Canada, 1990); 'Murder in Utopia' © *Crime Through Time III*, ed. Sharan Newman (Berkeley, New York, July 2000); 'Not Safe After Dark' © *Criminal Shorts*, ed. Howard Engel and Eric Wright (Macmillan: Toronto, Canada, 1992); 'Just My Luck' © *Bouchercon XXII Souvenir Programme Book*, Toronto, 1992; 'Anna Said. . .' © *Cold Blood IV*, ed. Peter Sellers (Mosaic Press: Oakville, Canada, 1992). An Inspector Banks story; 'Missing in Action' © *Ellery Queen's Mystery Magazine*, New York, November 2000; 'Memory Lane' © *Blue Lightning*, ed. John Harvey, Slow Dancer Press (UK), 1998; 'Carrion' © *No Alibi*, ed. Maxim Jakubowski (Ringpull: Manchester, 1995); 'April in Paris' © *Love and Death*, ed. Carolyn Hart (Berkeley, New York), February 2001; 'The Good Partner' © *Ellery Queen's Mystery Magazine*, New York, March 1994. An Inspector Banks story; 'Some Land in Florida' © *Ellery Queen's Mystery Magazine*, New York, Christmas issue, 1996; 'The Wrong Hands' © *Ellery Queen's Mystery Magazine*, New York, April 1998; 'The Two Ladies of Rose Cottage' © *Malice Domestic 6*, ed. Anne Perry (New York: Pocket Books, 1997); 'Lawn Sale' © *Cold Blood V*, ed. Peter Sellers and John North (Mosaic Press: Oakville, Canada, 1994); 'Gone to the Dawgs' © *The Mighty Johns*, ed. Otto Penzler (New Millennium Press, Beverly Hills, CA), summer 2002; 'In Flanders Fields' © 1998, first published in *Not Safe After Dark and Other Stories*, by Peter Robinson, Crippen & Landru (Virginia), October 1998; 'The Duke's Wife' © *Much Ado About Murder*, ed. Anne Perry (Berkeley, New York, December 2002).

'Going Back' first published 2004; © Eastvale Enterprise Inc.

SUMMER RAIN

AN INSPECTOR BANKS STORY

1

'**And exactly how** many times have you died, Mr Singer?'

'Fourteen. That's fourteen I've managed to uncover. They say that each human being has lived about twenty incarnations. But it's the last one I'm telling you about. See, I died by violence. I was murdered.'

Detective Constable Susan Gay made a note on the yellow pad in front of her. When she looked down, she noticed that she had doodled an intricate pattern of curves and loops, a bit like Spaghetti Junction, during the few minutes she had been talking to Jerry Singer.

She tried to keep the scepticism out of her voice. 'Ah-hah. And when was this, sir?'

'Nineteen sixty-six. July. That makes it exactly thirty-two years ago this week.'

'I see.'

Jerry Singer had given his age as thirty-one, which meant that he had been murdered a year before he was born.

'How do you know it was nineteen sixty-six?' Susan asked.

Singer leaned forward. He was a remarkably intense young man, Susan noticed, thin to the point of emaci-ation, with glittering green eyes behind wire-rimmed glasses. He looked as if the lightest breeze would blow

1

him away. His fine red hair had a gossamer quality that reminded Susan of spiders' webs. He wore jeans, a red T-shirt and a grey anorak, its shoulders darkened by the rain. Though he said he came from San Diego, California, Susan could detect no trace of suntan.

'It's like this,' he began. 'There's no fixed period between incarnations, but my channeller told me—'

'Channeller?' Susan interrupted.

'She's a kind of spokesperson for the spirit world.'

'A medium?'

'Not quite.' Singer managed a brief smile. 'But close enough. More of a mediator, really.'

'Oh, I see,' said Susan, who didn't. 'Go on.'

'Well, she told me there would be a period of about a year between my previous incarnation and my present one.'

'How did she know?'

'She just *knows*. It varies from one soul to another. Some need a lot of time to digest what they've learned and make plans for the next incarnation. Some souls just can't wait to return to another body.' He shrugged. 'After some lifetimes, you might simply just get tired and need a long rest.'

After some mornings, too, Susan thought. 'OK,' she said, 'let's move on. Is this your first visit to Yorkshire?'

'It's my first trip to England, period. I've just qualified in dentistry, and I thought I'd give myself a treat before I settled down to the daily grind.'

Susan winced. Was that a pun? Singer wasn't smiling. A New Age dentist, now there was an interesting combination, she thought. Can I read your tarot cards for you while I drill? Perhaps you might like to take a little astral

2

journey to Neptune while I'm doing your root canal? She forced herself to concentrate on what Singer was saying.

'So, you see,' he went on, 'as I've never been here before, it *must* be real, mustn't it?'

Susan realized she had missed something. 'What?'

'Well, it was all so familiar, the landscape, everything. And it's not only the *déjà vu* I had. There was the dream, too. We haven't even approached this in hypnotic regression yet, so—'

Susan held up her hand. 'Hang on a minute. You're losing me. What was so familiar?'

'Oh, I thought I'd made that clear.'

'Not to me.'

'The place. Where I was murdered. It was near here. In Swainsdale.'

2

Banks was sitting in his office with his feet on the desk and a buff folder open on his lap when Susan Gay popped her head around the door. The top button of his white shirt was undone and his tie hung askew.

That morning, he was supposed to be working on the monthly crime figures, but instead, through the half-open window, he listened to the summer rain as it harmonized with Michael Nyman's soundtrack from *The Piano*, playing quietly on his portable cassette. His eyes were closed and he was daydreaming of waves washing in and out on a beach of pure white sand. The ocean and sky were the brightest blue he could imagine, and tall palm trees dotted the landscape. The pastel village that straddled the steep hillside looked like a cubist collage.

'Sorry to bother you, sir,' Susan said, 'but it looks like we've got a right one here.'

Banks opened his eyes and rubbed them. He felt as if he were coming back from a very long way. 'It's all right,' he said. 'I was getting a bit bored with the crime statistics, anyway.' He tossed the folder onto his desk and linked his hands behind his head. 'Well, what is it?'

Susan entered the office. 'It's sort of hard to explain, sir.'

'Try.'

Susan told him about Jerry Singer. As he listened, Banks's blue eyes sparkled with amusement and interest. When Susan had finished, he thought for a moment, then sat up and turned off the music. 'Why not?' he said. 'It's been a slow week. Let's live dangerously. Bring him in.' He fastened his top button and straightened his tie.

A few moments later, Susan returned with Jerry Singer in tow. Singer looked nervously around the office and took the seat opposite Banks. The two exchanged introductions, then Banks leaned back and lit a cigarette. He loved the mingled smells of smoke and summer rain.

'Perhaps you'd better start at the beginning,' he said.

'Well,' said Singer, turning his nose up at the smoke, 'I've been involved in regressing to past lives for a few years now, partly through hypnosis. It's been a fascinating journey, and I've discovered a great deal about myself.' He sat forward and rested his hands on the desk. His fingers were short and tapered. 'For example, I was a merchant's wife in Venice in the fifteenth century. I had seven children and died giving birth to the eighth. I was only twenty-nine. In my next incarnation, I was an actor in a troupe of Elizabethan players, the Lord Chamberlain's

Men. I remember playing Bardolph in *Henry V* in 1599. After that, I—'

'I get the picture,' said Banks. 'I don't mean to be rude, Mr Singer, but maybe we can skip to the twentieth century?'

Singer paused and frowned at Banks. 'Sorry. Well, as I was telling Detective Constable Gay here, it's the least clear one so far. I was a hippie. At least, I think I was. I had long hair, wore a caftan, bell-bottom jeans. And I had this incredible sense of déjà vu when I was driving through Swainsdale yesterday afternoon.'

'Where, exactly?'

'It was just before Fortford. I was coming from Helmthorpe, where I'm staying. There's a small hill by the river with a few trees on it, all bent by the wind. Maybe you know it?'

Banks nodded. He knew the place. The hill was, in fact, a drumlin, a kind of hump-backed mound of detritus left by the retreating ice age. Six trees grew on it, and they had all bent slightly to the south-east after years of strong north-westerly winds. The drumlin was about two miles west of Fortford.

'Is that all?' Banks asked.

'All?'

'Yes.' Banks leaned forward and rested his elbows on the desk. 'You know there are plenty of explanations for déjà vu, don't you, Mr Singer? Perhaps you've seen a place very similar before and only remembered it when you passed the drumlin?'

Singer shook his head. 'I understand your doubts,' he said, 'and I can't offer concrete *proof*, but the *feeling* is unmistakable. I have been there before, in a previous life. I'm certain of it. And that's not all. There's the dream.'

'Dream?'

'Yes. I've had it several times. The same one. It's raining, like today, and I'm passing through a landscape very similar to what I've seen in Swainsdale. I arrive at a very old stone house. There are people and their voices are raised, maybe in anger or laughter, I can't tell. But I start to feel tense and claustrophobic. There's a baby crying somewhere and it won't stop. I climb up some creaky stairs. When I get to the top, I find a door and open it. Then I feel that panicky sensation of endlessly falling, and I usually wake up frightened.'

Banks thought for a moment. 'That's all very interesting,' he said, 'but have you considered that you might have come to the wrong place? We're not usually in the business of interpreting dreams and visions.'

Singer stood his ground. 'This is real,' he said. 'A crime has been committed. Against me.' He poked himself in the chest with his thumb. 'The crime of murder. The least you can do is do me the courtesy of checking your records.' His odd blend of naivety and intensity charged the air.

Banks stared at him, then looked at Susan, whose face showed sceptical interest. Never having been one to shy away from what killed the cat, Banks let his curiosity get the better of him yet again. 'All right,' he said, standing up. 'We'll look into it. Where did you say you were staying?'

3

Banks turned right by the whitewashed sixteenth-century Rose and Crown in Fortford, and stopped just after he had crossed the small stone bridge over the River Swain.

The rain was still falling, obscuring the higher green dale sides and their latticework of drystone walls. Lyndgarth, a cluster of limestone cottages and a church huddled around a small village green, looked like an Impressionist painting. The rain-darkened ruins of Devraulx Abbey, just up the hill to his left, poked through the trees like a setting for *Camelot*.

Banks rolled his window down and listened to the rain slapping against leaves and dancing on the river's surface. To the west he could see the drumlin that Jerry Singer had felt so strongly about.

Today it looked ghostly in the rain, and it was easy to imagine the place as some ancient barrow where the spirits of Bronze Age men lingered. But it wasn't a barrow; it was a drumlin created by glacial deposits. And Jerry Singer hadn't been a Bronze Age man in his previous lifetime; he had been a sixties hippie, or so he believed.

Leaving the window down, Banks drove through Lyndgarth and parked at the end of Gristhorpe's rutted driveway, in front of the squat limestone farmhouse. Inside, he found Gristhorpe staring gloomily out of the back window at a pile of stones and a half-completed drystone wall. The superintendent, he knew, had taken a week's holiday and hoped to work on the wall, which went nowhere and closed in nothing. But he hadn't bargained for the summer rain, which had been falling nonstop for the past two days.

He poured Banks a cup of tea so strong you could stand a spoon up in it, offered some scones, and they sat in Gristhorpe's study. A paperback copy of Trollope's *The*

Vicar of Bullhampton lay on a small table beside a worn and scuffed brown leather armchair.

'Do you believe in reincarnation?' Banks asked.

Gristhorpe considered the question a moment. 'No. Why?'

Banks told him about Jerry Singer, then said, 'I wanted your opinion. Besides, you were here then, weren't you?'

Gristhorpe's bushy eyebrows knit in a frown. 'Nine-teen sixty-six?'

'Yes.'

'I was here, but that's over thirty years ago, Alan. My memory's not what it used to be. Besides, what makes you think there's anything in this other than some New Age fantasy?'

'I don't know that there is,' Banks answered, at a loss how to explain his interest, even to the broad-minded Gristhorpe. Boredom, partly, and the oddness of Singer's claim, the certainty the man seemed to feel about it. But how could he tell his superintendent that he had so little to do he was opening investigations into the supernatural? 'There was a sort of innocence about him,' he said. 'And he seemed so sincere about it, so intense.'

'"The best lack all conviction, while the worst/Are full of passionate intensity." W. B. Yeats,' Gristhorpe replied.

'Perhaps. Anyway, I've arranged to talk to Jenny Fuller about it later today.' Jenny was a psychologist who had worked with the Eastvale police before.

'Good idea,' said Gristhorpe. 'All right, then, just for argument's sake, let's examine his claim objectively. He's convinced he was a hippie murdered in Swainsdale in summer, nineteen sixty-six, right?'

Banks nodded.

'And he thinks this because he believes in reincarnation, he had a déjà vu and he's had a recurring dream?'

'True.'

'Now,' Gristhorpe went on, 'leaving aside the question of whether you or I believe in reincarnation, or, indeed, whether there is such a thing – a philosophical speculation we could hardly settle over tea and scones, anyway – he doesn't give us a hell of a lot to go on, does he?'

'That's the problem. I thought you might remember something.'

Gristhorpe sighed and shifted in his chair. The scuffed leather creaked. 'In nineteen sixty-six, I was a thirty-year-old detective sergeant in a backwoods division. In fact, we were nothing but a subdivision then, and I was the senior detective. Most of the time I investigated burglaries, the occasional outbreak of sheep stealing, market-stall owners fencing stolen goods.' He sipped some tea. 'We had one or two murders – really interesting ones I'll tell you about someday – but not a lot. What I'm saying, Alan, is that no matter how poor my memory is, I'd remember a murdered hippie.'

'And nothing fits the bill?'

'Nothing. I'm not saying we didn't have a few hippies around, but none of them got murdered. I think your Mr Singer must be mistaken.'

Banks put his mug down on the table and stood up to leave. 'Better get back to the crime statistics, then,' he said.

Gristhorpe smiled. 'So *that's* why you're so interested in this cock and bull story? Can't say I blame you. Sorry I can't help. Wait a minute, though,' he added as they walked to the door. 'There was old Bert Atherton's lad. I suppose that was around the time you're talking about, give or take a year or two.'

Banks paused at the door. 'Atherton?'

'Aye. Owns a farm between Lyndgarth and Helm-thorpe. Or did. He's dead now. I only mention it because Atherton's son, Joseph, was something of a hippie.'

'What happened?'

'Fell down the stairs and broke his neck. Family never got over it. As I said, old man Atherton died a couple of years back, but his missis is still around.'

'You'd no reason to suspect anything?'

Gristhorpe shook his head. 'None at all. The Athertons were a decent, hard-working family. Apparently the lad was visiting them on his way to Scotland to join some commune or other. He fell down the stairs. It's a pretty isolated spot, and it was too late when the ambulance arrived, especially as they had to drive a mile down country lanes to the nearest telephone box. They were really devastated. He was their only child.'

'What made him fall?'

'He wasn't pushed, if that's what you're thinking. There was no stair carpet and the steps were a bit slippery. According to his dad, Joseph was walking around without his slippers on and he slipped in his stockinged feet.'

'And you've no reason to doubt him?'

'No. I did have one small suspicion at the time, though.'

'What?'

'According to the post-mortem, Joseph Atherton was a heroin addict, though he didn't have any traces of the drug in his system at the time of his death. I thought he might have been smoking marijuana or something up in

10

his room. That might have made him a bit unsteady on his feet.'

'Did you search the place?'

Gristhorpe snorted. 'Nay, Alan. There was no sense bringing more grief on his parents. What would we do if we found something, charge *them* with possession?'

'I see your point.' Banks opened the door and put up his collar against the rain. 'I might dig up the file anyway,' he called, running over to the car. 'Enjoy the rest of your week off.'

Gristhorpe's curse was lost in the sound of the engine starting up and the finale of Mussorgsky's 'Great Gate of Kiev' on Classic FM, blasting out from the radio, which Banks had forgotten to switch off.

4

In addition to the cells and the charge room, the lower floor of Eastvale Divisional Headquarters housed old files and records. The dank room was lit by a single bare light bulb and packed with dusty files. So far, Banks had checked nineteen sixty-five and sixty-six but found nothing on the Atherton business.

Give or take a couple of years, Gristhorpe had said. Without much hope, Banks reached for nineteen sixty-four. That was a bit too early for hippies, he thought, especially in the far reaches of rural North Yorkshire.

In nineteen sixty-four, he remembered, the Beatles were still recording ballads like 'I'll Follow the Sun' and old rockers like 'Long Tall Sally'. John hadn't met Yoko, and there wasn't a sitar within earshot. The Rolling Stones were doing 'Not Fade Away' and 'It's All Over

Now', the Kinks had a huge hit with 'You Really Got Me', and the charts were full of Dusty Springfield, Peter and Gordon, the Dave Clark Five and Herman's Hermits.

So nineteen sixty-four was a write-off as far as dead hippies were concerned. Banks looked anyway. Maybe Joseph Atherton had been way ahead of his time. Or perhaps Jerry Singer's channeller had been wrong about the time between incarnations. Why was this whole charade taking on such an aura of unreality?

Banks's stomach rumbled. Apart from that scone at Gristhorpe's, he hadn't eaten since breakfast, he realized. He put the file aside. Though there hardly seemed any point looking further ahead than nineteen sixty-six, he did so out of curiosity. Just as he was feeling success slip away, he came across it: Joseph Atherton. Coroner's verdict: accidental death. There was only one problem: it had happened in 1969.

According to the Athertons' statement, their son wrote to say he was coming to see them en route to Scotland. He said he was on his way to join some sort of commune and arrived at Eastvale station on the London train at three forty-five in the afternoon, 11 July 1969. By ten o'clock that night he was dead. He didn't have transport of his own, so his father had met him at the station in the Land Rover and driven him back to the farm.

Banks picked up a sheet of lined writing paper, yellowed around the edges. A separate sheet described it as an anonymous note received at the Eastvale police station about a week after the coroner's verdict. All it said, in block capitals, was, 'Ask Atherton about the red Volkswagen.'

Next came a brief interview report, in which a PC Wythers said he had questioned the Athertons about the car and they said they didn't know what he was talking about. That was that.

Banks supposed it was remotely possible that whoever was in the red Volkswagen had killed Joseph Atherton. But why would his parents lie? According to the statement, they spent the evening together at the farm eating dinner, catching up on family news, then Joseph went up to his room to unpack and came down in his stockinged feet. Maybe he'd been smoking marijuana, as Gristhorpe suggested. Anyway, he slipped at the top of the stairs and broke his neck. It was tragic, but hardly what Banks was looking for.

He heard a sound at the door and looked up to see Susan Gay.

'Found anything, sir?' she asked.

'Maybe,' said Banks. 'One or two loose ends. But I haven't a clue what it all means, if anything. I'm beginning to wish I'd never seen Mr Jerry Singer.'

Susan smiled. 'Do you know, sir,' she said, 'he almost had me believing him.'

Banks put the file aside. 'Did he? I suppose it always pays to keep an open mind,' he said. 'That's why we're going to visit Mrs Atherton.'

5

The Atherton farm was every bit as isolated as Gristhorpe had said, and the relentless rain had muddied the lane. At one point Banks thought they would have to get out and push, but on the third try the wheels caught and the car lurched forward.

The farmyard looked neglected: bedraggled weeds

poked through the mud; part of the barn roof had collapsed; and the wheels and tines of the old hayrake had
rusted.

Mrs Atherton answered their knock almost immediately. Banks had phoned ahead so their arrival wouldn't
frighten her. After all, a woman living alone in such a
wild place couldn't be too careful.

She led them into the large kitchen and put the kettle
on the Aga. The stone-walled room looked clean and tidy
enough, but Banks noted an underlying smell, like old
greens and meat rotting under the sink.

Mrs Atherton carried the aura of the sickroom about
with her. Her complexion was as grey as her sparse hair;
her eyes were dull yellow with milky blue irises; and the
skin below them looked dark as a bruise. As she made
the tea, she moved slowly, as if measuring the energy
required for each step. How on earth, Banks wondered,
did she manage up here all by herself? Yorkshire grit was
legendary, and often as close to foolhardiness as anything
else, he thought.

She put the teapot on the table. 'We'll just let it mash
a minute,' she said. 'Now, what is it you want to talk to
me about?'

Banks didn't know how to begin. He had no intention
of telling Mrs Atherton about Jerry Singer's 'previous lifetime', or of interrogating her about her son's death.
Which didn't leave him many options.

'How are you managing?' he asked first.

'Mustn't grumble.'

'It must be hard, taking care of this place all by yourself?'

'Nay, there's not much to do these days. Jack Crocker

keeps an eye on the sheep. I've nobbut got a few cows to milk.'

'No poultry?'

'Nay, it's not worth it any more, not with these battery farms. Anyway, seeing as you're a copper, I don't suppose you came to talk to me about the farming life, did you? Come on, spit it out, lad.'

Banks noticed Susan look down and smile. 'Well,' he said, 'I hate to bring up a painful subject, but it's your son's death we want to talk to you about.'

Mrs Atherton looked at Susan as if noticing her for the first time. A shadow crossed her face. Then she turned back to Banks. 'Our Joseph?' she said. 'But he's been dead nigh on thirty years.'

'I know that,' said Banks. 'We won't trouble you for long.'

'There's nowt else to add.' She poured the tea, fussed with milk and sugar, and sat down again.

'You said your son wrote and said he was coming?'

'Aye.'

'Did you keep the letter?'

'What?'

'The letter. I've not seen any mention of it anywhere. It's not in the file.'

'Well, it wouldn't be, would it? We don't leave scraps of paper cluttering up the place.'

'So you threw it out?'

'Aye. Bert or me.' She looked at Susan again. 'That was my husband, God rest his soul. Besides,' she said, 'how else would we know he was coming? We couldn't afford a telephone back then.'

'I know,' said Banks. But nobody had asked at the railway station whether Bert Atherton actually *had* met his son there, and now it was too late. He sipped some tea; it tasted as if the teabag had been used before. 'I don't suppose you remember seeing a red Volkswagen in the area around that time, do you?'

'No. They asked us that when it first happened. I didn't know owt about it then, and I don't know owt now.'

'Was there anyone else in the house when the accident occurred?'

'No, of course there weren't. Do you think I wouldn't have said if there were? Look, young man, what are you getting at? Do you have summat to tell me, summat I should know?'

Banks sighed and took another sip of weak tea. It didn't wash away the taste of decay that permeated the kitchen. He signalled to Susan and stood up. 'No,' he said. 'No, I've nothing new to tell you, Mrs Atherton. Just chasing will o' the wisps, that's all.'

'Well, I'm sorry, but you'll have to go chase 'em somewhere else, lad. I've got work to do.'

6

The Queen's Arms was quiet late that afternoon. Rain had kept the tourists away, and at four o'clock most of the locals were still at work in the offices and shops around the market square. Banks ordered a pork pie, then he and Jenny Fuller took their drinks to an isolated corner table and settled down. The first long draught of Theakston's bitter washed the archive dust and the taste of decay from Banks's throat.

'Well,' said Jenny, raising her glass of lager in a toast. 'To what do I owe the honour?'

She looked radiant, Banks thought: thick red hair tumbling over her shoulders, emerald green eyes full of humour and vitality, a fresh scent that cut through the atmosphere of stale smoke and made him think of childhood apple orchards. Though Banks was married, he and Jenny had once come very close to getting involved, and every now and then he felt a pang of regret for the road not taken.

'Reincarnation,' said Banks, clinking glasses.

Jenny raised her eyebrows. 'You know I'll drink to most things,' she said, 'but really, Alan, isn't this going a bit far?'

Banks explained what had happened so far that day. By the time he had finished, the barman delivered his pork pie, along with a large pickled onion. As Jenny mulled over what he had said, he sliced the pie into quarters and shook a dollop of HP Sauce onto his plate to dip them in.

'Fantasy,' she said finally.

'Would you care to elaborate?'

'If you don't believe in reincarnation, then there are an awful lot of strange phenomena you have to explain in more rational ways. Now, I'm no expert on parapsychology, but most people who claim to have lived past lifetimes generally become convinced through hypnosis, dreams and déjà vu experiences, like the ones you mentioned, or by spontaneous recall.'

'What's that?'

'Exactly what it sounds like. Remembering past lifetimes out of the blue. Children playing the piano without lessons, people suddenly speaking foreign languages, that kind of thing. Or any memory you have but can't explain, something that seems to have come from beyond your experience.'

'You mean if I'm walking down the street and I suddenly think of a Roman soldier and remember some sort of Latin phrase, then I'm recalling a previous lifetime?'

Jenny gave him a withering look. 'Don't be so silly, Alan. Of course *I* don't think that. Some people might, though. People are limitlessly gullible, it seems to me, especially when it comes to life after death. No, what I mean is that this is the kind of thing believers try to put forward as proof of reincarnation.'

'And how would a rational psychologist explain it?'

'She might argue that what a person recalls under hypnosis, in dreams, or wherever, is simply a web of fantasy woven from things that person has already seen or heard and maybe forgotten.'

'But he says he's never been here before.'

'There's television, books, films.'

Banks finished his pork pie, took a swig of Theakston's and lit a Silk Cut. 'So you're saying that maybe our Mr Singer has watched one too many episodes of *All Creatures Great and Small*?'

Jenny tossed back her hair and laughed, 'It wouldn't surprise me.' She looked at her watch, then drained her glass. 'Look, I'm sorry, but I must dash.' And with that, she jumped up, pecked him on the cheek and left. Jenny was always dashing, it seemed. Sometimes he wondered where.

Banks thought over what she had said. It made sense. More sense than Singer's reincarnation theory and more sense than suspecting Joseph Atherton's parents of covering up their son's murder.

But there remained the unsubstantiated story of the letter and the anonymous note about the red Volkswagen. If somebody else *had* driven Joseph Atherton to the farm, then his parents had been lying about the letter. Why? And who could it have been?

7

Two days later, sorting through his post, Banks found a letter addressed to him in longhand. It stood out like a sore thumb among the usual bundle of circulars and official communications. He spread it open on his desk in front of him and read.

Dear Mr Banks,

I'm not much of a one for letter writing so you must forgive me any mistakes. I didn't get much schooling due to me being a sickly child but my father always told us it was important to read and write. Your visit last week upset me by raking up the past I'd rather forget. I don't know what made you come and ask those questions but they made me think it is time to make my peace with God and tell the truth after all these years.

What we told the police was not true. Our Joseph didn't write to say he was coming and Bert didn't pick him up at the station. Joseph just turned up out of the blue one afternoon in that red car. I don't know who told the police about the car but I think it might have been Len Grimond in the farm down the road because he had fallen out with Bert over paying for repairs to a wall.

Anyway, it wasn't our Joseph's car. There was an American lass with him called Annie and she was driving. They had a baby with them that they said was theirs. I suppose that made him our grandson but it was the first time we ever heard about him. Our Joseph hadn't written or visited us for four years and we didn't know if he was alive or dead. He was a bonny little lad about two or three with the most solemn look on his face.

Well it was plain from the start that something was wrong. We tried to behave like good loving parents and welcome them into our home but the girl was moody and she didn't want to stay. The baby cried a lot and I don't think he had been looked after properly, though it's not my place to say. And Joseph was behaving very peculiar. His eyes looked all glassy with tiny pupils. We didn't know what was the matter. I think from what he said that he just wanted money.

They wouldn't eat much though I cooked a good roast for them, and Yorkshire puddings too, but our Joseph just picked at his food and the girl sat there all sulky holding the baby and wanting to go. She said she was a vegetarian. After we'd finished the dinner Joseph got very upset and said he had to go to the toilet. By then Bert was wondering what was going on and also a bit angry at how they treated our hospitality even if Joseph was our son.

Joseph was a long time in the toilet. Bert called up to him but he didn't answer. The girl said something about leaving him alone and laughed, but it wasn't a nice laugh. We thought something might be wrong with him so Bert went up and found Joseph with a piece of string tied around his arm heating something in a spoon with a match. It was one of our silver anniversary spoons he had taken from the kitchen without asking. We were just ignorant farmers and didn't know what was happening in crime and drugs and everything like you do, Mr Banks, but we knew our Joseph was doing something bad.

Bert lost his temper and pulled Joseph out of the toilet. When they were at the top of the stairs, Joseph started swearing at his father, using such words I've never heard before and would blush to repeat. That's when Bert lost his temper and hit him. On God's honour, he didn't mean to hurt him. Joseph was our only son and we loved him even though he was breaking my heart. But when Bert hit him Joseph fell down the stairs and when he got to the bottom his head was at such a funny angle I knew he must have broken his neck.

The girl started screaming then took the baby and ran outside and drove away. We have never seen her again or our grandson and don't know what has become of him. There was such a silence like you have never heard when the sound of the car engine vanished in the distance and Joseph was laying at the bottom of the stairs all twisted and broken. We tried to feel his pulse and Bert even put a mirror to his mouth to see if his breath would mist it but there was nothing.

I know we should have told the truth and we have

regretted it for all those years. We were always brought up to be decent honest folk respecting our parents and God and the law. Bert was ashamed that his son was a drug addict and didn't want it in the papers. I didn't want him to go to jail for what he had done because it was really an accident and it wasn't fair. He was suffering more than enough anyway because he had killed his only son.

So I said we must throw away all the drugs and needle and things and take our Joseph's shoes off and say he slipped coming down the stairs. We knew that the police would believe us because we were good people and we had no reason to lie. That was the hardest part. The laces got tied in knots and I broke my fingernails and in the end I was shaking so much I had to use the scissors.

And that is God's honest truth, Mr Banks. I know we did wrong but Bert was never the same after. Not a day went by when he didn't cry about what he'd done and I never saw him smile ever again. To this day we still do not know what has become of our grandson but whatever it is we hope he is healthy and happy and not as foolish as his father.

By the time you read this letter I'll be gone to my resting place too. For two years now I have had cancer and no matter what operations they do it is eating me away. I have saved my tablets. Now that I have taken the weight off my conscience I can only hope that the good Lord sees fit to forgive me my sins and take me unto his bosom.

Yours sincerely,
Betty Atherton

22

Banks put the letter aside and rubbed his left eye with the back of his hand. Outside, the rain was still falling, providing a gentle background for Finzi's Clarinet Concerto on the portable cassette. Banks stared at the sheets of blue vellum covered in Betty Atherton's crabbed hand, then he cursed, slammed his fist on the desk, went to the door and shouted for Susan Gay.

8

'**Her name is** Catherine Anne Singer,' said Susan the next afternoon. 'And she was relieved to talk to me as soon as I told her we weren't after her for leaving the scene of a crime. She comes from somewhere called Garden Grove, California. Like a lot of young Americans, she came over to "do" Europe in the sixties.'

The three of them – Banks, Susan and Jenny Fuller – sat over drinks at a dimpled, copper-topped table in the Queen's Arms listening to the summer rain tap against the diamonds of coloured glass.

'And she's Jerry Singer's mother?' Banks asked.

Susan nodded. 'Yes. I just asked him for her telephone number. I didn't tell him why I wanted it.'

Banks nodded. 'Good. Go on.'

'Well, she ended up living in London. It was easy enough to get jobs that paid under the counter, places where nobody asked too many questions. Eventually, she hooked up with Joseph Atherton and they lived together in a bedsit in Notting Hill. Joseph fancied himself as a musician then—'

'Who didn't?' said Banks. He remembered taking a few abortive guitar lessons himself. 'Sorry. Go on.'

'There's not a lot to add, sir. She got pregnant, wouldn't agree to an abortion, though apparently Joseph tried to persuade her. She named the child Jerry, after some guitarist Joseph liked called Jerry Garcia. Luckily for Jerry, Annie wasn't on heroin. She drew the line at hash and LSD. Anyway, they were off to join some Buddhist commune in the wilds of Scotland when Joseph said they should drop in on his parents on the way and try to get some money. She didn't like the idea, but she went along with it anyway.

'Everything happened exactly as Mrs Atherton described it. Annie got scared and ran away. When she got back to London, she decided it was time to go home. She sold the car and took out all her savings from the bank, then she got the first flight she could and settled back in California. She went to university and ended up working as a marine biologist in San Diego. She never married, and she never mentioned her time in England, or that night at the Atherton farm, to Jerry. She told him his father had left them when Jerry was still a baby. He was only two and a half at the time of Atherton's death, and as far as he was concerned he had spent his entire life in southern California.'

Banks drained his pint and looked at Jenny.

'Cryptomnesia,' she said.

'Come again?'

'Cryptomnesia. It means memories you're not consciously aware of, a memory of an incident in your own life that you've forgotten. Jerry Singer was present when his grandfather knocked his father down the stairs, but as far as he was concerned *consciously*, he'd never been to Swainsdale before, so how could he remember it? When he got mixed up in the New Age scene, these memories

24

he didn't know he had started to seem like some sort of proof of reincarnation.'

Sometimes, Banks thought to himself, things are better left alone. The thought surprised him because it went against the grain of both his job and his innate curiosity. But what good had come from Jerry Singer presenting himself at the station three days ago? None at all. Perhaps the only blessing in the whole affair was that Betty Atherton had passed away peacefully, as she had intended, in her pill-induced sleep. Now she wouldn't suffer any more in this world. And if there were a God, Banks thought, he surely couldn't be such a bastard as to let her suffer in the next one, either.

'Sir?'

'Sorry, Susan, I was miles away.'

'I asked who was going to tell him. You or me?'

'I'll do it,' said Banks, with a sigh. 'It's no good trying to sit on it all now. But I need another pint first. My shout.'

As he stood up to go to the bar, the door opened and Jerry Singer walked in. He spotted them at once and walked over. He had that strange naive, intense look in his eyes. Banks instinctively reached for his cigarettes.

'They told me you were here,' Singer said awkwardly, pointing back through the door towards the Tudor-fronted police station across the street. 'I'm leaving for home tomorrow and I was just wondering if you'd found anything out yet?'

FAN MAIL

The letter arrived one sunny Thursday morning in August, along with a Visa bill and a royalty statement. Dennis Quilley carried the mail out to the deck of his Beaches home, stopping by the kitchen on the way to pour himself a gin and tonic. He had already been writing for three hours straight and he felt he deserved a drink.

First he looked at the amount of the royalty cheque, then he put aside the Visa bill and picked up the letter carefully, as if he were a forensic expert investigating it for prints. Postmarked Toronto and dated four days earlier, it was addressed in a small, precise hand and looked as if it had been written with a fine-nibbed calligraphic pen. But the post code was different; that had been hurriedly scrawled in with a ballpoint. Whoever it was, Quilley thought, had probably got his name from the telephone directory and had then looked up the code in the post office just before mailing.

Pleased with his deductions, Quilley opened the letter. Written in the same neat and mannered hand as the address, it said:

Dear Mr Quilley,

Please forgive me for writing to you at home like this. I know you must be very busy, and it is inexcusable of me to intrude on your valuable time. Believe me, I would not do so if I could think of any other way.

I have been a great fan of your work for many years now. As a collector of mysteries, too, I also have first editions of all your books. From what I have read, I know you are a clever man and, I hope, just the man to help me with my problem.

For the past twenty years, my wife has been making my life a misery. I put up with her for the sake of the children, but now they have all gone to live their own lives. I have asked her for a divorce, but she just laughed in my face. I have decided, finally, that the only way out is to kill her and that is why I am seeking your advice.

You may think this is insane of me, especially saying it in a letter, but it is just a measure of my desperation. I would quite understand it if you went straight to the police, and I am sure they would find me and punish me. Believe me, I've thought about it. Even that would be preferable to the misery I must suffer day after day.

If you can find it in your heart to help a devoted fan in his hour of need, please meet me on the roof lounge of the Park Plaza Hotel on Wednesday, 19 August at two p.m. I have taken the afternoon off work and will wait longer if for any reason you are delayed. Don't worry, I will recognize you easily from your photo on the dust jacket of your books.

Yours, in hope,
A Fan

The letter slipped from Quilley's hand. He couldn't believe what he'd just read. He was a mystery writer – he specialized in devising ingenious murders – but for someone to assume that he did the same in real life was absurd. Could it be a practical joke?

He picked up the letter and read through it again. The man's whining tone and clichéd style seemed sincere enough, and the more Quilley thought about it, the more certain he became that none of his friends was sick enough to play such a joke.

Assuming that it was real, then, what should he do? His impulse was to crumple up the letter and throw it away. But should he go to the police? No. That would be a waste of time. The real police were a terribly dull and literal-minded lot. They would probably think he was seeking publicity.

He found that he had screwed up the sheet of paper in his fist, and he was just about to toss it aside when he changed his mind. Wasn't there another option? Go. Go and meet the man. Find out more about him. Find out if he was genuine. Surely there would be no obligation in that? All he had to do was turn up at the Park Plaza at the appointed time and see what happened.

Quilley's life was fine – no troublesome woman to torment him, plenty of money (mostly from American sales), a beautiful lakeside cottage near Huntsville, a modicum of fame, the esteem of his peers – but it had been rather boring of late. Here was an opportunity for adventure of a kind. Besides, he might get a story idea out of the meeting. Why not go and see?

He finished his drink and smoothed the letter on his knee. He had to smile at that last bit. No doubt the man would recognize him from his book-jacket photo, but it was an old one and had been retouched in the first place. His cheeks had filled out a bit since then and his thinning hair had acquired a sprinkling of grey. Still, he thought, he was a handsome man for fifty: handsome, clever and successful.

Smiling, he picked up both letter and envelope and went back to the kitchen in search of matches. There must be no evidence.

•

Over the next few days Quilley hardly gave a thought to the mysterious letter. As usual in summer, he divided his time between writing in Toronto, where he found the city worked as a stimulus, and weekends at the cottage. There he walked in the woods, chatted to locals in the lodge, swam in the clear lake and idled around getting a tan. Evenings, he would open a bottle of Chardonnay, reread P. G. Wodehouse and listen to Bach. It was an ideal life: quiet, solitary, independent.

When Wednesday came, though, he drove downtown, parked in the multi-storey at Cumberland and Avenue Road, then walked to the Park Plaza. It was another hot day. The tourists were out in force across Bloor Street by the Royal Ontario Museum, many of them Americans from Buffalo, Rochester or Detroit: the men in loud-checked shirts photographing everything in sight, their wives in tight shorts looking tired and thirsty.

Quilley took the elevator up to the nineteenth floor and wandered through the bar, an olde-worlde place with deep armchairs and framed reproductions of old Colonial scenes on the walls. It was busier than usual, and even though the windows were open, the smoke bothered him. He walked out onto the roof lounge and scanned the faces. Within moments he noticed someone looking his way. The man paused for just a split second, perhaps to translate the dust-jacket photo into reality, then beckoned Quilley over with raised eyebrows and a twitch of the head.

The man rose to shake hands, then sat down again, glancing around to make sure nobody had paid the two of them undue attention. He was short and thin, with sandy hair and a pale grey complexion, as if he had just come out of hospital. He wore wire-rimmed glasses and had a habit of rolling his tongue around in his mouth when he wasn't talking.

'First of all, Mr Quilley,' the man said, raising his glass, 'may I say how honoured I am to meet you.' He spoke with a pronounced English accent.

Quilley inclined his head. 'I'm flattered, Mr . . . er . . . ?'

'Peplow, Frank Peplow.'

'Yes . . . Mr Peplow. But I must admit I'm puzzled by your letter.'

A waiter in a burgundy jacket came over to take Quilley's order. He asked for an Amstel.

Peplow paused until the waiter was out of earshot. 'Puzzled?'

'What I mean is,' Quilley went on, struggling for the right words, 'whether you were serious or not, whether you really do want to—'

Peplow leaned forward. Behind the lenses, his pale blue eyes looked sane enough. 'I assure you, Mr Quilley, that I was, that I *am* entirely serious. That woman is ruining my life and I can't allow it to go on any longer.'

Speaking about her brought little spots of red to his

cheeks. Quilley held his hand up. 'All right, I believe you. I suppose you realize I should have gone to the police?'

'But you didn't.'

'I could have. They might be here, watching us.'

Peplow shook his head. 'Mr Quilley, if you won't help, I'd even welcome prison. Don't think I haven't realized that I might get caught, that no murder is perfect. All I want is a chance. It's worth the risk.'

The waiter returned with Quilley's drink and they both sat in silence until he had gone. Quilley was intrigued by this drab man sitting opposite him, a man who obviously didn't even have the imagination to dream up his own murder plot. 'What do you want from me?' he asked.

'I have no right to ask anything of you, I understand that,' Peplow said. 'I have absolutely nothing to offer in return. I'm not rich. I have no savings. I suppose all I want really is advice, encouragement.'

'If I were to help,' Quilley said, 'if I were to help, then I'd do nothing more than offer advice. Is that clear?'

Peplow nodded. 'Does that mean you will?'

'If I can.'

And so Dennis Quilley found himself helping to plot the murder of a woman he'd never met with a man he didn't even particularly like. Later, when he analysed his reasons for playing along, he realized that that was exactly what he had been doing – playing. It had been a game, a cerebral puzzle, just like thinking up a plot for a book, and he never, at first, gave a thought to real murder, real blood, real death.

Peplow took a handkerchief from his top pocket and wiped the thin film of sweat from his brow. 'You don't know how happy this makes me, Mr Quilley. At last I have a chance. My life hasn't amounted to much and I don't suppose it ever will. But at least I might find some peace and quiet in my final years. I'm not a well man.' He placed one hand solemnly over his chest. 'Ticker. Not fair, is it? I've never smoked, I hardly drink, and I'm only fifty-three. But the doctor has promised me a few years yet if I live right. All I want is to be left alone with my books and my garden.'

'Tell me about your wife,' Quilley prompted.

Peplow's expression darkened. 'She's a cruel and selfish woman,' he said. 'And she's messy, she never does anything around the place. Too busy watching those damn soap operas on television day and night. She cares about nothing but her own comfort, and she never over-looks an opportunity to nag me or taunt me. If I try to escape to my collection, she mocks me and calls me dull and boring. I'm not even safe from her in my garden. I realize I have no imagination, Mr Quilley, and perhaps even less courage, but even a man like me deserves some peace in his life, don't you think?'

Quilley had to admit that the woman really did sound awful – worse than any he had known, and he had met some shrews in his time. He had never had much use for women, except for occasional sex in his younger days. Even that had become sordid, and now he stayed away from them as much as possible. He found, as he listened, that he could summon up remarkable sympathy for Peplow's position.

'What do you have in mind?' he asked.

'I don't really know. That's why I wrote to you. I was hoping you might be able to help with some ideas. Your books . . . you seem to know so much.'

'In my books,' Quilley said, 'the murderer always gets caught.'

'Well, yes,' said Peplow, 'of course. But that's because the genre demands it, isn't it? I mean, your Inspector Baldry is much smarter than any real policeman. I'm sure if you'd made him a criminal, he would always get away.'

There was no arguing with that, Quilley thought. 'How do you want to do it?' he asked. 'A domestic accident? Electric shock, say? Gadget in the bathtub? She must have a hair curler or a dryer?'

Peplow shook his head, eyes tightly closed. 'Oh no,' he whispered, 'I couldn't. I couldn't do anything like that. No more than I could bear the sight of her blood.'

'How's her health?'

'Unfortunately,' said Peplow, 'she seems obscenely robust.'

'How old is she?'

'Forty-nine.'

'Any bad habits?'

'Mr Quilley, my wife has nothing *but* bad habits. The only thing she won't tolerate is drink, for some reason, and I don't think she has other men – though that's probably because nobody will have her.'

'Does she smoke?'

'Like a chimney.'

Quilley shuddered. 'How long?'

'Ever since she was a teenager, I think. Before I met her.'

'Does she exercise?'

'Never.'

'What about her weight, her diet?'

'Well, you might not call her fat, but you'd be generous in saying she was full-figured. She eats too much junk food. I've always said that. And eggs. She loves bacon and eggs for breakfast. And she's always stuffing herself with cream cakes and tarts.'

'Hmmm,' said Quilley, taking a sip of Amstel. 'She sounds like a prime candidate for a heart attack.'

'But it's me who—' Peplow stopped as comprehension dawned. 'Yes, I see. You mean one could be *induced*?'

'Quite. Do you think you could manage that?'

'Well, I could if I didn't have to be there to watch. But I don't know how.'

'Poison.'

'I don't know anything about poison.'

'Never mind. Give me a few days to look into it. I'll give you advice, remember, but that's as far as it goes.'

'Understood.'

Quilley smiled. 'Good. Another beer?'

'No, I'd better not. She'll be able to smell this one on my breath and I'll be in for it already. I'd better go.'

Quilley looked at his watch. Two-thirty. He could have done with another Amstel, but he didn't want to stay there by himself. Besides, at three it would be time to meet his agent at the Four Seasons, and there he would have the opportunity to drink as much as he wanted. To pass the time, he could browse in Book City. 'Fine,' he said, 'I'll go down with you.'

Outside on the hot, busy street, they shook hands and agreed to meet in a week's time on the back patio of the Madison Avenue Pub. It wouldn't do to be seen together twice in the same place.

Quilley stood on the corner of Bloor and Avenue Road among the camera-clicking tourists and watched Peplow walk off towards the St George subway station. Now that their meeting was over and the spell was broken, he wondered again what the hell he was doing helping this pathetic little man. It certainly wasn't altruism. Perhaps the challenge appealed to him; after all, people climb mountains just because they're there.

And then there was Peplow's mystery collection. There was just a chance that it might contain an item of great interest to Quilley and that Peplow might be grateful enough to part with it.

Wondering how to approach the subject at their next meeting, Quilley wiped the sweat from his brow with the back of his hand and walked towards the bookshop.

•

Atropine, hyoscyamine, belladonna . . . Quilley flipped through Dreisbach's *Handbook of Poisoning* one evening at the cottage. Poison seemed to have gone out of fashion these days, and he had only used it in one of his novels, about six years ago. That had been the old standby, cyanide, with its familiar smell of bitter almonds, which he had so often read about but never experienced. The small black handbook had sat on his shelf gathering dust ever since.

Writing a book, of course, one could generally skip over the problems of acquiring the stuff – give the killer a job as a pharmacist or in a hospital dispensary, for example. In real life, getting one's hands on poison might prove more difficult.

So far, he had read through the sections on agricultural poisons, household hazards and medicinal poisons. The problem was that whatever Peplow used had to be easily available. Prescription drugs were out. Even if Peplow could persuade a doctor to give him barbiturates, for example, the prescription would be on record and any death in the household would be regarded as suspicious.

Barbiturates wouldn't do, anyway, and nor would such common products as paint thinner, insecticides and weed killers – they didn't reproduce the symptoms of a heart attack.

Near the back of the book was a list of poisonous plants that shocked Quilley by its sheer length. He hadn't known just how much deadliness there was lurking in fields, gardens and woods. Rhubarb leaves contained oxalic acid, for example, and caused nausea, vomiting and diarrhoea. The bark, wood, leaves or seeds of the yew had a similar effect. Boxwood leaves and twigs caused convulsions; celandine could bring about a coma; hydrangeas contained cyanide; and laburnums brought on irregular pulse, delirium, twitching and unconsciousness. And so the list went on – lupins, mistletoe, sweet peas, rhododendron – a poisoner's delight. Even the beautiful poinsettia, which brightened up so many Toronto homes each Christmas, could cause gastroenteritis. Most of these plants were easy to get hold of, and in many cases the active ingredients could be extracted simply by soaking or boiling in water.

It wasn't long before Quilley found what he was looking for. Beside 'Oleander' the note read, 'See *digitalis*, 374.' And there it was, set out in detail. Digitalis occurred in all parts of the common foxglove, which grew on waste ground and woodland slopes, and flowered from June to September. Acute poisoning would bring about death from ventricular fibrillation. No doctor would consider an autopsy if Peplow's wife appeared to die of a heart attack, given her habits, especially if Peplow fed her a few smaller doses first to establish the symptoms.

Quilley set aside the book. It was already dark outside, and the downpour that the humid, cloudy day had been promising had just begun. Rain slapped against the asphalt roof tiles, gurgled down the drainpipe and pattered on the leaves of the overhanging trees. In the background, it hissed as it fell on the lake. Distant flashes of lightning and deep rumblings of thunder warned of the coming storm.

Happy with his solitude and his cleverness, Quilley linked his hands behind his head and leaned back in the chair. Out back, he heard the rustling of a small animal making its way through the undergrowth – a raccoon, perhaps, or even a skunk. When he closed his eyes, he pictured all the trees, shrubs and wild flowers around the cottage and marvelled at the deadly potential so many of them contained.

•

The sun blazed down on the back patio of the Madison, a small garden protected from the wind by high fences. Quilley wore his sunglasses and nursed a pint of Conner's Ale. The place was packed. Skilled and pretty waitresses came and went, trays laden with baskets of chicken wings and golden pints of lager.

The two of them sat out of the way at a white table in a corner by the metal fire escape. A striped parasol offered some protection, but the sun was still too hot and too bright. Peplow's wife must have given him hell about drinking the last time because today he had ordered only a Coke.

'It was easy,' Quilley said. 'You could have done it yourself. The only setback was that foxgloves don't grow wild here like they do in England. But you're a gardener; you grow them.'

Peplow shook his head and smiled. 'It's the gift of

clever people like yourself to make difficult things seem easy. I'm not particularly resourceful, Mr Quilley. Believe me, I wouldn't have known where to start. I had no idea that such a book existed, but you did because of your art. Even if I had known, I'd hardly have dared buy it or take it out of the library for fear that someone would remember. But you've had your copy for years. A simple tool of the trade. No, Mr Quilley, please don't underestimate your contribution. I was a desperate man. Now you've given me a chance at freedom. If there's anything at all I can do for you, please don't hesitate to say. I'd consider it an honour.'

'This collection of yours,' Quilley said. 'What does it consist of?'

'British and Canadian crime fiction, mostly. I don't like to boast, but it's a very good collection. Try me. Go on, just mention a name.'

'E. C. R. Lorac.'

'About twenty of the Inspector MacDonalds. First editions, mint condition.'

'Anne Hocking?'

'Everything but *Night's Candles.*'

'Trotton?'

Peplow raised his eyebrows. 'Good Lord, that's an obscure one. Do you know, you're the first person I've come across who's ever mentioned that.'

'Do you have it?'

'Oh, yes.' Peplow smiled smugly. 'X. J. Trotton, *Signed in Blood*, published 1942. It turned up in a pile of junk I bought at an auction some years ago. It's rare, but not very valuable. Came out in Britain during the war and probably died an immediate death. It was his only book, as far as I can make out, and there is no biographical information. Perhaps it was a pseudonym for someone famous?'

Quilley shook his head. 'I'm afraid I don't know. Have you read it?'

'Good Lord, no! I don't read them. It could damage the spines. Many of them are fragile. Anything I want to read – like your books – I also buy in paperback.'

'Mr Peplow,' Quilley said slowly, 'you asked if there was anything you could do for me. As a matter of fact, there *is* something you can give me for my services.'

'Yes?'

'The Trotton.'

Peplow frowned and pursed his thin lips. 'Why on earth . . . ?'

'For my own collection, of course. I'm especially interested in the war period.'

Peplow smiled. 'Ah! So that's how you knew so much about them? I'd no idea you were a collector too.'

Quilley shrugged modestly. He could see Peplow struggling, visualizing the gap in his collection. But finally the poor man decided that the murder of his wife was more important to him than an obscure mystery novel. 'Very well,' he said gravely. 'I'll mail it to you.'

'How can I be sure . . . ?'

Peplow looked offended. 'I'm a man of my word, Mr Quilley. A bargain is a bargain.' He held out his hand. 'Gentleman's agreement.'

'All right.' Quilley believed him. 'You'll be in touch when it's done?'

'Yes. Perhaps a brief note in with the Trotton, if you can wait that long. Say two or three weeks?'

'Fine. I'm in no hurry.'

Quilley hadn't examined his motives since the first

meeting, but he had realized, as he passed on the information and instructions, that it was the challenge he responded to more than anything else. For years he had been writing crime novels, and in providing Peplow with the means to kill his slatternly, overbearing wife, Quilley had derived some vicarious pleasure from the knowledge that he – Inspector Baldry's creator – could bring off in real life what he had always been praised for doing in fiction.

Quilley also knew that there were no real detectives who possessed Baldry's curious mixture of intellect and instinct. Most of them were thick plodders, and they would never realize that dull Mr Peplow had murdered his wife with a bunch of foxgloves, of all things. Nor would they ever know that the brains behind the whole affair had been none other than his, Dennis Quilley's.

The two men drained their glasses and left together. The corner of Bloor and Spadina was busy with tourists and students lining up for charcoal-grilled hot dogs from the street vendor. Peplow turned towards the subway and Quilley wandered among the artsy crowd and the rollerbladers on Bloor Street West for a while, then he settled at an open-air cafe over a daiquiri and a slice of kiwi-fruit cheesecake to read the *Globe and Mail*.

Now, he thought as he sipped his drink and turned to the arts section, all he had to do was wait. One day soon a small package would arrive for him. Peplow would be free of his wife, and Quilley would be the proud owner of one of the few remaining copies of X. J. Trotton's one and only mystery novel, *Signed in Blood*.

•

Three weeks passed and no package arrived. Occasionally, Quilley thought of Mr Peplow and wondered what had become of him. Perhaps he had lost his nerve after all. That wouldn't be surprising. Quilley knew that he would have no way of finding out what had happened if Peplow chose not to contact him again. He didn't know where the man lived or where he worked. He didn't even know if Peplow was his real name. Still, he thought, it was best that way. No contact. Even the Trotton wasn't worth being involved in a botched murder for.

Then, at ten o'clock one warm Tuesday morning in September, the doorbell chimed. Quilley looked at his watch and frowned. Too early for the postman. Sighing, he pressed the SAVE command on his PC and walked down to answer the door. A stranger stood there, an over-weight woman in a yellow polka-dot dress with short sleeves and a low neck. She had piggy eyes set in a round face and dyed red hair that looked limp and lifeless after a cheap perm. She carried an imitation crocodile-skin handbag.

Quilley must have stood there looking puzzled for too long. The woman's eyes narrowed and her rosebud mouth tightened so much that white furrows radiated from the red circle of her lips.

'May I come in?' she asked.

Stunned, Quilley stood back and let her enter. She walked straight over to a wicker armchair and sat down. The basketwork creaked under her. From there, she surveyed the room, with its waxed parquet floor, stone fireplace and antique Ontario furniture.

'Nice,' she said, clutching her handbag on her lap. Quilley sat down opposite her. Her dress was a size too small and the material strained over her red, fleshy upper arms and pinkish bosom. The hem rode up as she crossed her legs, exposing a wedge of fat, mottled thigh. Primly, she pulled it down again over her dimpled knees.

'I'm sorry to appear rude,' said Quilley, regaining his composure, 'but who the hell are you?'

'My name is Peplow,' the woman said. 'Gloria Peplow. I'm a widow.'

Quilley felt a tingling sensation along his spine, the way he always did when fear began to take hold of him.

He frowned and said, 'I'm afraid I don't know you, do I?'

'We've never met,' the woman replied, 'but I think you knew my husband.'

'I don't recall any Peplow. Perhaps you're mistaken?'

Gloria Peplow shook her head and fixed him with her piggy eyes. He noticed they were black, or as near as. 'I'm not mistaken, Mr Quilley. You didn't only know my husband, you also plotted with him to murder me.'

Quilley flushed and jumped to his feet. 'That's absurd! Look, if you've come here to make insane accusations like that, you'd better go.' He stood like an ancient statue, one hand pointing dramatically towards the door.

Mrs Peplow smirked. 'Oh, sit down. You look very foolish standing there like that.'

Quilley continued to stand. 'This is *my* home, Mrs Peplow, and I insist that you leave. Now!'

Mrs Peplow sighed and opened the gilded plastic clasp on her purse. She took out a Shoppers Drug Mart envelope, picked out two colour photographs and dropped them next to the Wedgwood dish on the antique wine table by her chair. Leaning forward, Quilley could see clearly what they were: one showed him standing with Peplow outside the Park Plaza, and the other caught the two of them talking outside the Scotiabank at Bloor and

42

Spadina. Mrs Peplow flipped the photos over, and Quilley saw that they had been date-stamped by the processors.

'You met with my husband at least twice to help him plan my death.'

'That's ridiculous. I do remember him now I've seen the picture. I just couldn't recollect his name. He was a fan. We talked about mystery novels. I'm very sorry to hear that he's passed away.'

'He had a heart attack, Mr Quilley, and now I'm all alone in the world.'

'I'm very sorry, but I don't see . . .'

Mrs Peplow waved his protests aside. Quilley noticed the dark sweat stain on the tight material around her armpit. She fumbled with the catch on her purse again and brought out a pack of Export Lights and a book of matches.

'I don't allow smoking in my house,' Quilley said. 'It doesn't agree with me.'

'Pity,' she said, lighting the cigarette and dropping the spent match in the Wedgwood bowl. She blew a stream of smoke directly at Quilley, who coughed and fanned it away.

'Listen to me, Mr Quilley,' she said, 'and listen good. My husband might have been stupid, but I'm not. He was not only a pathetic and boring little man, he was also an open book. Don't ask me why I married him. He wasn't even much of a man, if you know what I mean. Do you think I haven't known for some time that he was thinking of ways to get rid of me? I wouldn't give him a divorce because the one thing he did – the *only* thing he did – was provide for me and he didn't even do that very well. I'd have got half if we divorced, but half of what he earned isn't enough to keep a bag lady. I'd have had to go to work and I don't like that idea. So I watched him. He got more and more desperate, more and more secretive. When he started looking smug, I knew he was up to something.'

'Mrs Peplow,' Quilley interrupted, 'this is all very well, but I don't see what it has to do with me. You come in here and pollute my home with smoke, then you start telling me some fairy tale about your husband, a man I met casually once or twice. I'm busy, Mrs Peplow, and quite frankly I'd rather you left and let me get back to work.'

'I'm sure you would.' She flicked a column of ash into the Wedgwood bowl. 'As I was saying, I knew he was up to something, so I started following him. I thought he might have another woman, unlikely as it seemed, so I took my camera along. I wasn't really surprised when he headed for the Park Plaza instead of going back to the office after lunch one day. I watched the elevator go up to the nineteenth floor, the bar, so I waited across the street in the crowd for him to come out again. As you know, I didn't have to wait very long. He came out with you. And it was just as easy the next time.'

'I've already told you, Mrs Peplow, he was a mystery buff, a fellow collector, that's all—'

'Yes, yes, I know he was. Him and his stupid cata-logues and collection. Still,' she mused, 'it had its uses. That's how I found out who you were. I'd seen your pic-ture on the book covers, of course. If I may say so, it does you more than justice.' She looked him up and down as if he were a side of beef hanging in a butcher's window. He cringed. 'As I was saying, my husband was obvious. I knew he must be chasing you for advice. He spends so much time escaping to his garden or his little world of books that it was perfectly natural he would go to a mystery novelist for advice rather than to a real criminal. I imagine you were a bit more accessible, too. A little flattery and you were hooked. Just another puzzle for you to work on.'

'Look, Mrs Peplow—'

'Let me finish.' She ground out her cigarette butt in the bowl. 'Foxgloves, indeed! Do you think he could manage to brew up a dose of digitalis without leaving traces all over the place? Do you know what he did the first time? He put just enough in my Big Mac to make me a bit nauseous and make my pulse race, but he left the leaves and stems in the garbage! Can you believe that? Oh, I became very careful in my eating habits after that, Mr Quilley. Anyway, your little plan didn't work. I'm here and he's dead.'

Quilley paled. 'My God, you killed him, didn't you?'

'He was the one with the bad heart, not me.' She lit another cigarette.

'You can hardly blackmail me for plotting with your husband to kill you when *he's* the one who's dead,' said Quilley. 'And as for evidence, there's nothing. No, Mrs Peplow, I think you'd better go, and think yourself lucky I don't call the police.'

Mrs Peplow looked surprised. 'What are you talking about? I have no intention of blackmailing you for plotting to kill me.'

'Then what . . . ?'

'Mr Quilley, my husband was blackmailing you. That's why *you* killed *him*.'

Quilley slumped back in his chair. 'I what?'

She took a sheet of paper from her purse and passed it over to him. On it were just two words: 'Trotton – Quilley.'

He recognized the neat handwriting. 'That's a photocopy,' Mrs Peplow went on. 'The original's where I found it, slipped between the pages of a book called *Signed in Blood* by X. J. Trotton. Do you know that book, Mr Quilley?'

'Vaguely. I've heard of it.'

'Oh, have you? It might also interest you to know that along with that book and the slip of paper, locked away in my husband's files, is a copy of your own first novel. I put it there.'

Quilley felt the room spinning around him. 'I . . . I . . .' Peplow had given him the impression that Gloria was stupid, but that was turning out to be far from the truth.

'My husband's only been dead for two days. If the doctors look, they'll *know* that he's been poisoned. For a start, they'll find high levels of potassium and then they'll discover *eosinophilia*. Do you know what they are, Mr Quilley? I looked them up. They're a kind of white blood cell, and you find lots of them around if there's been any allergic reaction or inflammation. If I was to go to the police and say I'd been suspicious about my husband's behaviour over the past few weeks, that I had followed him and photographed him with you, and if they were to find the two books and the slip of paper in his files . . . Well, I think you know what they'd make of it, don't you? Especially if I told them he came home feeling ill after a lunch with you.'

'It's not fair,' Quilley said, banging his fist on the chair arm. 'It's just not bloody fair.'

'Life rarely is. But the police aren't to know how stupid and unimaginative my husband was. They'll just look at the note, read the books, and assume he was blackmailing you.' She laughed. 'Even if Frank had read the

Trotton book, I'm sure he'd have only noticed an "influence", at the most. But you and I know what really went on, don't we? It happens more often than people think. A few years ago I read in the newspaper about similarities between a book by Colleen McCullough and *The Blue Castle* by Lucy Maud Montgomery. I'd say that was a bit obvious, wouldn't you? It was much easier in your case, much less dangerous. You were very clever, Mr Quilley. You found an obscure novel and you didn't only adapt the plot for your own first book, you even stole the character of your series detective. There was some risk involved, certainly, but not much. Your book is better, without a doubt. You have some writing talent, which X. J. Trotton completely lacked. But he did have the germ of an original idea, and it wasn't lost on you, was it?'

Quilley groaned. Thirteen solid police procedurals, twelve of them all his own work, but the first, yes, a deliberate adaptation of a piece of ephemeral trash. He had seen what Trotton could have done and had done it himself. Serendipity, or so it had seemed when he found the dusty volume in a second-hand bookshop in Victoria years ago. All he had had to do was change the setting from London to Toronto, alter the names and set about improving upon the original. And now . . . ? The hell of it was that he would have been perfectly safe without the damn book. He had simply given in to the urge to get his hands on Peplow's copy and destroy it. It wouldn't have mattered, really. *Signed in Blood* would have remained unread on Peplow's shelf. If only the bloody fool hadn't written that note . . .

'Even if the police can't make a murder charge stick,' Mrs Peplow went on, 'I think your reputation would suffer if this got out. Oh, the great reading public might not care.

Perhaps a trial would even increase your sales – you know how ghoulish people are – but the plagiarism would at the very least lose you the respect of your peers. I don't think your agent and publisher would be very happy either. Am I making myself clear?'

Pale and sweating, Quilley nodded. 'How much?' he whispered.

'Pardon?'

'I said how much. How much do you want to keep quiet?'

'Oh, it's not your money I'm after, Mr Quilley, or may I call you Dennis? Well, not *only* money, anyway. I'm a widow now. I'm all alone in the world.'

She looked around the room, her piggy eyes glittering, then gave Quilley one of the most disgusting looks he'd ever had in his life.

'I've always fancied living near the lake,' she said, reaching for another cigarette. 'Live here alone, do you?'

INNOCENCE

Francis must be late, surely, Reed thought as he stood waiting on the bridge by the railway station. He was beginning to feel restless and uncomfortable; the handles of his holdall bit into his palm, and he noticed that the rain promised in the forecast that morning was already starting to fall.

Wonderful! Here he was, over two hundred miles away from home, and Francis hadn't turned up. But Reed couldn't be sure about that. Perhaps *he* was early. They had made the same arrangement three or four times over the past five years, but for the life of him Reed couldn't remember the exact time they'd met.

Reed turned and noticed a plump woman in a thread-bare blue overcoat come struggling against the wind over the bridge towards him. She pushed a large pram, in which two infants fought and squealed.

'Excuse me,' he called out as she neared him, 'could you tell me what time school gets out?'

The woman gave him a funny look – either puzzlement or irritation, he couldn't decide which – and answered in the clipped, nasal accent peculiar to the Midlands, 'Half past three.' Then she hurried by, giving Reed a wide berth.

He was wrong. For some reason he had got it into his mind that Francis finished teaching at three o'clock. It was only twenty-five past now, so there would be at least another fifteen minutes to wait before the familiar red Escort came into sight.

The rain was getting heavier and the wind lashed it hard against Reed's face. A few yards up the road from the bridge was the bus station, which was attached to a large modern shopping centre, all glass and escalators. Reed could stand in the entrance there just beyond the doors, where it was warm and dry, and still watch for Francis.

At about twenty-five to four, the first schoolchildren came dashing over the bridge and into the bus station, satchels swinging, voices shrill and loud with freedom. The rain didn't seem to bother them, Reed noticed: hair lay plastered to skulls; beads of rain hung on the tips of noses. Most of the boys' ties were askew, their socks hung loose around their ankles and their shoelaces snaked along the ground. It was a wonder they didn't trip over themselves. Reed smiled, remembering his own school-days.

And how alluring the girls looked as they ran smiling and laughing out of the rain into the shelter of the mall. Not the really young ones, the unformed ones, but the older, long-limbed girls, newly aware of their breasts and the swelling of their hips. They wore their clothes carelessly: blouses hanging out, black woolly tights twisted or torn at the knees. To Reed, there was something wanton in their disarray.

These days, of course, they probably all knew what was what, but Reed couldn't help but feel that there was also a certain innocence about them: a naive, carefree grace in the way they moved and a casual freedom in their laughter and gestures. Life hadn't got to them yet;

they hadn't felt its weight and seen the darkness at its core.

Mustn't get carried away, Reed told himself, with a smile. It was all very well to joke with Bill in the office about how sexy the schoolgirls who passed the window each day were, but it was positively unhealthy to mean it, or (God forbid!) attempt to do anything about it. He couldn't be turning into a dirty old man at thirty-five, could he? Sometimes the power and violence of his fantasies worried him, but perhaps everyone else had them too. It wasn't something you could talk about at work. He didn't really think he was abnormal; after all, he hadn't acted them out, and you couldn't be arrested for your fantasies, could you?

Where the hell was Francis? Reed peered out through the glass. Wind-blown rain lashed across the huge plate windows and distorted the outside world. All detail was obliterated in favour of the overall mood: grey-glum and dream-like.

Reed glanced at his watch again. After four o'clock. The only schoolchildren left now were the stragglers, the ones who lived nearby and didn't have to hurry for a bus. They sauntered over the bridge, shoving each other, playing tag, hopping and skipping over the cracks in the pavement, oblivious to the rain and the wind that drove it.

Francis ought to be here by now. Worried, Reed went over the arrangements again in his mind. He knew that he'd got the date right because he'd written it down in his appointment book. Reed had tried to call the previous evening to confirm, but no one had answered. If Francis had been trying to get in touch with him at work or at home, he would have been out of luck. Reed had been visiting another old friend – this one in Exeter – and Elsie, the office receptionist, could hardly be trusted to get her own name right.

When five o'clock came and there was still no sign of Francis, Reed picked up his holdall again and walked back down to the station. It was still raining, but not so fast, and the wind had dropped. The only train back home that night left Birmingham at nine-forty and didn't get to Carlisle until well after midnight. By then the local buses would have stopped running and he would have to get a taxi. Was it worth it?

There wasn't much alternative, really. A hotel would be too expensive. Still, the idea had its appeal: a warm room with a soft bed, shower, colour television and maybe even a bar downstairs, where he might meet a girl. He would just have to decide later. Anyway, if he did want to catch the train, he would have to take the eight-fifty from Redditch to get to Birmingham in time. That left three hours and fifty minutes to kill.

As he walked over the bridge and up towards the town centre in the darkening evening, Reed noticed two school-girls walking in front of him. They must have been kept in detention, he thought, or perhaps they'd just finished games practice. No doubt they had to do that, even in the rain. One looked dumpy from behind, but her friend was a dream: long wavy hair tumbling messily over her shoulders; short skirt flicking over her long, slim thighs; white socks fallen around her ankles, leaving her shapely calves bare. Reed watched the tendons at the back of her knees flex and loosen as she walked and thought of her struggling beneath him, his hands on her soft throat. They turned down a side street and Reed carried on ahead, shaking off his fantasy.

Could Francis have got lumbered with taking detention or games? he wondered. Or perhaps he had passed by without even noticing Reed sheltering from the rain. He didn't know where Francis's school was, or even what it was called. Somehow, the subject had just never come up. Also, the village where Francis lived was about eight miles away from Redditch and the local bus service was terrible. Still, he could phone. If Francis were home, he'd come out again and pick Reed up.

After phoning and getting no answer, Reed walked around town for a long time looking in shop windows and wondering about how to get out of the mess he was in. His holdall weighed heavy in his hand. Finally, he got hungry and ducked out of the light rain into the Tandoori Palace. It was still early, just after six, and the place was empty apart from a young couple absorbed in one another in a dim corner. Reed had the waiter's undivided attention. He ordered pakoras, tandoori and dhal. The food was very good and Reed ate it too fast.

After the spiced tea, he took out his wallet to pay. He had some cash, but he had decided to have a pint or two, and he might have to take a taxi home from the station. Best hang on to the paper money. The waiter didn't seem to mind taking plastic, even for so small a sum, and Reed rewarded him with a generous tip.

Next he tried Francis again, but the phone just rang and rang. Why didn't the bugger invest in an answering machine? Reed cursed. Then he realized he didn't even have one himself, hated the things. Francis no doubt felt the same way. If you were out, tough tittie; you were out and that was that.

Outside, the street lights reflected in oily puddles on the roads and pavements. After walking off his heartburn for half an hour, thoroughly soaked and out of breath, Reed ducked into the first pub he saw. The locals eyed him suspiciously at first, then ignored him and went back to their drinks.

'Pint of bitter, please,' Reed said, rubbing his hands together. 'In a sleeve glass, if you've got one.'

'Sorry, sir,' the landlord said, reaching for a mug. 'The locals bring their own.'

'Oh, very well.'

'Nasty night.'

'Yes,' said Reed. 'Very.'

'From these parts?'

'No. Just passing through.'

'Ah.' The landlord passed over a brimming pint mug, took Reed's money and went back to the conversation he'd been having with a round-faced man in a pin-stripe suit. Reed took his drink over to a table and sat down.

Over the next hour and a half he phoned Francis four more times, but still got no reply. He also changed pubs after each pint, but got very little in the way of a friendly greeting. Finally, at about twenty to nine, knowing he couldn't bear to wake up in such a miserable town even if he could afford a hotel, he went back to the station and took the train home.

•

Because of his intended visit to Francis, Reed hadn't planned anything for the weekend at home. The weather was miserable, anyway, so he spent most of his time indoors reading and watching television, or down at the local. He tried Francis's number a few more times, but still got no reply. He also phoned Camille, hoping that her warm, lithe body and her fondness for experiment might brighten up his Saturday night and Sunday morning, but all he got was her answering machine.

On Monday evening, just as he was about to go to bed after a long day catching up on boring paperwork, the phone rang. Grouchily, he picked up the receiver: 'Yes?'

'Terry?'

'Yes.'

'This is Francis.'

'Where the hell—'

'Did you come all the way down on Friday?'

'Of course I bloody well did. I thought we had an—'

'Oh God. Look, I'm sorry, mate, really I am. I tried to call. That woman at work – what's her name?'

'Elsie?'

'That's the one. She said she'd give you a message. I must admit she didn't sound as if she quite had her wits about her, but I'd no choice.'

Reed softened a little. 'What happened?'

'My mother. You know she's been ill for a long time?'

'Yes.'

'Well, she died last Wednesday. I had to rush off back to Manchester. Look, I really am sorry, but you can see I couldn't do anything about it, can't you?'

'It's me who should be sorry,' Reed said. 'To hear about your mother, I mean.'

'Yes, well, at least there'll be no more suffering for her. Maybe we could get together in a few weeks?'

'Sure. Just let me know when.'

'All right. I've still got stuff to do, you know, things to organize. How about if I call you back in a couple of weeks?'

'Great, I'll look forward to it. Bye.'

'Bye. And I'm sorry, Terry, really.'

Reed put the phone down and went to bed. So that was it – the mystery solved.

●

The following evening, just after he'd arrived home from work, Reed heard a loud knock at his door. When he opened it, he saw two strangers standing there. At first he thought they were Jehovah's Witnesses – who else came to the door in pairs, wearing suits? – but these two didn't quite look the part. True, one did look a bit like a bible salesman – chubby, with a cheerful, earnest expression on a face fringed by a neatly trimmed dark beard – but the other, painfully thin, with a long, pock-marked face, looked more like an undertaker, except for the way his sharp blue eyes glittered with intelligent suspicion.

'Mr Reed? Mr Terence J. Reed?' the cadaverous one said, in a deep, quiet voice, just like the way Reed imagined a real undertaker would speak. And wasn't there a hint of the Midlands nasal quality in the way he slurred the vowels?

'Yes, I'm Terry Reed. What is it? What do you want?' Reed could already see, over their shoulders, his neighbours spying from their windows: little corners of white net-curtain twitched aside to give a clear view.

'We're police officers, sir. Mind if we come in for a moment?' They flashed their identity cards, but put them away before Reed had time to see what was written there. He backed into the hallway and they took their opportunity to enter. As soon as they had closed the door behind them, Reed noticed the one with the beard start glancing around him, taking everything in, while the other continued to hold Reed's gaze. Finally, Reed turned and led them into the living room. He felt some kind of signal pass between them behind his back.

'Nice place you've got,' the thin one said, while the other prowled the room, picking up vases and looking inside, opening drawers an inch or two, then closing them again.

'Look, what is this?' Reed said. 'Is he supposed to be poking through my things? I mean, do you have a search warrant or something?'

'Oh, don't mind him,' the tall one said. 'He's just like that. Insatiable curiosity. By the way, my name's Bentley, Detective Superintendent Bentley. My colleague over there goes by the name of Inspector Rodmoor. We're from the Midlands Regional Crime Squad.' He looked to see Reed's reactions as he said this, but Reed tried to show no emotion at all.

'I still don't see what you want with me,' he said.

'Just routine,' said Bentley. 'Mind if I sit down?'

'Be my guest.'

Bentley sat in the rocker by the fireplace and Reed sat opposite on the sofa. A mug of half-finished coffee stood between them on the glass-topped table, beside a couple of unpaid bills and the latest *Radio Times*.

'Would you like something to drink?' Reed offered.

Bentley shook his head.

'What about him?' Reed glanced over nervously towards Inspector Rodmoor, who was looking through his bookcase, pulling out volumes that caught his fancy and flipping through them.

Bentley folded his hands on his lap: 'Just try to forget he's here.'

But Reed couldn't. He kept flicking his eyes edgily

from one to the other, always anxious about what Rodmoor was getting into next.

'Mr Reed,' Bentley went on, 'were you in Redditch on the evening of 9 November? Last Friday, that was.'

Reed put his hand to his brow, which was damp with sweat. 'Let me think now . . . Yes, yes, I believe I was.'

'Why?'

'What? Sorry . . . ?'

'I asked why. Why were you in Redditch? What was the purpose of your visit?'

He sounded like an immigration control officer at the airport, Reed thought. 'I was there to meet an old university friend,' he answered. 'I've been going down for a weekend once a year or so ever since he moved there.'

'And did you meet him?'

'As a matter of fact, no, I didn't.' Reed explained the communications breakdown with Francis.

Bentley raised an eyebrow. Rodmoor rifled through the magazine rack by the fireplace.

'But you still went there?' Bentley persisted.

'Yes. I told you, I didn't know he'd be away. Look, do you mind telling me what this is about? I think I have a right to know.'

Rodmoor fished a copy of *Mayfair* out of the magazine rack and held it up for Bentley to see. Bentley frowned and reached over for it. The cover showed a shapely blonde in skimpy pink lace panties and camisole, stockings and a suspender belt. She was on her knees on a sofa, and her round behind faced the viewer. Her face was also turned towards the camera, and she looked as if she'd just been licking her glossy red lips. The thin strap of the camisole had slipped over her upper arm.

'Nice,' Bentley said. 'Looks a bit young, though, don't you think?'

Reed shrugged. He felt embarrassed and didn't know what to say.

Bentley flipped through the rest of the magazine, pausing over the colour spreads of naked women in fetching poses.

'It's not illegal you know,' Reed burst out. 'You can buy it in any newsagent's. It's not pornography.'

'That's a matter of opinion, isn't it, sir?' said Inspector Rodmoor, taking the magazine back from his boss and replacing it.

Bentley smiled. 'Don't mind him, lad,' he said. 'He's a Methodist. Now where were we?'

Reed shook his head.

'Do you own a car?' Bentley asked.

'No.'

'Do you live here by yourself?'

'Yes.'

'Ever been married?'

'No.'

'Girlfriends?'

'Some.'

'But not to live with?'

'No.'

'Magazines enough for you, eh?'

'Now just a minute—'

'Sorry,' Bentley said, holding up his skeletal hand. 'Pretty tasteless of me, that was. Out of line.'

Why couldn't Reed quite believe the apology? He sensed very strongly that Bentley had made the remark on purpose to see how he would react. He hoped he'd passed the test. 'You were going to tell me what all this was about . . .'

'Was I? Why don't you tell me about what you did in Redditch last Friday evening first? Inspector Rodmoor will join us here by the table and take notes. No hurry. Take your time.'

And slowly, trying to remember all the details of that miserable, washed-out evening five days ago, Reed told them. At one point, Bentley asked him what he'd been wearing, and Inspector Rodmoor asked if they might have a look at his raincoat and holdall. When Reed finished, the heavy silence stretched on for seconds. What were they thinking about? he wondered. Were they trying to make up their minds about him? What was he supposed to have done?

Finally, after they had asked him to go over one or two random points, Rodmoor closed his notebook and Bentley got to his feet. 'That'll be all for now, sir.'

'For now?'

'We might want to talk to you again. Don't know. Have to check up on a few points first. We'll just take the coat and the holdall with us, if you don't mind, sir. Inspector Rodmoor will give you a receipt. Be available, will you?'

In his confusion, Reed accepted the slip of paper from Rodmoor and did nothing to stop them taking his things. 'I'm not planning on going anywhere, if that's what you mean.'

Bentley smiled. He looked like an undertaker consoling the bereaved. 'Good. Well, we'll be off then.' And they walked towards the door.

'Aren't you going to tell me what it's all about?' Reed asked again as he opened the door for them. They walked out onto the path, and it was Inspector Rodmoor who turned and frowned. 'That's the funny thing about it, sir,' he said, 'that you don't seem to know.'

'Believe me, I don't.'

Rodmoor shook his head slowly. 'Anybody would think you don't read your papers.' And they walked down the path to their Rover.

Reed stood for a few moments watching the curtains opposite twitch and wondering what on earth Rodmoor meant. Then he realized that the newspapers had been delivered as usual the past few days, so they must have been in with magazines in the rack, but he had been too disinterested, too tired, or too busy to read any of them. He often felt like that. News was, more often than not, depressing, the last thing one needed on a wet weekend in Carlisle. Quickly, he shut the door on the gawping neighbours and hurried towards the magazine rack.

He didn't have far to look. The item was on the front page of yesterday's paper, under the headline, MIDLANDS MURDER SHOCK. It read,

The quiet Midlands town of Redditch is still in shock today over the brutal slaying of schoolgirl Debbie Harrison. Debbie, 15, failed to arrive home after a late hockey practice on Friday evening. Police found her partially clad body in an abandoned warehouse close to the town centre early Saturday morning. Detective Superintendent Bentley, in charge of the investigation, told our reporter that police are pursuing some positive leads. They would particularly like to talk to anyone who was in the area of the bus station and noticed a strange man hanging around the vicinity late that afternoon. Descriptions are vague so far, but the man was wearing a light tan raincoat and carrying a blue holdall.

He read and reread the article in horror, but what was even worse than the words was the photograph that accompanied it. He couldn't be certain because it was a poor shot, but he thought it was the schoolgirl with the long wavy hair and the socks around her ankles, the one who had walked in front of him with her dumpy friend.

The most acceptable explanation of the police visit would be that they needed him as a possible witness, but the truth was that the 'strange man hanging around the vicinity' wearing 'a light tan raincoat' and carrying a 'blue holdall' was none other than himself, Terence J. Reed. But how did they know he'd been there?

•

The second time the police called Reed was at work. They marched right into the office, brazen as brass, and asked him if he could spare some time to talk to them down at the station. Bill only looked on curiously, but Frank, the boss, was hardly able to hide his irritation. Reed wasn't his favourite employee anyway; he hadn't been turning enough profit lately.

Nobody spoke during the journey, and when they got to the station one of the local policemen pointed Bentley towards a free interview room. It was a bare place: grey metal desk, ashtray, three chairs. Bentley sat opposite Reed, and Inspector Rodmoor sat in a corner, out of his line of vision.

Bentley placed the folder he'd been carrying on the desk and smiled his funeral director's smile. 'Just a few further points, Terry. Hope I don't have to keep you long.'

'So do I,' Reed said. 'Look, I don't know what's going on, but shouldn't I call my lawyer or something?'

'Oh, I don't think so. It isn't as if we've charged you or anything. You're simply helping us with our enquiries, aren't you? Besides, do you actually have a solicitor? Most people don't.'

Come to think of it, Reed didn't have one. He knew one, though. Another old university friend had gone into law and practised nearby. Reed couldn't remember what he specialized in.

'Let me lay my cards on the table, as it were,' Bentley said, spreading his hands on the desk. 'You admit you were in Redditch last Friday evening to visit your friend. We've been in touch with him, by the way, and he verifies your story. What puzzles us is what you did between, say, four and eight-thirty. A number of people saw you at various times, but there's at least an hour or more here and there that we can't account for.'

'I've already told you what I did.'

Bentley consulted the file he had set on the desk. 'You ate at roughly six o'clock, is that right?'

'About then, yes.'

'So you walked around Redditch in the rain between five and six, and between six-thirty and seven? Hardly a pleasant aesthetic experience, I'd imagine.'

'I told you, I was thinking things out. I looked in shops, got lost a couple of times . . .'

'Did you happen to get lost in the vicinity of Simmons Street?'

'I don't know the street names.'

'Of course. Not much of a street, really, more an alley. It runs by a number of disused warehouses—'

'Now wait a minute! If you're trying to tie me in to that

girl's murder, then you're way off beam. Perhaps I *had* better call a solicitor, after all.'

'Ah!' said Bentley, glancing over at Rodmoor. 'So you *do* read the papers?'

'I did. After you left. Of course I did.'

'But not before?'

'I'd have known what you were on about, then, wouldn't I? And while we're on the subject, how the hell did you find out I was in Redditch that evening?'

'You used your credit card in the Tandoori Palace,' Bentley said. 'The waiter remembered you and looked up his records.'

Reed slapped the desk. 'There! That proves it. If I'd done what you seem to be accusing me of, I'd hardly have been as daft as to leave my calling card, would I?'

Bentley shrugged. 'Criminals make mistakes, just like everybody else. Otherwise we'd never catch any. And I'm not accusing you of anything at the moment. You can see our problem, though, can't you? Your story sounds thin, very thin.'

'I can't help that. It's the truth.'

'What state would you say you were in when you went into the Tandoori Palace?'

'State?'

'Yes. Your condition.'

Reed shrugged. 'I was wet, I suppose. A bit fed up. I hadn't been able to get in touch with Francis. Hungry, too.'

'Would you say you appeared agitated?'

'Not really, no.'

'But someone who didn't know you might just assume that you were?'

'I don't know. Maybe. I was out of breath.'

'Oh? Why?'

'We'll I'd been walking around for a long time carrying my holdall. It was quite heavy.'

'Yes, of course. So you were wet and breathless when you ate in the restaurant. What about the pub you went into just after seven o'clock?'

'What about it?'

'Did you remain seated long?'

'I don't know what you mean.'

'Did you just sit and sip your drink, have a nice rest after a heavy meal and a long walk?'

'Well, I had to go the toilet, of course. And I tried phoning Francis a few more times.'

'So you were up and down, a bit like a yo-yo, eh?'

'But I had good reason! I was stranded. I desperately wanted to get in touch with my friend.'

'Yes, of course. Cast your mind back a bit earlier in the afternoon. At about twenty past three, you asked a woman what time the schools came out.'

'Yes. I . . . I couldn't remember. Francis is a teacher, so naturally I wanted to know if I was early or late. It was starting to rain.'

'But you'd visited him there before. You said so. He'd picked you up at the same place several times.'

'I know. I just couldn't remember if it was three o'clock or four. I know it sounds silly, but it's true. Don't you ever forget little things like that?'

'So you asked the woman on the bridge? That *was* you?'

'Yes. Look, I'd hardly have done that, would I, if . . . I mean . . . like with the credit card. I'd hardly have advertised my intentions if I was going to . . . you know . . .'

Bentley raised a beetle-black eyebrow. 'Going to *what*, Terry?'

Reed ran his hands through his hair and rested his elbows on the desk. 'It doesn't matter. This is absurd. I've done nothing. I'm innocent.'

'Don't you find schoolgirls attractive?' Bentley went on in a soft voice. 'After all, it would only be natural, wouldn't it? They can be real beauties at fifteen or six-teen, can't they? Proper little temptresses, some of them, I'll bet. Right prick-teasers. Just think about it – short skirts, bare legs, firm young tits. Doesn't it excite you, Terry? Don't you get hard just thinking about it?'

'No, it doesn't,' Reed said tightly. 'I'm not a pervert.'

Bentley laughed. 'Nobody's suggesting you are. It gets *me* going, I don't mind admitting. Perfectly normal, I'd say, to find a fifteen-year-old schoolgirl sexy. My Methodist inspector might not agree, but you and I know different, Terry, don't we? All that sweet innocence wrapped up in a soft, desirable young body. Doesn't it just make your blood sing? And wouldn't it be easy to get a bit carried away if she resisted, put your hands around her throat . . . ?'

'No!' Reed said again, aware of his cheeks burning.

'What about those women in the magazine, Terry? The one we found at your house?'

'That's different.'

'Don't tell me you buy it just for the stories.'

'I didn't say that. I'm normal. I like looking at naked women, just like any other man.'

'Some of them seemed very young to me.'

'For Christ's sake, they're models. They get paid for posing like that. I told you before, that magazine's freely available. There's nothing illegal about it.' Reed glanced over his shoulder at Rodmoor, who kept his head bent impassively over his notebook.

'And you like videos, too, don't you? We've had a little talk with Mr Hakim in your corner shop. He told us about one video in particular you've rented lately. Soft porn, I suppose you'd call it. Nothing illegal, true, at least not yet, but a bit dodgy. I'd wonder about a bloke who watches stuff like that.'

'It's a free country. I'm a normal single male. I have a right to watch whatever kind of videos I want.'

'*School's Out*,' Bentley said quietly. 'A bit over the top, wouldn't you say?'

'But they weren't *real* schoolgirls. The lead was thirty if she was a day. Besides, I only rented it out of curiosity. I thought it might be a bit of a laugh.'

'And was it?'

'I can't remember.'

'But you see what I mean, don't you? It looks bad: the subject-matter, the image. It all looks a bit odd. Fishy.'

'Well it's not. I'm perfectly innocent, and that's the truth.'

Bentley stood up abruptly and Rodmoor slipped out of the room. 'You can go now,' the superintendent said. 'It's been nice to have a little chat.'

'That's it?'

'For the moment, yes.'

'But don't leave town?'

Bentley laughed. 'You really must give up those American cop shows. Though it's a wonder you find time to watch them with all those naughty videos you rent. They warp your sense of reality – cop shows and sex films. Life isn't like that at all.'

'Thank you. I'll bear that in mind,' Reed said. 'I take it I *am* free to go?'

'Of course.' Bentley gestured towards the door.

Reed left. He was shaking when he got out onto the wet, chilly street. Thank God the pubs were still open. He went into the first one he came to and ordered a double Scotch. Usually he wasn't much of a spirits drinker, but these, he reminded himself as the fiery liquor warmed his belly, were unusual circumstances. He knew he should go back to work, but he couldn't face it: Bill's questions, Frank's obvious disapproval. No. He ordered another double, and after he'd finished that, he went home for the afternoon. The first thing he did when he got into the house was tear up the copy of *Mayfair* and burn the pieces in the fireplace one by one. After that, he tore up his video club membership card and burned that too. Damn Hakim!

•

'Terence J. Reed, it is my duty to arrest you for the murder of Deborah Susan Harrison . . .'

Reed couldn't believe this was happening. Not to him. The world began to shimmer and fade before his eyes, and the next thing he knew Rodmoor was bent over him offering a glass of water, a benevolent smile on his bible salesman's face.

The next few days were a nightmare. Reed was charged and held until his trial date could be set. There was no chance of bail, given the seriousness of his alleged crime. He had no money anyway, and no close family to support him. He had never felt so alone in his life as he did those long dark nights in the cell. Nothing terrible happened. None of the things he'd heard about in films and documentaries: he wasn't sodomized; nor was he forced to perform fellatio at knife point; he wasn't even beaten up. Mostly he was left alone in the dark with his fears. He felt all the certainties of his life slip away from him, almost to the point where he wasn't even sure of the truth any more: guilty or innocent? The more he proclaimed his innocence, the less people seemed to believe him. Had he done it? He might have done.

He felt like an inflatable doll, full of nothing but air, manoeuvred into awkward positions by forces he could do nothing about. He had no control over his life any more. Not only couldn't he come and go as he pleased, he couldn't even think for himself any more. Solicitors and barristers and policemen did that for him. And in the cell, in the dark, everything seemed to close in on him and some nights he had to struggle for breath.

When the trial date finally arrived, Reed felt relief. At least he could breathe in the large, airy courtroom, and soon it would be all over, one way or another.

In the crowded court, Reed sat still as stone in the dock, steadily chewing the edges of his newly grown beard. He heard the evidence against him – all circumstantial, all convincing.

If the police surgeon had found traces of semen in the victim, an expert explained, then they could have tried for a genetic match with the defendant's DNA, and that would have settled Reed's guilt or innocence once and for all. But in this case it wasn't so easy: there had been no seminal fluid found in the dead girl. The forensics people speculated, from the state of her body, that the killer had tried to rape her, found he was impotent and strangled her in his ensuing rage.

A woman called Maggie, with whom Reed had had a

brief fling a year or so ago, was brought onto the stand. The defendant had been impotent with her, it was established, on several occasions towards the end of their relationship, and he had become angry about it more than once, using more and more violent means to achieve sexual satisfaction. Once he had gone so far as to put his hands around her throat.

Well, yes he had. He'd been worried. During the time with Maggie, he had been under a lot of stress at work, drinking too much as well, and he hadn't been able to get it up. So what? Happens to everyone. And she'd wanted it like that, too, the rough way. Putting his hands around her throat had been her idea, something she'd got from a kinky book she'd read, and he'd gone along with her because she told him it might cure his impotence. Now she made the whole sordid episode sound much worse than it had been. She also admitted she had been just eighteen at the time, as well, and, as he remembered, she'd said she was twenty-three.

Besides, he had been impotent and violent only with Maggie. They could have brought on any number of other women to testify to his gentleness and virility, though no doubt if they did, he thought, his promiscuity would count just as much against him. What did he have to do to appear as normal as he needed to be, as he had once thought he was?

The witnesses for the prosecution all arose to testify against Reed like the spirits from Virgil's world of the dead. Though they were still alive, they seemed more like spirits to him: insubstantial, unreal. The woman from the bridge identified him as the shifty-looking person who had asked her what time the schools came out; the Indian waiter and the landlord of the pub told how agitated Reed had looked and acted that evening; other people had spotted him in the street, apparently following the murdered girl and her friend. Mr Hakim was there to tell the court what kind of videos Reed had rented lately – including *School's Out* – and even Bill told how his colleague used to make remarks about the schoolgirls passing by: 'You know, he'd get all excited about glimpsing a bit of black knicker when the wind blew their skirts up. It just seemed like a bit of a lark. I thought nothing of it at the time.' Then he shrugged and gave Reed a pitying look. And as if all that weren't enough, there was Maggie, a shabby Dido, refusing to look at him as she told the court of the way he had abused and abandoned her.

Towards the end of the prosecution case, even Reed's barrister was beginning to look depressed. He did his best in cross-examination, but the damnedest thing was that they were all telling the truth, or their versions of it. Yes, Mr Hakim admitted, other people had rented the same videos. Yes, he might have even watched some of them himself. But the fact remained that the man on trial was Terence J. Reed, and Reed had recently rented a video called *School's Out*, the kind of thing, ladies and gentlemen of the jury, that you wouldn't want to find your husbands or sons watching.

Reed could understand members of the victim's community appearing against him, and he could even comprehend Maggie's hurt pride. But why Hakim and Bill? What had he ever done to them? Had they never really liked him? It went on and on, a nightmare of distorted truth. Reed felt as if he had been set up in front of a funfair mirror, and all the jurors could see was his warped and twisted reflection. I'm innocent, he kept telling himself as he gripped the rail, but his knuckles turned whiter and whiter and his voice grew fainter and fainter.

Hadn't Bill joined in the remarks about schoolgirls? Wasn't it all in the spirit of fun? Yes, of course. But Bill wasn't in the dock. It was Terence J. Reed who stood accused of killing an innocent fifteen-year-old schoolgirl. *He* had been in the right place at the right time, and *he* had passed remarks on the budding breasts and milky thighs of the girls who had crossed the road in front of their office every day.

Then, the morning before the defence case was about to open – Reed himself was set to go into the dock, and not at all sure by now what the truth was – a strange thing happened.

Bentley and Rodmoor came softly into the courtroom, tiptoed up to the judge and began to whisper. Then the judge appeared to ask them questions. They nodded. Rodmoor looked in Reed's direction. After a few minutes of this, the two men took seats and the judge made a motion for the dismissal of all charges against the accused. Pandemonium broke out in court: reporters dashed for phones and the spectators' gallery buzzed with speculation. Amidst it all, Terry Reed got to his feet, realized *what* had happened, if not *how*, and promptly collapsed.

•

Nervous exhaustion, the doctor said, and not surprising after the ordeal Reed had been through. Complete rest was the only cure.

When Reed felt well enough, a few days after the trial had ended in uproar, his solicitor dropped by to tell him what had happened. Apparently, another schoolgirl had been assaulted in the same area, only this one had proved more than a match for her attacker. She had fought tooth and nail to hang onto her life, and in doing so had managed to pick up a half brick and crack the man's skull with it. He hadn't been seriously injured, but he'd been unconscious long enough for the girl to get help. When he was arrested, the man had confessed to the murder of Debbie Harrison. He had known details not revealed in the papers. After a night-long interrogation, police officers had no doubt whatsoever that he was telling the truth. Which meant Reed couldn't possibly be guilty. Hence motion for dismissal, end of trial. Reed was a free man again.

He stayed at home for three weeks, hardly venturing out of the house except for food, and even then he always went further afield for it than Hakim's. His neighbours watched him walk by, their faces pinched with disapproval, as if he were some kind of monster in their midst. He almost expected them to get up a petition to force him out of his home.

During that time he heard not one word of apology from the undertaker and the bible salesman; Francis still had 'stuff to do . . . things to organize'; and Camille's answering machine seemed permanently switched on.

At night Reed suffered claustrophobic nightmares of prison. He couldn't sleep well and even the mild sleeping pills the doctor gave him didn't really help. The bags grew heavier and darker under his eyes. Some days he wandered the city in a dream, not knowing where he was going, or, when he got there, how he had arrived.

The only thing that sustained him, the only pure, innocent, untarnished thing in his entire life, was when Debbie Harrison visited him in his dreams. She was alive then, just as she had been when he saw her for the first and only time, and he felt no desire to rob her of her innocence, only to partake of it himself. She smelled of apples in autumn and everything they saw and did together became a source of pure wonder. When she smiled, his heart almost broke with joy.

At the end of the third week, Reed trimmed his beard, got out his suit and went in to work. In the office he was met with an embarrassed silence from Bill and a redundancy cheque from Frank, who thrust it at him without a word of explanation. Reed shrugged, pocketed the cheque and left.

Every time he went into town, strangers stared at him in the street and whispered about him in pubs. Mothers held more tightly onto their daughters' hands when he passed them by in the shopping centres. He seemed to have become quite a celebrity in his home town. At first, he couldn't think why, then one day he plucked up the courage to visit the library and look up the newspapers that had been published during his trial.

What he found was total character annihilation, nothing less. When the headline about the capture of the real killer came out, it could have made no difference at all; the damage had already been done to Reed's reputation, and it was permanent. He might have been found innocent of the girl's murder, but he had been found guilty too, guilty of being a sick consumer of pornography, of being obsessed with young girls, unable to get it up without the aid of a struggle on the part of the female. None of it was true, of course, but somehow that didn't matter. It had been made so. As it is written, so let it be. And to cap it all, his photograph had appeared almost every day, both with and without the beard. There could be very few people in England who would fail to recognize him in the street.

Reed stumbled outside into the hazy afternoon. It was warming up towards spring, but the air was moist and grey with rain so fine it was closer to mist. The pubs were still open, so he dropped by the nearest one and ordered a double Scotch. The other customers looked at him suspiciously as he sat hunched in his corner, eyes bloodshot and puffy from lack of sleep, gaze directed sharply inwards.

Standing on the bridge in the misty rain an hour later, Reed couldn't remember making the actual decision to throw himself over the side, but he knew that was what he had to do. He couldn't even remember how he had ended up on this particular bridge, or the route he'd taken from the pub. He had thought, drinking his third double Scotch, that maybe he should go away and rebuild his life, perhaps abroad. But that didn't ring true as a solution. Life is what you have to live with, what you are, and now his life was what it had become, or what it had been turned into. It was what being in the wrong place at the wrong time had made it, and *that* was what he had to live with. The problem was he couldn't live with it; therefore, he had to die.

He couldn't actually see the river below – everything was grey – but he knew it was there. The River Eden, it was called. Reed laughed harshly to himself. It wasn't his fault that the river that runs through Carlisle is called the Eden, he thought; it was just one of life's little ironies.

Twenty-five to four on a wet Wednesday afternoon. Nobody about. Now was as good a time as any.

Just as he was about to climb onto the parapet, a figure emerged from the mist. It was the first girl on her

way home from school. Her grey pleated skirt swished
around her long, slim legs, and her socks hung over her
ankles. Under her green blazer, the misty rain had wet the
top of her white blouse so much that it stuck to her chest.
Reed gazed at her in awe. Her long blonde hair had darkened and curled in the rain, sticking in strands over her
cheek. There were tears in his eyes. He moved away from
the parapet.

As she neared him, she smiled shyly.

Innocence.

Reed stood before her in the mist and held his hands
out, crying like a baby.

'Hello,' he said.

MURDER IN UTOPIA

I had just finished cauterizing the stump of Ezekiel
Metcalfe's left arm, which I had had to amputate after it
was shredded in one of the combing machines, when
young Billy Ratcliffe came running in to tell me that a
man had fallen over the weir.

Believing my medical skills might be required, I left my
assistant Benjamin to take care of Ezekiel and tried to
keep up with young Billy as he led me down Victoria
Road at a breakneck pace. I was not an old man at that
time, but I fear I had led a rather sedentary life, and I was
panting by the time we passed the allotment gardens in
front of the mill. A little more slowly now, we crossed the
railway lines and the canal before arriving at the cast-iron
bridge that spanned the River Aire.

Several men had gathered on the bridge, and they were
looking down into the water, some of them pointing at a
dark shape that seemed to bob and twist in the current.
As soon as I got my first look at the scene, I knew that
none of my skills would be of any use to the poor soul,
whose coat had snagged on a tree root poking out from
the river bank.

'Did anyone see him fall?' I asked.

They all shook their heads. I picked a couple of stout
lads and led them down through the bushes to the river
bank. With a little manoeuvring, they were able to lie on
their bellies and reach over the shallow edge to grab hold

of an arm each. Slowly they raised the dripping body from the water.

When they had completed their task, a gasp arose from the crowd on the bridge. Though his white face was badly marked with cuts and bruises, there could be hardly a person present who didn't recognize Richard Ellerby, one of Sir Titus Salt's chief wool buyers.

•

Saltaire, where the events of which I am about to speak occurred in the spring of 1873, was then a 'model' village, a mill workers' Utopia of some four or five thousand souls, built by Sir Titus Salt in the valley of the River Aire between Leeds and Bradford. The village, laid out in a simple grid system, still stands, looking much the same as it did then, across the railway lines a little to the southwest of the colossal, six-storey woollen mill to which it owes its existence.

As there was no crime in Utopia, no police force was required, and we relied on constables from nearby townships in the unlikely event that any real unpleasantness or unrest should arise. There was certainly no reason to suspect foul play in Richard Ellerby's death, but legal procedures must be followed in all cases where the circumstances of death are not immediately apparent.

My name is Dr William Oulton, and I was then employed by the Saltaire hospital both as a physician and as a scientist, conducting research into the link between raw wool and anthrax. I also acted as coroner; therefore, I took it as my responsibility to enquire into the facts of Richard Ellerby's death.

In this case, I also had a personal interest, as the deceased was a close acquaintance of mine, and I had dined with him and his charming wife Caroline on a number of occasions. Richard and I both belonged to the Saltaire Institute – Sir Titus's enlightened alternative to the evils of public houses – and we often attended chamber-music concerts there together, played a game of billiards or relaxed in the smoking room, where we had on occasion discussed the possible health problems associated with importing wool. I wouldn't say I knew Richard *well* – he was, in many ways, reserved and private in my company – but I knew him to be an honest and industrious man who believed wholeheartedly in Sir Titus's vision.

My post-mortem examination the following day indicated only that Richard Ellerby had enough water in his lungs to support a verdict of death by drowning. Let me repeat: *there was no reason whatsoever to suspect foul play*. People had fallen over the weir and died in this way before. Assault and murder were crimes that rarely crossed the minds of the denizens of Utopia. That the back of Richard's skull was fractured, and that his face and body were covered with scratches and bruises, could easily be explained by the tumble he took over the weir. It was May and the thaw had created a spate of meltwater, which thundered down from its sources high in the Pennines with such force as easily to cause those injuries I witnessed on the body.

Of course, there *could* be another explanation, and that, perhaps, was why I was loath to let matters stand.

If you have imagined from my tone that I was less fully convinced of Saltaire's standing as a latterday Utopia than some of my contemporaries, then you may compliment yourself on your sensitivity to the nuances of the English language. As I look back on those days, though, I wonder if I am not allowing my present opinions to cloud the glass through which I peer at the past. Perhaps a little. I do know that I certainly believed in Sir Titus's absolute commitment to the idea, but I also think that even back then, after only thirty years on this earth, I had seen far too much of human nature to believe in Utopias like Saltaire.

Besides, I had another quality that would not permit me to let things rest: if I were a cat, believe me, I would be dead by now, nine lives notwithstanding.

•

It was another fine morning when I left Benjamin in charge of the ward rounds and stepped out of the hospital on a matter that had been occupying my mind for the past two days. The almshouses over the road made a pretty sight, set back behind their broad swathe of grass. A few pensioners sat on the benches smoking their pipes under trees bearing pink and white blossoms. Men of 'good moral character', they benefited from Sir Titus's largesse to the extent of free accommodation and a pension of seven shillings and six pence per week, but only as long as they continued to show their 'good moral character'. Charity, after all, is not for everyone, but only for those who merit it.

Lest you think I was a complete cynic at such an early age, I must admit that I found much to admire about Saltaire. Unlike the cramped, airless and filthy back-to-back slums of Bradford, where I myself had seen ten or more people sharing a dark, dank cellar that flooded every time it rained, Saltaire was designed as an open and airy environment. The streets were all paved and well drained, avoiding the filthy conditions that breed disease.

Each house had its own outdoor lavatory, which was cleared regularly, again averting the possibility of sickness caused by the sharing of such facilities. Sir Titus also insisted on special measures to reduce the output of smoke from the mill, so that we didn't live under a pall of suffocating fumes, and our pretty sandstone houses were not crusted over with a layer of grime. Still, there is a price to pay for everything, and in Saltaire it was the sense of constantly living out another man's moral vision.

I turned left on Titus Street, passing by the house with the 'spy' tower on top. This extra room was almost all windows, like the top of a lighthouse, and I had often spotted a shadowy figure up there. Rumour has it that Sir Titus employed a man with a telescope to survey the village, to look for signs of trouble and report any infringements to him. I thought I saw someone up there as I passed, but it could have been a trick of sunlight on the glass.

Several women had hung out their washing to dry across Ada Street, as usual. Though everyone knew that Sir Titus frowned on this practice – indeed, he had generously provided public wash houses in an attempt to discourage it – this was their little way of asserting their independence, of cocking a snook at authority.

As befitted a wool buyer, Richard Ellerby had lived with his wife and two children in one of the grander houses on Albert Road, facing westwards, away from the mill towards the open country. According to local practice after bereavement, the upstairs curtains were drawn.

I knocked on the door and waited. Caroline Ellerby opened it herself, wearing her widow's black, and bade me enter. She was a handsome woman, but today her skin was pale and her eyes red-rimmed from weeping.

When I was seated in her spacious living room, she asked me if I would care for a small sherry. While Sir Titus would allow no public houses in Saltaire, convinced that they encouraged vice, idleness and profligacy, he held no objection to people serving alcohol in their own homes. Indeed, he was known to keep a well-stocked wine cellar himself. On this occasion I declined, citing the earliness of the hour and the volume of work awaiting me back at the hospital.

Caroline Ellerby smoothed her voluminous black skirts and sat on the chesterfield. After I had expressed my sorrow over her loss and she had inclined her head in acceptance, I moved on to the business that had been occupying my thoughts.

'I need to ask you a few questions about Richard's accident,' I explained to her, 'only if, that is, you feel up to answering them.'

'Of course,' she said, folding her hands on her lap. 'Please continue.'

'When did you last see your husband?'

'The evening before . . . before he was discovered.'

'He was away from the house all night?'

She nodded.

'But surely you must have noticed he was missing?' I realized I was perhaps on the verge of being offensive, or even well beyond the verge, but the matter puzzled me, and when things puzzle me I worry away at them until they yield a solution. I could no more help myself than a tiger can change its stripes.

'I took a sleeping draught,' she said. 'I'm afraid I wouldn't have woken up if you'd set me down in the weaving shed.'

Given that the weaving shed contained twelve hundred

power looms, all thrumming and clattering at once, I suspected Caroline of hyperbole, but she got her point across.

'Believe me,' she went on, 'I have been tormenting myself ever since ... *If* I hadn't taken the sleeping draught. *If* I had noticed he hadn't come home. *If* I had tried to find him . . .'

'It wouldn't have helped, Caroline,' I said. 'His death must have been very swift. There was nothing you could have done. There's no use torturing yourself.'

'You're very kind, but even so . . .'

'When *did* you notice that Richard hadn't come home?'

'Not until George Walker from the office came to tell me.'

I paused before going on, uncertain how to soften my line of enquiry. 'Caroline, believe me, I don't mean to pry unnecessarily or to cause you any distress, but do you have any idea where Richard went that night?'

She seemed puzzled at my question. 'Went? Why, he went to the Travellers' Rest, of course, out on the Otley Road.'

It was my turn to be surprised. I thought I had known Richard Ellerby, but I didn't know he was a frequenter of public houses; the subject had simply never come up between us. 'The Travellers' Rest? Did he go there often?'

'Not *often*, no, but he enjoyed the atmosphere of a good tavern on occasion. According to Richard, the Travellers' Rest was a respectable establishment. I had no reason not to believe him.'

'Of course not.' I knew of the place, and had certainly heard nothing to blacken its character.

'You seem puzzled, Dr Oulton.'

'Only because your husband never mentioned it to me.'

Caroline summoned up a brief smile. 'Richard comes from humble origins, as I'm sure you know. He has worked very hard, both in Bradford and here at Saltaire, to achieve the elevated position he has attained. He is a great believer in Mr Samuel Smiles and his doctrine of self-help. Despite his personal success and advancement, though, he is not a snob. He has never lost touch with his origins. Richard enjoys the company of his fellow working men in the cheery atmosphere of a good tavern. That is all.'

I nodded. There was nothing unusual in that. I myself ventured to the Shoulder of Mutton, up on the Bingley Road, on occasion. After all, the village was not intended as a prison. It was beginning to dawn on me, though, that Richard probably assumed I was above such things as public houses because I was a member of the professional classes, or that I disapproved of them on health grounds because I was a doctor. I felt a pang of regret that we had never been able to get together over a pipe and a pint of ale. Now that he was dead, we never would.

'Did he ever overindulge?' I went on. 'I ask only because I'm searching for a reason for what happened. If Richard had, perhaps, had too much to drink that night and missed his footing . . .?'

Caroline pursed her lips and frowned, deep in thought for a moment. 'I'll not say he's *never* had a few too many,' she admitted, 'but I *can* say that he was not in the habit of overindulging.'

'And there was nothing on his mind, nothing that might tempt him to have more than his share that night?'

'There were many things on Richard's mind, especially

as regarded his work, but nothing unusual, nothing that would drive him to drink, of that I can assure you.' She paused. 'Dr Oulton, is there anything else? I'm afraid I'm very tired. Even with the sleeping draught . . . the past couple of nights . . . I'm sure you can understand. I've had to send the children to mother's. I just can't handle them at the moment.'

I got to my feet. 'Of course. You've been a great help already. Just one small thing?'

She tilted her head. 'Yes?'

'Did Richard have any enemies?'

'Enemies? No. Not that I know of. Surely you can't be suggesting someone did this to him?'

'I don't know, Caroline. I just don't know. That's the problem. Please, stay where you are. I'll see myself out.'

As I walked back to the hospital, I realized that *was* the problem: I *didn't know*. I also found myself wondering what on earth Richard was doing by the weir if he was coming home from the Travellers' Rest. The canal tow-path would certainly be an ideal route to the tavern and back, but the river was north of the canal, and Richard Ellerby's house was south.

•

On my way to the Travellers' Rest that evening, I considered the theory that Richard might have attracted the attention of a villain, or a group of villains, who had subsequently followed him, robbed him and tossed his body over the weir. The only problem with my theory, as far as I could see, was that he still had several gold sovereigns in his pocket, and no self-respecting thieves would have overlooked a haul that big.

As it turned out, the Travellers' Rest was as respectable

a tavern as Richard had told his wife, and as cheery a one as I could have hoped for after my gloomy thoughts. It certainly didn't seem to be a haunt of cutpurses and ruffians. On the contrary, the gas-lit public bar was full of warm laughter and conversation, and I recognized several groups of mill workers, many of whom I had treated for one minor ailment or another. Some of them looked up, surprised to see me there, and muttered sheepish hellos. Others were brash and greeted me more loudly, taking my presence as an endorsement of their own indulgence. Jack Liversedge was there, sitting alone in a corner nursing his drink. My heart went out to him; poor Jack had been severely depressed ever since he lost his wife to anthrax two months before, and there seemed nothing anyone could do to console him. He didn't even look up when I entered.

I made my way to the bar and engaged the landlord's attention. He was a plump man with a veined red nose, rather like a radish, which seemed to me to indicate that he was perhaps a whit too fond of his own product. He nodded a crisp greeting, and I asked for a pint of ale. When I had been served, noticing a slight lull in business, I introduced myself and asked him if he remembered Richard Ellerby's last visit. Once I had described my late colleague, he said that he did.

'Proper gentleman, Mr Ellerby was, sir. I were right sorry to hear about what happened.'

'I was wondering if anything unusual happened that evening.'

'Unusual?'

'Did he drink too much?'

'No, sir. Two or three ales. That's his limit.'

'So he wasn't drunk when he left here, unsteady in his gait?'

'No, sir. Excuse me a moment.' He went to serve another customer then came back. 'No, sir, I can't say as I've ever seen Mr Ellerby inebriated.'

'Were there any rough elements in here that night?'

He shook his head. 'Any rough elements I send packing, up to the Feathers on the Leeds Road. That's a proper rough sort of place, that is. But this is a respectable establishment.' He leaned forward across the bar. 'I'll tell thee summat for nowt, if Mr Salt won't have public houses in his village, there's no better place for his workers to pass an hour or two than the Travellers' Rest, and that's God's honest truth.'

'I'm sure you're right,' I said, 'but surely things must get a little out of hand on occasion?'

He laughed. 'Nothing I can't handle.'

'And you're sure nothing strange happened the last night Mr Ellerby was here?'

'You'd be better off asking him over there about that.' He nodded towards Jack Liversedge, who seemed engaged in a muttered dispute with himself. 'I've as much pity as the next man for a fellow who's lost his wife, poor beggar, but the way he's carrying on . . .' He shook his head.

'What happened?'

'They got into a bit of a barney.'

'What about?'

He shrugged. 'I heard Mr Liversedge call Mr Ellerby no better than a murderer, then he finished his drink and walked out.'

'How much longer before Mr Ellerby left?'

'Five minutes, mebbe. Not long.'

I mulled this over as he excused himself to serve more customers. Jack Liversedge's wife, Florence, a wool sorter, had died of anthrax two months ago. It is a terrible disease, and one we were only slowly coming to understand. Through my own research, I had been in correspondence with two important scientists working in the field: M. Casimir-Joseph Davaine, in France, and Herr Robert Koch, in Germany. Thus far we had been able to determine that the disease is caused by living microorganisms, most likely hiding in the alpaca wool of the South American llamas and the mohair of the Angora goats, both of which Sir Titus imported to make his fine cloths, but we were a long way from finding a prevention or a cure.

As I sipped my ale and looked at Jack Liversedge, I began to wonder. Richard Ellerby was a wool buyer. Had Jack, in his distraught and confused state, considered him culpable of Florence's death? Certainly from what I had seen and heard of Jack's erratic behaviour since her death, it was possible, and he was a big, strong fellow.

I was just about to go over to him, without having any clear plan in mind of what to say, when he seemed to come to a pause in his argument with himself, slammed his tankard down and left, bumping into several people on his way out. I decided to go after him.

•

I followed Jack down the stone steps to the towpath and called out his name, at which he turned and asked who I was. I introduced myself.

'Ah,' he said, ''tis thee, Doctor.'

The towpath was unlit, but the canal was straight, and

the light of a three-quarter moon lay on the still water like a shroud. It was enough to enable us to see our way.

'I saw you in the Travellers' Rest,' I said. 'You seemed upset. I thought we might share the walk home, if that's all right?'

'As you will.'

We walked in silence, all the while growing closer to the mill, which rose ahead in the silvery light, a ghostly block of sandstone against the black, starlit sky. I didn't know how to broach the subject that was on my mind, fearing that if I were right, Jack would put up a fight, and if I were wrong he would be justly offended. Finally, I decided to muddle along as best I could.

'I hear Richard Ellerby was in the Travellers' the other night, Jack.'

'Is that so?'

'Yes. I hear you argued with him.'

'Mebbe I did.'

'What was it about, Jack? Did you get into a fight with him?'

Jack paused on the path to face me, and for a moment I thought he was going to come at me. I braced myself, but nothing happened. The mill loomed over his shoulder. I could see a number of emotions cross his features in the moonlight, from fear and sorrow to, finally, resignation. He seemed somehow *relieved* that I had asked him about Richard.

'He were the wool buyer, weren't he?' he said, with gritted anger in his voice. 'He should've known.'

I sighed. 'Oh, Jack. Nobody could have known. He just buys the wool. There are no tests. There's no way of *knowing*.'

'It's not right. He bought the wool that killed her. Someone had to pay.'

He turned his back to me and walked on. I followed. We got to the bottom of Victoria Road, and I could hear the weir roaring to our right. Jack walked to the cast-iron bridge, where he stood gazing into the rushing water. I went and stood beside him. 'And whose place is it to decide who pays, Jack?' I asked, raising my voice over the water's roar. 'Whose job do you think it is to play God? Yours?'

He looked at me with pity and contempt, then shook his head and said, 'You don't understand.'

I looked down into the water, its foam tipped with moonlight. 'Did you kill him?' I asked. 'Did you kill Richard Ellerby because you blamed him for Florence's death?'

He said nothing for a moment, then gave a brief, jerky nod. 'There he were,' he said, 'standing there in his finest coat, drinking and laughing, while my Florence were rotting in her grave.'

'How did it happen?'

'I told him he were no better than a murderer, buying up wool that kills people. I mean, it weren't the first time, were it? He said it weren't his fault, that nobody could've known. Then, when I told him he should take more care, he said I didn't understand, that it were just a hazard of the job, like, and that she should've known she were taking a risk before she took it on.'

If Richard really *had* spoken that way to Jack, then he had certainly been guilty of exhibiting a gross insensitivity I had not suspected to be part of his character. Even if that was the case, we are all capable of saying the wrong thing at the wrong time, especially if we are pushed as far as Jack probably pushed Richard. What he had done had certainly not justified his murder.

'*How* did it happen, Jack?' I asked him.

After a short pause, he said, 'I waited for him on the towpath. All the way home we argued and in the end I lost my temper. There were a long bit of wood from a packing crate or summat by the bushes. He turned his back on me and started walking away. I picked it up and clouted him and down he went.'

'But why the weir?'

'I realized what I'd done.' He gave a harsh laugh. 'It's funny, you know, especially now it doesn't matter. But back then, when I'd just done it, when I knew I'd *killed* a man, I panicked. I thought if I threw his body over the weir then people would think he'd fallen. It weren't far, and he weren't a heavy man.'

'He wasn't dead, Jack,' I said. 'He had water in his lungs. That meant he was alive when he went into the water.'

'It's no matter,' said Jack. 'One way or another, it was me who killed him.'

The water roared in my ears. Jack turned towards me. I flinched and stepped back again, thrusting my arm out to keep him at a distance.

He shook his head slowly, tears in his eyes, and spoke so softly I had to strain to hear him. 'Nay, Doctor, you've nowt to fear from me. It's me who's got summat to fear from you.'

I shook my head. I really didn't know what to do, and my heart was still beating fast from the fear that he had been going to tip me over the railing.

'Well,' he said, 'all I ask is that you leave it till

morning. One more night in the house me and Florence shared. Will you do that for me, at least, Doctor?'

As I nodded numbly, he turned and began to walk away.

•

Early the following morning, after a miserable night spent tossing and turning, grappling with my conscience, I was summoned from the hospital to the works office building, attached to the west side of the mill. I hurried down Victoria Road, wondering what on earth it could be about, and soon found myself ushered into a large, well-appointed office with a thick Turkish carpet, dark wainscoting and a number of local landscapes hanging on the walls. Sitting behind the huge mahogany desk was Sir Titus himself, still a grand, imposing figure despite his years and his declining health.

'Dr Oulton,' he said, without looking up from his papers. 'Please sit down.'

I wondered what had brought him the twelve miles or so from Crows Nest, where he lived. He rarely appeared at the mill in those days.

'I understand,' he said in his deep, commanding voice, still not looking at me, 'that you have been enquiring into the circumstances surrounding Richard Ellerby's death?'

I nodded. 'Yes, Sir Titus.'

'And what, pray, have you discovered?'

I took a deep breath, then told him everything. As I spoke, he stood up, clasped his hands behind his back and paced the room, head hanging so that his grey beard almost reached his waist. Though his cheeks and eyes looked sunken, as if he was ill, his presence dominated the room. When I had finished, he sat down again and treated me to a long silence before he said, 'And what are we going to do about it?'

'The police will have to be notified.'

'As yet, then, you and I are the only ones who know the full truth?'

'And Jack himself.'

'Yes, of course.' Sir Titus stroked his beard. I could hear the muffled noise of the mill and feel the vibrations of the power looms shaking the office. It was a warm day, and despite the open window the room was stuffy. I felt the sweat gather on my brow and upper lip. I gazed out of the window and saw the weir, where Richard Ellerby had met his death. 'This is not good,' Sir Titus said finally. 'Not good at all.'

'Sir?'

He gestured with his arm to take in the whole of Saltaire. 'What I mean, Dr Oulton, is that this could be very bad for the village. Very bad. Do you have faith in the experiment?'

'The experiment, sir?'

'The moral experiment that is Saltaire.'

'I have never doubted your motive in wanting to do good, sir.'

Sir Titus managed a thin smile. 'A very revealing answer.' Another long silence followed. He got up and started pacing again. 'If a man visits a public house and becomes so intoxicated that he falls in a river and drowns, then that is an exemplary tale for all of us, wouldn't you say?'

'I would, sir.'

'And if a man, after visiting a public house, is followed by a group of ruffians who attack him, rob him and throw him in a river to drown, then again we have an exemplary – nay, a *cautionary* – tale, do we not?'

'We do, sir. But Richard Ellerby wasn't robbed.'

He waved his hand impatiently. 'Yes, yes, of course. I know that. I'm merely thinking out loud. Please forgive an old man his indulgence. This place – Saltaire – means the world to me, Dr Oulton. Can you understand that? The *world.*'

'I think I can, sir.'

'It's not just a matter of profits, though I'll not deny it's profitable enough. But I think I have created something unique. I call it my "experiment", of course, yet for others it is a home, a way of life. At least I hope it is. It was my aim to make Saltaire everything Bradford was not. It was designed to nurture self-improvement, decency, orderly behaviour and good health among my workers. I wanted to prove that making my own fortune was not incompatible with the material and spiritual wellbeing of the working classes. I saw it as my duty, my God-given duty. If the Lord looks so favourably upon me, then I take that as an obligation to look favourably upon my workers. Do you follow me?'

'Yes, sir.'

'And now this. Murder. Manslaughter. Call it what you will. It disrupts the fabric of things. It could destroy any trust that might have built up in the community. No doubt you remember the troubles we had over anthrax some years ago?'

'I do, sir.' In 1868 a man called Sutcliffe Rhodes had garnered much support from the village in his campaign against anthrax, and Sir Titus had been seriously embarrassed by the whole matter. 'But surely you can't expect me to ignore what I know, sir?' I said. 'To lie.'

Sir Titus smiled grimly. 'I could never ask a man to go against his beliefs, Doctor. All I ask is that you follow the dictates of your own conscience, but that you please bear in mind the consequences. If this issue surfaces again, especially in this way, then we're done for. Nobody will *believe* in the goodness of Saltaire any more, and I meant it to be a *good* place, a place where there would never be any reason for murder to occur.'

He shook his head in sadness and let the silence stretch again. Above the noise of the mill I suddenly heard men shouting. Someone hammered on the door and dashed into the office without ceremony. I couldn't be certain, but my first impression was that it was the same shadowy figure I had seen in the 'spy' tower.

'Sir Titus,' the interloper said, after a quick bow, 'my apologies for barging in like this, but you must come. There's a man on the mill roof.'

Sir Titus and I frowned at one another, then we followed him outside. I walked slowly, in deference to Sir Titus's age, and it took us several minutes to get around to the allotment gardens, from where we had a clear view.

The man stood atop the mill roof, full six storeys up, between its two decorative lanterns. I could also make out another figure inside one of the lanterns, perhaps talking to him. But the man on the roof didn't appear to be listening. He stood right at the edge and, even as we watched, he spread out his arms as if attempting to fly, then he sprang off the roof and seemed to hover in the air for a moment before falling with a thud to the forecourt.

It was a curious sensation. Though I knew in my heart and mind that I was witnessing the death of a fellow human being, there was a distant quality about the event. The figure was dwarfed by the mill, for a start, and just in front of us, a dog scratched at the dirt, as if digging for its bone, and it didn't cease during the man's entire fall to earth.

A mill hand came running up and told us that the man who had jumped was Jack Liversedge. Again it was an eerie feeling, but I suppose, in a way, I already knew that.

'An accident and a suicide,' muttered Sir Titus, fixing me with his deep-set eyes. 'It's bad enough, but we can weather it, wouldn't you say, Doctor?' There was hope in his voice.

My jaw tensed. I was tempted to tell him to go to hell, that his vision, his *experiment*, wasn't worth lying for. But I saw in front of me a sick old man who had at least tried to do *something* for the people who made him rich. Whether it was enough or not was not for me to say. Saltaire wasn't perfect – perfection is a state we will never find on this earth – but it was better than most mill towns.

Swallowing my bile, I gave Sir Titus a curt nod and set off back up Victoria Road to the hospital.

•

In the days and weeks that followed, I tried to continue with my work – after all, the people of Saltaire still needed a hospital and a doctor – but after Jack Liversedge's pointless death, my heart just didn't seem to be in it any more. Jack's dramatic suicide lowered the morale of the town for a short while – there were long faces everywhere and some mutterings of dissent – but eventually it was forgotten, and the townspeople threw themselves back into their work: weaving fine cloths of alpaca and mohair for those wealthy enough to be able to afford them.

Still, no matter how much I tried to convince myself to put the matter behind me and carry on, I felt there was something missing from the community; something more than a mere man had died the day Jack killed himself.

One day, after I had spent a wearying few hours tending to one of the wool sorters dying of anthrax, I made my decision to leave. A month later, after sorting out my affairs and helping my replacement settle in, I left Saltaire for South Africa, where I eventually met the woman who was to become my wife. We raised our three children, and I practised my profession in Cape Town for thirty years. After my retirement, we decided to move back to England, where we settled comfortably in a small Cornish fishing village. Now, my children are grown up, married and gone away, my wife is dead and I am an old man who spends his days wandering the cliffs above the sea watching the birds soar and dip.

And sometimes the sound of the waves reminds me of the roar of the Saltaire weir.

More than forty years have now passed since that night by the weir, when Jack Liversedge told me he had killed Richard Ellerby; more than forty years have passed since Sir Titus and I stood by the allotments and saw Jack's body fall and break on the forecourt of the mill.

Forty years. Long enough to keep a secret.

Besides, the world has changed so much since then that what happened that day long ago in Saltaire seems of little consequence now. Sir Titus died three years after Jack's fall, and his dream died with him. Fashions changed, and the ladies no longer wanted the bright, radiant fabrics that Sir Titus had produced. His son, Titus junior, struggled with the business until he, too, died in 1887, and the mill was taken over by a consortium of

Bradford businessmen. Today, Saltaire is no longer a moral experiment or a mill workers' Utopia; it is merely another business.

And today, in July 1916, nobody believes in Utopias any more.

NOT SAFE AFTER DARK

He had only gone out to the convenience store for cigarettes, but the park across the intersection looked inviting. It seemed to offer a brief escape from the heat and dirt and noise of the city. Cars whooshed by, radios blasting rock and funk and rap into the hot summer night. Street lights and coloured neons looked smeared and blurry in the humid heat. A walk among the trees by the lake might cool him down a little.

He knew he shouldn't, knew it was dangerous. What was it the guidebooks always said about big city parks? *Not safe after dark.* That was it. No matter which park they talked about – Central Park, Golden Gate Park – they were always *not safe after dark.*

He wondered why. Parks were quiet, peaceful places, a few acres of unspoilt nature in the heart of the city. People took their dogs for walks; children played on swings and teeter-totters. Parks provided retreats for meditation and the contemplation of nature, surely, not playgrounds for the corrupt and the delinquent.

There was more danger, he thought, among the dregs of humanity that haunted the vast urban sex and drug supermarkets like Times Square or the Tenderloin. There you got mugged, beaten up, raped, even murdered, for no good reason at all.

Hoodlums and thugs weren't into nature; they were happier idling on street corners harassing passers-by, starting fights in strip clubs or rock bars, and selling drugs in garbage-strewn alleys. If they wanted to mug someone, they had more chance downtown, where the crowds were thick and some fool always took a short cut down a dark alley. If they just wanted to scare and hurt people for the fun of it, crowded places like shopping malls guaranteed them both the victims and the audience.

Or so he found himself reasoning as he stood there by the traffic lights. Should he risk it? Over the road, the dark, tangled mass of branches tossed in the hot breeze like billowing black smoke against the starlit sky. A yellowish full moon, surrounded by a halo, gilded the tree tops. The traffic lights changed to green, and after only a moment's hesitation, he began to cross. Why not? What could possibly happen? The entrance, a long, tree-lined avenue, seemed rolled out like a tongue ready to lick him up and draw him into the park's dark mouth. Maybe he had a death wish, though he didn't think so.

Muted wrought-iron street lamps flanked the broad cinder path, which led under a small imitation Arc de Triomphe gate overgrown with weeds and lichen. Beyond that, the branches swayed slowly in the muggy gusts, leaves making a wet, hissing sound. The dimly lit path, he noticed, was lined with statues. He went over to see if he could make out any of the names. Writers: Shakespeare, Sir Walter Scott, Tennyson, Wordsworth. What on earth were they doing there?

The avenue ended at a small boating pool. In the water, a child's yacht with a white sail turned in slow circles. The sight brought a lump to his throat. He didn't know why, but somewhere, perhaps buried deep in his memories, was just such a feeling of loss or of drifting aimlessly in circles, never arriving. It made him feel suddenly, inexplicably sad.

Beyond the pond the park stretched, rising and falling down to the lake. Here were no broad avenues, only tarmac paths and dirt trails. He took one of the main paths that wound deeper into the woods. He could always take a side path later if he wanted. So far he had seen no one, and the traffic from the main road sounded more and more distant behind him. It was much darker now, away from the dim antique lights of the entrance. Only the jaundiced and haze-shrouded moon shone through the trees and slicked the path with oily gold. But as he walked, he found his eyes soon adjusted. At least he could make out shapes, if not details.

After he had been walking a few minutes, he noticed a playground to his left. There was nobody in it at this time of night, but one of the swings was rocking back and forth gently in the wind, creaking where its chains needed greasing. He felt like sitting on one of the wooden seats and shooting himself high, aiming his feet at the moon. But it would only draw unwelcome attention. Just being here was supposed to be dangerous enough, without asking for trouble. Somewhere, back on the road, he heard the whine of a police siren.

Off to the right, a path wound up the hillside between the trees. He took it. It was some kind of fitness trail. Every so often, he could make out wooden chin bars where the joggers were encouraged to pause and do a few pull-ups. Occasionally, he would hear a scuttling sound in the undergrowth. At first, it scared him, but he figured it was only a harmless squirrel, or a chipmunk running away.

The path straightened out at the top of the short hill,

and almost before he knew it he was in a clearing surrounded by trees. He thought he heard a different sound now, a low moan or a sigh. He pulled back quickly behind a tree. In the clearing stood a number of picnic benches, and at one of them he could just make out a couple of human figures. It took him a few seconds to focus clearly in the poor light, but when he realized what was happening, his throat constricted and his heart seemed to start thumping so loudly he was sure they could hear him.

There were two of them. One half-sat on the table edge, hands stretched behind, supporting himself as he arched backwards. The other knelt at his feet, head bowed forward. They seemed to freeze for a moment, as if they had heard him, then the one on the table said something he couldn't quite catch and the one on his knees continued slowly moving his head forward and back.

He felt sick and dizzy. He clutched onto the tree tightly and tried to control the swimming feeling in his head. He couldn't afford to faint – not here, not now, with those two so close. After a few deep breaths, he turned as quietly as he could and hurried down a dirt track that forked off in another direction.

After he had covered a good distance as fast as he dare go, he squatted in the ferns at the side of the trail, head in hands, and waited for his heart to still and his breathing to become regular. An insect crawled up his bare arm; he shuddered and brushed it off.

He was beginning to feel really scared now. He had no idea where he was, which direction he was travelling in. Like that yacht back in the pond a million miles away, he could be going in circles. Again he fought back the panic and walked on. Now he cursed his stupidity. Why had he come here? It hadn't been a good idea at all. He would wander round and round, then end up back where he started. He would collapse with exhaustion and those two men from the picnic table would find him and . . . Maybe he did have a death wish, after all. He should have taken notice of the guidebooks. He told himself to stop panicking and calm down.

Before he had got much further, he heard voices just off the path over to his left. He paused. Someone was singing an old Neil Young song. Someone else said 'Shut up,' then a girl giggled. After that came more singing, then a loud yell. They were drunk; that was it. As if to confirm his suspicions, he heard the sound of a bottle smashing on a road. He decided he had better lie low and keep out of their way. There was no telling what a gang of drunks might do to someone walking alone in the park. So he waited, behind a tree, as their voices faded slowly into the distance. He stayed where he was until he could hear them no longer, then set off again.

When he crested the next hill, he could see the lights of houses to his right and left. The park had narrowed to a kind of deep ravine now, and the path he was on ran parallel to its bottom, about halfway up one side. If he left the path and walked all the way up the side, he would probably soon find himself in someone's back garden.

He could see the moonlight gleaming on the surface of the narrow stream that flowed along the bottom. Across the other side, he could make out the lights of a police car flashing along a road that skirted the ravine's edge. The hillside was thickly wooded and the spaces between trees filled with ferns and shrubbery. At least now, he thought, he ought to be able to find his way back to civilization easily enough.

He heard a noise lower down the hillside and realized there was another path, running parallel to his, about fifty yards below, closer to the water. Again, he froze. This sound was far too loud to be a squirrel or a bird; it certainly wasn't the sound of a small animal running away, but more like a large one coming *towards* him.

He crouched by the edge of the dirt path and peered down through the bushes. He couldn't make much out at first, but something was moving through the undergrowth. A few moments later, his heart beating fast again, he saw the eyes, not more than thirty yards away down the slope. What was it? A fox? A wolf? Then he heard the woman's voice: 'Jason! Jason! Where are you, boy? Come on.' And she whistled. So it was a dog! But Jason took no notice of her. It seemed to have caught his scent and was making its way cautiously up the hillside to check him out.

He couldn't tell from that distance in the dark, but he was worried that it might be a pit bull or a Rottweiler. Surely no woman would go walking alone in the park at night without a vicious dog to guard her? He felt beside him on the path and his hand grasped a large stone, just small enough to hold. The dog came closer. 'Come on, Jason,' he whispered. 'Come on, boy!' The dog barked and made the last few yards in a dash. He swung the rock hard at its head, and the dog whimpered, then let out a low wail and collapsed.

'Jason?' the woman called from below. 'Jason! Where are you?' She sounded worried now. He could just about make her out in the faint light. She looked youngish, with long hair tied behind her neck in a ponytail, and she was wearing shorts and a T-shirt. She called for the dog again, then left the path and started climbing the hill through the shrubbery to the place she'd heard it wail.

Thirty yards. Twenty-five. Twenty. He could see the moonlight glint on her bracelet. Fifteen. He could hear her panting with effort. Ten. She ran the back of her hand over her brow and pushed back a stray tress of hair. 'Jason?' Five. He glanced around and listened. Nothing. So close to civilization, yet so far. There was nobody around but him and her.

Four. He held his breath. Three yards. She slipped back but managed to grasp a root and keep her balance. Two. He gripped the rock tight in his hand and felt it sticky and warm with the dog's blood. She was almost there now. Just a few more steps. One. He gripped the rock tighter, raising his arm. Suddenly he felt himself filled with strange joy and he knew he was grinning like an idiot. So this was why he had come. He didn't have a death wish, after all. What on earth had those fools who wrote the guidebooks meant? Of course it was safe after dark. Perfectly safe.

JUST MY LUCK

Los Angeles was the last place Walter Dimchuk would have chosen for the convention. A confirmed Torontonian, Walter had never been able to take California seriously. It seemed to him that the people there merely played at life under the palm trees and came up with loony-tune ideas.

Take the cuisine, if you could call it that: it was either Mexican, which gave Walter the runs, or so-called 'Californian': watercress, alfalfa sprouts and avocado with everything, even a burger. Faggot food, more like. He'd had a house salad just yesterday in which he hadn't recognized one single ingredient. Cilantro, arugula, fresh basil, sun-dried tomatoes and goat's cheese, the waiter had told him. With a dressing of tarragon, balsamic vinegar, cardamom oil and toasted pine nuts, for Christ's sake. Just his luck. Couldn't a person get a simple grilled cheese sandwich and a glass of milk in this state?

Smog, killer freeways, serial-killer bubblegum cards, earthquakes, Rodney King riots, more fruit loops per square mile than an asylum . . . the list went on. He hadn't been happy about leaving Kate and Maria alone in the house either. They might not be as close a family as they had once been – what could you expect after thirty-five years of marriage and three children grown up to adults – but they still got on all right, mostly thanks to

Maria, a late blessing when Kate was forty-five, and now a gawky thirteen-year-old.

The only good thing about the trip that Walter had been able to come up with on the plane over (Air Canada, three hours late, sweet Jesus, just Walter's fucking luck) was a brief respite from a cool Toronto October.

But he hadn't banked on the Santa Ana. When Toronto got hot, you sweated; here you dried to dust, dehydrated in seconds. He had once read a story about the hot, desert wind, the way it made meek wives feel the edge of the carving knife and study their husbands' necks. The writer was right: it *did* make you edgy and crazy. Walter felt as if he'd had a steel band around his forehead for two days. It was getting tighter.

'Wally!'

Walter came out of his reverie. He was sitting in the hotel lobby taking a smoke break between sessions. Nobody seemed to smoke these days. In California it was hardly surprising: you couldn't find many places where it was legal to do so. Damn government health warnings on everything now, even the wine. And he had seen the way the young hotshots with their white teeth turned up their noses when he lit up, even if they were sitting in a goddamn bar. Christ, who was this coming towards him, hand outstretched, teeth bared in a predatory smile? Should he remember? Awkwardly, he got to his feet.

'Hi, good to see you,' he said.

'Good to see *you*!' the stranger said. 'It's been years.'

'Yeah.' Walter scratched the side of his right eye and frowned. 'Now where the hell was it . . . ?'

'Baltimore. Baltimore, 'seventy-nine. Jimmy Lavalli. Remember, we closed down that bar together?'

'Yeah, of course. How you doing, Jimmy?'

And so it went on, the empty greetings, inane conversations, tales of triple bypasses, and all the time Walter knew, deep inside, that they were all out to get him, were all laughing at him. 'Oh, old Wally Woodchuk, Wally Dump-truck, Wally Up-chuck, fucking dinosaur, sales have been down for years.' No one had said it to his face, but they didn't need to. Wally knew. At fifty-nine, he was too old for the pool supplies business. And it was obvious from the number of tanned young men around the convention that the company thought so too. You'd almost think the new breed were chosen because they'd look good sitting around a swimming pool, like the way auto manufacturers used curvaceous women to sell cars. Wally's curves were in all the wrong places. Ungrateful bastards. He'd given his life to Hudson's Pools and Supplies, and this was how they paid him back. He felt like that salesman in the play must have done, the one that guy who'd been married to Marilyn Monroe – not the baseball player, one of the others – had written for Dustin Hoffman.

He had heard the talk around the office, noticed the muted conversations and insincere greetings as he passed couples chatting in the corridor. They were putting him out to pasture. That was why they sent him to California. He wouldn't be surprised if his office – if you could call a screened-off corner in an open plan an office – was cleaned out when he got back and someone else was sitting there in his place. Some tanned young asshole with white teeth and a wolfish smile. Maybe called Scott.

He got rid of Jimmy with promises to look him up if he was ever in Baltimore (not if he could help it!) and looked at his watch. Five o'clock. Shit. Time for another boring session, then up to get changed for the convention banquet. Tofu burgers again, most likely. Maybe grab a few minutes in between and call Kate . . .

●

Thank God that was over with, Walter thought, as he waved goodnight to the stragglers in the Pasadena Ballroom and headed for the elevator. What a fucking ordeal. And typical California, too – no smoking, not *any-where* in the dining hall. Not tofu burgers, but almost as bad: Cornish game hen or some such skinny little bird stuffed with grapes and olives and jalapeño peppers, basted in lemon, garlic and the ubiquitous cilantro, of course. And they had to put him at the table with that loud-mouthed jerk Carson, from United. Just his luck. Still, Walter had kept his end up. He had been nice to the right people, managed a smile, passed his company card around, even if the recipients did absently slip it into their side pockets where they'd throw it out with the lint and the hotel matches.

A funny business these conventions, he thought as he went into his room. Hours of manic glad-handing, hurried conversations in lobbies and men's rooms, talking business even with your dick in your hand, then when you finally got to be alone at the end of the night, all you felt was an incredible loneliness descend. At least Walter did.

So there you are in your strange hotel room alone miles from home after the party. Oh, the guys were setting up all-night poker sessions, planning trips to strip joints and bars, but Walter had had enough of all that, and of his colleagues. He wanted to *be* alone, but he didn't want to *feel* alone.

It was the wind, he thought, that goddamn Santa Ana.

And the air-conditioner had quit. Just his luck. He lay down on the bed with his hands behind his head and tried to relax. He couldn't. He hadn't drunk much. That was one thing he had under control these days. That was why he couldn't for the life of him remember closing any bar with Jimmy Lavalli in Baltimore. If those tanned bastards knew what they looked like after they'd had a few too many . . . anyway, those days were past. As he lay there restless in the heat, feeling the band tighten around his head, the heartburn start to kick in, the resentment and fear churn inside him, he became aware of one feeling he would never have expected. God dammit, Walter Dimchuk was horny!

Not that it had never happened before, of course, but never with such a keen, urgent edge, not for a long time. He remembered the outing he'd had with Al and Larry yesterday afternoon. Given a couple of spare hours, they had driven to Santa Monica, walked on the pier, the boardwalk towards Venice. And now as he lay trying to find sleep, all Walter could find were the disturbing images of those girls in their bikinis, all that smooth, firm, tanned flesh.

He turned over. This was ridiculous. His lust felt so strong it was gripping his heart, making him squirm. The images churned in his mind, spurring him on. It was the damn heat, he knew it. Maybe if he could get out for a while. Tell someone at the desk to fix his air-conditioning while he took a little drive around town.

He sat up and slid his shoes back on. Yeah, that was the thing to do. Maybe drive to the ocean and cool off a little. That or a cold shower. He looked at his watch. Still only eleven o'clock. OK, car keys, jacket . . .

•

Such romantic-sounding street names they had: La Cienega, Sepulveda, La Brea. But they weren't so fucking romantic when you were on them; they were either freeways or roads running past shitty little Spanish-style stucco houses with graffiti all over the stucco and postage-stamp gardens full of junk.

It was cool in the rental, but Walter still couldn't shake the horniness. He'd pass a row of stores set back from the road and see a gang of kids there, girls in cut-off jeans and halter tops drinking Coke from the bottle, breasts jutting out. It was getting worse, as if the Santa Ana somehow slipped in through the air-conditioning and messed with his brain.

He found himself on Hollywood Boulevard. Walter loved old movies, the black and white kind, and the real stars they had back then like Cary Grant, Garbo, Bogie, Gable, Jimmy Stewart. Christ, he must have seen *It's a Wonderful Life* about twenty times, and then they went and colourized the motherfucker. But the boulevard, with all those stars in the sidewalk, had gone to porn theatres, dirty bookstores with barred windows, hookers, pimps, muggers, losers.

He was stopped at a red light when he heard the tap on his window. If it had been a man, he would have burnt rubber driving away, even through a stop light. It wasn't. Nervously, he rolled down the window.

'Wann' good time, mister? Wann' have some fun?'

He looked at her. She must have been all of sixteen, going on forty, but she was pretty, a Latino with that honey skin and lustrous black hair. From what he could see of the rest of her, it looked pretty good too.

Walter hesitated. He had never been with a hooker before. He knew it happened at conventions, and somehow the guys thought it was all right, playing away from home like that. What the old lady doesn't know won't hurt her, hey Wally? But Walter had never done it. Now, though, with this girl hanging in his window practically spilling her tits onto his lap, with the lights changing, someone blowing a horn behind him and the desire sharp as knife cutting away inside him . . . Well, he opened the door.

The hooker got in and Walter drove off. She was wearing a short black skirt, way up around her thighs, and a tight pink halter made of material so thin he could see her nipples poking through. Her bare midriff was flat, with an outie belly button.

His mouth was dry. 'Where?' he croaked.

She directed him to a rundown hotel off Sunset, and he followed her up the stairs in a daze, aware only of the smell of disinfectant and rotting meat in the dim lobby and of the scuffed, stained linoleum on the stairs.

In the shaded light, the room didn't look too bad. What did it matter, anyway? She took his money first, then Walter watched as she wriggled out of the halter and her honey breasts with the dark hard nipples quivered as they fell free. Grinning at him, the tip of her tongue between her small, white teeth, she unzipped her skirt and let it fall. She was wearing only white panties now. He could see the dark shadow of her pubic hair, and some of the hairs curled around the edges of the silky material.

'You no undress?' she asked. 'Wann' me take your clothes off?'

Walter nodded. Deftly, she took off his jacket, shirt, pants.

'Oh, my, you so big,' she said, touching his erection. 'So big and hard. Safe,' she said, reaching for a condom from her bag. 'Always safe.'

Walter felt glad of that. AIDS had crossed his mind more than once between Hollywood Boulevard and the hotel, but if she always insisted on a condom she was bound to be clean, he thought. Desire seared like the sharp, hot desert wind inside him, driving him recklessly and thoughtlessly on.

She put her hands on his chest and pushed him gently down on the bed, then she straddled him, felt for his penis between her legs and thrust down on it slowly. Walter groaned and reached for her breasts as she moved back and forth on him. Dimly, he was aware of the bed springs creaking, but it didn't matter. Nothing mattered but this moist, warm tightness all around him, sucking him in, hooking onto his desire and channelling it, concentrating it. He couldn't have held back if he'd tried. It seemed like no time at all when everything burst and warmth flooded his veins. The woman moaned. He knew she was faking, but he didn't care.

Then it was all over. Walter thanked her and hurried out to his car and his shame. At first, he sat there breathing hard and cranked up the air-conditioner. His stomach clenched, his loins felt dry and empty, but the steel band was still there, tightening around his skull. Lighting a cigarette, he turned onto the boulevard and headed back to the hotel.

●

113

They still hadn't fixed the air-conditioning, he noticed, and when he phoned down to complain, the desk clerk said no one would be able to do it till the morning. Just his fucking luck. He should have felt better after sating his desire, he knew, but when he lay down and relived what he had just done he was appalled.

It was only midnight. No more than an hour ago he had been an innocent, a virtuous man. Now he had been tainted. How little time it took. And now he was worried, too. Condom or no condom, he could still get AIDS. That was a fact. The wind had done this to him, the wind and the palm trees and the hooker with the wonderful breasts and the sweet, warm place inside her. He'd been suckered. Jesus Christ, he wept, how could he face Kate and Maria again, after he'd been corrupted? That hooker hadn't been much older than his daughter. The goddamn hot wind had made him fuck his own daughter. Even if they didn't know, *he* knew. He couldn't face them. His marriage was over, his family broken, all because of some two-bit whore who had tempted him and given him a disease. He ground his teeth. The heat seemed to bore into his bones the way the damp cold did in England that time he went with Kate, so many years ago. He was burning up. Maybe he was already showing symptoms of whatever disease that whore had given him. But that was ridiculous. Maybe he'd got flu. Or maybe it was the Santa Ana.

He turned over and tried to sleep, but the steel band tightened and the guilt hammered away at him, making sleep impossible. His life was ruined. All because of fucking California. He couldn't think straight any more. Nothing but images shot through his mind, disjointed images: Kate crying; Maria slipping her panties off and rubbing her hand between her legs; the tanned assholes with the two-thousand-dollar smiles who were going to have his job. He couldn't take it any more. He had to do something. Christ, they'd walked over old Walter Dimchuk for long enough, pushed him around, used him for a doormat, laughed behind his back. Now they'd corrupted his soul. Goddammit, enough was enough. His luck was going to change.

Hardly thinking, he got dressed quickly and picked up his car keys. At the last moment, just before the door shut behind him, he went back and picked up the ice pick from the dish by the television.

•

This time it was a Caucasian girl: blonde hair, clean-cut looks, but the same style, tight short skirt and halter top. And she wanted to make a quick phone call before she got into his car and directed him to a different hotel. It was a step up from the last one, he noticed, for Wally was noticing things clearly now, like the old-fashioned bell on the wooden desk, the discreet damask armchairs in the lobby, the wood-panelling look, the hovering scent of sandalwood. In fact, Walter felt strangely calm and in control now he knew what he was going to do. The steel band had loosened.

He smiled to himself as she went through her undressing routine, a bit more elaborate and drawn out than the last one, with slow gestures and teasing glances. He felt no desire now; it was all gone. He let her continue.

Outside, the hot wind huffed and puffed at the windows. The halter revealed white, droopy breasts, the kind that fold over like envelope flaps. Her eyes were unfocused and dull, as if she were on drugs. She had a large bruise on the outside of her right thigh and a little scar just under her navel. Appendicitis? he wondered. But the appendix was further to the right, wasn't it? No matter. She stood naked before him finally, and he still felt no desire, only disgust and hatred. It wasn't the same one who had ruined him, corrupted him, but they were all the same underneath. Whores. They all shared the same tainted, rotten soul. She would do. He let her unbutton his shirt, then he moved her gently away and asked her to lie face down on the bed.

'Wanna come in from behind, hey, honey?' she said, and grinned lasciviously, lying down and hugging the pillow.

'No, that's not it.' Walter's voice felt strange – dry and stuck deep in his chest. 'That's not it at all.'

'S'OK by me.'

Walter slipped the ice pick from his jacket pocket and felt its point cool in his dry hand. He was just about to raise it above his head and plunge into the back of her neck when he heard a sound behind him.

Everything happened so fast. First, the door opened, and Walter saw a huge man blocking the exit, a giant with blond hair hanging over his massive shoulders, a tanned face carved of rock and veins thick as cables snaking down his thick arms. The man, he also noticed, was wearing a sleeveless white T-shirt and baggy, flowered pants held up by elastic.

Shit, Walter thought, glancing back at the girl for a second, then at his jacket over the back of a chair, they're going to rip me off, rob me. That's what the phone call was about. Just my fucking luck.

But what Walter didn't really register until it was much too late was that when he turned towards the doorway, he had an ice pick still raised above his head, and the other man had a gun.

Walter never did get a chance to explain. The giant raised his gun and, without a word, fired two shots right into Walter Dimchuk's angry, corrupt and unlucky heart.

ANNA SAID

AN INSPECTOR BANKS STORY

1

'**I'm not happy** with it, laddie,' said Dr Glendenning, shaking his head. 'Not happy at all.'

'So the super told me,' said Banks. 'What's the problem?'

They sat at a dimpled, copper-topped table in the Queen's Arms, Glendenning over a glass of Glenmorangie and Banks over a pint of Theakston's. It was a bitterly cold evening in February. Banks was anxious to get home and take Sandra out to dinner as he had promised, but Dr Glendenning had asked for help, and a Home Office pathologist was too important to brush off.

'One of these?' Glendenning offered Banks a Senior Service.

Banks grimaced. 'No. No thanks. I'll stick with tipped. I'm trying to give up.'

'Aye,' said Glendenning, lighting up. 'Me, too.'

'So what's the problem?'

'She should never have died,' the doctor said, 'but that's by the way. These things happen.'

'Who shouldn't have died?'

'Oh, sorry. Forgot you didn't know. Anna, Anna Childers is – was – her name. Admitted to the hospital this morning.'

'Any reason to suspect a crime?'

'No-o, not on the surface. That's why I wanted an informal chat first.' Rain lashed at the window; the buzz of conversation rose and fell around them.

'What happened?' Banks asked.

'Her boyfriend brought her in at about ten o'clock this morning. He said she'd been up half the night vomiting. They thought it was gastric flu. Dr Gibson treated the symptoms as best he could, but . . .' Glendenning shrugged.

'Cause of death?'

'Respiratory failure. If she hadn't suffered from asthma, she might have had a chance. Dr Gibson managed at least to get the convulsions under control. But as for the cause of it all, don't ask me. I've no idea yet. It could have been food poisoning. Or she could have taken something, a suicide attempt. You know how I hate guesswork.' He looked at his watch and finished his drink. 'Anyway, I'm off to do the post-mortem now. Should know a bit more after that.'

'What do you want me to do?'

'You're the copper, laddie. I'll not tell you your job. All I'll say is the circumstances are suspicious enough to worry me. Maybe you could talk to the boyfriend?'

Banks took out his notebook. 'What's his name and address?'

Glendenning told him and left. Banks sighed and went to the telephone. Sandra wouldn't like this at all.

2

Banks pulled up outside Anna Childers's large semi in south Eastvale, near the big roundabout, and turned off the tape of Furtwängler conducting Beethoven's Ninth. It was the 1951 live Bayreuth recording, mono but magnificent. The rain was still falling hard, and Banks fancied he could feel the sting of hail against his cheek as he dashed to the door, raincoat collar turned up.

The man who answered his ring, John Billings, looked awful. Normally, Banks guessed, he was a clean-cut, athletic type, at his best on a tennis court, perhaps, or a ski slope, but grief and lack of sleep had turned his skin pale and his features puffy. His shoulders slumped as Banks followed him into the living room, which looked like one of the package designs advertised in the Sunday colour supplements. Banks sat down in a damask-upholstered armchair and shivered.

'I'm sorry,' muttered Billings, turning on the gas fire. 'I didn't . . .'

'It's understandable,' Banks said, leaning forward and rubbing his hands.

'There's nothing wrong, is there?' Billings asked. 'I mean, the police . . . ?'

'Nothing for you to worry about,' Banks said. 'Just some questions.'

'Yes.' Billings flopped onto the sofa and crossed his legs. 'Of course.'

'I'm sorry about what happened,' Banks began. 'I just want to get some idea of how. It all seems a bit of a mystery to the doctors.'

Billings sniffed. 'You can say that again.'

'When did Anna start feeling ill?'

'About four in the morning. She complained of a headache, said she was feeling dizzy. Then she was up and down to the toilet the rest of the night. I thought it was a virus or something. I mean, you don't go running off to the doctor's over the least little thing, do you?'

'But it got worse?'

'Yes. It just wouldn't stop.' He held his face in his hands. Banks heard the hissing of the fire and the pellets of hail against the curtained window. Billings took a deep breath. 'I'm sorry. At the end she was bringing up blood, shivering, and she had problems breathing. Then . . . well, you know what happened.'

'How long had you known her?'

'Pardon?'

Banks repeated the question.

'A couple of years in all, I suppose. But only as a business acquaintance at first. Anna's a chartered accountant and I run a small consultancy firm. She did some auditing work for us.'

'That's how you met her?'

'Yes.'

Banks looked around at the entertainment centre, the framed Van Gogh print. 'Who owns the house?'

If Billings was surprised at the question, he didn't show it. 'Anna. It was only a temporary arrangement, my living here. I had a flat. I moved out. We were going to get married, buy a house together somewhere in the dale. Helmthorpe, perhaps.'

'How long had you been going out together?'

'Six months.'

'Living together?'

'Three.'

'Getting on all right?'

'I told you. We were going to get married.'

'You say you'd known her two years, but you've only been seeing each other six months. What took you so long? Was there someone else?'

Billings nodded.

'For you or her?'

'For Anna. Owen was still living with her until about seven months ago. Owen Doughton.'

'And they split up?'

'Yes.'

'Any bitterness?'

Billings shook his head. 'No. It was all very civilized. They weren't married. Anna said they just started going their different ways. They'd been together about five years and they felt they weren't really going anywhere together, so they decided to separate.'

'What did the two of you do last night?'

'We went out for dinner at that Chinese place on Kendal Road. You don't think it could have been that?'

'I really can't say. What did you eat?'

'The usual. Egg rolls, chicken chow mein, a Szechuan prawn dish. We shared everything.'

'Are you sure?'

'Yes. We usually do. Anna doesn't really like spicy food, but she'll have a little, just to keep me happy. I'm a curry nut, myself. The hotter the better. I thought at first maybe that was what made her sick, you know, if it wasn't the flu, the chillies they use.'

'Then you came straight home?'

'No. We stopped for a drink at the Red Lion. Got home just after eleven.'

'And Anna was feeling fine?'

'Yes. Fine.'

'What did you do when you got home?'

'Nothing much, really. Pottered around a bit, then we went to bed.'

'And that's it?'

'Yes. I must admit, I felt a little unwell myself during

the night. I had a headache and an upset stomach, but Alka-Seltzer soon put it right. I just can't believe it. I keep thinking she'll walk in the door at any moment and say it was all a mistake.'

'Did Anna have a nightcap or anything?' Banks asked after a pause. 'A cup of Horlicks, something like that?'

He shook his head. 'She couldn't stand Horlicks. No, neither of us had anything after the pub.'

Banks stood up. The room was warm now and his blotched raincoat had started to dry out. 'Thanks very much,' he said, offering his hand. 'And again, I'm sorry for intruding on your grief.'

Billings shrugged. 'What do you think it was?'

'I don't know yet. There is one more thing I have to ask. Please don't take offence.'

Billings stared at him. 'Go on.'

'Was Anna upset about anything? Depressed?'

He shook his head vigorously. 'No, no. Quite the opposite. She was happier than she'd ever been. She told me. I know what you're getting at, Inspector – the doctor suggested the same thing – but you can forget it. Anna would never have tried to take her own life. She just wasn't that kind of person. She was too full of life and energy.'

Banks nodded. If he'd had a pound for every time he'd heard that about a suicide he would be a rich man. 'Fair enough,' he said. 'Just for the record, this Owen, where does he live?'

'I'm afraid I don't know. He works at that big garden centre just off North Market Street, over from the Town Hall.'

'I know it. Thanks very much, Mr Billings.'

Banks pulled up his collar again and dashed for the car. The hail had turned to rain again. As he drove, windscreen wipers slapping, he pondered his talk with John Billings. The man seemed genuine in his grief, and he had no apparent motive for harming Anna Childers; but, again, all Banks had to go on was what he had been told. Then there was Owen Doughton, the ex live-in lover. Things might not have been as civilized as Anna Childers had made out.

The marvellous fourth movement of the symphony began just as Banks turned into his street. He sat in the parked car with the rain streaming down the windows and listened until Otto Edelmann came in with 'O Freunde, nicht diese Töne . . .', then turned off the tape and headed indoors. If he stayed out any longer he'd be there until the end of the symphony, and Sandra certainly wouldn't appreciate that.

3

Banks found Owen Doughton hefting bags of fertilizer around in the garden centre early the next morning. Doughton was a short, rather hangdog-looking man in his early thirties with shaggy dark hair and a droopy moustache. The rain had stopped overnight, but a brisk, chill wind was fast bringing in more cloud, so Banks asked if they could talk inside. Doughton led him to a small, cluttered office that smelled faintly of paraffin. Doughton sat on the desk and Banks took the swivel chair.

'I'm afraid I've got some bad news for you, Mr Doughton,' Banks started.

Doughton studied his cracked, dirty fingernails. 'I read about Anna in the paper this morning, if that's what you mean,' he said. 'It's terrible, a tragedy.' He brushed back a thick lock of hair from his right eye.

'Did you see much of her lately?'

'Not a lot, no. Not since we split up. We'd have lunch occasionally if neither of us was too busy.'

'So there were no hard feelings?'

'No. Anna said it was just time to move on, that we'd outgrown each other. We both needed more space to grow.'

'Was she right?'

He shrugged. 'Seems so. But I still cared for her. I don't want you to think I didn't. I just can't take this in.' He looked Banks in the eye for the first time. 'What's wrong, anyway? Why are the police interested?'

'It's just routine,' Banks said. 'I don't suppose you'd know anything about her state of mind recently?'

'Not really.'

'When did you see her last?'

'A couple of weeks ago. She seemed fine, really.'

'Did you know her new boyfriend?'

Doughton returned to study his fingernails. 'No. She told me about him, of course, but we never met. Sounded like a nice bloke. Probably better for her than me. I wished her every happiness. Surely you can't think she did this herself? Anna just wasn't the type. She had too much to live for.'

'Most likely food poisoning,' Banks said, closing his notebook, 'but we have to cover the possibilities. Nice talking to you, anyway. I don't suppose I'll be troubling you again.'

'No problem,' Doughton said, standing up.

Banks nodded and left.

NOT SAFE AFTER DARK

4

'If we split up,' Banks mused aloud to Sandra over an early lunch in the new McDonald's that day, 'do you think you'd be upset?'

Sandra narrowed her eyes, clear blue under the dark brows and blonde hair. 'Are you trying to tell me something, Alan? Is there something I should know?'

Banks paused, Big Mac halfway to his mouth, and laughed. 'No. No, nothing like that. It's purely hypothetical.'

'Well, thank goodness for that.' Sandra took a bite of her McChicken sandwich and pulled a face. 'Yuck. Have you really developed a taste for this stuff?'

Banks nodded. 'It's all right, really. Full of nutrition.' And he took a big bite as if to prove it.

'Well,' she said, 'you certainly know how to show a woman a good time, I'll say that for you. And what on earth are you talking about?'

'Splitting up. It's just something that puzzles me, that's all.'

'I've been married to you half my life,' Sandra said. 'Twenty years. Of course I'd be bloody upset if we split up.'

'You can't see us just going our separate ways, growing apart, needing more space?'

'Alan, what's got into you? Have you been reading those self-help books?' She looked around the place again, taking in the plastic decor. 'I'm getting worried about you.'

'Well, don't. It's simple really. I know twenty years hardly compares with five, but do you believe people can just disentangle their lives from one another and carry on with someone new as if nothing had happened?'

'Maybe they could've done in 1967,' Sandra answered. 'And maybe some people still can, but I think it cuts a lot deeper than that, no matter what anyone says.'

'Anna said it was fine,' Banks muttered, almost to himself. 'But Anna's dead.'

'Is this that investigation you're doing for Dr Glendenning, the reason you stood me up last night?'

'I didn't stand you up. I phoned to apologize. But, yes. I've got a nagging feeling about it. Something's not quite right.'

'What do you mean? You think she was poisoned or something?'

'It's possible, but I can't prove it. I can't even figure out how.'

'Then maybe you're wrong.'

'Huh.' Banks chomped on his Big Mac again. 'Wouldn't be the first time, would it?' He explained about his talks with John Billings and Owen Doughton. Sandra thought for a moment, sipping her Coke through a straw and picking at her chips, sandwich abandoned on her tray. 'Sounds like a determined woman, this Anna. I suppose it's possible she just made a seamless transition from one to the other, but I'd bet there's a lot more to it than that. I'd have a word with both of them again, if I were you.'

'Mmm,' said Banks. 'Thought you'd say that. Fancy a sweet?'

5

'The tests are going to take time,' Glendenning said over the phone, 'but from what I could see there's severe damage to the liver, kidneys, heart and lungs, not to mention the central nervous system.'

'Could it be food poisoning?' Banks asked.

'It certainly looks like some kind of poisoning. A healthy person doesn't usually die just like that. I suppose at a pinch it could be botulism,' Glendenning said. 'Certainly some of the symptoms match. I'll get the Board of Trade to check out that Chinese restaurant.'

'Any other possibilities?'

'Too damned many,' Glendenning growled. 'That's the problem. There's enough nasty stuff around to make you that ill if you're unlucky enough to swallow it: household cleaners, pesticides, industrial chemicals. The list goes on. That's why we'll have to wait for the test results.' And he hung up.

Cantankerous old bugger, Banks thought with a smile. How Glendenning hated being pinned down. The problem was, though, if someone – Owen, John or some undiscovered enemy – had poisoned Anna, how had he done it? John Billings could have doctored her food at the Chinese restaurant, or her drink in the pub, or perhaps there was something she had eaten that he had simply failed to mention. He certainly had the best opportunity.

But John Billings seemed the most unlikely suspect: he loved the woman; they were going to get married. Or so he said. Anna Childers was quite well off and upwardly mobile, but it was unlikely that Billings stood to gain, or even needed to gain, financially from her death. It was worth looking into, though. She had only been thirty, but she might have made a will in his favour. And Billings's consultancy could do with a bit of scrutiny.

Money wouldn't be a motive with Owen Doughton, though. According to both the late Anna and to Owen himself, they had parted without rancour, each content to get on with life. Again, it might be worth asking a few of their friends and acquaintances if they had reason to think any differently. Doughton had seemed gentle, reserved, a private person, but who could tell what went on in his mind? Banks walked down the corridor to see if either Detective Constable Susan Gay or Detective Sergeant Philip Richmond was free for an hour or two.

6

Two hours later, DC Susan Gay sat in front of Banks's desk, smoothed her grey skirt over her lap and opened her notebook. As usual, Banks thought, she was well dressed: tight blonde curls; just enough make-up; the silver hoop earrings; black scoop-necked top; and a mere whiff of Miss Dior cutting the stale cigarette smoke in his office.

'There's not much, I'm afraid,' Susan started, glancing up from her notes. 'No will, as far as I can discover, but she did alter the beneficiary on her insurance policy a month ago.'

'In whose benefit?'

'John Billings. Apparently she has no family.'

Banks raised his eyebrows. 'Who was the previous beneficiary?'

'Owen Doughton.'

'Odd that, isn't it?' Banks speculated aloud. 'A woman who changes her insurance policy with her boyfriends.'

'Well she wouldn't want it to go to the government, would she?' Susan said. 'And I don't suppose she'd want to make her ex rich either.'

'True,' said Banks. 'It's often easier to keep a policy going than let it lapse and apply all over again later. And they *were* going to get married. But why change it so soon? How much is it for?'

'Fifty thousand.'

Banks whistled.

'Owen Doughton's poor as a church mouse,' Susan went on, 'but he doesn't stand to gain anything.'

'But did he know that? I doubt Anna Childers would have told him. What about Billings?'

Susan gnawed the tip of her Biro and hesitated. 'Pretty well off,' she said. 'Bit of an up-and-comer in the consultancy world. You can see why a woman like Anna Childers would want to attach herself to him.'

'Why?'

'He's going places, of course. Expensive places.'

'I see,' said Banks. 'And you think she was a gold-digger?'

Susan flushed. 'Not necessarily. She just knew what side her bread was buttered on, that's all. Same as with a lot of new businesses, though, Billings has a bit of a cash-flow problem.'

'Hmm. Any gossip on the split up?'

'Not much. I had a chat with a couple of locals in the Red Lion. Anna Childers always seemed cheerful enough, but she was a tough nut to crack, they said, strong protective shell.'

'What about Doughton?'

'He doesn't seem to have many friends. His boss says he's noticed no real changes, but he says Owen keeps to himself, always did. I'm sorry. It's not much help.'

'Never mind,' Banks said. 'Look, I've got a couple of things to do. Can you find Phil for me?'

7

'Did you know that Anna had an insurance policy?' Banks asked Owen Doughton. They stood in the cold yard while Doughton stacked some bags of peat moss.

Doughton stood up and rubbed the small of his back. 'Aye,' he said. 'What of it?'

'Did you know how much it was for?'

He shook his head.

'All right,' Banks said. 'Did Anna tell you she'd changed the beneficiary, named John Billings instead of you?'

Doughton paused with his mouth open. 'No,' he said. 'No, she didn't.'

'So you know now that you stand to gain nothing, that it all goes to John?'

Doughton's face darkened, then he looked away and Banks swore he could hear a strangled laugh or cry. 'I don't believe this,' Doughton said, facing him again. 'I can't believe I'm hearing this. You think *I* might have killed Anna? And for money? This is insane. Look, go away, please. I don't have to talk to you, do I?'

'No,' said Banks.

'Well, bugger off then. I've got work to do. But remember one thing.'

'What's that?'

'I loved her. I loved Anna.'

8

John Billings looked even more wretched than he had the day before. His eyes were bloodshot, underlined by black smudges, and he hadn't shaved. Banks could smell alcohol on his breath. A suitcase stood in the hallway.

'Where are you going, John?' Banks asked.

'I can't stay here, can I? I mean, it's not my house, for a start, and . . . the memories.'

'Where are you going?'

He picked up the case. 'I don't know. Just away from here, that's all.'

'I don't think so.' Gently, Banks took the case from him and set it down. 'We haven't got to the bottom of this yet.'

'What do you mean? For Christ's sake, man!'

'You'd better come with me, John.'

'Where?'

'Police station. We'll have a chat there.'

Billings stared angrily at him, then seemed to fold. 'Oh, what the hell,' he muttered. 'What does it matter?' And he picked his coat off the rack and followed Banks. He didn't see DS Philip Richmond watching from the window of the cafe over the road.

9

It was after seven o'clock, dark, cold and windy outside. Banks decided to wait in the bedroom, on the chair wedged in the corner between the wardrobe and the dressing table. From there, with the door open, he could see the staircase, and he would be able to hear any sounds in the house.

He had just managed to get the item on the local news show at six o'clock, only minutes after Dr Glendenning had phoned with more detailed information: 'Poison suspected in death of Eastvale woman. Police baffled. No suspects as yet.' Of course, the killer might not have seen it, or might have already covered his tracks, but if Anna Childers *had* been poisoned, and Glendenning now seemed certain she had, then the answer had to be here.

Given possible reaction times, Glendenning had said in his late afternoon phone call, there was little chance she could have taken the poison into her system before eight o'clock the previous evening, at which time she had gone out to dine with John Billings.

The house was dark and silent save for the ticking of a clock on the bedside table and the howling wind rattling the window. Eight o'clock. Nine. Nothing happened except Banks got cramp in his left calf. He massaged it, then stood up at regular intervals and stretched. He thought of DS Richmond down the street in the unmarked car. Between them, they'd be sure to catch anyone who came.

Finally, close to ten o'clock, he heard it, a scraping at the lock on the front door. He drew himself deep into the chair, melted into the darkness and held his breath. The door opened and closed softly. He could see a torch beam sweeping the wall by the staircase, coming closer. The intruder was coming straight up the stairs. Damn! Banks hadn't expected that. He wanted whoever it was to lead him to the poison, not walk right into him.

He sat rigid in the chair as the beam played over the

threshold of the bedroom, mercifully not falling on him in his dark corner. The intruder didn't hesitate. He walked around the bed, within inches of Banks's feet, and over to the bedside table. Shining his torch, he opened the top drawer and picked something up. At that moment Banks turned on the light. The figure turned sharply, then froze.

'Hello, Owen,' said Banks. 'What brings you here?'

10

'**If it was** anyone, it had to be either you or him, John,' Banks said later back in his office, while Owen Doughton was being charged downstairs. 'Only the two of you were intimate enough with Anna to know her habits, her routines. And Owen had lived with her until quite recently. There was a chance he still had a key.'

John Billings shook his head. 'I thought you were arresting *me*.'

'It was touch and go, I won't deny it. But at least I thought I'd give you a chance, the benefit of the doubt.'

'And if your trap hadn't worked?'

Banks shrugged. 'Down to you, I suppose. The poison could have been anywhere, in anything. Toothpaste, for example. I knew if it wasn't you, and the killer heard the news, he'd try to destroy any remaining evidence. He wouldn't have had a chance to do so yet because you were in the house.'

'But I was at the hospital nearly all yesterday.'

'Too soon. He had no idea anything had happened at that time. This wasn't a carefully calculated plan.'

'But why?'

Banks shook his head. 'That I can't say for certain.

He's a sick man, an obsessed man. It's my guess it was his warped form of revenge. It had been eating away at him for some time. Anna didn't treat him very well, John. She didn't really stop to take his feelings into account when she kicked him out and took up with you. She just assumed he would understand, like he always had, because he loved her and had her welfare at heart. He was deeply hurt, but he wasn't the kind to make a fuss or let his feelings show. He kept it all bottled up.'

'She could be a bit blinkered, could Anna,' John mumbled. 'She was a very focused woman.'

'Yes. And I'm sure Doughton felt humiliated when she dumped him and turned to you. After all, he didn't have much of a financial future, unlike you.'

'But it wasn't that, not with Anna,' Billings protested. 'We just had so much in common. Goals, tastes, ambitions. She and Owen had nothing in common any more.'

'You're probably right,' Banks said. 'Anyway, when she told him a couple of weeks ago that she was going to get married to you, it was the last straw. He said she expected him to be happy for her.'

'But why did he keep on seeing her if it hurt him so much?'

'He was still in love with her. It was better seeing her, even under those circumstances, than not at all.'

'Then why kill her?'

Banks looked at Billings. 'Love and hate, John,' he said. 'They're not so far apart. Besides, he doesn't believe he did kill her, that wasn't really his intention at all.'

'I don't understand. You said he did. How did he do it?'

Banks paused and lit a cigarette. This wasn't going to

be easy. Rain blew against the window and a draught rattled the Venetian blind.

'How?' Billings repeated.

Banks looked at his calendar, trying to put off the moment; it showed a woodland scene, snowdrops blooming near The Strid at Bolton Abbey. He cleared his throat. 'Owen came to the house while you were both out,' Banks began. 'He brought a syringe loaded with a strong pesticide he got from the garden centre. Remember, he knew Anna intimately. Did you and Anna make love that night, John?'

Billings reddened. 'For Christ's sake—'

'I'm not asking whether the earth moved, I'm just asking if you did. Believe me, it's relevant.'

'All right,' said Billings after a pause. 'Yes, we did, as a matter of fact.'

'Owen knew Anna well enough to know that she was frightened of getting pregnant,' Banks went on, 'but she wouldn't take the pill because of the side effects. He knew she insisted on condoms, and he knew she liked to make love in the dark. It was easy enough to insert the needle into a couple of packages and squirt in some pesticide. Not much, but it's very powerful stuff, colourless and odourless, so even an infinitesimal coating would have some effect. The condoms were lubricated, so they'd feel oily anyway, and nobody would notice a tiny pinprick in the package. You absorbed a little into your system, too, and that's why you felt ill. You see, it's easily absorbed through skin or membranes. But Anna got the lion's share. Dr Glendenning would have found out eventually how the poison was administered from tissue samples, but further tests would have taken time. Owen could easily have nipped back to the house and removed the evidence by then. Or we might have decided that you had better access to the method.'

Billings paled. 'You mean it could just as easily have been me either killed or arrested for murder?'

Banks shrugged. 'It could have turned out any way, really. There was no way of knowing accurately what would happen, and certainly there was a chance that either you would die or the blame would fall on you. As it turned out, Anna absorbed most of it, and she had asthma. In Owen's twisted mind, he wanted your love-making to make you sick. That was his statement, if you like, after suffering so long in silence, pretending it was OK that Anna had moved on. But that's all. It was a sick joke, if you like. We found three poisoned condoms. Certainly if one hadn't worked the way it did, there could have been a build up of the pesticide, causing chronic problems. I did read about a case once,' Banks went on, 'where a man married rich women and murdered them for their money by putting arsenic on his condoms, but they were made of goatskin back then. Besides, he was French. I've never come across a case quite as strange as this.'

Billings shook his head slowly. 'Can I go now?' he asked.

'Where to?'

'I don't know. A hotel, perhaps, until . . .'

Banks nodded and stood up. As they went down the stairs, they came face to face with Owen Doughton, hand-cuffed to a large constable. Billings stiffened. Doughton glared at him and spoke to Banks. 'He's the one who killed her,' he said, with a toss of his head. 'He's the one you should be arresting.' Then he looked directly at Billings. 'You're going to have to live with that, you know,

Mr Moneybags. It was you who killed her. Hear that, Mr Yuppie Moneybags? *You* killed her. You killed Anna.'

Banks couldn't tell whether he was laughing or crying as the constable led him down to the cells.

MISSING IN ACTION

People go missing all the time in war, of course, but not usually nine-year-old boys. Besides, the war had hardly begun. It was only 20 September 1939 when Mary Critchley came hammering on my door at about three o'clock, interrupting my afternoon nap.

It was a Wednesday, and normally I would have been teaching the fifth-formers Shakespeare at Silverhill Grammar School (a thankless task if ever there was one), but the Ministry had just got around to constructing air-raid shelters there, so the school was closed for the week. We didn't even know if it was going to reopen because the plan was to evacuate all the children to safer areas in the countryside. Now I would be among the first to admit that a teacher's highest aspiration is a school without pupils, but in the meantime the government, in its eternal wisdom, put us redundant teachers to such complex, intellectual tasks as preparing ration cards for the Ministry of Food. (After all, *they* knew what was coming.)

All this was just a small part of the chaos that seemed to reign at that time. Not the chaos of war, the kind I remembered from the trenches at Ypres in 1917, but the chaos of government bureaucracies trying to organize the country for war.

Anyway, I was fortunate enough to become a Special Constable, which is a rather grandiose title for a sort of part-time dogsbody, and that was why Mary Critchley came running to me. That and what little reputation I had for solving people's problems.

'Mr Bashcombe! Mr Bashcombe!' she cried. 'It's our Johnny. He's gone missing. You musht help.'

My name is actually *Bascombe*, Frank Bascombe, but Mary Critchley has a slight speech impediment, so I forgave her the mispronunciation. Still, with half the city's children running wild in the streets and the other half standing on crowded station platforms clutching their Mickey Mouse gas-masks in little cardboard boxes, ready to be herded into trains bound for such nearby country havens as Graythorpe, Kilsden and Acksham, I thought perhaps she was overreacting a tad, and I can't say I welcomed her arrival after only about twenty of my allotted forty winks.

'He's probably out playing with his mates,' I told her.

'Not my Johnny,' she said, wiping the tears from her eyes. 'Not since . . . you know . . .'

I knew. Mr Critchley, Ted to his friends, had been a Royal Navy man since well before the war. He had also been unfortunate enough to serve on the aircraft carrier *Courageous*, which had been sunk by a German U-boat off the south-west coast of Ireland just three days before. Over five hundred men had been lost, including Ted Critchley. Of course, no body had been found, and probably never would be, so he was only officially 'missing in action'.

I also knew young Johnny Critchley, and thought him to be a serious boy, a bit too imaginative and innocent for his own good. (Well, many are at that age, aren't they, before the world grabs them by the balls and shakes some reality into them.) Johnny trusted everyone, even strangers.

'Johnny's not been in much of a mood for playing with his mates sinsh we got the news about Ted's ship,' Mary Critchley went on.

I could understand that well enough – young Johnny was an only child, and he always did worship his father – but I still didn't see what I could do about it. 'Have you asked around?'

'What do you think I've been doing sinsh he didn't come home at twelve o'clock like he was supposed to? I've ashked everyone in the street. Last time he was seen he was down by the canal at about eleven o'clock. Maurice Richards saw him. What can I do, Mr Bashcombe? Firsht Ted, and now . . . now my Johnny!' She burst into tears.

After I had managed to calm her down, I sighed and told her I would look for Johnny myself. There certainly wasn't much hope of my getting the other twenty winks now.

•

It was a glorious day, so warm and sunny you would hardly believe there was a war on. The late afternoon sunshine made even our narrow streets of cramped brick terraced houses look attractive. As the shadows lengthened, the light turned to molten gold. First, I scoured the local rec, where the children played cricket and football, and the dogs ran wild. Some soldiers were busy digging trenches for air-raid shelters. Just the sight of those long, dark grooves in the earth gave me the shivers. Behind the trenches, barrage balloons pulled at their moorings on the breeze like playful porpoises, orange and pink in the sun. I asked the soldiers, but they hadn't seen Johnny. Nor had any of the other lads.

After the rec, I headed for the derelict houses on Gallipoli Street. The landlord had let them go to rack and ruin two years ago, and they were quite uninhabitable, not even fit for billeting soldiers. They were also dangerous and should have been pulled down, but I think the old skinflint was hoping a bomb would hit them so he could claim insurance or compensation from the government. The doors and windows had been boarded up, but children are resourceful, and it wasn't difficult even for me to remove a couple of loose sheets of plywood and make my way inside. I wished I had my torch, but I had to make do with what little light slipped through the holes. Every time I moved, my feet stirred up clouds of dust, which did my poor lungs no good at all.

I thought Johnny might have fallen or got trapped in one of the houses. The staircases were rotten, and more than one lad had fallen through on his way up. The floors weren't much better, either, and one of the fourth-formers at Silverhill had needed more than fifteen stitches a couple of weeks before when one of his legs went right through the rotten wood and the splinters gouged his flesh.

I searched as best I could in the poor light, and I called out Johnny's name, but no answer came. Before I left, I stood silently and listened for any traces of harsh breathing or whimpering.

Nothing.

After three hours of searching the neighbourhood, I'd had no luck at all. Blackout time was seven forty-five p.m., so I still had about an hour and a half left, but if Johnny wasn't in any of the local children's usual haunts, I was at a loss as to where to look. I talked to the other boys I met here and there, but none of his friends had seen him since the family got the news of Ted's death. Little Johnny Critchley, it seemed, had vanished into thin air.

•

At half past six, I called on Maurice Richards, grateful for his offer of a cup of tea and the chance to rest my aching feet. Maurice and I went back a long time. We had both survived the first war, Maurice with the loss of an arm, and me with permanent facial scarring and a racking cough that comes and goes, thanks to the mustard gas leaking through my mask at the Third Battle of Ypres. We never talked about the war, but it was there, we both knew, an invisible bond tying us close together while at the same time excluding us from so much other, normal human intercourse. Not many had seen the things we had, and thank God for that.

Maurice lit up a Passing Cloud one-handed, then he poured the tea. The seven o'clock news came on the radio, some rot about us vowing to keep fighting until we'd vanquished the foe. It was still very much a war of words at that time, and the more rhetorical the language sounded, the better the politicians thought they were doing. There had been a couple of minor air skirmishes, and the sinking of the *Courageous*, of course, but all the action was taking place in Poland, which seemed as remote as the moon to most people. Some clever buggers had already started calling it the 'Bore War'.

'Did you hear Tommy Handley last night, Frank?' Maurice asked.

I shook my head. There'd been a lot of hoopla about Tommy Handley's new radio programme, *It's That Man Again*, or *ITMA*, as people called it. I was never a fan.

Call me a snob, but when evening falls I'm far happier curling up with a good book or an interesting talk on the radio than listening to Tommy Handley.

'Talk about laugh,' said Maurice. 'They had this one sketch about the Ministry of Aggravation and the Office of Twerps. I nearly died.'

I smiled. 'Not far from the truth,' I said. There were now so many of these obscure ministries, boards and departments involved in so many absurd pursuits – all for the common good, of course – that I had been thinking of writing a dystopian satire. I proposed to set it in the near future, which would merely be a thinly disguised version of the present. So far, all I had was a great idea for the title: I would reverse the last two numbers in the current year, so instead of 1939, I'd call it *1993*. (Well, *I* thought it was a good idea!)

'Look, Maurice,' I said, 'it's about young Johnny Critchley. His mother tells me you were the last person to see him.'

'Oh, aye,' Maurice said. 'She were round asking about him not long ago. Still not turned up?'

'No.'

'Cause for concern, then.'

'I'm beginning to think so. What was he doing when you saw him?'

'Just walking down by the canal, by old Woodruff's scrapyard.'

'That's all?'

'Yes.'

'Was he alone?'

Maurice nodded.

'Did he say anything.'

'No.'

144

'You didn't say anything to him?'

'No cause to. He seemed preoccupied, just staring in the water, like, hands in his pockets. I've heard what happened to his dad. A lad has to do his grieving.'

'Too true. Did you see anyone else? Anything suspicious?'

'No, nothing. Just a minute, though . . .'

'What?'

'Oh, it's probably nothing, but just after I saw Johnny, when I was crossing the bridge, I bumped into Colin Gormond, you know, that chap who's a bit . . . you know.'

Colin Gormond. I knew him all right. And that wasn't good news; it wasn't good news at all.

•

Of all the policemen they could have sent, they had to send Detective bloody Sergeant Longbottom, a big, brutish-looking fellow with a pronounced limp and a Cro-Magnon brow. Longbottom was thick as two short planks. I doubt he could have found his own arse even if someone nailed a sign on it, or detected his way out of an Anderson shelter if it were in his own back yard. But that's the calibre of men this wretched war has left us with at home. Along with good ones like me, of course.

DS Longbottom wore a shiny brown suit and a Silverhill Grammar School tie. I wondered where he'd got it from; he probably stole it from a schoolboy he caught nicking sweets from the corner shop. He kept tugging at his collar with his pink sausage fingers as we talked in Mary Critchley's living room. His face was flushed with the heat, and sweat gathered on his thick eyebrows and trickled down the sides of his neck.

'So he's been missing since lunchtime, has he?' DS Longbottom repeated.

Mary Critchley nodded. 'He went out at about half past ten, just for a walk like. Said he'd be back at twelve. When it got to three . . . well, I went to see Mr Bashcombe here.'

DS Longbottom curled his lip at me and grunted. 'Mr Bascombe. *Special* Constable. I suppose you realize that gives you no real police powers, don't you?'

'As a matter of fact,' I said, 'I thought it made me your superior. After all, you're not a *special* sergeant, are you?'

He looked at me as if he wanted to hit me. Perhaps he would have done if Mary Critchley hadn't been in the room. 'Enough of your lip. Just answer my questions.'

'Yes, sir.'

'You say you looked all over for this lad?'

'All his usual haunts.'

'And you found no trace of him?'

'If I had, do you think we'd have sent for you?'

'I warned you. Cut the lip and answer the questions. This, what's his name, Maurice Richards, was he the last person to see the lad?'

'Johnny's his name. And yes is the answer, as far as we know.' I paused. He'd have to know eventually, and if I didn't tell him, Maurice would. The longer we delayed, the worse it would be in the long run. 'There was someone else in the area at the time. A man called Colin Gormond.'

Mary Critchley gave a sharp gasp. DS Longbottom frowned, licked the tip of his pencil and scribbled something in his notebook. 'I'll have to have a word with him,' he said. Then he turned to her. 'Recognize the name, do you, ma'm?'

'I know Colin,' I answered, perhaps a bit too quickly.

DS Longbottom stared at Mary Critchley, whose lower lip started quivering, then turned slowly back to me. 'Tell me about him.'

I sighed. Colin Gormond was an oddball. Some people said he was a bit slow, but I'd never seen any real evidence of that. He lived alone and he didn't have much to do with the locals; that was enough evidence against him for some people.

And then there were the children.

For some reason, Colin preferred the company of the local lads to that of the rest of us adults. To be quite honest, I can't say I blame him, but in a situation like this it's bound to look suspicious. Especially if the investigating officer is someone with the sensitivity and understanding of a DS Longbottom.

Colin would take them trainspotting on the hill overlooking the main line, for example, or he'd play cricket with them on the rec, or hand out conkers when the season came. He sometimes bought them sweets and ice creams, even gave them books, marbles and comics.

To my knowledge, Colin Gormond had never once put a foot out of line, never laid so much as a finger on any of the lads, either in anger or in friendship. There had, however, been one or two mutterings from some parents – most notably from Jack Blackwell, father of one of Johnny's pals, Nick – that it somehow *wasn't right*, that it was *unnatural* for a man who must be in his late thirties or early forties to spend so much time playing with young children. There must be something not quite right in his head, he must be up to *something*, Jack Blackwell hinted, and as usual when someone starts a vicious rumour, there is no shortage of willing believers.

Such a reaction was only to be expected from someone, of course, but I knew it wouldn't go down well with DS Longbottom. I don't know why, but I felt a strange need to *protect* Colin.

'Colin's a local,' I explained. 'Lived around here for years. He plays with the lads a bit. Most of them like him. He seems a harmless sort of fellow.'

'How old is he?'

I shrugged. 'Hard to say. About forty, perhaps.'

DS Longbottom raised a thick eyebrow. 'About forty and he plays with the kiddies, you say?'

'Sometimes. Like a schoolteacher, or a youth club leader.'

'Is he a schoolteacher?'

'No.'

'Is he a youth club leader?'

'No. Look, what I meant—'

'I know exactly what you meant, Mr Bascombe. Now you just listen to what *I* mean. What we've got here is an older man who's known to hang around with young children, and he's been placed near the scene where a young child has gone missing. Now, don't you think that's just a wee bit suspicious?'

Mary Critchley let out a great wail and started crying again. DS Longbottom ignored her. Instead, he concentrated all his venom on me, the softie, the liberal, the defender of child molesters. 'What do you have to say about *that*, Mr Special Constable Bascombe?'

'Only that Colin was a friend to the children and that he had no reason to harm anyone.'

'*Friend*,' DS Longbottom sneered, struggling to his feet. 'We can only be thankful you're not regular police, Mr

Bascombe,' he said, nodding to himself, in acknowledgement of his own wisdom. 'That we can.'

'So what are you going to do?' I asked.

DS Longbottom looked at his watch and frowned. Either he was trying to work out what it meant when the little hand and the big hand were in the positions they were in, or he was squinting because of poor eyesight. 'I'll have a word with this here Colin Gormond. Other than that, there's not much more we can do tonight. First thing tomorrow morning, we'll drag the canal.' He got to the door, turned, pointed to the windows and said, 'And don't forget to put up your blackout curtains, ma'm, or you'll have the ARP man to answer to.'

Mary Critchley burst into floods of tears again.

•

Even the soft dawn light could do nothing for the canal. It oozed through the city like an open sewer, oil slicks shimmering like rainbows in the sun, brown water dotted with industrial scum and suds, bits of driftwood and paper wrappings floating along with them. On one side was Ezekiel Woodruff's scrapyard. Old Woodruff was a bit of an eccentric. He used to come around the streets with his horse and cart, yelling, 'Any old iron,' but now the government had other uses for scrap metal – supposedly to be used in aircraft manufacture – poor old Woodruff didn't have a way to make his living any more. He'd already sent old Nell the carthorse to the knacker's yard, where she was probably doing her bit for the war effort by helping to make the glue to stick the aircraft together. Old mangles and bits of broken furniture stuck up from the ruins of the scrapyard like shattered artillery after a battle.

On the other side, the bank rose steeply towards the

backs of the houses on Canal Road, and the people who lived there seemed to regard it as their personal tip. Flies and wasps buzzed around old hessian sacks and paper bags full of God knew what. A couple of buckled bicycle tyres and a wheel-less pram completed the picture.

I stood and watched as Longbottom supervised the dragging, a slow and laborious process that seemed to be sucking all manner of unwholesome objects to the surface – except Johnny Critchley's body.

I felt tense. At any moment I half expected the cry to come from one of the policemen in the boats that they had found him, half expected to see the small, pathetic bundle bob above the water's surface. I didn't think Colin Gormond had done anything to Johnny – nor Maurice, though DS Longbottom had seemed suspicious of him too – but I did think that, given how upset he was, Johnny might just have jumped in. He never struck me as the suicidal type, but I have no idea whether suicide enters the minds of nine-year-olds. All I knew was that he *was* upset about his father, and he *was* last seen skulking by the canal.

So I stood around with DS Longbottom and the rest as the day grew warmer, and there was still no sign of Johnny. After about three hours, the police gave up and went for bacon and eggs at Betty's Cafe over on Chadwick Road. They didn't invite me, and I was grateful to be spared both the unpleasant food and company. I stood and stared into the greasy water a while longer, unsure whether it was a good sign or not that Johnny wasn't in the canal, then I decided to go and have a chat with Colin Gormond.

•

'What is it, Colin?' I asked him gently. 'Come on. You can tell me.'

But Colin continued to stand with his back turned to me in the dark corner of his cramped living room, hands to his face, making eerie snuffling sounds, shaking his head. It was bright daylight outside, but the blackout curtains were still drawn tightly, and not a chink of light crept between their edges. I had already tried the light switch, but either Colin had removed the bulb or he didn't have one.

'Come on, Colin. This is silly. You know me. I'm Mr Bascombe. I won't hurt you. Tell me what happened.'

Finally Colin turned silent and came out of his corner with his funny, shuffling way of walking. Someone said he had a club foot, and someone else said he'd had a lot of operations on his feet when he was a young lad, but nobody knew for certain why he walked the way he did. When he sat down and lit a cigarette, the match light illuminated his large nose, shiny forehead and watery blue eyes. He used the same match to light a candle on the table beside him, and then I saw them: the black eye, the bruise on his left cheek. DS Longbottom. The bastard.

'Did you say anything to him?' I asked, anxious that DS Longbottom might have beaten a confession out of Colin, without even thinking that Colin probably wouldn't still be at home if that were the case.

He shook his head mournfully. 'Nothing, Mr Bascombe. Honest. There was nothing I *could* tell him.'

'Did you see Johnny Critchley yesterday, Colin?'

'Aye.'

'Where?'

'Down by the canal.'

'What was he doing?'

'Just standing there chucking stones in the water.'

'Did you talk to him?'

Colin paused and turned away before answering, 'No.'

I had a brief coughing spell, his cigarette smoke working on my gassed lungs. When it cleared up, I said, 'Colin, there's something you're not telling me, isn't there? You'd better tell me. You know I won't hurt you, and I just might be the only person who can help you.'

He looked at me, pale eyes imploring. 'I only called out to him, from the bridge, like, didn't I?'

'What happened next?'

'Nothing. I swear it.'

'Did he answer?'

'No. He just looked my way and shook his head. I could tell then that he didn't want to play. He seemed sad.'

'He'd just heard his dad's been killed.'

Colin's already watery eyes brimmed with tears. 'Poor lad.'

I nodded. For all I knew, Colin might have been thinking about *his* dad, too. Not many knew it, but Mr Gormond senior had been killed in the same bloody war that left me with my bad lungs and scarred face. 'What happened next, Colin?'

Colin shook his head and wiped his eyes with the back of his hand. 'Nothing,' he said. 'It was such a lovely day I just went on walking. I went to the park and watched the soldiers digging trenches, then I went for my cigarettes and came home to listen to the wireless.'

'And after that?'

'I stayed in.'

'All evening?'

'That's right. Sometimes I go down to the White Rose, but . . .'

'But what, Colin?'

'Well, Mr Smedley, you know, the air-raid precautions man?'

I nodded. 'I know him.'

'He said my blackout cloth wasn't good enough and he'd fine me if I didn't get some proper stuff by yester-day.'

'I understand, Colin.' Good-quality, thick, impenetrable blackout cloth had become both scarce and expensive, which was no doubt why Colin had been cheated in the first place.

'Anyway, what with that and the cigarettes . . .'

I reached into my pocket and slipped out a few bob for him. Colin looked away, ashamed, but I put it on the table and he didn't tell me to take it back. I knew how it must hurt his pride to accept charity, but I had no idea how much money he made, or how he made it. I'd never seen him beg, but I had a feeling he survived on odd jobs and lived very much from hand to mouth.

I stood up. 'All right, Colin,' I said. 'Thanks very much.' I paused at the door, uncertain how to say what had just entered my mind. Finally I blundered ahead. 'It might be better if you kept a low profile till they find him, Colin. You know what some of the people around here are like.'

'What do you mean, Mr Bascombe?'

'Just be careful, Colin, that's all I mean. Just be careful.'

He nodded gormlessly and I left.

•

As I shut Colin's front door, I noticed Jack Blackwell standing on his doorstep, arms folded, a small crowd of locals around him, their shadows intersecting on the cobbled street. They kept glancing towards Colin's house, and when they saw me come out they all shuffled off except Jack himself, who gave me a grim stare before going inside and slamming his door. I felt a shiver go up my spine, as if a goose had stepped on my grave, as my dear mother used to say, bless her soul, and when I got home I couldn't concentrate on my book one little bit.

●

By the following morning, when Johnny had been missing over thirty-six hours, the mood in the street had started to turn ugly. In my experience, when you get right down to it, there's no sorrier spectacle, nothing much worse or more dangerous, than the human mob mentality. After all, armies are nothing more than mobs, really, even when they are organized to a greater or lesser degree. I'd been at Ypres, as you know, and there wasn't a hell of a lot you could tell me about military organization. So when I heard the muttered words on doorsteps, saw the little knots of people here and there, Jack Blackwell flitting from door to door like a political canvasser, I had to do something, and I could hardly count on any help from DS Longbottom.

One thing I had learned both as a soldier and as a schoolteacher was that, if you had a chance, your best bet was to take out the ringleader. That meant Jack Blackwell. Jack was the nasty type, and he and I had had more than one run-in over his son Nick's bullying and poor performance in class. In my opinion, young Nick was the sort of walking dead loss who should probably have been drowned at birth, a waste of skin, sinew, tissue and bone, and it wasn't hard to see where he got it from. Nick's older brother, Dave, was already doing a long stretch in the Scrubs for beating a night watchman senseless during a robbery, and even the army couldn't find an excuse to spring him and enlist his service in killing Germans. Mrs Blackwell had been seen more than once walking with difficulty, with bruises on her cheek. The sooner Jack Blackwell got his call-up papers, the better things would be all around.

I intercepted Jack between the Deakins' and the Kellys' houses, and it was clear from his gruff, 'What do you want?' that he didn't want to talk to me.

But I was adamant.

'Morning, Jack,' I greeted him. 'Lovely day for a walk, isn't it?'

'What's it to you?'

'Just being polite. What are you up to, Jack? What's going on?'

'None of your business.'

'Up to your old tricks? Spreading poison?'

'I don't know what you're talking about.' He made to walk away, but I grabbed his arm. He glared at me but didn't do anything. Just as well. At my age, and with my lungs, I'd hardly last ten seconds in a fight. 'Jack,' I said, 'don't you think you'd all be best off using your time to look for the poor lad?'

'Look for him! That's a laugh. You know as well as I do where that young lad is.'

'Where? Where is he, Jack?'

'You know.'

'No, I don't. Tell me.'

'He's dead and buried, that's what.'

'Where, Jack?'

'I don't know the exact spot. If he's not in the canal, then he's buried somewhere not far away.'

'Maybe he is. But you don't *know* that. Not for certain. And even if you believe that, you don't know who put him there.'

Jack wrenched his arm out of my weakening grip and sneered. 'I've got a damn sight better idea than you have, Frank Bascombe. With all your *book* learning!' Then he turned and marched off.

Somehow I got the feeling that I had just made things worse.

•

After my brief fracas with Jack Blackwell, I was at a loose end. I knew the police would still be looking for Johnny, asking questions, searching areas of waste ground, so there wasn't much I could do to help them. Feeling impotent, I went down to the canal, near Woodruff's scrapyard. Old Ezekiel Woodruff himself was poking around in the ruins of his business, so I decided to talk to him. I kept my distance, though, for even on a hot day such as this Woodruff was wearing his greatcoat and black wool gloves with the fingers cut off. He wasn't known for his personal hygiene, so I made sure I didn't stand downwind of him. Not that there was much of a wind, but then it didn't take much.

'Morning, Ezekiel,' I said. 'I understand young Johnny Critchley was down around here the day before yesterday.'

'So they say,' muttered Ezekiel.

'See him, did you?'

'I weren't here.'

'So you didn't see him?'

'Police have already been asking questions.'

'And what did you tell them?'

He pointed to the other side of the canal, the back of the housing estate. 'I were over there,' he said. 'Sometimes people chuck out summat of value, even these days.'

'But you did see Johnny?'

He paused, then said, 'Aye.'

'On this side of the canal?'

Woodruff nodded.

'What time was this?'

'I don't have a watch, but it weren't long after that daft bloke had gone by.'

'Do you mean Colin Gormond?'

'Aye, that's the one.'

So Johnny was still alone by the canal *after* Colin had passed by. DS Longbottom had probably known this, but he had beaten Colin anyway. One day I'd find a way to get even with him. The breeze shifted a little and I got a whiff of stale sweat and worse. 'What was Johnny doing?'

'Doing? Nowt special. He were just walking.'

'Walking? Where?'

Woodruff pointed. 'That way. Towards the city centre.'

'Alone?'

'Aye.'

'And nobody approached him?'

'Nope. Not while I were watching.'

I didn't think there was anything further to be got from Ezekiel Woodruff, so I bade him good morning. I can't say the suspicion didn't enter my head that *he* might have had something to do with Johnny's disappearance, though I'd have been hard pushed to say exactly why or what. Odd though old Woodruff might be, there had never been any rumour or suspicion of his being overly interested in young boys, and I didn't want to jump to conclusions the way Jack Blackwell had. Still, I filed away my suspicions for later.

A fighter droned overhead. I watched it dip and spin through the blue air and wished I could be up there. I'd always regretted not being a pilot in the war. A barge full of soldiers drifted by, and I moved aside on the towpath to let the horse that was pulling it pass by. For my troubles I got a full blast of sweaty horseflesh and a pile of steaming manure at my feet. That had even Ezekiel Woodruff beat.

Aimlessly I followed the direction Ezekiel had told me Johnny had walked in – towards the city centre. As I walked, Jack Blackwell's scornful words about my inability to find Johnny echoed in my mind. *Book learning.* That was exactly the kind of cheap insult you would expect from a moron like Jack Blackwell, but it hurt nonetheless. No sense telling him I'd been buried in the mud under the bodies of my comrades for two days. No sense telling him about the young German soldier I'd surprised and bayoneted to death, twisting the blade until it snapped and broke off inside him. Jack Blackwell was too young to have seen action in the last war, but if there was any justice in the world, he'd damn well see it in *this* one.

The canal ran by the back of the train station, where I crossed the narrow bridge and walked through the crowds of evacuees out front to City Square. Mary Critchley's anguish reverberated in my mind, too: 'Mr Bashcombe! Mr Bashcombe!' I heard her call.

Then, all of a sudden, as I looked at the black facade of the post office and the statue of the Black Prince in the centre of City Square, it hit me. I thought I knew what had happened to Johnny Critchley, but first I had to go back to the street and ask just one important question.

•

It was late morning. The station smelt of damp soot and warm oil. Crowds of children thronged around trying to find out where they were supposed to go. They wore name tags and carried little cardboard boxes. Adults with clipboards, for the most part temporarily unemployed schoolteachers and local volunteers, directed them to the right queue, and their names were ticked off as they boarded the carriages.

Despite being neither an evacuated child nor a supervisor, I managed to buy a ticket and ended up sharing a compartment with a rather severe-looking woman in a brown uniform I didn't recognize, and a male civilian with a brush moustache and a lot of Brylcreem on his hair. They seemed to be in charge of several young children, also in the compartment, who couldn't sit still. I could hardly blame them. They were going to the alien countryside, to live with strangers, far away from their parents, for only God knew how long, and the idea scared them half to death.

The buttoned cushions were warm and the air in the carriage still and close, despite the open window. When we finally set off, the motion stirred up a breeze, which helped a little. On the wall opposite me was a poster of the Scarborough seafront, and I spent most of the journey remembering the carefree childhood holidays I had enjoyed there with my parents in the early years of the century: another world, another time. The rest of the trip I glanced out of the window, beyond the scum-scabbed canal, and saw the urban industrial landscape drift by: back gardens, where some people had put in Anderson shelters half-covered with earth to grow vegetables on; the dark mass of the town hall clock tower behind the city centre buildings; a factory yard, where several men were loading heavy crates onto a lorry, flushed and sweating in the heat.

Then we were in the countryside, where the smells of grass, hay and manure displaced the reek of the city. I saw small, squat farms, drystone walls, sheep and cattle grazing. Soon train tracks and canal diverged. We went through a long noisy tunnel, and the children whimpered. Later, I was surprised to see so many army convoys winding along the narrow roads, and the one big aerodrome we passed seemed buzzing with activity.

All in all, the journey took a little over two hours. Only about ten or eleven children were shepherded off at the small country station, and I followed as they were met and taken to the village hall, where the men and women who were to care for them waited. It was more civilized than some of the evacuation systems I'd heard about, which sounded more like the slave markets of old, where farmers waited on the platforms to pick out the strong lads, and local dignitaries whisked away the nicely dressed boys and girls.

I went up to the volunteer in charge, an attractive young country woman in a simple blue frock with a white lace collar and a belt around her slim waist, and asked her if she had any record of an evacuee called John, or Johnny, Critchley. She checked her records then shook her head, as I knew she would. If I were right, Johnny wouldn't be here under his own name. I explained my problem to the woman, who told me her name was

Phyllis Rigby. She had a yellow ribbon in her long wavy hair and smelled of fresh apples. 'I don't see how anything like that could have happened,' Phyllis said. 'We've been very meticulous. But there again, things *have* been a little chaotic.' She frowned in thought for a moment, then she delegated her present duties to another volunteer.

'Come on,' she said, 'I'll help you go from house to house. There weren't that many evacuees, you know. Far fewer than we expected.'

I nodded. I'd heard how a lot of parents weren't bothering to evacuate their children. 'They can't see anything happening yet,' I said. 'Just you wait. After the first air raid you'll have so many you won't have room for them all.'

Phyllis smiled. 'The poor things. It must be such an upheaval for them.'

'Indeed.'

I took deep, welcome breaths of country air as Phyllis and I set out from the village hall to visit the families listed on her clipboard. There were perhaps a couple of hundred houses, and less than fifty per cent had received evacuees. Even so, we worked up quite a sweat calling at them all. Or I did, rather, as sweating didn't seem to be in Phyllis's nature. We chatted as we went, me telling her about my school teaching, and she telling me about her husband, Thomas, training as a fighter pilot in the RAF. After an hour or so with no luck, we stopped in at her cottage for a refreshing cup of tea, then we were off again.

At last, late in the afternoon, we struck gold.

•

Mr and Mrs Douglas, who were billeting Johnny Critchley, seemed a very pleasant couple, and they were sad to hear that they could not keep him with them for a while longer. I explained everything to them and assured them that they would get someone else as soon as we had the whole business sorted out.

'He's *not* here,' Johnny said as we walked with Phyllis to the station. 'I've looked everywhere, but I couldn't find him.'

I shook my head. 'Sorry, Johnny. You know your mum's got a speech impediment. That was why I had to go back and ask her exactly what she said to you before I came here. She said she told you your father was missing in action, which, the way it came out, sounded like missing in *Acksham*, didn't it? That's why you came here, wasn't it, to look for your father?'

Young Johnny nodded, tears in his eyes. 'I'm sorry,' he said. 'I couldn't understand why *she* didn't come and look for him. She must be really vexed with me.'

I patted his shoulder. 'I don't think so. More like she'll be glad to see you. How did you manage to sneak in with the real evacuees, by the way?'

Johnny wiped his eyes with his grubby sleeve. 'At the station. There were so many people standing around, at first I didn't know . . . Then I saw a boy I knew from playing cricket on the rec.'

'Oliver Bradley,' I said. The boy whose name Johnny was registered under.

'Yes. He goes to Broad Hill.'

I nodded. Though I had never heard of Oliver Bradley, I knew the school; it was just across the valley from us. 'Go on.'

'I asked him where he was going, and he said he was being sent to Acksham. It was perfect.'

'But how did you get him to change places with you?'

'He didn't want to. Not at first.'

'How did you persuade him?'

Johnny looked down at the road and scraped at some gravel with the scuffed tip of his shoe. 'It cost me a complete set of "Great Cricketers" cigarette cards. Ones my dad gave me before he went away.'

I smiled. It would have to be something like that.

'And I made him promise not to tell anyone, just to go home and say there wasn't room for him, and he'd have to try again in a few days. I just needed enough time to find Dad . . . you know.'

'I know.'

We arrived at the station, where Johnny sat on the bench and Phyllis and I chatted in the late afternoon sunlight, our shadows lengthening across the tracks. In addition to the birds singing in the trees and hedgerows, I could hear grasshoppers chirruping, a sound you rarely heard in the city. I had often thought how much I would like to live in the country and, perhaps when I retired from teaching a few years in the future, I would be able to do so.

We didn't have long to wait for our train. I thanked Phyllis for all her help, told her I wished her husband well, and she waved to us as the old banger chugged out of the station.

•

It was past blackout when I finally walked into our street holding Johnny's hand. He was tired after his adventure and had spent most of the train journey with his head on my shoulder. Once or twice, from the depths of a dream, he had called his father's name.

I could sense that something was wrong as soon as I turned the corner. It was nothing specific, just a sudden chill at the back of my neck. Because of the blackout, I couldn't see anything clearly, but I got a strong impression of a knot of shifting shadows, just a little bit darker than the night itself, milling around outside Colin Gormond's house.

I quickened my step, and as I got nearer I heard a whisper pass through the crowd when they saw Johnny. Then the shadows began to disperse, slinking and sidling away, disappearing like smoke into the air. From somewhere, Mary Critchley lurched forward with a cry and took young Johnny in her arms. I let him go. I could hear her thanking me between sobs, but I couldn't stop walking.

The first thing I noticed when I approached Colin's house was that the window was broken and half the blackout curtain had been ripped away. Next I saw that the door was slightly ajar. I was worried that Colin might be hurt, but out of courtesy I knocked and called out his name.

Nothing.

I pushed the door open and walked inside. It was pitch dark. I didn't have a torch with me, and I knew that Colin's light didn't work, but I remembered the matches and the candle on the table. I lit it and held it up before me as I walked forward.

I didn't have far to look. If I hadn't had the candle, I might have bumped right into him. First I saw his face, about level with mine. His froth-specked lips had turned blue, and a trickle of dried blood ran from his left nostril.

The blackout cloth was knotted around his neck in a makeshift noose, attached to a hook screwed into the lintel over the kitchen door. As I stood back and examined the scene further, I saw that his down-turned toes were about three inches from the floor, and there was no sign of an upset chair or stool.

Harmless Colin Gormond, friend to the local children. Dead.

I felt the anger well up in me, along with the guilt. It was my fault. I shouldn't have gone dashing off to Acksham like that in search of Johnny, or I should at least have taken Colin with me. I knew the danger he was in; I had talked to Jack Blackwell before I left. How could I have been so stupid, so careless as to leave Colin to his fate with only a warning he didn't understand?

Maybe Colin *had* managed to hang himself somehow, without standing on a stool, though I doubted it. But whether or not Jack Blackwell or the rest had actually laid a finger on him, they were all guilty of driving him to it in my book. Besides, if Jack or anyone else from the street *had* strung Colin up, there would be evidence – fibres, fingerprints, footprints, whatever – and even DS bloody Longbottom wouldn't be able to ignore that.

I stumbled outside and made my way towards the telephone box on the corner. Not a soul stirred now, but as I went I heard one door – Jack Blackwell's door – close softly this time, as if he thought that too much noise might wake the dead, and the dead might have a tale or two to tell.

MEMORY LANE

MEMORY LANE

Another shitty gig. In more ways than one. I can smell the colostomy bags the minute we walk in the front doors. I shudder, as I always do when we enter a place like this. One day, and it might not be long, I know I won't be coming out.

The Recreation Director is waiting to greet us, crisp blue suit and Morningside accent. Why do RDs all have Scottish accents, even in Vancouver? A gold name tag just above the swell of her left breast tells me her name is Emily. Actually, if you look closely, our Emily's not that bad at all, despite the ill-fitting glasses and lifeless hair.

'You'll be the musicians, then?' Nervously eyeing her wristwatch.

Why does it sound like an insult?

'We'll be the musicians,' I admit. Then I introduce the band: Memory Lane. There are five of us, three of us expat Brits. Kit Stark, a washed-up hippie, is our drummer. Kit took one too many hits of acid on the Isle of Wight ferry nearly thirty years ago. When they'd fished him out of the Solent and done artificial respiration, he spent the next twenty years in and out of the nut house hallucinating plankton before washing up on the shores of Nova Scotia. Then there's Benny Leiberman, our morose, alcoholic bass player from Des Moines. Taffy Lloyd plays trumpet and trombone, and when he's not doing that, he's our vocalist. He looks like Harry Secombe but sounds more like one of the Spice Girls. The Hunchback of Notre Band, Geoff Carroll, plays piano, guitar and vibes and does most of our arrangements. He's so short-sighted that he has developed a permanent hunch from leaning over the keyboard to read the music.

Last but not least, there's me, Dex Hill (well, my real name is William Hill, but wouldn't *you* change that for something a bit more jazzy-sounding?), apple of my music teacher's eye, future clarinet soloist for the London Symphony Orchestra (failed), the next John Coltrane (failed) and husband to the beautiful, sexy and cruel Andrea (also failed).

Get the picture?

'I suppose you'd like to tune up, then?' suggests Emily.

Tune up? You don't tune up a clarinet or a saxophone. Or a trumpet for that matter. Perhaps Benny wants to mess around with his bass strings, though the way he's shaking he looks more as if he needs a drink.

I nod.

'Follow me. I'll show you the dressing room.'

We follow Emily's gently swaying hips down the corridor. If we exude a general aroma of booze and smoke, especially with those filthy French cigarettes Benny smokes, she affects not to notice. What does she go home to, my Emily, I wonder? How does she get the aura of death and disease out of her system when she leaves here? Sex? Drugs? Maybe I'll ask her.

Once we're settled in the broom closet they call a dressing room, Emily-less, Benny takes out a fifth of Jim Beam and inhales. He doesn't offer it around. He never does. Some people might think that's rude, but we're used to him and his strange lonely ways by now. Kit and

I share a spliff. Just another little smell lost among the faeces and sour sweat. Taffy, as is his wont, puffs on a Rothman's and does a few vocal exercises. Geoff studies the music as if it's the first time he's ever set eyes on it. He always does. In a way, I feel sorry for Geoff because wherever we go the poor sod *always* gets stuck with an out-of-tune piano. Still, he takes it in his stride. Very phlegmatic is Geoff. Lots of sangfroid. You have to have with a hunchback like his.

Anyway, after a few minutes of this and a chat about the order of songs, Emily returns and we're ready to face the chanting crowds.

'They've been looking forward to this all week, you know,' she says, with a tight, Morningside smile. 'A lot of them were in the war, with the Canadian armed forces, or with the RAF. It'll mean a lot to them, hearing those old songs played again.'

Well, there are about twenty people in the recreation room, which is quite a crowd for this sort of gig. I remember one RD apologizing – I think it was in Swift Current or Red Deer – that there would have been more people in the audience only two of them croaked during the night. That seemed a bit excessive to me. I mean, one, maybe, you might expect, but *two*?

There they sit, a pathetic bunch of losers waiting to die. It gives me the shivers just to look at them. Empty husks. Nothing left except bodily functions. Even those who have arses left probably need someone to wipe them. Most sit in wheelchairs, reptilian talons plucking at the tartan blankets spread over their knees. Some have the head shakes, some drool and twitch every now and then.

Still, I suppose I've seen worse audiences in Toronto jazz clubs.

A quick count, and we're off: 'Tennessee Waltz', always a nice easy swinger to start with. Intro done, Taffy comes in with the vocals, sounding more like Tiny Tim than Sporty Spice today. One, two, three, here we go . . . Hey up, there's one bloke on the nod already.

'I was dancing with my darling . . .'

•

I was the best dancer. That's why she chose me. I was the best dancer. She wasn't Carl's to start with. Wasn't anyone's. Just another girl at a forces dance on a Saturday night. Carl was the handsomest; he always got the pick of the girls. But not this time. I was the best dancer. Just put his nose out of joint a little, that's all. I didn't steal her from anyone. She melted in my arms, her shape moulded against me; we were missing halves of a whole and the purpose the music had been waiting for; we completed it, carried it away from its airy pointlessness to something more profound; we gave the music meaning.

Bullshit, O'Farrell. You stole your best friend's sweetheart, pure and simple. And all the rest, all this about profundity and meaning, is bullshit. Lust, that's all it was. Lust. And revenge for all those times when Carl got the girl. And look what happened. A two-week honeymoon, then you took her thousands of miles away from her family and friends, spent the next fifty years in and out of the bottle and drove the poor bitch to an early grave.

No . . . no . . . it wasn't like that. I'm tired, so tired of arguing with myself . . .

•

169

On the nod, just as we're going into 'Cheek to Cheek'. Christ, how stimulating we must be, what fucking exciting memories we must invoke. Still, he's twitching a bit in his wheelchair, so I suppose he must still be alive. His mouth seems to be moving. Maybe he's trying to sing along. Sometimes they do. But no, this one looks more as if he's having a conversation with himself, only half-mouthing the words, hardly daring to give them full breath. A little string of drool hangs from his chin. Shit, I hate this job. Solo time, man. Remember what Geoff told you, 'Stick real close to the melody line, Dex. You're not Coltrane playing "My Favourite Things", you know.' Thanks a lot, Geoff. And fuck you . . .

•

Heaven. I'm in heaven. Dancing cheek to cheek. A hot night in late July 1943. A little dance hall in a small town near the base, maybe used to be the church hall or the Women's Institute. A few rickety tables, a makeshift bar selling warm beer and weak scotch, weak beer and warm scotch, whatever. Dim air thick with smoke hanging in the lights: blue straight from the cigarette, grey when it comes out of the lungs. Everyone smoked then. All of us. It was the least of our worries. 'Cheek to Cheek' was the first song we danced to, the first time the magic hit.

But why does my memory smell of burning rubber and leather instead of her perfume? Why do flames and smoke blossom when I close my eyes and lean into her? I'm holding her close enough that she could almost be a part of me and I'm smelling hot metal and engine oil.

Bombenbrandschrumpfleichen.

My God, Carl, where did that come from? Not now. Not yet. That was later. Back to the dance. Holding her. Some of her face powder rubbed off when my lips brushed her cheek. It tasted like chalk. Carl was pissed, I could tell, but I was flying that night (funny, I was flying the night before, too) and it was my turn for once. They'd only been out together a couple of times. It wasn't serious. Besides, how was I to know that Mary and I would fall in love? It was just another dance, for crying out loud. We'd been to hundreds of them and Carl always got the best-looking women. But I was the best dancer and Carl had no chance this time when she and I were dancing cheek to cheek, me tasting chalk (or was it stardust?), smelling rubber burn and hearing those crackling noises arcing in my brain from ear to ear.

•

Christ, just look at them, will you? Half of them are asleep, about a third are deaf and three-quarters have no faculties left at all. What does that make? Is anyone out there listening at all? And that hunchbacked bastard Geoff gives me the evil eye for wandering too far on the 'Stardust' solo. As if anyone notices. Poor bastard's piano is so out of tune it sounds like a warped LP. Funny, all of a sudden I'm thinking of that bitch Andrea. Was 'Stardust' playing when we met, on our first date? I'm damned if I remember. 'Stairway to Heaven', more likely, or maybe 'Bitches Brew'. All I remember is ripping her panties off and fucking her hard up against the apartment door the minute we got back from the gig. Play it, Dex. 'All the Things You Are.' Bird, Trane, lead the way. And to hell with Geoff's evil eye . . .

•

Carl wouldn't talk to me. All the next day. And the next. He'd really wanted Mary the way a boy wants candy and he was jealous as hell. I didn't tell him anything. Didn't tell him about the softness of her body as we made love in the warm field that July night, the taste of the beet juice on her lips, the smooth warm skin, nipples hard as berries on my tongue, between her legs like warm, wet silk and how she cried out my name when she came. Not his. Mine. And clung to me afterwards for dear life as we lay against the drystone wall and watched squadron after squadron of Lancasters pass over the half-moon, blotting out its light like the plague of locusts, armadas from hell. Held me tighter as the roar of the bombers filled the sky.

Bombenbrandschrumpfleichen.

No. That wasn't till later. We didn't know then, the same way we didn't know smoking was killing us. We didn't know. But does that really make it any different in the end?

•

Another evil look from Geoff. Well, to hell with him. Let the miserable bastard fire me. I've had it with this, anyway. 'In the Middle of a Kiss.' Taffy always does a good job on this one. You just don't expect that alto voice to come out of someone so fat. Look at that guy, the way his head's swaying. If it's the shakes, at least he's in time with the music. Maybe some of them are capable of getting a little simple pleasure out of us, after all. Christ, if Andrea could see me now. She'd laugh until she pissed herself and tell me I'd found my true destiny. Here we go, man, 'Blowing Up a Storm'.

•

Firestorm. They had to invent new names for the way people died.

Bombenbrandschrumpfleichen.

Incendiary-bomb-shrunken bodies. Then there were the ones who melted, asphyxiated, baked or just plain roasted. And the human torches running down streets on fire, arms flailing.

These were the important factories and docks we were told we destroyed. The firestorm sucked in all the surrounding air, made winds rage fast as cyclones, suffocated all the people hiding in shelters, cellars and bunkers. Fifteen hundred degrees Fahrenheit at the core. Spontaneous combustion.

Bombenbrandschrumpfleichen.

And the night after that I stole my best friend's girl because I was the best dancer. That was the night we clung to one another watching the bombers set out again. Six raids. Day and night. Night and day. 41,800 killed. 37,439 injured, burned, maimed. Her skin warm and smooth, wet silk between her thighs, bombers blanking out the stars and the moon. Making Bombenbrandschrumpfleichen. *And the night after that, Carl bought it . . .*

•

'Blue Flame.' That should slow them down a bit before our fiery finale, and a nice searing blues solo for me. Most of them are asleep now anyway. There's even one old dear snoring in the far corner by the vase of flowers. And there's Emily, hands clasped on her lap, thin smile on her face. Is she enjoying us? As a matter of fact, I wouldn't mind fucking Emily, stick it to her hard, right up that tight Morningside arse of hers and take that smile off her face. Bet she's a screamer. That old guy's having a real struggle with himself now. Ought to be in a fucking nuthouse not a rest home. Drooling and muttering, arguing with himself . . .

•

It wasn't fair, we'd finished, we were heading home successful, looking forward to a hot cup of tea and a long sleep, no fighters in sight. But then it never is fair, is it? We'd dropped our load, made more Bombenbrand-schrumpfleichen, got out of the flack unscathed, and all of a sudden there it was, a lone Messerschmitt. Whether he was lost or just scavenging, looking for stragglers, I don't know, but he buzzed at us like an angry wasp and let rip. He could outmanoeuvre us easily and his machine-gun fire ripped through the plane as if our fuselage were made of paper. I could smell the fires breaking out behind us. Me and Clarky, my co-pilot. We started spewing smoke and losing altitude. One of our gunners hit the 'Schmitt and it exploded at ten o'clock. We were bucking and swinging to starboard like an old Short Stirling. God knows how we made it, but we did, Clarky and me, we came limping in the minute we got beyond the old white cliffs and crash-landed in a field. The tail section broke off and flames leapt up all around us. Within minutes we were surrounded by a crowd of gaping yokels right out of a Thomas Hardy novel. Whether they wore smocks and carried pitchforks I can't be certain, but that's how I see them when I look now. And when I went back to see how Carl was doing, that's when I found him. He was dead. Along with the others in back. All black and burned up, uniform and skin fused, welded into one, his knees crooked and his arms tightened up and fists clenched like a boxer, aimed at me. For one of those stupid moments, before reality's cold blade pierced the back of my brain, I thought he was getting ready to fight me. We hadn't spoken for three days because of Mary and I knew he was still pissed. But he was dead. Burned and shrivelled.

Bombenbrandschrumpfleichen.

Just like the people of Hamburg. Carl, you poor, sad, cocky, two-left-footed bastard. You were the handsomest, the most charming; you were the lady killer. But come waltz, tango or jitterbug, goddammit, I was the best dancer. I was the best dancer!

•

'I was the best dancer! I was the best dancer!'

One, two, three, and blow that bugle, Taffy! Let's wake the buggers up. 'Bugle Call Rag' and Jesus Christ, will you look at him, the old bastard's on his feet. Taffy flashes me a big grin and we get in the groove. I can feel Geoff's eyes boring into the back of my head. Fuck him. Things are jumping now. Taffy and I are trading licks like we haven't done in years. Trumpet and sax. Dizzy and Bird. Miles and Trane. Look at the guy go, he's out of his chair and jumping up and down, yelling at the top of his lungs, baggy pants slipping down his hips.

'I was the best dancer! I was the best dancer!'

Sure you were, buddy!

All of a sudden he seems to reach some sort of inner peak or crescendo as my sax and Taffy's trumpet join in some of the weirdest harmonies we've ever found. He's on tiptoe, stretching his arms as high as he can, reaching for the ceiling, or for heaven.

Then his whole body starts shaking. Taffy trails off to take a break and I blow harder, urging the old guy higher, but he's out of synch with us now. Whatever he's into, eyes closed, head tilted towards the ceiling, it's nothing to do with our music. His pants are down around his ankles, his shrivelled scrotum and shrunken penis there for all to see. I stop the solo and turn to catch Geoff's dagger gaze. I grin at him and shrug; he leads us back to the opening riff in a few spare, tight-assed chords.

The old man stiffens, then drops to the floor, spent. One by one, we let the music dribble away from us. Then there's the strangest sensation. The room seems to draw in on him, as if all its energy focuses on that single inert figure. Everything feels tight, like a corked bottle about to blow. The room fills with pressure, and it's hard against my eardrums, that deaf and fuzzy feeling before your ears pop on an airplane, everything silent and in slow motion.

Then it pops, the air hisses out, and he's just someone lying on the floor.

'Jesus,' whispers the man beside him. 'When I go, I want to go just like that.'

Then the smooth, practised staff breeze in like a team of office cleaners, or scene changers between the acts of a play, and start to tidy up the mess in a silence as heavy as prayer. Someone in white checks the old man's pulse and takes out a stethoscope. The other inmates, dazed, mumbling and drooling, are all wheeled back to their rooms. And it's getting to look like nothing ever happened.

Before they're done, Emily starts leading us back to the dressing room. 'I think it would probably be best all around if you left now, don't you think?' she says. 'Then we can get everyone calmed down. They take it hard, some of them, when one of them passes on, you know. See their own future, I suppose, poor things. Don't worry, you'll be paid your normal rate, of course. It wasn't your fault, after all, was it?'

I nod dumbly, walking beside her. She's right, of course. It wasn't our fault, no reason why we shouldn't get paid. But even so. *See their own future, I suppose.* Somehow that echoes, gets to me so much that I forget to ask for her phone number. And I remember it afterwards in the van. But this time Benny passes around the Jim Beam and Kit rolls another spliff and soon it's just another memory of just another shitty gig, after all, just another slice of turd on the nursing-home circuit.

CARRION

Isn't it strange the way two strangers might strike up a casual acquaintance due simply to a quirk of fate? And isn't it even stranger how that innocent meeting might so completely alter the life of one of them? That was exactly what happened when Edward Grainger and I met in a pub one wet September lunchtime, only weeks before his tragic loss.

I work in a bank in the City. It's a dull job, enlivened only by the occasional surge of adrenalin when the pound takes yet another plunge on the foreign exchange markets, and most lunchtimes I like to get out of the office and take refuge in the Mason's Arms.

As a rule, I will drink half a pint of Guinness with a slice of quiche or a cheese roll, say, and perhaps, once in a while, treat myself to a steak and kidney pie. As I eat, I work at the *Times* crossword, which I never seem able to finish before my glass is empty, and after my meal I enjoy a cigarette. I know the vile things are bad for me, but I can't quite seem to give them up. Besides, how bad can one cigarette a day be? And only five days a week, at that.

Given its location in the City, the Mason's Arms is generally busy, noisy and smoky by half past twelve on a weekday, and that suits me just fine. Lost in the crowd, buffeted by conversation and laughter that require no response on my part, I can concentrate on my crossword or allow my mind to drift in directions that the constant application of little grey cells to columns of figures precludes.

That particular lunchtime I found myself leaving the office a few minutes later than usual due to an important telephone conversation with an overseas client. The short walk also took longer because I had to struggle against the wind and rain with my rather flimsy umbrella. When I got to the Arms, as I had taken to calling it, I found my usual little corner table already taken by a stranger in a pinstripe suit. I could hardly tell him to sod off, so I carried my drink over and sat opposite him.

As he read his *Times*, I studied his features closely. I would guess his age at about forty-five – mostly because of the wrinkles around his eyes and the grey hair around his temples and ears – but having said that, I would have to admit that the overall effect of his face was one of youthfulness. He had bright blue eyes and a healthy, ruddy complexion, and he showed no sign of that dark, shadowy stubble that makes so many men look downright repulsive, not to mention sinister.

After I had finished my ham roll, I lit my cigarette and wrestled with eight down, letting the ebb and flow of conversation drift over me until a voice seemed to single itself out from the crowd and speak directly to me.

Startled, I noticed the man opposite looking at me in a way that suggested he had just spoken.

'Pardon?' I said. 'I was miles away.'

'"Crippen,"' he said. 'Eight down. "Quiet prince upset for this murderer." It's an anagram of "prince" and "p" for silent.'

'Yes, I do see that, thank you very much.' If my tone was a little frosty, it served the bugger right. I hate it when people solve my crossword clues for me, the same way I hate anyone reading over my shoulder. Takes all the fun out of it.

His face dropped when he saw the look I gave him.

'I'm sorry,' he said. 'Very rude of me. Didn't think.'

'It's all right.' I put the crossword aside and flicked a column of ash at the floor.

'Look, you wouldn't happen to know anything about septic tanks, would you?' he asked.

'I'm afraid not.' As far as conversational gambits went, this fellow wasn't exactly heading for the top of the class in my book.

'Oh. Pity. You see, we're having one installed in a couple of weeks, my wife Harriet and I. I'm just not sure what kind of mess to expect.'

'Well, I suppose they'll have to dig the garden up,' I told him. 'But I can't honestly say I've ever seen one, so I don't know how big they are.'

He smiled. 'Well, that's the point, isn't it? You're not supposed to *see* them. We're moving to the country, you know, to Hampshire.'

'Why are you moving?' I asked. And though I surprised myself by asking such a personal question of a complete stranger, it felt natural enough.

He sipped his gin and tonic before replying. 'It's for Harriet, mostly,' he said. 'Wants the country air. Not that I'd knock it, mind you. And it's a beautiful cottage, or it will be after the renovations. Seventeenth century. I'll keep the flat in town, of course, go down to the country at weekends. Yes, I'm sure it'll work out.'

'I hope so,' I told him. Then I excused myself and headed back to the bank, it being almost one-thirty and

Mr Beamish, the branch manager, being a real stickler for punctuality.

•

As time went on, our conversations became a regular feature of my lunchtime visits to the Arms, though I would be hard pushed now to think of everything we discussed: politics, of course, on which we disagreed; books, on which we agreed far more than we would have imagined; and marriage, about which we couldn't quite make up our minds. Sometimes, we would just work on the crossword together in silence.

He also talked about weekends at the country house, of autumn walks in the woods, the occasional hovercraft trip to the Isle of Wight, quiet nights with a good bottle of claret, a hefty volume of Trollope, and a log fire crackling in the hearth.

Though I had never fancied country living myself, I must admit that Edward's accounts made me quite envious. So much so that when Evelyn brought up the subject at home after watching a documentary on the Cotswolds, I thought it might become a real possibility for us, too, in a year or two's time.

Edward and I never met at any other times or places – ours was a purely casual arrangement – but I like to think that a sort of friendship developed. Sometimes he didn't turn up at all. He worked in international finance, he told me, and now and then he had to sacrifice his lunch hour for emergency meetings or telephone calls from strange time zones. Occasionally, he had to go abroad for a few days. But when he did come, we usually contrived to sit together and chat over our drinks and rolls for half an hour or so.

During that time, I didn't find out very much more about his private life, and if I were to come to any conclusions they would be due entirely to my reading between the lines.

I didn't ask Edward about his wife's occupation, for example, but somehow I got the impression that she spent most of her time at home cooking, cake-decorating, cleaning, sewing, knitting and such. What people used to call a 'housewife' in the old days. I suppose now she could call herself an 'estate manager' down in Hampshire. As far as their relationship went, it sounded perfectly normal to me.

Though I had never met Harriet, I'm sure you can imagine how shocked I was on that bright, windy Thursday in early October when Edward came in a quarter of an hour later than usual, looking drawn and haggard, and told me that his wife had disappeared.

•

Naturally, I tried to comfort him as best I could over the following weeks, at least as far as our brief and irregular meetings allowed. But there was little I could do. For the most part, I could only look on sadly as Edward lost weight and his former ruddy complexion turned wan. Soon he came to remind me of the wretched youth in Keats's poem: 'Alone and palely loitering'.

Weeks passed, and still there was no sign of Harriet. Theories as to her disappearance varied, as they do in cases like this. One tabloid speculated that she had been abducted by a serial killer, then chopped up and buried somewhere. A local doctor suggested that she could have suffered some form of amnesia. If so, he went on, she might easily have wandered off and ended up living on the streets of London with the thousands of other lost and lonely souls. One neighbour, Edward told me, speculated that Harriet could have been actually *planning* her escape for some time and had simply taken off for America, Ireland or France to start a new life under a new name. With a new man, of course. Astonishingly, Edward also told me that even *he* had come under police suspicion at one time, albeit not for long.

Christmas came and went. It was about as cheerful as a wet weekend in July, the way it usually is for families whose children have all grown up and left home. Edward seemed to have gained a little colour when I saw him after the holidays. Or perhaps the Arctic winds we had that January had rubbed his skin raw. Anyway, it was around then that he started dropping in at the Arms for lunch less and less frequently.

By the beginning of February I hadn't seen him for three weeks, and I was slipping easily back into my old routine of doing the crossword over lunch. I missed his company, of course, and I was certainly curious about Harriet, but we are creatures of habit, are we not? And old habits are deeply ingrained.

It was near the end of March when I saw him next, but it wasn't in the Arms. No, I had come into the West End to shop one Saturday afternoon, mostly to get out of the way while Evelyn was busy planting the herbaceous borders. I hate gardening, and if I'm around I usually get roped in.

Anyway, I was browsing downstairs in the fiction section of Waterstone's on Charing Cross Road, when I saw Edward across the table of new releases. It took me a moment to recognize him because he was wearing casual clothes and seemed to have done something to remove the grey from his hair. He was also fingering the new Will Self paperback, which one would hardly expect of a Trollope man.

On second glance, though, I realized it was definitely Edward and that the pretty young blonde with the prominent breasts didn't just happen to be standing beside him; she was *with* him. Surely this couldn't be the elusive Harriet?

Then a strange thing happened. Edward caught my eye as I walked over, and I saw a very odd look pass over his features. For a moment, I could have sworn, he wanted to turn tail and avoid me. But I got to him before he could retreat.

'Edward,' I said. 'It's good to see you.' Then I looked at the blonde. I could see her roots. 'I see Harriet has turned up, then,' I said with a smile.

Edward cleared his throat and the blonde merely frowned. 'Well . . . er . . .' he said. 'Not exactly. I mean, no, she hasn't. This is Joyce.' He put his arm around the blonde's shoulders and looked down at her with obvious pride and passion.

I said hello to Joyce as Edward haltingly explained our relationship, such as it was, then he made excuses and they hurried up the stairs as if the place were on fire. That was the last time I ever clapped eyes on Edward Grainger.

•

About a year after the incident in Waterstone's, something so profound, so shocking and so unexpected happened to me that my life was never to be the same again. I fell in love.

Like most people my age, I had long thought myself immune to powerful passions, long settled into a sedate and comfortable existence with little in the way of strong emotion to upset its even keel. If I have unsatisfied or unrequited hopes and wishes, then I am in good company, for who hasn't? If I regret some of the sacrifices I have made for the comforts I have gained, who doesn't? And if I sometimes feel that my life lacks adventure, lacks spice, then again, who doesn't? In all that, I felt, I was perfectly normal.

Life, it had come to seem to me, was a slow betrayal of the dreams of one's youth and a gradual decline from the desires of one's adolescence. Little did I know what a fragile illusion all that was until I met Katrina.

Imagine, if you can, my utter amazement when the bells started to ring, the earth moved and a sudden spring came into my step every time I saw her. Absurd, I told myself, she'll never pay the least attention to an old fuddy-duddy like you. But she did. Oh, indeed she did. Love truly must be blind if such a gorgeous creature as Katrina could give herself to me.

Katrina came to work for the branch in summer, and by autumn we were meeting clandestinely whenever we could. She lived alone in a tiny bedsit in Kennington, which was convenient, if a bit cramped. But what is a little discomfort to a pair of lovers? We were consumed with a passion that could no more be stopped than an avalanche or a tidal wave. It picked us up, tossed us about like rag dolls and threw us back on the ground dazed, dazzled and breathless. I couldn't get enough of her sad eyes, her soft red lips, her small breasts with the nipples hard as acorns when we made love, her skin like warm brown silk.

Needless to say, this affair made life very difficult both at work and at home, but I think I managed to cope well enough under the circumstances. I know I succeeded in hiding it from Evelyn, for I surely would have felt the repercussions had I not.

We went on meeting furtively for almost a year, during which time our passion did not abate in the least. Katrina never once asked me to abandon my marriage and live with her, but I wanted to. Oh God, how I wanted to. Only the thought of all the trouble, all the upheaval, that such a move would cause prevented me. For Evelyn wouldn't take it lying down. So, like many others embroiled in affairs, I simply let it run on, perhaps hoping vaguely that some *deus ex machina* would come along and solve my problems for me.

Then, one day, after an excruciatingly painful Christmas spent away from Katrina, Evelyn reminded me of a conversation we had had some time ago about getting a country cottage, and pointed out the ideal place in an estate agent's brochure: a rundown, isolated cottage in Oxfordshire, going for a song.

Furiously, I began to think of how such a move might prevent me from seeing Katrina as often as I needed to. We would have to sell the Dulwich house, of course, but the Oxfordshire cottage was indeed going for such an unbelievably low price that I might be able to afford a small flat in town.

At a pinch, however, Evelyn might suggest I could commute. The thought of that was unbearable. Though Katrina and I wouldn't be separated totally, anything other than a quick session after work before the train home would be impossible. And neither of us wanted to live like that. A quickie in the back of a car is so sordid, and we were passionately, romantically in love.

On the other hand, I could hardly crush Evelyn's

dreams of a place in the country without thinking up a damn good explanation as to why we should simply stay put. And I couldn't. The price was right, and we might not have another chance for years. Even with the renovations that would need to be done, we worked out, we could still easily afford it.

And so we took the plunge and bought the cottage. To say I was a soul in torment might sound like an exaggeration, but believe me, it doesn't even come close to describing how wretched I really felt as I signed on the dotted line.

•

We had sent Sam Halsey, a jack-of-all-trades in the renovation business, over to Oxfordshire on a number of occasions to assess what needed doing and how it could be done to our liking *and* to our budget. One of his complaints was that, due to its isolation and to the odd whims of its previous owners, the toilet arrangements were far from adequate.

After much deliberation, one afternoon at the house in Dulwich, Sam said, 'Of course, you could have a septic tank put in.'

'A what?' I said.

'A septic tank. Perfectly respectable. Lots of country folk have them. Of course, you'll need some carrion.'

'I'm sorry, Sam, I don't follow you.'

'Carrion. To get the whole process going. Now, some of the younger chaps in the business will tell you a bit of compost will do the job just fine, but don't believe them. Don't you believe them. My old boss told me—'

Sam's voice faded into the background as, suddenly, it hit me. I thought of my old lunchtime companion,

Edward Grainger, and that guilty look that flitted across his features the time I saw him in Waterstone's with Joyce, the blonde.

I remembered the tragedy of his wife's disappearance, and how, after that, I saw less and less of him.

And I remembered how the disappearance occurred around the time they were having a septic tank installed at their cottage in Hampshire. Carrion, indeed.

And then I thought of my Katrina, my beautiful, beautiful Katrina, who took my breath away with her sad eyes and her skin like warm brown silk.

And, lastly, I thought of Evelyn. Life just isn't fair, is it? Some people don't simply fade away quietly into the obscurity from whence they came when you want rid of them, do they? No, they have to cause trouble, create scenes, make unreasonable demands and generally do their damnedest to ruin your hopes of a decent and happy future without them. They just *won't go away*. Well, as I have already explained, Evelyn is one of those people. I'm certain of it.

On the other hand, people disappear all the time, don't they? And people change. Harriet changed into Joyce, didn't she? Sometimes you just have to give a little kick-start to get the process going, like the carrion in the septic tank, and then nature takes care of the rest.

'Penny for them?'

'What? Oh, I'm sorry, Sam. Miles away.'

'That's all right. I was just saying as how you'll need some carrion for the septic tank. My old boss swore by it, he did.'

At that moment, Evelyn passed by the open French windows in his shabby beige cardigan, secateurs in hand. Wisps of grey hair blew in the March wind like spiders' webs, and his glasses had slipped down his nose. Yes, people disappear all the time, don't they? And if it can happen to wives, I thought, then it can bloody well happen to husbands too.

'Yes, Sam,' I said slowly. 'Yes, I suppose we will. Don't worry. I'll take care of it.'

APRIL IN PARIS

The girl sitting outside the cafe reminds me of April. She has the same long hennaed hair, which she winds around her index finger in the same abstracted way. She is waiting for someone clearly – a lover perhaps – and as she waits she smokes, holding her cigarette in the same way, taking the same short, hurried puffs, that April used to do. With her free hand, she alternates between taking sips of milky *pastis* and tapping her cigarette packet on the table. She is smoking Marlboro, as everyone in Paris seems to do these days. Back then it was all Gitanes, Gauloises and Disque Bleus.

Still, it wasn't smoking that killed April; it was love.

•

It is late September, and though the weather is mild, it is still too cold outside for an old man like me, with blood as thin and as lacking in nutrients as workhouse gruel. Instead, I sit inside the little cafe on the Boulevard St Germain over a *pichet* of red wine, just watching the people come and go. The young people. I have spent most of my life surrounded by the young, and though I grow inexorably older every year, they always seem to stay young. *Immortal youth.* Like Tithonus, I am 'a white-haired shadow roaming like a dream'. But unlike Tennyson's luckless narrator, who gained eternal life but not eternal youth, I am not immortal.

Six months, perhaps less, the doctors say. Something is growing inside me; my cells are mutating. As yet I feel little pain, though my appetite has diminished and I often suffer from extreme weariness.

Dying, I find, lends an edge to living, gives a clarity and a special, golden hue to the quotidian scenes parading before me: a swarthy man with a briefcase, glancing at his watch, speeding up, late for an important appointment; a woman chastising her little girl at the corner, wagging her finger, the girl crying and stamping her foot; a distracted priest stumbling briefly as he walks up the steps to the church across the boulevard.

Dying accentuates the beauty of the young, sets their energy in relief, enhances the smooth glow of their unwrinkled skin. But dying does not make me bitter. I am resigned to my fate; I have come to the end of my three-score and ten; I have seen enough. If you wish to travel, my doctors told me, do it now while you're still strong enough. So here I am, revisiting the scene of my one and only great *amour*.

April. She always pronounced it *Ap-reel*. When I think of her, I still hear Thelonious Monk playing 'April in Paris', hesitantly at first, feeling his way into the song, reluctant to define the theme, then worrying away at it and, once finding it, altering it so much that the music becomes his own, only to be abandoned finally.

Of course, April didn't give a tinker's for Thelonious Monk. She listened to him dutifully, as they all did, for they were the heirs of Kerouac, Ginsberg and Burroughs, to whom Monk, Bird, Trane, Miles and Mingus were gods, sacred and cool. But April's generation had its own gods – the Doors, Cream, Jimi Hendrix, Bob Dylan – gods of words and images as well as of music, and it was they who provided the soundtrack to which I lived during my year as a visiting lecturer in American literature at the Sorbonne in 1968.

This cafe hasn't changed much. A lick of paint, perhaps, if that. It probably hasn't changed much since Hemingway and Fitzgerald used to hang out around here. Even the waiters are probably the same. It was here I first met April, of course (why else would I come here?), one fine evening towards the end of March that year, when I was still young enough to bear the slight chill of a clear spring evening.

•

That April was beautiful almost goes without saying. I remember her high cheekbones, her smooth, olive complexion, dark, watchful eyes and rich, moist lips, down-turned at the edges, often making her look sulky or petulant when she was far from it. I remember also how she used to move with grace and confidence when she remembered, but how the gaucheness of late adolescence turned her movements into a country girl's gait when she was at her most unselfconscious. She was tall, slim and long-legged, and her breasts were small, round and high. The breasts of a Cranach nude.

We met, as I say, one late March evening in 1968 at this cafe, the Café de la Lune, where I was then sitting with the usual group: Henri, Nadine, Brad, Brigitte, Alain and Paul. This was only days after Daniel Cohn-Bendit and seven other students had occupied the dean's office at Nanterre to protest against the recent arrest of six members of the National Vietnam Committee, an event that was to have cataclysmic effects on us all not long afterwards. Much of the time in those days we spoke of revolution, but that evening we were discussing, I remember quite clearly, F. Scott Fitzgerald's *Tender Is the Night*, when in she walked, wearing a woolly jumper and close-fitting, bell-bottomed jeans with flowers embroidered around the bells. She was carrying a bulky leather shoulder bag, looking radiant and slightly lost, glancing around for someone she knew.

It turned out that she knew Brad, an American backpacker who had attached himself to our group. People like Brad had a sort of fringe, outlaw attraction for the students. They seemed, with their freedom to roam and their contempt for rules and authority, to embody the very principles that the students themselves, with their heavy workloads, exams and future careers, could only imagine, or live vicariously. There were always one or two Brads around. Some dealt in drugs to make a living; Brad, though he spoke a good revolution, lived on a generous allowance wired regularly by his wealthy Boston parents via Western Union.

April went up to Brad and kissed him on both cheeks, a formal French gesture he seemed to accept with thinly veiled amusement. In his turn, Brad introduced her to the rest of us. That done, we resumed our discussion over another bottle of wine, the tang of Gauloises and *café noir* infusing the chill night air, and April surprised me by demonstrating that she had not only read *Tender Is the Night*, but that she had thought about it, too, even though she was a student of history, not of literature.

'Don't you think those poor young girls are terribly *used*?' she said. 'I mean, Nicole is Dick's *patient*. He should be healing her, not sleeping with her. And the way Rosemary is manipulated by her mother . . . I'd go so far as to say that the mother seems to be *pimping* for her.

Those films she made –' and here April gave her characteristic shrug, no more than a little shiver rippling across
her shoulders – 'they were no doubt made to appeal to
older men.' She didn't look at me as she said this, but my
cheeks burned nonetheless.

'Have you read *Day of the Locust*?' Henri, one of the
other students, chimed in. 'If you want to know about
how Hollywood warps people, that's your place to start.
There's a mother in there who makes Rosemary's look
like a saint.'

'Huxley?' asked Nadine, not our brightest.

'No,' said April. 'That was *After Many a Summer. Day
of the Locust* was Nathanael West, I think. Yes?'

Here, she looked directly at me, the professor, for the
first time, turned on me the full blaze of her beauty. She
knew she was right, of course, but she still deferred to
me out of politeness.

'That's right,' I said, smiling, feeling my heart lurch
and my soul tingle inside its chains of flesh. 'Nathanael
West wrote *Day of the Locust*.'

And from that moment on I was smitten.

•

I told myself not to be a fool, that April was far too young
for me, and that a beautiful woman like her couldn't possibly be interested in a portly, forty-year-old lecturer, even
if he did wear faded denim jeans, had a goatee and grew
those wisps of hair that remained a little longer than
some of his colleagues thought acceptable. But after that
first meeting I found myself thinking about April a lot. In
fact I couldn't get her out of my mind. It wasn't mere lust
– though, Lord knows, it was that too – but I loved the
sound of her voice, loved the way she twisted strands of

hair around her finger as she spoke, the way she smoked her cigarette, loved the passion of her arguments, the sparkle of her laughter, the subtle jasmine of her perfume.

Love.

That night, she had left the cafe after about an hour, arm in arm with Brad – young, handsome, rich, footloose and fancy-free Brad – and I had lain awake tormented by images of their passionate love making. I had never felt like that before, never felt so consumed by desire for someone and so racked by pain at the thought of someone else having her. It was as if an alien organism had invaded my body, my very soul, and wrought such changes there that I could hardly cope with more mundane matters, such as teaching and writing, eating and sleeping.

The second time I met her it was raining. I was walking along the *quai* across from Notre Dame, staring distractedly at the rain pitting the river's steely surface, thinking of her, when she suddenly ducked under my umbrella and took my arm.

I must have gasped out loud.

'Professor Dodgson,' she said. Not a question. She *knew* who I was. 'Sorry I startled you.'

But that wasn't why I gasped, I wanted to tell her. It was the sudden apparition of this beautiful creature I had been dreaming about for days. I looked at her. The driving rain had soaked her hair and face. Like Dick in *Tender Is the Night*, I wanted to drink the rain that ran from her cheeks. 'How did you recognize me under this?' I asked her.

She gave that little shrug that was no more than a ripple and smiled up at me. 'Easy. You're carrying the same old briefcase you had last week. It's got your initials on it.'

'How sharp of you,' I said. 'You should become a detective.'

'Oh, I could never become a fascist pig.' She said this with a completely straight face. People said things like that back then.

'Just a joke,' I said. 'Where are you going?'

'Nowhere special.'

'Coffee?'

She looked at me again, chewing on her lower lip for a moment as she weighed up my invitation. 'All right,' she said finally. 'I know a place.' And her gentle pressure on my arm caused me to change direction and enter the narrow alleys that spread like veins throughout the Latin Quarter. 'Your French is very good,' she said as we walked. 'Where did you learn?'

'School, mostly. Then university. I seem to have a facility for it. We used to come here when I was a child, too, before the war. Brittany. My father fought in the first war, you see, and he developed this love for France. I think the fighting gave him a sort of stake in things.'

'Do you, too, have this stake in France?'

'I don't know.'

She found the cafe she was looking for on the Rue St Séverin, and we ducked inside. 'Can you feel what's happening?' she asked me, once we were warm and dry, sitting at the zinc counter with hot, strong coffees before us. She lit a Gauloise and touched my arm. 'Isn't it exciting?'

I couldn't believe what I was hearing. *She* thought something was happening between us. I could hardly disguise my joy. But I was also so tongue-tied that I couldn't think of anything wise or witty to say. I probably sat there, my mouth opening and closing like a guppy's before saying, 'Yes. *Yes*, it is exciting.'

'There'll be a revolution before spring's over, you mark my words. We'll be rid of de Gaulle and ready to start building a new France.'

Ah, yes. *The revolution*. I should have known. It was the topic on everyone's mind at the time. Except mine, that is. I tried not to show my disappointment. Not that I wasn't interested – you couldn't be in Paris in the spring of 1968 and *not* be interested in the revolution one way or another – but I had been distracted from politics by my thoughts of April. Besides, as radical as I might have appeared to some people, I was still a foreign national, and I had to do my best to keep a low political profile, difficult though it was. One false step and I'd not only be out of a job but out of the country, and far away from April, for ever. And I had answered her question honestly; I didn't know whether I had a stake in France or not.

'What does Brad think?' I asked.

'Brad?' She seemed surprised by my question. 'Brad is an anarchist.'

'And you?'

She twisted her hair around her finger. 'I'm not sure. I know I want change. I think I'm an anarchist too, though I'm not sure I'd want to be completely without any sort of government at all. But we want the same things. Peace. A new, more equal society. He is an American, but they have had many demonstrations there, too, you know. Vietnam.'

'Ah, yes. I remember some of them.'

We passed a while talking about my experiences in California, which seemed to fascinate April, though I must admit I was far more interested in tracing the contours of her face and drinking in the beauty of her eyes and skin than I was in discussing the war in Vietnam.

In the end she looked at her watch and said she had to go to a lecture but would probably see me later at the cafe. I said I hoped so and watched her walk away.

●

You will have gathered that I loved April to distraction, but did she love me? I think not. She liked me well enough. I amused her, entertained her, and she was perhaps even flattered by my attentions, but ultimately brash youth wins out over suave age. It was Brad she loved. Brad, whose status in my mind quickly changed from that of a mildly entertaining, reasonably intelligent hanger-on to the bane of my existence.

He always seemed to be around, and I could never get April to myself. Whether this was deliberate – whether he was aware of my interest and made jealous by it – I do not know. All I know is that I had very few chances to be alone with her. When we were together, usually at a cafe or walking in the street, we talked – talked of what was happening in France, of the future of the university, of literature, of the Anarchists, Maoists, Trotskyists and Communists, talked about all these, but not, alas, of love.

Perhaps this was my fault. I never pushed myself on her, never tried to make advances, never tried to touch her, even though my cells ached to reach out and mingle with hers, and even though the most casual physical contact – a touch on the arm, for example – set me aflame with desire. After our first few meetings, she would greet me with kisses on each cheek, the way she greeted all her friends, and my cheeks would burn for hours afterwards.

One day she left a silk scarf at the cafe, and I took it home and held it to my face like a lovesick schoolboy, inhaling April's subtle jasmine perfume as I tried to sleep that night.

But I did not dare make a pass; I feared her rejection and her laughter far more than anything else. While we do not have the capacity to choose our feelings in the first place, we certainly have the ability to choose not to *act* on them, and that was what I was trying to do, admittedly more for my own sake than for hers.

•

When I did see April alone again it was late in the morning of 3 May, and I was still in bed. I had been up late the night before, trying to concentrate on a Faulkner paper I had to present at a conference in Brussels that weekend, and as I had no actual classes on Fridays I had slept in.

The soft but insistent tapping at my door woke me from a dream about my father in the trenches (why is it we never seem to dream at night about those we dream about all day?) and I rubbed the sleep out of my eyes.

I must explain that at the time, like the poor French workers, I wasn't paid very much and consequently, as I didn't need very much either, I lived in a small *pension* in a cobbled alley off the Boulevard St Michel, between the university and the Luxembourg Gardens. As I could easily walk from the *pension* to my office at the Sorbonne, as I usually ate at the university or at a cheap local bistro, and as I spent most of my social hours in the various bars and cafes of the Latin Quarter, I didn't really need much more than a place to lay my head at night.

I stretched, threw on my dressing gown and opened the door. I'm sure you can imagine my shock on finding

April standing there. *Alone*. She had been to the room only once previously, along with Brad and a couple of others for a nightcap of cognac after a Nina Simone concert, but she clearly remembered where I lived.

'Oh, I'm sorry, Richard—' She had started calling me by my first name, at my insistence, though of course she pronounced it in the French manner, and it sounded absolutely delightful to me every time she spoke it. 'I didn't know . . .'

'Come in,' I said, standing back. She paused a moment in the doorway, smiled shyly, then entered. I lay back on the bed, mostly because there was hardly enough room for two of us to sit together.

'Shall I make coffee?' she asked.

'There's only instant.'

She made a typical April moue at the idea of instant coffee, as any true French person would, but I directed her to the tiny kitchenette behind the curtain and she busied herself with the kettle, calling out over her shoulder as she filled it and turned on the gas.

'There's trouble at the university,' she said. 'That's what I came to tell you. It's happening at last. Everything's boiling over.'

I remembered that there was supposed to be a meeting about the 'Nanterre Eight', who were about to face disciplinary charges the following Monday, and I assumed that was what she meant.

'What's happening?' I asked, still not quite awake.

April came back into the bedroom and sat demurely on the edge of my only chair, trying not to look at me lying on the bed. 'The revolution,' she said. 'There's already a big crowd there. Students and lecturers together.

They're talking about calling the police. Closing down the university.'

This woke me up a little more. 'They're what?'

'It's true,' April went on. 'Somebody told me that the university authorities said they'd call in the police if the crowds didn't disperse. But they're not dispersing, they're getting bigger.' She lit a Gauloise and looked around for an ashtray. I passed her one I'd stolen from the Café de la Lune. She smiled when she saw it and took those short little puffs at her cigarette, hardly giving herself time to inhale and enjoy the tobacco before exhaling and puffing again. 'Brad's already there,' she added.

'Then he'd better be careful,' I said, getting out of bed. 'He's neither a student nor a French citizen.'

'But don't you see? This is everybody's struggle!'

'Try telling that to the police.'

'You can be so cynical sometimes.'

'I'm sorry, April,' I said, not wanting to offend her. 'I'm just concerned for him, that's all.' Of course, I was lying. Nothing would have pleased me better than to see Brad beaten to a pulp by the police or, better still, deported, but I could hardly tell April that. The kettle boiled and she gave me a smile of forgiveness and went to make the coffee. She only made one cup – for me – I noticed, and as I sipped it she talked on about what had happened that morning and how she could feel change in the air. Her animation and passion excited me and I had to arrange my position carefully to avoid showing any obvious evidence of my arousal.

Even in the silences she seemed inclined to linger, and in the end I had to ask her to leave while I got dressed, as there was nowhere for her to retain her modesty, and the thought of her standing so close to me, facing the wall, as I took off my dressing gown was too excruciating for me to bear. She pouted and left, saying she'd wait for me outside. When I rejoined her we walked to the Sorbonne together, and I saw that she was right about the crowds. There was defiance in the air.

We found Brad standing with a group of Anarchists, and April went over to take his arm. I spoke with him briefly for a while, alarmed at some of the things he told me. I found some colleagues from the literature department, and they said the police had been sent for. By four o'clock in the afternoon the university was surrounded by the Compagnies Républicaines de Sécurité – the CRS, riot police – and a number of students and lecturers had been arrested. Before long even more students arrived and started fighting with the CRS to free those who had been arrested. Nobody was backing down this time.

The revolution had begun.

•

I took the train to Brussels on Saturday morning and didn't come back until late on Tuesday, and though I had heard news of events in Paris, I was stunned at what awaited me on my return. The city was a war zone. The university was closed, and nobody knew when, or in what form, it would reopen. Even the familiar smell of the city – its coffee, cheese and something slightly overripe aroma – had changed, and it now smelled of fire, burnt plastic and rubber. I could taste ashes in my mouth.

I wandered the Latin Quarter in a dream, remnants of the previous day's tear gas stinging my eyes, barricades improvised from torn-up paving stones all over the place. Everywhere I went I saw the CRS, looking like invaders from space in their gleaming black helmets, with chin-straps and visors, thick black uniforms, jackboots and heavy truncheons. They turned up out of nowhere in coaches with windows covered in wire mesh, clambered out and blocked off whole streets apparently at random. Everywhere they could, people gathered and talked politics. The mood was swinging: you could taste it in the air along with the gas and ashes. This wasn't just another student demonstration, another Communist or Anarchist protest; this was civil war. Even the bourgeoisie were appalled at the violence of the police attacks. There were reports of pregnant women being beaten, of young men being tortured, their genitals shredded.

This was the aftermath of what later came to be known as 'Bloody Monday', when the 'Nanterre Eight' had appeared at the Sorbonne, triumphantly singing the 'Internationale', and sparked off riots.

I had missed April terribly while I was in Brussels, and now I was worried that she might have been hurt or arrested. I immediately tried to seek her out, but it wasn't easy. She wasn't at her student residence, nor at Brad's hotel. I tried the Café de la Lune and various other watering holes in the area, but to no avail. Eventually I ran into someone I knew, who was able to tell me that he thought she was helping one of the student groups produce posters, but he didn't know where. I gave up and went back to my room, unable to sleep, expecting her gentle rap on the door at any moment. It never came.

I saw her again on Thursday, putting up posters on the Rue St Jacques.

'I was worried about you,' I told her.

She smiled and touched my arm. For a moment I let myself believe that my concern actually mattered to her. I could understand her dedication to what was happening;

after all, she was young, and it was her country. I knew that all normal social activities were on hold, that the politics of revolution had little time or space for the personal, for such bourgeois indulgences as love, but still I selfishly wanted her, wanted to be with her.

My chance came at the weekend, when the shit really hit the fan.

•

All week negotiations had been going back and forth between the government and the students. The university stayed closed and the students threatened to 'liberate' it. De Gaulle huffed and puffed. The Latin Quarter remained an occupied zone. On Friday the workers threw in their lot with the students and called for a general strike the following Monday. The whole country was on its knees in a way it hadn't been since the German occupation.

Thus far I had been avoiding the demonstrations, not out of cowardice or lack of commitment, but because I was a British subject not a French one. By the weekend that no longer mattered. It had become a world struggle: us against them. We were fighting for a new world order. I was in. I had a stake. Besides, the university was closed so I didn't even have a job to protect any more. And perhaps, somewhere deep down, I hoped that heroic deeds on the barricades might win the heart of a fair lady.

So confusing was everything, so long running and spread out the battle, that I can't remember now whether it was Friday or Saturday. Odd that, the most important night of my life, and I can't remember what night it was. No matter.

It all started with a march towards the Panthéon, red and black flags everywhere, the 'Internationale' bolstering our courage. I had found April and Brad earlier, along with Henri, Alain and Brigitte, in the university quadrangle looking at the improvised bookstalls, and we went to the march together. April had her arm linked through mine on one side, and Alain on the other.

It was about half-past nine when things started to happen. I'm not sure what came first, the sharp explosions of the gas grenades or the flash of a Molotov cocktail, but all of a sudden pandemonium broke out, and there was no longer an organized march, only a number of battle fronts.

In the melee, April and I split off, losing Brad and the rest, and we found ourselves among those defending the front on the Boulevard St Michel. Unfortunate drivers, caught in the chaos, pressed down hard on their accelerators, honked their horns and drove through red lights to get away, knocking pedestrians aside as they went. The explosions were all around us now and a blazing CRS van silhouetted figures throwing petrol bombs and pulling up paving stones for the barricades. The restaurants and cafes were all closing hurriedly, waiters ushering clients out into the street and putting up the shutters.

The CRS advanced on us, firing gas grenades continuously. One landed at my feet and I kicked it back at them. I saw one student fall to them, about ten burly police kicking him as he lay and beating him mercilessly with their truncheons. There was nothing we could do. Clouds of gas drifted from the canisters, obscuring our view. We could see distant flames, hear the explosions and the cries, see vague shadows bending to pick up stones to throw at the darkness. The CRS charged. Some of us had come armed with Molotov cocktails and stones, but neither April nor I had any weapons, any means to defend ourselves, so we ran.

We got separated from the others, just the two of us now, and we were both scared. This was the worst the fighting had been so far. The demonstrators weren't just taking what the CRS dished out, they were fighting back, and that made the police even more vicious. They would show no quarter, neither with a woman nor a foreign national. We could hardly see for the tears streaming from our eyes as we tried to get away from the advancing CRS, who seemed to have every side street blocked off.

'Come on,' I said, taking April's hand in mine. 'This way.'

We jumped the fence and edged through the pitch-dark Luxembourg Gardens, looking for an unguarded exit. When we found one, we dashed out and across to the street opposite. A group of CRS saw us and turned. Fortunately, the street was too narrow and the buildings were too high for the gas guns. The police fired high in the air and most of the canisters fell harmlessly onto the roofs above us. Nobody gave chase.

Hand in hand, we made our way through the dark back streets to my *pension*, which, though close to the fighting, seemed so far unscathed. We ran up to my tiny room and locked the door behind us. Our eyes were streaming, and both of us felt a little dizzy and sick from the tear gas, but we also felt elated from the night's battle. We could still hear the distant explosions and see flashes and flames, like Guy Fawkes Night back in England. Adrenalin buzzed in our veins.

Just as I can't say exactly what night it was, I can't say exactly who made the first move. All I remember is that suddenly the room seemed too small for the two of us, our bodies were pressed together and I was tasting those moist, pink lips for the first time, savouring her small, furtive tongue in my mouth. My legs were like jelly.

'You know when I came here the other morning and you were in bed?' April said as she unbuttoned my shirt.

'Yes,' I said, tugging at her jeans.

She slipped my shirt off my shoulders. 'I wanted to get into bed with you.'

I unhooked her bra. 'Why didn't you?'

'I didn't think you wanted me.'

We managed to get mostly undressed before falling onto the bed. I kissed her breasts and ran my hands down her naked thighs. I thought I would explode with ecstasy when she touched me. Then she was under me, and I buried myself in her, heard her sharp gasp of pleasure.

At last, April was mine.

•

I lived on the memory of April's body, naked beside me, the two of us joined in love, while the country went insane. I didn't see her for three days, and even then we were part of a group; we couldn't talk intimately. That was what things were like then; there was little place for the individual. Everything was chaos. Normal life was on hold, perhaps never to be resumed again.

The university was closed, the campus hardly recognizable. The pillars in the square were plastered with posters of Marx, Lenin, Trotsky and Che Guevara. There was a general strike. Everything ground to a halt: the Metro, buses, coal production, railways. Everywhere I walked I saw burned-out vans and cars, gutted news kiosks, piles of paving stones, groups of truncheon-swinging CRS. People eating in the cafes had tears streaming down their faces from the remnants of tear gas in the morning-after air.

And every morning was a morning after.

I spotted Brad alone in a side street one night not long after dark, and as I had been wanting to talk to him about April, I thought I might never get a better opportunity. He was on his way to a meeting, he said, but could spare a few minutes. We took the steps down to the Seine by the side of the Pont St Michel, where we were less likely to get hassled by the CRS. It was dark and quiet by the river, though we could hear the crack of gas guns and explosions of Molotovs not so far away.

'Have you talked to April recently?' I asked him.

'Yes,' he said. 'Why?'

'I was wondering if . . . you know . . . she'd told you . . . ?'

'Told me what?'

'Well . . .' I swallowed. 'About us.'

He stopped for a moment, then looked at me and laughed. 'Oh, yes,' he said. 'Yes, she did, as a matter of fact.'

I was puzzled by his attitude. 'Well,' I said, 'is that all you have to say?'

'What do you want me to say?'

'Aren't you angry?'

'Why should I be angry? It didn't mean anything.'

I felt an icy fear grip me. 'What do you mean, *it didn't mean anything*?'

'You know. It was just a quickie, a bit of a laugh. She said she got excited by the street fighting and you happened to be the nearest man. It's not the first time, you know. I don't expect April to be faithful or any of that bourgeois crap. She's her own woman.'

'What did you say?'

'I said it didn't mean anything. You don't think she could be serious about someone like you, do you? Come off it, Richard, with your tatty jeans and your little goatee beard. You think you're a real hip intellectual, but you're nothing but a joke. That's all you were to her. A quickie. A laugh. A joke. She came straight to me afterwards for a real—'

The blow came from deep inside me and my fist caught him on the side of his jaw. I heard a sharp crack, distinct from the sound of a distant gas gun, and he keeled over into the Seine. We were under a bridge and it was very dark. I stopped, listened and looked around, but I could see no one, hear only the sounds of battle in the distance. Quickly, my blood turning to ice, I climbed the nearest stairs and re-entered the fray.

●

I had never imagined that love could turn to hatred so quickly. Though I had fantasized about getting rid of Brad many times, I had never really intended to harm him, and certainly not in the way, or for the reason, that I did. I had never thought of myself as someone capable of killing another human being.

They pulled his body out of the Seine two days later, and the Anarchists claimed that he had been singled out and murdered by the CRS. Most of the students were inclined to believe this, and another bloody riot ensued.

As for me, I'd had it. Had it with April, had it with the revolution and had it with Paris. If I could have, I would have left for London immediately, but the cross-Channel ferries weren't operating and Skyways had no vacancies for some days. What few tourists remained trapped in

Paris were queuing for buses to Brussels, Amsterdam or Geneva, anywhere as long as they got out of France.

Mostly, I felt numb in the aftermath of killing Brad, though this was perhaps more to do with what he had told me about April than about the act itself, which had been an accident, and for which I didn't blame myself.

April. How could she deceive me so? How could she be so cold, so cruel, so callous? I meant nothing to her, just the nearest man to scratch her itch.

A quickie. A joke.

I saw her only once more, near the Luxembourg Gardens, the same gardens we jumped into that marvellous night a million years ago, and as she made to come towards me I took off into a side street. I didn't want to talk to her again, didn't even want to see her. And it wasn't only April. I stayed away from all of them: Henri, Alain, Brigitte, Nadine, the lot of them. To me they had all become inextricably linked with April's humiliation of me, and I couldn't bear to be with them.

One day Henri managed to get me aside and told me that April had committed suicide. He seemed angry rather than sad. I stared at him in disbelief. When he started to say something more, I cut him off and fled. I don't think anyone knew that I had killed Brad, but clearly April lamented his loss so much that she no longer felt her life was worth living. He wasn't worth it, I wanted to say, remembering the things he had told me under the bridge that night. If anyone was the killer, it was Brad not me. He had killed my love for April, and now he had killed April.

I refused to allow myself to feel anything for her.

The people at Skyways said I might have some luck if I came out to the airport and waited for a vacancy on standby, which I did. Before I left, I glanced around my room one last time and saw nothing I wanted to take with me, not even April's silk scarf, which I had kept. So, in the clothes I was wearing, with the 500 francs that was all the Bank of France allowed to me withdraw, I left the country and never went back.

•

Until now.

I think it must be the memory of tear gas that makes my eyes water so. I wipe them with the back of my hand and the waiter comes to ask me if I am all right. I tell him I am and order another *pichet*. I have nowhere else to go except the grave; I might as well stay here and drink myself to death. What is the point of another miserable six months on earth anyway?

The girl who reminds me of April crushes out her cigarette and twists a strand of hair. Her lover is late. I dream of consoling her, but what have I to offer?

'Professor Dodgson? Richard? Is that you?'

I look up slowly at the couple standing over me. The man is grey-haired, distinguished looking, and there is something about him . . . His wife, or companion, is rather stout with grey eyes and short salt and pepper hair. Both are well dressed, healthy looking, the epitome of the Parisian bourgeoisie.

'Yes,' I say. 'I'm afraid you have me at a disadvantage.'

'Henri Boulanger,' he says. 'I was once your student. My wife, Brigitte, was also a student.'

'Henri? Brigitte?' I stand to shake his hand. 'Is it really you?'

He smiles. 'Yes. I wasn't sure about you at first. You

haven't changed all that much in the face, the eyes, but you . . . perhaps you have lost weight?'

'I'm ill, Henri. Dying, in fact. But please sit down. Be my guests. Let's share some wine. Waiter.'

Henri looks at Brigitte, who nods, and they sit. She seems a little embarrassed, uncomfortable, though I can't for the life of me imagine why. Perhaps it is because I told them I am dying. No doubt many people would feel uncomfortable sitting in a cafe drinking wine with death.

'Funnily enough,' I tell them, 'I was just thinking about you. What are you doing here?'

Henri beams. 'Now *I'm* the professor,' he says with great pride. 'I teach literature at the Sorbonne.'

'Good for you, Henri. I always believed you'd go far.'

'It's a pity you couldn't have stayed around.'

'They were difficult times, Henri. Interesting, as the Chinese say.'

'Still . . . It was a sad business about that girl. What was her name?'

'April?' I say, and I feel an echo of my old love as I say her name. *Ap-reel*.

'April. Yes. That was around the time you went away.'

'My time here was over,' I tell him. 'I had no job, the country was in a state of civil war. It wasn't my future.'

Henri frowns. 'Yes, I know. Nobody blames you for getting out . . . it's not that . . .'

'Blames me for what, Henri?'

He glances at Brigitte, who looks deep into her glass of wine. 'You remember,' he says. 'The suicide? I told you about it.'

'I remember. She killed herself over an American boy the CRS beat to death.'

'Brad? But that wasn't . . . I mean . . .' He stares at me, wide-eyed. 'You mean you don't *know*?'

'Don't know what?'

'I tried to tell you at the time, but you turned away.'

'Tell me what?'

Brigitte looks up slowly from her wine and speaks. 'Why did you desert her? Why did you turn your back on her?'

'What do you mean?'

'You rejected her. You broke her heart. The silly girl was in love with you, and you spurned her. *That's* why she killed herself.'

'That's ridiculous. She killed herself because of the American.'

Brigitte shakes her head. 'No. Believe me, it was you. She told me. She could talk only about you in the days before . . .'

'But . . . Brad?'

'Brad was jealous. Don't you understand? She was never more than a casual girlfriend to him. He wanted more, but she fell for you.'

I shake my head slowly. I can't believe this. Can't *allow* myself to believe this. The world starts to become indistinct, all shadows and echoes. I can't breathe. My skin tingles with pins and needles. I feel a touch on my shoulder.

'Are you all right? Richard? Are you all right?'

It is Henri. I hear him call for a brandy and someone places a cool glass in my hand. I sip. It burns and seems to dispel the mist a little. Brigitte rests her hand on my arm and leans forward. 'You mean you really didn't know?'

I shake my head.

'Henri tried to tell you.'

'Brad,' I whisper. 'Brad told me she just used me, that she thought I was a joke. I believed him.'

Henri and Brigitte look at one another, then back at me, concern and pity in their eyes. A little more than that in Henri's, too: suspicion. Maybe everybody wasn't convinced that the CRS had killed Brad after all.

'He was jealous,' Brigitte repeats. 'He lied.'

Suddenly, I start to laugh, which horrifies them. But I can't help myself. People turn and look at us. Henri and Brigitte are embarrassed. When the laughter subsides, I am left feeling hollow. I sip more brandy. Henri has placed his cigarettes on the table. Gauloises, I notice.

'May I?' I ask, reaching for the packet, even though I haven't smoked in twenty years.

He nods.

I light a Gauloise. Cough a little. What does it matter if I get lung cancer now? I'm already as good as dead. After a few puffs, the cigarette even starts to taste good, brings back, as tastes and smells do so well, even more memories of the cafes and nights of 1968. I begin to wonder whatever happened to that silk scarf I left in the drawer at my *pension*. I wish I could smell her jasmine scent again.

Outside, the girl's lover arrives. He is young and handsome and he waves his arms as he apologizes for being late. She is sulky at first, but she brightens and kisses him. He runs his hand down her smooth, olive cheek and I can smell tear gas again.

THE GOOD PARTNER

AN INSPECTOR BANKS STORY

1

The louring sky was black as a tax inspector's heart when Detective Chief Inspector Alan Banks pulled up outside 17 Oakley Crescent at eight o'clock one mid-November evening. An icy wind whipped up the leaves and set them skittering around his feet as he walked up the path to the glass-panelled door.

Detective Constable Susan Gay was waiting for him inside, and Peter Darby, the police photographer, was busy with his new video recorder. Between the glass coffee table and the brick fireplace lay the woman's body, blood matting the hair around her left temple. Banks put on his latex gloves, then bent and picked up the object beside her. The bronze plaque read, 'Eastvale Golf Club, 1991 Tournament. Winner: David Fosse.' There was blood on the base of the trophy. The man Banks assumed to be David Fosse sat on the sofa staring into space.

A pile of photographs lay on the table. Banks picked them up and flipped through them. Each was dated 13/11/93 across the bottom. The first few showed group scenes – red-eyed people eating, drinking and dancing at a banquet of some kind – but the last ones told a different story. Two showed a handsome young man in a navy blue suit, white shirt and garish tie, smiling lecherously at the photographer from behind a glass of whisky. Then the scene shifted to a hotel room, where the man had loosened his tie. None of the other diners were to be seen. In the last picture, he had also taken off his jacket. The date had changed to 14/11/93.

Banks turned to the man on the sofa. 'Are you David Fosse?' he asked.

There was a pause while the man seemed to return from a great distance. 'Yes,' he said finally.

'Can you identify the victim?'

'It's my wife, Kim.'

'What happened?'

'I . . . I was out taking the dog for a walk. When I got back I found . . .' He gestured towards the floor.

'When did you go out?'

'Quarter to seven, as usual. I got back about half past and found her like this.'

'Was your wife in when you left?'

'Yes.'

'Was she expecting any visitors?'

He shook his head.

Banks held out the photos. 'Have you seen these?'

Fosse turned away and grunted.

'Who took them? What do they mean?'

Fosse stared at the Axminster.

'Mr Fosse?'

'I don't know.'

'This date, 13 November. Last Saturday. Is that significant?'

'My wife was at a business convention in London last weekend. I assume they're the pictures she took.'

'What kind of convention?'

'She's involved in servicing home offices and small

businesses. *Servicing*,' he sneered. 'Now there's an apt term.'

Banks singled out the man in the gaudy tie. 'Do you know who this is?'

'No.' Fosse's face darkened and both his hands curled into fists. 'No, but if I ever get hold of him—'

'Mr Fosse, did you argue with your wife about the man in these photographs?'

Fosse's mouth dropped. 'They weren't here when I left.'

'How do you explain their presence now?'

'I don't know. She must have got them out while I was taking Jasper for a walk.'

Banks looked around the room and saw a camera on the sideboard, a Canon. It looked like an expensive auto-focus model. He picked it up carefully and put it in a plastic bag. 'Is this yours?' he asked Fosse.

Fosse looked at the camera. 'It's my wife's. I bought it for her birthday. Why? What are you doing with it?'

'It may be evidence,' said Banks, pointing at the expo-sure indicator. 'Seven pictures have been taken on a new film. I have to ask you again, Mr Fosse, did you argue with your wife about the man in these photos?'

'And I'll tell you again. How could I? They weren't there when I went out, and she was dead when I got back.'

The dog barked from the kitchen. The front door opened and Dr Glendenning walked in, a tall, imposing figure with white hair and a nicotine-stained moustache.

Glendenning glanced sourly at Banks and Susan and complained about being dragged out on such a night. Banks apologized. Though Glendenning was a Home Office patho-logist, and a lowly police surgeon could pronounce death,

Banks knew that Glendenning would never have forgiven them had they not called him.

As the Scene-of-Crime team arrived, Banks turned to David Fosse and said, 'I think we'd better carry on with this down at headquarters.'

Fosse shrugged and stood up to get his coat. As they left, Banks heard Glendenning mutter, 'A golf trophy. A bloody golf trophy! Sacrilege.'

2

'**Do you think** he did it, sir?' Susan Gay asked Banks.

Banks swirled the inch of Theakston's XB at the bottom of his glass and watched the patterns it made. 'I don't know. He certainly had means, motive and opportunity. But something about it makes me uneasy.'

It was almost closing time, and Banks and Susan sat in the warm glow of the Queen's Arms having a late dinner of microwaved steak and kidney pud, courtesy of Cyril, the landlord, who was used to their unsociable hours. Outside, rain lashed against the red and amber window panes.

Banks pushed his plate away and lit a cigarette. He was tired. The Fosse call had come in just as he was about to go home after a long day of paperwork and boring meetings.

They had learned little more during a two-hour interrogation at the station. Kim Fosse had left for London on Friday and returned on Monday with her business partner, Norma Cheverel. The convention had been held at the Ludbridge Hotel in Kensington.

David Fosse maintained his innocence, but sexual

jealousy made a strong motive, and now he was languishing in the cells under Eastvale Divisional Headquarters. *Languish* was perhaps too strong a word, as the cells were as comfortable as many bed and breakfasts, and the food and service much better. The only problem was that you couldn't open the door and go for a walk in the Yorkshire Dales when you felt like it.

They learned from the house-to-house that Fosse *did* walk the dog – several people had seen him – and not even Dr Glendenning could pinpoint time of death to within the forty-five minutes he was out of the house.

Fosse could have murdered his wife before he left or when he got home. He could also have nipped back around the rear, where a path ran by the river, got into the house unseen the back way, then resumed his walk.

'Time, ladies and gentlemen please,' called Cyril, ringing his bell behind the bar. 'And that includes coppers.'

Banks smiled and finished his beer. 'There's not a lot more we can do tonight, anyway,' he said. 'I think I'll go home and get some sleep.'

'I'll do the same.' Susan reached for her overcoat.

'First thing in the morning,' said Banks, 'we'll have a word with Norma Cheverel, see if she can throw any light on what happened in London last weekend.'

3

Norma Cheverel was an attractive woman in her early thirties with a tousled mane of red hair, a high freckled forehead and the greenest eyes Banks had ever seen. Contact lenses, he decided uncharitably, perhaps to diminish the sense of sexual energy he felt emanate from her.

She sat behind her desk in the large carpeted office, swivelling occasionally in her executive chair. After her assistant had brought coffee, Norma pulled out a long cigarette and lit up. 'One of the pleasures of being the boss,' she said. 'The buggers can't make you stop smoking.'

'You've heard about Kim Fosse, I take it?' Banks asked.

'On the local news last night. Poor Kim.' She shook her head.

'We're puzzled about a few things. Maybe you can help us?'

'I'll try.'

'Did you notice her taking many photographs at the convention?'

Norma Cheverel frowned. 'I can't say as I did, really, but there were quite a few people taking photographs there, especially at the banquet. You know how people get silly at conventions. I never could understand this mania for capturing the moment. Can you, Chief Inspector?'

Banks, whose wife, Sandra, was a photographer, could understand it only too well, though he would have quibbled with 'capturing the moment'. A good photographer, a *real* photographer, Sandra had often said, did much more than that; she transformed the moment. But he let the aesthetics lie.

Norma Cheverel was right about the photo mania, though. Banks had also noticed that since the advent of cheap, idiot-proof cameras every Tom, Dick and Harry had started taking photos indoors. He had been half-blinded a number of times by a group of tourists 'capturing the moment' in some pub or restaurant. It was almost as bad as the mobile-phone craze, though not quite.

'Did Kim Fosse share this mania?' he asked.

'She had a fancy new camera. She took it with her. That's all I can say, really. Look, I don't—'

'Bear with me, Ms Cheverel.'

'Norma, please.'

Banks, who reserved the familiarity of first-name terms to exercise power over suspects, not to interview witnesses, went on. 'Do you know if she had affairs?'

This time Norma Cheverel let the silence stretch. Banks could hear the fan cooling the microchip in her computer. She stubbed out her long cigarette, careful to make sure it wasn't still smouldering, sipped some coffee, swivelled a little, and said, 'Yes. Yes, she did. Though I wouldn't really describe them as affairs.'

'How would you describe them?'

'Just little flings, really. Nothing that really *meant* anything to her.'

'Who with?'

'She didn't usually mention names.'

'Did she have a fling in London last weekend?'

'Yes. She told me about it on the way home. Look, Chief Inspector, Kim wasn't a bad person. She just needed something David couldn't give her.'

Banks took a photograph of the man in the navy blue suit from his briefcase and slid it across the desk. 'Know him?'

'It's Michael Bannister. He's with an office-furnishings company in Preston.'

'And did Kim Fosse have a fling with him that weekend?'

Norma swivelled and bit her lip. 'She didn't tell me it was him.'

'Surprised?'

She shrugged. 'He's married. Not that that means much these days. I've heard he's very much in love with his wife, but she's not very strong. Heart condition, or something.' She sniffled, then sneezed and reached for a tissue.

'What did Kim tell you about last weekend?'

Norma Cheverel smiled an odd, twisted little smile from the corner of her lips. 'Oh, Chief Inspector, do you really want all the details? Girl talk about sex is so much *dirtier* than men's, you know.'

Though he felt himself reddening a little, Banks said, 'So I've been told. Did she ever express concern about her husband finding out?'

'Oh, yes. She told me under no circumstances to tell David. As if I would. He's very jealous and he has a temper.'

'Was he ever violent towards her?'

'Just once. It was the last time we went to a convention, as a matter of fact. Apparently he tried to phone her in her room after midnight – some emergency to do with the dog – and she wasn't there. When she got home he lost his temper, called her a whore and hit her.'

'How long had they been married?'

Norma sniffled again and blew her nose. 'Four years.'

'How long have you and Kim Fosse been in business together?'

'Six years. We started when she was still Kim Church. She'd just got her MBA.'

'How did the partnership work?'

'Very well. I'm on the financial side and Kim dealt with sales and marketing.'

'Are you married?'

'I don't see that it's any of your business, Chief Inspector, but no, I'm not. I guess Mr Right just hasn't turned up yet,' she said coldly, then looked at her gold wristwatch. 'Are there any more questions?'

Banks stood up. 'No, that's all for now. Thank you very much for your time.'

She stood up and walked around the desk to show him to the door. Her handshake on leaving was a little brisker and cooler than it had been when he arrived.

4

'**So Kim Fosse** was discreet, but she took photographs,' said Susan when they met up in Banks's office later that morning. 'Kinky?'

'Could be. Or just careless. They're pretty harmless, really.' The seven photographs from the film they had found inside the camera showed the same man in the hotel room on the same date, 14/11/93.

'Michael Bannister,' Susan read from her notes. 'Sales director for Office Comforts Ltd, based in Preston, Lancashire. Lives in Blackpool with his wife, Lucy. No children. His wife suffers from a congenital heart condition, needs constant pills and medicines, lots of attention. His workmates tell me he's devoted to her.'

'A momentary lapse, then?' Banks suggested. He walked over to his broken Venetian blind and looked out on the rainswept market square. Only two cars were parked there today. The gold hands on the blue face of the church clock stood at eleven thirty-nine.

'It happens, sir. Maybe more often than we think.'

'I know. Reckon we'd better go easy approaching him?'

'No sense endangering the wife's health, is there?'

'You're right. See if you can arrange to see him at his office.' Banks looked out of the window and shivered. 'I don't much fancy a trip to the seaside in this miserable weather anyway.'

5

The drive across the Pennines was a nightmare. All the way along the A59 they seemed to be stuck behind one lorry or another churning up gallons of filthy spray. Around Clitheroe, visibility was so poor that traffic slowed to a crawl. The hulking whale-shapes of the hills that flanked the road were reduced to faint grey outlines in the rain-haze. Banks played his Miles Davis *Birth of the Cool* tape, which Susan seemed to enjoy. At least, she didn't complain.

The office building on Ribbleton Lane, just east of the city centre, was three-storey red-brick. The receptionist directed them to Bannister's office on the second floor.

In the anteroom, a woman sat clicking away at a computer keyboard. Curly-haired, plump, in her forties. She came over and welcomed them. 'Hello, I'm Carla Jacobs. I'm Mr Bannister's secretary. He's in with someone at the moment, but he won't be a minute. He knows you're coming.'

Banks and Susan looked at the framed photographs of company products and awards on the walls as they waited. All the time, Banks sensed Carla Jacobs staring at the back of his head. After a couple of minutes, he turned around just in time to see her avert her gaze.

'Is anything wrong?' he asked.

She blushed. 'No. Well, not really. I mean, don't think I'm being nosy, but is Mr Bannister in some kind of trouble?'

'Why do you ask?'

'It's just that I'm a good friend of Lucy's, that's Mr Bannister's wife, and I don't know if you know, but—'

'We know about her health problems, yes.'

'Good. Good. Well . . .'

'Have you any reason to think Mr Bannister might be in trouble?'

She raised her eyebrows. 'Oh, no. But it's not every day we get the police visiting.'

At that moment the inner door opened and a small ferret-faced man in an ill-fitting suit flashed a smile at Carla as he scurried out. In the doorway stood the man in the photographs. Michael Bannister. He beckoned Banks and Susan in.

It was a large office, with Bannister's work desk, files and bookcases taking up one half and a large oval table for meetings in the other. They sat at the table, so well polished Banks could see his reflection in it, and Susan took out her notebook.

'I understand you attended a business convention in London last weekend?' Banks started.

'Yes. Yes, I did.'

'Did you meet a woman there called Kim Fosse?'

Bannister averted his eyes. 'Yes.'

Banks showed him a photograph of the victim, as she had been in life. 'Is this her?'

'Yes.'

'Did you spend the night with her?'

'I don't see what that's got—'

'Did you?'

'Look, for Christ's sake. My wife . . .'

'It's not your wife we're asking.'

'What if I did?'

'Did she take these photographs of you?' Banks fanned the photos in front of him.

'Yes,' he said.

'So you slept with Kim Fosse and she took some photographs.'

'It was just a lark. I mean, we'd had a bit to drink, I—'

'I understand, sir,' said Banks. 'You don't have to justify yourself to me.'

Bannister licked his lips. 'What's this all about? Will it go any further?'

'I can't say,' said Banks, gesturing for Susan to stand up. 'It depends. We'll keep you informed.'

'Good Lord, man,' said Bannister. 'Please. Think of my wife.' He looked miserably after them, and Banks caught the look of concern on Carla Jacobs's face.

'That was a bit of a wasted journey, wasn't it, sir?' Susan said on the way back to Eastvale.

'Do you think so?' said Banks, smiling. 'I'm not at all sure, myself. I think our Mr Bannister was lying about something. And I'd like to know what Carla Jacobs had on her mind.'

6

Sandra was out. After Banks hung up his raincoat, he went straight into the living room of his south Eastvale semi and poured himself a stiff Laphroaig. He felt as if the day's rain had permeated right to his bone marrow.

He made himself a cheese and onion sandwich, checked out all the television channels, found nothing worth watching, and put some Bessie Smith on the CD player.

But 'Woman's Trouble Blues' took a background role as the malt whisky warmed his bones and he thought about the Fosse case. Why did he feel so ill at ease? Because David Fosse sounded believable? Because he had felt Norma Cheverel's sexual power and resented it? Because Michael Bannister had lied about something? And was Carla Jacobs in love with her boss, or was she just protecting Lucy Bannister? Banks fanned out the photographs on the coffee table.

Before he could answer any of the questions, Sandra returned from the photography course she was teaching at the local college. When she had finished telling Banks how few people knew the difference between an aperture and a hole in the ground, which Banks argued was a poor metaphor because an aperture *was* a kind of a hole, she glanced at the photos on the coffee table.

'What are these, evidence?' she asked, stopping herself before she touched them.

'Go ahead,' said Banks. 'We've got all we need from them.'

Sandra picked up a couple of the group shots, six people in evening dress, each holding a champagne flute out towards the photographer, all with the red eyes characteristic of cheap automatic flash.

'Ugh,' said Sandra. 'What dreadful photos.'

'Snob,' said Banks. 'She doesn't have as good a camera as you.'

'Doesn't matter,' said Sandra. 'A child of five could do a better job with a Brownie than these. What kind of camera was it, anyway?'

'A Canon,' said Banks, adding the model number. The identification tag on the evidence bag was etched in his memory.

Sandra put the photos down and frowned. 'A what?'

Banks told her again.

'It can't be.'

'Why not?'

Sandra leaned forward, slipped her long blonde tresses behind her ears and spread out the photos. 'Well, they've all got red-eye,' she said. 'The camera you mentioned protects against red-eye.'

It was Banks's turn to look puzzled.

'Do you know what red-eye is?' Sandra asked.

'I don't know an aperture from a hole in the ground.'

She nudged him in the ribs. 'Be serious, Alan. Look, when you're in a dark room, your pupils dilate, the iris opens to let in more light so you can see properly, just like an aperture on a camera. Right? You know what it's like when you first walk into a dark place and your eyes slowly adjust?'

Banks nodded. 'Go on.'

'Well, when you're subjected to a sudden, direct flash of light, the iris doesn't have time to close. Red-eye is actually caused by the flash illuminating the blood vessels in the eye.'

'Why doesn't it happen with *all* flash photographs, then? Surely the whole point of flash is that you use it in the dark?'

'Mostly, yes, but red-eye only happens when the flash is pointed *directly* at your iris. It doesn't happen when the flash is held from *above* the camera. The angle's different. See what I mean?'

'Yes. But you don't usually see people with hand-held flashes using cameras like that.'

'That's right. That's because there's another way of getting rid of red-eye. The more expensive models, like the one you just mentioned to me, set off a series of quick flashes first, *before* the exposure, and that gives the iris a chance to close. Simple, really.'

'So you're saying that these photographs couldn't have been taken with that camera?'

'That's right.'

'Interesting,' said Banks. 'Very interesting.'

Sandra grinned. 'Have I solved your case?'

'Not exactly, no, but you've certainly confirmed some of the doubts I've been having.' Banks reached for the telephone. 'After what you've just told me, I think I can at least make sure that David Fosse sleeps in his own bed tonight.'

7

Norma Cheverel wasn't pleased to see Banks and Susan late the next morning. She welcomed them with all the patience and courtesy of a busy executive, tidying files on her desk as Banks talked, twice mentioning a luncheon appointment that was fast approaching. For a while, Banks ignored her rudeness, then he said, 'Will you stop your fidgeting and pay attention, Ms Cheverel?'

She gave him a challenging look. There was no 'Call me Norma' this time, and the sexual voltage was turned very low. But she sat as still as she could and rested her hands on the desk.

'Yes, *sir*,' she said. 'You know, you remind me of an old school-teacher.'

'Do you own a camera, Ms Cheverel?'

'Yes.'

'What model?'

She shrugged. 'I don't know. Just one of those cheap things everybody uses these days.'

'Does it have an automatic flash?'

'Yes. They all do, don't they?'

'What about red-eye?'

'What's that? A late-night flight?'

Banks explained. She started playing with the files again. 'I'd appreciate it if you'd let us examine your camera, Ms Cheverel.'

'Why on earth—'

'Because the photographs we found on the coffee table at the scene couldn't possibly have been taken by Kim Fosse's camera. That's why.' Banks explained what Sandra had told him, and what the result of tests earlier that morning had confirmed.

Norma Cheverel spread her hands. 'So someone else took them. I still don't see what that's got to do with me.'

Banks glanced over to Susan, who said, 'Ms Cheverel. Is it true that you lost almost fifty thousand pounds on a land speculation deal earlier this year?'

Norma Cheverel looked daggers at her and said to Banks through clenched teeth, 'My business deals are no—'

'Oh, but they are,' said Banks. 'In fact, Susan and I have been doing quite a bit of digging this morning. It seems you've made a number of bad investments these past couple of years, haven't you? Where's the money come from?'

'The money was mine. All mine.'

Banks shook his head. 'I think it came from the partnership.' He leaned forward. 'Know what else I think?'

'What do I care?'

'I think your cocaine habit is costing you a fortune, too, isn't it?'

'How dare you!'

'I noticed how jittery you were, how you couldn't keep still. And then there's the sniffling. Funny how your cold seems better this morning. How much? Say ten, twenty thousand a year up your nose?'

'I want my solicitor.'

'I think you were cheating the partnership, Ms Cheverel. I think you knew you'd gone so far it was only a matter of time before Kim Fosse found out about it. You dealt with the accounting, you told us, and she was on the marketing side. What could have been better? It would take her a while to discover something was wrong, but you couldn't keep it from your partner for ever, could you? So you came up with a plot to get rid of her and blame it on her husband. We only have *your* word for it that Kim Fosse was promiscuous. We only have your word that her husband was jealous enough to be violent.'

'Ask anyone,' said Norma Cheverel. 'They'll tell you. Everyone saw her black eye after the last convention.'

'We know about that. David Fosse told us this morning. It was something he regretted very much. But the only person Kim confided in was *you*, which gave you every opportunity to build a mountain of lies and suspicion on a small foundation of truth.'

'This is absurd.' Norma swivelled and reached for the phone. 'I'm calling my solicitor.'

'Go ahead,' said Banks. 'But you haven't been charged with anything yet.'

She held the phone halfway between her mouth and its cradle and smiled. 'That's right,' she said. 'You can make all the accusations you want but you can't prove anything. That business about the camera doesn't mean a thing, and you know that as well as I do.'

'It proves that Kim Fosse *didn't* take those photographs. Therefore, someone must have planted them to make it *look* as if she had been foolish as well as indiscreet.'

She put the phone down. 'You can't prove it was me. I defy you.'

Banks stood up. He was loath to admit it, but she was right. Short of finding someone who had seen her or her car in the vicinity of the Fosse house around the time of the murder, there was no proof. And Norma Cheverel wasn't the kind to confess. The bluff was over. But at least Banks and Susan *knew* as they walked out of the office that Norma Cheverel had killed Kim Fosse. The rest was just a matter of time.

8

The break took two days to come, and it came from an unexpected source.

The first thing Banks did after his interview with Norma Cheverel was organize a second house-to-house of Fosse's neighbourhood, this time to find out if anyone had seen Norma Cheverel or her car that evening. Someone remembered seeing a grey foreign car of some kind, which was about the closest they got to a sighting of Norma's silver BMW.

Next, he got a list of all 150 conventioneers and set a team to phone and find out if anyone remembered Norma Cheverel taking photos on the evening of the banquet. They'd got through seventy-one with no luck so far, when Banks's phone rang.

'This is Carla Jacobs, Inspector Banks. I don't know if you remember me. I'm Mr Bannister's secretary.'

'I remember you,' said Banks. 'What is it?'

'Well, I was going to ask you the same thing. You see, I've been talking to Lucy, and she's so worried that Michael is in trouble it's damaging her health.'

'Mr Bannister is in no trouble as far as I know,' said Banks. 'He just committed an unfortunate indiscretion, that's all. No blame.'

'But that's just it,' said Carla Jacobs. 'You see, she said he's been acting strangely. He's depressed. He shuts himself away. He doesn't talk to her. Even when he's with her she says he's withdrawn. It's getting her down. I thought if you could talk to her . . . just set her at ease.'

Banks sighed. Playing nursemaid. 'All right,' he said. 'I'll call her.'

'Oh, will you? Thank you. Thank you ever so much.' She lowered her voice. 'Mr Bannister is in his office now. She'll be by the phone at home.'

Lucy Bannister answered on the first ring. 'Yes?'

Banks introduced himself.

'I'm so worried about Michael,' she said, in that gushing manner of someone who's been waiting all week to pour it all out. 'He's never like this. Never. Has he done something awful? Are you going to arrest him? Please, you can tell me the truth.'

'No,' said Banks. 'No, he hasn't, and no we're not. He's simply been helping us with our enquiries.'

'That could mean anything. Enquiries into what?'

Banks debated for a moment whether to tell her. It would do no harm, he thought. 'He was at a business convention in London last weekend. We're interested in the movements of someone else who was there, that's all.'

'Are you sure that's all?'

'Yes.'

'And it's nothing serious?'

'Not for your husband, no.'

'Thank you. You don't know what this means to me.' He could hear the relief in her voice. 'Because of my heart condition, you see, Michael is a bit over-protective. I don't deny I'm weak, but sometimes I think he just takes too much upon himself.' She paused and gave a small laugh. 'I don't know why I'm telling you all this. It must be because I'm so relieved. He's a normal man. He has needs like any other man. I know he goes with other women and I never mention it because I know it would upset him and embarrass him. He thinks he keeps it from me to protect me from distress, and it's just easier to let him think that.'

'I can appreciate that,' Banks said, only half listening. Why hadn't he realized before? Now he knew what Michael Bannister had lied about, and why. 'Look, Mrs Bannister,' he cut in, 'you might be able to help us. Do you think you could talk to your husband, let him know you know?'

'I don't know. I don't want to upset him.'

Banks felt a wave of annoyance. The Bannisters were so damn busy protecting one another's feelings that there was no room for the truth. He could almost hear her chewing her lip over the line. He tried to keep the irritation out of his voice. 'It could be very important,' he said. 'And I'm sure it won't do any harm. If that's what he's feeling guilty about, you can help him get over it, can't you?'

'I suppose so.' Hesitant, but warming to the idea.

'I'm sure you'd be helping him, helping your relationship.' Banks cringed to hear himself talk. First a nursemaid, now a bloody marriage guidance counsellor.

'Perhaps.'

'Then you'll do it? You'll talk to him?'

'Yes.' Determined now. 'Yes, I will, Mr Banks.'

'And will you do me one more favour?'

'If I can.'

'Will you give him these telephone numbers and tell him that if he thinks of anything else he can call me without fear of any charges being made against him?' He gave her his work and home phone numbers.

'Ye-es.' She clearly didn't know what he meant, but that didn't matter.

'It's very important that you tell him there'll be no action taken against him and that he should talk to *me* personally. Is that clear?'

'Yes. I don't know what all this is about, but I'll do as you say. And thank you.'

'Thank you.' Banks headed for a pub lunch in the Queen's Arms. It was too early to celebrate anything yet, but he kept his fingers crossed as he walked in the thin November sunshine across Market Street.

9

Norma Cheverel's luxury flat was every bit as elegant and expensively furnished as Banks had expected. Some of the paintings on her walls were originals, and her

NOT SAFE AFTER DARK

furniture was all hand-crafted, by the look of it. She even had an oak table from Robert Thompson's workshop in Kilburn. Banks recognized the trademark: a mouse carved on one of the legs.

When Banks and Susan turned up at seven-thirty that evening, Norma had just finished stacking her dinner dishes in the machine. She had changed from her work outfit and wore black leggings, showing off her shapely legs, and a green woollen sweater that barely covered her hips. She sat down and crossed her legs, cigarette poised over the ashtray beside her.

'Well,' she said. 'Do I need my solicitor yet?'

'I think you do,' said Banks. 'But I'd like you to answer a few questions first.'

'I'm not saying a word without my solicitor present.'

'Very well,' said Banks. 'That's your right. Let me do the talking, then.'

She sniffed and flicked a half-inch of ash into the ashtray beside her. Her crossed leg was swinging up and down as if some demented doctor were tapping the reflex.

'I might as well tell you first of all that we've got Michael Bannister's testimony,' Banks began.

'I don't know what you're talking about.'

'I think you do. It was *you* who took those photographs at the banquet and in the hotel room afterwards. It was *you* who spent the night with Michael Bannister, not Kim Fosse.'

'That's ridiculous.'

'No, it's not. You told him later that if anyone asked he'd better say it was Kim Fosse he slept with or you'd tell his wife what he'd done. You knew Lucy had a weak heart, and that he thought such a shock might kill her.'

Norma had turned a shade paler. Banks scratched the

236

small scar beside his right eye. Often, when it itched, it was telling him he was on the right track. 'As it turns out,' he went on, 'Lucy Bannister was well aware that her husband occasionally slept with other women. It was just something they didn't talk about. He thought he was protecting her feelings; she thought she was protecting his. I suggested they talk about it.'

'Bastard,' Norma Cheverel hissed. Banks didn't know whether she meant him or Michael Bannister.

'You seduced Michael Bannister and you planted incriminating photographs on Kim Fosse's living-room table *after* you'd killed her in the hope that we would think her husband had done it in a jealous rage, a rage that you also helped set us up to believe. We've checked the processing services, too. I'm sure you chose Fotomat because it's busy, quick and impersonal, but the man behind the counter remembers *you* picking up a film on Wednesday, not Kim Fosse. Beauty has its drawbacks, Norma.'

Norma got up, tossed back her hair and went to pour herself a drink. She didn't offer Banks or Susan anything. 'You've got a nerve,' she said. 'And a hell of an imagination. You should work for television.'

'You knew that David Fosse walked the dog every evening, come rain or shine, between six forty-five and seven-thirty. It was easy for you to drive over to the house, park your car a little distance away, get the unsuspecting Kim to let you in, and then, still wearing gloves, hit her with the trophy and plant the photos. After that, all you had to do was convince us of her infidelity and her husband's violent jealousy. There was even a scrap of truth in it. Except you didn't bargain for Lucy Bannister, did you?'

'This is ridiculous,' Norma said. 'What about the film that was in the camera? You can't prove any of this.'

'I don't believe I mentioned that there was a film *in* the camera,' said Banks. 'I'm sure it seemed like a brilliant idea at the time, but *that* film couldn't possibly have been taken by Kim's camera, either, or Michael Bannister wouldn't have had red eyes.'

'This is just circumstantial.'

'Possibly. But it all adds up. Believe me, Norma, we've got a case and we've got a good chance of making it stick. The first film wasn't enough, was it? We might have suspected it was planted. But with a second film *in* the camera, one showing the same scene, the same person, then there was less chance we'd look closely at the photographic evidence. How did it happen? I imagine Kim had perhaps had a bit too much to drink that night and you put her to bed. When you did, you also took her room key. At some point during the night, when you'd finished with Michael Bannister, you rewound your second film manually in the dark until there was only a small strip sticking out of the cassette, then you went to Kim Fosse's room and you put it in her camera, taking out whatever film she had taken herself and dumping it.'

'Oh, I see. I'm that clever, am I? I suppose you found my fingerprints on this film?'

'The prints were smudged, as you no doubt knew they would be, and you wiped the photographs and camera. When you'd loaded the film, you advanced it in the dark with the flash turned off and the lens cap on. That way the double exposure wouldn't affect the already exposed film at all because no light was getting to it. When you'd wound it on so that the next exposure was set at number eight, you returned it to Kim Fosse's room.'

'I'm glad you think I'm so brilliant, Inspector, but I—'

'I don't think you're brilliant at all,' Banks said. 'You're as stupid as anyone else who thinks she can get away with the perfect crime.'

In a flash, Norma Cheverel picked up the ashtray and threw it at Banks. He dodged sideways and it whizzed past his ear and smashed into the front of the cocktail cabinet.

Banks stood up. 'Time to call that solicitor, Norma.'

But Norma Cheverel wasn't listening. She was banging her fists on her knees and chanting 'Bastard! Bastard!' over and over again.

SOME LAND IN FLORIDA

The morning they found Santa Claus floating face down in the pool, I had a hangover of gargantuan proportions. By midday I was starting to feel more human. By late afternoon, on my third Michelob at Chloe's, I was almost glad to be alive again. Almost. I was also coming to believe that Santa's death hadn't been quite the accident it appeared.

'Happy Hour' at Chloe's – a dim, horseshoe-shaped bar adjoining a restaurant – lasts from eleven a.m. to seven p.m., and by late afternoon the desperation usually starts to show through the cracks: the men tell the same joke for the third or fourth time; the women laugh just a little too loudly.

The afternoon after Santa's death I found myself sitting opposite his small coterie. They were an odd group, the three of them who formed the central core. There was a grey-haired man, about sixty, who always looked ill to me, despite his brick-red complexion; a size fourteen woman in her mid forties who wore size ten clothes; and a pretty blonde, no older than about twenty-five. Maybe I'm being sexist or ageist or whatever, but I could only wonder why she was hanging around with such a bunch of losers. Christ, didn't she know that if she played her cards right she could have me?

OK, so I'm no oil painting. But despite a bit of a beer gut, I'm reasonably well-preserved for a man of my age and drinking habits. I've still got a fine head of hair, even if it is grey. And I may be a bit grizzled and rough-edged, but I've been told I'm not without a certain cuddly quality.

Anyway, in my humble opinion, Santa – in reality Bud Schiller, a retired real estate agent from Kingston, Ontario – was a total asshole. Most people only needed to spend a couple of minutes in his company before heading for the hills. But not these three. Oh, no. They laughed at all his jokes; they hung on his every word. Of course, Schiller bought most of the drinks, but I thought his company was a hell of a price to pay for the occasional free beer.

'So, who do you think did it, then, Jack?'

Al French had slipped onto the empty stool beside me. Al was a cross between a loner and a social butterfly: he seemed to know everyone, but like a butterfly he never lit in any one place for long. He said he was a writer from Rochester, but I've never seen any of his books in the shops. If you ask him to be more specific, he just gets evasive.

Al tipped back his bottle and his Adam's apple bobbed as he swallowed. He was a skinny little guy with a long nose, slicked back hair and a perpetual five o'clock shadow. Today he was wearing a Hawaiian shirt and Bermuda shorts.

'It was an accident,' I said.

'Bullshit. And you know it.' Al put his bottle down and whispered in my ear. He sounded as if he'd had a few already. 'When a jerk like Bud Schiller dies, there has to be something more behind it than mere accident. Come on, buddy, you're supposed to be the private eye.'

'True. But I'm on vacation.'

'A real gumshoe never rests until he discovers the truth and sees that justice is done.'

I rolled my eyes. 'Where d'you read that, Al? An old *Black Mask* magazine?'

Al looked hurt. 'I didn't read it anywhere. I wrote it.'

'You write private eye stories?'

'We were talking about Bud Schiller's murder.'

See what I mean? Evasive. And persistent. I ordered another round of Michelob and offered Al a cigar.

'Cuban?' he asked.

'Uh-huh.'

Al shrugged and took the cigar. 'What they gonna do, huh? Arrest me for smoking?'

I laughed. 'Seriously, Al, the cop I talked to said it was an accident. She asked me if I'd seen or heard anything unusual, then she left.'

'Had you?'

'No.'

I wasn't going to tell Al, but I'd spent the evening sitting out in the lanai smoking a cigar, reading Robertson Davies and working my way through a bottle of Maker's Mark. I could hear the singalong in the distance, and I remember thinking there was something absurd about a bunch of adults singing 'Jingle Bells' and 'White Christmas' under the palms, especially with an asshole like Bud Schiller dressed as Santa leading them along. About nine-thirty, when the singalong ended, the print in my book was too blurred to read any more, and by ten o'clock or there-abouts, like most people in the Whispering Palms Condominium Estate, I was sawing logs.

'He'd been drinking,' I went on. 'Mary Pasquale, the girl in the office, she told me he was three sheets to the wind. He must have been carrying his piano away after the party when he tripped near the edge of the pool and pitched in, head first.'

Al just raised his eyebrows.

He had a point. Even as I repeated the official line, something nagged at the back of my mind. As an ex-cop turned PI, I've seen enough weird crime scenes in my time, like the guy they found dead on the subway tracks and couldn't find his head. But in this case, I had to ask myself two questions: first, wouldn't Schiller have dropped the piano as he flung his arms out to protect himself from the fall?

And second, perhaps more to the point, why on God's earth was Santa's electric piano *still plugged in*?

'I've noticed you talking to Schiller's cronies,' I said to Al quietly, so they wouldn't overhear. 'Do you know any of them well enough to think one of them killed him?'

Al shook his head. 'Not really. Just casting the nets, you know. Ed Brennan, the red-faced one, he's into the ponies. We went to the dog track at Naples once. But he's a sore loser. Too desperate. And I played golf with Schiller a couple of times a few years back. He cheats. Did you know that?'

I didn't rate cheating at golf as high on my list of motives for murder, but you never knew. 'What about the girl?'

Al raised his eyebrows. 'Ah-hah! *Cherchez la femme*, is it? Her name's Karen Lee. Kindergarten teacher, I think.'

'I wish my kindergarten teacher had looked like that.'

'You'd've been too young to appreciate it. Besides, if you've got any thoughts in that direction, Jack, forget them. I warn you, she's strictly an ice queen.'

I looked at Karen Lee. She was running her finger around the rim of a tall, frosted glass – abstractedly, rather than in any deliberately erotic way, but it still looked sexy as hell. She sure didn't look like an ice queen to me.

'How long has Schiller been coming here?' I asked.

'Longer than me, and I've been a regular for, what, nine, ten years now.'

'How did they all hook up with each other?'

'I don't know, except they're all from Canada. Every year Schiller would manage to gather a few luckless characters around him, but, like me, they didn't usually come back for more. Ed was the first one who did, about four years ago. The blonde was next, year after, I think, then Mama Cass showed up just last year.'

'What's her real name?'

'Ginny Fraser. Three time loser from Smith's Falls, far as I can gather. Single mother. Welfare.'

'How can she afford to come here?'

'Don't ask me.'

'What does Ed do?'

'Retired. Used to be a school caretaker in Waterloo.'

Kindergarten teacher; welfare case; retired caretaker. Not exactly high-paying jobs. And all Canadian. Still, that didn't mean much. Half of Canada rents condos in Florida in the winter – and Canada's a big country. I looked at them again, trying to read their faces for signs of guilt. Nothing. Karen was still running her finger around her glass rim. Ed was attempting to tell a joke, the kind, he said loudly, that he 'just knew old Bud would have appreciated'. Only Ginny was laughing, chins wobbling, tears in her eyes.

I finished my beer, said goodbye to Al and left. When I got back to the condo that evening with a bottle of Chilean wine and a pound of jumbo shrimp for the barbecue, I tried to put Al's suggestion of murder out of my mind.

But it wouldn't go away.

The problem was what, if anything, was I going to do about it? Back home, I'm a licensed private investigator, but down here I'm not even a citizen.

Still, that evening out on the lanai, after the wine and the shrimps, I decided to keep my bourbon intake down. A good night's sleep and no hangover would be the best bet for whatever tomorrow might bring.

•

The grass pricked my feet as I walked towards the pool the next morning for my pre-breakfast swim. Already the temperature was in the low seventies and the sky was robin's egg blue.

I stood for a moment on the bridge and looked down into the murky water for the huge turtles and catfish. Evenings, just before dark, I'd got in the habit of feeding them chunks of bread. But there was nobody around this morning.

A couple of hundred yards away, over the swathe of dry grass, the squat, brown condo units were strung out in a circle around the central island, connected to the mainland by a wooden bridge over the narrow moat. The pool, the office and the tennis courts were all on the island. And that was Whispering Palms. Someone had bought some land in Florida and got very rich.

An old man, fuzz of white body hair against leathery skin, was lying out on a lounge chair catching the early rays. The scent of coconut sun screen mingled with the whiff of chlorine. The pool was still marked off by yellow police tape.

I noticed that the office door was ajar, and when I popped my head inside, I saw Mary sitting at her desk, staring into space. I like Mary. She's about twenty-five, an athletic sort of girl with a swimmer's upper body and a runner's thighs. She has a shiny black pony tail and one of those open, friendly faces, the kind you trust on sight.

'Oh, Mr Erwin. You startled me. You weren't wanting to use the pool, were you?'

'I was. But I see it's still off-limits.'

A frown wrinkled Mary's smooth, tanned brow. 'Well, I mean, it's not on account of the cops or anything,' she said. 'It's just . . . well, I didn't think the residents would like it, you know, swimming in a dead man's water.' She turned her nose up. 'So I've called maintenance and they're gonna clean it out and refill it all fresh. Should be ready by this afternoon. Sorry.'

'No, you're right. It's a good idea,' I said.

Most people probably *would* be put off by swimming in the same water where an electrocuted Santa Claus had floated around all night alone in the dark, but it didn't bother me much. I had seen death close up more times than I cared to remember. Besides, people swam in the ocean all the time and thousands have died there over the centuries.

'Mary,' I asked, 'do you happen to know who the last people to see Mr Schiller alive were?'

'His friends. Mr Brennan, Miss Lee and Miss Fraser. They said he was fine when they left.'

Of course. The ubiquitous trio.

Mary shook her head. 'Never could understand what Miss Lee saw in that group, pretty girl like her.'

So I was vindicated for thinking exactly the same thing

yesterday. And if a young woman like Mary could think it too, it couldn't be either ageist or sexist, could it?

'Mind if I ask *you* something?' Mary said with a frown.

'Go ahead.'

'Mr Schiller was a Canadian citizen, right?'

'As far as I know.'

'Well, I was worried, you know, like his relatives might come down and make some sort of lawsuit. What do you think?'

Aha, the great American paranoia raises its ugly head: lawsuits. 'I'm no legal expert,' I said.

'You hear about things like that all the time, don't you? I mean, they could sue for millions. I could be liable. It would ruin me.' She laughed. 'Even if they sued for hundreds it would bankrupt me. I could lose my job. I need this job, Mr Erwin. I need the money to go back to school.'

I smiled as reassuringly as I could and told her I didn't think that would happen. We didn't even know if Schiller had any next of kin, for a start. And she couldn't be responsible for his behaviour when he was drunk.

'But the cops said he must have tripped over that crack in the tiles.'

'What crack?'

'Come on, I'll show you.'

We went outside. The old guy in the lounge chair was still working on his skin cancer. Near the side of the pool, Mary pointed out the crack. It didn't look like much to me. I put my foot in front of it and slid forward slowly. My big toe slipped right over the crack and the rest of my foot followed. I could hardly even feel the rough edge of the tile. 'It's hardly enough to trip over,' I said to Mary.

'He was wearing flip-flops.'

'Santa Claus was wearing flip-flops?'

She nodded.

'I suppose that might make a difference. Even so . . . It's still a long way from the water. Maybe six feet. Schiller was a little guy, only around five-four, wasn't he?'

'Yeah. I thought about that, too. But he must have been walking fast, or running, then he tripped and skidded in. Those tiles can get pretty slippery, especially if they're wet.'

'But wouldn't the piano just rip out of the socket?'

Mary shrugged. 'It was one of those ultra-light things,' she said. 'And it had a long cord.'

Still, I couldn't help but wonder why the hell Santa Claus should be running *towards* the swimming pool in the dark with a live electric piano in his arms, no matter how tight he was or how light the piano.

A heron landed by the side of the moat. Just for a moment, I felt a slight shiver run up my spine to the hairs at the back of my neck. It was a sign I recognized. I was being watched. And not by the heron or the sunbather.

Mary turned and walked back to the office, sandals clip-clopping against the tiles. I followed her, admiring the way her thigh muscles rippled with each step. I felt strangely detached, though; I could admire the sculpted, athletic beauty of her body, but I didn't feel attracted to her sexually. But, then, it had been a long time since I *had* been attracted to anyone sexually, except maybe Karen Lee.

Mary sat down at her desk again.

'Look,' I said, leaning forward and resting my hands on the warm wood, 'I know this might sound strange to you, but I'd like you to do me a favour without telling anyone or asking too many questions. Do you think you could do that?'

Mary nodded slowly, tentatively. 'Depends,' she said, 'on what it is.'

•

When I got back to the condo, it was time for breakfast, but without the swim, my appetite wasn't up to much. I put on a pot of coffee, drank a glass of orange juice and ate a bowl of high-fibre bran. The healthy life.

Usually I took my second cup out to the lanai and worked on one of the cryptics from the *Sunday Times* book of crosswords. That was one thing always annoyed me about American newspapers: you couldn't find a cryptic in any of them I'd seen. This morning, though, I took the two sheets of paper that Mary had printed out for me.

OK, so Schiller was alone at the pool after the sing-along, or so Ed, Karen and Ginny said. Anyone could have gone there in the dark, killed him and tried to make it look like an accident. And at least three people knew he was there: Ed, Karen and Ginny. Were they telling the truth?

There was some risk – there always is with murder – but it was minimal. Most of the residents are elderly and they're usually in bed by ten. This isn't like some of the places where you get kids drinking all night and skinny-dipping; there are no kids at Whispering Palms.

First, I looked over the list of condo owners I had persuaded Mary to print for me.

Schiller's unit was owned on paper by Gardiner Holdings, registered in Grand Cayman Island. If that didn't set alarm bells ringing in an old gumshoe's mind, what would? But I couldn't for the life of me figure out what it meant.

Ginny Fraser's unit was a timeshare, though Ginny herself wasn't listed as owning any time.

Ed Brennan's unit was registered to a Dr Joseph Brady in Waterloo, Canada, and Karen Lee's to a travel agency called *EscapeItAll*, based in Sarasota.

One way or another, these four had all ended up at Whispering Palms, Fort Myers, Florida, and I was damned if I could see any reason other than pure chance.

So which one of them did it? And why? Or was it someone else?

I pushed my glasses back up the bridge of my nose and reached for the telephone. Being a private investigator from Toronto has *some* advantages in Florida.

•

When I'd finished on the phone I felt the need to go out for a drive. Not far. Maybe over the skyway to Sanibel and Captiva. Lunch at the Mucky Duck. Seafood and Harp lager. After all, I was on vacation, whatever Al said about gumshoes and the search for truth and justice.

But when I walked out to the car, I saw Karen Lee bent over the front tyre of her red Honda rental just a few parking spots down, white cotton shorts stretched taut over her ass.

I stood and admired the view for a while then walked towards her and asked if she could use any help. Why not? She could only tell me to get lost, that she was perfectly capable of fixing the tyre herself. Or she could accept my offer graciously.

She did the latter.

Turning on her haunches and shielding her eyes from

the sun, she smiled and said, 'Why, thanks, yes. I'd appreciate that.' She had dimples at each corner of her mouth. Cute.

Then she stood up and brushed the dust off her hands. She was wearing a pink tank top, and a little sweat had darkened the cotton between her breasts.

'Flat,' she said.

A facetious reply formed in my mind, but before I could voice it she went on, 'The tyre. I should have done something about it last night. I thought something was wrong, maybe a slow leak. But I couldn't be bothered. Then, when I came out just now I saw it was flat.'

'No problem,' I said, and in no time we took off the flat and put on the spare.

'Thanks a lot,' said Karen, smiling. 'It's not that I'm helpless or anything. I mean, I know how to change a tyre. But—'

'Forget it,' I told her. 'My pleasure.'

'What I was going to say was it was nice to have a bit of company.' And she smiled again, giving me the full benefit of her dimples and baby blues. The front of her tank top was even damper now and I could see beads of moisture on the tops of her breasts, between the tiny hairs. She had her hair tied back and fixed with barrettes, but a few strands had come loose and stuck to her flushed face. Some ice queen.

'Hot, isn't it,' she said, waving her hand in front of her face. 'Look, why don't you come in and clean up? It's the least I can do.'

I could have gone to my own place, just a few buildings down, but I'm no fool. I followed her up the steps to her second-storey unit. Inside, it was pretty much the same layout as mine: open-plan kitchen and living room, two bedrooms – one with its own bathroom – guest bathroom, and the lanai out front.

'Sorry about the mess,' Karen said, picking up a few magazines scattered on the sofa. 'I wasn't expecting company. Please go ahead. Use the bathroom.'

The bathroom was full of the mysterious paraphernalia of feminine beauty – potions, eyebrow pencils, little sponges, cotton wool, Q-tips. I washed the sweat and grime off my hands and face and flushed the toilet, using the noise to cover up the sound as I went through the drawers and cupboards. There was nothing out of the ordinary: soap, deodorant, shampoo, talcum, tampons, Advil, Maalox. The only interesting item was a bottle of Prozac. These days it seems half the world's on Prozac.

When I got back to the living room, Karen had just finished tidying things into neat piles. She smiled. 'Cold drink?'

'A Coke would be great.'

'I'll just go freshen up.' She looked down at her body and spread her arms, then seemed embarrassed by the gesture. In fact, now we were inside, her manner had grown much more nervous and I didn't know how to put her at ease. Too many movies about the nice guy next door turning out to be a psycho, I suppose.

'I'll help myself,' I said. 'You go wash up.'

'OK . . . I'll . . . er . . . It's in the fridge. I won't be long. Are you sure you'll be OK?'

'I'll be fine. Don't worry.'

When she went into her bathroom, the lock clicked behind her. As soon as I heard the shower start up, I began a quick search, not knowing what the hell I was looking for. If Schiller had been murdered, Karen had to be a suspect. Much as I hoped she hadn't done it, she had been one of the three to know where he was after the sing-along. And how drunk he was.

All I found out was that Karen was halfway through *The Concrete Blonde*; that she more than likely slept alone; that she favoured casual clothes but had a couple of expensive dresses; that she didn't seem to watch videos very much; and that her musical tastes extended from Mozart to Alanis Morissette.

When she came out, she was wearing red shorts and a white shirt. Her hair was still damp from the shower and it hung in long hanks, framing her pale oval face.

'There,' she said, hoisting herself onto a stool at the kitchen counter. 'That's better. What a start to the day.'

I poured her a Coke. 'I guess you must still be pretty upset about your friend dying?' I said.

'Bud. Yes. How did you . . . ? Of course. I've seen you in Chloe's, haven't I? Always alone. No wife? Girlfriend?'

A definite hint of flirtation there, I thought. 'My wife died three years ago. Auto accident.'

'Oh, I'm so sorry. That must be terrible.'

I shrugged. 'There's good days and bad. Were you very close to Mr Schiller?'

She looked away. 'Not really.'

'I don't mean to pry or anything,' I said, 'but were you . . . I mean, what drew you to him?'

'I don't know. We weren't an item, if that's what you're getting at.' She blushed. 'I'd just been through a painful divorce. I was depressed. I suppose I came down here to escape . . . I don't know . . . I guess maybe I suc-ceeded. Bud and the others, they were my escape. It was all fun. No demands. Bud was a laugh. He never took anything seriously.'

'You were one of the last people to see him alive, weren't you?'

Karen nodded. 'Yes. With Ed and Ginny.'

'What happened?'

'We'd all had a bit too much to drink. When everyone else left after the carols, we started joking around by the pool. I fell in. I wanted to go home and change out of my wet clothes, so the three of us came to my place. Bud said he had a couple of things to do, then he was going to turn in.'

'Did he say what he had to do?'

'No. Just a couple of things.'

'Do you think he could have been meeting someone?'

'I suppose so . . . I . .' She looked me in the eye. 'Why?'

'Just curious. How did he seem?'

'He was very drunk.' She frowned, then went on. 'You know, I've thought time and time again that we should have done something, that I should have said something.'

. 'Like what?'

'Oh, made him come with us, something like that. Somehow I feel responsible.'

'Don't be silly. There's no way you could have known.'

'Even so . . . I can't help feeling guilty.' She held her hands up. 'Look, I don't know how we got into this, but it's a beautiful day out there and I don't want to get even more depressed.'

Interview over. 'You're right,' I said, getting up. 'I'd better be going myself.'

She walked me to the door. 'Thanks for the help. It was nice talking to you.'

'You too.' Before she could close the door on me, I turned. 'Don't think this too presumptuous of me,' I began, 'but how would you like to come out for dinner or a drink tonight?'

'Tonight?' Her face dropped. 'Oh, I can't. I'm busy.'

I started to turn away. 'It's OK. I understand. Believe me. My mistake, especially after what you said about the divorce and all. I'm sorry.'

But she rested her warm hand on my arm. 'It's nothing like that,' she said. 'I don't want you to think I'm making an excuse. I'm not. I really *do* have something on tonight. The three of us are having a sort of wake. I couldn't miss it.'

Maybe this wasn't the brush off, then. Heart thumping, fear of rejection bringing me out in a sweat, I persevered. 'How about tomorrow night then?'

She smiled. 'I'd love to. Really, I would.'

'Great. Do you like seafood?'

'Sure.'

'How about the Big Fin?'

'Fine. Look, I'll meet you at the bar there at seven. I've got some running around to do first, and I'm not sure if I'll have time to get back here. OK?'

'Fine. Big Fin. Bar. Seven.' I walked off, grinning like an idiot.

•

The phone started ringing, the way they do, the minute I stuck my key in the door that afternoon. I put the groceries I'd bought at Publix on the kitchen counter and picked up the extension.

'Jack, it's Mike.'

My partner. 'You were quick.'

'Well, partly it's a slow week.'

'And . . . ?'

'And partly there's not a hell of a lot to report.'

'Go ahead anyway.'

'Nothing on any of the people on the list. Squeaky clean, every one of them.'

'What about Schiller?'

'That's the only interesting part. As far as I can make out, nobody knows him. I checked out the Kingston address you gave me. It's owned by a couple called Renard. They confirmed that a man called Bud Schiller rents it from them and the cheques come in regularly.'

'Where from?'

'That they wouldn't tell me. Anyway, I got the name of the guy next door to the Schiller place, and he said the house is empty most of the time.'

Now what the hell did that mean? 'Anything else?'

'That doctor in Waterloo, Joseph Brady, he checks out. He's Edward Brennan's family doctor, has been for years, and he rented the condo to Ed for the first time a few years back. Apparently the poor guy needed to recuperate from some illness – nothing specific, you know doctors – but I got the impression this Ed character had suffered various health problems on and off over—'

'Mental or physical?'

'Can't say. But Brady's a family doctor, Jack, not a shrink.'

'OK. Go on.'

'So it was a kind of convalescent holiday. He liked it and kept coming back.'

'How about *EscapeItAll*?'

'Perfectly legit. They own a few condos down the Gulf Coast and rent them through local agencies. Quite a lot of the Toronto travel agents do business with them, and the ones I talked to said they never had any problems.'

'And the timeshare?'

'Also legit. There is one thing, though. Virginia Fraser, one of the names you gave me?'

'Right.' Ginny Fraser.

'I talked to the woman she rented from, and it turns out that the dates Fraser got weren't available originally.'

'So?'

'So she paid over the odds.'

'Ah-ha. On welfare, too. Is that all?'

'Just about. Gardiner Holdings, that company in the Caymans? Looks like it's the front of a front of a front. I couldn't get even get a whiff of the real movers and shakers behind it.'

'OK,' I said. 'Thanks a lot Mike. You did good work.' Then I hung up and mulled over what I'd learned.

•

'Gee, I dunno, Mr Erwin. I really shouldn't be doing this,' Mary said when she found the right key.

'It'll have to be cleaned out, anyway,' I said.

'Yeah, I know. It's just . . . Still, you *are* a licensed private investigator, right?'

'Right. And maybe we can check on next of kin, make sure no one's gonna come down and file a lawsuit against you.' I hated pressuring her that way, but I had to get inside Schiller's condo if I was to get any further. I was now more or less convinced that someone – either one of his three pals or someone he had arranged to meet – had gone to the pool and murdered him. It would help if I could find out whether he had anything to hide.

Still biting her lip, Mary turned the key in the lock.

Schiller certainly travelled light. A quick search of the master bedroom revealed only warm-climate clothes and a tattered Tom Clancy paperback on the bedside table. No papers in the drawers, no photographs, nothing. The cops must have taken his passport. The bathroom held only what a single man's bathroom would, and the guest bedroom was empty except for the bed, stripped down to its mattress. Kitchen and fridge contained the usual – milk, bread, condiments, a couple of TV dinners, cutlery, booze. By the looks of it, Schiller ate out a lot.

In the living room, the stereo, TV and VCR took up one corner. A cabinet under the VCR held a stock of tapes. One of the movies was from a local rental store, and it was overdue by two days. The tape was still in the machine.

'I'll take this back tomorrow,' I said to Mary, casually slipping the tape back in the box.

Mary just nodded and glanced nervously at the door.

'I think that's about all,' I said, 'if you want to go now.'

Mary was out the front door like a shot. 'You didn't find anything about next of kin?'

'Nothing. No news is good news. Don't worry.'

She flashed an anxious smile. 'I'll try not to.'

And I hurried back to call the courier company. It was late, but with luck, they could get a package to Mike overnight.

•

'Jack?'

'Uh-huh.'

'Mike.'

'Hang on . . . Just a minute . . .' I sat up quickly. It felt like I had to drag myself a long way back from God knew where. I rubbed my eyes and checked my watch. Three-thirty in the afternoon. I must have dozed off after lunch.

I opened the fridge and popped the tab on a can of Michelob, then picked up the phone again. 'Yeah, go ahead, Mike. Sorry about that.'

'No problem. I took the video down to Ident first thing this morning. It was a bit of a mess – must have been a popular movie down there – but Harry found a match you might be interested in.'

'Schiller's got a record?'

'Not Schiller. The only prints we could find on file belong to a Sherman Smith.'

'That rings a bell.'

'It should do,' he went on. 'Remember that land scam twenty years ago? Smith defrauded hundreds of people out of their life savings.'

'What was it, some land in Florida turned out to be swamp?'

'Something like that. Smith disappeared with the money and was never seen or heard of again. In all there must've been over two or three million bucks.'

I whistled. 'What happened?'

'The Mounties followed the paper trail for a while, then they lost it. Smith never surfaced again.'

Except as Schiller, I thought. He probably split his time between Florida and the Cayman Islands, travelling on a phony Canadian passport but not staying in Canada for long. Too risky. 'Do we recognize any of the victims' names?' I asked Mike.

I could almost hear him grinning over the phone. 'I thought you'd never ask. As a matter of fact we do: a Mr Edward Brennan.'

●

Karen was sitting at a stool at the bar sipping something colourful and cluttered through a candy-striped straw. She was wearing a green silk off-the-shoulder number, one I had seen in her closet, with her legs crossed. I caught an eyeful of slim, tanned thigh as I walked towards her. She smiled and said hello. Her shiny blonde hair fell over her shoulder on one side, and she had tucked the other side behind her ear, fixing it there with a pink flower that matched her lipstick. Nice touch.

I must admit I'd been relieved to find out it was Ed who had the connection with Smith, not Karen. It didn't mean he was the killer, of course, but it sure gave him one hell of a motive. I still had a lot of questions for Karen, though, and I wasn't sure how, or if, I could mix business and pleasure.

I ordered a bourbon on the rocks and we walked through to the table. It was a tacky-looking kind of restaurant, with nets hanging from the ceilings and old barrels converted into chairs, but the food was always superb.

Karen examined the menu, then she said, 'I'd like to start with some oysters. How about you?'

'Fine by me.' Oysters! For an ice queen? Maybe Al French had an agenda of his own? So we ordered a dozen oysters and a bottle of Californian champagne, followed by swordfish steak for me and coquilles Saint-Jacques for Karen. She avoided my eyes as the waiter lit candles on the table.

We chatted about this and that. Karen seemed nervous, on edge, attention all over the place, so much so that she seemed skittish. But just when I thought I'd lost her, she'd look me in the eye and come back with the kind of remark that showed she was there all the time, maybe even a step or two ahead.

'Did you know Bud, Ed or Ginny back home?' I asked when the subject came around to last night's wake.

She shook her head. 'One rule about a world you escape to is that neither it nor any of its inhabitants can exist in the world you regularly live in.' She fingered the napkin ring on the table as she spoke, shadows flitting in the depths of her eyes.

'I can understand that,' I said, thinking it sounded like something out of a computer-game manual. The oysters arrived and we helped ourselves. 'I suppose it's an escape for me too.'

'Is it? In what way?'

'I used to come down here with my wife.'

Karen frowned. 'Then it's not an escape you're after,' she said. 'It's *catharsis.*'

'Maybe you're right. If so, it hasn't happened yet.'

She put her hand lightly on mine. 'Give it time, Jack. Give it time.'

We finished the oysters, and the main courses arrived. I tried to find a way to steer the conversation back to Bud Schiller. As usual, I couldn't find a subtle way, so halfway through my swordfish, during a temporary lull, I said, 'Remember when you told me the three of you went to your room and Bud stayed out by the pool?'

She nodded. 'And you thought he might be meeting someone?'

'That's right. Did any of the others leave your room at any time?'

'Not until later.' She blushed. 'Ed must have passed out there. I found him on the couch in the morning.'

'Did Ed ever mention knowing Bud from before?'

Karen looked down at her plate and speared a scallop. 'No.' Then she looked back at me and her eyes widened.

'What are you suggesting? That Ed murdered Bud? You can't be serious?'

'I don't know, Karen. I'm just curious, that's all.'

'But why? Why are you interested? Are you a cop?'

'I'm a private investigator,' I told her, 'but I'm not licensed to operate down here.' I shrugged. 'It just seemed suspicious to me, that's all.'

I paused for a moment, then I jumped right in and told her about Schiller's true identity and the land scam, in which one Edward Brennan lost his life's savings. When I finished, Karen was pale. She excused herself to visit the washroom.

When she came back, she looked a lot better. She didn't wear much make-up, but she had given herself a fresh coat of the basics and looked good as new.

'I'm sorry for overreacting,' she said. 'Honestly, I'd never really considered that Bud's death could have been deliberate. I suppose I was too busy blaming myself. But Ed . . . ?'

'I can't be sure,' I said. 'But it doesn't look good. Are you certain he never left your condo?'

'He went over to his own unit to pick up some Scotch. I'd run out. But he wasn't gone for more than ten minutes.'

'Ten minutes was enough.'

'What are you going to do?'

'Tell the authorities, I suppose.'

She nodded slowly. 'That would be the right thing to do, of course. But poor Ed. I don't like the thought of him spending the rest of his life in jail. Can't you just . . . you know . . . let it go?'

'However much of an asshole Bud Schiller was, he didn't deserve to die like that.'

'You're right,' she whispered. 'I'd like to go home.'

As I followed Karen's Honda back to Whispering Palms, I was beginning to think that I'd blown my chances of a pleasant end to the evening. But she invited me up for a nightcap.

Once we were inside, she busied herself preparing the drinks, flitting nervously between fridge and cocktail cabinet, chattering brightly away. Ever since we got back, I'd sensed a certain tension between us and I thought it was sexual. When she walked past me to open the sliding glass door to the lanai, I put my hand out and touched her shoulder. She turned, gave me a swift peck on the cheek and said she had to go to the bathroom.

I gazed out at the dark island beyond the lanai, the Christmas lights on the bridge, drink in hand, waiting for her. What did the peck on the cheek mean? Was it promise or consolation? You're an old fool, Jack Erwin, I told myself. You should stick to your bourbon and blues.

Then I heard a door open behind me. Thinking it was Karen coming back, I turned around.

Ed Brennan stood there, a baseball bat in his hands.

Before I had time to react, the front door opened and Ginny Fraser walked in carrying a long kitchen knife.

Karen came out of the bathroom. She wasn't carrying any weapon and she looked as if she had been crying. 'Oh, Jack,' she said, shaking her head. 'I'm so sorry.'

'What are you going to do?' I asked, trying to sound more confident than I felt. 'Hit me on the head with the baseball bat then stab me and pretend it was an accident? Just to protect Ed here? Come on, Karen, he's not worth it.'

'You don't understand,' Karen said. 'You think you

know everything but you don't. You don't know anything.'

My breath caught in my throat. 'What the hell are you talking about?'

Then a strange thing happened. I saw Karen flash a quick, sad glance at Ed, and he just seemed to deflate right before my eyes. His baseball bat dropped to the floor. 'He's right, Karen,' he said. 'We can't do this. We're not killers.'

I looked at Ginny Fraser. She dropped the kitchen knife and flopped onto the sofa.

After I got my breath back, I turned to Karen and said, 'Right, now we've got that charade out of the way, will someone tell me what's going on here?'

•

'I'm sorry,' Ed said for the third time. 'I don't know what came over us. We were desperate. I still can't imagine what made us think we could kill an innocent man. When Karen phoned from the restaurant and told us you knew . . . we just panicked.'

'I'm sorry I deceived you,' Karen said. 'I admit I was trying to find out if you knew anything. After I saw you and the woman from the office looking at the pool yesterday, I thought you might be trouble. So I arranged the puncture.'

Well that makes two of us acting from impure motives, I thought. 'So you're all sorry,' I said. 'Whoop-a-de-doo-dah. Now would someone tell me why I shouldn't call the police right now?'

'We can't stop you,' Ed said. 'We *won't* stop you. In a way, it would be a relief.'

I poured three fingers of Karen's bourbon into my glass

and settled down on the sofa beside Ginny. Karen and Ed sat opposite in matching easy chairs. 'Just tell me what it's all about,' I said. 'Who really did kill Schiller?'

'We all did,' Ed answered.

I looked at Karen and Ginny, who both nodded.

Jesus Christ, I thought, it's *Murder on the Orient Express* all over again.

'Ginny and I pushed him into the pool,' Ed went on. 'He thought we were playing games. Karen plugged in the piano, and we all lowered it in after him. After that all we had to do was lie to the police and tell them he was still alive when we left him.'

'What I really don't understand,' I went on, 'is why. I know Smith cheated Ed out of his life's savings, but what did he ever do to you, Karen?'

'My father,' she said flatly. 'Vernon Connant. You'll find *his* name on your list. Lee's my married name. Smith swindled him out of every penny we had. When the news broke he killed my mother, then himself. With a shotgun. I was five at the time. Just before he put the gun in his mouth and pulled the trigger, he looked at me. He was going to kill me, too, but at the last moment, he couldn't do it. I'll never forget that look. I've spent my whole life trying, one shrink to another, pills, the lot. You can't tell me that Sherman Smith didn't deserve to die.'

I took a long sip of bourbon and let the fire fill my mouth before swallowing. 'What about you, Ginny? You weren't on the list, either.'

'My husband. Harvey Pellier. I went back to my maiden name.'

'What happened?'

Ginny gave a harsh laugh. 'Nothing quite so dramatic as Karen's story. Harvey lost everything, and it broke his spirit. He left us. Just walked out and never came back. We hadn't been really well off, but we'd been happy. When Harvey left, the family just fell apart. I couldn't hold it together. The kids did badly at school, started hanging with a bad crowd. You know the sort of thing. They drifted into drugs, street life. Will died of an overdose. Jane's still somewhere out on the streets. I haven't heard from her in years.'

After a few moments of silence, Ed ran his hands through his hair and said he wouldn't mind a drink. Karen got him a Scotch on the rocks. Then he began. 'I bumped into Smith about four years ago. Pure chance. Coincidence. I just couldn't believe it. I suppose, when you think about it, you never know who's going to be renting from who. Anyway, I saw him, after over fifteen years, and do you know what?'

I shook my head.

'He didn't recognize me. I mean, you ought to recognize people whose lives you ruined, don't you think? Because of him I had a nervous breakdown, I got hooked on the booze, lost job after job. You name it.' He thumped his chest with his fist. 'Then, when I began to relive what he'd done to me, I realized the anger was still there. Only now I had the advantage. But I couldn't kill him. Not alone.' He glanced at Karen and Ginny. 'When it first happened – I mean twenty years ago – lots of us had meetings with lawyers, and I became close to Karen's father and Ginny's husband. But Smith had never seen Karen or Ginny. So I got in touch with them, told them the situation and we planned what to do. We befriended him, one by one, pretended we didn't know each other, then we killed him.'

Ed fell silent and the others looked at me. It was hard

to imagine the havoc Sherman Smith had wreaked on these lives, hard not to sympathize with the three of them, but who was I to judge?

'It's up to you now, Jack,' Karen said, seeming to sense my dilemma. 'You know the whole story now. We're guilty of premeditated murder.' She glanced at Ed. 'If you want my honest opinion, I don't think it's helped any of us. I don't think it's going to make our lives any easier to bear – probably the opposite – but it's done and you're the only one who knows about it. We can't kill you, but we're not going to give ourselves up willingly, either. It's your decision.'

So whether I liked it or not, it *was* up to me. I finished my bourbon, then I nodded and went back to my condo.

•

Almost exactly one year to the day later, I found myself in Chloe's for 'Happy Hour'. There were one or two faces I recognized around the bar, but most of the people were strangers. I still didn't know why I kept coming back year after year. Especially this year. Maybe Karen had been right and I *was* looking for catharsis.

Or for Karen.

I looked across the bar at where I had first really noticed her last year, running her finger around the rim of a glass. Now a chain-smoking brunette with a hard face sat there instead.

'Hi, Shamus.'

Al French slipped onto the empty stool beside me.

'Beer?' I offered.

'My turn.' Al ordered two beers. 'Did you ever get to the bottom of that mysterious death?' he asked.

'Which one was that?'

'You know. Last year. That asshole Bud Schiller.'

'Oh, him.' I shook my head. 'I don't think there was anything mysterious about it at all. I think he was drunk, he tripped and he fell into the pool.'

'Yeah, and he pulled the piano in after him just for good measure. Come on, Jack.'

I shrugged. 'You know, Al, sometimes the strangest of accidents *do* happen. Did I ever tell you about the guy they found dead on the subway tracks and couldn't find his head?'

THE WRONG HANDS

'**Is everything in** order?' the old man asked, his scrawny fingers clutching the comforter like talons.

'Seems to be,' said Mitch.

Drawing up the will had been a simple enough task. Mr Garibaldi and his wife had the dubious distinction of outliving both their children, and there wasn't much to leave.

'Would you like to sign it now?' he asked, holding out his Mont Blanc.

The old man clutched the pen the way a child holds a crayon and scribbled his illegible signature on the documents.

'There . . . that's done,' said Mitch. He placed the papers in his briefcase.

Mr Garibaldi nodded. The movement brought on a spasm and such a coughing fit that Mitch thought the old man was going to die right there and then.

But he recovered. 'Will you do me a favour?' he croaked when he'd got his breath back.

Mitch frowned. 'If I can.'

With one bent, shrivelled finger, Mr Garibaldi pointed to the floor under the window. 'Pull the carpet back,' he said.

Mitch stood up and looked.

'Please,' said Mr Garibaldi. 'The carpet.'

Mitch walked over to the window and rolled back the carpet. Underneath was nothing but floorboards.

'One of the boards is loose,' said the old man. 'The one directly in line with the wall socket. Lift it up.'

Mitch felt and, sure enough, part of the floorboard was loose. He lifted it easily with his fingernails. Underneath, wedged between the joists, lay a package wrapped in old newspaper.

'That's it,' said the old man. 'Take it out.'

Mitch did. It was heavier than he had expected.

'Now put the board back and replace the carpet.'

After he had done as he was asked, Mitch carried the package over to the bed.

'Open it,' said Mr Garibaldi. 'Go on, it won't bite you.'

Slowly, Mitch unwrapped the newspaper. It was from 18 December 1947, he noticed, and the headline reported a blizzard dumping twenty-eight inches of snow on New York City the day before. Inside, he found a layer of oil-cloth. When he had folded back that too, a gun gleamed up at him. It was old, he could tell that, but it looked in superb condition. He hefted it into his hand, felt its weight and balance, pointed it towards the wall as if to shoot.

'Be careful,' said the old man. 'It's loaded.'

Mitch looked at the gun again, then put it back on the oilcloth. His fingers were smudged with oil or grease, so he took a tissue from the bedside table and wiped them off as best he could.

'What the hell are you doing with a loaded gun?' he asked.

Mr Garibaldi sighed. 'It's a Luger,' he said. 'First World War, probably. Old, anyway. A friend gave it to me many years ago. A German friend. I've kept it ever since. Partly as a memento of him and partly for protection. You know what this city's been getting like these past few years. I've maintained it, cleaned it, kept it loaded. Now I'm gonna die I want to hand it in. I don't want it to fall into the wrong hands.'

Mitch set the Luger down on the bed. 'Why tell me?' he asked.

'Because it's unregistered and I'd like you to hand it over for me.' He shook his head and coughed again. 'I haven't got long left. I don't want no cops coming round here and giving me a hard time.'

'They won't give you a hard time.' More like give you a medal for handing over an unregistered firearm, Mitch thought.

'Maybe not. But . . .' Mr Garibaldi grabbed Mitch's wrist with his talon. The fingers felt cold and dry, like a reptile's skin. Mitch tried to pull back a little, but the old man held on, pulled him closer and croaked, 'Sophie doesn't know. It would make her real angry to know we had a gun in the house the last fifty years and I kept it from her. I don't want to end my days with my wife mad at me. Please, Mr Mitchell. It's a small favour I ask.'

Mitch scratched the side of his eye. True enough, he thought, it *was* a small favour. And it might prove a profitable one, too. Old firearms were worth something to collectors, and Mitch knew a cop who had connections. All he had to say was that he had been entrusted this gun by a client, who had brought it to his office, that he had put it in the safe and called the police immediately. What could be wrong with that?

'OK,' he said, rewrapping the gun and slipping it in his briefcase along with the will. 'I'll do as you ask. Don't worry. You rest now. Everything will be OK.'

Mr Garibaldi smiled and seemed to sink into a deep sleep.

•

Mitch stood on the porch of the Garibaldi house and pulled on his sheepskin-lined gloves, glad to be out of the cloying atmosphere of the sickroom, even if it was minus ninety or something outside.

He was already wearing his heaviest overcoat over a suit and a wool scarf, but still he was freezing. It was one of those clear winter nights when the ice cracks underfoot and the breeze off the lake seems to numb you right to the bone. Reflected street lamps splintered in the broken mirror of the sidewalk, the colour of Mr Garibaldi's jaundiced eyes.

Mitch pulled his coat tighter around his scarf and set off, cracking the iced-over puddles as he went. Here and there, the remains of last week's snow had frozen into ruts, and he almost slipped and fell a couple of times on the uneven surface.

As he walked, he thought of old Garibaldi, with no more than a few weeks or days left to live. The old man must have been in pain sometimes, but he never complained. And he surely must be afraid of death? Maybe dying put things in perspective, Mitch thought. Maybe the mind, facing the eternal, icy darkness of death, had ways of dealing with its impending extinction, of discarding the dross, the petty and the useless.

Or perhaps not. Maybe the old man just lay there day after day running baseball statistics through his mind; or wishing he'd slept with his neighbour's wife when he had the chance.

As Mitch walked up the short hill, he cursed the fact that you could never get a decent parking spot in these residential streets. He'd had to park in the lot behind the drug store, the next street over, and the quickest way there was through a dirt alley just about wide enough for a garbage truck to pass through.

It happened as he cut through the alley. And it happened so fast that, afterwards, he couldn't be quite sure whether he felt the sharp blow to the back of his head before his feet slipped out from under him, or after.

•

When Mitch opened his eyes again, the first thing he saw was the night sky. It looked like a black satin bed-sheet with some rich woman's diamonds spilled all over it. There was no moon.

He felt frozen to the marrow. He didn't know how long he had been lying there in the alley – long enough to die of exposure it felt like – but when he checked his watch, he saw he had only been out a little over five minutes. Not surprising no one had found him yet. Not here, on a night like this.

He lay on the frozen mud and took stock. Despite the cold, everything hurt – his elbow, which he had cracked trying to break his fall; his tailbone; his right shoulder; and, most of all, his head – and the pain was sharp and spiky, not at all numb like the rest of him. He reached around and touched the sore spot on the back of his head. His fingers came away sticky with blood.

He took a deep breath and tried to get to his feet, but he could only manage to slip and skitter around like a newborn deer, making himself even more dizzy. There was no purchase, nothing to grip. Snail-like, he slid himself along the ice towards the rickety fence. There, by reaching out and grabbing the wooden rails carefully, he was able to drag himself to his feet, picking up only a few splinters for his troubles.

At first, he wished he had stayed where he was. His head started to spin and he thought it was going to split open with pain. For a moment, he was sure he was going to fall again. He held on to the fence for dear life and vomited, the world swimming around his head. After that, he felt a little better. Maybe he wasn't going to die.

The only light shone from a street lamp at the end of the alley, not really enough to search by, so Mitch used the plastic penlight attached to his key-ring to look for his briefcase. But it wasn't there. Stepping carefully on the ribbed ice, still in pain and unsure of his balance, Mitch extended the area of his search in case the briefcase had skidded off somewhere on the ice when he fell. It was nowhere to be found.

Almost as an afterthought, as the horrible truth was beginning to dawn on him, he felt for his wallet. Gone. So he'd been mugged. The blow had come *before* the fall. And they'd taken his briefcase.

Then Mitch remembered the gun.

•

The next morning was a nightmare. Mitch had managed to get himself home from the alley without crashing the car, and after a long, hot bath, a tumbler of Scotch and four extra-strength Tylenol, he began to feel a little better. He seemed to remember his mother once saying you shouldn't go to sleep after a bump on the head – he didn't know why – but it didn't stop him that night.

In the morning, he awoke aching all over.

When he had showered, taken more Tylenol and forced himself to eat some bran flakes, he poured a second cup of strong black coffee and sat down to think things out. None of his thoughts brought any comfort.

He hadn't gone to the cops. How could he, given what he had been carrying? Whichever way you looked at it, he had been in possession of an illegal, unregistered firearm when he was mugged. Even if the cops had been lenient, there was the Law Society to reckon with, and like most lawyers, Mitch feared the Law Society far more than he feared the police.

Maybe he could have sort of skipped over the gun in his account of the mugging. After all, he was pretty sure that it couldn't be traced either to him or to Garibaldi. But what if the cops found the briefcase and the gun was still inside it? How could he explain that?

Would that be worse than if the briefcase turned up and the gun was gone? If the muggers took it, the chances were someone might get shot with it. Either way, it was a bad scenario for Mitch, and it was all his fault. Well, maybe *fault* was too strong a word – he couldn't help getting mugged – but he still felt somehow responsible.

All he could do was hope that whoever took the gun would get rid of it, throw it in the lake, before anyone came to any harm.

Some hope.

•

Later that morning, Mitch remembered Garibaldi's will. That had gone, too, along with the briefcase and the gun. And it would have to be replaced.

There's only one true will – copies have no legal standing – and if you lose it you could have a hell of a mess on your hands. Luckily, he had Garibaldi's will on his computer. All he had to do was print it out again and hope to hell the old guy hadn't died during the night.

He hadn't. Puzzled, but accepting Mitch's excuse of a minor error he'd come across when proof-reading the document, Garibaldi signed again with a shaking hand.

'Is the gun safe?' he asked afterwards. 'You've got it locked away in your safe?'

'Yes,' Mitch lied. 'Yes, don't worry, the gun's perfectly safe.'

•

Every day Mitch scanned the paper from cover to cover for news of a shooting or a gun found abandoned somewhere. He even took to buying the *Sun* – which he normally wouldn't even use as toilet paper up at the cottage – because it covered more lurid local crime than the *Globe* or the *Star*. Anything to do with firearms was certain to make it into the *Sun*.

But it wasn't until three weeks and three days after the mugging – and two weeks after Mr Garibaldi's death 'peacefully, at home' – that the item appeared. And it was big enough news to make the *Globe and Mail*.

Mr Charles McVie was shot dead in his home last night during the course of an apparent burglary. A police spokesperson says Mr McVie was shot twice, once in the chest and once in the groin, while interrupting a burglar at his Beaches mansion shortly after midnight last night. He died of his wounds three hours later at East General Hospital. Detective Greg Hollins, who has been assigned the case, declined to comment on whether the police are following any significant leads at the moment, but he did inform our reporter that preliminary tests indicate the bullet was most likely fired from an old 9mm semi-automatic weapon, such as a Luger, unusual and fairly rare these days. As yet, police have not been able to locate the gun. Mr McVie, 62, made his fortune in the construction business. His wife, Laura, who was staying overnight with friends in Windsor when the shooting occurred, had no comment when she was reached early this morning.

The newspaper shook in Mitch's hands. It had happened. Somebody had died because of him. But while he felt guilt, he also felt fear. Was there really no way the police could tie the gun to him or Mr Garibaldi? Thank God the old man was dead, or he might hear about the shooting and his conscience might oblige him to come forward. Luckily, his widow, Sophie, knew nothing.

With luck, the Luger was in the deepest part of the lake for sure by now. Whether anyone else had touched it or not, Mitch knew damn well that *he* had, and that his greasy fingerprints weren't only all over the grip and the barrel, but on the wrapping paper, too. The muggers had probably been wearing gloves when they robbed him – it was a cold night – and maybe they'd had the sense to keep them on when they saw what was in the briefcase.

Calm down, he told himself. Even if the cops did find his fingerprints on the gun, they had no way of knowing *whose* prints they were. Mitch had never been finger-printed in his life, and the cops would have no reason to subject him to it now.

And they couldn't connect Charles McVie to either Mr Garibaldi or to Mitch.

Except for one thing.

Mitch had drawn up McVie's will two years ago, after his marriage to Laura, his second wife.

•

Mitch had known that Laura McVie was younger than her husband, but even that knowledge hadn't prepared him for the woman who opened the door to him three days after Charles McVie's funeral.

Black became her. Really became her, the way it set off her creamy complexion, long blonde hair, Kim Basinger lips and eyes the colour of a bluejay's wing.

'Yes?' she said, frowning slightly.

Mitch had put on his very best, most expensive suit, and he knew he looked sharp. He didn't want her to think he was some ambulance-chaser come after her husband's money.

As executor, Laura McVie was under no obligation to use the same lawyer who had prepared her husband's will to handle his estate. Laura might have a lawyer of her own in mind. But Mitch *did* have the will, so there was every chance that if he presented himself well she would choose him to handle the estate too.

And there was much more money in estates – especially those as big as McVie's – than there was in wills.

At least, Mitch thought, he wasn't so hypocritical as to deny that he had mixed motives for visiting the widow. Didn't everyone have mixed motives? He felt partly responsible for McVie's death, of course, and a part of him genuinely wanted to offer the widow help.

After Mitch had introduced himself, Laura looked him over, plump lower lip fetchingly nipped between two sharp, white teeth, then she flashed him a smile and said,

'Please come in, Mr Mitchell. I was wondering what to do about all that stuff. I really could use some help.' Her voice was husky and low-pitched, with just a subtle hint of that submissive tone that can drive certain men wild.

Mitch followed her into the high-ceilinged hallway, watching the way her hips swayed under the mourning dress.

He was in. All right! He almost executed a little jig on the parquet floor.

•

The house was an enormous heap of stone overlooking the ravine. It had always reminded Mitch of an English vicarage, or what he assumed an English vicarage looked like from watching PBS. Inside, though, it was bright and spacious and filled with modern furniture – not an anti-macassar in sight. The paintings that hung on the white walls were all contemporary abstracts and geometric designs, no doubt originals and worth a small fortune in themselves. The stereo equipment was state-of-the-art, as were the large screen TV, VCR and DVD player.

Laura McVie sat on a white sofa and crossed her legs. The dress she wore was rather short for mourning, Mitch thought, though he wasn't likely to complain about the four or five inches of smooth thigh it revealed. Especially as the lower part was sheathed in black silk stockings and the upper was bare and white.

She took a cigarette from a carved wooden box on the coffee table and lit it with a lighter that looked like a base-ball. Mitch declined the offer to join her.

'I hope you don't mind,' she said, lowering her eyes. 'It's my only vice.'

'Of course not.' Mitch cleared his throat. 'I just wanted

to come and tell you how sorry I was to hear about the . . . the tragic accident. Your husband was—'

'It wasn't an accident, Mr Mitchell,' she said calmly. 'My husband was murdered. I believe we should face the truth clearly and not hide behind euphemisms, don't you?'

'Well, if you put it like that . . .'

She nodded. 'You were saying about my husband?'

'Well, I didn't know him well, but I *have* done some legal work for him – specifically his will – and I am aware of his circumstances.'

'My husband was very rich, Mr Mitchell.'

'Exactly. I thought . . . well . . . there are some unscrupulous people out there, Mrs McVie.'

'Please, call me Laura.'

'Laura. There are some unscrupulous people out there, and I thought if there was anything I could do to help, perhaps give advice, take the burden off your hands . . .?'

'What burden would that be, Mr Mitchell?'

Mitch sat forward and clasped his hands on his knees. 'When someone dies, Mrs – Laura – there are always problems, legal wrangling and the like. Your husband's affairs seem to be in good order, judging from his will, but that was made two years ago. I'd hate to see someone come and take advantage of you.'

'Thank you,' Laura said. 'You're so sweet. And why shouldn't you handle the estate? Someone has to do it. I can't.'

Mitch had the strangest feeling that something was going awry here. Laura McVie didn't seem at all the person to be taken advantage of, yet she seemed to be swallowing his line of patter. That could only be, he decided, because it suited her, too. And why not? It *would* take a load off her mind.

'That wasn't the main reason I came, though,' Mitch pressed on, feeling an irrational desire to explain himself. 'I genuinely wanted to see if I could help in any way.'

'Why?' she asked, blue eyes open wide. 'Why should you? Mr Mitchell, I've come to learn that people do things for selfish motives. Self-interest rules. Always. I don't believe in altruism. Nor did my husband. At least we were agreed on that.' She turned aside, flicked some ash at the ashtray and missed. In contrast to everything else in the place, the tin ashtray looked as if it had been stolen from a lowlife bar. 'So you want to help me?' she said. 'For a fee, of course.'

Mitch felt embarrassed and uncomfortable. The part of him that had desperately wanted to make amends for his part in Charles McVic's death was being thwarted by the frankness and openness of the widow. Yes, he could use the money – of course he could – but that really *wasn't* his only reason for being there, and he wanted her to know that. How could he explain that he really wasn't such a bad guy?

'There are expenses involved in settling an estate,' Mitch went on. 'Disbursements. Of course, there are. But I'm not here to cheat you.'

She smiled at him indulgently. 'Of course not.'

Which definitely came across as, '*As if you could.*'

'But if you'll allow me to—'

She shifted her legs, showing more thigh. 'Mr Mitchell,' she said, 'I'm getting the feeling that you really do have another reason for coming to see me. If it's not that you're after my husband's money, then what are you after?'

Mitch swallowed. 'I . . . I feel. You see, I—'

'Come on, Mr Mitchell. You can tell me. You'll feel better.'

The voice that had seemed so submissive when Mitch first heard it now became hypnotic, so warm, so trustworthy, so easy to answer. And he had to tell someone.

'I feel partly responsible for your husband's death,' he said, looking into her eyes. 'Oh, I'm not the burglar, I'm not the killer. But I think I inadvertently supplied the gun.'

Laura McVie looked puzzled. Now he had begun, Mitch saw no point in stopping. If he could only tell this woman the full story, he thought, then she would understand. Perhaps she would even be sympathetic towards him. Forgive him. So he told her.

When he had finished, Laura stood up abruptly and walked over to the picture-window with its view of a back garden as big as Central Park. Mitch sat where he was and looked at her from behind. Her legs were close together and her arms were crossed. She seemed to be turned in on herself. He couldn't tell whether she was crying or not, but her shoulders seemed to be moving.

'Well?' he asked, after a while. 'What do you think?'

She let the silence stretch a moment, then dropped her arms and turned around slowly. Her eyes did look moist with tears. 'What do I think?' she said. 'I don't know. I don't know what to think. I think that maybe if you'd reported the gun stolen the police would have searched for it and my husband wouldn't have been murdered.'

'But I would have been charged, disbarred.'

'Mr Mitchell, surely that's a small price to pay for someone's life? I'm sorry. I think you'd better go. I can't think straight right now.'

'But I—'

'Please, Mr Mitchell. Leave.' She turned back to the window again and folded her arms, shaking.

Mitch got up off the sofa and headed for the door. He felt defeated, as if he had left something important unfinished, but there was nothing he could do about it. Only slink off with his tail between his legs feeling worse than when he had come. Why hadn't he just told her he was after handling McVie's estate. Money, pure and simple. Self-interest like that she would have understood.

●

Two days later, and still no developments reported in the McVie investigation, Laura phoned.

'Mr Mitchell?'

'Yes.'

'I'm sorry about my behaviour the other day. I was upset, as you can imagine.'

'I can understand that,' Mitch said. 'I don't blame you. I don't even know why I told you.'

'I'm glad you did. I've had time to think about it since then, and I'm beginning to realize how terrible you must feel. I want you to understand that I don't blame you. It's not the gun that commits the crime, after all, is it? It's the person who pulls the trigger. I'm sure if the burglar hadn't got that one, he'd have got one somewhere else. Look, this is very awkward over the telephone, do you think you could come to the house?'

'When?'

'How about this evening. For dinner?'

'Fine,' said Mitch. 'I'm really glad you can find it in your heart to forgive me.'

'Eight o'clock?'

'Eight it is.'

When he put down the phone, Mitch jumped to his feet, punched the air, shouted, 'Yes!'

•

'Dinner' was catered by a local Italian restaurant, Laura McVie not being, in her own words, 'much of a cook'. Two waiters delivered the food, served it discreetly, and took away the dirty dishes.

Mostly, Mitch and Laura made small talk in the candle-light over the pasta and wine, and it wasn't until the wait-ers had left and they were alone, relaxing on the sofa, each cradling a snifter of Courvoisier XO cognac, with mellow jazz playing in the background, that the conver-sation became more intimate.

Laura was still funereally clad, but tonight her dress, made of semi-transparent layers of black chiffon – more than enough for decency – fell well below knee height. There was still no disguising the curves, and the rustling sounds as she crossed her legs made Mitch more than a little hot under the collar.

Laura puckered her lips to light a cigarette. When she had blown the smoke out, she asked, 'Are you married?'

Mitch shook his head.

'Ever been?'

'Nope.'

'Just didn't meet the right girl, is that it?'

'Something like that.'

'You're not gay are you?'

He laughed. 'What on earth made you think that?'

She rested her free hand on his and smiled. 'Don't worry. Nothing made me think it. Nothing in particular. Just checking, that's all.'

'No,' Mitch said. 'I'm not gay.'

'More cognac?'

'Sure.' Mitch was already feeling a little tipsy, but he didn't want to spoil the mood.

She fetched the bottle and poured them each a generous measure. 'I didn't really *love* Charles, you know,' she said when she had settled down and smoothed her dress again. 'I mean, I respected him, I even liked him, I just didn't love him.'

'Why did you marry him?'

Laura shrugged. 'I don't know really. He asked me. He was rich and seemed to live an exciting life. Travel. Parties. I got to meet all kinds of celebrities. We'd only been married two years, you know. And we'd only known one another a few weeks before we got married. We hadn't even . . . you know. Anyway, I'm sorry he's dead . . . in a way.'

'What do you mean?'

Laura leaned forward and stubbed out her cigarette. Then she brushed back a long blonde tress and took another sip of cognac before answering. 'Well,' she said, 'now that he's dead, it's all mine, isn't it? I'd be a hypocrite and a fool if I said that didn't appeal to me. All this wealth and no strings attached. No responsibilities.'

'What responsibilities were there before?'

The left corner of her lips twitched in a smile. 'Oh, you know. The usual wifely kind. Charles was never, well . . . let's say he wasn't a very passionate lover. He wanted me more as a showpiece than anything else. A trophy. Something to hang on his arm that looked good. Don't get me wrong, I didn't mind. It was a small price to pay. And then we were forever having to entertain the most boring people. Business acquaintances. You know the sort of thing. Well, now that Charles is gone, I won't have to do that any more, will I? I'll be able to do what I want. Exactly what I want.'

Almost without Mitch knowing it, Laura had edged nearer towards him as she was speaking, and now she was so close he could smell the warm, acrid smoke and the cognac on her breath. He found it curiously intoxicating. Soon she was close enough to kiss.

She took hold of his hand and rested it on her breast. 'It's been a week since the funeral,' she said. 'Don't you think it's time I took off my widow's weeds?'

•

When Mitch left Laura McVie's house the following morning, he was beginning to think he might be on to a good thing. Why stop at being estate executor? he asked himself. He already knew that, under the terms of the will, Laura got everything – McVie had no children or other living relatives – and *everything* was somewhere in the region of five million dollars.

Even if he didn't love her – and how could you tell if you loved someone after just one night? – he certainly felt passionately drawn to her. They got on well together, thought alike, and she was a wonderful lover. Mitch was no slouch, either. He could certainly make up for her late husband in that department.

He mustn't rush it, though. Take things easy, see what develops . . . Maybe they could go away together for a while. Somewhere warm. And then . . . well . . . five million dollars.

Such were his thoughts as he turned the corner, just before the heavy hand settled on his shoulder and a deep voice whispered in his ear, 'Detective Greg Hollins, Mr

Mitchell. Homicide. I think it's about time you and I had a long talk.'

•

Relieved to be let off with little more than a warning in exchange for cooperating with the police, Mitch turned up at Laura's the next evening as arranged. This time they skipped the dinner and drinks preliminaries and headed straight for her bedroom.

Afterwards she lay with her head resting on his shoulder, smoking a cigarette.

'My God,' she said. 'I missed this when I was married to Charles.'

'Didn't you have any lovers?' Mitch asked.

'Of course I didn't.'

'Oh, come on. I won't be jealous. I promise. Tell me.'

She jerked away, stubbed out the cigarette on the bedside ashtray, and said, 'You're just like the police. Do you know that? You've got a filthy mind.'

'Hey,' said Mitch. 'It's me. Mitch. OK?'

'Still . . . They think I did it, you know.'

'Did what?'

'Killed Charles.'

'I thought you had an alibi.'

'I do, idiot. They think the burglary was just a cover. They think I hired someone to kill him.'

'Did you?'

'See what I mean? Just like the cops, with your filthy, suspicious mind.'

'What makes you think they suspect you?'

'The way they talked, the way they questioned me. I think they're watching me.'

'You're just being paranoid, Laura. You're upset. They

always suspect someone in the family at first. It's routine. Most killings are family affairs. You'll see, pretty soon they'll drop it.'

'Do you really think so?'

'Sure I do. Just you wait and see.'

And moments later they were making love again.

•

Laura seemed a little distracted when she let him in the next night. At first he thought she had something on the stove, but then he remembered she didn't cook.

She was on the telephone, as it turned out. And she hung up the receiver just as he walked into the living room.

'Who was that?' he asked. 'Not reporters, I hope?'

'No,' she said, arms crossed, facing him, an unreadable expression on her face.

'Who, then?'

Laura just stood there. 'They've found the gun,' she said finally.

'They've what? Where?'

'In your garage, under an old tarpaulin.'

'I don't understand. What are you talking about? When?'

She looked at her watch. 'About now.'

'How?'

Laura shrugged. 'Anonymous tip. You'd better sit down, Mitch.'

Mitch collapsed on the sofa.

'Drink?'

'A large one.'

Laura brought him a large tumbler of Scotch and sat in the armchair opposite him.

'What's all this about?' he asked, after the whisky had warmed his insides. 'I don't understand what you're saying. How could they find the gun in my garage? I told you what happened to it.'

'I know you did,' said Laura. 'And I'm telling you where it ended up. You're really not very bright, are you, Mitch? How do *you* think it got there?'

'Someone must have put it there.'

'Right.'

'One of the muggers? But . . .?'

'What does it matter? What matters is that it will probably have your fingerprints on it. Or the wrapping will. All those greasy smudges. And even if it doesn't, how are you going to explain its presence in your garage?'

'But why would the cops think *I* killed Charles?'

'We had a relationship. We were lovers. Like I told you, I'm certain they've been watching me, and they can't fail to have noticed that you've stayed overnight on more than one occasion.'

'But that's absurd. I hadn't even met you before your husband's death.'

'Hadn't you?' She raised her eyebrows. 'Don't you remember, honey, all those times we met in secret, made love cramped in the back of your car because we didn't even dare be seen signing in under false names in the Have-a-Nap Motel or wherever? We had to keep our relationship very, very secret. Don't you remember?'

'You'd tell them that?'

'The way they'll see it is that the relationship was more important to you than to me. You became obsessed by jealousy because I was married to someone else. You couldn't stand it any more. And you thought by killing my husband you could get both me and my money. After all, you did prepare his will, didn't you? You knew all about his finances.'

Mitch shook his head.

'I *would* like to thank you, though,' Laura went on. 'Without you, we had a good plan – a very good one – but *with* you we've got a perfect one.'

'What do you mean?'

'I mean you were right when you suggested I had a lover. I do. Oh, not you, not the one I'm handing over to the police, the one who became so obsessed with me that it unhinged him and he murdered my husband. No. I've been very careful with Jake. I met him on the Yucatan peninsula when Charles and I were on holiday there six months ago and Charles went down with Montezuma's revenge. I know it sounds like a romantic cliché, but it was love at first sight. We hatched the plan very quickly and we knew we had to keep our relationship a total secret. Nobody must suspect a thing. So we never met after that vacation. There were no letters or postcards. The only contact we had was through public telephones.'

'And what happens now?'

'After a decent interval – after you've been tried and convicted of my husband's murder – Jake and I will meet and eventually get married. We'll sell up here, of course, and live abroad. Live in luxury. Oh, please don't look so crestfallen, Mitch. Believe me, I *am* sorry. I didn't know you were going to walk into my life with that irresistible little confession, now, did I? I figured I'd just ride it out, the cops' suspicions and all. I mean they might suspect me, but they couldn't prove anything. I *was* in Windsor staying with friends. They've checked. And now they've got you into the bargain . . .' She shrugged. 'Why would they bother with little old me? I just couldn't look a gift horse in the mouth. You'll make a wonderful fall guy. But because I like you, Mitch, I'm at least giving you a little advance warning, aren't I? The police will be looking for you, but you've still got time to make a break, leave town.'

'What if I go to them, tell them everything you've told me?'

'They'll think you're crazy. Which you are. Obsession does that to people. Makes them crazy.'

Mitch licked his lips. 'Look, I'd have to leave everything behind. I don't even have any cash on me. Laura, you don't think you could—'

She shook her head. 'Sorry, honey. No can do. Nothing personal.'

Mitch slumped back in the chair. 'At least tell me one more thing. The gun. I still don't understand how it came to be the one that killed your husband.'

She laughed, showing the sharp, white teeth. 'Pure coincidence. It was beautiful. Jake happens to be . . .

•

. . . a burglar by profession, and a very good one. He has worked all over the States and Canada, and he's never been caught. We thought that if I told him about the security system at the house, he could get around it cleverly and . . . Of course, he couldn't bring his own gun here from Mexico, not by air, so he had to get one. He said that's not too difficult when you move in the circles he does. The kind of bars where you can buy guns and other stolen goods are much the same anywhere, in much the same sort of neighbourhoods. And he's done jobs up here before.

'As luck would have it, he bought an old Luger off

two inexperienced muggers. For a hundred bucks. I just couldn't believe it when you came around with your story. There couldn't be two old Lugers kicking around the neighbourhood at the same time, could there? I had to turn away from you and hold my sides, I was laughing so much. It made my eyes water. What unbelievable luck!'

'I'm so glad you think so,' said Mitch.

'Anyway, when I told Jake, he agreed it was too good an opportunity to miss, so he came back up here, dug the gun up from where he had buried it, safe in its wrapping, and planted it in your garage. He hadn't handled it without gloves on, and he thought the two young punks he bought it from had been too scared to touch it, so the odds were, after you told me your story, that your fingerprints would still be on it. As I said, even if they aren't . . . It's still perfect.'

Only tape hiss followed, and Detective Greg Hollins switched off the machine. 'That it?' he asked.

Mitch nodded. 'I left. I thought I'd got enough.'

'You did a good job. Jesus, you got more than enough. I was hoping she'd let something slip, but I didn't expect a full confession and her accomplice's name in the bargain.'

'Thanks. I didn't have a lot of choice, did I?'

The last two times Mitch had been to see Laura, he had been wearing a tiny but powerful voice-activated tape recorder sewn into the lining of his suit jacket. It had lain on the chair beside the bed when they made love, and he had tried to get her to admit she had a boyfriend, as Hollins had suspected. He had also been wearing it the night she told him the police were about to find the Luger in his garage.

The recorder was part of the deal. Why he got off with only a warning for not reporting the theft of an unregistered firearm.

'What'll happen to her now?' he asked Hollins.

'With any luck, both she and her boyfriend will do life,' said Hollins. 'But what do you care? After the way she treated you. She's a user. She chewed you up and spat you out.'

Mitch sighed. 'Yeah, I know . . .' he said. 'But it could have been worse, couldn't it?'

'How?'

'I could've ended up married to her.'

Hollins stared at him for a moment, then he burst out laughing. 'I'm glad you've got a sense of humour, Mitchell. You'll need it, what's coming your way next.'

Mitch shifted uneasily in his chair. 'Hey, just a minute! We made a deal. You assured me there'd be no charges over the gun.'

Hollins nodded. 'That's right. We did make a deal. And I never go back on my word.'

Mitch shook his head. 'Then I don't understand. What are you talking about?'

'Well, there's this lady from the Law Society waiting outside, Mitchell. And she'd *really* like to talk to you.'

THE TWO LADIES OF ROSE COTTAGE

In our village, they were always known as the 'Two Ladies of Rose Cottage': Miss Eunice with the white hair, and Miss Teresa with the grey. Nobody really knew where they came from, or exactly how old they were, but the consensus held that they had met in India, America or South Africa and decided to return to the homeland to live out their days together. And in 1939 they were generally believed to be in or approaching their nineties.

Imagine our surprise, then, one fine day in September, when the police car pulled up outside Rose Cottage, and when, in a matter of hours, rumours began to spread throughout the village: rumours of human bones dug up in a distant garden; rumours of mutilation and dismemberment; rumours of murder.

•

Lyndgarth is the name of our village. It is situated in one of the most remote Yorkshire Dales, about twenty miles from Eastvale, the nearest large town. The village is no more than a group of limestone houses with slate roofs clustered around a bumpy, slanted green that always reminded me of a handkerchief flapping in the breeze. We have the usual amenities – grocer's shop, butcher's, newsagent's, post office, school, a church, a chapel, three public houses – and proximity to some of the most beautiful countryside in the world.

I was fifteen in 1939, and Miss Eunice and Miss Teresa had been living in the village for twenty years, yet still they remained strangers to us. It is often said that you have to 'winter out' at least two years before being accepted into village life, and in the case of a remote place like Lyndgarth, in those days, it was more like ten.

As far as the locals were concerned, then, the two ladies had served their apprenticeship and were more than fit to be accepted as fully paid up members of the community, yet there was about them a certain detached quality that kept them ever at arm's length.

They did all their shopping in the village and were always polite to people they met in the street; they regularly attended church services at St Oswald's and helped with charity events; and they never set foot in any of the public houses. But still there was that sense of distance, of not quite being – or not *wanting* to be – a part of things.

•

The summer of 1939 had been unusually beautiful despite the political tensions. Or am I indulging in nostalgia for childhood? Our dale can be one of the most grim and desolate landscapes on the face of the earth, even in August, but I remember the summers of my youth as days of dazzling sunshine and blue skies. In 1939 every day was a new symphony of colour – golden buttercups, pink clover, mauve cranesbill – ever changing and recombining in fresh palettes. While the tense negotiations went on in Europe, while Ribbentrop and Molotov signed the Nazi-Soviet pact, and while there was talk of conscription and rationing at home, very little changed in Lyndgarth.

Summer in the dale was always a season for odd jobs – peat-cutting, wall-mending, sheep-clipping – and for entertainments, such as the dialect plays, the circus, fairs and brass bands. Even after war was declared on 3 September, we still found ourselves rather guiltily having fun, scratching our heads, shifting from foot to foot, and wondering when something really warlike was going to happen.

Of course, we had our gas masks in their cardboard boxes, which we had to carry everywhere; street lighting was banned, and motor cars were not allowed to use their headlights. This latter rule was the cause of numerous accidents in the dale, usually involving wandering sheep on the unfenced roads.

Some evacuees also arrived from the cities. Uncouth urchins for the most part, often verminous and ill-equipped for country life, they seemed like an alien race to us. Most of them didn't seem to have any warm clothing or Wellington boots, as if they had never seen mud in the city. Looking back, I realize they were far from home, separated from their parents, and they must have been scared to death. I am ashamed to admit, though, that at the time I didn't go out of my way to give them a warm welcome.

This is partly because I was always lost in my own world. I was a bookish child and had recently discovered the stories of Thomas Hardy, who seemed to understand and sympathize with a lonely village lad and his dreams of becoming a writer. I also remember how much he thrilled and scared me with some of the stories. After 'The Withered Arm' I wouldn't let anyone touch me for a week, and I didn't dare go to sleep after 'Barbara of the House of Grebe' for fear that there was a horribly disfigured statue in the wardrobe, that the door would slowly creak open and . . .

I think I was reading *Far from the Madding Crowd* that hot July day, and, as was my wont, I read as I walked across the village green, not looking where I was going. It was Miss Teresa I bumped into, and I remember thinking that she seemed remarkably resilient for such an old lady.

'Do mind where you're going, young man!' she admonished me, though when she heard my effusive apologies, she softened her tone somewhat. She asked me what I was reading, and when I showed her the book, she closed her eyes for a moment and a strange expression crossed her wrinkled features.

'Ah, Mr Hardy,' she said, after a short silence. 'I knew him once, you know, in his youth. I grew up in Dorset.'

I could hardly hold back my enthusiasm. Someone who actually *knew* Hardy! I told her that he was my favourite writer of all time, even better than Shakespeare, and that when I grew up I wanted to be a writer, just like him.

Miss Teresa smiled indulgently. 'Do calm down,' she said, then she paused. 'I suppose,' she continued, with a glance towards Miss Eunice, 'that if you are really interested in Mr Hardy, perhaps you might like to come to tea some day?'

When I assured her I would be delighted, we made an arrangement that I was to call at Rose Cottage the following Tuesday at four o'clock, after securing my mother's permission, of course.

•

That Tuesday visit was the first of many. Inside, Rose Cottage belied its name. It seemed dark and gloomy, unlike ours, which was always full of sunlight and bright flowers. The furnishings were antique, even a little shabby. I recollect no family photographs of the kind that embellished most mantelpieces, but there was a huge gilt-framed painting of a young girl working alone in a field hanging on one wall. If the place sometimes smelled a little musty and neglected, the aroma of Miss Teresa's fresh-baked scones more often than not made up for it.

'Mr Hardy was full of contradictions,' Miss Teresa told me on one occasion. 'He was a dreamer, of course, and never happier than when wandering the countryside alone with his thoughts. But he was also a fine musician. He played the fiddle on many social occasions, such as dances and weddings, and he was often far more gregarious and cheerful than many of his critics would have imagined. He was also a scholar, head forever buried in a book, always studying Latin or Greek. I was no dullard, either, you know, and I like to think I held my own in our conversations, though I had little Latin and less Greek.' She chuckled, then turned serious again. 'Anyway, one never felt one really *knew* him. One was always looking at a mask. Do you understand me, young man?'

I nodded. 'I think so, Miss Teresa.'

'Yes, well,' she said, staring into space as she sometimes did while speaking of Hardy. 'At least that was *my* impression. Though he was a good ten years older than me, I like to believe I got glimpses of the man behind the mask. But because the other villagers thought him a bit odd, and because he was difficult to know, he also attracted a lot of idle gossip. I remember there was talk about him and that Sparks girl from Puddletown. What was her first name, Eunice?'

'Tryphena.'

'That's right.' She curled her lip and seemed to spit out the name. 'Tryphena Sparks. A singularly dull girl, I always thought. We were about the same age, you know, she and I. Anyway, there was talk of a child. Utter rubbish, of course.' She gazed out of the window at the green, where a group of children were playing a makeshift game of cricket. Her eyes seemed to film over. 'Many's the time I used to walk through the wood-land past the house, and I would see him sitting there at his upstairs window seat, writing or gazing out on the garden. Sometimes he would wave and come down to talk.' Suddenly she stopped, then her eyes glittered, and she went on, 'He used to go and watch hangings in Dorchester. Did you know that?'

I had to confess that I didn't, my acquaintance with Hardy being recent and restricted only to his published works of fiction, but it never occurred to me to doubt Miss Teresa's word.

'Of course, executions were public back then.' Again she paused, and I thought I saw, or rather *sensed* a little shiver run through her. Then she said that was enough for today, that it was time for scones and tea.

I think she enjoyed shocking me like that at the end of her little narratives, as if we needed to be brought back to reality with a jolt. I remember on another occasion she looked me in the eye and said, 'Of course, the doctor tossed him aside as dead at birth, you know. If it hadn't been for the nurse he would never have survived. That must do something to a man, don't you think?'

We talked of many other aspects of Hardy and his work, and, for the most part, Miss Eunice remained silent, nodding from time to time. Occasionally, when Miss Teresa's memory seemed to fail her on some point, such as a name or what novel Hardy might have been writing in a certain year, she would supply the information.

I remember one visit particularly vividly. Miss Teresa stood up rather more quickly than I thought her able to, and left the room for a few moments. I sat politely, sipping my tea, aware of Miss Eunice's silence and the ticking of the grandfather clock out in the hall. When Miss Teresa returned, she was carrying an old book, or rather two books, which she handed to me.

It was a two-volume edition of *Far from the Madding Crowd*, and, though I didn't know it at the time, it was the first edition, from 1874, and was probably worth a small fortune. But what fascinated me even more than Helen Paterson's illustrations was the brief inscription on the flyleaf: *To Tess, With Affection, Tom.*

I knew that Tess was the diminutive of Teresa because I had an Aunt Teresa in Harrogate, and it never occurred to me to question that the 'Tess' in the inscription was the person sitting opposite me, or that the 'Tom' was none other than Thomas Hardy himself.

'He called you Tess,' I remember saying. 'Perhaps he had you in mind when he wrote *Tess of the d'Urbervilles*?'

Miss Teresa's face drained of colour so quickly I feared for her life, and it seemed that a palpable chill entered the room. 'Don't be absurd, boy,' she whispered. 'Tess Durbeyfield was hanged for murder.'

•

We had been officially at war for about a week, I think, when the police called. There were three men, one in uniform and two in plain clothes. They spent almost two hours in Rose Cottage, then came out alone, got in their car and drove away. We never saw them again.

The day after the visit, though, I happened to overhear our local constable talking with the vicar in St Oswald's churchyard. By a great stroke of fortune, several yews stood between us and I was able to remain unseen while I took in every word.

'Murdered, that's what they say,' said PC Walker. 'Bashed his 'ead in with a poker, then chopped 'im up in little pieces and buried 'em in t'garden. Near Dorchester, it were. Village called 'igher Bockhampton. People who lived there were digging an air-raid shelter when they found t'bones. 'Eck of a shock for t'bairns.'

Could they possibly mean Miss Teresa? That sweet old lady who made such delightful scones and had known the young Thomas Hardy? Could she really have bashed someone on the head, chopped him up into little pieces and buried them in the garden? I shivered at the thought, despite the heat.

But nothing more was heard of the murder charge. The police never returned, people found new things to talk about, and after a couple of weeks Miss Eunice and Miss Teresa reappeared in village life much as they had been before. The only difference was that my mother would no longer allow me to visit Rose Cottage. I put up token resistance, but by then my mind was full of Spitfires, secret codes and aircraft carriers anyway.

Events seemed to move quickly in the days after the police visit, though I cannot be certain of the actual time period involved. Four things, however, conspired to put the murder out of my mind for some time: Miss Teresa died, I think in the November of that same year; Miss

Eunice retreated into an even deeper silence than before; the war escalated; and I was called up to military service.

•

The next time I gave any thought to the two ladies of Rose Cottage was in Egypt, of all places, in September 1942. I was on night watch with the Eighth Army, not far from Alamein. Desert nights have an eerie beauty I have never found anywhere else since. After the heat of the day, the cold surprises one, for a start, as does the sense of endless space, but even more surprising is the desertscape of wrecked tanks, jeeps and lorries in the cold moonlight, metal wrenched and twisted into impossible patterns like some petrified forest or exposed coral reef.

To spoil our sleep and shatter our nerves, Rommel's Afrika Korps had got into the routine of setting up huge amplified speakers and blaring out 'Lili Marlene' over and over all night long. It was on a night such as this, while I was trying to stay warm and awake and trying to shut my ears to the music, that I struck up a conversation with a soldier called Sidney Ferris from one of the Dorset regiments.

When Sid told me he had grown up in Piddlehinton, I suddenly thought of the two ladies of Rose Cottage.

'Did you ever hear any stories of a murder around there?' I asked, offering Sid a cigarette. 'A place called Higher Bockhampton?'

'Lots of murder stories going around when I was a lad,' he said, lighting up, careful to hide the flame with his cupped hand. 'Better than the wireless.'

'This would be a wife murdering her husband.'

He nodded. 'Plenty of that and all. And husbands murdering their wives. Makes you wonder whether it's worth getting married, doesn't it? Higher Bockhampton, you say?'

'Yes. Teresa Morgan, I believe the woman's name was.'

He frowned. 'Name don't ring no bell,' he said, 'but I do recall a tale about some woman who was supposed to have killed her husband, cut him up in pieces and buried them in the garden. A couple of young lads found some bones when they was digging an air-raid shelter a few years back. Animal bones, if you ask me.'

'But did the villagers believe the tale?'

He shrugged. 'Don't know about anyone else, but I can't say as I did. So many stories like that going around, they can't all be true, or damn near all of us would be murderers or corpses. Stands to reason, doesn't it?' And he took a long drag on his cigarette, holding it in his cupped hand, like most soldiers, so the enemy wouldn't see the pinpoint of light.

'Did anyone say what became of the woman?' I asked.

'She went away some years later. There was talk of someone else seen running away from the farmhouse, too, the night they said the murder must have taken place.'

'Could it have been him? The husband?'

Sid shook his head. 'Too slight a figure. Her husband was a big man, apparently. Anyway, that led to more talk of an illicit lover. There's always a lover, isn't there? Have you noticed? You know what kind of minds these country gossips have.'

'Did anyone say who the other person might have been?'

'Nobody knew. Just rumours of a vague shape seen running away. These are old wives' tales we're talking about.'

'But perhaps there's some tru—'

But at that point I was relieved of my watch, and the next weeks turned out to be so chaotic that I never even saw Sid again. I heard later that he was killed at the Battle of Alamein just over a month after our conversation.

•

I didn't come across the mystery of Rose Cottage again until the early 1950s. At that time I was living in Eastvale, in a small flat overlooking the cobbled market square. The town was much smaller and quieter than it is today, though little about the square has changed, from the ancient market cross, the Queen's Arms on the corner, the Norman church and the Tudor-fronted police station.

I had recently published my first novel and was still basking in that exquisite sensation that comes only once in a writer's career: the day he holds the first printed and bound copy of his very first work. Of course, there was no money in writing, so I worked part-time in a bookshop on North Market Street, and on one of my mornings off, a market day as I remember, I was absorbed in polishing the third chapter of what was to be my second novel when I heard a faint tap at my door. This was enough to startle me, as I rarely had any visitors.

Puzzled and curious, I left my typewriter and went to open the door. There stood a wizened old lady, hunch-shouldered, white-haired, carrying a stick with a brass lion's head handle and a small package wrapped in brown paper, tied with string.

She must have noticed my confused expression because, with a faint smile, she said, 'Don't you recognize me, Mr Riley? Dear, dear, have I aged that much?'

Then I knew her, knew the voice.

'Miss Eunice!' I cried, throwing my door open. 'Please forgive me. I was lost in my own world. Do come in. And you must call me Christopher.'

Once we were settled, with a pot of tea mashing beside us – though, alas, none of Miss Teresa's scones – I noticed the dark circles under Miss Eunice's eyes, the yellow around the pupils, the parchment-like quality of her skin, and I knew she was seriously ill.

'How did you find me?' I asked.

'It didn't take a Sherlock Holmes. Everyone knows where the famous writer lives in a small town like East-vale.'

'Hardly famous,' I demurred. 'But thank you anyway. I never knew you took the trouble to follow my fortunes.'

'Teresa would have wished it. She was very fond of you, you know. Apart from ourselves and the police, you were the only person in Lyndgarth who ever entered Rose Cottage. Did you know that? You might remember that we kept ourselves very much to ourselves.'

'Yes, I remember that,' I told her.

'I came to give you this.'

She handed me the package and I untied it carefully. Inside was the Smith, Elder & Co. first edition of *Far from the Madding Crowd*, complete with Hardy's inscription to 'Tess'.

'But you shouldn't,' I said. 'This must be very valuable. It's a fir—'

She waved aside my objections. 'Please take it. It is what Teresa would have wished. And I wish it, too. Now listen,' she went on. 'That isn't the only reason I came. I have something very important to tell you, to do with why the police came to visit all those years ago. The thought of going to my grave without telling someone troubles me deeply.'

'But why me? And why now?'

'I told you. Teresa was especially fond of you. And you're a writer,' she added mysteriously. 'You'll understand. Should you wish to make use of the story, please do so. Neither Teresa nor I have any living relatives to offend. All I ask is that you wait a suitable number of years after my death before publishing any account. And that death is expected to occur at some point over the next few months. Does that answer your second question?'

I nodded. 'Yes. I'm sorry.'

'You needn't be. As you may well be aware, I have long since exceeded my three score and ten, though I can hardly say the extra years have been a blessing. But that is God's will. Do you agree to my terms?'

'Of course. I take it this is about the alleged murder?'

Miss Eunice raised her eyebrows. 'So you've heard the rumours?' she said. 'Well, there was a murder all right. Teresa Morgan murdered her husband, Jacob, and buried his body in the garden.' She held out her teacup and I poured. I noticed her hand was shaking slightly. Mine was, too. The shouts of the market vendors came in through my open windows.

'When did she do this?' was all I could manage.

Miss Eunice closed her eyes and pursed her cracked lips. 'I don't remember the exact year,' she said. 'But it really doesn't matter. You could look it up, if you wanted. It was the year the Queen was proclaimed Empress of India.'

I happened to know that was in 1877. I have always had a good memory for historical dates. If my calculations were correct, Miss Teresa would have been about twenty-seven at the time. 'Will you tell me what happened?' I asked.

'That's why I'm here,' Miss Eunice said rather sharply. 'Teresa's husband was a brute, a bully and a drunkard. She wouldn't have married him, had *she* had any choice in the matter. But her parents approved the match. He had his own small farm, you see, and they were only tenants. Teresa was a very intelligent girl, but that counted for nothing in those days. In fact, it was a positive disadvantage. As was her wilfulness. Anyway, he used to beat her to within an inch of her life – where the bruises wouldn't show, of course. One day she'd had enough of it, so she killed him.'

'What did she do?'

'She hit him with the poker from the fireplace and, after darkness had fallen, she buried him deep in the garden. She was afraid that if the matter went to court the authorities wouldn't believe her and she would be hanged. She had no evidence, you see. And Jacob was a popular man among the other fellows of the village, as is so often the case with drunken brutes. And Teresa was terrified of being publicly hanged.'

'But did no one suspect her?'

Miss Eunice shook her head. 'Jacob was constantly talking about leaving his wife and heading for the New World. He used to berate her for not bearing him any children – specifically sons – and threatened that one day she would wake up and he would be gone. Gone to another country to find a woman who could give him the children he wanted. He repeated these threats in the ale house so often that no one in the entire county of Dorset could fail to know about them.'

'So when he disappeared, everyone assumed he had followed through on his threats to leave her?'

'Exactly. Oh, there were rumours that his wife had murdered him, of course. There always are when such mysteries occur.'

Yes, I thought, remembering my conversation with Sid Ferris one cold desert night ten years ago: rumours and fancies, the stuff of fiction. And something about a third person seen fleeing from the scene. Well, that could wait.

'Teresa stayed on at the farm for another ten years,' Miss Eunice went on. 'Then she sold up and went to America. It was a brave move, but Teresa no more lacked for courage than she did for beauty. She was in her late thirties then, and even after a hard life, she could still turn heads. In New York, she landed on her feet and eventually married a financier. Sam Cotter. A good man. She also took a companion.'

'You?' I asked.

Miss Eunice nodded. 'Yes. Some years later Sam died of a stroke. We stayed on in New York for a while, but we grew increasingly homesick. We came back finally in 1919, just after the Great War. For obvious reasons, Teresa didn't want to live anywhere near Dorset, so we settled in Yorkshire.'

'A remarkable tale,' I said.

'But that's not all,' Miss Eunice went on, pausing only to sip some tea. 'There was a child.'

'I thought you said—'

She took one hand off her stick and held it up, palm out. 'Christopher, please let me tell the story in my own way. Then it will be yours to do with as you wish. You have no idea how difficult this is for me.' She paused and stared down at the brass lion's head for so long I feared she had fallen asleep, or died. Outside in the market square a butcher was loudly trying to sell a leg of mutton. Just as I was about to go over to Miss Eunice, she stirred. 'There was a child,' she repeated. 'When Teresa was fifteen, she gave birth to a child. It was a difficult birth. She was never able to bear any other children.'

'What happened to this child?'

'Teresa had a sister called Alice, living in Dorchester. Alice was five years older and already married with two children. Just before the pregnancy started to show, both Teresa and Alice went to stay with relatives in Cornwall for a few months, after it had been falsely announced that Alice was with child again. You would be surprised how often such things happened. When they came back, Alice had a fine baby girl.'

'Who was the father?'

'Teresa would never say. The one thing she did make clear was that no one had forced unwanted attentions on her, that the child was the result of a love match, an infatuation. It certainly wasn't Jacob Morgan.'

'Did she ever see the child again?'

'Oh, certainly. What could be more natural than visiting one's sister and seeing one's niece grow up? When the girl was a little older, she began to pay visits to the farm, too.' Miss Eunice stopped here and frowned so hard I thought her brow would crack like dry paper. 'That was when the problems began,' she said quietly.

'What problems?'

Miss Eunice put her stick aside and held out her teacup. I refilled it. Her hands steady now, she held the cup against her scrawny chest as if its heat were the only thing keeping her alive. 'This is the most difficult part,' she said in a faint voice. 'The part I didn't know whether I could ever tell anyone.'

'If you don't wish—'

She waved my objection aside. 'It's all right, Christopher, I didn't know how much I could tell you before I came here, but I know now. I've come this far. I can't go back now. Just give me a few moments to collect myself.'

Outside, the market was in full swing and during the ensuing silence I could hear the clamour of voices selling and buying, arguing over prices.

'Did I ever tell you that Teresa was an extremely beautiful young girl?' Miss Eunice asked after a while.

'I believe you mentioned it, yes.'

She nodded. 'Well, she was. And so was her daughter. When she began coming by herself to the house, she was about twelve or thirteen years of age. Jacob didn't fail to notice her, how well she was "filling out" as he used to say. One day Teresa had gone into the village for firewood and the child arrived in her absence. Jacob, just home from the ale house, was there alone to greet her. Need I say more, Mr Riley?'

I shook my head. 'I don't mean to excuse him in any way, but I'm assuming he didn't know the girl was his stepdaughter?'

'That is correct. He never knew. Nor did *she* know Teresa was her mother. Not until much later.'

'What happened next?'

'Teresa came in before her husband could have his way with the struggling, half-naked child. Everything else was as I said. She picked up the poker and hit him on the head. Not once, but six times. Then they cleaned up and waited until after dark and buried him deep in the garden. She sent her daughter back to her sister's and carried on as if her husband had simply left her, just as he had threatened to do.'

So the daughter was the mysterious third person seen leaving the farm in Sid Ferris's account. 'What became of the poor child?' I asked.

Miss Eunice paused again and seemed to struggle for breath. She turned terribly pale. I got up and moved towards her, but she stretched out her hand. 'No, no. I'm all right, Christopher. Please sit.'

A motor car honked outside and one of the street vendors yelled a curse. Miss Eunice patted her chest. 'That's better. I'm fine now, really I am. Just a minor spasm. But I do feel ashamed. I'm afraid I haven't been entirely truthful with you. It's so difficult. You see, I was, I *am*, that child.'

For a moment my mouth just seemed to flap open and shut and I couldn't speak. Finally, I managed to stammer, 'You? *You* are Miss Teresa's daughter? But you can't be. That's not possible.'

'I didn't mean to shock you,' she went on softly, 'but, really, you only have yourself to blame. When people see two old ladies together, all they see is two old ladies. When you first began calling on us at Rose Cottage fifteen years ago, Teresa was ninety and I was seventy-six. I doubt a fifteen-year-old boy could tell the difference. Nor could most people. And Teresa was always remarkably robust and well preserved.'

When I had regained my composure, I asked her to continue.

'There is very little left to say. I helped my mother kill Jacob Morgan and bury him. And we didn't cut him up into little pieces. That part is pure fiction invented by scurrilous gossipmongers. My foster parents died within a short time of one another, around the turn of the century, and Teresa wired me the money to come and live with her in New York. I had never married, so I had no ties to break. I think that experience with Jacob Morgan, brief and inconclusive as it was, must have given me a lifelong aversion to marital relations. Anyway, it was in New York that Teresa told me she was really my mother. She couldn't tell Sam, of course, so I remained there as her companion, and we always lived more as friends than as mother and daughter.' She smiled. 'When we came back to England, we chose to live as two spinsters, the kind of relationship nobody really questions in a village because it would be in bad taste to do so.'

'How did the police find you after so long?'

'We never hid our identities. Nor did we hide our whereabouts. We bought Rose Cottage through a local solicitor before we returned from America, so it was listed as our address on the all the official papers we filled in.' She shrugged. 'The police soon recognized that Teresa was far too frail to question, let alone put on trial, so they let the matter drop. And to be quite honest, they didn't really have enough evidence, you know. You didn't know it – and Teresa would never have told you – but she already knew she was dying before the police came. Just as I know I am dying now.'

'And did she really die without telling you who your father was?'

Miss Eunice nodded. 'I wasn't lying about that. But I always had my suspicions.' Her eyes sparkled for a moment, the way a fizzy drink does when you pour it. 'You know, Teresa was always unreasonably jealous of that Tryphena Sparks, and Mr Hardy did have an eye for the young girls.'

•

Forty years have passed since Miss Eunice's death, and I have lived in many towns and villages in many countries of the world. Though I have often thought of the tale she told me, I have never been moved to commit it to paper until today.

Two weeks ago, I moved back to Lyndgarth, and as I was unpacking I came across that first edition of *Far from the Madding Crowd*. 1874: the year Hardy married Emma Gifford. As I puzzled again over the inscription, words suddenly began to form themselves effortlessly in front of my eyes, and all I had to do was copy them down.

Now that I have finished, I suddenly feel very tired. It is a hot day, and the heat haze has muted the greens, greys and browns of the steep hillsides. Looking out of my window, I can see the tourists lounging on the village green. The young men are stripped to the waist, some bearing tattoos of butterflies and angels across their shoulder blades; the girls sit with them in shorts and T-shirts, laughing, eating sandwiches, drinking from pop or beer bottles.

One young girl notices me watching and waves cheekily, probably thinking I'm an old pervert, and as I wave back I think of another writer – a far, far greater writer than I could ever be – sitting at his window seat writing. He looks out of the window and sees the beautiful young girl passing through the woods at the bottom of the garden. He waves. She waves back. And she lingers, picking wild flowers, as he puts aside his novel and walks out into the warm summer air to meet her.

LAWN SALE

When Frank walked through to the kitchen, glass crunched under his feet, and he sent knives, forks and spoons skittering across the linoleum. He turned on the light. Someone had broken in while he had been at the Legion. They had cut the wire screen and smashed the glass in the kitchen door. They must have emptied the drawers looking for silverware because the cutlery was all over the place.

Someone had also been in the front room. Whoever it was had knocked or pushed over the tailor's dummy and the little table beside his armchair where he kept his reading glasses, book and coffee mug.

Suddenly afraid in case they were still in the house, Frank climbed on a stool to reach the high cupboard above the sink. There, at the back, where nobody would look beyond Joan's unused baking dishes, cake tins and cookie cutters shaped like hearts and lions, lay his old service revolver wrapped in an oily cloth. He had smuggled it back from the war and kept it all these years. Kept it loaded, too.

With the gun in his hand, he felt safer as he checked the rest of the house. Slowly, with all the lights on, he climbed the stairs. They had broken the padlock on Joan's room. Heart thumping, he turned on the light. When he saw the mess, he slumped against the wall.

They had emptied out all her dresser drawers, scatter-

ing underwear and trinkets all over the shiny pink cover-
let on the bed. And it looked as if someone had swept off
the lotions and perfumes from the dressing table right
onto the floor. One of the caps must have come loose
because he could smell Joan's sharp, musky perfume.

The lacquered jewellery case, the one he had bought
her in New York with the ballet dancer that spun to the
'Dance of the Sugar-Plum Fairy' when you opened it, lay
silent and empty on the bed. Frank sat down, gun hanging between his legs. They'd taken all Joan's jewellery.
Why? The stuff obviously wasn't valuable. Just trinkets,
really. None of it could possibly be worth anything
to them. They had even taken her wedding ring.

Frank remembered the day he bought it all those years
ago: the fairground across the street from the small jew-
eller's; the air filled with the smells of candyfloss and
fried onions and the sounds of children laughing and
squealing with delight. A little girl in a white frock with
pink smocking had smiled at him as she passed by, one
arm hugging a huge teddy bear and the other hand holding her mother's. How light his heart had been. Inside,
the ring was inscribed, 'FRANK AND JOAN. 21 JULY
1946. NO GREATER LOVE.' The bastards. It could mean
nothing to them.

Listlessly, he checked his own room. Drawers pulled
out, socks and underwear scattered on the bedclothes.
Nothing worth stealing except the spare change he kept
on his bedside table. Sure enough, it was gone, the $3.37
he had piled neatly into columns of quarters, dimes, nick-
els and pennies last night.

They didn't seem to have got far in the spare room,
where he kept his war mementos. Maybe they got disturbed, scared by a sound, before they could open the

lock on the cabinet. Anyway, everything was intact: his medals; the antique silver cigarette lighter that had never let him down; the bayonet; the Nazi armband; the tattered edition of *Mein Kampf*; the German dagger with the mother-of-pearl swastika inlaid in its handle.

Frank went downstairs and considered what to do. He knew he should put the gun back in its hiding place and call the police. But that would mean intrusion, questions. He valued his privacy and he knew that the neighbours thought he was a bit of an oddball. What would the police think of him, a man who kept the torso of a tailor's dummy in his living-room, along with yards of moth-eaten material and tissue-paper patterns? What if they found his gun?

No, he couldn't call the police; he couldn't have them trampling all over his house. They never caught burglars, anyway; everyone knew that. Weary, and still a little frightened, Frank nailed a piece of plywood over the broken glass, then carried his gun upstairs with him to bed.

•

The following morning was one of those light, airy days of early June, the kind that brings the whole city to the Beaches. The sky was robin's-egg blue, the sun shone like a pale yolk, and a light breeze blew off the lake to keep the temperature comfortable. In the gardens, apple and cherry blossom clung to the trees and the tulips were still in full bloom. It was a day for sprinklers, swimsuits, bar-becues, bicycle rides, volleyball and lawn sales.

Normally, Frank would have gone down to the board-walk, about the only exercise he got these days. Today, however, a change had come over him; a shadow had crept into his life and chilled him to the bone, despite the fine weather. He felt a deep lassitude and malaise. So much so that he delayed getting out of bed.

Maybe it was the dream made him feel that way. Though perhaps it wasn't right to call it a dream when it was so close to something that had really happened. It recurred every few months, and he had come to accept it now, much as one accepts the chronic pain of an old wound, as a kind of cross to bear.

Separated from his unit once in rural France during the Second World War, he had dragged himself out of a muddy stream, cigarettes tied up safely in army-issue condoms to keep them dry, and entered a forest. A few yards in, he had come face to face with a young German soldier, who looked as if he had also probably lost his comrades. They stared open-mouthed at each other for the split second before Frank, operating purely on survival instinct, aimed his revolver first and fired. The boy simply looked surprised and disappointed at the red patch that spread over his chest, then his face emptied of all expression for ever. Light-headed and numb, Frank moved on, looking for his unit.

It wasn't the first German he had killed, but it was the first he had looked in the eye. The incident haunted him all the way back to his unit, but a few hours later he had convinced himself that he had done the right thing and put it behind him.

After the war the memory surfaced from time to time in dreams. Details changed, of course. Each time the soldier had a different face, for example. Once, Frank even reached forward and put his finger into the bullet hole. The soft, warm flesh felt like half-set jelly. He was sure he had never touched it in real life.

Another time, the boy spoke to him. He spoke in

English and Frank couldn't remember what he said, though he was sure it was a poem, and the words 'I knew you in this dark' stuck in his mind. But Frank knew nothing of poetry.

This time the bullet had gone straight through, leaving a clean circle the size of a ring, and Frank had seen a winter landscape, all flat white and grey, through the hole.

He still had the gun he had used that day. It was the same one he had got down from the high cupboard last night when he thought the burglars might still be in the house. It was the one he felt for now under the pillow beside him.

•

Had he got up that day? He couldn't remember. He sat propped against pillows on his bed that night watching television as usual. He felt agitated, and whatever the figures on the screen were doing or saying didn't register. For some reason, he couldn't get the wedding ring out of his mind, the senselessness of its theft and the unimaginable value it had for him. He hadn't realized it fully until the ring was gone.

Then he thought he heard some noise outside. He turned the sound off with the remote and listened. Sure enough, he could hear voices. Beyond his back garden was a narrow alleyway, then came the backs of the stores and low-rise apartment buildings on Queen Street. Sometimes in this warm weather, when everyone had their windows open, you could hear arguments, television programmes and loud music. These were real voices, Frank could tell. Television voices sounded different. There were two of them, a woman's and a man's, hers getting louder.

'No, Daryl, it won't do!' he heard the woman shout. 'Haven't I told you before it's wrong to steal? Haven't I brought you up to respect other people's property? Haven't I?'

Frank couldn't hear the muffled answer, no matter how much he strained. He dragged himself up from the bed and went to the window.

'So if Marvin Johnson stuck his finger in a fire, you'd do that as well, would you? Christ, give me a break. How stupid can you get?'

Another inaudible reply.

'Right. So how do you think *they* feel, eh? The people whose house you broke into. Come on. What did you do with it?'

Frank couldn't hear the reply, though he held his breath.

'Don't lie to me. What do you think this is? It's a gold chain, isn't it? And what about these? Don't tell me you've suddenly started wearing earrings. I found these hidden in your room. You stole them, didn't you?'

Frank's heart knocked against his ribs. Joan had a gold chain and earrings, and they were among the items that had been stolen. But what about the ring? The ring?

'Shut up!' the woman yelled. 'I don't want to hear it. I want you to put together everything you stole and take it back, or so help me I'll call the police. I don't care if you are my son. Do you understand me?'

There came another inaudible reply followed by a sharp smack, then the sound of a door slamming. After that Frank heard a sound he didn't recognize at first. A cat in the garden, maybe? Then he realized it was the woman crying.

About five of the apartments in the building had lights

on at the back, and Frank hadn't been able to tell from which one the argument came. Now, though, he could see the silhouette of the woman with her head bowed and her hands held to her face. He thought he knew who she was. He had seen both her and her son on the street.

•

Frank sat in the coffee shop across from the apartment building early the next morning and watched people come and go. The building was one of those old places with a heavy wood and glass door, so warped by heat and time that it wouldn't shut properly. He knew who he was looking for, all right. It was that peroxide blonde, the one who looked like a hooker.

At about eight-thirty, her son, the thief, came out. He had a spotty face, especially around the nose and mouth, and he obviously had a skinhead haircut, or a completely shaved head, under the baseball hat he wore the wrong way around. He also wore a shiny silver jacket with a stylized black eagle on the back under some red writing. Below his baggy trousers, crotch right down to the knees, the laces of his sneakers trailed loose. At the corner, he hooked up with a couple of similarly dressed kids and they shuffled off, shoving each other, spitting and generally glaring down at the sidewalk as they went.

At about ten o'clock Frank had to move to the next coffee shop, a bit more up market, as he kept getting nasty looks from the owner. He ordered a cappuccino and a doughnut and sat by the window, watching.

At about a quarter to eleven, *she* came out, the boy's mother. She struggled with a shop cart of laundry through the front door and set off down the street.

Old though he was, Frank could still appreciate a

good figure when he saw one. She wore a white tube-top, tight over her heavy breasts, revealing a flat tummy, and even tighter white shorts cut sharp and high over long, tanned thighs. But she wore too much make-up and he could see the dark roots in her hair. Common as muck, Joan would have said, in the Lancashire accent that had never left her, no matter how long she'd been here. A real tart, a piece of white trash. No wonder her kid was a burglar, a ring thief, a robber of memories, defiler of all things decent and wholesome.

Frank watched her totter down the street on her ridiculous high heels and go into the laundromat. It took about half an hour for the wash cycle and about as long again to get things dry. That gave Frank an hour. He paid his bill, crossed the street and entered the apartment building.

•

He hadn't really formed a plan, even during the hours he had spent watching the building that morning. He knew from last night that the apartment was on the third floor at the back, right in the centre, which made it easy to find. The corridor smelled of soiled diapers and Pine-Sol. When he stood outside the door, he listened for a while. All he could hear was a baby crying on the next floor up and the bass boom of a stereo deep in the basement.

Frank had never broken the law in his life, and he was intelligent enough to recognize the irony of what he was about to do. But he was going to do it anyway because the absence of the ring was beginning to make his life hell. Nothing else really mattered.

For three days he had waited for the boy to return Joan's jewellery, as his mother had told him to do. Three days of nail-biting memories: dreaming about the German soldier he had killed again; reliving Joan's long illness and death; watching again, as if it were yesterday, the woman he had loved and lived with for nearly fifty years waste away in agony in front of his eyes. So thin did she become that one day the ring simply slipped off her finger onto the shiny pink quilt.

And now that he was on the brink of remembering the final horror, her death, the ring had assumed the potency of a talisman. He must have it back to keep his sanity, to keep the last memories at bay.

He had watched people on television open doors with credit cards, so he took out his seniors' discount card and tried to push it between the door and the lock. It wouldn't fit. He could get it part of the way in, then something blocked it; he waggled it back and forth, but still nothing happened. He cursed. This didn't happen on television. What was he going to do now? It looked as if he was destined to fail. He rested his head against the wood and tried to think.

'What the hell do you think you're doing?'

His heart jumped and he turned as quickly as he could.

'I said what do you think you're doing?'

It was her, the slut, standing there with her hands on her hips. It was disgusting, that bare midriff. He could see her belly button. He looked away.

'No, please.' He found his voice. 'Don't. I won't harm you.'

She laughed. 'You harm me!' she said. 'That's a laugh. Now go on, get out of here before I really *do* call the police. *Old* man.'

Frank had to admit she certainly didn't look scared.

'No, you don't understand,' he said. There was nothing for it now but to trust her. 'The robbery. I overheard. You see, it was *my* house your son broke into.'

She stared at him for a moment, her expression slowly softening, turning sad. She was quite pretty, really, he thought. She had a nice mouth, though her eyes looked a bit hard.

'You'd better come in, hadn't you?' she said, pushing past him and opening the door. 'I came back for more quarters. Just as well I did, isn't it, or who knows what might have happened?' She had a husky voice, probably from smoking too much.

The room was sparsely furnished, mostly from the Salvation Army or Goodwill, by the looks of it, but it was clean and the only unpleasant smell Frank noticed was stale tobacco. The woman pulled a packet of Rothmans from her bag, sat down on the wing of an armchair and lit up. She blew out a plume of smoke, crossed her legs and looked at Frank. 'Sit down, it'll hold your weight,' she said, nodding towards the threadbare armchair opposite her. He sat. 'Now what do you want? Is it money?'

'I just want what's mine,' Frank said. 'Your son stole my wife's jewellery. It's very important to me, especially the wedding ring. I'd like it back.'

She frowned. 'Wedding ring? There wasn't no wedding ring.'

'What?'

'I told you. There wasn't no wedding ring.' Sighing, she got up and went into another room. She came back with a handful of jewellery. 'That's all I found.'

Frank looked through it. The only pieces he recognized were the gold chain and the pair of cheap earrings. The rest, he supposed, must have been stolen from another house. 'I don't understand,' he said. 'What happened to the ring?'

'How should I know?' She stubbed her half-smoked cigarette out viciously. 'Maybe he sold it already, or threw it away. Look, I gotta go before someone steals the laundry. That's *all* I need.'

He grabbed her arm. 'No, wait. Can I talk to him? Maybe he'll tell me. I have to find that ring. I'm sorry . . . I . . .' He let her go, and before he knew it, he was crying.

She rubbed her arm. 'Oh, come on,' she said. 'There's no need for that. Shit. Listen, Daryl's a bit non-communicative these days. It's his age, just a phase he's going through. You know what teenagers are like. Basically, he's a good kid, it's just . . . well, with his father gone . . . Look, I'll talk to him again, OK? I promise. But I don't want you coming round here bothering us no more, you understand? I know he's done wrong, and he'll pay for it. Just leave it to me, huh? Take the chain and the earrings for now. For Christ's sake, take it all.'

'I only want the ring,' Frank said. 'He can keep the rest.'

'I told you, I'll talk to him. I'll ask him about it. OK? Here.'

Frank looked up to see her thrusting a handful of tissues towards him at arm's length. Her eyes had softened a little but still remained wary. He took the tissues and rubbed his face. 'I'm sorry,' he said. 'It's been such an ordeal. My wife died three years ago. Cancer. I keep a few of her things, for memories, you understand, and the ring's very important. I know it's sentimental of me, but we were happy all those years. I don't know how I've survived without her.'

'Yeah, tell me about it,' she said. 'Ain't life a bitch.

Look, I'm sorry, mister, really I am. But please, don't go to the police, OK? That's trouble I could do without right now. I promise I'll do what I can. All right? Give me your number. I'll call you.'

Frank watched the broken cigarette still smouldering in the ashtray. He couldn't think of anything else to say. He nodded, gave the woman his telephone number and shuffled out of the apartment. Only when he found himself holding the revolver in his hand at home in the early evening did he realize he didn't even know the woman's name.

•

A day passed. Nothing. Another day. Nothing. Long gaps between the memories, when nothing seemed to be happening at all. Most of the time Frank sat at his bedroom window, lights out, watching the apartment. He cleaned his gun. There were no more rows. Mostly the place was dark and empty at night.

At first, he thought they'd moved, but on the second night he saw the light come on at about midnight and glimpsed the boy cross by the window. Then it went dark again until about two, when he saw the woman. She must work in a bar or something, he thought. It figured. The next thing he knew it was morning and he couldn't remember why he had been sitting by the window all night. The sun was up, the birds were singing, and his joints were so stiff he could hardly stand up.

Still he heard nothing from the mother. He had been a fool to trust her.

After three days he decided to confront her again. Rather, he found himself walking into her building, for that was the way things seemed to be happening more

325

and more these days. He could never remember the point at which he decided to do something; he just found himself doing it.

Halfway up the stairs to her apartment, he suddenly had no idea where he was or why he was there. He stopped, heart heavy and chest tight with panic. Then the memory flooded back in the image of the ring, burnished gold, bright as fire in his mind's eye, slightly tilted so he could read the inscription clearly: 'NO GREATER LOVE.' He walked on.

He hammered on the door so hard that people came out of other apartments to see what was going on, but nobody answered.

'My ring!' he shouted at the door. 'I want my ring.'

'Get out before I call the police,' one of the neighbours said. Frank turned and glared. The frightened woman backed into her apartment and slammed the door. He felt the sweat bead on his wrinkled forehead and ran his hand over his sparse grey hair. Slowly, he walked away.

•

Finally his telephone rang. He snatched up the receiver. 'Yes? Hello,' he said.

'It's me.' It was the woman's voice, husky and low. He heard her blow out smoke before she went on. 'I heard you come over here again. You shouldn't of done that. Look, I've talked to Daryl and I'm sorry. He said he threw the ring away because it had writing on it and he didn't think he'd be able to sell it. I know how important it was to you, but—'

'Where did he throw it?'

'He says he doesn't remember. Look, mister, give us a break here, please. Things are tough enough as it is. He's

not a real criminal, otherwise he'd of known he could sell
it to someone who'd melt it down, wouldn't he? He won't
do anything like that again, honest.'

'That won't bring my ring back, will it?'

'I'm sorry. If I could bring it back, I would. What can
I do? I'll save up. I'll give you some money.' He heard her
inhale the smoke again and blow it out, then he thought
he heard her sniffle. 'Look, maybe we can even come to
some . . . arrangement . . . if you know what I mean. You
must be lonely, aren't you? I saw the way you were looking at me when I found you outside my door. Just give
Daryl a chance. Don't go to the police. Please, I'm beg—'

Frank slammed the phone down. If only he could think
clearly. Things had gone too far. This whore and her evil
offspring had conspired to ruin what little peace he had
left in his life: his memories of Joan. What did they know
about his marriage, about the happy years, the shock of
Joan's illness and the agony of her death, the agony he
suffered with her? How could a woman like that know
how much the ring meant to him? She probably hadn't
even *tried* to find it.

The next thing he knew, he was walking along the
boardwalk. When he took stock of his surroundings and
saw the ruffled blue of the lake and the tilted white sails
of boats, heard the seagulls screech and the children play,
he felt as if he were in one of those jump-frame videos he
had seen on television once, with no idea how he got
from one frame to the next, and with seconds, minutes,
hours missing in between.

•

It was dark. That much he knew. Dark and the boy was
at home. She was at work. He knew because he had

followed her to the bar where she worked, watched her put on her apron and start serving drinks. He didn't know where he had been or what he had done or dreamed all day, but now it was dark, the boy was at home and the gun lay heavy and warm in his pocket.

The boy, Daryl, simply opened the door and let him in. Such arrogance. Such cockiness. Frank could hardly believe it. The music was deafening.

'Turn it off,' he said.

Daryl shrugged and did so. 'What do you want?' he asked. 'My mother told me you've been pestering her. We should call the law on you. I'll bet you're one of those dirty old men, aren't you? Are you trying to get in my mother's pants? Or are you a pervert? Is it young boys you like?' He struck a parody of a sexy pose.

Out of the window, Frank could see the upstairs light he had left on in his house over the laneway. Daryl was smoking, his free hand slapping against his baggies in time to some imaginary music. He wouldn't keep still, kept walking up and down the room. Frank just stood there, by the door.

'How old are you?' Frank asked.

'What's it to you, pervert?'

'Have you been taking drugs?'

'What if I have? What are you going to do about it?'

'Where's my ring?'

He curled his upper lip back and laughed. 'Bottom of the lake. Or maybe in the garbage. I don't remember.'

'Please,' said Frank. 'Where is it? It's all I have left of her.'

'Tough shit. Get a life, old man.'

'You don't understand.'

Daryl stopped pacing and thrust his chin out towards

Frank. The tendons in his neck stood out like cables. 'Yes, I do. You think I'm a fucking retard, don't you, just like the teachers do? Well, fuck the lot of you. It was your wife's ring. It's all you've got to remember her by. Read my lips. *I don't fucking care!*'

Blinking back the tears, Frank stuck his hand in his pocket for the gun. He actually felt his hand tighten around the handle and his finger slip into the trigger guard before he relaxed his grip and let go. At the time he didn't know why he was doing it, but the next thing he knew he was walking down the stairs.

'And stay away from us!' he heard Daryl shout after him.

Out in the street, with no memory of going out the door, he found himself on the boardwalk again. It was dark and there was nobody else around except a man walking his dog. Frank went and sat out on the rocks. The lake stretched like black satin ahead of him, smudged with thin white moonlight. Water slopped around the rock at his feet and splashed over his ankles. He thought he could see lights over on the American side.

The next thing Frank knew he was at home and something like a thunderbolt cracked inside his head, filling it with light. It was all so clear now. It was time to let go. He laughed. So simple. From his window, he could see Daryl light another cigarette, hear the loud music. What did his feelings matter to Daryl or his mother? They didn't. And why should they? Nothing really mattered now, but at least he knew what he had to do. He had known the moment he got close enough to Daryl to see the tattoo of a swastika on his cheek below his left eye.

●

329

Even though it was dark, Frank managed to arrange the stuff on his lawn. He was thinking clearly now. His life had regained its sense of continuity. No more jump-frame reality. The memory he had tried so hard to deny had forced itself on him now the ring was gone, the talisman that had protected him for so long. It wasn't such a bad thing. In a way, he was free. It was all over.

It was a warm night. A raccoon snuffled around the neighbour's garbage. It stopped and looked at Frank with its calm, black-ringed eyes. He moved forward and stamped his foot on the sidewalk to make it go away. It simply stared at him until it was ready to go, then it waddled arrogantly along the street. Far in the distance, a car engine revved. Other shapes detached themselves from the darkness and proved even more difficult to chase away than the raccoon, but Frank held his ground.

Carefully, he arranged the objects around him on the dark lawn. By the time he had finished, the sun was coming up, promising a perfect day for a lawn sale. Now that everything was neatly laid out, the memory was complete; he could keep nothing at bay.

What a death Joan's had been. She had spent ten years doing it, in and out of hospital, one useless operation after another, night after sleepless night of agony despite the pills. He remembered now the times she had begged him to finish her, saying she would do it herself if she had the strength, if she could move without making the knives twist and cut up her insides.

And every time he let her down. He couldn't do it, and he didn't really know why. Surely if he really loved her, he told himself, he would have killed her to stop her suffering? But that argument didn't work. He knew that he loved her, but he still couldn't kill her.

Once, he stood over her for ten minutes holding a pillow in his hands, and he felt her willing him to push it down over her face. Her tongue was swollen, her gums had receded and her teeth were falling out. Every time he smoothed her head with his hand, tufts of dry hair stuck to his palm.

But he had thrown the cushion aside and run out of the house. Why couldn't he do it? Because he couldn't imagine life without her, no matter how much pain and anguish she suffered to stay with him, no matter how little she now resembled the wife he had married? Perhaps. Selfishness? Certainly. Cowardice? Yes.

At last she had gone. Not with a quiet whisper like a candle flame snuffed out, not gently, but with convulsions and loud screams as if fish hooks had ripped a bloody path through her insides.

And he remembered her last look at him, the bulging eyes, the blood trickling from her nose and mouth. How could he forget that look? Through all the final agony, through the knowledge that the release of death was only seconds away, the hard glint of accusation in her eyes was unmistakable.

Frank wiped the tears from his stubbly cheeks and held the gun on his lap as the sun grew warmer and the city came to life around him. Soon he would find the courage to do to himself what he hadn't been able to do for the wife he loved, what he had only been able to do to some nameless German soldier who haunted his dreams. Soon.

By the time the tourists got here all they would see was an old man asleep amid the detritus of his life: the torso of a tailor's dummy; yards of moth-eaten fabrics and folded patterns made of tissue paper; baking dishes; cake tins; cookie cutters shaped like hearts and lions; a silver cigarette lighter; a Nazi armband; a tattered copy of *Mein Kampf*; medals; a bayonet; a German dagger with a mother-of-pearl swastika inlaid in its handle.

GONE TO THE DAWGS

It was the penultimate week of the NFL football pool and Charlie Firth was ahead by ten points. Nothing could stop the smug bastard from winning again now. Nothing short of murder.

Such was the uncharitable thought that crossed the mind of Calvin Bly as he sat with the usual crowd in the local bar watching the Monday night game, St Louis at Tampa Bay. Outside, in the east end of Toronto, the wind was howling, piling up snow in the side streets and swirling it in surreal patterns across the main roads, but inside it was warm, and the occasional single malt between pints of Guinness helped make it even warmer.

There were six of them at the table, the usual crowd, all in the pool. Calvin was second, having come up with a complicated system of mathematical checks and balances that had earned him solid eights and nines all season, plus the occasional eleven. Behind him by six points was Marge, the only girl in the group. Well, woman really, he supposed, seeing as she was in her fifties. The other three, Chris, Jeff and Brad, weren't even in the running.

'How's your mother, Calvin?' Charlie's loud voice boomed across the table. Calvin looked away from his conversation with Marge and saw the sneer on Charlie's face, the baiting grin, the arrogant, disdaining eyes.

'She's fine, thank you,' he said.

Charlie looked at his watch. 'Only it's getting late. I'm surprised she lets you stay out this long.'

He laughed and some of the others joined in, but more because it was the thing to do than because they had any heart for it. Truth be told, nobody really found Charlie's sense of humour funny. Vicious, yes. Cutting and hurtful, yes. But funny, no way.

Perhaps it wasn't worth murdering someone for two thousand dollars, Calvin thought, but it might be worth it just to clear the world of the loud-mouthed fucker. People would probably thank him for it. Three years in a row Charlie Firth had won that NFL pool, and he hadn't let a soul forget it. Twice Calvin had come in second, and Charlie wasn't about to let him forget that either. The teasing would go on well into the baseball season.

Yes, if he got rid of Charlie, he would be doing the world a favour.

The Buccs threw a touchdown pass to take the lead in the dying seconds of the game, and Calvin shook himself free of his dark thoughts. Of course he wouldn't murder Charlie. He'd never harmed a soul in his life, didn't have the guts for it. It was nothing but a pleasant, harmless fantasy.

Got that one, thought Calvin when the game was over, and Charlie had picked the Rams. He was still nine points ahead of the field, though, pretty much impossible to catch, and Marge was still six behind as they went into the final week. It had been a weekend of upsets – the Seahawks beat the Raiders, the Chiefs beat the Broncos and the Lions beat the Jets – but Calvin had come away with nine points.

'Say hi to your mom from me,' Charlie called out as

Calvin bundled up and headed out to clear the snow off his car. He didn't bother answering.

•

Calvin hadn't been home five minutes, was watching the news quietly on TV, when the banging started. Mother had a walking stick which she didn't use to walk with as she rarely bothered to walk, but to bang on the floor of her bedroom to summon her son, calling out his name. With a sigh, Calvin hauled himself out of the La-Z-Boy and climbed up the stairs.

He hated Mother's sick room, the unpleasant smells – she never opened the window and didn't bathe very often – the way she lay there looking frail, hands like talons clutching the sheet tight around her neck as if he were going to rape her or something, when the very idea of her nakedness disgusted him.

'Yes, Mother?'

'You were out late.'

'It was a long game.'

'Anything could have happened to me. I could have had a seizure. What would I have done, then?'

'Mother, you're not going to have a seizure. The doctor told you yesterday your health's just fine.'

'Doctor, schmoctor. What does that quack know?' Her tone became wheedling, flirtatious. 'Calvin, baby, I can't sleep. I'm having one of my bad nights. Make Mommy some hot milk and bring my pills, Little Calvin. Pull-leeeease.'

Calvin went back downstairs and poured some milk into a saucepan, enough for two, as he decided he might as well treat himself to some hot chocolate if he was heating up milk anyway. While he listened to the hiss of the gas flame and watched the milk's surface change as it heated, he thought again how pleasant it would be if he had the guts to do something about Charlie Firth.

The man was insufferable. For a start, he was well off and always made a point of letting you know how much his possessions cost, from the Porsche to his leather Italian loafers. Women, of course, just wouldn't leave him alone. He had a big house on Kingswood, prime Beach property – all to himself, as he had never married, probably because no woman in her right mind could stand his company for more than a night – and as well as winning the NFL pool, he had been his company's real-estate agent of the year more than once. A success. And Calvin, what had he got? Nothing. Unemployment benefits. A savings account that was thinning out as quickly as his hair, a pot belly that seemed to be getting bigger, a hypochondriac mother who would probably live to torment him for ever, a small, gloomy, draughty row house on the wrong side of Victoria Park. Nothing. Sweet fuck all.

Bubbles started to surface on the milk. Time to turn down the heat. Mother hated it when he burnt the milk. Before he had even got the mugs out of the cupboard he heard the banging on the ceiling again. As if the silly old cow thought banging with that stick of hers would make milk boil any faster. He burned himself as he slopped the hot milk into the cup, forgot about his hot chocolate and hurried upstairs.

●

In the light of the next day, killing Charlie didn't seem like such a good idea. Given Calvin's luck, he was bound to get caught for a start. And, technically, Charlie would still be the winner. If you didn't phone your picks in on time, the administrator assigned you the underdogs, and even with the DAWGS, as they were called, Charlie would still beat the field. He would be too dead to collect his winnings, of course, and Calvin supposed they would go to whoever came second.

The way the pool worked was every Wednesday before five o'clock you phoned in your picks, based on that day's point spread, to the administrator, who ran the whole thing from his desk at one of the major newspapers downtown. You always got his answering machine with its curt message: 'I'm away from my desk right now. Please leave your message after the beep.' There were over a hundred people in the pool, at a hundred bucks each for the season, and in addition to the grand prize of $2000, there were also smaller weekly prizes. Calvin had actually covered this year's entry fee on one weekly win. Usually by Friday evening a photocopy of everyone's picks, along with the weekly and accumulated scores, was faxed to Jeff, who made copies and distributed them in the bar.

Calvin liked to see which teams everyone else had chosen – especially Charlie – but this week he would miss it. On Thursday he had to accompany Mother down to Fort Myers, where they would spend Christmas with their only living relatives, his Aunt Vicky and Uncle Frank, who had retired there seven years ago and were generous enough to help out with the airfare.

The Florida trip used to be the highlight of Calvin's year. Not because he liked the place. Three or four days was about all he could stand. It was too hot and too full of old people, or people who didn't speak English, as if Toronto wasn't bad enough that way. No, what Florida used to mean to him was freedom, glorious freedom! Mother used to stay down there for at least six weeks, and as soon as she was 'settled' Calvin was allowed to go home alone. God only knew how Vicky and Frank put up with the old bat, Calvin thought, but they did. Now she was too worried about getting sick and not being able to afford US medical bills, so they were both returning on the following Wednesday.

That Tuesday morning at breakfast Calvin checked the sports section to see if the spreads had changed since Monday. He liked to do that, factor it into his calculations. Sometimes you could guess a lot just by the ways the spreads were changing. After that, his day followed its usual dull routine. He cleared the driveway of snow, did household chores, did some food shopping and took care of Mother. But on Tuesday evening Calvin had a date.

This was one thing nobody knew about him – at least, so he believed. Calvin had a secret girlfriend. Heidi. Probably no one would believe it if he told them that a pudgy, balding, boring fifty-one-year-old man like him could have an attractive blonde forty-year-old woman as a girlfriend. Sometimes he could hardly believe it himself. They had met six months ago in HMV downtown, both looking at the selection of show tunes. A common interest in film musicals led them to venture to a local coffee shop together, where they found they enjoyed one another's company immensely. A loner by nature – apart from the easy and informal gregariousness of the bar – Calvin found it hard to talk to her at first, but Heidi had a way of drawing him out of his shell. There was, of course, a big problem.

Heidi was married.

Slowly, piece by piece, it emerged over furtive meetings in the city centre, first just for coffees, then regular lunches at Red Lobster, that Heidi was not exactly happy with her marriage. Her children had both left home, one for Winnipeg, poor sod, and the other for southern California, so it was only a matter of time, she told Calvin, before the separation occurred. Until then, they had to be very careful and keep their relationship a secret. Her husband worked shifts for a security company, and this week he was working evenings. Calvin would go over to the west end, where Heidi lived, not far from High Park, and they would talk and make love until midnight, at which time he would dress and sneak out of the back door to where he had parked his car several blocks away.

That Tuesday Heidi did not seem to be in her usual good spirits.

'What's wrong?' Calvin asked, after he had suspected her of counting cracks in the ceiling while they made love.

'Nothing,' she said.

'Come on. I can tell there's something bothering you.'

'I told you, it's nothing. Leave it.'

'Maybe I can help.'

Heidi turned, propped herself on her elbow and looked at him. 'I don't think I can go on,' she said after a pause.

Calvin felt his chest tighten, his heart race. 'What do you mean?'

'This. You and me. I don't think I can go on.'

'But why?'

'It's not that I don't like you, Calvin.' She stroked his cheek. 'It's just . . . oh, everything, the lies, the guilt. Joe and I had a really long talk the other night.'

'For God's sake, Heidi, you didn't tell him . . . ?'

'No. No, of course not. What sort of a fool do you

think I am? No, we just . . . well, he realized he'd been neglecting me, and I realized I missed him more than I thought. We decided . . . you know . . . to try to make a go of things.'

'Make a go of things?'

'Yes.' She smiled. 'We're going to start with a trip to Mexico. A sort of second honeymoon. We're going for New Year.'

'B-but . . .'

'Oh, Calvin. Don't be upset. Please don't be upset. You had fun while it lasted, didn't you?'

'Yes, but . . . but I thought . . .'

'You thought what?'

'I mean, just now, even when you knew this, you . . . we . . .' He shook his head.

'Was that so unfair of me, Calvin? Just to have you one last time? Was that too selfish of me?'

'It's not that.'

'Then what?'

'It just seems so sudden, so abrupt, that's all.' Calvin sat on the edge of the bed and reached for his clothes.

'But you knew it had to end one day.'

'I sort of hoped that when you and Joe split up, we might . . . you know . . .'

'Oh, Calvin, that's sweet. That's *too* sweet.'

'I gather you didn't?'

Heidi lay back on the pillow. 'I never thought, really, not beyond the next time. I've hurt you, haven't I?'

'It's all right. I'll mend.'

'I'm sorry, Calvin.'

'Don't worry about it. I'll go now.'

'You'll be careful? Make sure no one sees you?'

'I'll be careful.'

Calvin bent over to give her a goodnight kiss, as he always did. She turned her head and offered him her cheek. He kissed it lightly and found it surprisingly cool, then he went downstairs and sneaked out of the back door. He thought of making a lot of noise, but Calvin wasn't the type to draw too much attention to himself.

•

He was OK to drive, he told himself as he headed out of the nearest bar – to which he had gone as soon as he'd left Heidi's – he'd only had two pints and a shot of whisky, and he felt in control. Sad, hurt, but in control.

The city crews had been through the neighbourhood and the roads were pretty clear. He headed down Roncesvalles towards Lakeshore and the Gardiner, noting how quiet the roads were. Hardly surprising, as it was going on for half past one on a cold, miserable Tuesday evening.

It was all over with Heidi. He couldn't believe it, couldn't believe the callous way she had treated him. How could she? He had even fantasized a real life for them: restaurants, theatres, musicals, weekends together. Now this.

Almost home. He stopped at a red light. Nobody around. Lights from TV sets in a couple of windows. Christmas trees. Lights.

As he neared the next set of traffic lights, he saw someone come out of a bar alone and start to cross just as the lights were changing. It was Charlie. There was no mistaking that expensive leather jacket, the hand-tooled cowboy boots. He was clearly a bit pissed, not falling down drunk, but definitely unsteady. And unobservant. Calvin was driving slowly enough to stop, but something, he couldn't say what, some demon, some inner compulsion, seemed to take control of him. A quick glance to make sure there were no other cars visible ahead or behind, nobody on the street in seeing distance, and almost unbidden his foot pressed down on the gas pedal as if it was made of lead.

Charlie knew something was wrong, saw it coming at the last moment, but was too late to do anything about it. Calvin saw the horrified expression on his face, even fancied he saw recognition there, too, then the car hit him with a satisfying, meaty smack and threw him away from the car. Calvin felt the shuddering bump and crunch as he ran over the body. No stopping now. He sped off and turned the first corner, heading into the maze of residential streets that would eventually take him home, heart in his mouth, blood pulsing hard through his veins, but alive, alive at last.

•

Calvin didn't sleep at all that night and spent the next day in terror of the knock upon his door. The newspaper reported Charlie's death and asked anyone who might have seen anything to contact them. Calvin was almost certain that no one had seen him, but there was still room for doubt, and that doubt bred fear. If the police came to check out his car, they would see the damage Charlie's body had caused to the radiator and the headlight. They could probably even match paint chips from the body to his car; he had seen them do it on TV.

So terrified was he that he almost forgot to phone in his picks. Almost. At four-thirty he picked up the phone with trembling hands and dialled the administrator's number. Just as the answering machine cut in, Mother's stick banged on the floor above. He automatically held the phone at arm's length and put his hand over the mouthpiece, even though there wasn't a real person on the other end, and shouted up that he was busy and would be with her in a few moments. When he got back to the phone, he was just in time to hear the familiar beep. He began: 'Giants, Broncos, Bills, Jets, Rams, Bears . . .'

•

The journey to Fort Myers on Thursday morning was a nightmare for Calvin. Not because of the weather, though the flight was delayed more than an hour and the wings had to be de-iced. Not even because of Mother, despite the fact that she never stopped complaining for one moment until the plane took off, when she immediately fell asleep. No, it was because he expected to be arrested at every stage of the journey. At the check-in he noticed two airline officials huddled to one side talking, and occasionally they seemed to be looking in his direction. Sweat beaded on his forehead. But nothing happened. Next, at US Immigration, just when he expected the firm hand on his shoulder, the hushed 'Please step this way, Mr Bly,' the immigration officer wished him and Mother happy holidays after barely a glance at their passports.

Could getting away with murder really be that easy? Calvin wondered when he disembarked at Fort Myers and found no policemen waiting for him, only Frank and Vicky in the crowd waving, ready to drive him and Mother back to the condo. Nothing had happened. Nobody had come for him. He must have got away with it.

Though the locals thought the weather cold and farmers were worried about the citrus crop, Calvin found it comfortable enough to sit out on the deck. As he poured himself a Jack Daniels and looked out over the long strip of beach to the blue-green sea, Charlie's murder began to seem distant and unreal. After a few hours and three or four bourbons, he could almost believe it hadn't happened, that it had merely been a bad dream, and the following morning he imagined that when he got back to Toronto and walked into the bar they would all be waiting there, as usual, including Charlie, flashing his winnings.

In the late afternoon Florida sun, how easy it was to believe that snowy Tuesday night in Toronto had never happened.

•

By Christmas Eve, Calvin was already two games up, having picked the Bills to beat a three-point spread against the Seahawks and the Broncos to win plus seven over the 49ers on Saturday. He'd lost the Giants–Jaguars game, but even with his system he could never expect to win them all.

He was sipping a Jack Daniels on the rocks and watching Miami against New England, hoping the Pats would beat the spread, when during the half-time break came a brief interview with a convicted killer called Leroy Cody, scheduled to be electrocuted early in the New Year. Instead of pushing the mute button, Calvin turned the sound up a notch or two and leaned forward in his chair. He'd read about Cody in USA Today and found his curiosity piqued by the man's nonchalant, laconic manner and his total lack of remorse.

The interview was a special from death row, Leroy in

his cell in drab prison clothes, hair cropped close to his skull, no emotion in his eyes, his face all sharp angles.

'You shot a liquor store clerk for fifteen dollars, is that right?' the interviewer asked.

'I didn't know he'd only got a lousy fifteen dollars when I shot him, now, did I?' Leroy answered in his slow, surprisingly high-pitched drawl.

'But you shot him, and fifteen dollars is all you got?'

'Yessir. Sure was a disappointment, let me tell you.'

'And then you shot a pregnant woman and dragged her out of her car to make your escape.'

'I didn't know she was pregnant.'

'But you shot the woman and stole her car?'

Leroy spat on the floor of his cell. 'Hell, I had to make a fast getaway. I don't have no car of my own. I had to take a goddamn cab to the store, but I was damned if I was gonna hang around and try to flag one after I done robbed the place.'

'And you feel no remorse for any of this?'

'Remorse?'

'Regrets.'

'Regrets? Nope. No regrets. I'm a killer. That's what I am.'

'You regret nothing at all?'

Leroy smiled; it looked like an eclipse of the sun moving slowly across his features. 'Only getting caught,' he said.

Calvin's attention wandered as the presenter started to comment, and then they were back at the half-time show, catching up on scores. But even as he checked the numbers, part of Calvin's mind stayed with Leroy Cody. 'I'm a killer. That's what I am.' He liked that. It was honest, direct, had a ring to it.

Calvin tried it out loud: 'I'm a killer. That's what I am.' It sounded good. He let the fantasy wander, trying on his new self and finding it a perfect fit. 'I'm a killer. That's what I am. Me and Leroy. Yeah, man.' And if he was a killer, he could kill again. Why stop at Charlie? He could kill Heidi's husband. Could even kill that bitch Heidi herself, maybe make her beg a little first. He could kill . . .

There was no upstairs in the condo, but he heard the click-click of Mother's walking stick on the tile floor before he heard her voice. 'Leroy,' she said (he was sure she called him Leroy), 'are you going to just sit here and watch this garbage all Christmas? Why don't you come and play cribbage with the old folks for a while?' Calvin sighed, picked up the remote, turned off the game and muttered, 'Coming, Mother.'

•

There were no cops waiting at the airport when Calvin and Mother got back to Toronto on Wednesday. It was over a week since Charlie's death, and still nothing to fear.

After settling Mother at home, against her protests, Calvin decided to drop in at the bar. As he had suspected, the usual crowd was there. Minus Charlie.

'Calvin,' said Marge, patting his arm when he sat down beside her. 'Welcome home. You've heard the news?'

Calvin nodded sadly. 'Heard just before we left for Florida. It's tragic, isn't it?'

'I still can't believe it,' said Marge. 'He always seemed so . . .'

'Alive?' Calvin suggested.

'Yes. Alive. That's it. Alive.'

'Is there any progress?' he asked the table in general.

'No,' Jeff answered. 'You know the cops. They've put

it down as a hit and run, asked for the public's co-operation, and that's the last you'll hear of it.'

'Unless someone comes forward,' Calvin said.

'Yes,' Jeff agreed. 'Unless someone comes forward. By the way,' he went on, 'here's the final scores on the pool.' He handed Calvin the sheets of paper.

Kelly, the waitress with the walk out of a forties' *noir* movie, finally came over with his drink. Calvin desperately wanted to see the final scores, but he didn't want to appear too anxious. After all, Charlie *was* dead. So he sipped some beer, talked a little about his Christmas, and then, casually, glanced down at the sheets.

The first thing that caught his eye was his weekend's score: 5. That had to be wrong. Calvin had checked the game scores after the cribbage game and found he had nine. He had also won the evening game, the Raiders over the Panthers, *and* the Monday evening game, when the Titans had creamed the Cowboys. So how could he end up with *five*? He had *eleven*.

He turned to the column of picks and noticed scrawled across the line where his should be, the word 'DAWGS'. Charlie, of course, had got the same. It meant they hadn't got their picks in on time.

But Calvin *had* got his picks in; he remembered phoning them. It was late in the afternoon, four-thirty to be precise, but definitely *before* the five o'clock deadline. So what was going on?

'Calvin?'

The voice came as if from a long way. 'Huh? Sorry. What?'

'Just that you've gone pale. Are you OK?' It was Marge, and her hand was on his arm.

'I'm fine,' he said. 'Must be . . . you know . . . Charlie . . . delayed shock.'

Marge nodded. 'I don't suppose it seemed real until you got back here, did it?' she said.

'Something like that. What's happening with the pool?'

Marge frowned. 'Well,' she said, 'with Charlie gone and you forgetting to phone in . . . er . . . I won.'

'You?'

Marge laughed nervously. 'Well, don't look so surprised, Calvin. I've been up there with the best of you all season.'

'I know. It's not that . . .'

'What, then?'

'Never mind. Congratulations, Marge.' Calvin knew he couldn't complain Whatever had gone wrong here, however he had gone from eleven to five, there was nothing he could do about it, and getting upset about the result would only look suspicious.

'Thanks,' said Marge. 'I know it must be a disappointment, you being so close and all.' She managed a weak smile. 'I only beat you by one, if that means anything at all. It was my best week of the whole season. Twelve.'

Calvin laughed. He couldn't help himself. 'So what are you going to do with your winnings?'

Marge looked at the others, then said, 'I decided – well, we all decided, really – that I'd use the money for a wake, you know, to pay for a wake here. For Charlie. He would have liked that.'

'Yes,' said Calvin, still quaking with laughter inside while he tried to keep a straight face. 'Yes, I think he would.'

•

When Calvin got home he poured himself a large whisky and tried to figure out what had gone wrong. *Five*. The *DAWGS*. It was an insult, a slap in the face.

He cast his mind back to that Wednesday afternoon and remembered first that his hand had been shaking as he dialled. He had, after all, just killed Charlie the previous evening. Could he have misdialled? The first three numbers were all the same, and connected him to the newspaper the administrator worked for. The last four were 4697. It would have been easy, say, to transpose the six and the nine, or even to dial seven first rather than four, given that he was upset at the time. He tried both and got the same message: 'I'm away from my desk right now. Please leave a message after the beep.' The only difference was that 7694 was a woman's voice and 4967 was a man's. So that was what had happened. In his disturbed state of mind, Calvin had dialled the wrong number. Why had it happened like that? Why hadn't he listened to the message, noticed the difference in voice and realized what he had done?

Then he remembered. Just as he had got through, Mother had knocked on the bedroom floor for him. He had held the phone at arm's length and covered the mouthpiece, as you do, and yelled up that he was coming in a minute. He *hadn't heard* the administrator's message, only vaguely recognized it was a man's voice on the answering machine, heard the usual beep and left his picks with someone else at the paper.

Someone who hadn't a clue what he was talking about.

Calvin held his head in his hands. *The wrong number.* All for nothing. He drank some more whisky. Well, maybe not *all* for nothing, he thought after a while. Hadn't he already decided that, nice as it would have been, he hadn't killed Charlie only for the money? Wasn't $2000 a paltry sum to murder for? More than $15, but still . . . he knew he had had more reason than the money. Winning the pool was a part of it, of course, but that wasn't to be. So what was left? What could he salvage from this disaster?

'I'm a killer. That's what I am.'

The voice seemed to come into his head from nowhere, and slowly as the whisky warmed his insides, understanding dawned on Calvin.

'I'm a killer. That's what I am.'

The sound of a heavy stick hammering on the ceiling above broke into his thoughts. He could hear her muffled yelling. 'Leroy! Leroy! I need my hot milk, Leroy!'

Calvin put his glass down, looked up at the ceiling and got to his feet. 'Coming, Mother,' he said softly.

IN FLANDERS FIELDS

I considered it the absolute epitome of irony that, with bombs falling around us, someone went and bludgeoned Mad Maggie to death.

To add insult to injury, she lay undiscovered for several days before Harry Fletcher, the milkman, found her. Because milk was rationed to one or two pints a week, depending on how much the children and expectant mothers needed, he didn't leave it on her doorstep the way he used to do before the war. Even in a close community like ours, a bottle of milk left unguarded on a doorstep wouldn't have lasted five minutes.

These days, Harry walked around with his float, and people came out to buy. It was convenient, as we were some way from the nearest shops, and we could always be sure we were getting fresh milk. However mad Maggie might have been, it wasn't like her to miss her milk ration. Thinking she might have slept in, or perhaps have fallen ill with no one to look after her, Harry knocked on her door and called her name. When he heard no answer, he told me, he made a tentative try at the handle and found that the door was unlocked.

There she lay on her living-room floor in a pool of dried blood dotted with flies. Poor Harry lost his breakfast before he could dash outside for air.

Why Harry came straight to me when he found Mad Maggie's body I can't say. We were friends of a kind, I suppose, of much the same age, and we occasionally passed a pleasurable evening together playing dominoes and drinking watery beer in the Prince Albert. Other than that, we didn't have a lot in common: I was a school-teacher – English and history – and Harry had left school at fourteen; Harry had missed the first war through a heart ailment, whereas I had been gassed at Ypres in 1917; I was a bachelor, and Harry was married with a stepson, Thomas, who had just come back home on con-valescent leave after being severely wounded during the Dunkirk evacuation. Thomas also happened to be my godson, which I suppose was the main thing Harry and I had in common.

Perhaps Harry also came to me because I was a Special Constable. I know it sounds impressive, but it isn't really. The services were so mixed up that you'd have the police putting out fires, the Home Guard doing police work, and anyone with two arms carrying the stretchers. A Special Constable was simply a part-time policeman, without any real qualifications for the job except his willingness to take it on. The rest of the time I taught what few pupils remained at Silverhill Grammar School.

As it turned out, I was glad that Harry did call on me because it gave me a stake in the matter. The regular police were far more concerned with lighting offences and the black market than they were with their regular duties, and one thing nobody had time to do in the war was investigate the murder of a mad, mysterious, cantan-kerous old woman.

Nobody except me, that is.

Though my position didn't grant me any special pow-ers, I pride myself on being an intelligent and perceptive sort of fellow, not to mention nosy, and it wasn't the first time I'd done a spot of detective work on the side. But first, let me tell you a little about Mad Maggie . . .

•

I say *old* woman, but Maggie was probably only in her mid-forties, about the same age as me, when she was killed. Everyone just called her *old*; it seemed to go with *mad*. With a certain kind of woman, it's not so much a matter of years, anyway, but of demeanour, and Maggie's demeanour was old.

Take the clothes she wore, for a start: most women were trying to look like one of the popular film stars like Vivien Leigh or Deanna Durbin, with her bolero dresses, but even for a woman of her age, Maggie wore clothes that could best be described as old-fashioned, even antique: high, buttoned boots, long dresses with high collars, ground-sweeping cloaks and broad-brimmed hats with feathers.

Needless to say, the local kids – at least those whose parents hadn't packed them off to the countryside already – used to follow her down the street in gangs and chant, 'Mad Maggie, Mad Maggie, she's so mad, her brain's all claggy . . .' Children can be so cruel. Most of the time she ignored them, or seemed oblivious to their taunts, but once in a while she wheeled on them, eyes blazing, and started waving her arms around and yelling curses, usually in French. The children would squeal with exaggerated horror, then turn tail and run away.

Maggie never had any visitors; none of us had ever been inside her house; nobody in the community even knew what her real name was, where she had come from, or how she had got to be the way she was. We simply accepted her. There were rumours of course. Some gossip-mongers had it that she was an heiress cut off by her family because she went mad; others said she had never recovered from a tragic love affair; still others said she was a rich eccentric and kept thousands of pounds stuffed in her mattress.

Whoever and whatever Mad Maggie was, she managed to take care of life's minutiae somehow; she paid her rent, she bought newspapers, and she handled her ration coupons just like the rest of us. She also kept herself clean, despite the restriction to only five inches of bath water. Perhaps her eccentricity was just an act, then, calculated to put people off befriending her for some reason? Perhaps she was shy or antisocial? All in all, she was known as Mad Maggie only because she never talked to anyone except herself, because of the old clothes she wore, because of her strange outbursts in French and because, as everyone knew, she never went to the shelters during air-raids, but would either stay indoors alone or walk the blacked-out streets muttering and arguing with herself, waving her arms at the skies as if inviting the bombs to come and get her.

•

When Harry called that Monday morning, I was lying in bed grappling with one of my frequent bouts of insomnia, waiting for the birds to sing me back to sleep. I couldn't even tell if it was daylight or not because of the heavy blackout curtains. I had been dreaming, I remembered, and had woken at about half-past four, gasping for air, from my recurring nightmare about being sucked down into a quicksand.

I heard Harry banging at my door and calling my name, so I threw on some clothes and hurried downstairs. I thought at first that it might be something to do with

Tommy, but when I saw his pale face, his wide eyes and the thin trickle of vomit at the corner of his mouth, I worried that he was having the heart attack he had been expecting daily for over twenty years.

He turned and pointed down the street. 'Frank, please!' he said. 'You've got to come with me.'

I could hear the fear in his voice, so I followed him as quickly as I could to Maggie's house. It was a fine October morning, with a hint of autumn's nip in the air. He had left the door ajar. Slowly, I pushed it open and went inside. My first impression was more surprise at how clean and tidy the place was than shock at the bloody figure on the carpet. In my defence, lest I sound callous, I had fought in the first war and, by some miracle, survived the mustard gas with only a few blisters and a nasty coughing fit every now and then. But I had seen men blown apart; I had been spattered with the brains of my friends; I had crawled through trenches and not known whether the soft, warm, gelatinous stuff I was putting my hands in was mud or the entrails of my comrades. More recently, I had also helped dig more than one mangled or dismembered body from the ruins, so a little blood, a little death, never bothered me much. Besides, despite the pool of dried blood around her head, Mad Maggie looked relatively peaceful. More peaceful than I had ever seen her in life.

Funny, but it reminded me of that old Dracula film I saw at the Crown, the one with Bela Lugosi. The count's victims always became serene after they had wooden stakes plunged through their hearts. Mad Maggie hadn't been a vampire, and she didn't have a stake through her heart, but a bloodstained posser lay by her side, the concave copper head and wooden handle both covered in blood. A quick glance in the kitchen showed only one puzzling item: an unopened bottle of milk. As far as I knew, Harry's last round had been the morning of the air raid, last Wednesday. I doubted that Maggie would have been able to get more than her rations; besides, the bottle top bore the unmistakable mark of the dairy where Harry worked.

Harry waited outside, unwilling to come in and face the scene again. Once I had taken in what had happened, I told him to fetch the police, the real police this time.

They came.

•

And they went.

One was a plainclothes officer, Detective Sergeant Longbottom, a dull-looking bruiser with a pronounced limp, who looked most annoyed at being called from his bed. He asked a few questions, sniffed around a bit, then got the ambulance men to take Maggie away on a stretcher.

One of the questions Sergeant Longbottom asked was the victim's name. I told him that, apart from 'Mad Maggie', I had no idea. With a grunt, he rummaged around in the sideboard drawer and found her rent book. I was surprised to discover that she was called Rose Faversham, which I thought was actually quite a pretty name. Prettier than Mad Maggie, anyway. Sergeant Longbottom also asked if we'd had any strangers in the area. Apart from an army unit billeted near the park where they were carrying out training exercises, and the gypsy encampment in Silverhill Woods, we hadn't.

'Ah, gypsies,' he said, and wrote something in his little black notebook. 'Is anything missing?'

I told him I didn't know, as I had no idea what *might* have been here in the first place. That seemed to confuse him. For all I knew, I went on, the rumour might have been right, and she could have had a mattress stuffed with banknotes. Sergeant Longbottom checked upstairs and came back scratching his head. 'Everything *looks* normal,' he said, then he poked around a bit more, noting the canteen of sterling silver cutlery, and guessed that Mad Maggie had probably interrupted the thief, who had killed her and fled the scene – probably back to the gypsy encampment. I was on the point of telling him that I thought the Nazis were supposed to be persecuting gypsies, not us, but I held my tongue. I knew it would do no good.

Of course, I told him how everyone in the neighbourhood knew Mad Maggie paid no attention to air raids, how she even seemed to enjoy them the way some people love thunderstorms, and how Tom Sellers, the ARP man, had remonstrated with her on many occasions, only to get a dismissive wave and the sight of her ramrod-stiff back walking away down the street. Maggie had also been fined more than once for blackout infringements, until she solved that one by keeping her heavy black curtains closed night *and* day.

I also told Longbottom that, in the blackout, anyone could have come and gone easily without being seen. I think that was what finally did it. He hummed and hawed, muttered 'Gypsies' again, made noises about a continuing investigation, then put his little black notebook away, said he had pressing duties to attend to and left.

•

And there things would have remained had I not become curious. No doubt Mad Maggie would have been fast forgotten and some poor, innocent gypsy would have been strung up from the gallows. But there was something about the serenity of Mad Maggie's features in death that haunted me. She looked almost saintlike, as if she had sloughed off the skin of despair and madness that she had inhabited for so long and reverted to the loving, compassionate Christian woman she must have once been. She had a real name now, too: *Rose Faversham*. I was also provoked by Detective Sergeant Longbottom's gruff manner and his obvious impatience with the whole matter. No doubt he had more important duties to get back to, such as the increased traffic in black market onion substitutes.

I would like to say that the police searched Maggie's house thoroughly, locked it up fast and put a guard on the door, but they did nothing of the kind. They did lock the front door behind us, of course, but that was it. I imagined that, as soon as he found out, old Grasper, the landlord, would slither around, rubbing his hands and trying to rent the place out quickly again, for twice as much, before the army requisitioned it as a billet.

One thing I had neglected to tell Detective Sergeant Longbottom, I realized as I watched his car disappear around a pile of rubble at the street corner, was about Fingers Finnegan, our local black marketeer and petty thief. Human nature is boundlessly selfish and greedy, even in wartime, and air raids provided the perfect cover for burglary and black market deals. The only unofficial people on the streets during air raids were either mad, like Maggie, or up to no good, like Fingers. We'd had a spate of burglaries when most decent, law-abiding people were in St Mary's church crypt, or at least in their damp and smelly backyard Anderson shelters, and Fingers was my chief suspect. He could be elusive when he wanted to be, though, and I hadn't seen him in a number of days.

Not since last Wednesday's air raid, in fact.

•

After the police had gone, Harry and I adjourned to my house, where, despite the early hour, I poured him a stiff brandy and offered him a Woodbine. I didn't smoke, myself, because of that little bit of gas that had leaked through my mask at Ypres, but I had soon discovered that it was wise to keep cigarettes around when they were becoming scarce. Like all the rationed items, they became a kind of currency. I also put the kettle on, for I hadn't had my morning tea yet, and I'm never at my best before my morning tea. Perhaps that may be one reason I have never married; most of the women I have met chatter far too much in the morning.

'What a turn up,' Harry said, after taking a swig and coughing. 'Mad Maggie, murdered. Who'd imagine it?'

'Her killer, I should think,' I said.

'Gypsies.'

I shook my head. 'I doubt it. Oh, there's no doubt they're a shifty lot. I wouldn't trust one of them as far as I could throw him. But killers? A defenceless woman like Maggie? I don't think so. Besides, you saw her house. It hadn't been touched.'

'But Sergeant Longbottom said she might have interrupted a burglar.'

I sniffed. 'Sergeant Longbottom's an idiot. There was

no evidence at all that her killer was attempting to burgle the place.'

'Maybe she was one of them once – a gypsy – and they came to take her back?'

I laughed. 'I must say, Harry, you certainly don't lack imagination, I'll grant you that. But no, I rather fancy this is a different sort of matter altogether.'

Harry frowned. 'You're not off on one of your Sherlock Holmes kicks again, are you, Frank? Leave it be. Let the professionals deal with it. It's what they're paid for.'

'*Professionals!* Hmph. You saw for yourself how interested our Detective Sergeant Longbottom was. Interested in crawling back in his bed, more like it. No, Harry, I think that's the last we've seen of them. If we want to find out who killed poor Maggie, we'll have to find out for ourselves.'

'Why not just let it be, Frank?' Harry pleaded. 'We're at war. People are getting killed every minute of the day and night.'

I gave him a hard look, and he cringed a little. 'Because this is different, Harry. While I can't say I approve of war as a solution to man's problems, at least it's socially sanctioned murder. If the government, in all its wisdom, decides that we're at war with Germany and we should kill as many Germans as we can, then so be it. But nobody sanctioned the killing of Mad Maggie. When an individual kills someone like Maggie, he takes something he has no right to. Something he can't even give back or replace, the way he could a diamond necklace. It's an affront to us all, Harry, an insult to the community. And it's up to us to see that retribution is made.' I'll admit I sounded a little pompous, but Harry could be extremely obtuse on occasion, and his using the war as an excuse for so outrageous a deed as Rose's murder brought out the worst in me.

Harry seemed suitably cowed by my tirade, and when he'd finished his brandy he shuffled off to finish his deliveries. I never did ask him whether there was any milk left on his unattended float.

•

I had another hour in which to enjoy my morning tea before I had to leave for school, but first I had to complete my ritual and drop by the newsagent's for a paper. While I was there, I asked Mrs Hope behind the counter when she had last seen Mad Maggie. Last Wednesday, she told me, walking down the street towards her house just before the warning siren went off, muttering to herself. That information, along with the unopened milk and the general state of the body, was enough to confirm for me that Rose had probably been killed under cover of the air raid.

That morning, I found I could neither concentrate on *Othello*, which I was supposed to be teaching the fifth form, nor could I be bothered to read about the bombing raids, evacuation procedures and government pronouncements that passed for news in these days of propaganda and censorship.

Instead, I thought about Mad Maggie, or Rose Faversham, as she had now become for me. When I tried to visualize her as she was alive, I realized that had I looked closely enough, had I got beyond the grim expressions and the muttered curses, I might have seen her for the handsome woman she was. *Handsome*, I say, not pretty or beautiful, but I would hazard a guess that twenty years ago she would have turned a head or two. Then I remembered that it was about twenty years ago when she first arrived in the neighbourhood, and she had been Mad Maggie right from the start. So perhaps I was inventing a life for her, a life she had never had, but certainly when death brought repose to her features, it possessed her of a beauty I had not noticed before.

When I set off for school, I saw Tommy Markham, Harry's stepson, going for his morning constitutional. Tommy's real dad, Lawrence Markham, had been my best friend. We had grown up together and had both fought in the Third Battle of Ypres, between August and November 1917. Lawrence had been killed at Passchendaele, about nine miles away from my unit, while I had only been mildly gassed. Tommy was in his mid twenties now. He never knew his real dad, but worshipped him in a way you can worship only a dead hero. Tommy joined up early and served with the Green Howards as part of the ill-fated British Expeditionary Force in France. He had seemed rather twitchy and sullen since he got back from the hospital last week, but I put that down to shattered nerves. The doctors had told Polly, his mother, something about nervous exhaustion and about being patient with him.

'Morning, Tommy,' I greeted him.

He hadn't noticed me at first – his eyes had been glued to the pavement as he walked – but when he looked up, startled, I noticed the almost pellucid paleness of his skin and the dark bruises under his eyes.

'Oh, good morning, Mr Bascombe,' he said. 'How are you?'

'I'm fine, but you don't look so good. What is it?'

'My nerves,' he said, moving away as he spoke. 'The doc said I'd be all right after a bit of rest, though.'

'I'm glad to hear it. By the way, did your fath—, sorry, did Harry tell you about Mad Maggie?' I knew Tommy was sensitive about Harry not being his real father.

'He said she was dead, that's all. Says someone clobbered her.'

'When did you last see her, Tommy?'

'I don't know.'

'Since the raid?'

'That was the day after I got back. No, come to think of it, I don't think I have seen her since then. Terrible business, in'it?'

'Yes, it is.'

'Anyway, sorry, must dash. Bye, Mr Bascombe.'

'Bye, Tommy.'

I stood frowning and watched him scurry off, almost crabwise, down the street.

•

There was another air raid that night, and I decided to look for Fingers Finnegan. By then I had talked to enough people on the street to be certain that no one had seen Rose since the evening of the last raid.

We lived down by the railway, the canal and the power station, so we were always copping it. The Luftwaffe could never aim accurately, though, because the power station sent up clouds of appalling smoke as soon as they heard there were enemy planes approaching. If the bombs hit anything of strategic value, it was more by good luck than good management.

The siren would go off, wailing up and down the scale for two minutes, and it soon became an eerie fugue as you heard the sirens from neighbouring boroughs join in, one after another. The noise frightened the dogs and cats and they struck up, wailing and howling, too. At first, you could hardly see a thing outside, only hear the droning of the bombers high above and the swishing and whistling sound of the bombs as they fell in the distance. Then came the explosions, the hailstone of incendiaries on roofs like a rain of fire, the flames crackling, blazing through the smoke. Even the sounds seemed muffled, the distant explosions no more than dull, flat thuds, like a heavy book falling on the floor, the crackle of anti-aircraft fire like fat spitting on a griddle. Sometimes you could even hear someone scream or shout out a warning. Once I heard a terrible shrieking that still haunts my night-mares.

But the city had an eldritch beauty during an air raid. In the distance, through the smoke haze, the skyline seemed lit by a dozen suns, each a slightly different shade of red, orange or yellow. Searchlights criss-crossed one another, making intricate cat's cradles in the air, and ack-ack fire arced into the sky like strings of Christmas lights. Soon, the bells of the fire engines became part of the symphony of sound and colour. The smoke from the power station got in my eyes and up my nose, and with my lungs, it brought on a coughing fit that seemed to shake my ribs free of their moorings. I held a handker-chief to my face, and that seemed to help a little.

It wasn't too difficult to get around, despite the black-out and the smoke. There were white stripes painted on the lampposts and along the kerbside, and many people had put little dots of luminous paint on their doorbells, so you could tell where you were if you knew the neigh-bourhood well enough.

I walked along Lansdowne Street to the junction with Cardigan Road. Nobody was abroad. The bombs were distant but getting closer, and the smell from a broken sewage pipe was terrible, despite my handkerchief. Once, I fancied I saw a figure steal out of one of the houses, look this way and that, then disappear into the smoky darkness. I ran, calling out after him, but when I got there he had vanished. It was probably Fingers, I told myself. I'd have a devil of a time catching him now I had scared him off. My best chance was to run him down in one of the back-street cafes where he sold his stolen goods the next day.

So instead of pursuing my futile task, and because it was getting more and more difficult to breathe, I decided that my investigation might next benefit best from a good look around Rose's empty house.

It was easy enough to gain access via the kitchen window at the back, which wasn't even latched, and after an undignified and painful fall from the sink to the floor, I managed to regain my equilibrium and set about my business. It occurred to me that if I had such an easy time getting in, then her killer would have had an easy time, too. Rose had been killed with the posser, which would most likely have been placed near the sink or tub in which she did her washing.

Because of the blackout curtains, I didn't have to worry about my torch giving me away; nor did I have to cover it with tissue paper, as I would outside, so I had plenty of light to see by. I stood for a few moments, adjusting to the room. I could hear fire-engine bells not too far away.

I found little of interest downstairs. Apart from necessities, such as cutlery, pans, plates and dishes, Rose seemed to own nothing. There were no framed photographs on the mantelpiece, no paintings on the drab walls. There wasn't even a wireless. A search of the sideboard revealed only the rent book that Longbottom had already discovered, a National Identity Card, also in the name of Rose Faversham, her ration book, various coupons, old bills and about twenty pounds in banknotes. I did find two bottles of gin, one almost empty, in the lower half of the china cabinet. There were no letters, no address books, nothing of a personal nature. Rose Faversham's nest was clean and tidy, but it was also quite sterile.

Wondering whether it was worth bothering, I finally decided to go upstairs to finish my search. The first of the two bedrooms was completely bare. Most people use a spare room to store things they no longer use but can't bear to throw out just yet; there was nothing like this in Rose's spare bedroom, just some rather austere wallpaper and bare floorboards.

I felt a tremor of apprehension on entering Rose's bedroom. After all, she had lived such a private, self-contained life that any encroachment on her most intimate domain seemed a violation. Nonetheless, I went inside.

Apart from the ruffled bedclothes, which I assumed were the result of Detective Sergeant Longbottom's cursory search, the bedroom was every bit as neat, clean and empty as the rest of the house. The one humanizing detail was a library book on her bedside table: Samuel Butler's *The Way of All Flesh*. So Rose Faversham had been an educated woman. Butler's savage and ironic attack on Victorian values was hardly common bedtime reading on our street.

I looked under the mattress and under the bed, and found nothing. The dressing table held those few items deemed essential for a woman's appearance and hygiene, and the chest of drawers revealed only stacks of carefully folded undergarments, corsets and the like, among which I had no desire to go probing. The long dresses hung in the wardrobe beside the high-buttoned blouses.

About to give up and head home to bed, I tried one last place – the top of the wardrobe, where I used to keep my secret diaries when I was a boy – and there I found the shoebox. Even a brief glance inside told me it was the repository of whatever past and personal memories Rose Faversham might have wanted to hang on to. Instead of sitting on the bedspread to read by torchlight, I went back downstairs and slipped out of the house like a thief in the night, which I suppose I was, with Rose's shoebox under my arm. A bomb exploded about half a mile away as I sidled down the street.

•

I should have gone to one of the shelters, I know, but I was feeling devil-may-care that night, and I certainly didn't want anyone to know I had broken into Rose's house and stolen her only private possessions. Back in my own humble abode, I made sure my curtains were shut tight, poured a large tumbler of brandy – perhaps, apart from nosiness and an inability to suffer fools gladly, my only vice – then turned on the standard lamp beside my armchair and settled down to examine my haul. There was a certain excitement in having pilfered it, as they say, and for a moment I imagined I had an inkling of that illicit thrill Fingers Finnegan must get every time *he* burgles someone's house. Of course, this was different; I hadn't broken into Rose's house for my own benefit, to line my own pockets, but to solve the mystery of her murder.

The first thing the shoebox yielded was a photograph of three smiling young women standing in front of an old van with a cross on its side. I could tell by their uniforms that they were nurses from the First World War. On the back, in slightly smudged ink, someone had written 'Midge, Rose and Margaret – Flanders, 30 July 1917. Friends Inseparable For Ever!'

I stared hard at the photograph and, though my imagination may have been playing tricks on me, I thought I recognized Rose as the one in the middle. She had perfect dimples at the edges of her smile, and her eyes gazed, pure and clear, directly into the lens. She bore little resemblance to the Rose I had known as Mad Maggie, or indeed to the body of Rose Faversham as I had seen it. But I think it was her.

I put the photograph aside and pulled out the next item. It was a book of poetry: *Severn and Somme* by Ivor Gurney. One of my favourite poets, Gurney was gassed at St Julien, near Passchendaele, and sent to a war hospital near Edinburgh. I heard he later became mentally disturbed and suicidal, and he died just two or three years ago, after nearly twenty years of suffering. I have always regretted that we never met.

I opened the book. On the title page, someone had written, 'To My Darling Rose on her 21st Birthday, 20 March 1918. Love, Nicholas.' So Rose was even younger than I had thought.

I set the book aside for a moment and rubbed my eyes. Sometimes I fancied the residual effects of the gas made them water, though my doctor assured me that it was a foolish notion, as mustard gas wasn't a lachrymator.

I hadn't been in the war as late as March 1918. The injury that sent me to a hospital in Manchester, my 'Blighty', took place the year before. Blistered and blinded, I had lain in bed there for months, unwilling to get up. The blindness passed, but the scarring remained, both inside and out. In the small hours, when I can't sleep, I relive those early days of August 1917 in Flanders: the driving rain, the mud, the lice, the rats, the deafening explosions. It was madness. We were doomed from the start by incompetent leaders, and as we struggled waist deep through mud, with shells and bullets flying all around us, we could only watch in hopeless acceptance as our own artillery sank in the mud, and our tanks followed it down.

Judging by the words on the back of the photograph, Rose had been there, too: *Rose*, one of the angels of mercy who tended the wounded and the dying in the trenches of Flanders' fields.

I opened the book. Nicholas, or Rose, had underlined the first few lines of the first poem, 'To the Poet Before Battle':

Now, youth, the hour of thy dread passion comes;
Thy lovely things must all be laid away;
And thou, as others, must face the riven day
Unstirred by rattle of the rolling drums
Or bugles' strident cry.

Perhaps Nicholas had been a poet, and Gurney's call for courage in the face of impending battle applied to him, too? And if Nicholas had been a poet, was Rose one of the 'lovely things' he had to set aside?

Outside, the all-clear sounded and brought me back to

earth. I breathed a sigh of relief. Spared again. Still, I had been so absorbed in Rose's treasures that I probably wouldn't have heard a bomb if one fell next door. They say you never hear the one with your name on.

I set the book down beside the photograph and dug around deeper in the shoebox. I found a medal of some sort – I think for valour in wartime nursing – and a number of official papers and certificates. Unfortunately, there were no personal letters. Even so, I managed to compile a list of names to seek out and one or two official addresses where I might pursue my enquiries into Rose Faversham's past. No time like the present, I thought, going over to my escritoire and taking out pen and paper.

•

I posted my letters early the following morning, when I went to fetch my newspaper. I had the day off from school, as the pupils were collecting aluminium pots and pans for the Spitfire Fund, so I thought I might slip into Special Constable mode and spend an hour or two scouring Fingers Finnegan's usual haunts.

I started at Frinton's, on the High Street, where I also treated myself to two rashers of bacon and an egg. By mid-morning, I had made my way around most of the neighbouring cafes, and it was lunchtime when I arrived at Lyon's in the city centre. I didn't eat out very often, and twice a day was almost unheard of. Even so, I decided to spend one and threepence on roast beef and Yorkshire pudding. There was a lot of meat around then because the powers that be were slaughtering most of the farm animals to turn the land over to crops. I almost felt that I was doing my national duty by helping eat some before it went rotten.

As I waited, I noticed Finnegan slip in through the door in his usual manner, licking his lips, head half-bowed, eyes flicking nervously around the room trying to seek out anyone who might be after him, or to whom he might have owed money. I wasn't in uniform, and I was pretending to be absorbed in my newspaper, so his eyes slid over me. When he decided it was safe, he sat down three tables away from me.

My meal came, and I tucked in with great enthusiasm, managing to keep Finnegan in my peripheral vision. Shortly, another man came in – dark-haired, red-faced – and sat with Finnegan. The two of them put their heads together, all the time Finnegan's eyes flicking here and there, looking for danger signs. I pretended to pay no attention but was annoyed that I couldn't overhear a word. Something exchanged hands under the table, and the other man left: Finnegan fencing his stolen goods again.

I waited, lingering over my tea and rice pudding, and when Finnegan left, I followed him. I hadn't wanted to confront him in the restaurant and cause a scene, so I waited until we came near a ginnel not far from my own street, then I speeded up, grabbed him by the shoulders and dragged him into it.

Finnegan was not very strong – in fact, he was a scrawny, sickly sort of fellow, which is why he wasn't fit for service – but he was slippery as an eel, and it took all my energy to hang on to him until I got him where I wanted him, with his back to the wall and my fists gripping his lapels. I slammed him against the wall a couple of times to take any remaining wind out of his sails, then when he went limp, I was ready to start.

'Bloody hell, Constable Bascombe!' he said when he'd

got his breath back. 'I didn't recognize you at first. You didn't have to do that, you know. If there's owt you want to know why don't you just ask me? Let's be civilians about it.'

'The word is *civilized*. With you? Come off it, Fingers.'

'My name's Michael.'

'Listen, Michael, I want some answers and I want them now.'

'Answers to what?'

'During last night's air raid I saw you coming out of a house on Cardigan Road.'

'I never.'

'Don't lie to me. I know it was you.'

'So what? I might've been at my cousin's. He lives on Cardigan Road.'

'You were carrying something.'

'He gave me a couple of kippers.'

'You're lying to me, Fingers, but we'll let that pass for the moment. I'm interested in the raid before that one.'

'When was that, then?'

'Last Wednesday.'

'How d'you expect me to remember what I was doing that long ago?'

'Because murder can be quite a memorable experience, Fingers.'

He turned pale and slithered in my grip. My palms were sweaty. 'Murder? Me? You've got to be joking! I've never killed nobody.'

I didn't bother pointing out that that meant he must have killed *somebody* – linguistic niceties such as that being as pointless with someone of Finnegan's intelligence as speaking loudly to a foreigner and hoping to be understood – so I pressed on. 'Did you break into Rose Faversham's house on Aston Place last Wednesday during the raid?'

'Rose Faversham. Who the bloody hell's she when she's at home? Never heard of her.'

'You might have known her as Mad Maggie.'

'*Mad Maggie*. Now why would a bloke like me want to break into *her* house? That's assuming he did things like that in the first place, hypnotically, like.'

Hypnotically? Did he mean *hypothetically*? I didn't even ask. 'To rob her, perhaps?'

'Nah. You reckon a woman who went around looking like she did would have anything worth stealing? Hypnotically, again, of course.'

'Of course, Fingers. This entire conversation is *hypnotic*. I understand that.'

'Mad Maggie hardly draws attention to herself as a person worth robbing. Not unless you're into antiques.'

'And you're not?'

'Wouldn't know a Chippendale from a Gainsborough.'

'Know anybody who is?'

'Nah.'

'What about the thousands of pounds they say she had hidden in her mattress?'

'And pigs can fly, Constable Bascombe.'

'What about silverware?'

'There's a bob or two in a nice canteen of cutlery. Hypnotically, of course.'

The one thing that might have been of value to someone other than herself was Rose's silverware, and that had been left alone. Even if Fingers had been surprised by her and killed her, he would hardly have left his sole prize behind when he ran off. On the other hand, with a murder charge hanging over it, the silverware might have turned out to be more of a liability than an asset. I looked at his face, into his eyes, trying to decide whether he was telling the truth. You couldn't tell anything from Finnegan's face, though; it was like a ferret mask.

'Look,' he said, licking his lips, 'I might be able to help you.'

'Help me?'

'Yeah. But . . . you know . . . not standing here, like this . . .'

I realized I was still holding him by the lapels, and I had hoisted him so high he had to stand on his tiptoes. I relaxed my grip. 'What do you have in mind?'

'We could go to the Prince Albert, have a nice quiet drink. They'll still be open.'

I thought for a moment. The hard way hadn't got me very far. Maybe a little diplomacy was in order. Though it galled me to be going for a drink with a thieving illiterate like Fingers Finnegan, there were larger things at stake. I swallowed my pride and said, 'Why not?'

•

Nobody paid us a second glance, which was all right by me. I bought us both a pint, and we took a quiet table by the empty fireplace. Fingers brought a packet of Woodbines out of his pocket and lit up. His smoke burned my lungs and caused me a minor coughing fit, but he didn't seem concerned by it.

'What makes you think you can help me?' I asked him when I'd recovered.

'I'll bet you're after Mad Maggie's murderer, aren't you?'

'How do you know that?'

'Word gets around. The *real* police think it was gypsies, you know. They've got one of them in the cells right now. Found some silver candlesticks in his possession.'

'How did they know whether Rose had any silver candlesticks?'

He curled his lip and looked at me as if I were stupid. 'They don't, but they don't know that she didn't, do they? All they need's a confession, and he's a brute in the interrogation room is that short-arse bastard.'

'Who?'

'Longbottom. It's what we call him. Longbottom. Short-arse. Get it?'

'I'm falling off my chair with laughter. Have you got anything interesting to tell me or haven't you?'

'I might have seen someone, mightn't I?'

'Seen someone? Who? Where?'

He rattled his empty glass on the table. 'That'd be telling, wouldn't it?'

I sighed, pushed back the disgust I felt rising like vomit in my craw and bought him another pint. He was smirking all over his ferret face when I got back.

'Ta very much, Constable Bascombe. You're a true gentleman, you are.'

The bugger was *enjoying* this. 'Fingers,' I said, 'you don't know how much your praise means to me. Now, to get back to what you were saying.'

'It's Michael. I told you. And none of your Micks or Mikes. My name's Michael.'

'Right, Michael. You know, I'm a patient man, but I'm beginning to feel just a wee bit let down here. I'm thinking that perhaps it might not be a bad idea for me to take you to Detective Sergeant Longbottom and see if he can't persuade you to tell him what you know.'

Fingers jerked upright. 'Hang on a minute. There's no need for anything drastic like that. I'm just having my little bit of fun, that's all. You wouldn't deny a fellow his little bit of fun, would you?'

'Heaven forbid,' I muttered. 'So now you've had your fun, Fin— er . . . Michael, perhaps we can get back to business?'

'Right . . . well . . . theatrically speaking, of course, I might have been in Aston Place on the night you're talking about.'

Theatrically? Let it go, Frank. 'Last Wednesday, during the air raid?'

'Right. Well I might have been, just, you know, being a concerned citizen and all, going round checking up all the women and kids was in the shelters, like.'

'And the old people. Don't forget the old people.'

'Especially the old people. Anyway, like I said, I just *might* have been passing down Aston Place during the air raid, seeing that everyone was all right, like, and I *might* just have seen someone coming out of Mad Maggie's house.'

'Did you?'

'Well, it was dark, and that bloody smoke from the power station doesn't make things any better. Like a real pea-souper, that is. Anyway, I might just have seen this figure, like, a quick glimpse.'

'I understand. Any idea who it was?'

'Not at first I hadn't, but now I've an idea. I just hadn't seen him for a long time.'

'Where were you?'

'Coming out of— Can't have been more than two or three houses away. When I saw him he gave me a real fright, so

I pressed myself back in the doorway, like, so he couldn't see me.'

'But you got a look at him?'

'Not a good one. First thing I noticed, though, is he was wearing a uniform.'

'What kind of uniform?'

'I don't know, do I? Soldier's, I suppose.'

'Anything else?'

'Well, he moved off sort of sideways, like.'

'Crabwise?'

'Come again?'

'Like a crab?'

'If you say so, Constable Bascombe.'

Something about all this was beginning to make sense, but I wasn't sure I liked the sense it made. 'Did you notice anything else?'

'I saw him go into a house across the street.'

'Which one?' I asked, half of me not wanting to know the answer.

'The milkman's,' he said.

•

I didn't want to, but I had to see this through. *Tommy Markham.* My own godson. All afternoon I thought about it, and I could see no way out of confronting Harry and Tommy. No matter how much thinking I did, I couldn't come up with an explanation, and if Tommy *had* murdered Rose Faversham, I wanted to know why. He had certainly been acting oddly since he came back from the army hospital, but I had acted rather strangely myself after they released me from the hospital in Manchester in 1918. I knew better than to judge a man by the way he reacts to war.

I consoled myself with the fact that Tommy might not have killed Rose, that she was already dead when he went to see her, but I knew in my heart that didn't make sense. Nobody just dropped in on Mad Maggie to see how she was doing, and the idea of two people going to see her in one night was absurd. No, I knew that the person Fingers had seen coming out of Rose's house had to be her killer, and he swore that person was Tommy Markham.

Fingers could have been lying, but that didn't make sense, either. For a start, he wasn't that clever. He must also know that I would confront Tommy and that, one way or another, I'd find out the truth. No, if Fingers had killed Mad Maggie and wanted to escape blame, all he had to do was deny that he had been anywhere near her house and let the gypsy take the fall.

I steeled myself with a quick brandy, then I went around to Harry's house just after eight o'clock. They were all listening to a variety programme on the Home Service, and someone was torturing 'A Nightingale Sang in Berkeley Square'. As usual, Tommy was wearing his army uniform, even though he was on extended leave. He still looked ill, pale and thin. His mother, Polly, a stout, silent woman I had known ever since she was a little girl, offered to make tea and disappeared into the kitchen.

'What brings you out at this time of night, then?' Harry asked. 'Want some company down at the Prince Albert?'

I shook my head. 'Actually, it's your Tommy I came to see.'

A shadow of fear crossed Harry's face. 'Tommy? Well, you'd better ask him yourself, then. Best of luck.'

Tommy hadn't moved yet, but when I addressed him, he slowly turned to face me. There was a look of great disappointment in his eyes, as if he knew he had had something valuable in his grasp only to have it taken from him at the last minute. Harry turned off the radio.

'Tommy,' I said, speaking as gently as I could, 'did you go to visit Mad Maggie last Wednesday night, the night of the air raid?'

Harry was staring at me, disbelief written all over his face. 'For God's sake, Frank!' he began, but I waved him down.

'Did you, Tommy? Did you visit Mad Maggie?'

Slowly, Tommy nodded.

'You don't have to say any more,' Harry said, getting to his feet. He turned to me as if I were his betrayer. 'I've considered you a good friend for many years, Frank, but you're pushing me too far.'

Polly came back with the teapot and took in the scene at a glance. 'What's up? What's going on?'

'Sit down, Polly,' I said. 'I'm asking your Tommy a few questions, that's all.'

Polly sat. Harry remained standing, fists clenched at his sides, then Tommy's voice broke the deadlock. 'It's all right, Mum,' he said to Polly. 'I want to tell him. I want to get it off my chest.'

'I don't know what you're talking about, son,' she said.

Tommy pointed at Harry. 'He does. He's not as daft as he looks.'

I looked at Harry, who sat down again and shook his head.

Tommy turned back to me. 'Did I go visit Mad Maggie? Yes I did. Did I kill her? Yes, I did. I got in through the back window. It wasn't locked. I picked up the posser and went through into the living room. She was sitting in the dark. Didn't even have a wireless. She must have heard me, but she didn't move. She looked at me just once before I hit her, and I could swear she knew why I was doing it. She understood and she knew it was right. It was *just*.'

As Tommy spoke, he became more animated and his eyes started to glow with life again, as if his prize were once more within his grasp.

'Why did you do it, Tommy?' I asked. 'What did she ever do to harm you?'

He looked at Harry. 'She killed my dad.'

'She what?'

'I told you. She killed my dad. My real dad.'

Polly flopped back in her armchair, tea forgotten, and put her hand to her heart. 'Tommy, what are you saying?'

'He knew,' he said, looking at Harry again. 'Or at least he suspected. I told him about the field, about the villagers, the madwoman.'

Harry shook his head. 'I *didn't* know,' he said. 'You never told me it was *her*. All I knew was that you were upset, you were saying crazy things and acting strange. Especially when you came in from the raid that night. I was worried, that's all. If I ever suspected you, that's the only reason, son, I swear it. When I found her body, I thought if there was the remotest possibility . . . That's why I went for Frank. I told him to lay off it, to let the gyppos take the blame. But he wouldn't.' Harry pointed his finger at me, red in the face. 'If you want to blame anyone, blame him.'

'Calm down, Harry,' I told him. 'You'll give yourself a heart attack.'

'It's not a matter of blame,' Tommy said. 'It's about justice. And justice has been served.'

'Better tell me about it, Tommy,' I said. The air-raid siren went off, wailing up and down the scale. We all ignored it.

Tommy paused and ran his hand through his closely cropped hair. He looked at me. 'You should understand, Mr Bascombe. You were there. He was your best friend.'

I frowned. 'Tell me, Tommy.'

'Before Dunkirk, a group of us got cut off and we were in this village near Ypres for a few days, before the Germans got too close. We almost didn't make it to the coast in time for the evacuation. The people were frightened about what the Germans might do if they found out we were there, but they were kind to us. I became quite friendly with one old fellow who spoke very good English, and I told him my father had been killed somewhere near here in the first war. Passchendaele. I said I'd never seen his grave. One day, the old man took me out in his horse and cart and showed me some fields. It was late May, and the early poppies were just coming out among the rows of crosses. It looked beautiful. I knew my father was there somewhere.' Tommy choked for a moment, looked away and wiped his eyes.

'Then the old man told me a story,' he went on. 'He said there was a woman living in the village who used to you . . . you know . . . with the British soldiers. But she was in love with a German officer, and she passed on any information she could pick up from the British directly to him. One soldier let something slip about some new trench positions they were preparing for a surprise attack, and before anyone knew what had hit them, the trenches were shelled and the Germans swarmed into them. They killed every British soldier in their path. It came to hand to hand combat in the end. Bayonets. And the woman's German lover was one of the last to die.'

Tommy paused, glanced at his mother and went on, 'He told me she never recovered. She went mad, and for a while after the armies had moved on she could be heard wailing for her dead German lover in the poppy fields at night. Then nothing more was heard of her. The rumour was that she had gone to England, where they had plenty of other madwomen to keep her company. I thought of Mad Maggie right from the start, of course, and I remembered the way she used to burst into French every now and then. I asked him if he had a photograph, and he said he thought he had an old one. We went back to his house, and he rummaged through his attic and came down with an old album. There she was. The same sort of clothes. That same look about her. Much younger and very beautiful, but it was *her*. It was Mad Maggie. And she had killed my father. He was in one of those trenches.'

'What happened next, Tommy?'

'I don't remember much of the next couple of months. The Germans got too close and we had to make a hasty departure. That's when I was wounded. I was lucky to make it to Dunkirk. If it hadn't been for my mates . . . They carried me most of the way. Anyway, for a while I didn't know where I was. In and out of consciousness. To be honest, half the time I preferred to be out of it. I had dreams, nightmares, visions, and I saw myself coming back and avenging my father's death.'

His eyes shone with pride and righteousness as he spoke. Outside, the bombs were starting to sound alarmingly close. 'Let's get down to the shelter,' Harry suggested.

'No,' said Tommy, holding up his hand. 'Hear me out now. Wait till I'm done.' He turned to me. 'You should understand, Mr Bascombe. She killed my dad. He was your best friend. You should understand. I only did what was right.'

I shook my head. 'There's no avenging deaths during wartime, Tommy. It's every man for himself. Some German bullet or bayonet had Larry's name on it, and that was that. Wrong place, wrong time. It could just as easily have been me.'

Tommy stared at me in disbelief.

'Besides,' I went on, getting a little concerned at the explosions outside, 'are you sure it was her, Tommy? It seems an awful coincidence that she should end up living on our street, don't you think?'

'I'm sure. I saw the photograph. I've still got it.'

'Can I have a look?'

Tommy opened his top pocket and handed me a creased photograph. There was no doubt about the superficial resemblance between the woman depicted there, leaning against a farmer's fence, wearing high buttoned boots, smiling and holding her hand to her forehead to keep the sun out of her eyes. But it wasn't the same woman whose photograph I had found in Rose Faversham's shoebox. In fact, it wasn't any of the three – Midge, Rose or Margaret. There were no dimples, for a start, and the eyes were different. We all have our ways of identifying people, and with me it's always the eyes. Show me someone at six, sixteen and sixty and I'll know if it's the same person or not by the eyes.

Another bomb landed far too close for comfort, and the whole house shook. Then a split second later came a tremendous explosion. Plaster fell off the ceiling. The lights and radio went off. I could hear the drone of the bombers slowly disappearing to the south-east, on their way home again. We were all shaken, but I pulled myself to my feet first and suggested we go outside to see if anyone needed help.

I didn't really think he'd make a run for it, but I stuck close to Tommy as we all went outside. The smell was awful; the bitter, fiery smell of the explosive and a whiff of gas from a fractured pipe mixed with dust from broken masonry. The sky was lit up like Guy Fawkes night. It was a terrible sight that met our eyes, and the four of us could only stand and stare.

A bomb had taken out about three houses on the other side of the street. The middle one, now nothing but a pile of burning rubble, was Mad Maggie's.

•

When the answers to my letters started trickling in a couple of weeks after Tommy's arrest, I picked up some more leads, one of which eventually led me to Midge Livesey, now a mother of two boys – both in the RAF – who was living only thirty miles away, in the country. I telephoned her, and she seemed pleased to hear from someone who had known Rose, though she was saddened by the news of Rose's death, and she suggested I be her guest for the weekend.

Though it was late October, the weather was fine when I got off the train at the tiny station. It was a wonderful feeling to be out in the country again. I had been away for so long I had almost forgotten what the autumn leaves looked like and how many different varieties of birdsong there are. The sweet, acrid scent of burning leaves from someone's garden made a fine change from the stink of the air raids.

Midge and her husband, Arthur, welcomed me at the door of their cottage and told me they had already prepared the spare room. After I had laid out my things on the bed, I opened the window. Directly outside stood an apple tree, and beyond that I could see the landscape undulating to the north, where the large anvil shapes of peaks and fells were visible in the distance. I took in a deep breath of fresh air – as deep as I could manage with my poor lungs – and for once it didn't make me cough. Perhaps it was time I left the city, I thought. But no, there were police duties to attend to, and I loved my teaching job. After the war, perhaps, I would think about it again, see if I could get a job in a village school.

When I showed Midge the photograph of the three of them over dinner that evening, a sad smile played across her features, and she touched the surface with her fingers, as if it could send out some sort of message to her.

'Yes,' she said, 'that was Rose. And that was Margaret. Poor Margaret, she died in childbirth ten years ago. The war wasn't all bad for us. We did have some good times. But I think the day that photograph was taken marked the beginning of the end. It was the day before the third Ypres battle started, and we were field nurses. We used to go onto the fields and into the trenches to clean up after the battles.' She shook her head and looked at Arthur, who tenderly put his hand on top of hers. 'You've never . . . well, I suppose you have.' She looked at her husband. 'Arthur understands, too. He was wounded at Arras. I worry about my boys. Just remembering, just thinking about it, makes me fear for them terribly. Does that make sense?'

'Yes,' I said.

She paused for a moment and poured us all tea. 'Anyway, Rose was especially sensitive,' she went on. 'She wrote poetry and wanted to go to university to study English literature when it was all over. French, too. She spoke French very well and spent a lot of time talking to the poor wounded French soldiers. Often they were with the English, you know, and there was nobody could talk to them. Rose did. She fell in love with a handsome young English lieutenant. Nicholas, his name was.' She smiled. 'But we were young. We were always falling in love back then.'

'What happened to her?' I asked.

'Rose? She broke under the strain. Shell shock, I suppose you'd call it. You hear a lot about the poor boys, the breakdowns, the self-inflicted wounds, but you never hear much about the women, do you? Where are we in the history books? We might not have been shooting at the Germans and only in minimal danger of getting shot at ourselves – though there were times – but we were *there*. We saw the slaughter first hand. We were up to our elbows in blood and guts. Some people just couldn't take it, the way some of the boys couldn't take combat. I'll say this, though, I think it was Nicholas's death that finally sent Rose over the edge. It was the following year, 1918, the end of March, near a little village on the Somme called St Quentin. She found him, you know, on the field. It was pure chance. Half his head had been blown away. She was never the same. She used to mutter to herself in French and go into long silences. Eventually, she tried to commit suicide by taking an overdose of morphine, but a doctor found her in time. She was invalided out in the end.'

'Do you know what happened next?'

'I visited her as soon as the war was over. She'd just come out of the hospital and was living with her parents. They were wealthy landowners – very posh, you might say – and they hadn't a clue what to do with her. She was an embarrassment to them. In the end they set up a small fund for her, so she would never have to go without, and left her to her own devices.'

After a moment or two's silence, I showed Midge the book of poetry. Again, she fingered it like a blind person looking for meaning. 'Oh, yes. Ivor Gurney. She was always reading this.' She turned the pages. 'This was her favourite.' She read us a short poem called 'Bach and the Sentry', in which the poet on sentry duty hears his favourite Bach prelude in his imagination and wonders how he will feel later, when he actually plays the piece again in peacetime. Then she shook her head. 'Poor mad Rose. Nobody knew what to do with her. Do tell me what became of her.'

I told her what I knew, which wasn't much, though for some reason I held back the part about Tommy and his mistake. I didn't want Midge to know that my godson had mistaken her friend for a traitor. It seemed enough to lay the blame at the feet of a gypsy thief and hope that Midge wasn't one of those women who followed criminal trials closely in the newspapers.

Nor did I tell her that Rose's house had been destroyed by a bomb almost a week after the murder and that she would almost certainly have been killed anyway. Midge didn't need that kind of cruel irony. She had suffered enough; she had enough bad memories to fuel her nightmares, and enough to worry about in the shape of her two boys.

I simply told her that Rose was a very private person, certainly eccentric in her dress and her mannerisms, and that none of us really knew her very well. She was a part of the community, though, and we all mourned her loss.

So Mad Maggie was another of war's victims, I thought, as I breathed in the scent of the apple tree before getting into bed that night. One of the uncelebrated ones. She came to our community to live out her days in anonymous grief and whatever inner peace she could scrounge for herself, her sole valuable possessions a book of poetry, an old photograph and a nursing medal.

And so she would have remained, a figure to be mocked by the children and ignored by the adults, had it not been for another damn war, another damaged soul and the same poppy field in Flanders.

Requiescat in pace, Rose, though I am not a religious man. *Requiescat in pace*.

•

It should never have happened, but they hanged Tommy Markham for the murder of Rose Faversham at Wandsworth Prison on 25 May 1941, at eight o'clock in the morning.

Everyone said Tommy should have got off for psychiatric reasons, but his barrister had a permanent hangover, and the judge had an irritable bowel. In addition, the *expert* psychiatrist hired to evaluate him didn't know shell shock from an Oedipus complex.

The only thing we could console ourselves with was

that Tommy went to the gallows proud and at peace with himself for having avenged his father's death.

I hadn't the heart to tell him that he was wrong about Mad Maggie, that she wasn't the woman he thought she was.

THE DUKE'S WIFE

I **was absolutely** speechless. After everything that had happened, there he stood, bold as brass, telling all the world we were going to be married. *Married!* You would have been speechless, too.

Let me give you a little background. My name is Isabella, and until that moment I had been all set to enter a convent. I fear I have a wayward and impulsive nature that needs to be kept in check, and the convent I had in mind, the votarists of St Clare, was one of strict restraint. Imagine my feelings when, head swimming from the twists and turns of recent events, I heard I was to be married to the duke!

But there's more, much more.

A short while ago the duke realized that he had become lax in his duties, being of too mild and gentle a nature to enforce the laws of the land to their fullest. Of special concern to him, because it ate away at the very institution of marriage itself, was the law that forbade, on pain of death, a man to live with a woman to whom he was not married.

Fearing that the people would revolt if he were suddenly to change course and start enforcing the law rigorously himself, the duke thought it better to slip away for a while and leave his deputy, Angelo, in charge. Thus, Angelo was invested with all the duke's powers and charged with cleaning up Vienna.

Mistake. Big mistake.

Where do I come into all this? you might be wondering. Well, it so happens that my brother Claudio had plighted his troth to his fiancée Juliet, and they were sleeping together. The problem was that they had kept their marriage contract a secret in the hope that Juliet's family would in time come to favour their union and provide a dowry, and this brought them within the scope of the law against fornication.

Now, Angelo *could* have exercised mercy, realizing that this was a very minor infringement indeed, and that the two were, in all but the outward ceremony itself, legally married, but Angelo is a cold fish and a sadistic, ruthless dictator. He likes to hurt people and make them squirm; it gives him pleasure. Believe me, I *know*.

Finding himself so suddenly and inexplicably condemned to death, Claudio asked me to intercede with Angelo on his behalf and see if I could secure a pardon. This I did, with disastrous results: Angelo told me he was in love with *me*, and he would only let Claudio go if I slept with *him*.

Now, while I do realize that in many people's eyes to give up one's virginity for one's brother's life might not seem too much to ask, you must bear in mind that I was to join the votarists of St Clare. I was to be married to God. This was my life, my destiny, and all of that – my very soul itself – would be sacrificed if I gave in to Angelo's base demands.

And don't think I didn't care about Claudio. Don't think for a moment that the thought of complying didn't cross my mind, but I wasn't going to give in to that kind of blackmail. I didn't trust Angelo anyway. For all I knew, he might take my virginity *and* have Claudio executed as well – which, as it turned out, was exactly what he had in mind.

The whole process was degrading, me pleading passionately for my brother's life, going down on my knees on the cold stone to beg, Angelo making it clear that only by yielding up my body to his will could I save Claudio. Humiliating.

When I told him my decision, Claudio wasn't at all understanding. Of everyone, he should have been the one to see how important my virginity was, but no. He even had the effrontery to suggest that I should reconsider and commit this vile sin to save his life. Claudio was afraid of death, and all he could talk about was his fear of dying when *I* was facing a much greater enemy than death.

I told him he would find his comfort in the bosom of the Lord. He didn't seem to agree.

Where was the wily duke during all this? You may well ask. As it turns out he was secretly directing events, disguised as a friar, and he was the one who came up with a cunning plan. He may be of a tender and mild disposition, but he has a devious mind and he likes to play games. Nor does he always stop to think who might get hurt by them.

Angelo had once been betrothed to a woman called Mariana, but her dowry went down on the same ship as her brother Frederick, and Angelo left her in tears, pretending he had discovered some stain on her honour when it was, in fact, the loss of the dowry that turned him against her. If you needed any more evidence of his worthlessness, that's the kind of person he is.

Now, if I were to go back to Angelo and pretend to agree to his demands, the friar suggested, we could arrange things so that Mariana went to his chamber in my stead, breaking no laws and saving both my virginity and Claudio's life.

It seemed a very good plan, and it worked, though the friar did have to do a little juggling with severed heads later on to convince Angelo that Claudio had indeed been beheaded. Then, for reasons of his own, the friar let me go on believing that Claudio had been executed – I did say he likes to play games, didn't I? – until the final scenes had been played out.

He had Mariana beg for Angelo's life, and the poor woman importuned *me* to beg with her! Thus, I found myself on my knees for a second time, this time pleading for the life of a man I hated, the man who, I thought, had killed my brother even though, he thought, he had enjoyed the treasures of my body.

So is it any wonder I was speechless when in walked Claudio, as alive as you or I, and the duke announced that I was to be his duchess?

•

I could have said no, I suppose, but at the time I was too stunned to say anything, and the next thing I knew we were married.

Though it took me many months, I got over the shock of it all and adapted myself as best I could to my new life. I hadn't actually taken my vows, so there was no legal problem with the marriage. The duke took over Vienna again and enforced the law himself, tempered with mercy and charity, and things were back on an even keel. I'm not saying that fornication ceased. That could never happen here. We Viennese are an odd lot, our lives full of secret vices and lies, and anyone with an interest in the human mind and perverse behaviour would have a field day studying us.

Being the duke's wife had many advantages, I soon found, though I did have some trouble adjusting to his husbandly demands. He wasn't a young man, but he was certainly vigorous, though he needed certain props to help him perform those functions he liked so much. In particular, he liked to dress as a friar and intone Latin vespers when he took me from behind, as was his wont. That, I could deal with, but I drew the line when he asked *me* to dress as a nun. That would have been far too much of a travesty for me to take, given everything that had happened.

So time passed, and on the whole I quite enjoyed the life of idleness and luxury. I loved my horses, enjoyed the theatre and the frequent grand balls, and I came to rely on the kind attentions of my maids and the delicious concoctions of my cooks. As I say, the sacrifices were bearable. Once in a while, I had a wistful thought for the life I might have led, but I must confess that when I hosted a magnificent banquet or walked the grounds and gardens of our wonderful palace, the thought of a bare, cold, tiny cloister lost much of its appeal. Mind you, I still attended church regularly and prayed every night, and we gave generously to the votarists of St Clare.

•

You might be interested in knowing what happened to the others. Claudio and Juliet were married, after which they moved to the country. By all accounts they are happy enough, though we don't see them very often. Angelo and Mariana were also married – it was *her* wish, the duke's dictate, and in accord with the law – but their story didn't end happily at all. Well, how could it with an evil, sadistic pervert like Angelo for a husband? Mariana is very sweet, but she is *such* a naif when it comes to men. Even back when I was headed for the convent I had more idea than she did.

So I wasn't at all surprised when she came to me in tears about six months after her marriage.

'Dry your eyes, dear,' I said to her, 'and let's walk in the garden.' It was a beautiful spring day, with a warm gentle breeze wafting the scents of flowers through the mild air.

'I can't go on,' she said.

'What's wrong?'

'It's Angelo.'

'What about him?'

'He doesn't love me any more.'

He never did love her, I could have said, but I held my tongue. I doubted that was what she wanted to hear at the moment. 'What makes you think that?' I asked.

She looked around, then leaned in towards me and lowered her voice. 'He has other women.'

I could have laughed out loud. Just about every husband in Vienna has other women. I suspect even my own duke has one from time to time, but if it spares me the friar's costume and the Latin vespers for a night, who am I to complain? But Mariana, I could see, was really upset. 'It's just men, Mariana,' I told her. 'They're like that. They can't help themselves. It's their nature. Every time they see an attractive woman they just have to conquer her.'

'But am *I* not attractive?'

'That's neither here nor there. You're his *wife*. That's all that counts.'

'Yes, I am his wife, so why does he have to sleep with

other women? I'll sleep with him any time he wants. I'll do *anything* he wants me to, even if it hurts me, even that disgusting thing with the—'

'Mariana! I told you, it's just their nature. You'll have to learn to live with it or your life will be a very unhappy one.'

'But I *am* unhappy already. I can't live with it. I want to die.'

I took her arm. 'Don't be so histrionic, Mariana,' I said. 'You'll get used to it.'

She broke away. 'I won't! Never! I want to die. I'm going to kill myself.'

I sighed. 'Over a man? There must be better reasons. Look, who is this woman he's been seeing?'

Mariana looked at me. Her eyes were so full of pain that my heart cried for her, even though I thought she was being foolish. 'It's not just *one* woman.'

'How many?'

'I don't know.'

'Two, three?'

'I told you. I don't know.'

'You must have some idea. Is it three, four, or five?'

'About three. I think that's about right.'

'So he's sleeping with three other women?'

'Three a week. Yes.'

'*What?*'

'He has them sent to him. There's a man called Pandarus, a Greek I think, a despicable human being, and Angelo pays him to procure young women. Usually young virgins from the provinces who are new in town and haven't settled into employment. They're so young. They don't . . . I mean they don't all know what to expect.'

'He forces them?'

Mariana nodded. 'I've heard cries. Screams, sometimes, and he swears they will die terribly if they ever speak of what happened.'

Mariana's story was starting to interest me. I had heard of this Pandarus, though I had never met him, and I knew that he affected a respectable enough surface and was able to move among varying levels of society. Procuring wasn't new to Vienna, even among the higher echelons – nothing to do with sex is new to Vienna – but this Pandarus intrigued me all the same. 'How do you know all this?' I asked.

'A dear friend told me. She had a conversation with one . . . with one of the girls.'

'And you're certain it's true?'

Mariana nodded. 'One night I lay in wait, hiding in the bushes, and watched. We have always had separate quarters, and Angelo maintains the same chamber he used . . . do you remember, that night when I went to him in your stead?'

I nodded. It wasn't a memory I cared to dwell on. Not one of my finest moments.

'They come in the darkest of night, and he burns no candles. Everything is just as it was that night.'

'I see,' I said. I had hated Angelo long and deeply enough for what he had inflicted on me that, even as we spoke, the beginnings of a plan began to form itself effortlessly in my mind.

'What can I do, dear Isabel? Pray, tell me, what can I do?'

I took her hand. 'Do nothing,' I said. 'At least not for the moment. I know it pains you, but bear with it. I'm certain there's a solution and I promise that your suffering will come to an end ere long.'

Her eyes widened and lit up at that little sliver of hope. 'Really? You promise? Oh, Isabel, is it possible I can be happy again?'

'We'll see,' I said, busy thinking. 'We'll see.'

•

I was finally satisfied enough with my changed appearance and the peasant clothes I had painstakingly made to venture out into the city streets in the guise of a country girl seeking employment. Through further, cautious questioning of Mariana, I had already determined that Pandarus tended to prey on his victims in the busy public square near the coach station, often approaching them the very moment they arrived in the city. He had, I imagined, a skilled eye and knew exactly who was vulnerable to his approach and who best to leave alone. I affected to look lost and weak, and on my second visit a man came up to me. His clothes and his bearing signified a certain level of wealth and influence in society, and his general manner was that of a gentleman.

'Are you new here?' he asked.

'Me?' I responded shyly, keeping my head down. 'Yes, sir.'

'Where are you from?'

I named a distant village I had once heard one of my husband's ministers mention.

'And what, may I ask, brings you to Vienna?'

'I seek employment, sir.'

'You do, do you? And what skills do you possess?'

'I can cook, sir, and wash, and mend clothes.'

'Valuable skills, indeed. Come, walk with me.'

I couldn't just go with him, not that easily. I had to play the shy country girl. 'I cannot, sir.'

'Cannot? Why not?'

'I don't know, sir. It just seems so . . . forward. I don't know you.'

'Forward? Walking alongside a perfect gentleman in a public place?' He smiled. He really did have a warm smile, the kind that leads you to trust a person. 'Come, come, don't be silly.'

So I walked beside him. He offered his arm, but I didn't take it. That didn't seem to upset him too much. 'You know, I think I might be able to help you,' he said, stroking his moustache.

'Help me, sir? You mean *you* require my services?'

He laughed. 'Me? Oh, no. Not me. A friend of mine. And I will speak for you.'

'But you don't know me, sir. How can you speak for me? You don't even know my name.'

He stopped walking and put his fingers under my chin, lifting my face. He was taller than I, so I had to look up, though I tried to keep my eyes down under my fluttering lashes. I felt myself blush. 'I am an excellent judge of character,' he said. 'I believe you to be an honest country maiden, and I believe you are exactly what he has in mind.' He let me go and carried on walking. This time I picked up my pace to keep up with him, showing interest. 'He does, however, have one peculiarity I must mention,' he went on.

'What might that be, sir?'

'He prefers to conduct his business at night.'

'That is strange, indeed, sir.'

He shrugged. 'It is a mere trifle.'

'If you say so, sir.' As a country girl, I could, of course, have no idea of the ways of city folk.

'So, should you be interested – and he is a most kind,

considerate and bountiful master – you must go to him through his garden at night and he will acquaint you with his needs. You need have no fears. He is an honourable man, and I shall be close by.'

Again, I had to remind myself that I was playing the role of a simple country girl. 'If you think so, sir.'

'Tonight, then?'

I hesitated for just as long as necessary. 'Tonight,' I whispered finally.

'Meet me here,' he said, then he melted into the crowds.

•

My plan was simple enough. I intended to gain entry to Angelo's chamber under cover of darkness and . . . Well, I hadn't really thought much past that, except that I planned to confront him and expose him for what he was. If necessary, I would claim that I went to visit my friend Mariana and that he attempted to ravage me, but I doubted it would come to that. One of the many advantages of being the duke's wife is that subjects tend to fear my husband's power, and I had no doubt that Angelo would give up his nightly escapades if faced with their possible political consequences. A wife's railing is easy enough to ignore, but the power of the duke is another matter entirely.

I could not help but feel restless all evening as I waited for the appointed hour. After the usual antics with cassock and vespers, I slipped a sleeping draught into the duke's nightcap, and he went out like a snuffed candle. When the servants were all in bed, I donned my disguise and slipped out of the house.

The dark streets frightened me, as I had not gone out

alone at night before, and I feared lest some drunken peasant or soldier should molest me. In case of just such an incident, I carried a dagger concealed about my person, a present to the duke from a visiting diplomat. But either the denizens of the night are better behaved than I had imagined, or I was blessed by fortune, for I made my way to the square without any hindrance whatsoever. When I got there, I was surprised at how many people were still out and about at such a late hour, lounging by the fountain, talking and laughing by the light of braziers and flaming torches. I had no idea that such a world of shadows existed, and I found that the discovery oddly excited me.

Pandarus appeared at my side as if by magic, wrapped in dark robes, his head hooded, as was mine.

'Are you ready?' he asked.

I nodded.

'Then come with me.'

I followed him through the narrow alleys and across the broad cobbled courtyards to Angelo's quarters, where we paused at a gate in the high wall surrounding the garden.

'This gate is unlocked,' said Pandarus. 'Cross the garden directly to the chamber before you, where you will find the door also unlocked. Enter, and all will be explained.'

I managed to summon up one last show of nerves. 'I'm not certain, sir. I mean . . . I do not . . .'

'There's nothing to fear,' he said softly.

'Will you accompany me, sir?'

'I cannot. My friend prefers to conduct his business in private.'

He stood there while I gathered together all my strength, took a deep breath and opened the gate. There

were no lights showing beyond the garden, so I had to
walk carefully to make sure I didn't trip and fall. Finally,
I reached the door of Angelo's chamber, and it opened
when I pushed it gently, hinges creaking a little. By this
time I could make out the varying degrees of shadows, so
I was aware of the large canopied bed and of the silhouette standing before me: Angelo.

'Come in, my little pretty one,' he said. 'Make yourself
comfortable. Has my friend Pandarus told you what you
must do?'

I curtsied. 'Yes, sir. He told me you might have a position for me, but that you only conduct interviews at
night.'

Angelo laughed. 'He's a fine dissembler, my Pandarus.
But in that, he is not all wrong. I do, indeed, have a *position* for you.'

With this he moved towards me, and I felt his lizard-
like hand caress my cheek. I should have drawn back, I
know, and at that moment told him who I was and why
I was there, but something in me, some innate curiosity
compelled me to continue my deception.

Angelo led me slowly to the bed and bade me sit, then
he sat beside me and began his caresses again, this time
venturing into more private territory than before. I took
hold of his hand and moved it away, but he was persistent, growing rougher. Before I knew it, he had me on my
back on the bed and his hand was groping under my
skirts, rough fingers probing me. I struggled and tried to
tell him who I was, but he put his other hand over my
mouth to silence me.

All the time he manhandled me thus, he was calling
out my name. 'Isabella . . . Oh, my beautiful Isabella! Do it
for me, Isabella. Please do it for me!' At first this confused

me, for I was certain he hadn't recognized me. Then I realized with a shock that he *didn't* know who I was, but that this must be what he said to all his night-time visitors. He called them *all* Isabella.

And then I understood.

The whole thing, the re-creation of the exact same conditions as the night I was to visit him in exchange for Claudio's life – the hour, the insistence on absolute darkness. Though Mariana had gone to him in my stead, Angelo either refused to believe this, or thought that by duplicating the trappings he could enjoy the treasures of my body time after time in the darkness of his vile imagination.

As we struggled there on the bed, disgust and outrage overcame any simple desire I harboured for justice, and I knew then what I had been planning to do all along. Angelo's behaviour just made it all that much easier.

I slipped out my dagger and plunged it into his back with as much force as I could muster. He stiffened, as if stung by a wasp, and reared back, hand behind him trying to staunch the flow of blood.

Then I plunged the dagger into his chest and said, 'This for Mariana!'

He croaked my name: 'Isabella . . . my Isabella . . .'

'Yes, it's me,' I said, 'but I'm *not* yours.' And I plunged the dagger in again. 'This is for me!' I said, and he rolled to the floor, pleading for his life. I knelt over him and plunged the dagger in one more time, into his black heart. 'And this is for not being able to tell us apart in the dark!'

After that he lay still. I didn't move for several minutes, but knelt there over Angelo's body catching my breath until I was sure that no one had heard. The house remained silent.

Knowing that Pandarus was probably still lurking by the garden gate, I left by the front door and hurried home through the dark streets. Nobody accosted me; I saw not a soul. When I got home, in the light of a candle in my chamber, I saw that my clothing was bloodstained. No matter. I would burn it. As soon as that was done and I was washed clean of Angelo's blood, all would be well. Mariana might shed a tear or two for her miserable, faithless husband, but she would get over him in time and he would never hurt her or anyone else again.

And as for me, as I believe I have already told you, there are many advantages to be gained from being the duke's wife, not the least of which is the unlikelihood of being suspected of murder.

GOING BACK

AN INSPECTOR BANKS NOVELLA

1

Banks pulled up outside his parents' council house and parked his Renault by the side of the road. He wondered if it would be safe left out overnight. The estate had had a bad reputation even when he grew up there in the sixties, and it had only got worse over recent years. Not that there was any alternative, he realized, as he made sure it was locked and the security system was working; his parents didn't own a garage.

He couldn't very well remove the CD player for the weekend, but to be on the safe side he stuffed the CDs themselves into his overnight bag. He didn't think any young joyriders would want to steal Thelonious Monk, Cecilia Bartoli or the Grateful Dead, but you couldn't be too careful. Besides, he had a portable disc player now, and he liked to listen to music in bed as he drifted off to sleep.

Banks's parents' house stood near the western edge of the estate, close to the arterial road, across from an abandoned factory and a row of shops. Banks paused for a moment and took in the red-brick terrace houses – rows of five, each with a little garden, low wall and privet hedge. His family had moved here from the tiny, grim back-to-back when he was twelve, when the houses were new.

It was a Friday afternoon near the end of October, and Banks was home for the weekend of his parents' golden wedding anniversary that Sunday, only his second overnight stay since he had left home at the age of eighteen to study business at London Polytechnic. When that didn't work out, and when the sixties lost their allure in the early seventies, he joined the police. Since then, long hours, hard work, and his parents' overt disapproval of his career choice had kept him away. Visiting home was always a bit of a trial, but they *were* his mother and father, Banks reminded himself; he owed them more than he could ever repay, he had certainly neglected them over the years, and he knew they loved him in their way. They weren't getting any younger either.

He took a deep breath, opened the gate, walked up the path and knocked on the scratched red door, a little surprised by the loud music coming from the next house. He saw his mother approach through the frosted-glass pane. She opened the door, rubbed her hands together as if drying them and said, 'Alan, lovely to see you. Come on in, love, come in.'

Banks dropped his overnight bag in the hall and followed his mother through to the living room. It stretched from the front of the house to the back, and the back area, next to the kitchen, was permanently laid out as a dining room. The wallpaper was a wispy brown autumn leaves pattern, the three-piece suite a matching brown velveteen, and a sentimental autumn landscape hung over the electric fire.

His father was sitting in his usual armchair, the one with the best straight-on view of the television. He didn't get up, just grunted, 'Son, nice of you to come.'

'Hello, Dad. How are you doing?'

'Mustn't complain.' Arthur Banks had been suffering from mild angina for years, ever since he'd been made redundant from the sheet-metal factory, and it seemed to get neither better nor worse as time went on. He took pills for the pain and didn't even need an inhaler. Other than that, and the damage booze and fags had wreaked on his liver and lungs over the years, he had always been as fit as a fiddle. Hollow-chested and skinny, he still sported a head of thick dark hair with hardly a trace of grey. He wore it slicked back with lashings of Brylcreem.

Banks's mother, Ida, plump and nervy, fussed a little more about how thin Banks was looking, then the kitchen door opened and a stranger walked into the room.

'Kettle's on, Mrs B. Now, who have we got here? Let me guess.'

'This is our son, Geoff. We told you he was coming. For the party, like.'

'So this is the lad who's done so well for himself, is it? The Porsche and the mews house in South Kensington?'

'No, that's Roy, the other one. He's not coming till Sunday afternoon. He's got important business. No, this is our eldest, Alan. I'm sure I told you about him. The one in that picture.'

The photograph she pointed to, half-hidden by a pile of women's magazines on one of the cabinet shelves, showed Banks at the age of sixteen, when he captained the school rugby team for a season. There he stood in his purple and yellow strip, holding the ball, looking proud. It was the only photograph of him they had ever put on display.

'This is Geoff Salisbury,' said Ida Banks. 'Geoff lives up the street at number fifty-five.'

Geoff moved forward, hand stretched out like a

weapon. He was a small, compact man, with lively, slightly watery eyes and cropped grey hair, about Banks's age. His smile revealed what looked to Banks like a set of perfect false teeth. His handshake was firm, and his hands callused and ingrained with oil or grease from manual labour.

'Pleased to meet you, Alan,' he said. 'I'd love to stay and chat, but I can't just now.' He turned to Banks's mother. 'Have you got that shopping list, Mrs B? I'll be off to Asda now.'

'Only if you're sure it's no trouble.'

'Nothing's too much trouble for you, you know that. Besides, I have to go there myself.'

Banks's mother picked up her handbag, took out her purse and gave Geoffrey a handwritten list and a twenty-pound note. 'Will that cover it?'

'Easily, Mrs B. Easily. I'll be back in a tick. Coach and Horses tonight, Arthur?'

'Maybe. We'll see how I feel,' said Banks's father. On closer examination, he did look tired and drawn, Banks thought. More than when he had last seen him in the summer. His eyes had the look of milky marbles and his skin was the colour of porridge. It could be the strain of preparing for the upcoming party – Arthur Banks, while gregarious enough in the pub, had never liked a house full of relatives – but most of the organization, Banks guessed, would have fallen to his mother. Perhaps it was simple old age catching up fast.

Geoff Salisbury left, and Banks saw him go up to the red Fiesta with the rusted chassis, parked behind Banks's Renault. Geoff paused and looked Banks's car over before getting into his own and driving off.

'Who's that?' Banks asked his mother.

'I told you. Geoff Salisbury. He's a neighbour.'

'He seems at home here.'

'I don't know what we'd do without him,' said Mrs Banks. 'He's just like a son to us. Anyway, sit yourself down. Have a cuppa.'

Banks sat and his mother poured. 'So Roy's not coming till Sunday, then?' he said.

'No. He rang us last night, didn't he, Arthur?' She said it as if it were some momentous event. Arthur Banks nodded. 'He's got an important business meeting all day Saturday,' she went on. 'Something to do with some Yanks flying in, and they have to be back in New York by evening . . . I don't know. Anyway, he says he should be here by Sunday lunchtime.'

'Good of him to bother,' Banks muttered.

His mother cast him a long-suffering glance. Banks knew she had been used to the brothers' bickering when they both lived at home, and it was no surprise whose side she usually took. 'What time are you planning on starting the party?' Banks asked.

'We told everyone to come about six o'clock. That'll give us time to clear up and get things ready after lunch. By the way, I don't suppose you've heard yet, but Mrs Summerville passed away.' She announced it in the sort of soft and solemn tones generally reserved for those who had *passed away*.

'I'm sorry to hear it,' said Banks. Mrs Summerville was the mother of the first girl he had ever slept with, though he had always believed that neither the late Mrs Summerville nor his own mother knew that. 'What did she die of?'

'It wasn't anything suspicious, if that's what you're thinking.'

'Perish the thought.'

His mother studied him, frowning. 'Yes . . . well, it was a blessing really. She'd been very poorly. Died in her sleep, according to Alice Green.'

'Still—' said Banks, uncertain what to say. He sipped some tea. As usual, it was milky and sweet, though he had stopped taking milk and sugar twenty years ago.

'And how are the Marshalls?' he asked. The Marshalls were the parents of Banks's school friend Graham, who had disappeared at the age of fourteen and whose body had been discovered the previous summer. Banks had come down to help the locals work on the case and the solution hadn't pleased anyone. It was during that time he had met Detective Inspector Michelle Hart, whom he had been seeing on and off ever since. Pity she wasn't around this weekend, he thought.

'Same as ever, I suppose,' said Mrs Banks. 'We don't see much of them, do we, Arthur?'

Arthur Banks shook his head.

'It's as if they've shut themselves away since you were last down.' Banks's mother cast him an accusing glance, as if their becoming recluses were his fault. And maybe it was, in a way. The truth is rarely as liberating as people would have us believe; it often binds more than it frees.

'I'm sorry to hear that,' he said.

'You know,' his mother went on, 'while you're here, you ought to go and see Mrs Green. She keeps asking about you, and she was very put out you didn't drop by and see her in the summer. She still thinks very fondly of you, though I can't see why, the noise you lot used to make at her house.'

Banks smiled. He remembered Mrs Green fondly, too. She was the mother of an old school friend, Tony Green, whom Banks hadn't seen since he left home. Tony hadn't been one of the real in-crowd, but he had been in the rugby team with Banks, and Banks had always liked Mrs Green. Most of the kids did. She didn't stop them from smoking in her house, and she didn't mind them playing the sort of music – the Beatles and the Rolling Stones mostly – that most adults hated. Once or twice she had given Banks and Tony half a crown apiece and sent them off to the pictures out of her way. She had also been very pretty, with the kind of bosom young boys dream about, and she certainly had a mouth on her. Mrs Green had a reputation for speaking her mind, nobody ruffled her feathers and got away with it. Tony had gone off to Canada, Banks remembered. And Mr Green had died of emphysema about nine months ago. His mother had told him over the telephone, and he had sent a sympathy card. Yes, he would pay Mrs Green a visit.

2

So Banks sipped tea with his mother and father, catching up on the local gossip. The usual stuff: another school friend had emigrated to Australia, an old neighbour, who had moved into a home a year ago, had died, and the Venables lad from number sixty-six had been sent to Borstal for mugging a pensioner. Banks didn't bother telling his mother that it wasn't called 'Borstal' any more but 'detention centre' or 'youth custody centre'. They weren't much interested in what he'd been doing, outside of the divorce from Sandra. They were more interested in Brian and Tracy, and they expressed regret that neither could come to the party on Sunday: Brian's band was playing an important series of gigs in Germany, and Tracy had flu. Not entirely convinced this wasn't some excuse, Banks had dropped by and offered to drive her from her university residence in Leeds, but when he saw her, he took pity and said he'd look in again on his way back. Fortunately, she had friends there who would feed her chicken noodle soup and Lemsip in the meantime.

'Have you seen who's moved in next door?' Mrs Banks asked.

'No,' said Banks, 'but I heard them.'

'Not that side. The other. A Paki family, that's who. I must say, though,' she went on, 'they seem really nice. Very quiet they are, even the kids, aren't they, Arthur? And polite. Always say good morning and ask how you're doing. Talk just like us, they do. Makes a change from that lot on the other side.'

'Who are they?' Banks asked.

She shook her head. 'I don't even know their name. They moved in about two weeks ago. They're not very friendly neighbours. Don't know how many of them live there, either. Shifty-looking lot. Comings and goings all hours of the day and night. Noise. And the place is a pigsty.'

It sounded like a drug house. Banks made a mental note to keep his eyes open. If he noticed anything suspicious, he'd get on to the local police.

Banks's father picked up the remote control and turned the television on at half-past five, as Banks remembered he did every weekday. 'Is that the time?' said Ida Banks. 'I'd better get the tea on. Pork chops, peas and chips all right?'

'Fine,' said Banks, his stomach sinking. As if there was a choice.

'And a nice bit of steamed pudding and custard for sweet.'

'I'll help.' Banks followed her into the kitchen.

True to his word, Geoff Salisbury came back from Asda with a bag of groceries. He dumped it on the kitchen table and handed Ida Banks two pound coins in change, then they went through to the living room. Banks, peeling potatoes at the time, started to unload the groceries. As he did so, he came across the printed receipt stuck by condensation to the side of a bottle of chilled apple juice.

The print was a little blurred, but even so he could see that the total came to £16.08, which left a discrepancy of £1.92 between that and the £2 Geoff had handed his mother. Holding the receipt, Banks went into the living room.

'I think you've got the change wrong,' he said, holding out the receipt for Geoff to see.

Banks's mother frowned. 'Alan! Must you?' Then she turned to Geoff. 'I'm so sorry. Our Alan's in the police and he can't seem to let us forget it,' she said with a dismissive sniff.

'One of the boys in blue, eh?'

'CID, actually,' said Banks.

'Ah. All that Sherlock Holmes stuff.'

'Something like that.'

'Let's see, then.' Geoff took a pair of bifocals from his shirt pocket and squinted at the list. 'Bloody hell, you're right,' he admitted, blushing. He showed the receipt to Ida Banks. 'It's a fair cop. See there, Mrs B? It looks like an eight to me but it's really a six. That's what comes of being too vain to wear my glasses in the supermarket.'

Ida Banks laughed and slapped him on the arm

playfully. 'Oh, get away with you, Geoff. Anyone could make a mistake like that.'

Geoff counted out the rest of the change into her hand. He glanced sideways at Banks, still slightly red with embarrassment. 'I can see I'll have to watch myself now there's a copper around,' he joked.

'Yes,' said Banks, not laughing. 'I think you better had.'

3

'**There was no** need for that, Alan,' Banks's mother said after Geoff Salisbury had left. 'Embarrassing us all.'

'I wasn't embarrassed,' Banks said. 'Besides, he tried to cheat you.'

'Don't be silly. It's like he said, he couldn't see the figures properly.'

'Does he do this often?'

'Do what?'

'Go shopping for you.'

'Yes. We can't get around like we used to, you know, what with your dad's angina and my legs and feet.'

'Legs and feet?'

'My varicose veins and bunions. Getting old is no treat, Alan, I can tell you that much. You'll find out yourself one day. Anyway, he's been good to us, has Geoff, and now you've gone and upset him.'

'I don't think he's upset at all.'

'Only here five minutes, and there's trouble already.'

'Mum, I really don't think I upset him. Maybe he'll just be more careful in future.'

'And maybe we'll have to find *someone else* who'll do

our shopping for us and give the place a good dust and a vacuum every now and then. Fat chance of that.'

'I'm sure he'll be fine.'

'Well, I just hope you'll apologize next time you see him.'

'Apologize?'

'Yes. You as good as called the man a thief.'

'Fine,' said Banks, raising his hands in surrender. 'I'll apologize.'

His mother gave another disapproving little sniff. 'I'd better see to those pork chops.' Then she strode off into the kitchen and shut the door behind her.

4

The Coach and Horses, about a hundred yards away on the main road, was one of those pubs that had hardly changed at all in the past forty years or so. True, they'd got in a jukebox and a few video machines, and the brewery had forked out for a minor facelift sometime in the eighties, hoping to pull in a younger, freer-spending crowd. But it didn't take. The people who drank at the Coach and Horses had, for the most part, been drinking there most of their lives. And their fathers had supped there before them.

Though there were few young people to be seen, it still managed to be a warm and lively pub, Banks noticed as he walked in with his father just after eight o'clock that night, the steamed pudding and custard still weighing heavy in his stomach. His father had managed the walk without too much puffing and wheezing, which he put down to having stopped smoking two years ago. Banks, who had only stopped that summer, still felt frequent and powerful urges.

'Arthur! Arthur! Come on, lad, come on over.'

It was Geoff Salisbury. He was sitting at a table with an elderly couple Banks didn't recognize and two other men in their sixties he remembered from his previous visit. They cleared a little space when Banks and his father walked over to join them.

'My shout,' said Geoff. 'Name your poison.'

'No,' said Banks, still standing. 'I'm the visitor. Let me buy the first round.'

That got no argument, so Banks wandered off to the bar. He hardly had to fight his way through the crowds of impatient drinkers. The bartender, the same one Banks remembered when he had last been in the Coach that summer, nodded a curt greeting and proceeded to pull the pints. When Banks carried the tray back to the table, his father was already talking football with one of his old pals, Harry Finnegan. Harry looked up and said hello to Banks, asked him how he was doing.

'Fine,' said Banks. 'You're looking well yourself.'

'Fair to middling. Sorry to hear about you and that young lass of yours splitting up.'

Sandra. No secrets here. He wondered if they also knew about Sean and the imminent baby. 'Well,' said Banks, 'these things happen.' More to his generation than theirs, he realized. Theirs tended to stick at marriage even when all the love had gone out of it. He didn't know if that was better or worse than changing wives every decade. Probably best not to get married at all, he suspected.

But his mother and father still loved one another, or so he believed. Fifty years together meant they probably didn't have much new to say to one another any more, and the passion might have disappeared from their relationship years ago, but they were comfortable together. Besides, passion is transitory and infinitely transferable, anyway, Banks believed. What his parents had was stronger, deeper, more permanent; it was what he would never get to experience with Sandra: growing old together. He was used to the loss by now, but every now and then he still felt a pang of regret for what might have been and a lump came to his throat.

Harry introduced Banks to the couple at the table, Dick and Mavis Conroy. The other man, Jock McFall, said hello and shook hands.

'I hear you're a Leeds United supporter these days, Alan,' said Harry, a twinkle in his eye.

Banks nodded. 'For my sins. Not that I get the chance to go to Elland Road very often. *Match of the Day* is usually the closest I get.'

'*Elland Road,*' his father said. 'You'd not be able to bloody afford it on what a copper earns, son.' They all laughed.

Banks laughed with them. 'Too true.'

As the conversations went on in that vein, people started to pair off: Dick and Mavis talking to Jock McFall about the latest supermarket price wars; Harry and Arthur Banks discussing Peterborough United's miserable performance that season. Banks edged his chair closer to Geoff Salisbury's.

'Sorry about that business with the change,' said Geoff. 'My eyesight's not what it used to be. Honest mistake.'

Banks nodded. 'Honest mistake. No offence,' he said, though he still wasn't convinced. It was the closest he was willing to get to an apology, so it would just have to do.

There was certainly no point in antagonizing Geoff and upsetting his mother even more. After all, he was only down for the weekend; these people had to live close to one another day in day out. And if Banks couldn't be around to help his parents with their shopping and house-cleaning, then it was a good thing Geoff Salisbury was.

'How long have you lived on the estate, Geoff?' Banks asked.

'About a year.'

'Where did you live before?'

'Oh, here and there. Bit of a wanderer, really.'

'What made you settle down?'

Geoff laughed and shrugged. 'My age, I suppose. I don't know. Wandering lost its appeal.'

'Well, there's something to be said for knowing you've always got a roof over your head.'

'There is that.' Geoff took a stick of chewing gum from his pocket. When he had unwrapped it and put it in his mouth, he folded the silver paper time and time again until it was just a tiny square, which he set down in the ashtray. He noticed Banks watching him and laughed. 'Habit,' he said. 'Stopped smoking five years ago and got addicted to this bloody stuff. Wish I'd stuck with cigarettes sometimes.'

'You're probably better off as you are,' Banks said. 'What line of work are you in?'

'Odd jobs, mostly.'

'What? Fixing things? Carpentry?'

'Cars, mostly. Tinkering with engines. I used to be a mechanic.'

'Not any more?'

'Got made redundant from the last garage I worked at, and I just couldn't seem to get taken on anywhere else.

My age, I suppose. Again. They can get young kids still wet behind the ears and pay them bugger all to do the same job.'

'I suppose so,' Banks said. 'So you work for yourself now?'

'I don't need much, just enough to keep the wolf from the door.'

'And you help out Mum and Dad?'

'Grand folk, Arthur and Ida,' Geoff said. 'Been like a mother and father to me, they have.'

If there was any irony intended in the remark, Geoff didn't seem aware of it.

'How long have you known them?' Banks asked.

'Since not long after you'd left this summer. They told me about that business with the missing lad. Terrible. Anyway, they always said hello right from the start, you know, like, when they saw me in the street. Invited me in for a cup of tea. That sort of thing. And with them not being . . . well, you know what I mean, not as able to get around as well as they used to do, I started doing them little favours. Just washing, cleaning, shopping and the like, helping them out with their finances. I like to help people.'

'Finances?'

'Paying bills on time, that sort of thing. They do get a bit forgetful sometimes, just between you and me. And taking the rent down to the council office. It's an awful bother for them.'

'I'm sure they appreciate it, Geoff.'

'I think they do.' He nodded. 'Another?'

Banks looked at his empty glass. 'Yes,' he said. 'Go on, then. One more.' He looked over at his father. 'All right, Dad?'

Arthur Banks nodded and went back to his conversation with Harry Finnegan. The pub had filled up in the last half hour or so, and Banks thought he recognized some of the faces. One or two people looked at him as if they knew him, then decided perhaps they didn't, or didn't want to. Banks watched Geoff Salisbury at the bar. He seemed to know everyone; he was shaking more hands and patting more backs than a politician on election day. Popular fellow.

Geoff came back with the drinks and excused himself to talk to someone else. Banks chatted with Dick and Mavis for a while – they wanted to know if he'd helped catch the Yorkshire Ripper – then, after his second drink, his father said he was tired and would like to go home. 'You can stay if you like,' he said to Banks.

'No, I'll walk back with you. I'm feeling a bit tired myself.'

'Suit yourself.'

They said their goodbyes and walked out into the cool autumn night. It was mild for the time of year, Banks thought: light jacket weather rather than overcoats, but the leaves were changing colour, winter was in the air and the weather forecast said they had a shower or two in store. Neither Banks nor his father had anything to say on the way home, but then Arthur Banks needed all his breath for walking.

5

Banks's bedroom, he had been amazed to discover that summer, was almost exactly as it had been when he first left home. Only the wallpaper, curtains and bedding had been changed. The bed itself was also the same one he had had since he was about twelve.

As he squeezed himself between the tightly tucked sheets on his narrow bed, he remembered how he used to hold the old transistor radio to his ear under the sheets, listening to Radio Luxembourg amidst the whistles and crackles. First, Jimmy Saville playing the latest top-ten hit from 'member number 11321', Elvis Presley. Then, a few years later, came the pirate stations, with even more static and interference: John Peel playing the Mothers of Invention, Jefferson Airplane and Country Joe and the Fish, names from another world, music so startling and raw it transcended even the poor radio reception.

Banks's eyes were too tired and scratchy from the smoky pub to read his Graham Greene, so he put on the Cecilia Bartoli CD of Gluck arias and listened as he drifted towards sleep.

As he lay there, he couldn't help but think about Geoff Salisbury. Something about the man put Banks on his guard. It wasn't just the wrong change – that *could* have been an honest mistake – but the manner in which he seemed to have insinuated himself into the lives of Banks's parents, the ease with which he breezed in and out of the house. Banks wouldn't be surprised if Geoff had a key. He switched off the CD and turned on his side, trying to shake off the uneasy feeling, telling himself he was being too mistrusting, and that he probably only felt this way because he felt guilty he wasn't taking care of his ageing parents himself. He knew he ought to be glad that *someone* was doing the job; he only wished that someone wasn't Geoff Salisbury.

6

Banks awoke with a start the following morning and experienced a moment of absolute panic when he had no idea who or where he was. It was as if he had woken from a coma after many years, all memory gone and the world around him totally changed, or as if he had been abducted and had woken up in an alien spaceship.

But it only lasted a second or two, thank God, and after that he managed to orient himself and his heartbeat slowed to normal. He was in his old bedroom, of course, the room he had slept in between the ages of twelve and eighteen. It was at the back of the house and looked over back yards, an alleyway and a stretch of waste ground to the north, where he and his friends used to play. When Banks looked out of his window, he noticed that the builders had moved in since his last visit and laid the foundations for yet more houses. As if Peterborough needed to grow any more. Since the mid-sixties, when the developers decided to make it a catchment area for London's overcrowded suburbs, it had done nothing but grow, swamping outlying villages with housing estates and business parks. The planners and promoters said it blended old and new in unique and interesting ways. Even so, Banks thought, King Paeda, who had founded the city, would turn in his grave.

On a Saturday morning, the building site was deserted; concrete mixers sat idle and quiet, and the thick sheets of polythene covering pallets of bricks or boards flapped in the wind. It was another grand autumn morning: sunshine, bright blue sky and a cool wind to make everything look and feel fresh. Banks checked his watch. It was after nine o'clock, and he was surprised he had slept so long and so deeply; he couldn't remember having any dreams at all. He listened for sounds of life from downstairs and thought he could hear talking on the radio and dishes rattling in the sink. They were up.

Desperate for tea or coffee, Banks dressed quickly and made his way downstairs. In the living room, his father looked up from his paper and grunted, 'Morning, son.'

'Morning, Dad,' Banks replied, glancing out of the window to make sure his car was still there. It was. His father's newspaper rustled back into position, and the local radio station, according to the DJ, was about to play a request for 'Memories Are Made of This' by Val Doonican, for Mrs Patricia Gaitskell, of 43 Wisteria Drive, Stamford. Jesus, thought Banks, he could have been caught in a time warp while he slept, back to the B-side of 1967. Perhaps that was why he had felt so disorientated the minute he awoke.

He walked through to the kitchen, where his mother, washing the breakfast dishes, gave him a cursory glance and said, 'Well, you've decided to get up at last, have you?' It was exactly what she used to say when he was a teenager and liked to lie in bed most of the morning. The only thing that saved him from seriously doubting his sanity was the little television on the kitchen table showing a breakfast programme. That hadn't been there all those years ago; nor had breakfast television.

Banks made some comment about having had a long drive and put on the kettle. 'Want a cup of tea?' he asked his mother.

'No, thanks. We had ours ages ago.'

'Well, you could have another.'

She gave him a withering look, and he busied himself looking for the tea bags, telling himself that his parents really weren't being especially nasty to him. They had their routine; it just took a little getting used to.

'They're where they've always been,' his mother told him.

That didn't help much, as he couldn't remember where they'd always been. A terracotta jar in the cupboard with TEA engraved on the front looked promising, but it turned out to be empty. Beside it, however, Banks found a jar of instant coffee. Might as well, he thought. As long as you convince yourself it's a different drink, not really coffee at all, then it doesn't taste too bad. The kettle boiled and Banks made himself a cup of instant coffee. Specks of undissolved powder floated on the surface no matter how much he stirred it.

'Don't you want any breakfast?' his mother asked, drying her hands on her pinafore. 'We got some Sugar Puffs in for you specially. You always used to like Sugar Puffs.'

When I was about twelve, thought Banks. 'I'll give them a miss this morning,' he said. 'Maybe tomorrow.'

He wandered into the living room again, his mother not far behind. Val Doonican had given way to the Searchers singing 'Some Day We're Gonna Love Again'. An improvement, Banks thought. Funny how the Searchers were exactly the kind of 'pop rubbish' his parents dismissed thirty-five years ago, but now they were as acceptable as Val Doonican.

Banks needed a newspaper to complete his morning ritual. His father was still buried deep in the *Daily Mail*, which, being a Labour man, he only read so he could find things to complain about. The *Mail* wasn't Banks's kind of paper anyway. No real meat on its bones. Especially at the weekend. He needed something with a bit more writing and fewer pictures, like the *Independent* or the *Guardian*.

'I'm off to the newsagent's for a paper,' he announced. 'Anything I can get for you?'

'You'll be lucky if they've got any left at this time,' his mother said. His father just grunted.

Banks took their responses as a 'no' and set off. In the house next door the upstairs windows were all open and music thudded out. It definitely wasn't Val Doonican or the Searchers; more like Nine Inch Nails or Metallica. Banks studied the house. There were no curtains on the windows, and the front door was wide open. As he was looking, a scruffy couple walked out onto the overgrown path. They looked like Fred and Rosemary West on acid. The man's eyes, in particular, reminded Banks of the opening of *Vertigo*.

'Morning,' said Banks. 'Lovely day, isn't it?'

They looked at him as if he were from Mars – or as if they were *on* it – so he shrugged and walked down to the newsagent's across the main road. The short strip of shops there, set back from the road by a stretch of tarmac, had gone through dozens of changes over the years. When he first moved to the estate, Banks remembered, there had been a fish and chip shop, a ladies' hairdresser, a butcher's, a greengrocer's and a launderette; now there was a video-rental shop, a takeaway pizza and tandoori place called Caesar's Taj Mahal, a minimart and a unisex hair salon. The only constants were the fish and chip shop, which now sold takeaway Chinese food, too, Banks noticed, and Walker's, the newsagent's.

Banks waited to cross the busy road. On the other side, lower down from the shops, stood the remains of the old ball-bearing factory. The gates were chained and padlocked shut and it was surrounded by high wire-mesh fencing with barbed wire on top, the windows beyond covered by rusty grilles. Despite these security precautions, most of them were broken anyway, and the front of the blackened brick building was covered in colourful graffiti.

Banks remembered when the place was in production, lorries coming and going, factory whistle blowing and crowds of workers waiting at the bus stop. A lot of them were young women, or girls scarcely out of school, and he had a crush on one of them. Called Mandy by her friends, she used to stand at the bus stop smoking, a far-away look in her eyes, scarf done up like a turban on her head. She had pale smooth skin and lips like Julie Christie, whom Banks had gone to see in *Darling* with a couple of school friends because she did a nude scene in it. They had only been fourteen or fifteen at the time, but the bored woman in the ticket office at the local fleapit hardly even looked at them before issuing their one and threepennies. The nude scene was terrific, but he didn't understand much of the rest of the film; it didn't make the same sense as *Billy Liar* did for him when he saw it only a few months later. Escaping a boring environment was something he could easily relate to.

One day Mandy started wearing an engagement ring, and a few weeks later she no longer stood at the bus stop with the others, and he never saw her again. He spent ages in his room moping, and even a few years later, when he bought *Beggars Banquet* and listened to 'Factory Girl', he thought of her.

Banks went into the newsagent's. Mrs Walker moved much more slowly now, and the joints on her left hand were swollen. Arthritis by the look of it. There was still a small pile of *Independent*s under the magazine rack, so Banks picked one up and took it to the counter.

'You're the Banks lad back again, aren't you?' she said.

'That's me,' said Banks.

'I thought so. My body might be falling to pieces but my mind's still all right. Haven't seen you since that business in the summer. How are you doing?'

'Fine, thanks. I see you're still soldiering on.'

'I'll be here till I drop.'

'I'm surprised you can manage all by yourself.'

'Oh, I've got help. Some local lads help with the papers, and there's Geoff helps with going to wholesalers, stocktaking and whatnot.'

'Geoff?'

'Geoff Salisbury. Nice lad. Well, I say "lad", but he's probably your age or older. Always there when you need him is Geoff. And with a smile on his face, too. There's not too many folk you can say that about these days.'

'True enough,' Banks agreed. So the ubiquitous Geoff Salisbury had his feet under Mrs Walker's table, too. Still, he did say he did odd jobs, and Banks assumed Mrs Walker paid him for his 'help'. He had to make a living somehow. It didn't seem that one could go far around the estate, though, without finding some traces of its patron saint, Geoff bloody Salisbury.

The bell jangled and someone else walked into the shop. Banks half-expected it to be Salisbury himself, but when he turned he was gobsmacked by who he saw. It was Kay Summerville. And looking hardly a day older than when he had last seen her thirty years ago. That was an exaggeration, of course – her eyes had gathered a few crow's feet, and the long blonde hair that still cascaded over her shoulders now showed evidence of dark roots – but she still had her figure and her looks.

A hoarse 'Kay' was about all he could manage.

She seemed equally stunned. 'Alan.'

'Are you two going to stand there gawping at one another all afternoon or are you going to step aside, young man, and let the lady get what she's come for?' said Mrs Walker.

'Of course.' Banks moved aside.

Kay smiled. She was wearing a thin white T-shirt under a blue denim jacket, and hip-hugging blue jeans. The hips looked as if they were worth hugging. She caught him looking at her and gave him a shy smile.

'Packet of Polo mints, please, Mrs Walker, and –' she turned to the magazine rack and picked out a copy of *Marie Claire* – 'and I'll take this, too.'

Banks stood by the door and loitered, pretending to be looking at a display of anniversary cards. When Kay had finished, she walked towards him.

'Walk back with you?' he said.

She did a little curtsy. 'Why, thank you, kind sir.'

Banks laughed. He had been sixteen when he had first met Kay, and just about to go into the lower sixth. Kay had been fifteen, about to enter her O level year. Her family had just moved up from north London, and Banks had seen her walking along the street in her blue jeans and orange jacket, or in her school uniform – white blouse, maroon jacket, grey skirt probably just a couple of inches too short for the principal's liking – pouty lips, pale skin, head in the air, and her long blonde hair trailing halfway down her back.

She had seemed unobtainable, ethereal, like Mandy from the factory and, if truth be told, like most of the women or girls Banks lusted after, but one day they met in the newsagent's, just like today, both wanting the latest issue of *New Musical Express*. There was only one copy left, so Banks, being the gentleman, let Kay take it. They walked back to the estate together, chatting about pop music. Both were Cream fans, upset about the band splitting up that summer. Both loved Canned Heat's 'On the Road Again' and hated Mary Hopkins's 'Those Were the Days'. Kay said she would lend her *NME* to Banks when she had finished with it. He asked her when that would be, and she said probably Saturday. Emboldened, he went on and asked if she'd like to go to the pictures with him on Saturday night. He could have dropped in his tracks when she said yes.

They went to see *Here We Go Round the Mulberry Bush*, on a double bill with *I'll Never Forget Whatshisname*, and that was it, the start of Banks's first serious relationship.

'I heard about your mother,' Banks said, holding the door for her. 'I'm sorry.'

Kay pushed a stray tress of hair from her forehead. 'Thank you. She'd been ill for a long time. She was riddled with cancer and her heart wasn't strong. I know it's a cliché, but in this case it really was a blessing.'

'Is that why you're up here?'

'Yes. I've got to deal with the house before the council relets it. The rent's paid up till the end of the month, so I thought I'd take a few days and get it all sorted. You?'

'It's Mum and Dad's golden wedding tomorrow.'

'That's marvellous.'

'It is pretty remarkable, isn't it? Fifty years. What kind of work do you do?'

'Investment banking.'

'Oh.'

Kay laughed. 'Yes, that's usually the reaction. Quite a conversation stopper.'

'I'm sorry, it's just . . . I don't . . .'

She smiled at him. 'It's OK. Most people don't. Even the ones who *do* it. What about you? I seem to remember Mum saying you had something to do with the police.'

'True. Detective Chief Inspector, CID, Major Crimes.'

'Well, well, well. I *am* impressed. Just like Morse.'

It was Banks's turn to laugh. 'Except I'm not on telly. I'm real. And I'm still alive. Like your job, it's usually a conversation stopper. You must be the first person who hasn't jumped a mile when I told them what I do for a living. No skeletons in your closet?'

She wiggled her eyebrows. 'That's for me to know and you to find out.'

They reached Banks's parents' house and stopped on the pavement, both a little awkward, embarrassed. It was one of those moments, Banks felt, like the one thirty years ago when he had asked her out for the first time. 'Look,' he said, 'seeing as we're both up here this weekend, would you like to go out tonight, maybe find a country pub, have a bite to eat or a drink, do a bit of catching up? I mean, bring your husband, by all means, you know—'

Kay smiled at his discomfort. 'Sorry, there's only me,' she said. 'And yes, I'd love to. Pick me up at half past seven?'

'Good. Great, I mean.' Banks grinned. 'OK, then, see you this evening.'

Banks watched Kay walk away, and he could have sworn she had a bit of a spring in her step. He definitely had one in his, which couldn't be dampened even by the sight of Geoff Salisbury talking to his mother in the hall when he opened the front door.

'Morning, Alan,' Geoff said. 'Have a good time last night?'

'Fine,' said Banks.

'That the Summerville girl you were talking to?'

'Yes,' said Banks. 'We're old friends.'

Geoff frowned. 'I was sorry to hear about her poor mother. Anyway, must dash. Just a passing visit.' He turned back to Ida Banks. 'Right, then, Mrs B, don't you fret. I'll pick up everything we need for tomorrow, and I'll pop around in the morning and do a bit of tidying and vacuuming for you. How's that?'

'It's all right,' said Banks. 'I can do that.'

'Don't be silly,' his mother chided him. 'You don't know one end of a vacuum cleaner from the other.' Which might have been true at one time but certainly wasn't any more. 'That'll be just dandy, Geoff,' she said, handing him a plastic card, which he put quickly in his pocket. 'I know we can always rely on you.'

It was too late to argue. With a smile and a wave, Geoff Salisbury was halfway down the path, whistling 'Colonel Bogey' as he went.

'I mean it,' said Banks. 'Anything needs doing, just ask me.'

His mother patted his arm. 'I know, son,' she said. 'You mean well. But Geoff's . . . well we're *used* to having him around. He knows where everything is.'

Does he, indeed? thought Banks. 'By the way,' he asked, 'what was that you just gave him?'

'What?'

'You know. The card.'

'Oh, yes. That's the Abbeylink card. He'll need some cash, won't he, if he's going to get the food and drink in for tomorrow?'

Banks almost choked. 'You mean he knows your PIN number?'

'Well, of course he does, silly. A fat lot of use the card would be to him without it.' Shaking her head, she edged past Banks towards the living room. 'And what's this about you and Kay Summerville?' she asked, turning. 'Didn't you two used to go out together?'

'That was a long time ago. Actually, we're going to have dinner together tonight.'

His mother's face dropped. 'But I was going to make us toad-in-the-hole. Your favourite.'

True, Banks had once expressed an enthusiasm for toad-in-the-hole when he was about fourteen. 'I'm sorry,' he said, 'but it's the only chance we'll get to catch up.'

'Well,' his mother said, that familiar, hurt, hard-done-by tone in her voice. 'I suppose if that's really what you want to do. I must say, she always seemed like a nice lass. Her mother and me weren't close at all, just to say hello to in passing, like, but you tell her she's welcome to drop by tomorrow, for the party. I'd like to offer her my condolences.'

'I'll ask her,' said Banks, then he hurried upstairs.

7

With his bedroom window open, Banks could hear the polythene from the building site flapping in the breeze and the cars whooshing by on the main road. He could also hear a dull, bass rumbling from next door along with the occasional shout and bang. Their back garden, he noticed, was full of rubbish like a tip: broken furniture, rocks, a dismantled bicycle. Maybe there was even a body or two buried there.

His knees cracked as he squatted to read the spines of the books in the old glass-fronted bookcase. There they were, a cross-section of his early years' reading, starting with the large, illustrated *Black Beauty*, which his mother had read to him when he was small, old *Beano*, *Dandy* and *Rupert* annuals, and Noddy books – the originals, where Noddy and Big Ears slept together, hung out with Golliwog, and 'gay' meant 'cheerful'. He must have kept Enid Blyton in luxury almost single-handed, he thought, as he had moved on to the Famous Five and the Secret Seven.

Then came his high school reading: Billy Bunter, Jennings and William, followed by war stories such as Biggles, *The Wooden Horse*, *The Guns of Navarone* and *Camp on Blood Island*. Next to these were several editions of the *Pan Book of Horror Stories*, from a phase he went through in his teens, along with some H. P. Lovecraft and M. R. James. There wasn't much crime fiction, but he did still have a few dog-eared old Saint paperbacks, the Father Brown stories and a complete Sherlock Holmes. The James Bond books were all there, too, of course, and a few Sexton Blakes.

There were also history books, the kind with lots of illustrations, some Oxford and Penguin anthologies of poetry and those children's illustrated encyclopaedias that came out with a letter a week, none of which he'd got beyond C or D.

In addition, on the bottom shelf, there were books about his many hobbies, including photography, coins, birds, stamps and astronomy, and several Observer books of cars, aircraft, geology, trees, music and pond life. He'd seen these old editions in second-hand book shops and some of them were worth a bit now. Maybe he should take them back up to Yorkshire with him, he thought. Would that upset his parents? Were his books and his room some sort of virtual umbilical cord that was all that tied him to them now? It was a depressing thought.

One book stood out. Sitting between Enid Blyton's *The River of Adventure* and *The Mountain of Adventure* was a used, orange-spined Penguin edition of *Lady Chatterley's Lover*, a 1966 reprint with Richard Hoggart's introduction. Curious, Banks picked it out. He didn't remember buying it and was surprised when he opened it up and saw written on the flyleaf: 'Kay Summerville, London, June 7th, 1969'. Banks remembered that day well. Smiling, he put it aside. He would give it back to her tonight.

The more he thought about his 'date' with Kay the more he looked forward to it. Not only was she an extremely attractive woman, she was also intelligent and she shared some of his past with him. He didn't imagine the date would lead to anything of a sexual nature – he certainly wasn't out to seduce her – but you never knew. He wondered how he would feel about that. Michelle Hart was on holiday in Tuscany. Besides, they had made no commitments, and Michelle always seemed to be holding back, on the verge of ending the tenuous relationship they did have. Banks didn't know why, but he sensed she had deep and painful secrets she didn't want to share. It seemed that all the women he had met since parting with Sandra – including Annie Cabbot back up in Yorkshire – shied away from intimacy.

Banks stood up and looked down at the books. Well, there they all were, for what they were worth, like those strata of different coloured rock or the layers of antiquities at an archaeological dig. His mother called up: 'Alan, are you coming down? Lunch is on the table. It's potted meat sandwiches.'

Banks sighed. 'Coming,' he shouted. 'I just have to wash my hands. I'll be right there.' True, he had once loved potted meat, the same way he had liked Sugar Puffs and toad-in-the-hole, when he was a teenager, but he hadn't touched the stuff in years.

8

The people next door were out in force, Banks noticed, on his way to see Mrs Green after lunch. There was an unmarked delivery van outside their house, and two strapping young lads were carrying what looked like a fifty-inch television set up the path. It hardly looked as if it would fit through the door. Fred and Rosemary stood on the lawn, rubbing their hands together in glee, practically salivating at the sight, and their various children, aged between about five and fifteen, milled about beside them. Banks hadn't seen so many shaved heads since the nit nurse had visited his school. He tried wishing them good morning again, but everyone was far too intent on the imminent television even to notice him. He would have bet a pound to a penny it was stolen.

The wind had picked up even more, Banks noticed, bringing a few fast-flying clouds and a chill with it, and there was a smell of rain in the air. Banks zipped his leather jacket all the way up and walked the short distance to the close, where Mrs Green lived. She answered Banks's knock and expressed delight at seeing him again. She had certainly aged – thickened at the waist, drooped at the bosom – but she had lost none of her sprightliness, and she fussed around making tea and bringing out a plate of scones. Her living room was sparsely decorated – plain cream wallpaper, no prints or paintings – and a few framed family photographs stood on the mantelpiece.

'How's Tony doing?' Banks asked. 'I've always regretted we didn't manage to stay in touch.'

'These things happen,' said Mrs Green. 'People drift apart over the years. It's only natural. It doesn't mean they don't share good memories, though.'

'I suppose not.'

'Anyway, Tony's doing fine. He lives in Vancouver now, you know. He's a tax lawyer. This is him about two years ago.' She picked up one of the photographs and handed it to Banks. It showed the smile he remembered, the mischief in the eyes, surrounded by a bald head on a pudgy body in brightly coloured shorts and a red T-shirt. Tony stood with a relaxed, smiling woman Banks took to be his wife, and two bored and/or cool-looking teenage children. They were on a beach and there were cloud-topped mountains in the background. 'I'll let him know you were asking about him,' Mrs Green said.

'Please do.' Banks replaced the photo on the mantelpiece. 'I've been to Toronto, but never Vancouver.'

'You should go if you get a chance. Bill and I visited him there five years ago. It's a lovely city. I'm sure Tony and Carol would be happy to have you stop with them. They've got a big house.'

'Maybe I will,' said Banks.

'We don't see you down here very often, do we?'

'Well,' said Banks, feeling guilty he hadn't made time for Mrs Green on his previous visit, 'I keep pretty busy up north. You know how it is.' He sipped some tea.

'Your parents are really very proud of you, you know.'

Banks almost choked on his tea. Where had that come from?

Mrs Green considered him through her tortoiseshell glasses. 'You might not think so,' she said, 'and they might not admit it, but they are. Especially since that business last summer.'

'What makes you say that?'

'Oh, don't think I don't know about your differences. They never did approve of what you chose to do with your life, did they? Your dad thought you'd joined the enemy and your mother thought you'd let her down. That was clear enough to anyone who knew them.'

'Was it?'

'Oh, yes. And I knew where they were coming from, of course.'

'What do you mean?'

She smiled. 'Oh, don't be so obtuse, Alan. You always did have that infuriating habit of pretending not to see the obvious. You wouldn't have got far in your chosen career if you couldn't even add together the basics. You had all the opportunities; they had none. They had to settle for their lot in life. And the Thatcher years were pretty tough around here. How do you think your dad felt when he saw coppers laying into workers on the news? Miners, whatever they were, they were still working men, like himself. How do you think he felt when he saw the police in riot gear waving their overtime pay in the faces of men who'd lost everything? Do you think he actually enjoyed working at that factory every day of his life? I'd say it was a cause for celebration when they made him redundant, but for him it was a blow to his pride. And your mother, cleaning up other folk's messes? They made a lot of sacrifices for you, so you could do better than they had. And what did you do? You joined the police force. You must have known how people around here felt about the police.'

'I'd say they expect us to make sure their cars are safe and keep the muggings and gang fights to a minimum.'

'You always were a cheeky young beggar, Alan Banks. Perhaps now they do. But not back then.'

'I know what you mean,' said Banks.

'But what I'm telling you is they know you've done well for yourself now. Every time you got a promotion they told me, and you should have heard the pride in their voices. "Our Alan's a detective *sergeant* now," they'd say. Or "They've made Alan detective *chief* inspector now!" I got sick of hearing about you. It just took them a long time to work it out, and they don't find it easy to express. It also helped that you came down on the right side last time you were here. Of course, they always did dote on that useless brother of yours.'

'Roy.'

'Yes. I'm sorry, but you know I've always spoken my mind, and I can't say I ever took to him. Sly, he seemed to me, two-faced, always up to something behind your back. You were no angel, mind, but you weren't sly.'

Banks smiled as he buttered his scone, thinking about the time he had orchestrated going to bed with Kay while his parents were visiting his granny, and the time he and Tony Green had drunk some of Mr Green's whisky and topped the bottle up with water. Whether he spotted it or not they never knew. Sly? All kids are sly, Banks thought; they have to be in their constant struggle with the inexplicable and unreasonable rules and regulations imposed on them by adults. But Banks knew how to take a compliment when he was offered one, even at the expense of his brother.

'Thanks,' he said. 'Roy could be a bit of a handful.'

'To say the least. Anyway, I don't see much of your mum and dad any more, except when I bump into Ida on the street,' Mrs Green went on. 'That's how I knew about the golden wedding. She invited me. It's sad, though. People seem to isolate themselves when they get old. They don't get out as much, and I don't go to the Coach and Horses. How are they?'

'Same as ever,' said Banks. 'Mum's complaining about varicose veins and her bunions, but she doesn't seem to do too badly. Dad's still got his angina, but it doesn't seem any worse. There's a neighbour helps out. Bloke called Geoff Salisbury. Know him?'

Banks couldn't swear to it, but he thought Mrs Green's expression darkened for a moment. Her lips certainly tightened.

'I know him,' she said.

Banks leaned forward in his armchair. 'You don't sound so thrilled about it.'

'Can't say as I am. Oh, he's a charmer all right is Geoff Salisbury. Bit too much of one for my liking.'

'How did you meet him?'

'He seems to have some sort of radar for all the old folks in trouble on the estate. He turns up everywhere at one time or another. Usually when you need help.'

'What do you mean?'

'More tea?'

'Please.' Banks held out his cup.

'You know, you can smoke if you like.' She smiled. 'If I let you do it when you were fifteen, I can hardly stop you now you're . . . what would it be?'

'A lot older.' Banks put his hand to his left temple. 'Can't you tell by the grey?'

Mrs Green laughed and touched her own head. 'You call *that* grey?' It was true, she had an entire head of fluffy grey hair.

'Anyway,' Banks said, remembering what Mr Green had died of, 'thanks, but I've stopped.'

'I won't say that's not good news. If only we'd all known all along what it was doing to us.'

'You were saying? About Geoff Salisbury.'

'I was, wasn't I?' She sat back in her chair, tea and saucer resting on her lap. 'Oh, you know me. I tend to go off half-cocked on things.'

'I'd still be interested to hear your thoughts,' said Banks. 'To be honest, I haven't really taken to him myself, and he seems to be spending an awful lot of time around Mum and Dad.'

She waved a hand. 'It's nothing, really. He started coming around when Bill was sick. It was near the end and Bill was in a wheelchair, breathing from that horrible oxygen tank.'

'What did he want?'

'Want? Nothing. He never asked for a thing. Only to help. Give him his due, he's a hard and willing worker, and he was certainly useful at the time. He fixed a few things around the house, ran errands.'

'So what was the problem?'

'You'll think I was imagining things.'

'Not necessarily.'

'Well, it wasn't any one thing, really. Just little things. The wrong change, or one of Bill's tools would go missing. Nothing you could really put your finger on.'

Banks remembered the short change Geoff Salisbury had handed his mother yesterday evening. 'Anything else?'

'Ooh, just listen to us,' said Mrs Green, refilling her teacup. 'I'm being questioned by a policeman.'

Banks smiled. 'I'm sorry, I didn't mean it to seem like that. Comes with the territory, I suppose.'

She laughed. 'It's all right, Alan. I was only teasing. But it's hard to talk about. It was only a feeling.'

'What feeling?'

She clasped the collar of her frock. 'That he was . . . hovering . . . like the Angel of Death or something. Listen to me now. What a fool I sound.'

'You don't think Geoff Salisbury had anything to do with your husband's death, do you?'

'Of course not. No, it's nothing like that. It was a faulty valve, they said, on the oxygen tank.' She gave a harsh laugh. 'Someone told me if we'd been living in America I'd have got millions of dollars in compensation.'

'That's probably true.'

'Yes, well, if we'd been living in America we probably wouldn't have been able to afford the medical treatment in the first place, and Bill would have died a lot sooner.'

'Also true,' said Banks. 'Can you explain a bit more clearly? About this feeling you had.'

'I'm not sure. I felt as if he were, you know, waiting, waiting in the wings until Bill died.'

'For what?'

'I don't know. So he could take over more, maybe, manipulate me more.'

Banks smiled at her. 'He obviously didn't know who he was dealing with.'

She didn't smile back. 'You'd be surprised how easy it is to take advantage when people are vulnerable.' She looked at him. 'Or maybe you wouldn't. You probably see a lot of it in your job. Anyway, I felt as if he was hovering, waiting for Bill to die so that he could be more in control.'

'But what could possibly have been in it for him?'

'I don't know. Like I said, I was probably imagining things anyway.'

'I don't suppose you won the lottery recently?'

'Never bought a ticket.'

'And you don't have a million pounds hidden in the mattress or anything?'

She laughed. 'Wish I had. No, there's nothing, really. Bill's insurance policy. Old-age pension. I'm not complaining, mind you. It's enough to get by on.'

'What happened?'

'After Bill died, I gave Geoff Salisbury his marching orders. I was nice about it. I thanked him for his help, but said I was perfectly capable of managing by myself and I'd prefer it if he didn't come around any more. It wasn't that I couldn't still have used the sort of help he had to offer, but I just didn't feel comfortable having him around. Maybe I was being oversensitive as well as ungrateful.'

'I don't know,' said Banks. 'As I said, I haven't taken to him myself and I'm not sure why.'

'You'll be feeling guilty because he's looking after your parents while you're not there to do it.'

'Perhaps. Partly, yes. But there's more. I don't trust him. I don't know what he's up to, but I don't trust him. Maybe it's copper's instinct.'

'Well, I can tell you one thing for a start: you'll get no thanks around these parts for going after Geoff Salisbury.'

'Popular, is he?'

'To hear some talk, you'd think the sun shone out of his . . . well, you know what.'

Banks smiled. 'I think I can guess. How did he take your rejection?'

Mrs Green shrugged. 'Well enough, I suppose. At least he didn't bother me after that. Oh, I see him around now and then, and he always smiles and says hello as if nothing ever happened. It's just that—'

'What?'

'Oh, probably me being silly again. But it feels just skin deep, as if underneath it all, if you were just to strip off the surface that, well, you'd find something else entirely under there. Something very nasty indeed.'

9

Banks decided to pay a quick visit to the city centre that afternoon. He needed to pick up a couple of things from the shops for tomorrow, such as a nice anniversary card and some candles. He asked his parents if they needed anything, but they said no (implying, Banks thought, that Geoff Salisbury was taking care of everything), so off he went. Rather than search the side streets for a vacant parking space, he parked in the short stay behind the town hall and walked through to Bridge Street.

Of course, the city centre had changed quite a lot since his schooldays. Most cities *had* changed a lot in the past thirty years, but Peterborough more so than many others. Gone were the small record shop in the back alley, where he used to buy a new single nearly every week and LPs whenever he could afford them – usually only Christmas and birthdays – and the musty used book shop, where he

used to browse for hours among the dog-eared paperbacks, the one where the sour-faced woman behind the
counter used to watch him like a hawk the entire time he
was in there. The open-air market had closed; some of
the pubs he used to drink in when he was sixteen and
seventeen had disappeared and new ones had sprung up;
an old cinema, after several years as a bingo hall, was
now a nightclub; department stores had disappeared,
moved or been given facelifts; Cathedral Square was now
a pedestrian precinct.

Only yards from the Queensgate Centre stood the
ancient cathedral itself. Throughout Banks's childhood,
the majestic structure had simply *been there*. It didn't
dominate the city the way York Minster did, and like most
of the other local kids he had paid it scant attention
unless school projects and organized visits demanded
otherwise. After all, what kid was interested in a boring
old cathedral where boring old farts had gone to pray and
where even more boring ones were buried? But now he
found himself admiring the west front, with its three soaring Gothic arches flanked by twin-pinnacled towers, the
stone cream-coloured in the autumn sunshine.

In the Queensgate Centre, Banks bought an expensive golden anniversary card and some gold candles, then
he browsed around for a while and picked up a CD he
thought Kay would enjoy listening to on their way to dinner. It was one oldie he didn't have, and he had been
aware of the gap in his collection for some time.

He looked at his watch. Four o'clock. He thought he
just had time for a quick walk by the river before driving
back to his parents' house.

As he walked down Bridge Street past the Magistrates'
Court and the police station, he realized that he hadn't

been able to put Geoff Salisbury out of his thoughts completely. Something about the man was still nagging away
at him. Mrs Green had been partly right; of course he felt
guilty that Geoff was doing all the things for his ageing
parents that a good and dutiful son ought to be doing. But
also, as the astute Mrs Green had realized, there was
more to it than that. If nothing worse, he certainly got the
impression that Geoff Salisbury was a petty thief.

He glanced towards the old Customs House with its
light on top to guide the ships navigating the River
Nene, then he made his way down to the footpath that
ran along the Nene Way. There he found a bench and,
away from the crowds, took out his mobile and phoned
the detectives' room back at Eastvale. DI Annie Cabbot
and DC Winsome Jackman were on weekends at Western
Area HQ, and it was Annie who answered.

'DCI Banks, what a pleasant surprise. Can't leave us
alone for a minute, can you, sir?'

'I take it you're not alone in the office?'

'That's right, sir. Just Winsome and I, as per the duty
roster.'

'Everything all right?'

'Fine. Business as usual. Couple of fights after closing
time last night and a sexual assault on the East Side
Estate. We've got a man in for questioning.'

'Is that all?'

'Honestly, we're on top of it. Relax. Enjoy yourself.'

'I'm trying, Annie, I'm trying. Actually, I wasn't calling
to check up on you. I'm sure everything's under control.
I need you to do a little detective work for me.'

'Detective work?'

'Yes. I want you to check on a name for me. See if you
come up with anything.'

'I don't believe it. Even at your parents' golden wedding anniversary you're still on the job?'

'You know the rules, Annie, we can't ignore wrongdoing whether we're on or off duty.'

'Oh, what a load of bollocks. OK. Go ahead.'

Banks gave her Geoff Salisbury's name and address, along with the number of his Fiesta, which he had memorized, for good measure.

'What's it about?' Annie asked.

'I don't know yet,' said Banks. 'Probably nothing. Just a suspicious character in the neighbourhood. I want to know if he's got form, first of all, then anything else you can dig up on him.'

'Will do. Where can I get in touch with you?'

'Call my mobile number. I'll leave it switched on.' Banks didn't want the call arriving at his parents' house. 'If there's no answer, don't worry. Leave a message and I'll get back to you.'

'OK. Will do.'

Feeling vaguely guilty, though he had done nothing to feel in the least bit guilty about, Banks put the phone in his pocket and walked back towards his car.

10

Bath water was always at a premium, even now they had a house with a real bathroom, and Banks had to be careful not to use all the hot water. After a short soak and a shave, he was ready. Not expecting to be going out on a date, he hadn't brought a great selection of clothes with him, so he had to settle for some casual grey cotton trousers and a blue button-down Oxford shirt. He first checked the pockets of his sports jacket for car keys and wallet, then slipped in the copy of *Lady Chatterley's Lover* he had found in his bookcase before he went downstairs.

Annie hadn't rung back yet, and given that it was past seven on a Saturday evening, Banks guessed she probably wouldn't until tomorrow. He certainly didn't want his mobile ringing in the restaurant, so he turned it off for the evening. There was no real urgency about the matter, anyway; he just wanted to know if Geoff Salisbury had form.

'Here,' his mother said, 'you'd better take a key. You'll probably be late back.'

'I shouldn't think so,' said Banks.

'Take one anyway. I don't want you hammering on the door waking us up at some ungodly hour in the morning.'

Banks pocketed the key. 'We're only going out for dinner.'

'And be quiet when you do come in,' his mother went on. 'You know your father's a light sleeper.'

The only thing Banks knew was that his *mother* had always complained of being a light sleeper, but he said nothing except goodnight and that he wouldn't be late.

11

Kay came to the door in a long, dark, loose skirt, white blouse tucked in the waistband, soft suede jacket on top. Banks complimented her on her appearance, feeling for all the world like that awkward teenager taking her to the ABC to see *Here We Go Round the Mulberry Bush*. The film had only exacerbated his teenage angst about living in a provincial town – and a 'New Town' at that – but the music, mostly by Traffic and the Spencer Davis Group, was as good as it got and, what's more, a young and lovely Judy Geeson starred in it.

The main attraction of the evening, of course, had been Kay Summerville.

There, on the back row with the other would-be lovers, Banks had somehow found the bottle to put his arm around Kay, and she hadn't seemed to mind. After a while, though, his arm had started to ache like hell, then he had felt it going numb, but he was damned if he was going to remove it after all the courage it had taken to put it there in the first place. Some of his school friends had told him that they had unbuttoned their girlfriends' blouses and felt their breasts in that very cinema, but Banks hadn't the nerve to try that. Not on their first time out together.

On their way home, they had held hands and necked for a while in the bus shelter, and that was as far as things had gone that night. Banks remembered it all vividly as Kay arranged herself next to him in the car: the warm, slightly hazy evening smearing the city lights; noise from a nearby pub; the fruity, chemical taste of her lipstick; the softness of her neck just below her ear; the way it made him tingle and turn hard as he touched her; the warmth of her small breasts crushed against him.

'Any ideas?' Kay asked.

'Ideas? What ideas?'

'About where to go. I'm almost as much a stranger to these parts as you are.'

'Oh, that. I thought I'd just drive out Fotheringhay way. It's not too far, and we ought to be able to find somewhere decent to eat.'

Kay laughed. 'It'll probably be called the Mary Queen of Scots or something.'

'She certainly did get around, that woman.'

'Didn't have much choice, did she? What a miserable existence.'

'Never wanted to be royalty?'

Kay shook her head. 'Not me. I'm happy being a commoner.'

Banks slipped the Blind Faith CD he had bought that afternoon into the stereo and Stevie Winwood's 'Had to Cry Today' came out as crisp and heart-rending as the day it was cut.

'That's not—' Kay began, then she put her head back. 'My God, I haven't heard that in decades. You still listen to this sort of stuff?'

'A lot of old sixties and early seventies stuff, yes,' said Banks. 'I reckon those eight or nine years or so between "Love Me Do" and the time everyone died produced about the best rock we'll ever hear.'

'That's a very sweeping statement. What about punk?'

'Too much noise and not enough talent. The Clash were all right, though.'

'Roxy Music? Bowie? REM? The Pretenders?'

'There are exceptions to every rule.'

Kay laughed. 'And what else, these days?'

'I'm a hip-hop fan, myself. What about you?'

Kay nudged him in the ribs. 'Seriously.'

'Mostly jazz and classical. But I still listen to a fair bit of rock and folk: Sheryl Crow, Lucinda Williams, Beth Orton.'

'I'm afraid I don't listen to much at all these days,' said Kay. 'Don't have the time. I have the radio on sometimes while I'm in the bath, but I hardly notice what's being played. I suppose if I had to pick something I'd choose a string quartet or some sort of chamber music. Schubert, perhaps.'

'Nothing wrong with old Franz. What about this place?'

By the time the band had got to 'Can't Find My Way Home', one of Banks's favourites, he had wandered off the main road, and they were passing through a small village of grey stone, thatched cottages clustered around a broad green. Lights shone behind curtains, and here and there a television set flickered. The pub was not called the Mary Queen of Scots but a far more lowly Fox and Hounds. Banks parked the car out front and turned off the music.

Banks and Kay ducked as they walked under the low beam of the door. Already the place was busy, emanating that rosy glow of a village pub popular with the city crowd. They went up to the bar, where Banks ordered a pint of bitter and Kay a vodka and tonic, then a young girl, who looked no more than about sixteen, seated them in the dining area and pointed out that the evening's menu was written on the blackboard by the window. Just one glance told Banks they'd come to the right sort of place: a wide selection of real ale and good food beyond basic pub fare, but nothing too ambitious. The noise level was perfect, only the buzz of conversation from other tables, the thud of darts in the board at the opposite end, sometimes accompanied by a mild oath or a cheer, and the sounds of the cash register.

'Cheers,' said Banks when they'd sat down and had a good look at the blackboard. 'To – to—'

'To times gone by,' said Kay.

'To times gone by.'

They clinked glasses and each took a sip. Banks felt the need for a cigarette, partly from nerves and partly from habit – he *was* in a pub, after all – but he rode out the craving and soon forgot about it.

'Do you remember that concert?' he asked.

Kay's eyes sparkled. 'Of course I do. Well, not so much the music . . . I mean, if you asked me I couldn't tell you what they played or who else was on . . . but the occasion . . . yes, how could I forget? My mother wouldn't let me out of the door for a week afterwards, except to go to school.'

Banks laughed. 'Mine, too.'

On 7 June 1969, earlier on the day Kay had bought *Lady Chatterley's Lover* at a second-hand book shop on Charing Cross Road, Banks and Kay had taken the train to London for the free Blind Faith concert in Hyde Park. Through a combination of circumstances – partly to do with going off to smoke dope in a flat in Chelsea with some people they met – they had missed their train back and ended up getting home very early the following morning. Needless to say, parental recriminations had been severe.

'So,' said Kay, 'tell me about the last thirty years. I suppose you're married? Children?'

'Two children: one girl at university, and one boy in a rock band. And don't say it serves me right.'

Kay laughed. 'Heaven forbid. Maybe he'll make enough money to keep you in your old age.'

'That's what I'm banking on.'

'What about your wife?'

The waitress came over, notepad in hand. 'Have you decided yet?'

Banks glanced at Kay, who nodded and ordered the sole and salad. Banks went for venison medallions in port and mushroom sauce.

'More drinks?'

Banks looked at his half-full glass and shook his head. Kay asked for a glass of white wine with her meal.

'You were saying?' Kay went on when the waitress had gone away. 'About your wife.'

Banks paused. 'I'm divorced.'

'How long?'

'Two years. She's already remarried.'

Kay whistled. 'That's pretty fast. Usually you'd expect some sort of . . . well . . . I don't know . . .'

'Period of mourning?'

'That's not the term I was looking for, but I suppose it'll do.'

'It took me by surprise too. I can't say I'm in any hurry to get married again.'

'Is there someone?'

Banks thought of Michelle and Annie, and experienced another pang of guilt as he said, 'No one serious. It's too soon for that.'

'Uh-huh.'

'You?'

'Me? What?'

'Are you still married?'

'Not for the past five years.'

'I'm sorry.'

'You needn't be. He ran away with his secretary.'

'That must have been tough.'

'At the time, yes, I'd say it was a bit of a blow to the old self-esteem. She was much younger than me, of course. But I'm over it now.'

'Someone new?'

'No one special.' Kay smiled and gave a slight blush as she picked up her glass and sipped. It was the same smile and blush Banks remembered from all those years ago when he had first asked her out. What had happened to them? he asked himself. Why had they split up? But he knew the answer: it had been his fault.

Their meals arrived and Kay's glass of wine soon followed. Banks stuck with his one pint, as he had to drive. 'How are you coping about your mother?' he asked, after they had both eaten a couple of mouthfuls.

'Not bad. I think. I've got most of it done except the cleaning.' She smiled. 'Never was my strong suit, not even in my own home. I'll probably do it tomorrow. Anyway, a local dealer's coming to take away the furniture on Monday morning. Didn't offer much for it, but what the hell . . . The rest is already packed and ready to go to my house.' She shook her head. 'It was difficult going through someone's life like that. Your own mother's memories. Do you know, I found letters to her from a young man – this was before she and Dad met, of course – but they were love letters. Quite spicy, too, one or two of them.'

'It *is* hard to imagine your parents having lives of their own, isn't it?'

Kay nodded. 'There was lots of other stuff, too. Old photos. Me when I was a kid at the seaside. Letters from me, too, when I was at university. Full of energy and ambition.' Tears glistened in her eyes.

'And now?'

Kay wiped away the tears. 'Oh, I suppose I'm still ambitious enough. I work practically all the hours God sends. I know I neglected Mum, especially after Dad died.' Banks remembered hearing that Kay's father had been killed ten years ago in a car accident, an accident her mother survived. It had been the talk of the estate for weeks, so his mother had told him. Kay laughed and made a dismissive gesture. 'I don't know, maybe there's something Freudian about it – I always was Daddy's little girl – but my career really started to take off around then, too. Life was exciting at last: lots of travel, parties, financial success. I hardly ever made time to come home and help Mum, even when she was ill. For crying out loud, I was in Zurich when she died. I barely managed to get back in time for the funeral. Some daughter. Some mother, too. Even my kids say they never see me.'

'Kids?'

'Three girls. All married. I'm a grandmother, Alan. Can you believe it? A bloody grandmother.'

'It's hard to believe, looking at you.'

She blushed and smiled again. 'Why, thank you. I'll tell you, though, it takes a lot of hard work and a lot of investment in potions and salves these days. Remember when we were kids? We thought we were immortal, that we'd be young for ever.'

'True enough,' Banks agreed. 'I'm still waiting for the wisdom that's supposed to come with age.'

'Me, too.'

They paused to eat in comfortable silence. Banks watched Kay break off flakes of moist sole with the edge of her fork. His venison was good, tender and tasty. He decided he could risk one more drink and asked the waitress to bring him a glass of red wine.

'How are *your* parents?' Kay asked.

'Fine. Oh, that reminds me: Mum asked me to invite you to drop by tomorrow, if you want.'

Kay nodded slowly. 'Yes. All right, that would be nice.'

'About six, OK?'

'Fine. Just for half an hour or so.' Kay frowned. 'You know, there is one thing that puzzles me a bit about Mum,' she said.

'Oh?'

'It's nothing, really, but I was going through her finances yesterday, and I noticed she'd withdrawn a hundred pounds from the cash machine the day she died, but I can't find it. There's only about six or seven pounds in her purse, and she wasn't the type to hide her money under the mattress.'

The little scar beside Banks's right eye began to itch. 'Maybe she had bills to pay, or she owed it to someone?'

'Neither a lender nor a borrower be. That was Mum's motto. And all her bills had been paid. No, it's a mystery. What do you have to say, O great detective?'

'I still think there's probably a logical explanation.'

'Probably. The other thing that puzzles me, though, is how did she get it?'

'What do you mean?'

'Well, she was bedridden for the last few days. There was a nurse on call twenty-four hours a day, of course, and Dr Grenville dropped by quite often, but . . . I just don't see how she could even have *got* to the cash machine.'

The itch got stronger. Banks scratched the side of his eye. 'Have you ever heard of a fellow called Geoff Salisbury?' he asked her.

Kay frowned. 'The name sounds vaguely familiar. I think he introduced himself to me at the funeral. A neighbour. Why?'

'Oh, nothing,' said Banks. 'Nothing important. Dessert?'

12

'Would you like some music on?' Kay asked. They were back at her parents' house, and Banks had accepted her invitation to come in for a nightcap – a half-bottle of 'medicinal' brandy that Kay had found while tidying out the kitchen cupboards. They drank it out of cracked teacups that she had been about to put in the dustbin.

'Sure,' said Banks.

Kay walked over to the old stereo system. 'Let's see,' she said, flipping through a box of LPs. 'I packed these last night but I didn't really pay much attention. There's probably not a lot of choice. Dad only liked the stuff he used to listen to in the war, and Mum wasn't much interested in music at all. As you can see, they don't own a CD player. I think the last LP they bought was in 1960.'

Banks went over and joined her, looking at the old-fashioned covers. At least he could read what was written on the backs of them, unlike the tiny print on CDs. 'That's after 1960,' he said, pointing to *Beatles for Sale*.

'That must be one of mine,' Kay said. 'I didn't even notice it.'

Banks flipped open the cover. Written inside, in tiny blue ballpoint over the photograph, were some words. They were hard to make out, but he thought they said, 'Kay Summerville loves Alan Banks.' Banks passed it to Kay, who blushed and put it away. 'I lent it to Susan Fish,' she said. 'The sneaky devil. I didn't know she'd done that.' She pulled out another LP. 'Ah, this will do fine.'

The needle crackled as it hit the groove, a sound that gave Banks an unexpected frisson of delight and nostalgia, and then Billie Holiday started singing 'Solitude'.

'Couldn't do much better,' he said.

'Dance?' Kay asked.

'I don't know,' said Banks. 'Remember the vicar wouldn't allow dancing at the youth club because he said it led to sex?'

Kay laughed. 'Yes, I remember.'

Then she was in his arms, Billie was singing about solitude, and they were doing what passed for dancing.

13

'**A wise man,** that vicar,' said Banks about an hour later, as he lay back on the sofa, Billie Holiday long finished, a naked Kay half on top of him, her head resting on his chest, fingertips trailing languorously over his skin. It had been good – no doubt much better than their youthful fumblings, which he could scarcely remember now – though there had been something a little melancholy and desperate about it, as if both had been straining to capture something that eluded them.

'What happened to us?' Kay asked. 'All those years ago.'

'We were just kids. What did we know?'

'I suppose so. But have you ever wondered what would have happened? You know, if we hadn't—'

'Of course I have.'

'And?'

'I don't know. It's hard for me to imagine a life without Sandra and the kids.'

'I know that. I mean, even though it ended badly, me and Keith had some good times. And the kids are marvellous. It's just a game. Imagining. You know, sometimes I've been places or experienced things and thought I'd have liked you there to share it.'

'You have?'

'Yes. Haven't you ever felt the same?'

'I can't say I have,' said Banks, who had.

She nudged him in the ribs. 'Bastard.'

'There's something I never told you before,' Banks said, stroking her silky blonde hair and touching the soft skin on her neck, just below her ear.

'And you want to tell me now?'

'Yes.'

'Are you sure that's a good idea?'

'The timing seems right.'

'Why?'

'No particular reason.'

Kay shifted position. 'OK. Go ahead.'

'You know that first time when my parents were out and you came over to the house? The day we'd decided we were finally going to do it?'

'How could I forget? I was about to lose my virginity. I was scared silly.'

'Me too. On both counts. Nervous as hell.'

Banks remembered that, as the months went on, he and Kay had graduated from kissing in the bus shelter to touching above the waist, first with clothing intact, then under her jumper, with only the thin bra between his hands and her bare, swollen flesh. After a few weeks of that, and much trouble fumbling with the clasp that held the thing on, he got beyond the bra to the unimaginably firm and tender mounds beneath.

They had been going out nearly a year before the subject of moving to below the waist came up, and both were understandably a bit nervous about it. This might have been the swinging sixties, when kids were making love openly at Woodstock, but Banks and Kay were young, unsophisticated, provincial kids, and the antics of drug-taking pop stars and free-loving hippies seemed as fantastic as Hollywood films.

But they had done it.

'Well,' Banks went on. 'I had to go and get some . . .
you know . . . Durex.'

'Rubber Johnnies? Yes, I suppose you did. Do you
know, I never really thought about that.'

'Well, I couldn't very well go to the local chemist's or
the barber's, could I? They knew me there. Someone
would have been bound to tell my parents.'

Kay propped herself on one elbow and leaned over
him, her nipple hard against his chest. He could smell
white wine and cheap brandy on her breath, see sparks
of light dancing in her dark blue eyes. 'So what did you
do? Where did you go?' she asked.

'I walked miles and miles to the other side of town and
found a barber's where I was certain no one would recognize me.'

Kay giggled. 'Oh, how sweet.'

'I'm not finished yet.'

'Go on.'

'Do you know how the old barbers' shops had a sort
of hallway with a counter between the outer and inner
door, nice and private, where you could buy shampoo
and razor blades and stuff?'

'And rubber Johnnies?'

'And rubber Johnnies.'

'I remember. My dad used to take me to the barber's
with him sometimes when I was a little girl.'

'Right,' Banks went on. 'Well, as I said, I'd walked halfway to Cambridge and there I was, bold as brass, outside
a barber's on a street where not a soul could possibly
know who I was.'

Kay smiled. 'What happened?' She moved her head
and her hair tickled his chest.

'Well, wouldn't you know it, but this particular establishment didn't have a discreet sales area. Oh no. I opened the front door and I found myself standing right by the barber's chair. He was giving a bloke a shave, I remember, and the place was full of grown men. I mean, every chair in the waiting area was taken, and I swear that the minute I walked in there they all looked up from their newspapers and every eye was on me.'

'My God! What did you do?'

'What could I do? I'd gone too far to turn back. I stood my ground and I said, in as deep a voice as I could manage, "Packet of three, please."'

Kay put her hand to her mouth to hold back the laughter. 'Oh, no!' she said. 'You're joking?'

'No word of a lie.'

'What did he say? The barber.'

'Not a word. He stopped mid-shave, straight-blade razor in his hand, and he went to his cabinet and got them for me. But you should have heard the other buggers laugh and cheer. You'd think Peterborough United had won a game. I went red as a beet.'

Kay burst into a fit of laughter and couldn't stop. Banks started laughing with her, holding her against his chest, and after a while laughter turned to lust.

14

It was after two o'clock when Banks slipped the key into the door of his parents' house and turned the lock as quietly as he could. He shut the door slowly behind him, without making much noise, and made sure the chain and bolt were on. The stairs creaked a little as he tiptoed up to bed. He couldn't very well go and brush his teeth as he would have to put the bathroom light on and the tap would make a noise. He thought he could just about manage to undress and crawl into bed in the dark. The bed would creak too, but that couldn't be helped. Fortunately, he'd had the foresight to use the toilet before leaving Kay's.

The minute he got to the landing he heard his mother muttering something to his father, who muttered something back. He couldn't catch the words but knew they were about him, how late he was. He felt himself blushing. Christ, it really didn't matter how quiet he had tried to be; she'd been lying awake until he came home, just like she used to do when he was a teenager.

15

Despite his late night, Banks woke early on Sunday morning to the sound of rain blowing in sharp gusts against his bedroom window. The rest of the house was quiet, and he didn't think his parents were awake yet. His first thought on finding consciousness was to wonder what the hell he and Kay had thought they were up to last night, but the more he remembered the less he regretted. Blame it on Billie Holiday, if you will, on dancing, the old estate and the romance of the past, but whatever it was, it was something special and he refused to feel guilty.

He only hoped Kay felt the same way in the damp grey of dawn.

Two memories assailed him almost simultaneously as he got out of bed and went over to the wardrobe for his overnight bag: that he had forgotten to give Kay her old copy of *Lady Chatterley's Lover* and that he was certain he had seen a tiny, neatly folded square of silver paper in the bathroom waste bin. Perhaps Mrs Summerville had taken to chewing gum in her final days, though he doubted it, or maybe Kay did, though he had seen no evidence of it last night, and he remembered that she had bought mints at the newsagent's, not gum. Which left him with the strongest suspicion that Geoff Salisbury had been there sometime over the past few weeks, leaving Banks little doubt as to where the hundred pounds had gone.

What to do about him, that was the question.

Banks stretched as he pulled out his bag and decided to start the day dressed simply, in jeans and a polo-neck sweater. He would change for the party later. Today was his parents' big day, and Roy was due to come up from London. Banks resolved to be nice to Roy for his parents' sake.

As Banks put his bag back in the wardrobe, he noticed some cardboard boxes on the far side. On his previous visit he had found some old records and diaries, which were still there, but now it looked as if there was more. Curious, he opened the other door and lifted a box out. The flaps were shut, but not sealed, and written across the top, in his mother's inimitable scrawl, was his name: *Alan*. More childhood stuff, then.

On top he found yet more old school reports, from the grammar school this time, most of them urging him to try harder and assuring him he could do better if he only put his shoulder to the wheel etc. The reports were handwritten in black ink, and Banks occasionally had difficulty reading the comments. He remembered some of the teachers' names – Mr Newman, Mr Phelps, Mr Hawtry – but most of them were a blur.

Along with the reports was a class photograph dated 14

May 1967. There they all were, three rows of teenage boys in their school uniforms. Banks remembered several of the faces: Steve Hill, Paul Major, Dave Grenfell, his best friends, then Tony Green, John McLeod, the school bully, and Ian Marston, who, so Banks's mother had told him, committed suicide seven or eight years ago after his courier business failed. The rest of them he hardly remembered except for the odd feature here and there, such as a long, freckled face, a big nose, or prominent ears, but he couldn't put a name to them. He had met up with Dave Grenfell and Paul Major on his previous visit, and he had found out then that Steve Hill had died of lung cancer, but what had become of everyone else he had no idea. Others would be dead, some would be dying, some would be successful, some would be failures, some would be criminals, many would be divorced. There was one angry-looking kid glaring into the camera with a cocky expression on his face, black hair just a little bit too long, tie slightly askew, top button undone against school regulations. Himself. Even more of a mystery than all the rest.

Next came a few school exercise books full of sums and compositions. One of them contained some poems Banks had written when he went through that stage of adolescence in which poetry was an acceptable means of expression as long as you kept it to yourself. It was with excruciating embarrassment that he looked over them again now, with the autumn rain starting to spatter against his bedroom window.

There were lines about the awkwardness of being an adolescent, love poems to Julie Christie and Judy Geeson, poems about how phony the world was. None of them rhymed, of course, nor were any overly concerned with metrics; the lines simply ended where he had decided to end them, for no other reason than that it looked like poetry on the page. There were no capital letters, either. Still, Banks reflected, from what he had seen that wasn't a hell of a lot different from the sort of thing most published poets did today. Awful lines and images jumped out at him, such as 'I feel like a corpse/in the coffin of your mind.' What on earth had prompted him to write that? About what? He couldn't even remember whose mind was supposed to be the coffin. And then there was a poem marked, 'For Kay', in which these immortal lines appeared:

> i skimmed across
> your life
> like a pebble
> on the water's surface
> i sank
> quickly
> the tide went out

What had he been thinking of? There was another image about her being 'naked/on a sheepskin/by the crackling fire', but as far as Banks could remember, they had never lain on a sheepskin rug, and electric fires, which everyone on the estate had, didn't crackle. Poetic licence?

He remembered that first time up in this same room while his parents were out. The event was awkward and far less momentous for both of them than his imagination had convinced him it would be, but it went well enough in the end and they decided they liked it and would certainly try again. They got better and better over the next few months, stealing an hour or two here and there while parents were absent. Once they almost got caught when Kay's mother came home sooner than expected from a dental appointment. They just managed to get their clothes on and tidy up the bed in time to tell her they'd been listening to records, though judging by the expression on Mrs Summerville's face when she saw her daughter's dishevelled hair, Banks didn't think she was convinced. Kay told him later that that very evening she had got a lecture about the dangers of teenage pregnancy and what men think of women who haven't 'saved themselves' for marriage, though no overt mention was made of Banks or that afternoon's events, and nobody tried to stop them seeing one another.

Smiling at the memory, Banks slipped the exercise book of poetry into his overnight bag, determined to remember to feed it to the fire when he got back to his Gratly cottage. As he moved it, a newspaper cutting slipped out from between some of the unfilled pages. It was a report in the local paper on the disappearance of Graham Marshall, a school friend of Banks's, and the reason for his visit home in the summer. Alongside the article was a photograph of Graham with his fair hair, melancholy expression and pale face, like some fin de siècle poet.

Banks moved on to the bottom of the box, where he found more old forty-fives, ones he had forgotten he had: Procol Harum's 'A Whiter Shade of Pale', 'Juliet' by the Four Pennies, 'Hippy Hippy Shake' by the Swinging Blue Jeans, the Lovin' Spoonful's 'Summer in the City', 'Devil in Disguise' by Elvis Presley and 'Still I'm Sad' by the Yardbirds.

Banks put the box back on top of one marked *Roy* and tiptoed downstairs into the kitchen for a cup of tea. His heart almost stopped when he saw Geoff Salisbury sitting at the kitchen table eating buttered toast.

'Morning, Alan,' Geoff said. 'I've come to do some cleaning up. Already took your em and pee a cup of tea up, bless 'em. It's a big day for them, you know. Like a cuppa yourself?'

Banks felt like saying he would make his own tea, but he remembered he hadn't been able to find the tea bags. Instead, he got himself a mug. 'Thanks,' he grunted.

'Not much of a morning person?' Geoff asked. 'Still, I imagine after a late night like you had you must be feeling even more tired. Your poor old mum was lying awake worrying where you'd got to.' Salisbury winked. 'Having a good time with that Summerville girl, were you?'

So Banks's mother had already told Geoff that her son had been out with Kay Summerville and had not returned home until the early hours of the morning. He knew all this, and it wasn't even nine o'clock yet. Geoff Salisbury was starting to get *really* annoying. Even though Banks hadn't had a chance to call Annie back about criminal records, he decided that now would be as good a time as any to go on the offensive and make a couple of things clear to him.

'I'm glad you're here, actually,' Banks said. 'I've been wanting to have a quiet word with you.'

'Oh? What about?'

'Your sticky fingers.'

'Come again?'

'You know what I'm talking about. Don't come the innocent. It doesn't work with me.'

'I understand that your job must make you cynical, but why are you picking on me? What have I done?'

'You know what you've done.'

'Look, if it's that business about the change, I thought I'd already made it clear to you it was a genuine mistake. I thought we'd put it behind us.'

'I might have done if it hadn't been for a few other interesting titbits I've heard since I've been down here.'

'It's that Summerville girl, isn't it? If she's been saying things, she's lying. She doesn't like me.'

'Well,' said Banks, 'that at least shows good taste on her part. It doesn't matter who's been saying what. The point is that I've been hearing from a number of independent sources about things sort of disappearing when you're in the vicinity. Money, for example.'

Salisbury turned red. 'I resent that.'

'I should imagine you do. But is it true?'

'Of course it isn't. I don't know who's—'

'I told you, it doesn't matter who.'

Salisbury stood up. 'Well, it does to me. You might not believe it, but there are people who have it in for me. Not everybody appreciates what I do for the decent folk around here, you know.'

'What do you mean?'

'Never you mind. Now, if you've finished with your groundless accusations, I've got work to do. Your parents' golden wedding might not be important to you, but it is to me. Arthur and Ida mean a lot to me.'

Before Banks could say another word, Salisbury had gone into the front room and started up the vacuum. Irritated both by Salisbury's reaction and his own tumbling accusation, Banks went across to the newsagent's to see if he could pick up a *Sunday Times*.

16

Banks went to the Bricklayer's Inn by himself for a quiet pint on Sunday lunchtime, taking the newspaper with him and promising to be back by two o'clock for lunch. It felt like his first real break that weekend, and he made the most of it, even getting the crossword three-quarters done, which was good for him without Annie's help. On his way home he took cover in the rain-lashed bus shelter by the gates of the derelict factory to call Annie in Eastvale. Though the shelter hadn't been there all those years ago, Banks still couldn't help but think of Mandy, with her Julie Christie lips and the faraway look in her eyes. He wondered what had happened to her, whether she had ever found that distant thing she had seemed to be dreaming of. Probably not; most people didn't. Though it seemed like another age, she would only be in her early fifties, after all, and that no longer sounded very old to Banks.

DC Winsome Jackman answered his ring. 'Is DI Cabbot not in?' Banks asked.

'I'm afraid not, sir,' said Winsome. 'She's out on the East Side Estate interviewing neighbours about that sexual assault.'

'Do you know when she'll be back?'

'No, sir. Sorry, but you'll just have to make do with me.'

Banks could hear teasing humour in her voice, the way it tinged her lilting Jamaican speech. Did she know that Annie and he used to have a thing? He wouldn't be surprised. No matter how much you try to keep something like that a secret, there are always people who seem able to pick up on it intuitively.

'DI Cabbot did leave a message for you, though, sir,' Winsome went on.

'Yes?'

'That man you were asking about, Geoffrey Salisbury.'

'Right. Any form?'

'Yes, sir. One conviction. Six years ago. Served eighteen months.'

'What for?'

'Fraud, sir. To put it in a nutshell, he tried to swindle a little old lady out of her life savings, but she was a lot smarter than he reckoned on.'

'Did he indeed?' Banks said. 'What a surprise.'

'Sir?'

'Nothing. Where did this happen?'

'Loughborough, sir.'

That wasn't very far away, Banks thought. 'Thanks a lot,' he said. 'And thank DI Cabbot. That's a great help.'

'There's more, sir. DI Cabbot said she's going to try to talk to the local police, the ones who handled the case. She said it looks like there might be more to it than meets the eye.'

'What did she mean by that?'

'Don't know, sir. Shall I ask her to ring you when she's been in touch with Loughborough police?'

'If you would, Winsome. And thanks again.'

'No problem, sir. Enjoy the party.'

17

Roy didn't turn up in time for Sunday lunch, which was pretty much what Banks had expected. They ate without him, Ida Banks fretting and worrying the whole time, unable to enjoy her food. Arthur tried to calm her, assuring her that nothing terrible had happened and that Roy wasn't trapped in a burning car wreck somewhere on the M1. Banks said nothing. He knew his mother well enough to realize that anything he said regarding Roy would only succeed in adding fuel to the fire. Instead, he ate his roast beef and Yorkshires like a good boy – and a fine lunch it was, too, especially if you liked your meat and vegetables overcooked – and counted his blessings. In the first place his mother was far too distracted to go on at him for being late home last night, and in the second place Geoff bloody Salisbury had buggered off home and wasn't eating with them, though he had promised to come back early to help set up for the party.

The phone finally rang at about half past two, just as they were starting their jam roly-poly, and Banks's mother leapt up and dashed into the hall to answer it. When she came back she was much calmer, and she informed Banks and his father that poor Roy had had a devil of a job getting away on time and the rain had caused some terrible delays. There was also a pile-up on the M25, so he was stuck in traffic there at the moment and would arrive as soon as he could.

'There you are, you see,' Arthur said. 'All that fretting for nothing. I told you he was all right.'

'But you never know, do you?' she said.

Banks offered to do the dishes and his offer was, to his surprise, accepted. His father had a nap with the open newspaper unread on his lap, and his mother went for a short lie-down to calm her nerves. When Banks had finished the dishes, he sneaked a couple of fingers of his father's Johnnie Walker to calm *his* nerves. He had no sooner downed it than the explosion went off.

At least that was what it sounded like at first. Eventually, Banks's ears adjusted enough to discern that it was music coming from next door. Heavy-metal gangsta rap, music only if you used the term very loosely indeed. Banks's father stirred in his armchair. 'At it again,' he grumbled. 'Never get a moment's peace.'

Banks sat by him on the arm. 'Does this happen a lot?' he asked.

His father nodded. 'Too often for me. Oh, I've tried having a word, but he's an ignorant bugger. If I were twenty or thirty years younger—'

Banks heard his mother's footsteps on the landing. 'At it again, I hear,' she called down.

'It's bad for her nerves,' Arthur Banks said.

'Have you talked to the council?'

'We've tried, but they say, apart from issuing a warning, they can't do anything.'

'What about Geoff Salisbury?'

'Geoff's got his strengths, but he's not got a lot of bottle. Proper tough guy him next door.'

'Right,' said Banks, standing up. 'Give me a few minutes.'

'Where are you going, Alan?' his mother asked, coming down the stairs as he got to the front door.

'Just off to have a quiet word with next door, that's all.'

'Don't you go causing any trouble. Do you hear? You just be careful. And remember we have to live here after you've gone, you know.'

Banks patted his mother's arm. 'Don't worry, Mum,' he said. 'I know what I'm doing. I'll make sure I don't cause you any trouble.'

It was still raining outside. Banks knocked on the door, but got no answer. Hardly surprising, as he supposed nobody could hear him over the music. The windows were all open and the angry heavy-metal rap spilled out into the street, someone bragging about raping a bitch and offing a pig.

Banks tried the front door. It was open. He found himself in a small hallway, where the stairs led up to the bedrooms. The wallpaper was peeling and something that looked like a sleeping bag lay on the staircase. Banks nudged it with his foot. It was empty.

He didn't like just walking in unannounced, but it seemed the only option. He called out a few times while he stood still in the hallway but he could hardly even hear his own shouts.

Finally, he went through into the living room. Now he knew why they kept the windows open; the smell was overwhelming. It was a mixture of things – human smells, definitely, such as sweat and urine, but also rotten vegetables, burnt plastic and marijuana. There were piles of old newspapers and other rubbish on the floor and it looked as though a dog had chewed up the furniture, though there wasn't one in evidence. Thankful for small mercies, Banks thought; they probably had a pit bull. Three people were slumped on sofas and armchairs, and one of them stood up when Banks walked in.

'Who the fuck do you think you are?' he shouted.

'I'm not a lip-reader,' Banks said, stepping over to the mound of stereo equipment and turning the volume down. 'That's better.'

It was the man of the house – Fred West to a T, eyebrows and all. The woman Banks assumed was his wife watched from one of the chairs. A girl Banks guessed to be about thirteen or fourteen sat in the other chair staring blankly at him.

The man squared up to Banks and gestured to the door with his thumb. 'Right, mate,' he said. 'I'm done being polite. On your bike.'

'I came to ask you to turn down the music,' Banks said. 'We can hardly hear ourselves think next door.'

'What's it to you? You're not from around here.'

'I was here a long time before you came on the scene. I grew up here. It's my parents' house and today's their wedding anniversary.'

'Well, bully for you. Sorry we forgot to buy them a present. Now just fuck off before I do you some real damage.'

'You don't understand,' said Banks, slipping his warrant card out. 'I'm a police officer and I'm asking you nicely to keep the noise down.'

The man actually leaned forward and scrutinized the card. 'North Yorkshire!' he said. 'You've got no powers down here. You're out of your jurisdiction, mate.'

'Big word that. I'm surprised you didn't choke on it.'

'I'm not scared of you. Now fuck off!'

'You should be,' said Banks.

The man walked over to the stereo and cranked up the volume again. The girl and the woman hadn't moved. They were just watching. Banks guessed they were stoned on something or other. He thought he could see a crack pipe half-hidden under a newspaper on the floor, but it wasn't crack they were on. These two weren't jerky or manic; they were practically comatose. Downers or smack, most likely.

With a sigh, Banks walked over to the stereo, picked up the CD player, ripped out the wires and dropped it on the floor. The music stopped. The women still didn't move, but Fred came right at him. He was a couple of inches taller than Banks, and thickset, muscular in the upper body. But Banks had his wiry and deceptive strength and speed going for him. He grabbed the man's wrist and twisted it so that he soon had him on his knees, arm up his back, foot placed solidly on his left kidney. By exerting just a little more pressure on the arm, Banks could make the pain excruciating. Even more pressure and the arm would snap or the shoulder joint would pop. The women just looked on, goggle-eyed. They'd never seen anything like this before.

'I'll do you for this!' the man yelled. 'I'll see you bloody locked up, copper or no. You've got no right going around destroying a man's private property.'

'Oh, give it a rest, Fred,' said Banks. 'It was probably nicked, anyway.'

'My name's Lenny. You've got the wrong bloke.'

'My mistake. Sorry, Lenny. Are you listening?'

'I'm still not scared of—'

Banks gave a little twist and Lenny screamed. Banks let him relax a moment and then repeated his question.

'All right,' said Lenny. 'All right, I'm listening. Let go.'

Banks didn't. 'I'm sorry about your CD player,' he said. 'I'm a music lover, myself, so it hurt me almost as it hurt you. I'm sure it'll be OK; it's just had rather a nasty shock, that's all. If it's not, then I'm sure you'll have no problem lifting another. But first I'd like a promise out of you.'

'What promise?'

Banks gave another little twist. Lenny screamed, his face red with pain. The woman Banks assumed was his wife lit a cigarette and contemplated the scene before her with great interest, as if she was watching a television programme. The girl started buffing her nails. Banks listened in the silence after the CD player's sudden demise, but he could hear no other sounds coming from anywhere in the house. A good sign. No ambush imminent.

'I'd like you to promise me that you won't ever, ever, play your music so loud again that it disturbs my mum and dad next door. Do you think you can do that, Lenny?'

'It's my house. I'll do what I like in my own fucking house.'

Twist. Scream.

'Lenny, you're not listening. If you really mean what you just said, you ought to consider moving to a detached house, you know, miles away from your nearest neighbours. Besides, it's not your house. It's the council's house. You just rent it.'

'You're a bastard, you are,' Lenny said, gasping. 'You're worse than the fucking criminals you put away. Filth!' He spat on the floor.

'Yeah, yeah. It's all been said before. But we're not talking about me, we're talking about your promise.'

'What promise? I haven't made any fucking promise.'

'But you're going to, aren't you?'

Lenny said nothing. The woman frowned as she looked at him. Banks could tell the suspense was killing her. *Will he or won't he?* The young girl got up and made to leave the room.

'Where are you going?' Banks asked her.

'Bog,' she said, making a squatting gesture.

Banks was a little concerned that she might reappear with a weapon. 'Hold on a minute, love,' he said. 'Wait till I'm finished here.'

'I'll piss myself.'

'I said hold on. You'll live with it.'

'These are me new jeans.'

Banks turned back to Lenny. The girl slumped against the doorpost, legs crossed. Banks kept a close eye on her. She chewed on her lower lip and looked sulky.

'Right, Lenny, the quicker you give me your promise, the quicker your lass here will get to go to the toilet.'

'She's not *my* lass. Let her piss herself. I don't care. Won't be the first time.'

Banks gave a harder twist and Lenny cursed. 'What I want you to promise,' Banks said slowly, 'is that you won't play your music so loud that it upsets my mum and dad, remember?'

'I remember.'

'And if you do,' Banks said, 'I'll have the local drugs squad over here before you can flush a tab of E down the toilet. Is that clear?'

'It's clear.'

'Is it a promise?'

'I—'

Banks twisted again. 'Is it a promise?'

'All right, all right! Jesus Christ, yes, it's a fucking promise!'

'And if you do anything – anything at all – to harm or intimidate them in any way, I'll consider that promise broken. And I deal with broken promises myself. North Yorkshire's not that far away. Got it?'

'Got it. Let me go.'

Banks let go and Lenny squirmed on the floor for a while, rubbing his arm and his shoulder before subsiding into his armchair and lighting a cigarette with shaking hands.

'You're a nutter, you are,' he said. 'You ought to be locked up.'

'You've got that right.'

'Is it over?' the girl by the door asked. 'Are you done? Are you? 'Cos I'm bleeding bursting here.'

'It's over, love,' said Banks. 'Off you go.'

'About fucking time.' She dashed upstairs. The woman on the sofa looked at Lenny with contempt, but still said nothing.

'You in charge here, Lenny?' Banks asked, catching her look. 'Because there's no point my talking to the monkey, if you catch my drift.'

'I'm in fucking charge,' he said, glaring at the woman. 'They know that.'

She sniffed, but Banks could see fear in her eyes, the first emotion he had noticed in her. Lenny was in charge all right, and he probably used the same tactics Banks had just used to rule his roost. That didn't make Banks feel particularly good, but needs must. He wondered what other sorts of abuse went on in this house, in addition to drugs. The young girl, for example, or the other kids, wherever they were. Nothing would have surprised him. Maybe he'd call in the drugs squad, anyway, and the social. Someone ought to keep a close eye on this lot, that was for certain.

He heard the toilet flush as he left.

18

Roy's arrival at about four o'clock broke the tension for Banks. Until then he had been helping Geoff set up the bar and buffet on tables in the kitchen, keeping a tight rein on his temper for his parents' sake, even though Geoff treated him like an employee. 'Now, Alan, if you wouldn't mind just moving that over there . . . That's a good lad . . . If you could nip over to the shops and pick up . . .' And so on. He had also been wanting to get Geoff alone and have another go at him in the light of Winsome's information, but his mother was always around issuing instructions too. Wisely, his father had gone upstairs to 'rest'.

When the doorbell rang, Ida Banks practically ran to the front door, and Banks heard her shouts of glee as she greeted Roy. After divesting himself of his raincoat, the man himself came through to the living room, clutching a bottle-shaped bag, and with a young woman in tow. She looked about twenty, Banks thought, with short, shaggy hair, black streaked with blonde, a pale, pretty face, with beautiful eyes the colour and gleam of chestnuts in September. She also had a silver stud just below her lower lip. She was wearing jeans and a short woolly jumper, exposing a couple of inches of bare, flat midriff and a navel with a ring in it.

'This is Corinne,' said Roy. 'Say hello to my brother, Alan, Corinne.'

Corinne shook Banks's hand and said hello. She gave him a shy smile and averted her eyes.

Roy looked at Geoff, free hand stretched out, smiling like a salesman. 'And you are—?'

'Geoff. Geoff Salisbury.'

'Geoff. Of course! Pleased to meet you, Geoff. I've heard a lot about you. Mum and Dad say they'd be lost without you.'

Geoff beamed and shifted from foot to foot. 'Well . . . that's probably a bit of an exaggeration.'

Very 'umble, Banks thought.

'Not at all,' said Roy. 'Not at all.' He gave Geoff a firm

handshake and clapped him on the shoulder. 'Good to meet you at last.'

Geoff basked in the glow of Roy's charm like a child in his mother's embrace.

All this time, Ida Banks had stood by, smiling on. Roy turned to her again and gave her a hug. Then he handed over the package he'd been carrying. Ida Banks opened it. It was a bottle of Veuve Clicquot champagne. Vintage.

She turned to her husband. 'Ooh, look at this, Arthur! Champagne.'

'It's the real stuff, too,' Roy said, with a wink at Banks. 'None of your Spanish *cava* or New World sparklers.'

Arthur Banks grunted. Banks happened to know that his father hated champagne, as much because it was a symbol of the upper classes as for its taste.

'I'd better put it away for a special occasion,' said his mother, taking it through the kitchen and placing it into the dark depths of the larder, where it would probably remain. Banks thought to mention that today was as special an occasion as they were likely to have in a while, but he knew it was best to keep quiet when Roy was in full benevolent swing. He'd bought a few cans of beer and lager, himself, and he knew that *they* would be emptied that very evening, without a doubt.

'Now, then,' said Ida Banks, rubbing her hands together and reaching out to touch Corinne's shoulder, 'what about a drink for everyone? Corinne, love, what'll you have?'

'Lager and lime?'

'Right you are, love. And you, Roy?'

'Just a Perrier for me, Mum,' said Roy. 'Driving.'

'Of course.' Ida Banks frowned. 'What did you say? Perrier? I don't think we have any of that, do we, Alan?'

Banks shook his head. 'Only tap water.'

'Well, that won't do, will it?' his mother said scornfully.

'It's all right, Mrs B,' chimed in Geoff, 'I'll just nip over the road. Old Ali's bound to have some. He sells everything.' And before anyone could stop him he was off.

Ida Banks turned to Roy again. 'You won't be driving for ages yet, I hope, son. Won't you have a glass of something a bit stronger first?'

'Oh, go on, then,' said Roy. 'You've twisted my arm. I'll have a glass of white wine.'

Banks's mother gave him a questioning glance. 'We've got that, Mum,' he said, then looked at his brother. 'Screw top OK, Roy?'

'Whatever,' said Roy, his lip curling.

Banks and his father both opted for beer.

'Come on, then, Corinne, love,' said Ida Banks, taking Corinne by the arm. 'You can keep me company and help me pour.'

Banks couldn't believe it. His mother was fawning all over Roy's twenty-something bit of fluff, the sort of girl who'd have been granted no more than a sniff of distaste if Banks had brought her home. Still, he should have expected it. Roy was Banks's younger brother by five years. He had grown up watching Banks do everything wrong and getting caught for it – staying out too late as a teenager, listening to the radio under the bedsheets when he should have been asleep, smoking, leaving home to go to college in London, joining the police – and Roy had keenly observed his parents' reactions. Roy had learned well from his brother's mistakes, and he had done everything right. Now, in his mother's eyes, Roy could do no wrong, and even Arthur Banks, not given to expressions of any kind, didn't seem to disapprove of Roy as much as he did of Banks. Which was odd, indeed, Banks thought, as Roy was the consummate capitalist.

Roy sat down, first pulling at the razor-sharp crease of his black suit trousers. 'So how's life at the cop shop?' he asked, looking away even before he'd got the words out, indicating to Banks that he didn't have the slightest iota of interest.

'Fine,' said Banks.

'Is that your Renault out there?'

'Yes. Why?'

'Not bad. Only it looks new. Been on the take?'

'Oh, you know me, Roy. A few thousand here, a few thousand there.'

Roy laughed. Corinne and Ida Banks, best friends now, came through with the drinks on a tray at the same time Geoff came back from the shop. 'Sorry, they didn't have any Perrier,' he said. 'I got this other stuff Ali recommended. St . . . something or other . . . I can't pronounce it. OK?'

'It'll do,' said Roy. 'Be a good bloke and pop it in the fridge, would you, Geoff?'

Geoff seemed only too pleased to oblige.

'Isn't this lovely?' said Ida Banks, handing out the drinks. 'We can have our own little family party before the rest of our guests arrive. Corinne tells me she's an accountant, Roy.'

'That's right, Mum. Saved me a fortune in taxes.'

Corinne sat on the floor near his feet and rested her head against his thigh. He stroked her hair the way one would a faithful dog. 'She's very good with figures, aren't you, Corinne?'

Corinne blushed. 'If you say so, Roy.'

She really did seem like a 'nice' girl to Banks, and that

made him wonder all the more what she was doing with Roy. Not that Roy wasn't handsome or charming. In fact he possessed both of those attributes in spades. Under his suit, he wore a pale blue silk polo-neck. His hair, not quite so black as Banks's, was long, over his ears and collar, expensively cut, and he had a small shaving nick near the cleft of his chin. His energetic blue eyes resembled Banks's, except that they were predatory and calculating, whereas Banks's were curious and intense.

Banks had thought more than once that his brother Roy fitted the classic definition of the psychopath: he was glib and superficial, egocentric, manipulative, shallow and completely lacking in any feelings of remorse, empathy or guilt. Certainly all his behaviour and his emotional responses were learned, assumed through close observation of others as the best way to get on in the world. Underneath it all, Banks guessed, the only things that mattered to him were his needs, and how he could meet them, and his success, measured, of course, by money and power. Perhaps that was why he had already gone through three wives.

'Oops, mustn't forget,' Roy said, putting his glass down and getting suddenly to his feet. Corinne almost fell over sideways. 'Sorry, love.' He patted her shoulder. 'Just got to nip down to the Porsche. Forgot something. Wouldn't want to leave it out there too long. You never know on an estate like this. Give us a hand, will you, Geoff?'

Geoff, returned from the kitchen, beer in hand, stated that he was only too willing to do anything for Roy, and set his glass down on the table. Corinne smiled shyly as the two of them went out. Banks hadn't heard her speak yet and wondered what her voice was like, her accent. 'Where are you from?' he asked, just to find out.

'Canterbury,' she said. 'Well, I grew up there. After that I went to Manchester University.'

She didn't have much of a regional accent, Banks learned. She was well spoken, clearly educated, and her voice was pleasant, soft and musical, a little reedy.

'How long have you known Roy?'

'About three months.'

'They're getting engaged,' Ida Banks said. 'So now we've *really* got something to celebrate.'

Corinne blushed.

'That true?' Banks asked.

She smiled and nodded. He felt like warning her off. Roy had been married three times and two of his wives had ended up confiding in Banks about what an unfaithful, cruel bastard Roy was. He had never actually hit either of them – so they both swore – but he curtailed their freedom and terrorized them psychologically. The second, a particularly bright neurosurgeon called Maria, ended up seeing a psychiatrist for years after they split up, trying to splice together the frayed strands of her self-esteem. Banks had seen her change – albeit at infrequent intervals – from a secure, confident young doctor into an apologetic, tongue-tied wreck whose hands shook so much she couldn't thread a needle. The third wife, thank God, had seen the signs before it got too late and left Roy in time.

Roy and Geoff came back carrying large cardboard boxes, which they set down on the living-room floor. 'Happy anniversary,' Roy said. 'Go on. Open them.'

Banks's parents looked at one another, then his mother got some scissors from the kitchen drawer and came back and knelt by the largest box. Roy and Geoff helped, and soon between them had managed to drag out the computer monitor, processor unit and keyboard.

'It's a computer,' said Ida Banks, clearly at a loss.

'Now you'll be able to go on the Internet,' said Roy. 'We'll be able to send each other email.'

'Will we?'

'Yes.'

'But it's so . . . so expensive.'

'Oh, it's nothing. Everyone should have a computer these days. They're the future.'

Ida Banks reached out and touched it gingerly, as if it might bite. 'The future—'

'We'd better get it out of the way for the time being,' said Arthur Banks. 'Our guests will be arriving soon.'

'Right.'

Between them, Geoff, Roy and Banks took the computer upstairs and set it up on the desk in the spare room.

'That'll be nice for them,' said Geoff.

Banks thought it was the stupidest present he could think of. His parents were in their seventies; they weren't going to learn how to use a computer. His own present, a particularly moody Yorkshire landscape painting he had found in an antique shop in Richmond, had met with polite praise, but he felt it was probably destined for the back of the wardrobe. The computer, he suspected, would sit at this desk, not even plugged in, just gathering dust. Unless Geoff Salisbury decided to use it.

Just as the three of them started downstairs, the front doorbell rang.

'Here come the first guests,' said Geoff. 'It's started.'

19

First to arrive were Uncle Frank and Aunt Harriet, and after that Banks began to lose track. Here came relatives he hadn't seen for years, cousins he never even knew existed. It was only to be expected with both his mother and father coming from large families – six and four respectively – but it was a shock nonetheless.

Geoff took to bartending duties like a fish to water, and Roy worked the room like a politician, all hail-fellow-well-met, as if these people he had probably never seen before meant more to him than his own life. If the truth were known, he had been home even less often than Banks and hardly ever in touch with the more distant relatives.

Arthur Banks seemed bewildered by it all, tired, sticking to his armchair, glass of beer at hand, though Ida got into the party spirit and Banks fancied she even became a little tipsy. Music played quietly in the background, mostly crooners and big bands, though pop entered the mix when someone found an old compilation album. It was pretty much the same stuff as Banks had found in his room, or at least softer stuff from the same period – Cliff Richard, Eden Kane, Frank Ifield, Billy Fury, the Bachelors and the ubiquitous Val Doonican – but it was only for background, wallpaper music.

In a lull after the first few guests had arrived, Banks managed to get Roy alone for a few minutes while a couple of young cousins, similarly bedecked, admired Corinne's body-piercing.

'I've been wanting a word in your ear,' Banks said. 'It's about that Geoff Salisbury.'

'What about him? Seems like a decent chap. Takes good care of Mum and Dad.'

'That's just it. I think he steals from them.'

'Oh, come on, Alan. It's that suspicious copper's mind of yours working overtime again.'

'No. It's more than that.' Banks told him about the short change.

'Could have been any reason for that,' Roy said. 'A genuine mistake. You don't always have to think the worst of people, you know.'

'He's got their PIN number. They give him their Abbeylink card.'

'He takes care of their finances. For crying out loud, *somebody's* got to do it. I mean it's not as if you're around much, is it?'

Banks realized he was fighting a losing battle. Roy didn't want to believe that Geoff was anything other than a godsend, and he would resist any evidence to the contrary. 'He's got a criminal record,' Banks went on nevertheless, pissing against the wind. 'Swindling old folk out of their life savings.'

Roy just laughed. 'Mum and Dad haven't got anything worth swindling. You know that. And besides, don't you believe in rehabilitation? I assume he's paid his debt to society?'

'Yes, but—'

'Well, then.'

'For Christ's sake, Roy. I caught him red-handed.'

'Listen, big brother. So what if he's pocketing a bob or two here and there? He practically does all their shopping for them, house cleaning, too. Isn't it worth it?'

'That's not the point. If he wants paying for what he does, that's different.'

486

'Maybe it's just his way.'

'It's a funny bloody way.'

Roy shrugged and laid his arm across Banks's shoulders. 'Like I said, it's not as if you're around to do it, is it, eh? I say count your blessings and let sleeping dogs lie. Look, there's Uncle Ken. See you later.'

Banks muttered to himself under his breath. He should have known approaching Roy was a waste of time. Anybody suspected of swindling a penny out of *him* and he'd probably put a contract out on them, but his own parents . . . On the other hand, was Roy right? Was Banks making too much out of all this? Being a party pooper? He looked at his parents. They seemed happy enough – his mother did, anyway – what right had he got to challenge that? What gave him the moral justification to come down here once in a blue moon and spoil what little good fortune they had going for them? His mother clearly adored Geoff – he could tell by the way she looked at him and talked about him – and having him around made life a hell of a lot easier for his father, too. Roy was right. Banks had been interfering too much, and it was about time he backed off and left people to get on with their lives.

'Penny for them?'

Banks turned. It was Kay. 'I didn't hear you come in,' he said. 'Nice to see you.'

She smiled and touched his arm. 'Nice to see you, too. I was just talking to your mother. She offered her condolences.'

She was wearing a lemon summer dress, which fell to just below her knees and she had her hair tied up and held in place with a patterned leather barrette.

'You look wonderful,' Banks said.

Kay blushed. 'Thank you. How about a drink for the lady?'

'Of course. Vodka and tonic?'

'That'll do nicely.' She took hold of his arm. 'And don't go too far away. I don't know anyone else here.'

'Of course you do,' said Banks. 'You know my parents.'

'I haven't seen them for years.'

'And my brother Roy.'

'He was just a little kid when we were together. Around too often, if I remember correctly.'

Banks nodded. He remembered being blackmailed into giving Roy money to get lost on more than one occasion. 'You know Geoff Salisbury,' he said, nodding to where Geoff stood by the fireplace talking to some cousin whose name Banks couldn't remember.

Kay gave a little shudder. 'Yuck. I don't know about you, but he gives me the creeps.'

They got their drinks.

'Come on,' Banks said to Kay. 'Let's get some fresh air.'

They went out to the back step. Banks could hear music next door, but only softly. The rain had stopped earlier that afternoon and it had turned into a pleasant evening. The sky was already darkening and the stars coming out. There was even a pale quarter moon low in the sky. Banks leaned against the wall. Kay stood quietly beside him.

'Last night—' he began.

But Kay hushed him, putting a finger to his lips. 'No. Don't say anything. That was marvellous. Special. Let's leave it at that, shall we?'

'If you like,' Banks said. He'd been thinking the same thing. What had happened had been about the past, unfinished business, passing magic. It had been time out of time. Tomorrow they would both go back to their real lives and probably never see one another again. Banks thought about how their relationship had ended all those years ago, and how he had believed he would never see her again after he went to London. This was enough. This was more than enough. It had to be.

They went back inside. The party went on, as these things do. Banks and Kay talked to Mrs Green for a while, and Banks promised not to be such a stranger. Aunt Florence regaled him with her cataracts, and Aunt Lynn went on about her gall-bladder operation. He also heard about Cousin Patrick's prostate problems, Uncle Gerald's haemorrhoids and Cousin Louise's manic depression. It was enough to make him want to kill himself before he got old. Then there was Cousin Beth's divorce, Nick and Janet's third baby, a girl they had named Shania, Sharon's promotion, Gail's miscarriage and Ayesha's boob job. All the while Kay stood politely by, asking questions and making sympathetic comments or noises. Roy continued to work the room, seemingly indefatigable.

Inevitably, Uncle Ted fell asleep. Cousin Angie had too much to drink and was sick in the kitchen sink, dislodging a nose stud in the process, which she nearly inhaled. Uncle Gerald and Uncle Frank almost came to blows. Aunt Ruth wet herself, and young, lovely, anorexic Cousin Sue, with all the self-esteem of a blade of grass, became tearful and made a pathetic attempt to seduce Banks.

All in all, it was just another typical family do.

Roy and Corinne left early. They sought out Banks and Kay to say their goodbyes, and as usual Roy invited Banks to the South Kensington house, said they really must see more of one another and that he hoped Banks could make it to the wedding next year. Banks promised he would try, gave the blushing bride-to-be a chaste kiss on her pale, cool cheek, and they were gone.

When Banks looked around, he noticed that Geoff Salisbury had left too. Only one or two relatives remained, and they were either very close or very drunk. Banks found his mother having a heart-to-heart with her sister, Flo, and said he'd see Kay home and be right back.

The street was quiet, the evening air cool. They saw only a few people as they walked the short distance to Kay's house.

'I'd better not come in,' he said at the doorstep.

'No.'

He wondered what would happen if he leaned forward and kissed her on the lips. Would their resolve melt? Somehow, he didn't think it was very strong.

'Anyway,' he said, 'if you're ever up Eastvale way—'

'Of course I will.' She gave him the sort of smile that said she never would be, then after a quick kiss on the cheek, the door opened and closed and Banks was left standing there alone.

He didn't want to go back to the dregs of the party immediately, didn't want to face the drunken relatives desperately sobering up for the drive home, didn't want to face the mess of spilled drinks and food smeared on the carpets. He knew he would have to – he owed it to his parents to help clean up at least – but he could put it off for a little while longer.

The moon was higher now and Banks could see stars, planets, constellations even, beyond the amber glow of the street lights. He wandered the quiet Sunday night streets of the estate feeling oddly melancholy, past the maisonettes where he used to deliver newspapers, past the house where his old, late friend Steve Hill used to live. Steve had kept toads in a bell jar at the bottom of the garden, Banks remembered, but he was forgetful, and one summer he neglected them for so long that they shrivelled up and died. They looked like dried mushrooms. That was what happened to living things you were supposed to love and care for but neglected.

His melancholy was probably something to do with Kay, he realized, though he hadn't really wanted to repeat last night, either. Last night had had a magic about it that any attempt at repetition would fall well short of. He remembered how their relationship had fallen apart all those years ago. His fault.

It had all started to change when Kay left school at sixteen and got a job at Lloyd's bank in the town centre. She made new friends, had money to spare, started going for drinks with the office crowd regularly after work on a Friday. Banks was still at school, having stayed on for his A levels, and somehow a schoolboy had less appeal than these slightly older, better dressed, more sophisticated men of the world at the office. They had more money to flash around and, even more important, some of them had cars. One pillock called Nigel, with a plummy accent and a Triumph MG, particularly got up Banks's nose. Kay insisted there was no hanky-panky going on, but Banks became tortured with jealousy, racked by imagined infidelities, and in the end Kay walked away. She couldn't stand his constant harping on about who she was seeing and what she was doing, she said, and the way he got stroppy if she even so much as *looked at* another man.

The irony was, given that his A level results weren't good enough for university – the first bone of contention between him and his parents – he might as well not have bothered staying on. He'd spent far too much time with Kay, away from his studies, listening to Hendrix, Dylan and Pink Floyd, reading books that weren't on the syllabus.

Shortly after the break up, Banks moved to London and went to pursue business studies at the poly. A year or two after that and several brief, unsatisfactory, casual relationships later, he met Sandra.

A dog barked as he reached the edge of the estate by the railway lines. A local train rattled by, one or two silhouettes visible through the windows. Banks started towards home. He had only got a few yards when the mobile in his pocket rang. He had forgotten to turn it off.

'Alan? I hope I'm not disturbing your party.'

It was Annie Cabbot. Banks wondered how he would have felt if he had gone in with Kay and the phone had rung just as they were . . . it didn't bear thinking about.

'No,' he said quietly. He happened to be passing the telephone boxes at the end of the street, so he decided to stand inside one and take the call. That way he didn't seem like one of those silly buggers walking around talking to his girlfriend on his mobile phone.

'I'm sorry to call so late,' Annie said.

'That's all right. Aren't you off duty?'

'Yes, but I was waiting to hear from DS Ryan in Loughborough. He was out at the pictures.'

'DS Ryan? So this is about Geoff Salisbury?'

'Yes. What's wrong, Alan? You sound funny. Distant.'

'So would you if you were standing in the middle of a council estate talking on your mobile.'

Annie laughed. 'Oh, I don't know. I'm not quite as conservative as you are.'

'OK. Point taken. What did this DS Ryan come up with?'

'It's interesting, actually,' said Annie. 'At least, I thought you'd want to know.'

'Fill me in.'

'As Winsome told you, Salisbury was actually convicted of fraud. It was a neighbour, an elderly woman, and he started by helping out around the place, that sort of thing.'

'Sounds familiar,' said Banks. 'Go on.'

'Seems he managed to come between her and her children and get himself written into her will. She didn't have much. Only a few hundred quid and an insurance policy, but he copped for most of it.'

'What happened?'

'The family contested it. Undue influence, that sort of thing. Hard to prove. Anyway, in the end Mr Salisbury won out.'

'Where does the conviction come in?'

'Just getting to that. During proceedings, it came out that Geoff Salisbury had persuaded the woman to invest in a non-existent business venture of his. A garage.'

'Ah-hah.'

'Again, it wasn't much. Only two hundred quid.'

'Doesn't matter,' said Banks. 'Is a man who preys on the poor any less guilty than one who preys on the rich?'

'I'm afraid that's a bit too philosophical for me at this time on a Sunday evening, but at a guess I'd say even more so, wouldn't you?'

'I would. Thanks a lot, Annie. Above and beyond, and all that.'

'Oh, that's not all.'

'Really?'

'Really. While all this was going on, Mr Salisbury's mother died. Well, she was old and—'

'Sick?'

'How did you guess? She had diabetes. Anyway, she died. Or—'

Banks felt a tingle go up his spine. 'Or what?'

'Or he helped her on her way. Nothing was ever proven. There weren't even any charges. But DS Ryan was one of the investigating officers, and he says he was suspicious enough to ask for an autopsy. Negative. The woman was old, she went hypoglycaemic, and that was that.'

'What's that?'

'Hypoglycaemic? It's something that happens to diabetics, apparently, caused by too much insulin or low food intake.'

'He gave her an overdose of insulin?'

'No evidence of that.'

'But someone could have brought it about, this hypoglycaemic coma?'

'Yes. Hard to prove, though.'

'What did DS Ryan say?'

'DS Ryan said that his older sister is a diabetic and she always keeps her bedside drawer full of Mars bars or chocolate of some kind for just that sort of eventuality.'

'But I thought diabetics had to avoid sugar like the plague?'

'So did I. Apparently, they do. Unless they go hypoglycaemic. Then they need a hit of sugar.'

'Or?'

'Coma. Death. And in this case there were other complications. Weak heart, for example.'

'And DS Ryan says?'

'DS Ryan says the doctor didn't find any traces of sugar products close to Mrs Salisbury's bed, and he found that in itself suspicious. In his opinion – DS Ryan's, that is – Geoff Salisbury was responsible, knowing it was just a matter of time before she'd need a sugar fix.'

'He killed his own mother. Is that what you're saying?'

'Mercy killing, but killing all the same.'

'Bloody hell,' said Banks. 'This changes things.'

'It does?'

'I'd been thinking of leaving well alone.'

'But not now?'

'Not now. Thanks a lot, Annie.'

'My pleasure. See you tomorrow?'

'OK. And thanks again.'

Missing Mars bars. A faulty oxygen-tank valve. Banks wondered who else Geoff Salisbury had assisted in their final moments on earth. He also wondered how long it would be before his own father suffered that fatal angina attack and was unable to find his nitroglycerine tablets in time. Putting his phone in his pocket, he headed straight for Geoff Salisbury's house.

20

'Look, I can see you're not going to let this drop, are you?' said Salisbury when Banks had told him he knew about the conviction. 'So I've been to prison. It's nothing to be ashamed of. I served my time.'

'As a matter of fact,' said Banks, 'it is something to be ashamed of. But those who've been there rarely seem to think so. Innocent, were you, like everyone else?'

'No. I did it. I was desperate and she didn't need the

money, so I conned her. I'm not saying I'm proud of *that*, what I did, but like I said, I served my time, paid my debt to society.'

Debt to society. Roy's words exactly and an odd phrase when you really thought about it. 'Would that it were as simple as that,' Banks said. Salisbury's living room wasn't quite as clean and tidy as he had expected, but perhaps he used all his energy on other people's homes and had none left for his own. Dust gathered in the corners, the carpet was threadbare and lumps of mould floated on the half-empty coffee cup on the table.

'All right,' said Salisbury, 'suppose, just *suppose* that I was ripping people off. Some people might actually believe I'm a power for good around here.'

'What do you mean?'

'An estate like this, the old folks need someone on their side, someone to look out for them. They die off, you see, and when they do it's mostly young 'uns come in off the waiting list. You know the sort. Young lasses barely out of school with three kids and no father in sight. Or that lot next door to your mum and dad's. Scum. Now you're a copper, Alan, you tell me if he doesn't have prison written all over him. And as for the kids, well, it'll only be a matter of time. And if it's not scum like that it's foreigners. Gyppos. Darkies. Pakis. Them with the turbans. All with their funny ways, slaughtering goats in the street and whatever, not giving a toss for our customs and traditions and way of life. See, the old folks, they get frightened when everything around them starts to feel threatening and *unfamiliar*. Their world's changing so fast and their bodies can't do what they used to do, so they end up feeling lost and scared. That's where someone like me comes in. I reassure them, do odd jobs, give them a friendly and familiar face to relate to. So what if I make a few bob out of it? Hypothetically.'

'I'd say, hypothetically, that it makes you a thief.'

'Words, Alan, just words.'

'Actually, no. Legal concepts.'

'Well, you would say that, wouldn't you?'

'Here's another one to try on for size. *Murder*.'

Salisbury blinked and stared at him. 'What?'

'You heard me, Geoff. Oh, you might have a more fancy name for it, something high-sounding and moral, such as *mercy* killing, but in my eyes it's murder plain and simple.'

Salisbury sat back in his chair. 'I don't know what you're talking about.'

'Oh, I think you do. There was your own mother for a start. Don't tell me a woman who's been a diabetic for a good part of her life doesn't know to keep some sugar on hand in case she goes hypoglycaemic.'

Salisbury banged his fist on the chair arm. 'That's over and done with,' he said. 'I wasn't there. Nobody ever proved anything against me!'

'I'm not saying you haven't been clever, Geoff. You never were there, were you? Mr Green's faulty valve, for example. Wouldn't be difficult for a car mechanic, would it? And what about Mrs Summerville, Geoff, gentle pillow over the face as she slept, was it? Nobody would ask too many questions. Or perhaps a little too much morphine? She was alone. You had a key. They always give you a key, don't they? And what about the hundred quid you drew out with her bank card the day she died. Mistake, that. She couldn't get it herself, remember – she was bedridden – and her daughter could find no sign of the money.'

Salisbury got to his feet. 'You can't prove a damn thing. Get out of here! Go on, get out!'

Banks didn't move. 'You don't get away with it that easily, Geoff, especially not when it's my parents you're playing with now. I saw the piece of silver paper you folded and dropped in the bin at Mrs Summerville's house. I'll bet it has your prints on it.'

'So I went there. I helped her. Like I helped the others. So what? That doesn't prove anything.'

'I'll bet if we exhumed the body, though, we'd find some evidence of tampering, some evidence of what you did. She hasn't been dead as long as the others, Geoff. There'll be forensic evidence. In the house, too.'

For the first time, Banks saw Salisbury falter and sit down again. He knew he had been guessing, taking a stab in the dark, but it seemed to have touched a nerve. 'She had cancer and a weak heart,' Banks went on. 'All it took was a little pressure. She didn't even have the strength to fight back, did she?'

'What do you mean *forensic* evidence?' Geoff asked. 'They'd never dig her up.'

'Oh yes, they would. On my say-so. And you know exactly what they'd find, don't you?'

'But the doctor signed the death certificates. There wasn't even an inquest, nothing suspicious at all.'

'Why would there be, Geoff? Don't you know how it goes? All your victims were medically attended during their illnesses, they'd all been seen by their doctors within fourteen days of death, and they were all terminally ill, likely to die at any time. There were no grounds for a coroner's inquest. And remember: none of them was alone with family members when they died. Not even your mother. You made sure you were out of the house that night, didn't you?'

'This is absurd. They'll never open up her coffin.'

'Yes, they will. We'd just better thank the Lord that she was buried and not cremated, don't you think? What will they find? Tell me.'

Salisbury licked his lips, staring at Banks, and said nothing for a long time. 'You think you're clever, don't you?' he said at last. 'You don't know nothing about it.'

'About what?'

'Suffering.'

'Tell me about it, Geoff. I want to know.'

'Why should I? You wouldn't understand.'

'Believe me, I'll try. And it'll go better for you if you do. If we don't have to exhume the body. That's a lot of work. And messy. Nobody wants to do it. I think we'd be able to prove a case against you, Geoff, I really do, but if you help us, if you tell me about it, it'll go a lot easier for you.'

'Why do you think they let me cheat them, take their money?'

Banks frowned. 'Come again?'

'You don't think they didn't know what I was doing, do you? They knew all right and they let it go on. Payment. That's what it was. They just couldn't come right out and say it. What they really wanted me to do. But it was their way of paying me, of letting me know what they wanted me to do.'

'Hang on a minute, Geoff,' said Banks. 'Let me get this straight. Did you kill Mr Green and Mrs Summerville?'

'Yes. No. I put them to sleep. I ended their suffering.'

'And your mother?'

'It was what she wanted. It was what they all wanted. It was beautiful.'

'What was?'

Salisbury's eyes shone. 'The transformation. From pain to peace. Suffering to grace. It was like being God.'

'Did either Mrs Green or anyone from the Summerville family suggest that you do what you did?'

'Not in so many words, no.'

'But that was how you interpreted their actions in letting you get away with stealing money?'

'Like I said, they knew. It was their way of paying for what they wanted done. Close family couldn't do it, could they? They'd soon be suspects, or they didn't care enough and were never around, like you and that Summerville girl. You don't see their suffering. I do. Day in, day out. I was their saviour. Somebody had to be.'

Banks got up.

'What are you doing?'

'I'm going to ring the local police now, and I want you to tell them what you've just told me. Tell them everything. Maybe you're sick. Maybe you need help. I don't know.' All I do know, Banks thought as he took out his mobile, is that I want you off this estate and as far away from my parents as possible.

21

It was about an hour later when two uniformed constables and one detective sergeant, grumpy at being dragged out of the Sunday night pub darts match, arrived at Geoff Salisbury's house.

'You know, with all due respect to your rank and all, sir,

we don't particularly appreciate North Yorkshire CID poking around on our patch, doing our job for us,' said the surly DS, whose name was Les Kelly and who was going prematurely bald. Luckily, Banks hadn't encountered DS Kelly on his last trip to Peterborough.

Banks smiled to himself. It would probably have been his reaction, too, had Kelly come up north. At least it would have been *if* he had been a DS and ten years younger.

'Believe me, DS Kelly, it wasn't my intention,' he said. 'I just came for the party.'

'You what?'

Banks sighed. 'I was brought up around here. Down the street. I came home for my parents' golden wedding and this is what I found going on.' He gestured towards Salisbury, who was giving his statement to the uniformed officers.

'How about we go outside for a minute?' said Kelly. 'The uniforms can deal with his statement, and I fancy a smoke.'

Banks and Kelly stood on the path. Kelly lit a cigarette and Banks craved one. A few locals had noted the arrival of the police and a small crowd had gathered just beyond the patrol car. Not that police cars were a novelty on the estate, but it *was* nearly bedtime on a Sunday.

'I was winning, too,' said Kelly.

'What?'

'The darts match.'

Banks smiled. 'Oh. Sorry.'

'Never mind. We never sleep. Always ready to bring another wrongdoer to justice. I just transferred here from West Midlands, myself. You say you're from around these parts?'

'Uh-huh. Long time ago. Came here when I was twelve. Grew up just down the street. Used to go out with the girl whose mother that bastard killed.'

'They'll put him in the nut house.'

'Likely. As long as he's locked up.'

Kelly looked around and sniffed the air, then he took a deep drag on his cigarette and blew out a long plume of smoke. 'I grew up on an estate pretty much like this one,' he said. 'Barrow-in-Furness.'

'Not a part of the world I know.'

'Don't bother.'

'Look, while you're here,' said Banks, 'there is another small matter you might be able to help with.'

'Oh? And what's that?'

'The family that lives next to my parents,' said Banks. 'I don't know their names but the bloke looks like Fred West—'

'Ah, the Wyatts.'

'Is that their name?'

'Well, it's easier that way. To be honest, though, I think he's the only true Wyatt there. She's a Fisher. Had kids with a Young and Harrison and a Davies. Need I go on?'

'How many of them are there?'

'According to the council, only five. That's all the place is big enough for.'

'I saw a sleeping bag on the staircase.'

'You were in there?'

'Noise complaint.'

'Ah, yes. Well, our latest estimation is about twelve, give or take a couple.'

'Can you do anything?'

'About what?'

'Drugs, for a start. And I wouldn't be surprised if some of those kids are being sexually abused.'

'Nor me.' Kelly finished his cigarette and stamped it out on the path. 'It's only a matter of time,' he said. 'You know how these things can drag on. But we've got an eye on them, and the social's investigating them, too, so sooner or later one of us will come up with something.'

'And then?'

Kelly laughed. 'And then? You know as well as I do. Then the farce just begins. They'll end up on another estate much like this one, most likely, and it'll start all over again.'

The uniforms came out with Geoff Salisbury, slump-shouldered, between them. 'Done,' one of them said. Salisbury gave Banks a look that was half pleading for understanding and forgiveness, and half pure hatred. Banks didn't know which half he liked less.

'Right.' Kelly clapped his hands. 'Let's go see what the custody sergeant has to say, shall we? And I'll say goodnight to you, for the moment, DCI Banks. We might need you again.'

Banks smiled. 'I'm only a phone call away.'

22

By Monday morning, when Banks awoke to sunshine and the sound of birds beyond his thin curtains, news of Geoff Salisbury's arrest had spread around the entire estate. When he went down for breakfast, he found his parents sitting quietly at the table. He poured himself a cup of tea. His mother wouldn't look at him when he walked into the room.

'You've heard, then?' he asked.

'About Geoff?' she said, tears in her eyes. 'Mrs Wilkins came to tell me. That was your doing, wasn't it?'

'I'd no choice, Mum,' said Banks, resting his hand on her arm. She jerked it away.

'How could you do that? You know what he meant to us.'

'Mum, Geoff Salisbury was a murderer. He killed Mr Green and he killed Kay's mother.' Not to mention his own mother, Banks thought. 'I don't see how you can defend him. You *knew* those people. They were your neighbours.'

Mrs Banks shook her head. 'I don't believe it. Not Geoff. He wouldn't do anything like that. He's gentle as a kitten.'

'He admitted it.'

'You must have forced him. Interrogated him until he didn't know what he was saying.'

'I don't work like that, Mum. Believe me, he did it. He might have thought he was doing good, doing the families a favour, but he did it.'

Banks looked at his father, who caught his eye. He knew right away that they were thinking the same thing: who was next?

Banks stood up. 'Look, Mum, I've got to go now.'

'All you brought was trouble. It was supposed to be a happy occasion. Now look what you've gone and done. Spoiled it all, as usual. I wish our Roy was here.'

Banks's heart felt heavy, but there was nothing more he could say. There was as much point in telling his mother that Roy didn't give a shit as there was in telling her that Geoff Salisbury was a cold-blooded murderer.

'I'm sorry, Mum,' he said, then dashed upstairs to

throw his few belongings in his bag. He looked at the boxes of records and exercise books again and decided to leave them. All he took was the poetry.

Let go.

He was standing at the door of his room when he saw his father come slowly up the stairs. They stood on the landing facing one another. 'She's upset,' said Arthur Banks. 'She doesn't know what she's saying. I'll take care of her. I'll make sure she knows what's what.'

'What *is* what, Dad? I'm not even sure I know. Did I do the right thing?'

'Only you know that for certain, lad. But you did your job. You'd no choice. You're a copper and he was a bad 'un. Your mother'll get over it. She really liked him, that's all. He was useful around the house. And he could be a right charmer.'

'I know,' said Banks. 'His type usually is.'

'You know she never likes admitting she's wrong about people. But if he killed those people, you were right. You were only doing your job. I don't mind a bob or two here and there – and don't think I didn't notice, I just kept quiet for your mother's sake – but I draw the line at killing.' He laughed. 'Who's to say it wouldn't have been me next, eh?'

They both knew there was a lot more truth in that fear than either cared to explore.

'Bye, Dad,' Banks said. 'I'll be in touch.'

'Don't be a stranger, son. And don't worry. Your mother'll get over it. I'll tell her to ring you in a day or so, shall I?'

'Please do.'

His father smiled. 'Or send you an email?'

Banks moved forward impulsively and hugged him. It

was quick, and he felt only the slightest pressure of his father's hand on the back of his shoulder, but it was enough.

Banks dashed down the stairs and walked down the path to his car, tears prickling his eyes. He felt a weight in the side pocket of his jacket and realized it was Kay's copy of *Lady Chatterley's Lover*. Now he decided he might as well keep it. Maybe he would even get around to reading it, over thirty years after he'd borrowed it.

When he got to the driver's side of his car, he cursed out loud. Some bastard had taken a coin or a nail and made a deep scratch along the paintwork all the way from back to front. He thought he saw someone watching from an upstairs window of the Wyatt house.

Bugger them. Bugger the lot of them, he thought, and got into his car and drove away.

A NECESSARY END

**For Martin, Chris, Steve and Paul – old friends
who all contributed**

1

ONE

The demonstrators huddled in the March drizzle outside Eastvale Community Centre. Some of them held home-made placards aloft, but the anti-nuclear slogans had run in the rain like the red lettering at the beginning of horror movies. It was hard to make out exactly what they said any more. By eight thirty, everyone was thoroughly soaked and fed up. No television cameras recorded the scene, and not one reporter mingled with the crowd. Protests were passé, and the media were only interested in what was going on inside. Besides, it was cold, wet and dark out there.

Despite all the frustration, the demonstrators had been patient so far. Their wet hair lay plastered to their skulls and water dribbled down their necks, but still they had held up their illegible placards and shifted from foot to foot for over an hour. Now, however, many of them were beginning to feel claustrophobic. North Market Street was narrow and only dimly lit by old-fashioned gas lamps. The protestors were hemmed in on all sides by police, who had edged so close that there was nowhere left to spread out. An extra line of police stood guard at the top of the steps by the heavy oak doors, and opposite the hall more officers blocked the snickets that led to the winding back streets and the open fields beyond Cardigan Drive.

Finally, just to get breathing space, some people at the edges began pushing. The police shoved back hard. The agitation rippled its way to the solidly packed heart of the crowd, and suppressed tempers rose. When someone brought a placard down on a copper's head, the other demonstrators cheered. Someone else threw a bottle. It smashed harmlessly, high against the wall. Then a few people began to wave their fists in the air and the crowd started chanting, 'We want in! Let us in!' Isolated scuffles broke out. They were still struggling for more ground, and the police pushed back to contain them. It was like sitting on the lid of a boiling pot; something had to give.

Later, nobody could say exactly how it happened, or who started it, but most of the protestors questioned claimed that a policeman yelled, 'Let's clobber the buggers!' and that the line advanced down the steps, truncheons out. Then all hell broke loose.

TWO

It was too hot inside the Community Centre. Detective Chief Inspector Alan Banks fidgeted with his tie. He hated ties, and when he had to wear one he usually kept the top button of his shirt undone to alleviate the choking feeling. But this time he toyed with the loose knot out of boredom as well as discomfort. He wished he was at home with his arm around Sandra and a tumbler of good single malt Scotch in his hand.

But home had been a cold and lonely place these past two days because Sandra and the children were away. Her father had suffered a mild stroke, and she had gone down to Croydon to help her mother cope. Banks wished she were back. They had married young, and he found that the single life, after almost twenty years of (mostly) happy marriage, had little to recommend it.

But the main cause of Banks's ill humour droned on and on, bringing to the crowded Eastvale Community Centre a particularly nasal brand of Home Counties monetarism. It was the Honourable Honoria Winstanley, MP, come to pour oil on the troubled waters of North–South relations. Eastvale had been blessed with her presence because, though not large, it was the biggest and most important town in that part of the country between York and Darlington. It was also enjoying a period of unprecedented and inexplicable growth, thus marking itself out as a shining example of popular capitalism at work. Banks was present as a gesture of courtesy, sandwiched between two taciturn Special Branch men. Superintendent Gristhorpe had no doubt assigned him, Banks thought, because he had no desire to listen to the Hon. Honoria himself. If pushed, Banks described himself as a moderate socialist, but politics bored him and politicians usually made him angry.

Occasionally, he glanced left or right and noticed the restless eyes of the official bodyguards, who seemed to be expecting terrorist action at any moment. For want of their real names, he had christened them Chas and Dave. Chas was the bulky one with the rheumy eyes and bloated red nose, and Dave was blessed with the lean and hungry look of a Tory cabinet minister. If a member of the audience shifted in his or her seat, raised a fist to muffle a cough or reached for a handkerchief, either Chas or Dave would slip his hand under his jacket towards his shoulder holster.

It was all very silly, Banks thought. The only reason anyone might want to kill Honoria Winstanley would be for inflicting a dull speech on the audience. As motives for murder went, that came a long way down the list – though any sane judge would certainly pronounce it justifiable homicide.

Ms Winstanley paused and took a sip of water while the audience applauded. 'And I say to you all,' she continued in all-out rhetorical flight, 'that in the fullness of time, when the results of our policies have come to fruition and every vestige of socialism has been stamped out, all divisions will be healed, and the North, that revered cradle of the Industrial Revolution, will indeed prosper every bit as much as the rest of our glorious nation. Once again this will be a *united* kingdom, united under the banner of enterprise, incentive and hard work. You can already see it happening around you here in Eastvale.'

Banks covered his mouth with his hand and yawned. He looked to his left and noticed that Chas had become so enrapt by Honoria that he had momentarily forgotten to keep an eye open for the IRA, the PLO, the Baader-Meinhof group and the Red Brigade.

The speech was going down well, Banks thought, considering that members of the same government had recently told the North to stop whining about unemployment and had added that most of its problems were caused by poor taste in food. Still, with an audience made up almost entirely of members of the local Conservative Association – small businessmen, farmers and landowners, for the most part – such whole-hearted enthusiasm was only to be expected. The people in the hall had plenty of money, and no doubt they ate well, too.

It was getting even hotter and stuffier, but the Hon. Honoria showed no signs of flagging. Indeed, she was off on a laudatory digression about share-owning, making it sound as if every Englishman could become a millionaire overnight if the government continued to sell off nationalized industries and services to the private sector.

Banks needed a cigarette. He'd been trying to give up again lately, but without success. With so little happening at the station and Sandra and the children away, he had actually increased his intake. The only progress he had made was in switching from Benson & Hedges Special Mild to Silk Cut. He'd heard somewhere that breaking brand loyalty was the first step towards stopping entirely. Unfortunately he was beginning to like the new brand more than the old.

He shifted in his seat when Honoria moved on to the necessity of maintaining, even expanding, the American military presence in Britain, and Chas gave him a challenging glance. He began to wonder if perhaps this latest digression was a roundabout way of approaching the issue many people present wanted to hear about.

There had been rumours about a nuclear power station across the North York Moors on the coast, only about forty miles from Eastvale. With Sellafield to the west, that was one too many, even for some of the more right-wing locals. After all, radioactivity could be quite nasty when you depended on the land for your prosperity. They all remembered Chernobyl, and its tales of contaminated milk and meat.

And as if the peaceful use of nuclear power weren't bad enough, there was also talk of a new American air force base in the area. People were already fed up with low-flying jets breaking the sound barrier day in, day out. Even if the sheep did seem to have got used to them, they were bad for the tourist business. But it looked as if Honoria was going to skirt the issue in true politician's fashion and dazzle everyone with visions of a new golden age. Maybe the matter would come up in question time.

Honoria's speech ended after a soaring paean to education reform, law and order, the importance of military strength, and private ownership of council housing. She had made no reference at all to the nuclear power station or to the proposed air base. There was a five-second pause before the audience realized it was all over and began to clap. In that pause, Banks thought he heard signs of a commotion outside. Chase and Dave seemed to have the same notion too; their eyes darted to the doors and their hands slid towards their left armpits.

THREE

Outside, police and demonstrators punched and kicked each other wildly. Parts of the dense crowd had broken up into small skirmishes, but a heaving struggling central mass remained. Everyone seemed oblivious to all but his or her personal battle. There were no individuals, just fists, wooden sticks, boots and uniforms. Occasionally, when a truncheon connected, someone would scream in agony, fall to his knees and put his hands to the flow of blood in stunned disbelief. The police got as good as they gave, too; boots connected with groins, fists with heads. Helmets flew off and demonstrators picked them up to swing them by the straps and use as weapons. The fallen on both sides were trampled by the rest; there was no room to avoid them, no time for compassion.

One young constable, beset by two men and a woman, covered his face and flailed blindly with his truncheon; a girl, blood flowing down the side of her neck, kicked a policeman, who lay in the rain curled up in the foetal position. Four people, locked together, toppled over and crashed through the window of Winston's Tobacco Shop, scattering the fine display of Havana cigars, bowls of aromatic pipe tobacco and exotic Turkish and American cigarette packets onto the wet pavement.

Eastvale Regional Police Headquarters was only a hundred yards or so down the street, fronting the market square. When he heard the noise, Sergeant Rowe dashed outside and sized up the situation quickly. He then sent out two squad cars to block off the narrow street at both ends, and a Black Maria to put the prisoners in. He also phoned the hospital for ambulances.

When the demonstrators heard the sirens, most of them were aware enough to know they were trapped. Scuffles ceased and the scared protestors broke for freedom. Some managed to slip by before the car doors opened, and two people shoved aside the driver of one car and ran to freedom across the market square. A few others hurled themselves at the policemen who were still trying to block off the snickets, knocked them out of the way, and took off into the safety and obscurity of the back alleys. One muscular protestor forced his way up the steps towards the community centre doors with two policemen hanging on to the scruff of his neck trying to drag him back.

FOUR

Loud and prolonged applause drowned out all other sounds, and the Special Branch men relaxed their grips on their guns. The Hon. Honoria beamed at the audience and raised her clasped hands above her head in triumph.

Banks still felt uneasy. He was sure he'd heard sounds of an argument or a fight outside. He knew that a small demonstration had been planned, and wondered if it had turned violent. Still, there was nothing he could do. At all costs, the show must go on, and he didn't want to create a stir by getting up and leaving early.

At least the speech was over. If question time didn't go on too long he'd be able to get outside and smoke a cigarette in half an hour or so. An hour might see him at home with that Scotch and Sandra on the other end of the telephone line. He was hungry, too. In Sandra's absence, he had decided to have a go at haute cuisine, and though it hadn't worked out too well so far – the curry had lacked spiciness, and he'd overcooked the fish casserole – he was making progress. Surely a Spanish omelette could present no real problems?

The applause died down and the chairman announced question time. As the first person stood up and began to ask about the proposed site of the nuclear power station, the doors burst open and a hefty bedraggled young man lurched in with two policemen in tow. A truncheon cracked down, and the three fell on to the back row. The young man yelped in pain. Women screamed and reached for their fur coats as the flimsy chairs toppled and splintered under the weight of the three men.

Chas and Dave didn't waste a second. They rushed to Honoria, shielding her from the audience, and with Banks in front, they left through the back door. Beyond the cluttered storerooms, an exit opened on to a complex of back streets, and Banks led them down a narrow alley where the shops on York Road dumped their rubbish. In no time at all the four of them had crossed the road and entered the old Riverview Hotel, where the Hon. Honoria was booked to stay the night. For the first time that evening, she was quiet. Banks noticed in the muted light of the hotel lobby how pale she had turned.

Only when they got to the room, a suite with a superb view over the terraced river-gardens, did Chas and Dave relax. Honoria sighed and sank into the sofa, and Dave locked the door and put the chain on while Chas headed over to the cocktail cabinet.

'Pour me a gin and tonic, will you, dear?' said Honoria in shaky voice.

'What the hell was all that about?' Chas asked, also pouring out two stiff shots of Scotch.

'I don't know,' Banks said. 'There was a small demonstration outside. I suppose it could have—'

'Some bloody security you've got here,' said Dave, taking his drink and passing the gin and tonic to Honoria.

She gulped it down and put her hand to her brow. 'My God,' she said. 'I thought there was nobody but farmers and horse trainers living up here. Look at me, I'm shaking like a bloody leaf.'

'Look,' Banks said, hovering at the door, 'I'd better go and see what's happening.' It was obvious he wasn't going to get a drink, and he was damned if he was going to stand in as a whipping boy for the security organizers. 'Will you be all right?'

'A damn sight safer than we were back there,' Dave said. Then his tone softened a little and he came to the door with Banks. 'Yes, go on. It's your problem now, mate.' He smiled and lowered his voice, twitching his head in Honoria's direction. 'Ours is her.'

In the rush, Banks had left his raincoat in the community centre, and his cigarettes were in the right-hand pocket. He noticed Chas lighting up as he left, but hadn't

9

the audacity to ask for one. Things were bad enough already. Flipping up his jacket collar against the rain, he ran down to the market square, turned right in front of the church and stopped dead.

The wounded lay groaning or unconscious in the drizzle, and police still scuffled with the ones they'd caught, trying to force them into the backs of the cars or into the Black Maria. Some demonstrators, held by their hair, wriggled and kicked as they went, receiving sharp blows from truncheons for their efforts. Others went peacefully. They were frightened and tired now; most of the fight had gone out of them.

Banks stood rooted to the spot and watched the scene. Radios crackled; blue lights spun; the injured cried in pain and shock while ambulance attendants rushed around with stretchers. It defied belief. A full-blown riot in East-vale, admittedly on a small scale, was near unthinkable. Banks had got used to the rising crime rate, which affected even places as small as Eastvale, with just over four-teen thousand people, but riots were surely reserved for Birmingham, Liverpool, Leeds, Manchester, Bristol or London. It couldn't happen here, he had always thought as he shook his head over news of Brixton, Toxteth and Tottenham. But now it had, and the moaning casualties, police and demonstrators alike, were witness to that hard truth.

The street was blocked off at the market square to the south and near the Town Hall, at the junction with Elmet Street, to the north. The gas lamps and illuminated window displays in the twee tourist shops full of Yorkshire woollen wear, walking gear and local produce shone on the chaotic scene. A boy, no more than fifteen or sixteen, cried out as two policemen dragged him by his hair along the glistening cobbles; a torn placard that had once defiantly read NO NUKES flapped in the March wind as the thin rain tapped a faint tattoo against it; one policeman, helmet gone and hair in disarray, bent to help up another, whose moustache was matted with blood and whose nose lay at an odd angle to his face.

In the revolving blue lights, the aftermath of the battle took on a slow-motion, surrealistic quality to Banks. Elongated shadows played across walls. In the street, odd objects caught the light for a second, then seemed to vanish: an upturned helmet, an empty beer bottle, a key ring, a half-eaten apple browning at the edges, a long white scarf twisted like a snake.

Several policemen had come out of the station to help, and Banks recognized Sergeant Rowe standing behind a squad car by the corner.

'What happened?' he asked.

Rowe shook his head. 'Demo turned nasty, sir. We don't know how or why yet.'

'How many were there?'

'About a hundred.' He waved his hand at the scene. 'But we didn't expect anything like this.'

'Got a cigarette, Sergeant?'

Rowe gave him a Senior Service. It tasted strong after Silk Cut, but he drew the smoke deep into his lungs nonetheless.

'How many hurt?'

'Don't know yet, sir.'

'Any of ours?'

'Aye, a few, I reckon. We had about thirty or so on crowd control duty, but most of them were drafted in from York and Scarborough on overtime. Craig was there, and young Tolliver. I haven't seen either of them yet. It'll be busy in the station tonight. Looks like we've nicked about half of them.'

Two ambulance attendants trotted by with a stretcher between them. On it lay a middle-aged woman, her left eye clouded with blood. She turned her head painfully and spat at Sergeant Rowe as they passed.

'Bloody hell!' Rowe said. 'That was Mrs Campbell. She takes Sunday school at Cardigan Drive Congregationalist.'

'War makes animals of us all, Sergeant,' Banks said, wishing he could remember where he'd heard that, and turned away. 'I'd better get to the station. Does the super know?'

'It's his day off, sir.' Rowe still seemed stunned.

'I'd better call him. Hatchley and Richmond, too.'

'DC Richmond's over there, sir.' Rowe pointed to a tall, slim man standing near the Black Maria.

Banks walked over and touched Richmond's arm.

The young detective constable flinched. 'Oh, it's you, sir. Sorry, this has got me all tense.'

'How long have you been here, Phil?'

'I came out when Sergeant Rowe told us what was happening.'

'You didn't see it start, then?'

'No, sir. It was all over in fifteen minutes.'

'Come on. We'd better get inside and help with the processing.'

Chaos reigned inside the station. Every square inch of available space was taken up by arrested demonstrators, some of them bleeding from minor cuts, and most of them complaining loudly about police brutality. As Banks and Richmond shouldered their way towards the stairs, a familiar voice called out after them.

'Craig!' Banks said, when the young constable caught

up with them. 'What happened?'

'Not much, sir,' PC Craig shouted over the noise. His right eye was dark and puffed up, and blood oozed from a split lip. 'I got off lucky.'

'You should be at the hospital.'

'It's nothing, sir, really. They took Susan Gay off in an ambulance.'

'What was she doing out there?'

'They needed help, sir. The men on crowd control. We just went out. We never knew it would be like this . . .'

'Is she hurt badly?'

'They think it's just concussion, sir. She got knocked down, and some bastard kicked her in the head. The hospital just phoned. A Dr Partridge wants to talk to you.'

A scuffle broke out behind them and someone went flying into the small of Richmond's back. He fell forward and knocked Banks and Craig against the wall.

Banks got up and regained his balance. 'Can't anyone keep these bloody people quiet!' he shouted to the station in general. Then he turned to Craig again. 'I'll talk to the doctor. But give the super a call, if you're up to it. Tell him what's happened and ask him to come in. Sergeant Hatchley, too. Then get to the hospital. You might as well have someone look at your eye while you pay a sick call on Susan.'

'Yes, sir.' Craig elbowed his way back through the crowd, and Banks and Richmond made their way upstairs to the CID offices.

First Banks reached into his desk drawer, where he kept a spare packet of cigarettes, then he dialled Eastvale General Infirmary.

Reception paged the doctor, who picked up the phone about a minute later.

'Are there any serious injuries?' Banks asked.

'Most of them are just cuts and bruises. A few minor head wounds. On the whole, I'd say it looks worse than it is. But that's not—'

'What about PC Gay?'

'Who?'

'Susan Gay. The policewoman.'

'Oh, yes. She's all right. She's got concussion. We'll keep her in overnight for observation, then after a few days' rest she'll be right as rain. Look, I understand your concern, Chief Inspector, but that's not what I wanted to talk to you about.'

'What is it, then?' For a moment, Banks felt an icy prickle of irrational fear. Sandra? The children? The results of his last chest X-ray?

'There's been a death.'

'At the demonstration?'

'Yes.'

'Go on.'

'Well, it's more of a murder, I suppose.'

'Suppose?'

'I mean that's what it looks like. I'm not a pathologist. I'm not qualified—'

'Who's the victim?'

'It's a policeman. PC Edwin Gill.'

Banks frowned. 'I've not heard the name. Where's he from?'

'One of the others said he was drafted in from Scarborough.'

'How did he die?'

'Well, that's the thing. You'd expect a fractured skull or some wound consistent with what went on.'

'But?'

'He was stabbed. He was still alive when he was brought in. I'm afraid we didn't . . . There was no obvious wound at first. We thought he'd just been knocked out like the others. He died before we could do anything. Internal bleeding.'

Banks put his hand over the receiver and turned his eyes up to the ceiling. 'Shit!'

'Hello, Chief Inspector? Are you still there?'

'Yes. Sorry, Doctor. Thanks for calling so quickly. I'll send down some more police guards. Nobody's to leave, no matter how minor their injuries. Is there anyone from Eastvale station there? Anyone conscious, that is.'

'Just a minute.'

Dr Partridge came back with PC Tolliver, who had accompanied Susan Gray in the ambulance.

'Listen carefully, lad,' Banks said. 'We've got a bloody crisis on our hands back here, so you'll have to handle the hospital end yourself.'

'Yes, sir.'

'There'll be more men down there as soon as I can round some up, but until then do the best you can. I don't want anyone from tonight's fracas to leave there, do you understand?'

'Yes, sir.'

'And that includes our men, too. I realize some of them might be anxious to get home after they've had their cuts dressed, but I need statements, and I need them while things are fresh in their minds. OK?'

'Yes, sir. There's two or three more blokes here without serious injuries. We'll see to it.'

'Good. You know about PC Gill?'

'Yes, sir. The doctor told me. I didn't know him.'

'You'd better get someone to identify the body formally. Did he have a family?'

'Don't know, sir.'

'Find out. If he did, you know what to do.'

'Yes, sir.'

'And get Dr Glendenning down there. We need him to examine the body. We've got to move quickly on this, before things get cold.'

'I understand, sir.'

'Good. Off you go.'

Banks hung up and turned to Richmond, who stood in the doorway nervously smoothing his moustache. 'Go downstairs, would you, Phil, and tell whoever's in charge to get things quietened down and make sure no one sneaks out. Then call York and ask if they can spare a few more men for the night. If they can't, try Darlington. And you'd better get someone to rope off the street from the market square to the Town Hall, too.'

'What's up?' Richmond asked.

Banks sighed and ran a hand through his close-cropped hair. 'It looks like we've got a murder on our hands and a hundred or more bloody suspects.'

2

ONE

The wind chimes tinkled and rain hissed on the rough moorland grass. Mara Delacey had jut put the children to bed and read them Beatrix Potter's *Tale of Squirrel Nutkin*. Now it was time for her to relax, to enjoy the stillness and isolation, the play of silence and natural sound. It reminded her of the old days when she used to meditate on her mantra.

As usual, it had been a tiring day; washing to do, meals to cook, children to take care of. But it had also been satisfying. She had managed to fit in a couple of hours throwing pots in the back of Elspeth's craft shop in Relton. If it was her lot in life to be an earth mother, she thought with a smile, better to be one here, away from the rigid rules and self-righteous spirituality of the ashram, where she hadn't even been able to sneak a cigarette after dinner. She was glad she'd left all that rubbish behind.

Now she could enjoy some time to herself without feeling she ought to be out chasing after converts or singing the praises of the guru – not that many did now he was serving his stretch in jail for fraud and tax evasion. The devotees had scattered: some, lost and lonely, had gone to look for new leaders; others, like Mara, had moved on to something else.

She had met Seth Cotton a year after he had bought the

place near Relton, which he had christened Maggie's Farm. As soon as he showed it to her, she knew it had to be her home. It was a typical eighteenth-century Dales farmhouse set in a couple of acres of land on the moors above the dale. The walls were built of limestone, with gritstone corners and a flagstone roof. Recessed windows looked north over the dale, and the heavy door head, supported on stacked quoins, bore the initials T.J.H. – standing for the original owner – and the date 1765. The only addition apart from Seth's workshop, a shed at the far end of the back garden, was a limestone porch with a slate roof. Beyond the back garden fence, about fifty yards east of the main house, stood an old barn, which Seth had been busy renovating when she met him. He had split it into an upper studio-apartment, where Rick Trelawney, an artist, lived with his son, and a one-bedroom flat on the ground floor, occupied by Zoe Hardacre and her daughter. Paul, their most recent tenant, had a room in the main house.

Although the barn was more modern inside, Mara preferred the farmhouse. Its front door led directly into the spacious living room, a clean and tidy place furnished with a collection of odds and sods: an imitation Persian carpet, a reupholstered 1950s sofa, and a large table and four chairs made of white pine by Seth himself. Large beanbag cushions lay scattered against the walls for comfort.

On the wall opposite the stone fireplace hung a huge tapestry of a Chinese scene. It showed enormous mountains, their snow-streaked peaks sharp as needles above the pine forests. In the middle distance, a straggling line of tiny human figures moved up a winding path. Mara looked at it a lot. There was no overhead light in the room. She kept the shaded lamps dim and supplemented them with fat red candles because she liked the shadows the flames cast on the tapestry and the whitewashed stone walls. Her favourite place to curl up was near the window in an old rocking chair Seth had restored. There she could hear the wind chimes clearly as she sipped wine and read.

In her early days, she had devoured Kerouac, Burroughs, Ginsberg, Carlos Castaneda and the rest, but at thirty-eight she found their works embarrassingly adolescent, and her tastes had reverted to the classics she remembered from her university days. There was something about those long Victorian novels that suited a place as isolated and slow-moving as Maggie's Farm.

Now she decided to settle down and lose herself in *The Mill on the Floss*. A hand-rolled Old Holborn and a glass of Barsac would also go down nicely. And maybe some music. She walked to the stereo, selected Holst's *The Planets*, the side with 'Saturn', 'Uranus' and 'Neptune', then nestled in the chair to read by candlelight. The others were all at the demo, and they'd be sure to stop off for a pint or two at the Black Sheep in Relton on the way back. The kids were sleeping in the spare room upstairs, so she wouldn't have to keep nipping out to the barn to check on them. It was half past nine now. She could probably count on at least a couple of hours to herself.

But she couldn't seem to concentrate. The hissing outside stopped. It was replaced by the steady dripping of rain from the eaves-troughs, the porch and the trees that protected Maggie's Farm from the harsh west winds. The chimes began to sound like warning bells. There was something in the air. If Zoe were home, she'd no doubt have plenty to say about psychic forces – probably the moon.

Shrugging off her feeling of unease, Mara returned to her reading: 'And this is Dorlcote Mill. I must stand a

minute or two here on the bridge and look at it, though the clouds are threatening, and it is far on in the afternoon . . .'
It was no good; she couldn't get into it. George Eliot's spell just wasn't working tonight. Mara put down the book and concentrated on the music.

As the ethereal choir entered the end of 'Neptune', the front door rattled open and Paul rushed in. His combat jacket was dark with rain and his tight jeans stuck to his stick-insect legs.

Mara frowned. 'You're back early,' she said. 'Where are the others?'

'I don't know.' Paul was out of breath and his voice sounded shaky. He took off his jacket and hung it on the hook at the back of the door. 'I ran back by myself over the moors.'

'But that's more than four miles. What's wrong, Paul? Why didn't you wait for Seth and the others? You could have come back in the van.'

'There was some trouble,' Paul said. 'Things got nasty.' He took a cigarette from his pack of Players and lit it, cupping it in his hands the way soldiers do in old war films. His hands were trembling. Mara noticed again how short and stubby his fingers were, nails bitten to the quick. She rolled another cigarette. Paul started to pace the room.

'What's that?' Mara asked, pointing in alarm to the fleshy spot at the base of his left thumb. 'It looks like blood. You've hurt yourself.'

'It's nothing.'

Mara reached out, but he pulled his hand away.

'At least let me put something on it.'

'I told you, it's nothing. I'll see to it later. Don't you want to hear what happened?'

Mara knew better than to persist. 'Sit down, then,' she

said. 'You're driving me crazy pacing around like that.'

Paul flopped on to the cushions by the wall, taking care to keep his bloodied hand out of sight.

'Well?' Mara said.

'The police set on us, that's what. Fucking bastards.'

'Why?'

'They just laid into us, that's all. Don't ask me why. I don't know how cops think. Can I have some wine?'

Mara poured him a glass of Barsac. He took a sip and pulled a face.

'Sorry,' she said. 'I forgot you don't like the sweet stuff. There's some beer in the fridge.'

'Great.' Paul hauled himself up and went through to the kitchen. When he came back he was carrying a can of Carlsberg lager and he'd stuck an Elastoplast on his hand.

'What happened to the others?' Mara asked.

'I don't know. A lot of people got arrested. The police just charged into the crowd and dragged them off left, right and centre. There'll be plenty in hospital, too.'

'Weren't you all together?'

'We were at first, right up at the front, but we got separated when the fighting broke out. I managed to sneak by some cops and slip down the alley, then I ran all the way through the back streets and over the moor. I'm bloody knackered.' His Liverpudlian accent grew thicker as he became more excited.

'So people did get away?'

'Some, yes. But I don't know how many. I didn't hang around to wait for the others. It was every man for himself, Mara. The last I saw of Rick he was trying to make his way to the market square. I couldn't see Zoe. You know how small she is. It was a bleeding massacre. They'd everything short of water cannons and rubber bullets. I've seen some bother in my time, but I never expected anything like this, not in Eastvale.'

'What about Seth?'

'Sorry, Mara. I've no idea what became of him. Don't worry, though; they'll be all right.'

'Yes.' Mara turned and looked out of the window. She could see her own reflection against the dark glass streaked with rain. It looked like a candle flame was burning from her right shoulder.

'Maybe they got away,' Paul added. 'They might be on their way back right now.'

Mara nodded. 'Maybe.'

But she knew there'd be trouble. The police would soon be round, bullying and searching, just like when Seth's old friend Liz Dale ran away from the nut house and hid out with them for a few days. They'd been looking for heroin then – Liz had a history of drug abuse – but as far as Mara remembered they'd just made a bloody mess of everything in the place. She resented that kind of intrusion into her world and didn't look forward to another one.

She reached for the wine bottle, but before she started pouring, the front door burst open again.

TWO

When Banks went downstairs, things were considerably quieter than they had been earlier. Richmond had helped the uniformed men to usher all the prisoners down to the cellar until they could be questioned, charged and released. Eastvale station didn't have many cells, but there was plenty of unused storage space down there.

Sergeant Hatchley had also arrived. Straw-haired, head

and shoulders above the others, he looked like a rugby prop forward gone to seed. He leaned on the reception desk looking bewildered and put out as Richmond explained what had happened.

Banks walked up to them. 'Super here yet?'

'On his way, sir,' Richmond answered.

'Can you get everyone together while we're waiting?' Banks asked. 'There's a few things I want to tell them right now.'

Richmond went into the open-plan office area, the domain of the uniformed police at Eastvale, and rounded up everyone he could. The men and women sat on desks or leaned against partitions and waited for instructions. Some of them still showed signs of the recent battle: a bruised cheekbone, torn uniform, black eye, cauliflower ear.

'Does anyone know exactly how many we've got in custody?' Banks asked first.

'Thirty-six, sir.' It was a constable with a split lip and the top button torn off his jacket who answered. 'And I've heard there's ten more at the hospital.'

'Any serious injuries?'

'No, sir. Except, well, Constable Gill.'

'Yes. So if there were about a hundred at the demo, there's almost a fifty-fifty chance we've already caught our killer. First, I want everyone searched, fingerprinted and examined for Gill's bloodstains. Constable Reynolds, will you act as liaison with the hospital?'

'Yes, sir.'

'The same procedure applies there. Ask the doctor to check the ten patients for blood. Next we've got to find the murder weapon. All we know so far is that PC Gill was stabbed. We don't know what kind of knife was used, so anything with a blade is suspicious, from a kitchen knife to a stiletto. There's some extra men on the way from York, but I want a couple of you to start searching the street thoroughly right away, and that includes having a good look down the grates, too. Clear so far?'

Some muttered, 'Yes, sir.' Others nodded.

'Right. Now we get to the hard work. We'll need a list of names: everyone we've got and anyone else we can get them to name. Remember, about sixty people got away, and we have to know who they were. If any of you recall seeing a familiar face we don't have here or at the hospital, make a note of it. I don't suppose the people we question will want to give their friends away, but lean on them a bit, do what you can. Be on the lookout for any slips. Use whatever cunning you have. We also want to know who the organizers were and what action groups were represented.

'I want statements from everyone, even if they've nothing to say. We're going to have to divide up the interrogations, so just do the best you can. Stick to the murder; ask about anyone with a knife. Find out if we've got any recorded troublemakers in the cells; look up their files and see what you come up with. If you think someone's lying or being evasive, push them as far as you can, then make a note of your reservations on the statement. I realize we're going to be swamped with paperwork, but there's no avoiding it. Any questions?'

Nobody said a word.

'Fine. One last thing: we want statements from all witnesses, too, not just the demonstrators. There must have been some people watching from those flats overlooking the street. Do the rounds. Find out if anyone saw anything. And rack your own brains. You know there'll be some kind of official inquiry into why all this happened in the first place, so all of you who were there might as well make a statement now, while the events are fresh in your minds. I want all statements typed and on Superintendent Gristhorpe's desk first thing in the morning.'

Banks looked at his watch. 'It's nine thirty now. We'd better get cracking. Anything I've overlooked?'

Several officers shook their heads; others stood silent. Finally a policewoman put her hand up. 'What are we to do with the prisoners, sir, after we've got all the statements?'

'Follow normal procedure,' Banks said. 'Just charge them and let them go unless you've got any reason to think they're involved in PC Gill's death. They'll appear before the magistrate as soon as possible. Is that all?' He paused, but nobody said anything. 'Right. Off you go then. I want to know about any leads as soon as they come up. With a bit of luck we could get this wrapped up by morning. And would someone take some of the prisoners upstairs? There'll be three of us interviewing up there when the super arrives.' He turned to Richmond. 'We'll want you on the computer, Phil. There'll be a lot of records to check.'

'The super's here now, sir.' PC Telford pointed to the door, which was out of Banks's line of vision.

Superintendent Gristhorpe, a bulky man in his late fifties with bushy grey hair and eyebrows, a red pock-marked face and a bristly moustache, walked over to where the three CID men were standing by the stairs. His eyes, usually as guileless as a baby's, were clouded with concern, but his presence still brought an aura of calm and unhurried common sense.

'You've heard?' Banks asked.

'Aye,' said Gristhorpe. 'Not all the details, but enough.

Let's go upstairs and you can tell me about it over a cup of coffee.' He put his hand on Banks's arm gently.

Banks turned to Sergeant Hatchley. 'You might as well get started on the interviews,' he said. 'We'll help you out in a minute when I've filled the super in.' Then the four CID men trudged upstairs and PC Telford ushered a brace of wet frightened demonstrators up after them.

THREE

'Zoe! Thank God you're all right!'

Paul and Mara stared at the slight figure in the glistening red anorak. Her ginger hair was stuck to her skull, and the dark roots showed. Rain dripped on to the straw mat just inside the doorway. She slipped off her jacket, hung it next to Paul's and walked over to hug them both.

'You've told her what happened?' she asked Paul.

'Yes.'

Zoe looked at Mara. 'How was Luna?'

'No trouble. She fell asleep when Squirrel Nutkin started tickling Mr Brown with a nettle.'

Zoe's face twitched in a brief smile. She went over to the bookcase. 'I threw an I Ching this morning,' she said, 'and it came up "Conflict". I should have known what would happen.' She opened the book and read from the text: '"Conflict. You are being sincere and are being obstructed. A cautious halt halfway brings good fortune. Going through to the end brings misfortune. It furthers one to see the great man. It does not further one to cross the great water."'

'You can't take it so literally,' Mara said. 'That's the problem. It didn't tell you what would happen, or how.'

Though she was certainly interested in the I Ching and tarot cards herself, Mara often thought that Zoe went too far.

'It's clear enough to me. I should have known something like this would happen: "Going through to the end brings misfortune." You can't get any more specific than that.'

'What if you *had* known?' Paul said. 'You couldn't call it off, could you? You'd still have gone. Things would still have worked out the same.'

'Yes,' Zoe muttered, 'but I should have been prepared.'

'How?' asked Mara. 'Do you mean you should have gone armed or something?'

Zoe sighed. 'I don't know. I just should have been prepared.'

'It's easy to say that now,' Paul said. 'The truth is nobody had the slightest idea the demo would turn nasty, and there wasn't a damn thing they could do about it when it did. There were a lot of people involved, Zoe, and if they'd've all done the I Ching this morning they'd've all got different answers. It's a load of cobblers, if you ask me.'

'Sit down,' said Mara. 'Have a glass of wine. Did you see what happened to the others?'

'I'm not sure.' Zoe sat cross-legged on the carpet and accepted Paul's glass. 'I think Rick got arrested. I saw him struggling with some police at the edge of the crowd.'

'And Seth?'

'I don't know. I couldn't see.' Zoe smiled sadly. 'Most people were bigger than me. All I could see was shoulders and necks. That's how I managed to get away, because I'm so little. That and the rain. One cop grabbed my anorak, but his hand slipped off because it was wet. I'm a Pisces, a slippery fish.' She paused to sip her Barsac. 'What'll happen to them, Mara, the ones who got caught?'

Mara shrugged. 'I should imagine they'll be charged and let go. That's what usually happens. Then the magistrate decides what to fine them or whether to send them to jail. Mostly they just get fined or let off with a caution.'

Mara wished she felt as confident as she sounded. Her uneasiness had nothing to do with the message Zoe had got from the I Ching, but the words of the oracle somehow emphasized it and gave her disquietude a deeper dimension of credibility: 'Going through to the end brings misfortune. It furthers one to see the great man.' Who was the great man?

'Shouldn't we do something?' Paul asked.

'Like what?'

'Go down there, down to the police station and find out what's happened. Try and get them out.'

Mara shook her head. 'If we do that, it's more likely they'll take us in for obstructing justice or something.'

'I just feel so bloody powerless, so useless, not being able to do a damn thing.' Paul's fists clenched, and Mara could read the words jaggedly tattooed just below his knuckles. Instead of the more common combination, LOVE on one hand and HATE on the other, his read HATE on both hands. Seeing the capitalized word so ineptly tattooed there reminded Mara how hard and violent Paul's past had been and how far he had come since they'd found him sleeping in the open early last winter on their way to a craft fair in Wensleydale.

'If we had a phone we could at least call the hospital,' Zoe said. 'Maybe one of us should walk down to Relton and do it anyway.'

'I'll go,' Mara said. 'You two have had enough for one

night. Besides, the exercise will do me good.'

She got to her feet before either of the others could offer
to go instead. It was only a mile down to Relton, a village
high on the southern slope of Swainsdale, and the walk
should be a pleasant one. Mara looked out of the window.
It was drizzling lightly again. She took her yellow cyclist's
cape and matching rainhat out of the cupboard and
opened the door. As she left, Paul was on his way to the
fridge for another beer, and Zoe was reaching for her tarot
cards.

Zoe worried Mara sometimes. Not that she wasn't a
good mother, but she did seem too offhand. True, she had
asked about Luna, but she hadn't wanted to go and look
in on her. Instead she had turned immediately to her
occult aids. Mara doted on both children: Luna, aged four,
and Julian, five. Even Paul, just out of his teens, seemed
more like a son than anything else at times. She knew she
felt especially close to them because she had no children
of her own. Many of her old schoolfriends would probably
have kids Paul's age. What an irony, she thought, heading
for the track – a barren earth mother!

The rain was hardly worth covering up for, but it gave
an edge to the chill already present in the March air, and
Mara was glad of the sweater she wore under her cape.
The straight narrow track she followed was part of an old
Roman road that ran diagonally across the moors above
the dale right down to Fortford. Just wide enough for the
van, it was drystone on both sides and covered with gravel
and small chips of stone that crunched and crackled
underfoot. Mara could see the lights of Relton at the
bottom of the slope. Behind her the candle glowed in the
window, and Maggie's Farm looked like an ark adrift on a
dark sea.

She shoved her hands through the slits in her cape, deep into the pockets of her cords, and marched the way she imagined an ancient Roman would have done. Beyond the clouds, she could make out the pearly sheen of a half moon.

The great silence all around magnified the little sounds – the clatter of small stones, the rhythmic crunch of gravel, the swishing of her cords against the cape – and Mara felt the strain on her weak left knee that she always got going downhill. She raised her head and let the thin cool rain fall on her closed eyelids and breathed in the wet-dog smell of the air. When she opened her eyes, she saw the black bulk of distant fells against a dark grey sky.

At the end of the track, Mara walked into Relton. The change from gravel to the smooth tarmac of Mortsett Lane felt strange at first. The village shops were all closed. Television sets flickered behind drawn curtains.

Just to be sure, Mara first popped her head inside the Black Sheep, but neither Seth nor Rick was there. A log fire crackled in the corner of the cosy public bar, but the place was half empty. The landlord, Larry Grafton, smiled and said hello. Like many of the locals, he had come to accept the incomers from Maggie's Farm. At least, he had once told Mara, they weren't like those London yuppies who seemed to be buying up all the vacant property in the Dales these days.

'Can I get you anything?' Grafton called out.

'No. No, thanks,' Mara said. 'I was looking for Seth. You haven't seen him, have you?'

Two old men looked up from their game of dominoes, and a trio of young farm labourers paused in their argument over subsidies and glanced at Mara with faintly curious expressions on their faces.

'No, lass,' Grafton said. 'They've not been in since lunch time. Said they were off to that there demonstration in Eastvale.'

Mara nodded. 'That's right. There's been some trouble and they haven't come back yet. I was just wondering—'

'Is it right, then?' one of the farm labourers asked. 'Tommy Exton dropped in half an hour sin' and said there'd been some fighting in Market Street.'

Mara told him what little she knew, and he shook his head. 'It don't pay to get involved in things like that. Best left well alone,' he said, and returned to his pint.

Mara left the Black Sheep and headed for the public telephone box on Mortsett Lane. Why they didn't have a phone installed at the farm she didn't know. Seth had once said he wouldn't have one of the things in the house, but he never explained why. Every time he needed to make a few calls he went down to the village, and he never once complained. At least in the country you could usually be sure the telephones hadn't been vandalized.

The receptionist at Eastvale General Infirmary answered and asked her what she wanted. Mara explained that she was interested in news of a friend of hers who hadn't come home from the demonstration. The receptionist said, 'Just a minute,' and the phone hiccuped and burped a few times. Finally a man's voice came on.

'Can I help you, miss?'

'Yes. I'd like to know if you have a patient called Seth Cotton and one called Rick Trelawney.'

'Who is this calling?'

'I . . . I'd rather not say,' Mara answered, suddenly afraid that if she gave her name she would be inviting trouble.

'Are you a relation?'

'I'm a friend. A very close friend.'

'I see. Well, unless you identify yourself, miss, I'm afraid I can't give out any information.'

'Look,' Mara said, getting angry, 'this is ridiculous. It's not as if I'm asking you to break the Official Secrets Act or anything. I just want to know if my friends are there and, if so, how badly they're injured. Who are you, anyway?'

'Constable Parker, miss. If you've any complaints you'd better take them up with Chief Inspector Banks at Eastvale CID headquarters.'

'Chief Inspector Banks? CID?' Mara repeated slowly. She remembered the name. He was the one who had visited the farm before, when Liz was there. 'Why? I don't understand. What's going on? I only want to know if my friends are hurt.'

'Sorry, miss. Orders. Tell me your name and I'll see what I can do.'

Mara hung up. Something was very wrong. She'd done enough damage already by mentioning Seth and Rick. The police would surely take special note of their names and push them even harder than the rest. There was nothing to do but wait and worry. Frowning, she opened the door and walked back into the rain.

FOUR

'Fell like a broke-down engine, ain't got no drivin' wheel,' sang Blind Willie McTell.

'I know exactly what you mean, mate,' Banks mumbled to himself as he poured a Laphroaig single malt, an indulgence he could scarcely afford. It was almost two in the morning and the interrogations had produced no results so far. Tired, Banks had left the others to it and come home for a few hours' sleep. He felt he deserved it. *They* hadn't had to spend the morning in court, the afternoon on a wild-goose chase after a stolen tractor, and the evening listening to the Hon. Honoria, who would no doubt by now be sleeping the sleep of the truly virtuous before heading back, with great relief, down south in the morning.

Banks put his feet up, lit a cigarette and warmed the glass in his palm. Suddenly the doorbell rang. He jumped to his feet and cursed as he spilled a little valuable Scotch on his shirt front. Rubbing it with the heel of his hand, he walked into the hall and opened the door a few inches on the chain.

It was Jenny Fuller, the psychologist he had met and worked with on his first case in Eastvale. More than that, he had to admit; there had been a mutual attraction between them. Nothing had come of it, of course, and Jenny had even become good friends with Sandra. The three of them had often been out together. But the attraction remained, unresolved. Things like that didn't seem to go away as easily as they arrived.

'Jenny?' He slipped off the chain and opened the door wider.

'I know. It's two o'clock in the morning and you're wondering what I'm doing at your door.'

'Something like that. I assume it's not just my irresistible charm?'

Jenny smiled. The laugh lines around her green eyes crinkled. But the smile was forced and short-lived.

'What is it?' Banks asked.

'Dennis Osmond.'

'Who?'

'A friend. He's in trouble.'

'Boyfriend?'

'Yes, boyfriend.' Jenny blushed. 'Or would you prefer beau? Lover? Significant other? Look, can I come in? It's cold and raining out here.'

Banks moved aside. 'Yes, of course. I'm sorry. Have a drink?'

'I will, if you don't mind.' Jenny walked into the front room, took off her green silk scarf and shook her red hair. The muted trumpet wailed and Sara Martin sang 'Death Sting Me Blues'.

'What happened to opera?' Jenny asked.

Banks poured her a Laphroaig. 'There's a lot of music in the world,' he said. 'I want to listen to as much as I can before I shuffle off this mortal coil.'

'Does that include heavy metal and middle of the road?'

Banks scowled. 'Dennis Osmond. What about him?'

'Ooh, touchy, aren't we?' Jenny raised her eyes to the ceiling and lowered her voice. 'By the way, I hope I haven't disturbed Sandra or the children?'

Banks explained their absence. 'It was all a bit sudden,' he added, to fill the silence that followed, which seemed somehow more weighty than it should. Jenny expressed her sympathy and shifted in her seat. She took a deep breath. 'Dennis was arrested during that demonstration tonight. He managed to get in a phone call to me from the police station. He's not come back yet. I've just been there and the man on the desk told me you'd left. They wouldn't tell me anything about the prisoners at all. What's going on?'

'Where hasn't he come back to?'

'My place.'

'Do you live together?'

Jenny's eyes hardened and drilled into him like emerald

34

laser beams. 'That's none of your damn business.' She drank some more Scotch. 'As a matter of fact, no, we don't. He was going to come round and tell me about the demonstration. It should have been all over hours ago.'

'You weren't there yourself?'

'Are you interrogating me?'

'No. Just asking.'

'I believe in the cause – I mean I'm against nuclear power and American missile bases – but I don't see any point standing in the rain in front of Eastvale Community Centre.'

'I see.' Banks smiled. 'It *was* a nasty night, wasn't it?'

'And there's no need to be such a cynic. I had work to do.'

'It was a pretty bad night inside, too.'

Jenny raised her eyebrows. 'The Hon. Hon?'

'Indeed.'

'You were there?'

'I had that dubious honour, yes. Duty.'

'You poor man. It might have been worth a black eye to get out of that.'

'I take it you haven't heard the news, then?'

'What news?'

'A policeman was killed at that peaceful little demonstration tonight. Not a local chap, but one of us, nonetheless.'

'Is that why Dennis is still at the station?'

'We're questioning people, yes. It's serious, Jenny. I haven't seen Dennis Osmond, never even heard of him. But they won't let him go till they've got his statement, and we're not giving out any information to members of the public yet. It doesn't mean he's under suspicion or anything, just that he hasn't been questioned yet.'

'And then?'

'They'll let him go. If all's well you'll still have some of the night left together.'

Jenny lowered her head for a moment, then glared at him again. 'You're being a bastard, you know,' she said. 'I don't like being teased that way.'

'What do you want me to do?' Banks asked. 'Why did you come?'

'I . . . I just wanted to find out what happened.'

'Are you sure you're not trying to get him special treatment?'

Jenny sighed. 'Alan, we're friends, aren't we?'

Banks nodded.

'Well,' she went on, 'I know you can't help being a policeman, but if you don't know where your job ends and your friendships begin . . . Need I go on?'

Banks rubbed his bristly chin. 'No. I'm sorry. It's been a rough night. But you still haven't answered my question.'

'I'd just hoped to get some idea of what might have happened to him, that's all. I got the impression that if I'd lingered a moment longer down at the station they'd have had me in for questioning, too. I didn't know about the death. I suppose that changes things?'

'Of course it does. It means we've got a killer on the loose. I'm sure it's nothing to do with your Dennis, but he'll have to answer the same questions as the rest. I can't say exactly how long he'll be. At least you know he's not in hospital. Plenty of people are.'

'I can't believe it, Alan. I can understand tempers getting frayed, fists flying, but not a killing. What happened?'

'He was stabbed. It was deliberate; there's no getting around that.'

Jenny shook her head.

'Sorry I can't be any more help,' Banks said. 'What was Dennis's involvement with the demo?'

'He was one of the organizers, along with the students' union and those people from Maggie's Farm.'

'That place up near Relton?'

'That's it. The local women's group was involved, too.'

'WEEF? Dorothy Wycombe?'

Jenny nodded. Banks had come up against the Women of Eastvale for Emancipation and Freedom before – Dorothy Wycombe in particular – and it gave him a sinking feeling to realize that he might have to deal with them again.

'I still can't believe it,' Jenny went on. 'Dennis told me time and time again that the last thing they wanted was a violent confrontation.'

'I don't suppose anybody wanted it, but these things have a way of getting out of hand. Look, why don't you go home? I'm sure he'll be back soon. He won't be mistreated. We don't suddenly turn into vicious goons when things like this happen.'

'*You* might not,' said Jenny. 'But I've heard how you close ranks.'

'Don't worry.'

Jenny finished her drink. 'All right. I can see you're trying to get rid of me.'

'Not at all. Have another Scotch if you want.'

Jenny hesitated. 'No,' she said finally. 'I was only teasing. You're right. It's late. I'd better get back home.' She picked up her scarf. 'It was good, though. The Scotch. So rich you could chew it.'

Banks walked her to the door. 'If there are any problems,' he said, 'let me know. And I could do with your help, too. You seem to know a bit about what went on behind the scenes.'

Jenny nodded and fastened her scarf.

'Maybe you could come to dinner?' Banks suggested on impulse. 'Try my gourmet cooking?'

Jenny smiled and shook her head. 'I don't think so.'

'Why not? It's not that bad. At least—'

'It's just . . . it wouldn't seem right with Sandra away, that's all. The neighbours . . .'

'OK. We'll go out. How does the Royal Oak in Lyndgarth suit you?'

'It'll do fine,' Jenny said. 'Give me a call.'

'I will.'

She pecked him on the cheek and he watched her walk down the path and get into her Metro. They waved to each other as she set off, then he closed his door on the wet chilly night. He picked up the Scotch bottle and pulled the cork, thought for a moment, pushed it back and went upstairs to bed.

3

ONE

COP KILLED IN DALES DEATH DEMO, screamed the tabloid headlines the next morning. As he glanced at them over coffee and a cigarette in his office, Banks wondered why the reporter hadn't gone the whole hog and spelled cop with a k.

He put the paper aside and walked over to the window. The market square looked dreary and desolate in the grey March light, and Banks fancied he could detect a shell-shocked atmosphere hovering around the place. Shoppers shuffled along with their heads hung low and glanced covertly at the site of the demonstration as they passed, as if they expected to see armed guards wearing gas masks, and tear gas drifting in the air. North Market Street was still roped off. The four officers sent from York had arrived at about four in the morning to help the local men search the area, but they had found no murder weapon. Now they were trying again in what daylight there was.

Banks looked at the calendar on his wall. It was March 17, St Patrick's Day. The illustration showed the ruins of St Mary's Abbey in York. Judging by the sunshine and the happy tourists, it had probably been taken in July. On the real March 17, his small heater coughed and hiccuped as it struggled to take the chill out of the air.

He turned back to the newspapers. The accounts varied

a great deal. According to the left-wing press, the police had brutally attacked a peaceful crowd without provocation; the right-wing papers, however, maintained that a mob of unruly demonstrators had provoked the police into retaliation by throwing bottles and stones. In the more moderate newspapers, nobody seemed to know exactly what had happened, but the whole affair was said to be extremely unfortunate and regrettable.

At eight thirty, Superintendent Gristhorpe, who had been up most of the night interviewing demonstrators and supervising the search, called Banks in. Banks stubbed out his cigarette – the super didn't approve of smoking – and wandered into the book-lined office. The shaded table lamp on Gristhorpe's huge teak desk cast its warm glow on a foot-thick pile of statements.

'I've been talking to the assistant chief constable,' Gristhorpe said. 'He's been on the phone to London and they're sending a man up this morning. I'm to cover the preliminary inquiry into the demo for the Police Complaints Authority.' He rubbed his eyes. 'Of course, someone'll no doubt accuse me of being biased and scrap the whole thing, but they want to be seen to be acting quickly.'

'This man they're sending,' Banks asked, 'what's he going to do?'

'Handle the murder investigation. You'll be working with him, along with Hatchley and Richmond.'

'Do you know who he is?'

Gristhorpe searched for the scrap of paper on his desk. 'Yes . . . let me see . . . It's a Superintendent Burgess. He's attached to a squad dealing with politically sensitive crimes. Not exactly Special Branch, but not quite your regular CID, either. I'm not even sure we're allowed to know *what* he is. Some sort of political troubleshooter, I suppose.'

'Is that Superintendent Richard Burgess?' Banks asked.

'Yes. Why? Know him?'

'Bloody hell.'

'Alan, you've gone pale. What's up?'

'Yes, I know him,' Banks said. 'Not well, but I worked with him a couple of times in London. He's about my age, but he's always been a step ahead.'

'Ambitious?'

'Very. But it's not his ambition I mind so much,' Banks went on. 'He's slightly to the right of . . . Well, you name him and Burgess is to the right.'

'Is he good, though?'

'He gets results.'

'Isn't that what we need?'

'I suppose so. But he's a real bastard to work with.'

'How?'

'Oh, he plays his cards close to his chest. Doesn't let the right hand know what the left hand's doing. He takes short cuts. People get hurt.'

'You make him sound like he doesn't even have a left hand,' Gristhorpe said.

Banks smiled. 'We used to call him Dirty Dick Burgess.'

'Why?'

'You'll find out. It's nothing to do with his sexual activities, I can tell you that. Though he did have a reputation as a fairly active stud about town.'

'Anyway,' Gristhorpe said, 'he should be here around midday. He's taking the early Intercity to York. There's too long a wait between connections, so I'm sending Craig to meet him at the station there.'

'Lucky Craig.'

Gristhorpe frowned. Banks noticed the bags under his eyes. 'Yes, well, make the best of it, Alan. If Superintendent

Burgess steps out of line, I won't be far away. It's still our patch. By the way, Honoria Winstanley called before she left – at least one of her escorts did. Said all's well, apologized for his brusqueness last night and thanked you for handling things so smoothly.'

'Wonders never cease.'

'I've booked Burgess into the Castle Hotel on York Road. It's not quite as fancy or expensive as the Riverview, but then Burgess isn't an MP, is he?'

Banks nodded. 'What about office space?'

'We're putting him in an interview room for the time being. At least there's a desk and a chair.'

'He'll probably complain. People like Burgess get finicky about offices and titles.'

'Let him,' Gristhorpe said, gesturing around the room. 'He's not getting this place.'

'Any news from the hospital?'

'Nothing serious. Most of the injured have been sent home. Susan Gay's on sick leave for the rest of the week.'

'When you were going through the statements,' Banks asked, 'did you come across anything on a chap called Dennis Osmond?'

'The name rings a bell. Let me have a look.' Gristhorpe leafed through the pile. 'Yes, I thought so. Interviewed him myself. One of the last. Why?'

Banks explained about Jenny's visit.

'I took his statement and sent him home.' Gristhorpe read through the sheet. 'That's him. Belligerent young devil. Threatened to bring charges against the police, start an inquiry of his own. Hadn't seen anything, though. Or at least he didn't admit to it. According to records he's a CND member, active in the local anti-nuclear group. Amnesty International, too – and you know what Mrs Thatcher thinks of *them* these days. He's got connections with various other groups as well, including the International Socialists. I should imagine Superintendent Burgess will certainly want to talk to him.'

'Hmmm.' Banks wondered how Jenny would take that. Knowing both her and Burgess as he did, he could guarantee sparks would fly. 'Did anything turn up in the statements?'

'Nobody witnessed the stabbing. Three people said they thought they glimpsed a knife on the road during the scuffles. It must have got kicked about quite a bit. Nothing I've heard so far brings order out of chaos. The poor lighting didn't help either. You know how badly that street is lit. Dorothy Wycombe's been pestering us about it for weeks. I keep putting her on to the council, but to no avail. She says it's an invitation to rape, especially with all those unlit side alleys, but the council says the gas lamps are good for the tourist business. Anyway, PC Gill was found just at the bottom of the community centre steps, for what that's worth. Maybe if we can find out the names of the people on the front line we'll get somewhere.'

Banks went on to tell Gristhorpe what he'd discovered from Jenny about the other organizers.

'The Church for Peace group was involved, too,' Gristhorpe added. 'Did I hear you mention Maggie's Farm, that place near Relton?'

Banks nodded.

'Didn't we have some trouble with them a year or so ago?'

'Yes,' Banks said. 'But it was a storm in a teacup. They seemed a harmless enough bunch to me.'

'What was it? A drug raid?'

'That's right. Nothing turned up, though. They must

have had the foresight to hide it, if they had anything. We were acting on a tip from some hospital social workers. I think they were overreacting.'

'Anyway,' Gristhorpe said, 'that's about it. The rest of the people we picked up were just private citizens who were there because they feel strongly about nuclear power, or about government policy in general.'

'So what do we do now?'

'You'd better look over these statements,' Gristhorpe said, shoving the tower of paper towards Banks, 'and wait for the great man. Sergeant Hatchley's still questioning those people in the flats overlooking the street. Not that there's much of anything there. They can't have seen more than a sea of heads. If only the bloody TV cameras had been there we'd have had it on video. Those buggers in the media are never around when you need them.'

'Like policemen,' Banks said with a grin.

The phone rang. Gristhorpe picked it up, listened to the message and turned back to Banks. 'Sergeant Rowe says Dr Glendenning's on his way up. He's finished his preliminary examination. I think you'd better stay for this.'

Banks smiled. 'It's a rare honour indeed, the good doctor setting foot in here. I didn't know he paid house calls.'

'I heard that,' said a gruff voice with distinct Edinburgh accent behind him. 'I hope it wasn't meant to be sarcastic.'

The tall white-haired doctor looked down sternly at Banks, blue eyes twinkling. His moustache was stained yellow with nicotine, and a cigarette hung from the corner of his mouth. He was wheezing after climbing the stairs.

'There's no smoking in here,' Gristhorpe said. 'You ought to know better; you're a doctor.'

Glendenning grunted. 'Then I'll go elsewhere.'

'Come to my office,' Banks said. 'I could do with a fag myself.'

'Fine, laddie. Lead the way.'

'Bloody traitor.' Gristhorpe sighed and followed them.

After they'd got coffee and an extra chair, the doctor began. 'To put it in layman's terms,' he said, 'PC Gill was stabbed. The knife entered under the ribcage and did enough damage to cause death from internal bleeding. The blade was at least five inches long, and it looks like it went in to the hilt. It was a single-edged blade with a very sharp point. Judging by the wound, I'd say it was some kind of flick knife.'

'Flick knife?' echoed Banks.

'Aye, laddie. You know what a flick knife is, don't you? They come in all shapes and sizes. Illegal here, of course, but easy enough to pick up on the Continent. The cutting edge was extremely sharp, as was the point.'

'What about blood?' Gristhorpe asked. 'Nobody conveniently covered in Gill's type, I suppose?'

Dr Glendenning lit another Senior Service and shook his head. 'No. I checked the tests. And I'd have been very surprised if there had been,' he said. 'What most people don't realize is that unless you open a major vein or artery – the carotid or the jugular, for example – there's often very little external bleeding with knife wounds. I'd say in this case that there was hardly any, and what there was would've been mostly absorbed by the man's clothing. The slit closes behind the blade, you see – especially a thin one – and most of the bleeding is internal.'

'Can you tell if it was a professional job?' Gristhorpe asked.

'I wouldn't care to speculate. It could have been, but it

could just as easily have been a lucky strike. It was a right-handed up-thrust wound. With a blow like that on a dark night, I doubt that anybody would have noticed, unless they saw the blade flash, and there's not enough light for that on North Market Street. It would have looked more like a punch to the solar plexus than anything else, and from what I hear there was plenty of that going on. Now if he'd raised his hand above his head and thrust downwards . . .'

'People aren't usually so obliging,' Banks said.

'If we take into account the kind of knife used,' Gristhorpe speculated, 'it could easily have been a spontaneous act. Pros don't usually use flick knives – they're street weapons.'

'Aye, well,' said Gristhorpe, standing to leave, 'that's for you fellows to work out. I'll let you know if I find anything more at the post-mortem.'

'Who identified the body?' Banks asked him.

'Sister. Pretty upset about it, too. A couple of your lads did the paperwork. Luckily, Gill didn't have a wife and kids.' A quarter-inch of ash fell on to the linoleum. Glendenning shook his head slowly. 'Nasty business all round. Be seeing you.'

When the doctor had left, Gristhorpe stood up and flapped his hand theatrically in front of his face. 'Filthy bloody habit. I'm back to my office where the air's clean. Does this Burgess fellow smoke, too?'

Banks smiled. 'Cigars, if I remember right.'

Gristhorpe swore.

TWO

Over the valley from Maggie's Farm, mist clung to the hill-sides and limestone scars, draining them of all colour. Soon after breakfast, Seth disappeared into his workshop to finish restoring Jack Lippett's Welsh dresser; Rick did some shopping in Helmthorpe, then went to his studio in the converted barn to daub away at his latest painting; Zoe busied herself in her flat with Elsie Goodbody's natal chart; and Paul went for a long walk on the moors.

In the living room, Mara kept an eye on Luna and Julian while she mended the tears in Seth's jacket. The children were playing with Lego bricks and she often glanced over, awed by the look of pure concentration on their faces as they built. Occasionally an argument would break out, and Julian would complain that the slightly younger Luna wasn't doing things right. Then Luna would accuse him of being bossy. Mara would step in and give them her advice, healing the rift temporarily.

There was nothing to worry about really, Mara told herself as she sewed, but after what Seth and Rick had said about the dead policeman, she knew they could expect to come under close scrutiny. After all, they were different. While not political in the sense of belonging to any party, they certainly believed in protection of the environment. They had even allowed their house to be used as a base for planning the demo. It would only be a matter of time before the knock at the door. There was something else bothering Mara, too, hovering at the back of her mind, but she couldn't quite figure out what it was.

Seth and Rick had been tired and hungry when they got back just after two in the morning. Seth had been charged with threatening behaviour and Rick with obstructing a police officer. They hadn't much to add to what Mara had heard earlier except for the news of PC Gill's murder, which had soon spread around the police station.

In bed, Mara had tried to cheer Seth up, but he had been difficult to reach. Finally, he said he was tired and went to sleep. Mara had stayed awake listening to the rain for a long time and thinking just how often Seth seemed remote. She'd been living with him for two years now, but she hardly felt she knew him. She didn't even know if he really was asleep now or just pretending. He was a man of deep silences, as if he were carrying a great weight of sadness within him. Mara knew that his wife, Alison, had died tragically just before he bought the farm, but really she knew nothing else of his past.

How different from Rick he was, she thought. Rick had tragedy in his life, too – he was involved in a nasty custody suit with his ex-wife over Julian – but he was open and he let his feelings show, whereas Seth never said much. But Seth was strong, Mara thought – the kind of person everyone else looked up to as being really in command. And he loved her. She knew she had been foolish to feel such jealousy when Liz Dale had run away from the psychiatric hospital and come to stay. But Liz had been a close friend of Alison's and had known Seth for years; she was a part of his life that was shut off from Mara, and that hurt. Night after night Mara had lain awake listening to their muffled voices downstairs until the small hours, gripping the pillow tightly. It had been a difficult time, what with Liz, the plague of social workers and the police raid, but she could look back and laugh at the memory of her jealousy now.

As she sat and sewed, watching the children, Mara felt

lucky to be alive. Most of the time these days she was happy; she wouldn't change things for the world. It had been a good life so far, though a confusing one at times. After her student days, she had thrown herself into life – travel, communal living, love affairs, drugs – all without a care in the world.

Then she had spent four years with the Resplendent Light Organization, culminating in nine long months in one of their ashrams, where all earnings were turned over to the group and freedom was severely limited. There were no films, no evenings in the pub, no frivolous chatty gatherings around the fire; there was very little laughter. Mara had soon come to feel trapped, and the whole episode had left her with a bitter taste in her mouth. She felt she had been cheated into wasting her time. There had been no love there, no special person to share life with. But that was all over now. She had Seth – a solid dependable man, however distant he could be – Paul, Zoe, Rick and, most important of all, the children. After wandering and searching for so long, she seemed at last to have found the stability she needed. She had come home.

Sometimes, though, she wondered what things would be like if her life had been more normal. She'd heard of business executives dropping out in the 1960s; they took off their suits and ties, dropped acid and headed for Woodstock. But sometimes Mara dreamed of dropping in. She had a good brain; she had got a first in English Literature at the University of Essex. At times she could see herself all crisp and efficient in a business suit, perhaps working in advertising, or standing in front of a blackboard reading Keats or Coleridge to a class of spellbound children.

But the fantasies never lasted long. She was thirty-eight years old, and jobs were hard to come by even for the qualified and experienced. All those opportunities had passed her by. She knew also that she would no more be able to work in the everyday world, with its furious pace, its petty demands and its money-grubbing mentality, than she would be able to join the armed forces. Her years on the fringes of society had distanced her from life inside the system. She didn't even know what people talked about at work these days. The new BMW? Holidays in the Caribbean? All she knew was what she read in the papers, where it seemed that people no longer lived their lives but had 'lifestyles' instead.

The closest she came to a normal middle-class existence was working in Elspeth's craft shop in Relton three days a week in exchange for the use of the pottery wheel and kiln in the back. But Elspeth was hardly an ordinary person; she was a kindly old silver-haired lesbian who had been living in Relton with her companion, Dottie, for over thirty years. She affected the tweedy look of a country matron, but the twinkle in her eyes told a different story. Mara loved both of them very much, but Dottie was rarely to be seen these days. She was ill – dying of cancer, Mara suspected – and Elspeth bore the burden with her typical gruff stoicism.

At twelve o'clock, Rick knocked and came in through the back door, interrupting Mara's wandering thoughts. He looked every inch the artist: beard, paint-stained smock and jeans, beer belly. His whole appearance cried out that he believed in himself and didn't give a damn what other people thought about him.

'All quite on the western front?' he asked.

Mara nodded. She'd been half listening for the sound of a police car above the wind chimes. 'They'll be here, though.'

'It'll probably take them a while,' Rick said. 'There were a lot of others involved. We might not be as important as we think we are.'

He picked up Julian and whirled him around in the air. The child squealed with delight and wriggled as Rick rubbed his head against his face. Zoe tapped at the door and came in from the barn to join them.

'Stop it, Daddy!' Julian screamed. 'It tickles. Stop it!'

Rick put him down and tousled his hair. 'What are you two building?' he asked.

'A space station,' answered Luna seriously.

Mara looked at the jumble of Lego and smiled to herself. It didn't look like much of anything to her, but it was remarkable what children could do with their imaginations.

Rick laughed and turned to Zoe. 'All right, kiddo?' he asked, slipping his arm around her shoulder. 'What do the stars have to say today?'

Zoe smiled. She obviously adored Rick, Mara thought; otherwise she would never put up with being teased and treated like a youngster at the age of thirty-two. Could there be any chance of them getting together, she wondered. It would be good for the children.

'Elsie Goodbody's wasted as a housewife,' said Zoe. 'By the looks of her chart she should be in politics.'

'She's in domestic politics,' Rick said, 'and that's even worse. Anyone for the pub?'

They usually all walked down to the Black Sheep on Saturday and Sunday lunchtimes. The landlord was good about the children as long as they kept quiet, and Zoe took along colouring books to occupy them. Mara fetched Seth from his workshop, Julian got up on his father's shoulders, and Luna held Zoe's hand as they walked out to the track.

'Just a minute, I'll catch you up,' Mara said, dashing back into the house. She wanted to leave a note for Paul to tell him where they were; a formality really, an affectionate gesture. But as she wrote and her mind turned back to him, she suddenly realized what had been nagging her all morning.

Last night, Paul's hand had been bleeding and he had put an Elastoplast on it. This morning, when he came down, the plaster had slipped off, probably when he was washing, and the base of his thumb was as smooth as ever. There was no sign of a cut at all.

Mara's heart beat fast as she hurried to catch up with the others.

THREE

'Detective Superintendent Burgess, sir,' PC Craig said, then left.

The man who stood before them in Gristhorpe's office looked little different from the Burgess that Banks remembered. He wore a scuffed black leather sports jacket over an open-necked white shirt and close-fitting navy blue cords. The handsome face with its square determined jaw hadn't changed much, even if his slightly crooked teeth were a little more tobacco-stained. The pouches under his cynical grey eyes still suited him. His dark hair, short and combed back, was touched with grey at the temples, and by the look of it he still used Brylcreem. He was about six feet tall, well-built but filling out a bit, and looked as if he still played squash twice a week. The most striking thing about his appearance was his deep tan.

'Barbados,' he said, catching their surprise. 'I'd

recommend it highly, especially at this time of year. Just got back when this business came up.'

Gristhorpe introduced himself, then Burgess looked over at Banks and narrowed his eyes. 'Banks, isn't it? I heard you'd been transferred. Looking a bit pasty-faced, aren't you? Not feeding you well up here?'

Banks forced a smile. It was typical of Burgess to make the transfer sound like a punishment and a demotion. 'We don't get much sun,' he said.

Burgess looked towards the window. 'So I see. If it's any consolation, it was pissing down in London when I left.' He clapped his hands together sharply. 'Where's the boozer, then? I'm starving. Didn't dare risk British Rail food. I could do with a pint, as well.'

Gristhorpe excused himself, claiming a meeting with the assistant chief commissioner, and Banks led Burgess over to the Queen's Arms.

'Not a bad-looking place,' Burgess said, glancing around and taking in the spacious lounge with its dimpled copper-topped tables with black wrought-iron legs and deep armchairs by the blazing fire. Then his eyes rested on the barmaid. 'Yes. Not bad at all. Let's sit at the bar.'

Some of the locals paused in their conversations to stare at them. They knew Banks already, and Burgess's accent still bore traces of his East End background. As right-wing as he was, he didn't come from the privileged school of Tories, Banks remembered. His father had been a barrow boy, and Burgess had fought his way up from the bottom. Banks also knew that he felt little solidarity with those of his class who hadn't managed to do likewise. To the locals, he was obviously the London bigwig they'd been expecting after the previous night's events.

Banks and Burgess perched on the high stools. 'What'll

you have?' Burgess asked, taking a shiny black leather wallet from his inside pocket. 'I'm buying.'

'Thanks very much. I'll have a pint of Theakston's bitter.'

'Food?'

'The hotpot is usually good.'

'I think I'll stick to plaice and chips,' Burgess said. He ordered the food and drinks from the barmaid. 'And a pint of Double Diamond for me, please, love.' He lit a Tom Thumb cigar and poked it at Banks's glass. 'Can't stand that real ale stuff,' he said, rubbing his stomach and grimacing. 'Always gives me the runs. Ah, thank you, love. What's your name?'

'Glenys,' the barmaid said. She gave him a coy smile with his change and turned to serve another customer.

'Nice,' Burgess said. 'Not exactly your buxom barmaid type, but nice nonetheless. Lovely bum. A fiver says I'll bonk her before this business is over.'

Banks wished he would try. The muscular man drying glasses at the far end of the bar was Glenys's husband, Cyril. 'You're on,' he said, shaking hands. Though how Burgess would prove it if he won, Banks had no idea. Perhaps he'd persuade Glenys to part with a pair of panties as a trophy? The most likely outcome, though, would be a black eye for Burgess and a fiver in Banks's pocket.

'So, I hear you had a riot on your hands last night.'

'Not quite a riot,' Banks said, 'but bad enough.'

'It shouldn't have been allowed.'

'Sure. It's easy to say that from hindsight, but we'd no reason to expect trouble. A lot of people around here have sympathy with the cause and they don't usually kill policemen.'

Burgess's eyes narrowed. 'Including you? Sympathy with the cause?'

Banks shrugged. 'Nobody wants any more airbase activity in the Dales, and I'm no great fan of nuclear power.'

'A bloody bolshie on the force, eh? No wonder they sent you up here. Like getting sent to Siberia, I'll bet?' He chuckled at his own joke, then sank about half a pint in one gulp. 'What have you got so far, then?'

Banks told him about the statements they'd taken and the main groups involved in organizing the protest, including the people at Maggie's Farm. As he listened, Burgess sucked on his lower lip and tapped his cigar on the side of the blue ashtray. Every time Glenys walked by, his restless eyes followed her.

'Seventy-one names,' he commented when Banks had finished. 'And you think there were over a hundred there. That's not a lot, is it?'

'It is in a murder investigation.'

'Hmmm. Got anyone marked out for it?'

'Pardon?'

'Local troublemaker, shit-stirrer. Let's be honest about this, Banks. It doesn't look like we'll get any physical evidence unless someone finds the knife. The odds are that whoever did it was one of the ones who got away. You might not even have his name on your list. I was just wondering who's your most likely suspect.'

'We don't have any suspects yet.'

'Oh, come on! No one with a record of political violence?'

'Only the local Conservative member.'

'Very good,' Burgess said, grinning. 'Very good. It seems to me,' he went on, 'that there are two possibilities.

One: it happened in the heat of the moment; someone lost his temper and lashed out with a knife. Or two: it was a planned deliberate act to kill a copper, an act of terrorism calculated to cause chaos, to disrupt society.'

'What about the knife?' Banks said. 'The killer couldn't be sure of getting away, and we've found no traces of it in the area. I'd say that points more towards your first theory. Someone lost his temper and didn't stop to think of the consequences, then just got lucky.'

Burgess finished his pint. 'Not necessarily,' he said. 'They're kamikaze merchants, these bloody terrorists. They don't care if they get caught or not. Like you said, whoever it was just got lucky this time.'

'It's possible, I suppose.'

'But unlikely?'

'In Eastvale, yes. I told you, most of the people involved were fairly harmless; even the groups they belonged to have never been violent before.'

'But you don't have everyone's name.'

'No.'

'Then that's something to work on. Sweat the ones you've got and get a full list.'

'DC Richmond's working on it,' Banks said, though he could hardly see Philip Richmond sweating anyone.

'Good.' Burgess gestured to the barmaid. 'Another two pints, Gladys, love,' he called out.

'It's Glenys,' she said, then she blushed and lowered her head to keep an eye on the pint she was pulling.

'Sorry, love, I'm still train-lagged. Have one for yourself too, Glenys.'

'Thank you very much.' Glenys smiled shyly at him and took the money for a gin and tonic. 'I'll have it later when we're not so busy, if you don't mind.'

'As you will.' Burgess treated her to a broad smile and winked. 'Where were we?' he asked, returning to Banks.

'Names.'

'Yes. You must have a list of local reds and whatnot? You know the kind I mean – anarchists, skinheads, bum punchers, women's libbers, uppity niggers.'

'Of course. We keep it on the back of a postage stamp.'

'You mentioned three organizations earlier. What's WEEF?'

'Women of Eastvale for Emancipation and Freedom.'

'Oh, very impressive. Touch of the Greenham Common women, eh?'

'Not really. They mostly stick to local issues like poor streetlighting and sexual discrimination in jobs.'

'Still,' Burgess said, 'it's a start. Get your man – Richmond, is it? – to liaise with Special Branch on this. They've got extensive files on bolshies everywhere. He can do it through the computer, if you've got one up here.'

'We've got one.'

'Good. Tell him to see me about access.' Their food arrived, and Burgess poured salt and vinegar on his fish and chips. 'We can set them against each other, for openers,' he said. 'Simple divide and conquer tactics. We tell those WEEF people that the students' union has fingered them for the murder, and vice versa. That way if anyone does know anything they'll likely tell us out of anger at being dropped right in it. We need results, and we need them quick. This business can give us a chance to look good for once. We're always looking like the bad guys these days – especially since that bloody miners' strike. We need some good press for a change, and here's our chance. A copper's been killed – that gets us plenty of public sympathy for a start. If we can come up with some pinko terrorist we've got it made.'

'I don't think setting the groups against each other will get us anywhere,' Banks said. 'They're just not that aggressive.'

'Don't be so bloody negative, man. Remember, *somebody* knows who did it, even if it's only the killer. I'll get myself acclimatized this afternoon, and tomorrow' – Burgess clapped his hands and showered his plate with ash – 'we'll swoop into action.' He had a nasty habit of sitting or standing motionless for ages, then making a sudden jerky movement. Banks remembered how disconcerting it was from their previous meetings.

'Action?'

'Raids, visits, call them what you will. We're looking for documents, letters, anything that might give us a clue to what happened. Any trouble getting warrants up here?'

Banks shook his head.

Burgess speared a chip. 'Nothing like a Sunday morning for a nice little raid, I always say. People have funny ideas about Sundays, you know. Especially churchy types. They're all comfortable and complacent after a nice little natter with the Almighty, and then they get pissed off as hell if something interrupts their routine. Best day for raids and interrogations, believe me. Just wait till they get their feet up with the Sunday papers. You mentioned some dropouts at a farm earlier, didn't you?'

'They're not dropouts,' Banks said. 'They just try to be self-sufficient, keep to themselves. They call the place Maggie's Farm,' he added. 'It's the title of an old Bob Dylan song. I suppose it's a joke about Thatcher, too.'

Burgess grinned. 'At least they've got a sense of humour. They'll bloody need it before we're through.

We'll pay them a visit, keep them on their toes. Bound to be drugs around, if nothing else. How about dividing up the raids? Any suggestions?'

Banks had no desire to tangle with Dorothy Wycombe again, and sending Sergeant Hatchley to WEEF headquarters would be like sending a bull into a china shop, as would sending Burgess up to Maggie's Farm. On the other hand, he thought, meeting Ms Wycombe might do Dirty Dick some good.

'I'll take the farm,' he said. 'Let Hatchley do the church group, Richmond the students, and you can handle WEEF. We can take a couple of uniformed men to do the searches while we ask the questions.'

Burgess's eyes narrowed suspiciously, then he smiled and said, 'Right, we're on.'

He knows I'm setting him up, Banks thought, but he's willing to go along anyway. Cocky bastard.

Burgess washed down the last of his plaice and chips. 'I'd like to stay for another,' he said, 'and feast my eyes more on the lovely Glenys, but duty calls. Let's hope we'll have plenty of reason to celebrate tomorrow lunch time. Why don't you catch up on a bit of paperwork this afternoon? There's not a lot we can do yet. And maybe this evening you can show me some of these quaint village pubs I've read about in the tourist brochures?'

The prospect of a pub crawl with Dirty Dick Burgess, following hot on the heels of an evening with the Hon. Honoria Winstanley, appealed to Banks about as much as a slap in the face with a wet fish, but he agreed politely. It was a job, after all, and Burgess was his senior officer. They'd be working together for a few days, probably, and it would do no harm to get on as good terms as possible. Make the best of it, Gristhorpe had said. And Banks did have a vague recollection that Burgess wasn't such bad company after a few jars.

Burgess slid off his chair and strode towards the door. 'Bye, Glenys, love,' he called out over his shoulder as he left. Banks noticed Cyril scowl and tighten his grip on the pump he was pulling.

Banks pushed his empty plate aside and lit a Silk Cut. He felt exhausted. Just listening to Burgess reminded him of everything he had hated about his days on the Met. But Burgess was right, of course; they were looking into a political murder, and the first logical step was to check out local activist groups.

It was the obvious relish with which the superintendent contemplated the task that irked Banks and reminded him so much of his London days. And he remembered Burgess's interrogation technique, probably learned from the Spanish Inquisition. There were hard times ahead for a few innocent people who simply happened to believe in nuclear disarmament and the future of the human race. Burgess was like a pit bull terrier; he wouldn't let go until he got what he wanted.

Oh, for a nice English village murder, Banks wished, just like the ones in books: a closed group of five or six suspects, a dodgy will, and no hurry to solve the puzzle. No such luck. He drained his pint, stubbed out the cigarette and went back across the street to read more statements.

FOUR

Mara sipped at her half of mild without really tasting it. She couldn't seem to relax and enjoy the company as usual. Seth sat at the bar chatting with Larry Grafton about some old furniture the landlord had inherited from his great-grandmother, and Rick and Zoe were arguing about astrology. By the window, the children sat colouring quietly.

What did it mean? Mara wondered. When she had tackled Paul about the blood on his hand the previous evening, he had gone into the kitchen and put on a plaster without showing her the cut. Now it turned out there was no cut. So whose blood had it been?

Of course, she told herself, anything could have happened. He could have accidentally brushed against somebody who had been hurt in the demo, or even tried to help someone. But he had clearly run all the way home; when he had arrived he had been upset and out of breath. And if the explanation was an innocent one, why had he lied? Because that's what it came down to in the end. Instead of telling the simple truth, he had let her go on believing he was hurt, albeit not badly, and she couldn't come up with a convincing reason why he had done that.

'You're quiet today,' Seth said, walking over with more drinks.

It's easy for you, she felt like saying. You can cover up your feelings and talk about hammers and planes and chisels and bevels and chamfering as if nothing has happened, but I don't have any small talk. Instead, she said, 'It's nothing. I'm just a bit tired after last night, I suppose.'

Seth took her hand. 'Didn't you sleep well?'

No, Mara almost said, No, I didn't bloody sleep well. I was waiting for you to share your feelings with me, but you never did. You never do. You can talk about work to any Tom, Dick and Harry, but not about anything else, not about anything important. But she didn't say any of that. She squeezed his hand, kissed him lightly and said she was all right. She knew she was just irritable, worried about Paul, and the mood would soon pass. No point starting a row.

Rick, his conversation with Zoe finished, turned to the others. Mara noticed streaks of orange and white paint in his beard. 'They were all talking about the Eastvale demo,' he said. 'Plenty of tongues started clucking in the grocer's when I walked in.'

'What did they think about it?' Mara asked.

Rick snorted. 'They don't think. They're just like the sheep they raise. They're too frightened to come out with an opinion about anything for fear it'll be the wrong one. Oh, they worry about nuclear fallout. Who doesn't? But that's about all they do, worry and whine. When push comes to shove they'll just put up with it like everything else and bury their heads in the ground. The wives are even worse. All they can do if anything upsets the nice, neat, comfortable little lives they've made for themselves is say tut-tut-tut, isn't it a shame.'

The door cracked open and Paul walked in.

Mara watched the emaciated figure, fists bunched in his pockets, walk over to them. With his hollow bony face, tattooed fingers and the scars, needle tracks and self-inflicted cigarette burns that Mara knew stretched all the way up his arms, Paul seemed a frightening figure. The only thing that softened his appearance was his hairstyle. His blond hair was short at the back and sides but long on top, and the fringe kept slipping down over his eyes. He'd brush it back impatiently and scowl but never mention having it cut.

Mara couldn't help thinking about his background. Right from childhood, Paul's life had been rough and hard. He never said much about his real parents, but he'd told

Mara about the emotionally cold foster home where he had been expected to show undying gratitude for every little thing they did for him. Finally, he had run away and lived a punk life on the streets, done whatever he'd had to to survive. It had been a life of hard drugs and violence and, eventually, jail. When they had met him, he had been lost and looking for some kind of anchor in life. She wondered just how much he really had changed since he'd been with them.

Remembering the blood on his hand, the way he had lied and the murdered policeman, she began to feel frightened. What would he do if she were to question him? Was she living with a killer? And if she was, what should she do about it?

As the conversation went on around her, Mara began to feel herself drifting off on a chaotic spate of her own thoughts. She could hear the sounds the others were making, but not the words, the meaning. She thought of confiding in Seth, but what if he took some kind of action? He might be hard on Paul, even drive him away. He could be very stern and inflexible at times. She didn't want her new family to split apart, imperfect as she knew it was. It was all she had in the world.

No, she decided, she wouldn't tell anyone. Not yet. She wouldn't make Paul feel as if they were ganging up on him. The whole thing was probably ridiculous anyway. She was imagining things, filling her head with stupid fears. Paul would never hurt her, she told herself, never in a million years.

4

ONE

Sunday morning dawned clear and cold. A brisk March wind blew, restoring the sun and the delicate colours of early spring to the lower hillsides. Women hung on to their hats and men clutched the lapels of their best suits as they struggled to church along Mortsett Lane in Relton. The police car, a white Fiesta Popular, with the official red and blue stripes on its sides, turned and made its way up the bumpy Roman road to Maggie's Farm. PC McDonald drove, with Craig silent beside him and Banks cramped in the back.

The view across the dale was superb. Banks could see Fortford on the valley bottom and Devraulx Abbey below Lyndgarth on the opposite slope. Behind them all the northern daleside rose, baring along its snowy heights scars of exposed limestone that looked like rows of teeth gleaming in the light.

Banks felt refreshed after an evening at home reading *Madame Bovary*, followed by a good night's sleep. Luckily, Dirty Dick had phoned to cancel their pub crawl, claiming tiredness. Banks suspected he had decided to drop in at the Queen's Arms – just around the corner from his hotel – to work on Glenys, but Burgess looked relatively unscathed the next morning. He seemed tired though, and his grey eyes were dull, like champagne that had lost its fizz. Banks wondered how he was getting on with Dorothy Wycombe.

As the car pulled on to the gravel outside the farmhouse, someone glanced through the window. When Banks got out, he could hear the wind chimes jingling like a piece of experimental music, harmonizing strangely with the wind that whistled around his ears. He had forgotten how high on the moorland Maggie's Farm was.

His knock was answered by a tall slender woman in her mid to late thirties wearing jeans and a rust-coloured jumper. Banks thought he remembered her from his previous visit. Her wavy chestnut hair tumbled over her shoulders, framing a pale heart-shaped face, free of make-up. Perhaps her chin was a little too pointed and her nose a bit too long, but the whole effect was pleasing. Her clear brown eyes looked both innocent and knowing at once.

Banks presented his warrant and the woman moved aside wearily. They knew we were coming sometime, he thought; they've just been waiting to get it over with.

'They'd better not damage anything,' she said, nodding towards McDonald and Craig.

'Don't worry, they won't. You won't even know they've been here.'

Mara sniffed. 'I'll get the others.'

The two uniformed men started their search, and Banks sat in the rocking chair by the window. Turning his head sideways, he scanned the titles in the pine bookcase beside him. They were mostly novels – Hardy, the Brontës, John Cowper Powys, Fay Weldon, Graham Greene – mixed in with a few more esoteric works, such as an introduction to Jung's psychology and a survey of the occult. On the lower shelves rested a number of older well-thumbed paperbacks – *The Teachings of Don Juan, Naked Lunch, The Lord of the*

Rings. In addition, there were the obligatory political texts: Marcuse, Fanon, Marx and Engels.

On the floor beside Banks lay a copy of George Eliot's *The Mill on the Floss*. He picked it up. The bookmark stood at the second page; that was about as far as he'd ever got with George Eliot himself.

Mara came back from the barn with the others, three of them vaguely familiar to Banks from eighteen months ago: Zoe Hardacre, a slight freckle-faced woman with frizzy ginger hair and dark roots; Rick Trelawney, a big bear of a man in a baggy paint-smeared T-shirt and torn jeans; and Seth Cotton, in from his workshop, wearing a sand-coloured lab coat, tall and thin with mournful brown eyes and neatly trimmed dark hair and beard framing a dark-complexioned face. Finally came a skinny, hostile-looking youth Banks hadn't seen before.

'Who are you?' he asked.

'Paul's not been here long,' Mara said quickly.

'What's your last name?'

Paul said nothing.

'He doesn't have to say,' Mara argued. 'He's done nothing.'

Seth shook his head. 'Might as well tell him,' he said to Paul. 'He'll find out anyway.'

'He's right, you know,' Banks said.

'It's Boyd, Paul Boyd.'

'Ever been in trouble, Paul?'

Paul smiled. It was either that or a scowl, Banks couldn't decide. 'So what if I have? I'm not on probation or parole. I don't have to register at the local nick everywhere I go, do I?' He fished for a cigarette in a grubby packet of Players. Banks noticed that his stubby fingers were trembling slightly.

'Just like to know who we've got living among us,' Banks said pleasantly. He didn't need to pursue the matter. If Boyd had a record, the Police National Computer would provide all the information he wanted.

'So what's all this in aid of?' Rick said, leaning against the mantelpiece. 'As if I need ask.'

'You know what happened on Friday night. You were arrested for obstructing a police officer.' Rick laughed. Banks ignored him and went on. 'You also know that a policeman was killed at that demonstration.'

'Are you saying you think one of us did it?'

Banks shook his head. 'Come on,' he said, 'you know the rules as well as I do. A situation like this comes up, we check out all political groups.'

'We're not political,' Mara said.

Banks looked around the room. 'Don't be so naive. Everything you have here, everything you say and do, makes a political statement. It doesn't matter whether or not any of you belongs to an official party. You know that as well as I do. Besides, we've got to act on tips we get.'

'What tip?' Rick asked. 'Who's been talking?'

'Never mind that. We just heard you were involved, that's all.' Burgess's trick seemed at least worth a try.

'So we were there,' Rick said. 'Seth and me. You already know that. We gave statements. We told you all we knew. Why come back pestering us now? What are you looking for?'

'Anything we can find.'

'Look,' Rick went on, 'I still don't see why you're persecuting us. I can't imagine who's been telling you things or what they've been saying, but you're misinformed. Just because we employed our right to demonstrate for a cause we happen to believe in, it doesn't give you the right to come around with these Gestapo tactics and harass us.'

'The Gestapo didn't need a search warrant.'

Rick sneered and scratched his straggly beard. 'With a JP like the one you've got in your pocket, I'd hardly consider that a valid argument.'

'Besides,' Banks went on, 'we're not persecuting you or harassing you. Believe me, if we were, you'd know it. Do any of you remember anything else about Friday night?'

Seth and Rick shook their heads. Banks looked around at the others. 'Come on, I'm assuming you were all there. Don't worry, I can't prove it. I'm not going to arrest you if you admit it. It's just one of you might have seen something important. This is a murder investigation.'

Still silence. Banks sighed. 'Fine. Don't blame me if things get rough. We've got a man up from London. A specialist. Dirty Dick, his friends call him. He's a hell of a lot nastier than I am.'

'Is that some kind of threat?' Mara asked.

Banks shook his head. 'I'm just letting you know your options, that's all.'

'How can we tell you we saw something if we didn't?' Paul said angrily. 'You say you know we were there. OK. Maybe we were. I'm not saying we were, but maybe. That doesn't mean we saw anything or did anything wrong. It's like Rick says, we had a right to be there. It's not a fucking police state yet.' He turned away sullenly and drew on his cigarette.

'Nobody's denying your right to be there,' Banks said. 'I just want to know if you saw anything that could help us solve this murder.'

Silence.

'Does anyone here own a flick knife?'

Rick said no and the others shook their heads.

'Ever seen one around? Know anyone who does have one?'

Again nothing. Banks thought he saw an expression of surprise flit across Mara's face, but it could have been a trick of the light.

In the following silence, Craig and McDonald came downstairs, shook their heads and went to search the out-buildings. Two small children walked in from the kitchen and hurried over to Mara, each taking a hand. Banks smiled at them, but they just stared at him, sucking their thumbs.

He tried to imagine Brian and Tracy, his own children, growing up under such conditions, isolated from other children. For one thing, there didn't seem to be a television in the place. Banks disapproved of TV in general, and he always tried to make sure that Brian and Tracy didn't watch too much, but if children saw none at all, they would have nothing to talk to their pals about. There had to be a compromise somewhere; you couldn't just ignore the blasted idiot box in this day and age, much as you might wish you could.

On the other hand, these children certainly showed no signs of neglect, and there was no reason to assume that Rick and the rest weren't good parents. Seth Cotton, Banks knew, had a reputation as a fine carpenter, and Mara's pottery sold well locally. Sandra even had a piece, a shapely vase glazed in a mixture of shades: green, ultra-marine and the like. He didn't know much about Rick Trelawney's paintings, but if the local landscape propped up by the fireplace was his, then he was good, too. No, he had no call to impose his own limited perspective on them. If the children grew up into creative, free-thinking adults, their mind unpolluted by TV and mass culture, what could be so wrong about that?

Apart from the sounds of the wind chimes, they sat in silence until Rick finally spoke. 'Do you know,' he said to Banks, 'how many children come down with leukaemia and rare forms of cancer in areas around Sellafield and other nuclear power stations? Do you have any idea?'

'Look,' said Banks. 'I'm not here to attack your views. You're entitled to them. I might even agree. The thing is, what happened on Friday night goes beyond all that. I'm not here to argue politics or philosophy; I'm investigating a murder. Why can't you get that into your heads?'

'Maybe they can't be as neatly separated as you think,' Rick argued. 'Politics, philosophy, murder – they're all connected. Look at Latin America, Israel, Nicaragua, South Africa. Besides, the police started it. They kept us penned in like animals, then they charged with their truncheons out, just like some Chilean goon squad. If some of them got hurt too, they bloody well deserved it.'

'One of them got killed. Is that all right?'

Rick turned away in disgust. 'I never said I was a pacifist,' he muttered, looking at Seth. 'There'll be a local police inquiry,' he went on, 'and the whole thing'll be rigged. You can't expect us to believe there's going to be any objectivity about all this. When it comes to the crunch you bastards always stick together.'

'Believe what you like,' Banks said.

Craig and McDonald came back in through the kitchen. They'd found nothing. It was eleven o'clock. At twelve Banks was to meet Burgess, Hatchley and Richmond in the Queen's Arms to compare notes. There was nothing to be gained by staying to discuss nuclear ethics with Rick, so he stood up and walked over to the door.

As he held his jacket closed and pushed against the wind to the car, he felt someone staring at his back through the window. He knew he had sensed fear in the house. Not just fear of a police raid they'd been expecting, but something different. All was not as harmonious as it should have been. He filed away his uneasiness to be mulled over later along with the thousand other things – concrete or nebulous – that lodged themselves in his mind during an investigation.

TWO

'Nothing,' Burgess growled, grinding out his cigar viciously in the ashtray at the centre of the copper-topped table. 'Absolutely bugger all. And that woman's crazy. I'll swear I thought she was going to bite me.'

For the first time ever Banks felt a sudden rush of affection for Dorothy Wycombe.

All in all, though, the morning had been disappointing for everyone. Not surprisingly, the searches had produced no murder weapon or documents attesting to the terrorist plot that Burgess suspected; none of the witnesses had changed their statements and the reaction to Burgess's divide and conquer tactic had been negligible.

Sergeant Hatchley reported that the Church for Peace group seemed stunned by the murder and had even offered prayers for PC Gill in their service that morning. The students' union, according to DC Richmond, who had visited the leaders – Tim Fenton and Abha Sutton – at their flat, thought it typical of the others to blame them for what had happened, but insisted that assassination was not part of their programme for a peaceful revolution. While Burgess thought Dorothy Wycombe quite capable of murder – especially of a member of the male species – she had stuck to her guns and ridiculed any such suggestion.

'So it's back to square one,' Hatchley said. 'A hundred suspects and not one scrap of evidence.'

'I did find out from one of the lads on duty,' said Richmond, 'that Dorothy Wycombe, Dennis Osmond and some of the people from Maggie's Farm were close to the front at one time. But he said everything went haywire when the fighting started. He also said he noticed a punkish-looking kid with them.'

'That'd be Paul Boyd,' Banks said. 'He seems to live up at the farm, too. Run him through the computer, will you, Phil, and see what comes up. I wouldn't be surprised if he's done time. While you're at it, find out what you can about the lot of them up there. I've got a funny feeling that something's not quite right about that place.'

He glanced at Burgess, who seemed to be staring abstractedly over at Glenys. Her husband was nowhere in sight.

'Maybe we should have a look into Gill's background,' Banks suggested.

Burgess turned. 'Why?'

'Someone might have had a reason for wanting him dead. We'll get nowhere on means and opportunity unless the knife turns up, but if we could find a motive—'

Burgess shook his head. 'Not in a crime like this. Whether it was planned or spur of the moment, the victim was random. It could have happened to any of the coppers on duty that night. It was just poor Gill's bad luck, that's all.'

'But still,' Banks insisted, 'it's something we can do. Maybe the demo was just used as a cover.'

'No. It'll look bad, for a start. What if the papers find out we're investigating one of our own? We've got enough trouble already with an inquiry into the whole bloody mess. That'd give the press enough ammo to take a few cheap shots at us without making things easier for them. Jesus, there's enough weirdos and commies to investigate already without bringing a good copper into it. What about this Osmond character? Anyone talked to him yet?'

'No,' said Banks. 'Not since Friday night.'

'Right, this is what we'll do. Get another round in, Constable, would you?' Burgess handed Richmond a fiver.

Richmond nodded and went to the bar. Burgess had switched from Double Diamond to double Scotch, claiming it was easier on his stomach, but Banks thought he was just trying to impress Glenys with his largesse. And now he was showing her he was too important to leave the conference and that he had the power to order others to do things for him. Good tactics, but would they work on her?

'You and I, Banks,' he said, 'will pay this Osmond fellow a visit this afternoon. DC Richmond can check up on those dropouts you went to see and feed a few more names into the PNC. Sergeant Hatchley here can start making files on the leaders of the various groups involved. We want every statement cross-checked with the others for inaccuracies, and all further statements checked against the originals. Someone's going to slip up at some point, and we're going to catch the bugger at it. Bottoms up.' He drank his Scotch and turned to wink at Glenys. 'By the way,' he said to Banks, 'that bloody office you gave me isn't big enough to swing a dead cat in. Any chance of another?'

Banks shook his head. 'Sorry, we're pushed for space. It's either that or the cells.'

'What about yours?'

'Too small for two.'

'I was meaning for one. Me.'

'Forget it. I've got all my files and records in there. Besides, it's cold and the blind doesn't work.'

'Hmmm. Still . . .'

'You could do most of the paperwork in your hotel room,' Banks suggested. 'It's close enough, big enough and there's a phone.' And you'll be out of my way, too, he thought.

Burgess nodded slowly. 'All right. It'll do for now. Come on!' He jumped into action and clapped Banks on the back. 'Let's see if anything's turned up at the station first, then we'll set off and have a chat with Mr Dennis Osmond, CND.'

Nothing had turned up, and as soon as Richmond had located Paul Boyd's record and Banks had had a quick look at it, the pair set off for Osmond's flat in Banks's white Cortina.

'Tell me about this Boyd character,' Burgess asked as Banks drove.

'Nasty piece of work.' Banks slipped a Billie Holiday cassette in the stereo and turned the volume down low. 'He started as a juvenile – gang fights, assault, that kind of thing – skipping school and hanging around the streets with the rest of the deadbeats. He's been nicked four times, and he drew eighteen months on the last one. First it was drunk and disorderly, underage, then assaulting a police officer trying to disperse a bunch of punks frightening shoppers in Liverpool city centre. After that it was a drugs charge, possession of a small amount of amphetamines. Then he got nicked breaking into a chemist's to steal pills. He's been clean for just over a year now.'

Burgess rubbed his chin. 'Everything short of soccer

A NECESSARY END

hooliganism, eh? Maybe he's not the sporting type.
Assaulting a police officer, you say?'

'Yes. Him and a couple of others. They didn't do any
real damage, so they got off lightly.'

'That's the bloody trouble,' Burgess said. 'Most of them
do. Any political connections?'

'None that we know of so far. Richmond hasn't been on
to the Branch yet, so we haven't been able to check on his
friends and acquaintances.'

'Anything else?'

'Not really. Most of his probation officers and social
workers seemed to give up on him.'

'My heart bleeds for the poor bastard. It looks like
we've got a likely candidate. This Osmond is a social
worker, isn't he?'

'Yes.'

'Maybe he'll know something about the kid. Let's
remember to ask him. Where's Boyd from?'

'Liverpool.'

'Any IRA connections?'

'Not as far as we know.'

'Still . . .'

Dennis Osmond lived in a one-bedroom flat in north-
east Eastvale. It had originally been council-owned, but
the tenants had seized their chance and bought their
units cheaply when the government started selling them
off.

A shirtless Osmond answered the door and led Banks
and Burgess inside. He was tall and slim with a hairy chest
and a small tattoo of a butterfly on his upper right arm. He
wore a gold crucifix on a chain around his neck. With his
shaggy dark hair and Mediterranean good looks, he looked
the kind of man who would be attractive to women. He

75

moved slowly and calmly, and didn't seem at all surprised by their arrival.

The flat had a spacious living room with a large plate-glass window that overlooked the fertile plain to the east of Swainsdale: a chequerboard of ploughed fields, bordered by hedgerows, rich brown, ready for spring. The furniture was modern – tubes and cushions – and a large framed painting hung on the wall over the fake fireplace. Banks had to look very closely to make sure the canvas wasn't blank; it was scored with faint red and black lines.

'Who is it?' A woman's voice came from behind them. Banks turned and saw Jenny Fuller poking her head round a door. From what he could tell, she was wearing a loose dressing gown, and her hair was in disarray. His eyes caught hers and he felt his stomach tense up and his chest tighten. Meeting her in a situation like this was something he hadn't expected. He was surprised how hard it hit.

'Police,' Osmond said. But Jenny had already turned back and shut the door behind her.

Burgess, who had watched all this, made no comment. 'Can we sit down?' he asked.

'Go ahead.' Osmond gestured to the armchairs and pulled a black T-shirt over his head while they made themselves as comfortable as possible. The design on the front showed the CND symbol – a circle with a wide-spread inverted Y inside it, each branch touching the circumference – with NO NUKES written in a crescent under it.

Banks fumbled for a cigarette and looked around for an ashtray.

'I'd rather you didn't,' Osmond said. 'Second-hand smoke can kill, you know.' He paused and looked Banks over. 'So you're Chief Inspector Banks, are you? I've heard a lot about you.'

'Hope it was good,' Banks said, with more equilibrium than he felt. What had Jenny been telling him? 'It'll save us time getting acquainted, won't it?'

'And you're the whizz-kid they sent up from London,' Osmond said to Burgess.

'My, my, how word travels.' Dirty Dick smiled. He had the kind of smile that made most people feel nervous, but it seemed to have no effect on Osmond. As Banks settled into the chair, he could picture Jenny dressing in the other room. It was probably the bedroom, he thought gloomily, and the double bed would be rumpled and stained, the *Sunday Times* review section spread out over the creased sheets. He took out his notebook and settled down as best he could for the interrogation.

'What do you want?' Osmond asked, perching at the edge of the sofa and leaning forward.

'I hear you were one of the organizers of Friday's demonstration,' Burgess opened.

'So what if I was?'

'And you're a member of the Campaign for Nuclear Disarmament and the International Socialists, if I'm not mistaken.'

'I'm in Amnesty International as well, in case you don't have that in your file. And as far as I'm aware it's not a crime yet.'

'Don't be so touchy.'

'Look, can you get to the point? I haven't got all day.'

'Oh yes, you have,' Burgess said. 'And you've got all night, too, if I want it like that.'

'You've no right—'

'I've every right. One of your lot – maybe even you – killed a good honest copper on Friday night, and we don't like it at all. I'm sorry if we're keeping you from your fancy woman, but that's the way it is. Whose idea was it?'

Osmond frowned. 'Whose idea was what? And I don't like you calling Jenny names like that.'

'You don't?' Burgess narrowed his eyes. 'There'll be a lot worse names than that flying around, sonny, if you don't start to cooperate. Whose idea was the demonstration?'

'I don't know. It just sort of came together.'

Burgess sighed. ' "It just sort of came together," ' he repeated mockingly, looking at Banks. 'Now what's that supposed to mean? Men and women come together, if they're lucky, but not political demonstrations – they're planned. What are you trying to tell me?'

'Exactly what I said. There are plenty of people around here opposed to nuclear arms, you know.'

'Are you telling me that you all just happened to meet outside the community centre that night? Is that what you're trying to say? "Hello, Fred, fancy meeting you here. Let's have a demo." Is that what you're saying?'

Osmond shrugged.

'Well, balls is what I say, Osmond. Balls to that. This was an organized demonstration, and that means somebody organized it. That somebody might have also arranged for a little killing to spice things up a bit. Now, so far the only somebody we know about for sure is you. Maybe you did it all by yourself, but I'm betting you had some help. Whose tune do you dance to, Mr Osmond? Moscow's? Peking's? Or is it Belfast?'

Osmond laughed. 'You've got your politics a bit mixed up, haven't you? A socialist is hardly the same as a Maoist. Besides, the Chairman's out of favour these days. And as for the IRA, you can't seriously believe—'

'I seriously believe a lot of things that might surprise

you,' Burgess cut in. 'And you can spare me the fucking lecture. Who gave you your orders?'

'You're wrong,' Osmond said. 'It wasn't like that at all. And even if there was somebody else involved, do you think I'm going to tell you who it was?'

'Yes, I do,' Burgess said. 'There's nothing more certain. The only question is when you're going to tell me, and where.'

'Look,' Banks said, 'we'll find out anyway. There's no need to take it on yourself to carry the burden and get done for withholding information in a murder investigation. If you didn't do it and you don't think your mates did either, then you've nothing to worry about, have you?' Banks found it easy to play the nice guy to Burgess's heavy, even though he felt a strong instinctive dislike for Osmond. When he questioned suspects with Sergeant Hatchley, the two of them switched roles. But Burgess only had one method of approach: head on.

'Listen to him,' Burgess said. 'He's right.'

'Why don't you find out from someone else then?' Osmond said to Banks. 'I'm damned if I'm telling you anything.'

'Do you own a flick knife?' Burgess asked.

'No.'

'Have you ever owned one?'

'No.'

'Know anybody who does?'

Osmond shook his head.

'Did you know PC Gill?' Banks asked. 'Had you any contact with him before last Friday?'

Osmond looked puzzled by the question, and when he finally answered no, it didn't ring true. Or maybe he was just thrown off balance. Burgess didn't seem to notice anything, but Banks made a mental note to check into the possibility that Osmond and Gill had somehow come into contact.

The bedroom door opened and Jenny walked out. She'd brushed her hair and put on a pair of jeans and an over-sized check shirt. Banks bet it belonged to Osmond and tried not to think about what had been going on earlier in the bedroom.

'Hello, love,' Burgess said, patting an empty chair beside him. 'Come to join us? What's your name?'

'In the first place,' Jenny said stiffly, 'I'm not "love", and in the second, I don't see as my name's any of your damn business. I wasn't even there on Friday.'

'As you like,' Burgess said. 'Just trying to be friendly.'

Jenny glanced at Banks as if to ask, 'Who is this bastard?' and Burgess caught the exchange.

'Do you two know each other?' he asked.

Banks cursed inwardly and felt himself turning red. There was no way out. 'This is Dr Fuller,' he said. 'She helped us on a case here a year or so back.'

Burgess beamed at Jenny. 'I see. Well, maybe you can help us again, Dr Fuller. Your boyfriend here doesn't want to talk to us, but if you've helped the police before—'

'Leave her alone,' Osmond said. 'She had nothing to do with it.' Banks had felt the same thing – he didn't want Burgess getting his claws into Jenny – and he resented Osmond for being able to defend her.

'Very prickly today, aren't we?' Burgess said. 'All right, sonny, we'll get back to you, if that's the way you want it.' But he kept looking at Jenny, and Banks knew he was filing her away for future use. Banks now found it hard to look her in the eye himself. He was only a chief inspector and Burgess was a superintendent. When things were going his way, Burgess wouldn't pull rank, but if Banks let any of his special feeling for Jenny show, or tried in any way to protect her, then Burgess would certainly want to humiliate him. Besides, she had her knight in shining armour in the form of Osmond. Let him take the flak.

'What were you charged with on Friday?' Burgess asked.

'You know damn well what I was charged with. It was a trumped-up charge.'

'But what was it? Tell me. Say it. Just to humour me.' Burgess reached into his pocket and took out his tin of Tom Thumbs. Holding Osmond's eyes with his own all the time, he slowly took out a cigar and lit it.

'I said I don't want you smoking in here,' Osmond protested on cue. 'It's my home and—'

'Shut up,' Burgess said, just loudly enough to stop him in his tracks. 'What was the charge?'

'Breach of the peace,' Osmond mumbled. 'But I told you, it was trumped up. If anyone broke the peace, it was the police.'

'Ever heard of a lad by the name of Paul Boyd?' Banks asked.

'No.' It was a foolish lie. Osmond had answered before he'd had time to register the question. Banks would have known he was lying even if he hadn't already learned, via Jenny, that Osmond was acquainted with the people at Maggie's Farm.

'Look,' Osmond went on, 'I'm starting an inquiry of my own into what happened on Friday. I'll be taking statements and, believe me, I'll make sure your behaviour here today goes into the final report.'

'Bully for you,' said Burgess. Then he shook his head slowly. 'You don't get it, do you, sonny? You might be able to pull those outraged-citizen tactics with the locals, but they won't wash with me. Do you know why not?'

Osmond scowled and kept silent.

'I said, do you know why not?'

'All right, no, I don't bloody well know why not!'

'Because I don't give a flying fuck for you or for others like you,' Burgess said, stabbing the air with his cigar. 'As far as I'm concerned, you're shit, and we'd all be a hell of a lot better off without you. And people I work with, they feel the same way. It doesn't matter if Chief Inspector Banks here has the hots for your Dr Fuller and wants to go easy on her. It doesn't matter that he's got a social conscience and respects people's rights, either. I don't, and my bosses don't. We don't piss around, we get things done; and you'd do well to remember that, both of you.'

Jenny was flushed and speechless with rage; Banks himself felt pale and impotent. He should have known that nothing would slip by Burgess.

'I can't tell you anything,' Osmond repeated wearily. 'Why can't you believe me? I don't know who killed that policeman. I didn't see it, I didn't do it, and I don't know who did.'

A long silence followed. At least it seemed long to Banks, who was aware only of the pounding of his heart. Finally Burgess stood up and walked over to the window, where he stubbed out his cigar on the white sill. Then he turned and smiled. Osmond gripped the tubular arms of his chair tightly.

'OK,' Burgess said, turning to Banks. 'We'll be off then, for the moment. Sorry to spoil your afternoon in bed. You can get back to it now, if you like.' He looked at Jenny and licked his lips. 'That's a fetching shirt you've got on, love,' he said to her. 'But you didn't need to leave it half unbuttoned just for me. I've got plenty of imagination.'

Back in the car, Banks was fuming. 'You were way out of line in there,' he said. 'There was no reason to insult Jenny, and there was especially no need to bring me into it the way you did. What the hell were you trying to achieve?'

'Just trying to stir them up a bit, that's all.'

'So how does making me out to be a bloody lecher stir them up?'

'You're not thinking clearly, Banks. We make Osmond jealous, maybe he lets his guard down.' Burgess grinned. 'Anyway, there's nothing in it, is there, you and her?'

'Of course there isn't.'

'Methinks this fellow doth protest too much.'

'Fuck off.'

'Oh, come on,' Burgess said calmly. 'Don't take it so seriously. You use what you need to get results. Christ, I don't blame you. I wouldn't mind tumbling her myself. Lovely pair of tits under that shirt. Did you see?'

Banks took a deep breath and reached for a cigarette. There was no point, he realized, in going on. Burgess was an unstoppable force. However angry and disorientated Banks felt, it would do no good to let more of it show. Instead, he put his emotions in check, something he knew he should have done right from the start. But the feelings still rankled as they knotted up below the surface. He was furious with Burgess, he was furious with Osmond, he was furious with Jenny, and he was furious with, most of all, himself.

Starting the car with a lurch, he shoved the cassette back in and turned up the volume. Billie Holiday sang 'God Bless the Child', and Burgess whistled blithely along as they sped through the bright blustery March day back to the market square.

THREE

They were all a bit drunk, and that was unusual at Maggie's Farm. Mara certainly hadn't been so tipsy for a long time. Rick was sketching them as they sat around the living room. Paul drank lager from the can, and even Zoe had turned giggly on white wine. But Seth was the worst. His speech was slurred, his eyes were watery, and his coordination was askew. He was also getting maudlin about the 1960s, something he never did when he was sober. Mara had seen him drunk only once before, the time he had let slip about the death of his wife. Mostly, he was well guarded and got on with life without moaning.

Things had begun well enough. After the police visit, they had all walked down to the Black Sheep for a drink. Perhaps the feeling of relief, of celebration, had encouraged them to drink more than usual, and they had splurged on a few cans of Carlsberg Special Brew, some white wine and a bottle of Scotch to take home. Most of the afternoon Seth and Mara had lounged about over the papers or dozed by the fire, while Paul messed about in the shed, Rick painted in his studio, and Zoe amused the children. Early in the evening they all got together, and the whisky and wine started making the rounds.

Seth stumbled over to the stereo and sought out a scratchy old Grateful Dead record from his collection. 'Those were the days,' he said. 'All gone now. All people care about today is money. Bloody yuppies.'

Rick looked up from his sketch pad and laughed. 'When was it ever any different?'

'Isle of Wight, Knebworth . . .' Seth went on, listing the rock festivals he'd been to. 'People really shared back then . . .'

Mara listened to him ramble. They had been under a lot of stress since the demo, she thought, and this was clearly Seth's way of getting it out of his system. It was easy to fall under the spell of nostalgia. She remembered the sixties, too – or more accurately the late sixties, when the hippie era had really got going in England. Things *had* seemed better back then. Simpler. More clear cut. There was us and them, and you knew *them* by the shortness of their hair.

'. . . Santana, Janis, Hendrix, the Doors. Jesus, even the Hare Krishnas were fun back then. Now they all wear bloody business suits and wigs. I remember one time—'

'It's all crap!' Paul shouted, banging his empty can on the floor. 'It was never like that. It's just a load of cobblers you're talking, Seth.'

'How would you know?' Seth sat up and balanced unsteadily on his elbow. 'You weren't there, were you? You were naught but a twinkle in your old man's eye.'

'My mum and dad were hippies,' Paul said scornfully. 'Fucking flower children. She OD'd, and he was too bloody stoned to take care of me, so he gave me away.'

Mara was stunned. Paul had never spoken about his true parents before, only about the way he had been badly treated in his foster home. If it was true, she thought, did he really see Seth and her in the same light? They were about the right age. Did he hate them too?

But she couldn't believe that. There was another side to the coin. Maybe Paul was looking for what he had lost, and he had found at least some of it at Maggie's Farm. They didn't take drugs and, while she and Seth might have grown up in the 1960s and tried to cling on to some of its ideals, they neither looked nor acted like hippies any longer.

'We're not like that,' she protested, looking over at Zoe for support. 'You know it, Paul. We care about you. We'd never desert you. It was fun back then for a lot of people. Seth's only reminiscing about his youth.'

'I know,' Paul said grudgingly. 'I can't say I had one worth reminiscing about, myself. Anyway, I'm only saying, Mara, that's all. It wasn't all peace and love like Seth tells it. He's full of shit.'

'You're right about that, mate,' Rick agreed, putting down his sketch pad and pouring another shot of Scotch. 'I never did have much time for hippies myself. Nothing but a moaning, whining bunch of little kids, if you ask me. Seth's just pissed, that's all. Look at him, anyway – he's a bloody landowner, a landlord even. Pretty soon it'll be baggy tweeds and out shooting pheasant every afternoon. Sir Seth Cotton, squire of Maggie's Farm.'

But Seth had slumped back against a beanbag and seemed to have lost all interest in the conversation. His eyes were closed, and Mara guessed that he was either asleep or absorbed in the soaring Jerry Garcia guitar solo.

'Where's your father now?' Mara asked Paul.

'I don't fucking know. Don't fucking care, either.' Paul ripped open another can of lager.

'But didn't he ever get in touch?'

'Why should he? I told you, he was too zonked out to notice me even when I was there.'

'It's still no reason to say everyone was like that,' Mara said. 'All Seth was saying was that the spirit of love was strong back then. All that talk about the Age of Aquarius meant something.'

'Yeah, and what's happened to it now? Two thousand years of this crap I can do without, thanks very much. Let's just forget the fucking past and get on with life.' With that, Paul got up and left the room.

Jerry Garcia played on. Seth stirred, opened one blood-shot eye, then closed it again.

Mara poured herself and Zoe some more white wine, then her mind wandered back to Paul. As if she weren't confused enough already, the hostility he'd shown tonight and the new information about his feelings for his parents muddied the waters even more. She was scared of approaching him about the blood on his hand, and she was beginning to feel frightened to go on living in the same house as someone she suspected of murder. But she hated herself for feeling that way about him, for not being able to trust him completely and believe in him.

What she needed was somebody to talk to, somebody she could trust from outside the house. She felt like a woman with a breast lump who was afraid to go to the doctor and find out if it really was cancer.

And what made it worse was that she'd noticed the knife was missing: the flick knife Seth said he had bought in France years ago. Everybody else must have noticed, too, but no one had mentioned it. The knife had been lying on the mantelpiece for anyone to use ever since she'd been at Maggie's Farm, and now it was gone.

FOUR

Banks ate the fish and chips he had bought on the way home, then went into the living room. Screw gourmet cooking, he thought. If that irritating neighbour, Selena Harcourt, didn't turn up with some sticky dessert to feed him up 'while the little woman's away', he'd have the evening to relax instead of mixing up sauces that never turned out anyway.

He had calmed down soon after leaving Burgess at the station. The bastard had been right. What had happened at Osmond's, he realized, had not been particularly serious, but his shock at finding Jenny there had made him exaggerate things. His reaction had been extreme, and for a few moments, he'd lost his detachment. That was all. It had happened before and it would happen again. Not the end of the world.

He poured a drink, put his feet up and turned on the television. There was a special about the Peak District on Yorkshire TV. Half watching, he flipped through Tracy's latest copy of *History Today* and read an interesting article on Sir Titus Salt, who had built a utopian community called Saltaire, near Bradford, for the workers in his textile mills. It would be a good place to visit with Sandra and the kids, he thought. Sandra could take photographs; Tracy would be fascinated; and surely even Brian would find something of interest. The problem was that Sir Titus had been a firm teetotaller. There were no pubs in Saltaire. Obviously one man's utopia is another man's hell.

The article made him think of Maggie's Farm. He liked the place and respected Seth and Mara. They had shown antagonism towards him, but that was only to be expected. In his job, he was used to much worse. He didn't take it personally. Being a policeman was like being a vicar in some ways; people could never be really comfortable with you even when you dropped into the local for a pint.

The TV programme finished, and he decided there was no point putting off the inevitable. Picking up the phone, he dialled Jenny's number. He was in luck; she answered on the third ring.

'Jenny? It's Alan.'

There was a pause at the other end. 'I'm not sure I want to talk to you,' she said finally.

'Could you be persuaded to?'

'Try.'

'I just wanted to apologize for this afternoon. I hadn't expected to see you there.'

Only the slight crackle of the line filled the silence. 'It surprised me, too,' Jenny said. 'You keep some pretty bad company.'

I could say the same for you, too, Banks thought. 'Yes,' he said. 'I know.'

'I do think you should keep him on a leash in future. You could maybe try a muzzle as well.' She was obviously warming to him again; he could tell.

'Love to. But he's the boss. How did Osmond take it?' The name almost stuck in his throat.

'He was pissed off, all right. But it didn't last. Dennis is resilient. He's used to police harassment.'

There was silence again, more awkward this time.

'Well,' Banks said, 'I just wanted to say I was sorry.'

'Yes. You've said that already. It wasn't your fault. I'm not used to seeing you in a supporting role. You're not at your best like that, you know.'

'What did you expect me to do? Jump up and hit him?'

'No, I didn't mean anything like that. But when he said what he did about us I could see you were ready to.'

'Was it so obvious?'

'It was to me.'

'I blew up at him in the car.'

'I thought you would. What did he say?'

'Just laughed it off.'

'Charming. I could have killed him when he said that about my shirt being undone.'

'It was though.'

'I dressed in a hurry. I wanted to know what was going on.'

'I know. I'm not trying to make out you did it on purpose or anything. It's just that, well, with a bloke like him around you've got to be extra careful.'

'Now I know. Though I hope I won't have the pleasure again.'

'He doesn't give up easily,' Banks said gloomily.

'Nor do I. Where are you? What are you doing?'

'At home. Relaxing.'

'Me too. Is Sandra back?'

'No.' The silence crackled again. Banks cleared his throat. 'Look,' he said, 'when I mentioned dinner the other day, before all this, I meant it. How about tomorrow?'

'Can't tomorrow. I've got an evening class to teach.'

'Tuesday?'

Jenny paused. 'I suppose I can break my date,' she said. 'It had better be worth it though.'

'The Royal Oak is always worth it. My treat. I need to talk to you.'

'Business?'

'I'm hoping you can help me get a handle on some of those Maggie's Farm people. Seth and Mara are about my age. It's funny how we all grew up in the sixties and turned out so different.'

'Not really. Everybody's different.'

'I liked the music. I just never felt I fitted in with the long-haired crowd. Mind you, I did try pot once or twice.'

'Alan! You didn't?'

'I did.'

'And here's me thinking you're so strait-laced. What happened?'

'Nothing, the first time.'

'And the second?'

'I fell asleep.'

Jenny laughed.

'Still,' Banks mused, 'Burgess is about my age, too.'

'He was probably sitting around in jackboots and a leather overcoat pulling the wings off flies.'

'Probably. Anyway, dinner. Eight o'clock all right?'

'Fine.'

'I'll pick you up.'

Jenny said goodnight and hung up. Still friends. Banks breathed a sigh of relief.

He went back to his armchair and his drink, but he suddenly felt the need to call Sandra.

'How's your father?' he asked.

Sandra laughed. 'Cantankerous as ever. But Mother's coping better than I'd hoped.' The line was poor and her voice sounded far away.

'How much longer will you be down there?'

'A few more days should do it. Why? Are you missing us?'

'More than you know.'

'Hang on a minute. We had a day in London yesterday and Tracy wants to tell you about it.'

Banks talked to his daughter for a while about St Paul's and the Tower of London, then Brian cut in and told him how great the record shops were down there. There was exactly the guitar he'd been looking for . . . Finally, Sandra came back on again.

'Anything happening up there?'

'You could say that.' Banks told her about the demo and the killing.

Sandra whistled. 'I'm glad I'm out of it. I can imagine how frantic things are.'

'Thanks for the support.'

'You know what I mean.'

'Remember Dick Burgess? Used to be a chief inspector at the Yard?'

'Was he the one who pawed the hostess and threw up in the geraniums at Lottie's party?'

'That's the one. He's up here, in charge.'

'God help you. Now I'm really glad I'm down here. He had his eyes on me too, you know, if not his hands.'

'I'd like to say it was good taste, but don't flatter yourself, love. He's like that with everyone in a skirt.'

Sandra laughed. 'Better go now. Brian and Tracy are at it again.'

'Give them my love. Take care. See you soon.'

After he'd hung up, Banks felt so depressed that he almost regretted phoning in the first place. Why, he wondered, does a phone call to a distant loved one only intensify the emptiness and loneliness you were feeling before you called?

At a loose end, he turned off the television in the middle of a pop music special that Brian would have loved and put on the blues tape an old colleague had sent him from London. The Reverend Robert Wilkins sang 'Prodigal Son' in his eerie voice, unusually thin and high-pitched for a bluesman. Banks slouched in the armchair by the gas fire and sipped his drink. He often did his best thinking while drinking Scotch and listening to music, and it was time to put some of his thoughts about Gill's murder in order.

A number of things bothered him. There were demonstrations all the time, much bigger than the one in Eastvale, and while opposing sides sometimes came to blows, policemen didn't usually get stabbed. Call it statistics, probability or just a hunch, but he didn't believe in Burgess's view of the affair.

And that was a problem, because it didn't leave much else to choose from. He still had uneasy feelings about some of the Maggie's Farm crowd. Paul Boyd was as dangerous character if ever he'd met one, and Mara had seemed extremely keen to come to his defence. Seth and Zoe had been especially quiet, but Rick Trelawney had expressed more violent views than Banks had expected. He didn't know what it added up to, but he felt that somebody knew something, or thought they did, and didn't want to communicate their suspicions to the police. It was a stupid way to behave, but people did it all the time. Banks just hoped that none of them got hurt.

As for Dennis Osmond, putting personal antipathy aside, Banks had caught him on two lies. Osmond had said he didn't know Paul Boyd when he clearly did, and Banks had also suspected him of lying when he denied knowing PC Gill. It was easy enough to see why he might have lied: nobody wants to admit a connection with a murdered man or a convicted criminal if he doesn't have to. But Banks had to determine if there was anything more sinister to it than that. How could Osmond have known PC Gill? Maybe they'd been to school together. Or perhaps Gill had had occasion to arrest Osmond at some previous anti-nuclear protest. If so, it should be on the files. Richmond would have the gen from Special Branch in the morning.

Nothing so far seemed much like a motive for murder though. If he was really cautious, he might be able to get something out of Jenny on Tuesday. She didn't usually resent his trying to question her, but she was bound to be especially sensitive where Osmond was concerned.

Perhaps he had reacted unprofessionally on finding

Jenny in Osmond's bedroom and to Burgess's approach to interrogation. But, he reminded himself, Dirty Dick had made him look a proper wally, and what was more he had insulted Jenny. Sometimes Banks thought that Burgess's technique was to badger everyone involved in a case until someone was driven to try to throttle him. At least then he could lay a charge of attempted murder.

Halfway through his third Laphroaig and the second side of the tape, Banks decided that there was only one way to get back at the bastard, and that was to solve the case himself, in his own way. Burgess wasn't the only one who could play his cards close to his chest. Let him concentrate on the reds under the bed. Banks would do a bit of discreet digging and see if he could come up with anyone who had a motive for wanting PC Edwin Gill, and not just any copper, dead.

But if Gill the person rather than Gill the policeman was the victim, it raised a number of problems. For a start, how could the killer know that Gill was going to be at the demo? Also, how could he be sure that things would turn violent enough to mask a kill? Most puzzling of all was how could he have been certain of an escape? But at least these were concrete questions, a starting point. The more Banks thought about it, the more the thick of a political demonstration seemed the ideal cover for murder.

5

ONE

The funeral procession wound its way from Gordon Street, where Edwin Gill had lived, along Manor Road to the cemetery. Somehow, Banks thought, the funeral of a fellow officer was always more solemn and grim than any other. Every policeman there knew it could just as easily have been him in the coffin; every copper's wife lived with the fear that her husband, too, might end up stabbed, beaten or, these days shot; and the public at large felt the tremor and momentary weakness in the order of things.

For the second time in less than a week, Banks found himself uncomfortable in a suit and tie. He listened to the vicar's eulogy, the obligatory verses from the *Book of Common Prayer*, and stared at the bristly necks in front of him. At the front, Gill's immediate family – mother, two sisters, uncles and aunts, nephews and nieces – snuffled and slipped each other wads of Kleenex.

When it was over, everyone filed out and waited for the cars to take them to the funeral lunch. The oaks and beeches lining the cemetery drive shook in the brisk wind. One moment the sun popped out from behind the clouds, and the next a five-minute shower took everyone by surprise. It was that kind of day: chameleon, unpredictable.

Banks stood with DC Richmond by the unmarked black police Rover – his own white Cortina was hardly the thing for a funeral – and waited for someone to lead the way. He wore a light grey raincoat over his navy blue suit, but his head was bare. With his close-cropped black hair, scar beside the right eye and lean angular features, he thought he must look a suspicious figure as he held his raincoat collar tight around his throat to keep out the cold wind. Richmond, rangy and athletic, wearing a camel hair overcoat and trilby, stood beside him.

It was early Tuesday afternoon. Banks had spent the morning reading over the records Richmond had managed to gather on Osmond and the Maggie's Farm crowd. There wasn't much. Seth Cotton had once been arrested for carrying an offensive weapon (a bicycle chain) at a mods and rockers debacle in Brighton in the early 1960s. After that, he had one marijuana bust to his credit – only a quid deal, nothing serious – for which he had been fined.

Rick Trelawney had been in trouble only once, in St Ives, Cornwall. A tourist had taken exception to his drunken pronouncements on the perfidy of collecting art, and a rowdy argument turned into a punch-up. It had taken three men to drag Rick off, and the tourist had ended up with a broken jaw and one permanently deaf ear.

The only other skeleton in Rick's cupboard was the wife from whom he had recently separated. She was an alcoholic, which made it easy enough for Rick to get custody of Julian. But she was now staying with her sister in London while undergoing treatment, and there was a legal battle brewing. Things had got so bad at one point that Rick had applied for a court order to prevent her from coming near their son.

There was nothing on Zoe, but Richmond had checked the birth registry and discovered that the father of her child, Luna, was one Lyle Greenberg, an American student who had since returned to his home in Eau Claire, Wisconsin.

On Mara there was even less. Immigration identified her as Moira Delacey, originally from Dublin. With her parents, she had come to England at the age of six, and they had settled in Manchester. No known Republican connections.

Most interesting and disturbing of all was Dennis Osmond's criminal record. In addition to arrests for his part in anti-government demonstrations – with charges ranging from breach of the peace to theft of a police officer's helmet – he had also been accused of assault by a live-in girlfriend called Ellen Ventner four years ago. At the woman's insistence, the charges had later been dropped, but Ventner's injuries – two broken ribs, a broken nose, three teeth knocked out and concussion – had been clearly documented by the hospital, and Osmond came out of the affair looking far from clean. Banks wasn't sure whether to bring up the subject when he met Jenny for dinner that evening. He wondered if she already knew. If she didn't she might not take kindly to his interference. Somehow, he doubted that Osmond had told her.

They were still waiting for the information from Special Branch, who had files on Osmond, Tim Fenton, the student leader, and five others known to have been at the demo. Apparently, the Branch needed Burgess's personal access code, password, voice-print and genetic fingerprint, or some equally ludicrous sequence of identification. Banks didn't expect much from them, anyway. In his own experience, Special Branch kept files on everyone who had ever brought a copy of *Socialist Weekly*.

Today, while Banks and Richmond were attending Gill's funeral, Burgess was taking Sergeant Hatchley to do the rounds again. They intended to revisit Osmond,

Dorothy Wycombe, Tim Fenton and Maggie's Farm. Banks wanted to talk to the students himself, so he decided to call on them when he got back that evening – if Burgess hadn't alienated them beyond all communication by then.

Burgess had been practically salivating at the prospect of more interrogations, and even Hatchley had seemed more excited about work than usual. Perhaps it was the chance to work with a superstar that thrilled him, Banks thought. The sergeant had always found *The Sweeney* much more interesting than the real thing. Or maybe he was going to suck up to Dirty Dick in the hope of being chosen for some special Scotland Yard squad. And the devil of it was, perhaps he would be, too.

Banks had mixed feelings about that possibility. He had got used to Sergeant Hatchley sooner than he'd expected to, and they had worked quite well together. But Banks had no real feeling for him. He couldn't even bring himself to call Hatchley by his first name, Jim.

In Banks's mind, Hatchley was a sergeant and always would be. He didn't have that extra edge needed to make inspector. Phil Richmond did, but unfortunately there wasn't anywhere for him to move up to locally unless Hatchley was promoted too. Superintendent Gristhorpe wouldn't have that, and Banks didn't blame him. If Burgess liked Hatchley enough to suggest a job in London, that would solve all their problems. Richmond had already passed his sergeant's exam – the first stage on the long road to promotion – and perhaps PC Susan Gay, who had shown remarkable aptitude for detective work, could be transferred in from the uniformed branch as a new detective constable. PC Craig would be opposed, of course. He still called policewomen 'wopsies', even though the gender-specific designation, WPC, had been dropped in favour of the neutral PC as far back as 1975. But that was Craig's problem; Hatchley was everyone's cross to bear.

Finally, the glossy black cars set off. Banks and Richmond followed them through the dull deserted streets of Scarborough to the reception. There was nowhere quite as gloomy as a coastal resort in the off-season. If it hadn't been for the vague whiff of sea and fish in the air, nobody would have guessed they were at the seaside.

'Fancy a walk on the prom after lunch?' Banks asked.

Richmond sniffed. 'Hardly the weather for that, is it?'

'Bracing, I'd say.'

'Maybe I'll wait for you in a nice cosy pub, if you don't mind, sir.'

Banks smiled. 'And put your notes in order?' He knew how fussy Richmond was about notes and reports.

'I'll have to, won't I? It'll not stick in my memory that long.'

On the way to Scarborough, Banks had put forward his theory about Gill's murder not being quite what it seemed. While Richmond had expressed reservations, he had agreed that it was at least worth pursuing. They had decided to chat up Gill's colleagues at the reception and see what they could pick up about the man. Burgess, of course, was to know nothing about this.

Richmond had argued that even if there was something odd about Gill, none of his mates would say so at his funeral. Banks disagreed. He thought funerals worked wonders on the conscience. The phony platitudes often stuck in people's craws and made them want to tell someone the truth. After all, it wasn't as if they were trying to prove corruption or anything like that against Gill; they just wanted to know what kind of man he was and whether he might have made enemies.

The procession pulled into the car park of the Crown and Anchor, where a buffet had been arranged in the banquet room, and the guests hurried through a heavy shower to the front doors.

TWO

'Bloody hell! What stone did you crawl out from under?' Burgess said when Paul Boyd walked into the front room to see what was going on.

Paul scowled. 'Piss off.'

Burgess strode forward and clipped him around the ear. Paul flinched and stumbled back. 'Less of your cheek, sonny,' Burgess said. 'Show a bit of respect for your elders and betters.'

'Why should I? You didn't show any fucking respect for me, did you?'

'Respect? For you?' Burgess narrowed his eyes. 'What makes you think you deserve any respect? You're an ugly little pillock with a record as long as my arm. And that includes assaulting a police officer. And while we're at it, mind your tongue. There's ladies present. At least, I think there are.'

Mara felt cold as Burgess ran his eyes up and down her body.

Burgess turned back to Paul, who stood in the doorway holding his hand to his ear. 'Come on, who put you up to it?'

'Up to what?'

'Killing a police officer.'

'I never. I wasn't even there.'

'It's true, he wasn't,' Mara burst out. 'He was here with

me all evening. Somebody had to stay at home and look after the children.'

She had held her tongue so far, trying to figure Burgess out. He didn't seem as mild-mannered as Banks, and she was afraid of attracting his attention. Even as she spoke, her stomach muscles tensed.

Burgess looked at her again and shook his head. His eyes were as sharp as chipped slate. 'Very touching, love. Very touching. Didn't your mother and father teach you not to tell lies? He was spotted in the crowd. We know he was there.'

'You must have been mistaken.'

Burgess glanced at Paul, then looked at Mara again. 'Mistaken! How could anyone mistake this piece of garbage for someone else? You need your mouth washing out with soap and water, you do, love.'

'And don't call me love.'

Burgess threw up his arms in mock despair. 'What's wrong with you lot? I thought everyone called each other love up north. Anyway, I can't for the life of me see why you're defending him. He's got a limited vocabulary and, with a body like that, I doubt if he's much good in bed.'

'Bastard,' Mara said between clenched teeth. There was going to be no reasoning with this one, that was certain. Best just stick it out.

'That's right, love,' Burgess said. 'Get it off your chest. You'll feel all the better for it.' He eyed her chest, as if to prove his point, and turned to Paul again. 'What did you do with the knife?'

'What knife?'

'The one you used to stab PC Gill. The flick knife. Just your kind of weapon, I'd say.'

'I didn't stab anyone.'

'Oh, come on! What did you do with it?'

'I didn't have no fucking knife.'

Burgess wagged a finger at him. 'I warned you, watch your tongue. Are you getting all this, Sergeant Hatchley? The kid's denying everything.'

'Yes, sir.' Hatchley was sitting on the beanbag cushions, looking, Mara thought, rather like a beached whale.

'All we need is the knife,' Burgess said. 'Once we trace it back to you, you'll be in the nick before your feet can touch the ground. With your record, you won't have a chance. We've already placed you at the scene.'

'There were about a hundred other people there, too,' Paul said.

'Count them, did you? I thought you said you weren't there.'

'I wasn't.'

'Then how did you know?'

'Read it in the papers.'

'Read? You? I doubt you'd get past the comics.'

'Very funny,' Paul said. 'But you can't prove nothing.'

'You might just be right about that,' Burgess said. 'But remember, if I can't prove nothing, it means I *can* prove something. And when I do . . . when I do . . .' He left the threat hanging and turned to the room at large. They were all gathered in the house except Rick, who had taken the children to town for new clothes. 'The rest of you are just as guilty,' he went on. 'When we build a case against dick-head here, you'll all get done for withholding information and for being accessories. So if any of you know anything, you'd best tell us now. Think about it.'

'We don't know anything,' Seth said quietly.

'Well, there we are then.' Burgess sighed and ran his free hand through his hair. 'Stalemate.'

'And don't think we won't complain about the way you've treated us and how you hit Paul,' Mara said.

'Do it, love. See if I care. Want me to tell you what'll happen? If you're lucky, it'll get passed down the line back to my boss at the Yard. And do you know what? He's an even bigger bastard than I am. No, your best bet's to come clean, tell the truth.'

'I told you,' Paul said. 'I don't know anything about it.'

'All right.' Burgess dropped his cigar stub into a teacup balanced on the arm of a chair. The hot ash sizzled as it hit the dregs. 'But don't say I didn't warn you. Come on, Sergeant. We'll leave these people to think about it a bit more. Maybe one of them'll come to his senses and get in touch with us.'

Hatchley struggled to his feet and joined Burgess by the door. 'We'll be back, don't worry,' Burgess said. As they walked out of the small porch, he reached up, slapped the wind chimes and snarled, 'Bloody tuneless racket.'

THREE

Banks waited, glass of sherry in hand, until the crowd around the buffet had dwindled before he collected his own paper plateful of cold meat and salad.

'Ee, it's a bit of all right this, i'n't it,' a grey-haired woman in a powder-blue crêpe dress was saying to her friend.

'Aye,' the other said. 'Better'n old Ida Latham's do. Nobbut them little sarnies wi' t'crusts cuts off. No bigger'n a postage stamp they weren't. Cucumber, too. It allus gives me gas, cucumber does.'

'Chief Inspector Banks?'

The man who suddenly materialized beside Banks was about six foot two with a shiny bald head, fuzzy white hair above the ears and a grey RAF moustache. He wore a black armband over his dark grey suit and a black tie. Even the rims of his glasses were black. Banks nodded.

'Thought it must be you,' the man went on. 'You don't look like a relation, and I've never see you around here before. Superintendent Gristhorpe sent word you were coming.' He stretched out his hand. 'Detective Chief Inspector Blake, Scarborough CID.' Banks managed to balance his sherry glass on his plate and shake hands.

'Pleased to meet you,' he said. 'Shame it has to be at something like this.'

They walked over to a quieter and less crowded part of the hall. Banks put down his plate on a table – after all, he couldn't eat while talking – and took out a cigarette.

'How's the investigation going?' Blake asked.

'Nothing yet. Too many suspects. Anything could have happened in a situation like that.' He looked around the hall. 'Lot of people here. PC Gill must have been a popular bloke.

'Hmmm. Didn't know him well, myself. It's a big station.'

'Keen though,' Banks said. 'Volunteering for overtime on a Friday night. Most of our lads would've rather been at the pub.'

'It's more likely he needed the money. You know how half the bloody country lives on overtime. Has to, the wages we get paid.'

'True. Fond of money, was he?'

Chief Inspector Blake frowned. 'Are you digging?'

'We don't know anything about Gill,' Banks admitted.

'He wasn't one of ours. Every little bit helps. I'm sure you know that.'

'Yes. But this is hardly a normal case, is it?'

'Still . . .'

'As I said, I didn't really know him. I hear you've got a whizz-kid from the Yard in charge.'

Banks stubbed out his cigarette and picked up his plate. He knew he wasn't going to get anything out of Blake, so he ate his lunch while exchanging small talk. From the corner of his eye, he noticed Richmond talking to one of the uniformed pallbearers, probably one of the locals who had been bussed in with Gill to the demo. They had all given statements, of course, but none had seen Gill get stabbed. He hoped that Richmond was doing better than he was.

Chief Inspector Blake drifted away after about five minutes, and Banks took the opportunity to refill his sherry glass. At the bar, he found himself standing next to another pallbearer.

Banks introduced himself. 'Sad occasion,' he said.

'Aye,' PC Childers replied. He was young, perhaps in his early twenties. Banks felt irritated by his habit of looking in another direction while speaking.

'Popular bloke, PC Gill, by the look of it,' Banks said.

'Oh, aye. A right card, old Eddie was.'

'That right? Keen on his work?'

'You could say that. Certain parts of it, anyway.'

'I'll bet the overtime came in handy.'

'It's always good to have a bit extra,' Childers said slowly. Banks could tell he was holding back; whether out of friendship, a sense of occasion or out of simply duty, he couldn't be sure. But something was wrong. Childers was getting edgier, staring at the far wall. Finally, he excused himself abruptly and went to talk to his sergeant.

Banks was beginning to feel his mission had been wasted. He was also aware that very soon he would become an unwelcome guest if Childers and Blake mentioned his probings to others. Christ, he thought, they were a bloody sensitive lot here. It made him wonder if they'd got something to hide.

Back at the table for a helping of trifle, Banks manoeuvred himself next to a third pallbearer, a moon-faced lad with bright blue eyes and fine thinning hair the colour of wheat. Taking a deep breath, he smiled and introduced himself.

'I know who you are, sir,' the PC said. 'Ernie Childers told me. I'm PC Grant, Tony Grant. Ernie warned me. Said you were asking questions about Eddie Gill.'

'Just routine,' Banks said. 'Like we do in all murder investigations.'

Grant glanced over his shoulder. 'Look, sir,' he said, 'I can't talk to you here.'

'Where then?' Banks felt his heart speed up.

'Do you know the Angel's Trumpet?'

Banks shook his head. 'Don't know the place well. Only been here once before.'

'It'll take too long to explain,' Grant said. They finished helping themselves to dessert and turned around just in time to spot one of Grant's colleagues walking towards them.

'Marine Drive then, just round from the funfair,' Banks said quickly out of the corner of his mouth. It was the only place he could think of offhand. 'About an hour.'

'Fine,' Grant said as a uniformed sergeant joined them.

'Good of you to come, Chief Inspector,' the sergeant

said, holding out his hand. 'We appreciate it.'

Grant had merged back into the crowd, and as Banks exchanged trivialities with the sergeant, his mind was on the meeting ahead and the nervous covert way in which it had been arranged.

FOUR

'He made me feel dirty,' Mara said to Seth. 'The way he looked at me.'

'Don't let it get to you. That's just his technique. He's trying to goad you into saying something you'll regret.'

'But what about Paul? You saw the way he was picking on him. What can we do?'

Paul had taken off as soon as Burgess and Hatchley left. He had said he was feeling claustrophobic and needed a walk on the moors to calm down after the onslaught. He hadn't objected to Zoe's company, so Seth and Mara were left alone.

'What is there to do?' Seth said.

'But you saw the way that bastard went at him. I wouldn't put it past him to frame Paul if it came down to it. He *has* got a record.'

'They'd still need evidence.'

'He could plant it.'

'He couldn't just plant any old knife. It'd have to be the one that fitted the wound. They have scientists working for them. You can't put things across on that lot so easily, you know.'

'I suppose not.' Mara bit her lip and decided to take the plunge. 'Seth? Have you noticed that the knife's missing? That old flick knife from the mantelpiece.'

Seth looked at her in silence for a while. His brown eyes were sad, and the bags under them indicated lack of sleep. 'Yes,' he said, 'I have. But I didn't say anything. I didn't want to cause any alarm. It'll probably turn up.'

'But what if . . . what if that was the knife?'

'Oh come on, Mara. Surely you can't believe that. There are plenty of flick knives in the country. Why should it be that one? Somebody's probably borrowed it. It'll turn up.'

'Yes. But what if? I mean Paul could have taken it, couldn't he?'

Seth drummed his fingers on the chair arm. 'You know how many people were around on Friday afternoon,' he said. 'Any one of them could have taken it. When did you last notice it, for example?'

'I don't remember.'

'See? And it still doesn't mean it was the knife that was used. Someone might just have borrowed it and forgot to say anything.'

'I suppose so.' But Mara wasn't convinced. It seemed too much of a coincidence that a flick knife had been used to kill the policeman and the flick knife from the mantelpiece was missing. She thought Seth was grasping for straws in trying to explain it away as he was, but she wanted to believe him.

'There you are then,' he said. 'Why assume it's Paul just because he has a violent past? He's changed. You're thinking like the police.'

Mara wanted to, but she couldn't bring herself to tell Seth about the blood. Somehow, along with everything else, that information seemed so final, so damning.

She had decided to get in touch with that friend of Dennis Osmond's, Jenny. Mara liked her, though she wasn't too sure about Osmond himself. And Jenny was a professional psychologist. Mara could put her a theoretical case, using Paul's background, and ask if such a person was likely to be dangerous. She could say it was a part of some research she was doing for a story or something. Jenny would believe her.

'Maybe he should go away,' Seth said after a while.

'Paul? But why?'

'It might be best for him. For all of us. Till it's over. You can see how all this is getting to him.'

'It's getting to all of us,' Mara said. 'You, too.'

'Yes, but—'

'Where would he go? You know he hasn't got anybody else to turn to.' Despite her fears, Mara couldn't help but want to protect Paul. She didn't understand her feelings, but as much as she suspected him, she couldn't just give up and send him away.

Seth stared at the floor.

'It could look bad, too,' Mara argued. 'The police would think he was running away because he was guilty.'

'Let him stay, then. Just make up your mind.'

'Don't you care about him?'

'Of course I care about him. That's why I suggested he get away. Come on, Mara, which way do you want it? If I suggest he goes, I'm being cruel, and if he stays he might have to put up with a hell of a lot more from that fascist bastard we had round this afternoon. What do you want? Do you think he can take it? Look how he reacted to today's little chat. That was a picnic compared to what'll happen if they decide to take him in for questioning. And we can't protect him. Well? How much do you think he can take?'

'I don't know.' Things had suddenly got even more complicated for Mara. 'I want what's best for Paul.'

'Let's ask him, then. We can't make his decisions for him.'

'No! We've got to stand by him. If we approach him, he might think we believe he's guilty and want him out of the way.'

'But we'd have to approach him to ask if he'd like to go away for a while, until things settle down.'

'So we do nothing. If he wants to stay, he stays, and we stand by him, whatever. If he goes, then it's his decision. We don't force him out. He's not stupid, Seth. I'm sure he knows he's in for a lot of police harassment. The last thing he needs is to feel that we're against him, too.'

'OK.' Seth nodded and stood up. 'We'll leave it at that, I've got to go and do some work on that old sideboard now. I'm already late. You all right?'

Mara looked up at him and smiled. 'I'll manage.'

'Good.' He bent and kissed her, then went out to his workshop.

But Mara wasn't all right. Left to herself, she began to imagine all kinds of terrible things. The world of Maggie's Farm had seemed at first to offer the stability, love and freedom she had always been searching for, but now it had broken adrift. The feeling was like that she remembered having during a mild earthquake in California, when she'd travelled around the States with Matthew, aeons ago. Suddenly, the floor of the room, the house's foundations, the solid earth on which they were built, had seemed no more stable than water. A ripple had passed fleetingly under her, and what she had always thought durable turned out to be flimsy, untrustworthy and transient. The quake had only lasted for ten seconds and hadn't registered above five on the Richter scale, but the impression had remained with her ever since. Now it was coming back stronger than ever.

On the mantelpiece, among the clutter of seashells, pebbles, fossils and feathers, she could see the faint outline of dust around where the knife had been. As she wiped the surface clean, she thanked her lucky stars that the police had been looking for material things, not absences.

FIVE

Banks drove along Foreshore Road and Sandside by the Old Harbour. The amusement arcades and gift shops were all closed. In season, crowds of holidaymakers always gathered around the racks of cheeky postcards, teenagers queued for the ghost train, and children dragged their parents to the booths that sold candyfloss and Scarborough rock. But now the prom was deserted. Even on the seaward side, there were no stalls selling cockles, winkles and boiled shrimp. A thick high cloud cover had set in, and the sea sloshed at the barnacle-crusted harbour walls like molten metal. Fishing boats rocked at their moorings, and stacks of lobster pots teetered on the quayside. Towering over the scene, high on its promontory, the ruined castle looked like something out of a black and white horror film.

Banks dropped Richmond off at a pub near the West Pier and carried on along Marine Drive, parking just beyond the closed funfair. He buttoned up his raincoat tight and walked along the road that curved around the headland between the high cliff and the sea. Signs on the hillside warned of falling rocks. Waves hit the sea wall and threw up spray onto the road.

Tony Grant was already there, leaning on the railing

and staring out to the point where sea and sky merged in a uniform grey. He wore a navy duffel coat with the hood down, and his baby-fine hair fluttered in the wind. A solitary oil tanker was moving slowly across the horizon.

'I like it best like this,' he said as Banks joined him. 'If you don't mind getting a bit wet.'

They both looked out over the ruffled water. Salt spray filled the air and Banks felt the ozone freshen his lungs as he breathed deep. He shivered and asked, 'What is it you want to tell me?'

Grant hesitated. 'Look, sir,' he said after staring at the oil tanker for half a minute, 'I don't want you to get me wrong. I'm not a grass or anything. I've not been long on the force, and mostly I like it. I didn't think I would, not at first, but I do now. I want to make a career out of it.' He looked at Banks intensely. 'I'd like to join the CID. I'm not stupid; I've got brains. I've been to university, and I could maybe have got into teaching – that's what I thought I wanted to do – but, well, you know the job situation. Seems all that's going these days is the police force. So I joined. Anyway, as I said, I like it. It's challenging.'

Banks took out a cigarette and cupped his hand around his blue Bic lighter. It took him four attempts to get a flame going long enough. He wished Grant would get to the point, but he knew he had to be patient and listen. The kid was about to go against his peers and squeal on a colleague. Listening to the justification, as he had listened to so many before, was the price Banks had to pay.

'It's just that,' Grant went on, 'well . . . it's not as clean as I expected.'

Naive bugger, Banks thought. 'It's like anything else,' he said, encouraging the lad. 'There's a lot of bastards out there, whatever you do. Maybe our line of work attracts more than the usual quota of bullies, lazy sods, sadists and the like. But that doesn't mean we're all like that.' Banks sucked on his cigarette. It tasted different, mixed with the sea air. A wave broke below them and the spray wet their feet.

'I know what you're saying,' Grant said, 'and I think you're right. I just wanted you to know what side I'm on. I don't believe that the end justifies the means. With me they're innocent until proven guilty, as the saying goes. I treat people with respect, no matter what colour they are or how they dress or wear their hair. I'm not saying I approve of some of the types we get, but I'm not a thug.'

'And Gill was?'

'Yes.' A big wave started to peak as it approached the wall, and they both stepped back quickly to avoid the spray. Even so, they couldn't dodge a mild soaking, and Banks's cigarette got soggy. He threw it away.

'Was this common knowledge?'

'Oh, aye. He made no bones about it. See, with Gill it wasn't just the overtime, the money. He liked it well enough, but he liked the job more, if you see what I mean.'

'I think I do. Go on.'

'He was handy with his truncheon, Gill was. And he enjoyed it. Every time we got requests for manpower at demos, pickets and the like, he'd be first to sign up. Got a real taste for it during the miners' strike, when they bussed police in from all over the place. He was the kind of bloke who'd wave a roll of fivers at the striking miners to taunt them before he clobbered them. He trained with the Tactical Aid Group.'

The TAG, Banks knew, was a kind of force within a force. Its members trained together in a military fashion and learned how to use guns, rubber bullets and tear gas.

When their training was over, they went back to normal duties and remained on call for special situations like demos and picket lines. The official term for them had been changed to PSU – Police Support Unit – as the TAGs got a lot of bad publicity and sounded too obviously martial. But it was about as effective as changing the name of Windscale to Sellafield; a nuclear power station by another name . . .

'Is that how he behaved in Eastvale?' Banks asked.

'I wouldn't swear to it, but I'm pretty sure it was Gill who led the charge. See, things were getting a bit hairy. We were all hemmed in so tight. Gill was at the top of the steps with a few others, just looking down at people pushing and shoving – not that you could see much, it was so bloody dark with those old-fashioned street lamps. Anyway, one of the demonstrators chucked a bottle, and someone up there, behind me, yelled, "Let's clobber the bastards." I think I recognized Gill's voice. Then they charged down and . . . well, you know what happened. It needn't have – that's what I'm saying. Sure, there was a bit of aggro going on, but we could have sat on it if someone had given the order to loosen up a bit, give people room to breathe. Instead, Gill led a fucking truncheon charge. I know we coppers are all supposed to stick together, but . . .' Grant looked out to sea and shivered.

'There's a time to stick together,' Banks said, 'and this isn't it. Gill got himself killed, remember that.'

'But I couldn't swear to anything. I mean, officially . . .'

'Don't worry. This is off the record.' At least it is for now, he told himself. If anything came of their discussion, young Grant might find himself with a few serious decisions to make. 'How did the others feel about Gill?' he asked.

'Oh, most of them thought it was all a bit of a joke, a lark. I mean, there'd be Gill going on about clobbering queers and commies. I don't think they really took him seriously.'

'But it wasn't just talk? You say he liked smashing skulls.'

'Yes. He was a right bastard.'

'Surely they knew it?'

'Yes, but . . .'

'Did they approve?'

'Well, no, I wouldn't say that. Some, maybe . . . but I didn't, for one.'

'But nobody warned him, told him to knock it off?'

Grant pulled up his collar. 'No.'

'Were they scared of him?'

'Some of the lads were, yes. He was a bit of hard case.'

'What about you?'

'Me? Well, I wouldn't have taken him up on anything, that's for sure. I'm scarcely above regulation height myself, and Gill was a big bugger.'

A seagull screeched by them, a flash of white against the grey, and began circling over the water for fish. The tanker had moved far over to the right of the horizon. Banks felt the chill getting to him. He put his hands deep in his pockets and tensed up against the cold wet wind.

'Did any of the others actually like him?' he asked. 'Did he have any real mates at the station?'

'I wouldn't say so, no. He wasn't a very likeable bloke. Too big-headed, too full of himself. I mean, you couldn't have a conversation with him; you just had to listen. He had views on everything, but he was thick. I mean, he never really thought anything out. It was all down to Pakis and Rastas and students and skinheads and unemployed yobbos with him.'

'So he wasn't popular around the station?'

'Not really, no. But you know what it's like. A few of the lads get together in the squad room – especially if they've had TAG training – and you get all that macho tough-guy talk, just like American cop shows. He was good at that, Gill was, telling stories about fights and taking risks.'

'Are there any more like him in your station?'

'Not as bad, no. There's a few that don't mind a good punch-up now and then, and some blokes like to pull kids in on a sus just to liven up a boring night. But nobody went as far as Gill.'

'Did he have any friends outside the station?'

'I don't know who he went about with off duty.'

'Did he have a girlfriend?'

'I don't know. He never mentioned anyone.'

'So he didn't brag about having women like he did about thumping people?'

'No. I never heard him. Whenever he did talk about women it was always like they were whores and bitches. He was a foul-mouthed bastard. He'd hit them too, at demos. It was all the same to him.'

'Do you think he could have been the type to mess around with someone else's girlfriend or wife?'

Grant shook his head. 'Not that I know of.'

The seagull flew up towards the cliffs behind them, a fish flapping in its beak. The sea had settled to a rhythmic slapping against the stone wall, hardly sending up any spray at all. Banks risked another cigarette.

'Did Gill have any enemies that you know of?'

'He must have made plenty over the years, given his attitude towards the public,' Grant said. 'But I couldn't name any.'

'Anyone on the force?'

'Eh?'

'You said nobody at the station really liked him. Had anyone got a good reason to dislike him? Did he owe money, cheat people, gamble? Any financial problems?'

'I don't think so. He just got people's backs up, that's all. He talked about betting on the horses, yes, but I don't think he did it that much. It was just the macho sort of thing that went with his image. He never tried to borrow any money off me, if that's what you mean. And I don't think he was on the take. At least he was honest on that score.'

Banks turned his back to the choppy water and looked up towards the sombre bulk of the ruined castle. He couldn't see much from that angle; the steep cliff, where seabirds made their nests, was mottled with grass, moss and bare stone. 'Is there anything else you can tell me?' he asked.

'I don't think so. I just wanted you to know that all that crap at the funeral was exactly that. Crap. Gill was a vicious bastard. I'm not saying he deserved what happened to him, nobody deserves that, but those who live by the sword . . .'

'Did you have any particular reason to dislike Gill?'

Grant seemed startled by the question. 'Me? What do you mean?'

'What I say. Did he ever do you any harm personally?'

'No. Look, if you're questioning my motives, sir, believe me, it's exactly like I told you. I heard you were asking questions about Gill and I thought someone should tell you the truth, that's all. I'm not the kind to go around speaking ill of the dead just because they're not here to defend themselves.'

Banks smiled. 'Don't mind me, I'm just an old cynic. It's a long time since I've come across a young idealist like you on the force.' Banks thought of Superintendent Gristhorpe, who had managed to hang on to a certain amount of idealism over the years. But he was one of the old guard; it was a rare quality in youth these days, Banks had found, especially in those who joined the police. Even Richmond could hardly be called an idealist. Keen yes, but as practical as the day was long.

Grant managed a thin smile. 'It's nice of you to say that, but it's not exactly true. After all,' he said, 'I laid into them with the rest last Friday, didn't I? And do you know what?' His voice caught in his throat and he couldn't look Banks in the eye. 'After a while, I even started to enjoy myself.'

So, Banks thought, maybe Grant had told all because he felt ashamed of himself for acting like Gill and enjoying the battle. Getting caught up in the thrill of action was hardly unusual; the release of adrenalin often produced a sense of exhilaration in men who would normally run a mile from a violent confrontation. But it obviously bothered Grant. Perhaps this was his way of exorcizing what he saw as Gill's demon inside him. Whatever his reasons, he'd given Banks plenty to think about.

'It happens,' Banks said by way of comfort. 'Don't let it worry you. Look, would you do me a favour?' They turned and started walking back to their cars.

Grant shrugged. 'Depends.'

'I'd like to know a bit more about Gill's overtime activities – like where he's been and when. There should be a record. It'd also be useful if I could find out about any official complaints against him, and anything at all about his private life.'

Grant frowned and pushed at his left cheek with his

tongue as if he had a ulcer. 'I don't know,' he said finally, fiddling in his duffel coat pocket for his car keys. 'I wouldn't want to get caught. They'd make my life a bloody misery here if they knew I'd even talked to you like this. Can't you just request his record?'

Banks shook his head. 'My boss doesn't want us to be seen investigating Gill. He says it'll look bad. But if we're not seen . . . Send it to my home address, just to be on the safe side.' Banks scribbled his address on a card and handed it over.

Grant got into his car and opened the window. 'I can't promise anything,' he said slowly, 'but I'll have a go.' He licked his lips. 'If anything important comes out of all this . . .' He paused.

Banks bent down, his hand resting on the wet car roof.

'Well,' Grant went on, 'I don't want you to think I'm after anything, but you will remember I said I wanted to join the CID, won't you?' And he smiled a big broad innocent open smile.

Bloody hell, there were no flies on this kid. Banks couldn't make him out. At first he'd taken such a moral line that Banks suspected chapel had figured strongly somewhere in his background. But despite all his idealism and respect for the law, he might well be another Dirty Dick in the making. On the other hand, that damn smiling moon-face looked so bloody cherubic . . .

'Yes,' Banks said, smiling back. 'Don't worry, I won't forget you.'

6

ONE

In the cross-streets between York Road and Market Street, near where Banks lived, developers had converted terraces of tall Victorian family houses into student flats. In one of these, in a two-room attic unit, Tim Fenton and Abha Sutton lived.

If Tim and Abha made an unlikely-looking couple, they made an even more unlikely pair of revolutionaries. Tim had all the blond good looks of an American preppie, with dress sense to match. Abha, half-Indian, had golden skin, beetle-black hair and a pearl stud through her left nostril. She was studying graphic design; Tim was in the social sciences. They embraced Marxism as the solution to the world's inequalities, but were always quick to point out that they regarded Soviet Communism as an extreme perversion of the prophet's truth. Both were generally well mannered, and not at all the type to call police pigs.

They sat on a beat-up sofa under a Che Guevara poster while Banks made himself comfortable on a second-hand office swivel chair at the desk. The cursor blinked on the screen of an Amstrad PC, and stacks of paper and books overflowed from the table to the floor and on to any spare chairs.

After getting back from Scarborough, Banks had just had time to drop in at the station and see what Special

Branch had turned up. As usual, their files were as thin as Kojak's hair and gathered on premisses as flimsy as a stripper's G-string. Tim Fenton was listed because he had attended a seminar in Slough sponsored by *Marxism Today*, and some of the speakers there were suspected of working for the Soviets. Dennis Osmond had attracted the Branch's attention by writing a series of violently anti-government articles for various socialist journals during the miners' strike, and by organizing a number of political demonstrations, especially against the American military presence in Europe. As Banks had suspected, their crimes against the realm hardly provided grounds for exile or execution.

Tim and Abha were predictably hostile and frightened after Burgess's visit. Banks had previously been on good terms with the two after successfully investigating a series of burglaries in student residences the previous November. Even Marxists, it appeared, valued their stereos and television sets. But now they were cautious and guarded. It took a lot of small talk to get them to relax and open up. When Banks finally got around to the subject of the demo, they seemed to have stopped confusing him with Burgess.

'Did you see anything?' Banks asked first.

'No, we couldn't,' Tim answered. 'We were right in the thick of the crowd. One of the cops shouted something and that was that. When things went haywire we were too busy trying to protect ourselves to see what was happening to anyone else.'

'You were involved in organizing the demo, right?'

'Yes. But that doesn't mean—'

Banks held up his hand. 'I know,' he said. 'And that's not what I'm implying. Did you get the impression that anyone involved – anyone at all – might have had more on his mind than just protesting Honoria Winstanley's visit?'

They both shook their heads. 'When we got together up at the farm,' Abha explained, 'everyone was just so excited that we could organize a demo in a place as conservative as Eastvale. I know there weren't many people there, but it seemed like a lot to us.'

'The farm?'

'Yes. Maggie's Farm. Do you know it?'

Banks nodded.

'They invited us up to make posters and stuff,' Tim said. 'Friday afternoon. They're really great up there; they've really got it together. I mean, Seth and Mara, they're like the old independent craftsmen, doing their own thing, making it outside the system. And Rick's a pretty sharp Marxist.'

'I thought he was an artist.'

'He is,' Tim said, looking offended. 'But he tries not to paint anything commercial. He's against art as a saleable commodity.'

So that pretty watercolour Banks had noticed propped by the fireplace at Maggie's Farm couldn't have been one of Rick's.

'What about Paul Boyd?'

'We don't know him well,' Abha said. 'And he didn't say much. One of the oppressed, I suppose.'

'You could say that. And Zoe?'

'Oh, she's all right,' Tim said. 'She goes in for all that bourgeois spiritual crap – bit of a navel-gazer – but she's OK underneath it all.'

'Do you know anything about their backgrounds, where they come from?'

They shook their heads. 'No,' Tim said finally. 'I mean

122

we just talk about the way things are now, how to change them, that kind of thing. And a bit of political theory. Rick's pissed off about his divorce and all that, but that's about as far as the personal stuff goes.'

'And you know nothing else about them?'

'No.'

'Who else was there?'

'Just us and Dennis.'

'Osmond?'

'That's right.'

'Do either of you recall seeing a flick knife that day, or hearing anyone mention one?'

'No. That's what the other bloke went on about,' Tim said, getting edgy. 'Bloody Burgess. He went on and on about a flick knife.'

'He almost came right out and accused us of killing that policeman, too,' Abha said.

'That's just his style. I wouldn't worry about it. Did anyone at the meeting mention PC Gill by name?'

'Not that I heard,' Tim said.

'Nor me,' said Abha.

'Have you ever heard anyone talk about him? Dennis Osmond, for example? Or Rick?'

'No. The only thing we knew about him,' Abha said, 'was that he'd trained with the TAG groups and he liked to work on crowd control. You know – demos, pickets and such.'

The chair creaked as Banks swivelled sharply. 'How did you know that?'

'Word gets around,' Abha said. 'We keep—'

Tim nudged her in the ribs and she shut up.

'What she means,' he said, 'is that if you're politically involved up here, you soon get to know the ones to watch out for. You lot keep tabs on us, don't you? I'm pretty sure Special Branch has a file on me, anyway.'

'Fair enough,' Banks said, smiling to himself at the absurdity of it all. Games. Just little boys' games. 'Was this fairly common knowledge? Could anyone have known to expect Gill at the demo that night?'

'Anyone involved in organizing it, sure,' Tim said. 'And anyone who'd been to demos in Yorkshire before. There aren't many like him, thank God. He did have a bit of a reputation.'

'Did you *know* he was going to be on duty?'

'Not for certain, no. I mean, he could have had flu or broke his leg.'

'But short of that?'

'Short of that he was rarely known to miss. Look, I don't know what all this is in aid of,' Tim said, 'but I think you should know we're still going to do our own investigation.'

'Into the murder?'

Tim gave him a puzzled glance. 'No. Into the police brutality. We're all getting together again up at the farm in a few days to compare notes.'

'Well, if you find anything out about PC Gill's death, let me know.'

Banks looked at his watch and stood up. It was time he went and got ready for his evening out with Jenny. After he'd said goodbye and walked back down the gloomy staircase to the street, he reflected how odd it was that wherever he went all roads seemed to lead to Maggie's Farm. More than that, almost anyone involved could have known that Gill was likely to be there that night. If Gill cracked heads in Yorkshire for a hobby, then the odds were that one or two people might hold a strong grudge against him. He wished Tony Grant would hurry up and send the information from Scarborough.

TWO

Mara put on her army surplus greatcoat and set off down the track for Relton. It was dark now and the stars were glittering flecks of ice in the clear sky. Distant hills and scars showed only as muted silhouettes, black against black. The crescent moon was up, hanging lopsided like a backdrop to a music-hall song. Mara almost expected a man with a top hat, cape and cane to start dancing across it way up in the sky. The gravel crackled under her feet, and the wind whistled through gaps in the lichen-covered drystone wall. In the distance, the lights of cottages and villages down in the dale twinkled like stars.

She would talk to Jenny, she decided, thrusting her hands deeper into her pockets and hunching up against the chill. Jenny knew Chief Inspector Banks, too. Though she distrusted all policemen, Mara had to admit that he was a hell of a lot better than Burgess. Perhaps she might also be able to find out what the police really thought, and if they were going to leave Paul alone from now on.

Mara's mind strayed back to the I Ching, which she had consulted before setting off. What the hell was it all about? It was supposed to be an oracle, to offer words of wisdom when you really needed them, but Mara wasn't convinced. One problem was that it always answered questions obliquely. You couldn't ask, 'Did Paul kill that policeman?' and get a simple yes or no. This time, the oracle had read: 'The woman holds the basket, but there are no fruits in it. The man stabs the sheep, but no blood flows. Nothing that acts to further.' Did that mean Paul hadn't killed anyone, that the blood on his hand had come from somewhere else? And what about the empty basket? Did that have something to do with Mara's barren womb? If there was any practical advice at all, it was to do nothing, yet here she was, walking down the track on her way to call Jenny. All the book had done was put her fears into words and images.

At the end of the track, Mara walked along Mortsett Lane, past the closed shops and the cottages with their television screens flickering behind curtains. In the dimly lit phone booth, she rang Jenny's number. She heard a click followed by a strange disembodied voice that she finally recognized as Jenny's. The voice explained that its owner was out, but that a message could be left after the tone. Mara, who had never dealt with an answering machine before, waited nervously, worried that she might miss her cue. But it soon came, the unmistakable high-pitched bleep. Mara spoke quickly and loudly, as people do to foreigners, feeling self-conscious about her voice: 'This is Mara, Jenny. I hope I've got this thing right. Please, will you meet me tomorrow lunch time in the Black Sheep in Relton? It's important. I'll be there at one. I hope you can come.' She paused for a moment and listened to the silence, feeling that she should add something, but she could think of nothing more to say.

Mara put the phone back gently. It had been rather like sending a telegram, something she had done once before. The feeling that every word cost money was very inhibiting, and so, in a different way, was the sense of a tape winding around the capstan past the recording head as she talked.

Anyway, it was done. Leaving the booth, she hurried

towards the Black Sheep, feeling lighter in spirit now that she had at least taken a practical step to deal with her fears.

THREE

Banks and Jenny sat in the bar over aperitifs while they studied the menu. The Royal Oak was a cosy place with muted lights, mullioned windows and gleaming copperware in little nooks and crannies. Fastened horizontally between the dark beams on the ceiling was a collection of walking sticks of all lengths and materials: knobbly ashplants, coshers, swordsticks and smooth canes, many with ornate brass handles. On a long shelf above the bar stood a row of toby jugs with such faces as Charles II, Shakespeare and Beethoven; some, however, depicted contemporaries like Margaret Thatcher and Paul McCartney.

Jenny sipped a vodka and tonic, Banks a dry sherry, as they tried to decide what to order. Finally, after much self-recrimination about the damage it would do to her figure, Jenny settled for steak *au poivre* with a wine and cream sauce. Banks chose roast leg of lamb. Much as he liked to watch the little blighters frolic around the dale every spring, he enjoyed eating them almost as much. They'd only grow up into sheep anyway, he reasoned.

They followed the waitress into the dining room, pleased to find only one other table occupied, and that by a subdued couple already on dessert. Mozart's Clarinet Quintet played quietly in the background. Banks watched Jenny walk ahead of him. She was wearing a loose top, cut square across the collarbone, which looked as if it had been tie-dyed in various shades of blue and red. Her pleated skirt was plain rust-red, the colour of her tumbling wavy hair, and came to midway down her calves. The tights she wore had some kind of pattern on them, which looked to Banks like a row of bruises up the sides of her legs. Being a gentleman, though, he had complimented her on her appearance.

The waitress lit the candle, took their orders and moved off soundlessly, leaving them with the wine list to study. Banks lit a cigarette and smiled at Jenny.

Despite the claims of *Playboy*, the Miss World contest and other promoters of the feminine image to men, Banks often found it was the most insignificant detail that made a woman physically attractive to him: a well-placed mole, a certain curve of the lips or turn of the ankle; or a mannerism, such as the way she picked up a glass, tilted her head before smiling or fiddled with a necklace while speaking.

In the case of Sandra, his wife, it was the dark eyebrows and the contrast they made with her naturally ash-blonde hair. With Jenny, it was her eyes, or rather the delta of lines that crinkled their outer edges, especially when she smiled. They were like a map whose contours revealed a sense of humour and a curious mixture of toughness and vulnerability that Banks himself felt able to identify with. Her beautiful red hair and green eyes, her shapeliness, her long legs and full lips were all very well, but they were just icing on the cake. It was the lines around the eyes that did it.

'What are you thinking?' Jenny asked, looking up from the list.

Banks gave her the gist of it.

'Well,' she said, after a fit of laughter, 'I'll take that as a compliment, though there are many women who wouldn't. What shall we have?'

'They've got a nice Séguret 1980 here, if I remember rightly. And not too expensive, either. That's if you like Rhône.'

'Fine by me.'

When the waitress returned with their smoked salmon and melon first course, Banks ordered the wine.

'So what's all this decadence in aid of?' asked Jenny, her eyes twinkling in the candle flame. 'Are you planning to seduce me, or are you just softening me up for questioning?'

'What if I said I was planning to seduce you?'

'I'd say you were going about it the right way.' She smiled and looked around the room. 'Candlelight, romantic music, nice atmosphere, good food.'

The wine arrived, shortly followed by their main courses, and soon they were enjoying the meal to the accompaniment of the Flute Quartets.

Over dinner, Jenny complained about her day. There had been too many classes to teach, and she was tired of the undergraduates' simplistic assumptions about psychology. Sometimes, she confessed, she was even sick of psychology itself and wished she'd studied English literature or history instead.

Banks told her about the funeral, careful to leave out his meeting with Tony Grant. It would be useful to have something in reserve later, if he could steer her around to talking about Osmond. He also mentioned his visit to Tim and Abha and how Burgess's approach had soured the pitch.

'Your Dirty Dick is a real jerk,' Jenny said, employing an Americanism the man himself would have been proud of. 'Dare I ask about dessert?' she asked, pushing her empty plate aside.

'It's *your* figure.'

'In that case, I think I'll have chocolate mousse. Absolutely no calories at all. And coffee and cognac.'

When the waitress came, Banks ordered Jenny's dessert and brandy along with a wedge of Stilton and a glass of Sauternes for himself. 'You didn't really answer my question, you know,' he said.

'What question's that?'

'The one about seducing you.'

'Oh, yes. But I did. I said you were going about it the right way.'

'But you didn't say whether I'd get anywhere or not.'

Jenny's eyes crinkled. 'Alan! Are you feeling the itch because Sandra's away?'

Banks felt foolish for bringing the subject up in the first place. Flirting with Jenny might be fun, but it also had a serious edge that neither really wanted to get too close to. If it hadn't been for that damned incident at Osmond's flat, he thought, he'd never have been so silly as to start playing games like this. But when he had seen Jenny look round Osmond's bedroom door like that – the robe slipping off her shoulder, the tousled hair, the relaxed unfocused look that follows lovemaking – it hadn't only made him jealous, it had also inflamed old desires. He had felt that nobody else should enjoy what he couldn't enjoy himself. And he couldn't; of that there was no doubt. So he played his games and ended up embarrassing both of them.

He lit a cigarette to hide behind and poured the last of the Séguret. 'Change the subject?'

Jenny nodded. 'A good idea.'

The dessert arrived at the same time as a noisy party of businessmen. Fortunately, the waitress seated them at the far end of the room.

'This is delicious,' Jenny said, spooning up the chocolate mousse. 'I suppose you're going to question me now? I've got a feeling that seduction would probably have been a lot more fun.'

'Don't tempt me,' Banks said. 'But you're right. I would like your help on a couple of things.'

'Here we go. Can I just finish my sweet first?'

'Of course.'

When the dishes were empty, Jenny sipped some cognac. 'All right,' she said, saluting and sitting up to attention. 'I'm all ears.'

'Were you there?' Banks asked.

'Where?'

'At the demo. You came to see me at two in the morning. You said you'd been waiting at your house for your boyfriend—'

'Dennis!'

'Yes, all right. Dennis.' Banks wondered why he hated the sound of the name so much. 'But you could have been at the demo, too.'

'You mean I could have been lying?'

'That's not what I'm getting at. You might have just failed to mention it.'

'Surely you don't think I'm a suspect now? Being seduced by Quasimodo would be more fun than this.'

Banks laughed. 'That's not my point. Think about it. If you were there with Osmond right up until the time he got arrested, then you'd be a witness that he didn't stab PC Gill.'

'I see. So Dennis is a prime suspect as far as you're concerned?'

'He is as far as Burgess is concerned. And that's what counts.'

Banks wondered if he too wanted Osmond to be guilty. Part of him, he had to admit, did. He was also wondering whether or not to tell Jenny about the assault charges. It would be a mean thing to do right now, he decided, because he couldn't trust his motives. Would he be telling her for her own good, or out of the jealousy he felt, out of a desire to hurt her relationship with Osmond?

'I see what you mean,' Jenny said finally. 'No, I wasn't at the demo. I don't know what happened. Dennis has talked to me about it, of course, and, by the way, he's going ahead with his own inquiry into the thing, you know, along with Tim and Abha. And Burgess is going to come off pretty badly. Apparently he was around again today with Hatchley.'

Banks knew that. He also knew that the dirty duo had got no more out of anyone than they had the first time round. They'd probably be drowning their sorrows in the Queen's Arms by now, and with a bit of luck Dirty Dick would push it too far with Glenys and her Cyril would thump him.

'Back to the demo,' Banks said. 'What exactly has Dennis said?'

'He doesn't know what happened to that policeman. Do you think I'd be sitting here talking to you, answering your questions, if I wasn't trying to convince you that he had nothing to do with it?'

'So he saw nothing?'

'No. He said he heard somebody shout – he didn't catch the words – and after that it was chaos.'

That seemed to square with what Tony Grant and Tim and Abha had said about the riot's origin. Banks took a sip of Sauternes and watched it make legs down the inside of his glass.

'Did he ever mention PC Gill to you?'

Jenny shrugged. 'He may have done. I didn't have much to do with the demo, as I said.'

'Did you ever hear the name?'

'I don't know.' Jenny was getting prickly. 'I can't say I pay much attention to Dennis's political concerns. And if you're going to make a crack about that, forget it. Unless you want a lap full of hot coffee.'

Banks decided it was best to veer away from the subject of Osmond. 'You know the people at Maggie's Farm, don't you?' he asked.

'Yes. Dennis got friendly with Seth and Mara. We've been up a few times. I like them, especially Mara.'

'What's the set-up there?'

Jenny swirled the cognac and took another sip. 'Seth bought the place about three years ago,' she said. 'Apparently, it was in a bit of a state, which was why he got it quite cheaply. He fixed it up, renovated the old barn and rented it out. After Mara, Rick came next, I think, with Julian. He was having some problems with his wife.'

'Yes, I've heard about his wife,' Banks said. 'Do you know anything else about her?'

'No. Except according to Rick her name must be Bitch.'

'What about Zoe?'

'I'm not sure how she met up with them. She came later. As far as I know she's from the east coast. She seems like a bit of a space cadet, but I suspect she's quite shrewd, really. You'd be surprised how many people are into that New Age stuff these days. Looking for something, I suppose . . . Reassurance . . . I don't know. Anyway, she makes a good living from it. She does the weekly horoscope in the *Gazette* too, and takes a little booth on the coast on summer weekends for doing tarot readings and whatnot. You know, Madame Zoe, Gypsy Fortune Teller . . .'

'The east coast? Could it be Scarborough?'

Jenny shook her head. 'Whitby, I think.'

'Still,' Banks muttered, 'it's not far away.'

'What isn't?'

The waitress brought coffee, and Banks lit another cigarette, careful to keep the smoke away from Jenny.

'Tell me about Mara.'

'I like Mara a lot. She's bright, and she's had an interesting life. She was in some religious organization before she came to the farm, but she got disillusioned. She seems to want to settle down a bit now. For some reason, we get along quite well. Seth, as I say, I don't know much about. He grew up in the sixties and he hasn't sold out – I mean he hasn't become a stockbroker or an accountant, at least. His main interest is his carpentry. There's also something about a woman in his past.'

'What woman?'

'Oh, it was just something Mara said. Apparently Seth doesn't like to talk about it. He had a lover who died. Maybe they were even married, I don't know. That was just before he bought the farm.'

'What was her name?'

'Alison, I think.'

'How did she die?'

'Some kind of accident.'

'What kind?'

'That's all I know, really. I'm not being evasive. Mara said it's all she knows, too. Seth only told her because he got drunk once. Apparently he's not much of a drinker.'

'And that's all you know?'

'Yes. It was some kind of motor accident. She got knocked down or something.'

'Where was he living then?'

'Hebden Bridge, I think. Why does it matter?'

'It probably doesn't. I just like to know as much as I can about who I'm dealing with. They were involved in the demo, and every time I question someone, Maggie's Farm comes up.'

It would be easy enough to check the Hebden Bridge accident records, though where Gill might come into it, Banks had no idea. Perhaps he had been on traffic duty at the time? He would hardly have been involved in a religious organization either, unless he felt a close friend or relation had been brainwashed by such a group.

'What about Paul Boyd?' he asked.

Jenny paused. 'He's quite new up there. I can't say I know him well. To tell you the truth – and to speak quite unprofessionally – he gives me the creeps. But Mara's very attached to him, like he's a younger brother, or a son even. There's about seventeen years between them. He's another generation, really – punk, post sixties. Mara thinks he just needs tender loving care, something he's never had much of, apparently.'

'What do you think of Paul professionally?'

'It's hard to answer that. As I said, I haven't really talked to him that much. He seems angry, antisocial. Maybe life at the farm will give him some sense of belonging. If you think about it, what reason does he have to love the world? No adult has ever given him a break, nor has society. He feels worthless and rejected, so he makes himself look like a reject; he holds it to him and shouts it out, as people do. And that,' Jenny said with a mock bow, 'is Dr Fuller's humble opinion.'

Banks nodded. 'It makes sense.'

'But it doesn't make him a killer.'

'No.' He couldn't think of any more questions without returning to the dangerous territory of Dennis Osmond, and things had gone so well for the past half-hour or so that he didn't want to risk ending the evening on a sour note. Jenny was bound to be guarded if he really started pushing about Osmond again.

Banks picked up the bill, which Jenny insisted on sharing, and they left. The drive home went smoothly, but Banks felt guilty because he was sure he was a bit over the limit, and if anyone ought to know better about drunken driving, it was a policeman. Not that he felt drunk. After all, he hadn't had much to drink, really. He was perfectly in control. But that's what they all said when the crystals changed colour. Jenny told him not to be silly, he was quite all right. When he dropped her off, there was no invitation to come in for a coffee, and he was glad of that.

Luckily, he thought as he tried to fall asleep, Jenny hadn't pushed him about his own theories. If she had, he would have told her – and trusted her to make sure it got no further – about his little chat with Tony Grant on Marine Drive, the implications of which put a different light on things.

On the one hand, what Grant had told him made the possibility of a personal motive for killing Gill much more likely. He didn't know who might have had such a motive yet, but according to what Tim and Abha had said, almost any of the demonstrators – especially the organizers or people close to them – would have known to expect Gill at the demo. And if Gill was there, wasn't it a safe bet that violence would follow?

On the other hand, Banks found himself thinking that if

Gill had enemies within the force, perhaps a fellow police-man, not a demonstrator, might have taken the oppor-tunity to get rid of him: someone whose wife or girlfriend Gill had fooled around with, for example; or a partner in crime, if he had been on the take. Tony Grant hadn't thought so, but he was only a naive rookie, after all.

It wasn't an idea Banks would expect Burgess to entertain for a moment; for one thing, it would blow all political considerations off the scene. But another police-man would have expected Gill to cause trouble, could have arranged to be on overtime with him and could have been sure of getting away. None of which could be said for any of the demonstrators. Nobody searched the police; nobody checked their uniforms for Gill's blood.

Maybe it was the kind of far-fetched theory one usually got on the edge of sleep and would seem utterly absurd in the morning light. But Banks couldn't quite rule it out. He'd known men on the Metropolitan force more than capable of murdering fellow officers, and in many cases, the loss would hardly have diminished the quality of the human gene pool. The only way to find out about the angle, though, was to press Tony Grant even further into service. If there was anything in it, the fewer people who knew about Banks's line of investigation, the better. It could be dangerous.

And so, the Sauternes still warm in his veins and a stretch of cold empty bed beside him, Banks fell asleep thinking of the victim, convinced that someone not too far away had had a very good reason for wanting PC Edwin Gill dead.

7

ONE

Banks turned up the track to Gristhorpe's old farmhouse above Lyndgarth, wondering what the superintendent was doing at home on a Wednesday morning. The message, placed on his desk by Sergeant Rowe, had offered no explanation, just an invitation to visit.

Pulling up in front of the squat solid house, he stabbed out his cigarette and ejected the Lightning Hopkins cassette he'd been listening to. Breathing in the fresh cold air, he looked down over Swainsdale and was struck by the way Relton and Maggie's Farm, directly opposite on the south side of the dale, formed almost a mirror image of Lyndgarth and Gristhorpe's house. Like the latter, Maggie's Farm stood higher up the hillside than the village it was close to – so high it was on the verge of the moorland that spread for miles on the heights between dales.

Looking down the slope from the farmhouse, Banks could see the grey-brown ruins of Devraulx Abbey, just west of Lyndgarth. On the valley bottom, Fortford marked the western boundary of the river meadows. Swainsdale was at its broadest there, where the River Swain meandered through the flats until it veered south-east to Eastvale and finally joined the Ouse outside York.

In summer, the lush green meadows were speckled with golden buttercups. Bluebells, forget-me-nots and wild garlic grew by the riverside under the shade of ash and willow. The Leas, as they were called locally, were a favourite spot for family picnics. Artists set up their easels there too, and fishermen spent idle afternoons on the riverbank and waded in the shallows at dusk. Now, although the promise of spring showed in the grass and clung like a green haze around the branches of the trees, the meadows seemed a haunted and desolate spot. The snaking river sparkled between the trees, and a brisk wind chased clouds over from the west. Shadows flitted across the steep green slopes with a speed that was almost dizzying to watch.

Gristhorpe answered the door and led Banks into the living room, where a peat fire burned in the hearth, then disappeared into the kitchen. Banks took off his sheepskin-lined car coat and rubbed his hands by the flames. Outside the back window, a pile of stones stood by the unfinished drystone wall that the superintendent worked on in his spare time. It fenced in nothing and went nowhere, but Banks had enjoyed many hours placing stones there with Gristhorpe in companionable silence. Today, though, it was too cold for such outdoors activity.

Carrying a tray of tea and scones, Gristhorpe returned and sat down in his favourite armchair to pour. After small talk about the wall and the possibility of yet more snow, the superintendent told Banks his news: the inquiry into the demo had been suspended.

'I'm on ice, as our American cousins would put it,' he said. 'The assistant chief commissioner's been talking to the PCA about getting an outsider to finish the report. Maybe someone from Avon and Somerset division.'

'Because we're too biased?'

'Aye, partly. I expected it. They only set me on it in the

first place to make it look like we were acting quickly.'

'Did you find anything out?'

'It looks like some of our lads overreacted.'

Banks told him what he'd heard from Jenny and Tim and Abha.

Gristhorpe nodded. 'The ACC doesn't like it. If you ask me, I don't think there'll be an official inquiry. It'll be postponed till it's no longer an issue. What he's hoping is that Superintendent Burgess will come up with the killer fast. That'll satisfy everyone, and people will just forget about the rest.'

'Where does that leave you?'

'I'm taking a few days' leave, on the ACC's advice. Unless anything else comes up – something unconnected to Gill's death – then that's how I'll stay. He's right, of course. I'd only get in the way. Burgess is in charge of that investigation, and it wouldn't do to have the two of us treading on each other's toes. But don't let the bugger near my office with those foul cigars of his! How are you getting on with him?'

'All right, I suppose. He's got plenty of go, and he's certainly not stupid. Trouble is, he's got a bee in his bonnet about terrorists and lefties in general.'

'And you see things differently?'

'Yes.' Banks told him about the meeting with Tony Grant and the possibilities it had opened up for him. 'And,' he added, 'you'd think Special Branch would have known if there'd been some kind of terrorist action planned, wouldn't you?'

Gristhorpe digested the information and mulled it over for a few moments, then turned his light blue eyes on Banks and rubbed his chin. 'I'll not deny you might be right,' he said, 'but for Christ's sake keep your feet on the ground. Don't go off half-cocked on this or you could bring down a lot of trouble on yourself, and on me. I appreciate you want to follow your own nose – you'd be a poor copper if you didn't – and maybe you'd like to show Dirty Dick a thing or two. But be careful. Just because Gill turned out to be a bastard, it doesn't follow that's why he was killed. Burgess could be right.'

'I know that. It's just a theory. But thanks for the warning.'

Gristhorpe smiled. 'Think nothing of it. But keep it under your hat. If Burgess finds out you've been pursuing a private investigation, he'll have your guts for garters. And it won't be just him. The ACC'll have your balls for billiards.'

'I don't know as I've got enough body parts to go round,' Banks said, grinning.

'And this conversation hasn't taken place. I know nothing about what you're up to, agreed?'

'Agreed.'

'But keep me posted. God, how I hate bloody politics.'

Banks knew that the superintendent came from a background of Yorkshire radicals – Chartists, the anti-Corn Laws crowd – and there was even a Luddite lurking in the family tree. But Gristhorpe himself was conservative with a small c. He was, however, concerned with the preservation of human rights that had been fought for and won over the centuries. That was how he saw his job – as a defender of the people, not an attacker. Banks agreed, and that was one reason they got along so well.

Banks finished his tea and looked at his watch. 'Talking of Dirty Dick, I'd better be off. He's called a conference in the Queen's Arms for one o'clock.'

'Seems like he's taken up residence there.'

'You're not far wrong.' Banks explained about Glenys and put on his car coat. 'Besides that,' he added, 'he drinks like a bloody fish.'

'So it's not only Glenys and her charms?'

'No.'

'Ever seen him pissed?'

'Not yet.'

'Well, watch him. Drinking's an occupational hazard with us, but it can get beyond a joke. The last thing you need is a piss artist to rely on in a tight spot.'

'I don't think there's anything to worry about,' Banks said, walking to the car. 'He's always been a boozer. And he's usually sharp as a whippet. Anyway, what can I do if I think he is overdoing it? I can just see his face if I suggest a visit to AA.'

Gristhorpe stood by the car. Banks rolled the window down, slipped Lightning Hopkins back in the slot, and lit a cigarette.

The superintendent shook his head. 'It's about time you stopped that filthy habit, too,' he said. 'And as for that racket you call music . . .'

Banks smiled and turned the key in the ignition. 'Do you know something?' he said. 'I do believe you're becoming an insufferable old fogey. I know you're tone-deaf and wouldn't know Mozart from the Beatles, but don't forget, it wasn't that long ago you gave up smoking yourself. Have you no bad habits left?'

Gristhorpe laughed. 'I gave them all up years ago. Are you suggesting I should take some up again?'

'Wouldn't be a bad idea.'

'Where do you suggest I start?'

Banks rolled up the window before he said, 'Try sheep-shagging.' But judging by the raised eyebrows and the startled smile, Gristhorpe could obviously read lips. Grinning, Banks set off down the track, the still, deserted river meadows spread out below him, and headed for the Eastvale road.

TWO

Jenny was already five minutes late. Mara nursed her half of mild and rolled a cigarette. It was Wednesday lunch time, and the Black Sheep was almost empty. Apart from the landlord reading his *Sun*, and two old men playing dominoes, she was the only other customer in the cosy lounge.

Now that the time was close, she was beginning to feel nervous and foolish. After all, she didn't know Jenny *that* well, and her story did sound a bit thin. She couldn't put the real problem into words. How could she say that she suspected Paul had killed the policeman and that she was even beginning to be afraid living in the same house, but despite it all she wouldn't give him away and still wanted to keep him there? It sounded insane without the feelings that went with it. And to tell Jenny that she just wanted information for a story she was writing hardly ranked as the important reason for the meeting she had claimed on the telephone. Perhaps Jenny wasn't going to come. Maybe Mara hadn't responded to the answering machine properly and she hadn't even got the message.

All she could hear was the sound of asthmatic breathing from one of the old men, the occasional rustling of the newspaper, and the click of dominoes as they were laid on the hard surface. She swirled the beer in the bottom of her half-pint glass and peered at her watch again. Quarter past one.

'Another drink, love?' Larry Grafton called out.

Mara flashed a smile and shook her head. Why was it that she didn't mind being called love by the locals, but when Burgess had said it, her every nerve had bristled with resentment? It must be something in the tone, she decided. The old Yorkshiremen who used the word were probably as chauvinistic as the rest – in fact, sex roles in Dales family life were as traditional as anywhere in England – but when the men called women love it carried at least overtones of affection. With Burgess, though, the word was a weapon, a way of demeaning the woman, of dominating her.

Jenny arrived and interrupted her train of thought.

'Sorry I'm late,' she said breathlessly. 'Class went on longer than I expected.'

'It's all right,' Mara said. 'I haven't been here long. Drink?'

'Let me get them.'

Jenny went to the bar, and Mara watched her, a little intimidated, as usual, by her poise. Jenny always seemed to wear the right expensive-looking clothes. Today it was a waist-length fur jacket (fake, of course – Jenny wouldn't be caught dead wearing real animal fur), a green silk blouse, close-fitting rust cords and well polished knee-length boots. Not that Mara would want to dress like that – it wouldn't suit her personality – but she did feel shabby in her moth-eaten sweater and muddy wellingtons. Her jeans hadn't been artificially aged like the ones teenagers wore either; they had earned each stain and every faded patch.

'Quiet, isn't it?' Jenny said, setting the drinks down. 'You looked thoughtful when I came in. What was it?'

Mara told her her feelings about being called love.

'I know what you mean. I could have throttled Burgess when he did it to me.' She laughed. 'Dorothy Wycombe once chucked her drink at a stable lad for called her love.'

'Dorothy doesn't have much to do with us,' Mara said. 'I think we're too traditional for her tastes.'

Jenny laughed. 'You should count yourself lucky, then.' She took off her jacket and made herself comfortable. 'I heard she made mincemeat of Burgess. She gave Alan a hard time once, too. He gives her a wide berth now.'

'Alan? Is that the policeman you know? Chief Inspector Banks?'

Jenny nodded: 'He's all right. Why? Is that what you wanted to talk about?'

'What do you mean?'

'Don't be so cagey. I know you've come in for a lot of police attention since the demo. I just wondered if that was what was on your mind. Your message wasn't exactly specific, you know.'

Mara smiled. 'I'm not used to answering machines, that's all. Sorry.'

'No need. You just came across as frightfully worried and serious. Are you?'

A domino clicked loudly on the board, obviously a winning move. 'Not as much as I probably sounded, no,' Mara said. 'But it is about the demo. Partly, anyway.' She had decided that, as Jenny had mentioned Banks, she might as well begin by seeing if she could find anything out about the investigation, what the police were thinking.

'Go ahead, then.'

Mara took a deep breath and told Jenny about recent events at the farm, especially Burgess's visit.

'You ought to complain,' Jenny advised her.

Mara sniffed. 'Complain? Who to? He told us what

would happen if we did. Apparently his boss is a bigger bastard than he is.'

'Try complaining locally. Superintendent Gristhorpe isn't bad.'

Mara shook her head. 'You don't understand. The police would never listen to a complaint from people like us.'

'Don't be so sure about that, Mara. Alan wants to understand. It's only the truth he's after.'

'Yes, but . . . I can't really explain. What do they really think about us, Jenny? Do they believe that one of us killed that policeman?'

'I don't know. Really I don't. They're interested in you, yes. I'd be a liar if I denied that. But as far as actually suspecting anyone . . . I don't think so. Not yet.'

'Then why do they keep pestering us? When's it going to stop?'

'When they find out who the killer is. It's not just you, it's everyone involved. They've been at Dennis, too, and Dorothy Wycombe and the students. You'll just have to put up with it for the time being.'

'I suppose so.' The old men shuffled dominoes for another game, and a lump of coal shifted in the fire, sending out a shower of sparks and a puff of smoke. Flames rose up again, licking at the black chimney back. 'Look,' Mara went on, 'do you mind if I ask you a professional question, something about psychology? It's for a story I'm working on.'

'I didn't know you wrote.'

'Oh, it's just for my own pleasure really. I mean, I haven't tried to get anything published yet.' Even as she spoke, Mara knew that her excuse didn't ring true.

'OK,' Jenny said. 'Let me get another round in first.'

'Oh no, it's my turn.' Mara went to the bar and bought

another half for herself and a vodka and tonic for Jenny. If only she could get away with some of her fears about Paul allayed – without giving them away, of course – then she knew she would feel a lot better.

'What is it?' Jenny asked when they'd settled down with their drinks again.

'It's just something I'd like to know, a term I've heard that puzzles me. What's a sociopath?'

'A sociopath? Good Lord, this is like an exam question. Let me think for a bit. I'll have to give you a watered-down answer, I'm afraid. I don't have the textbook with me.'

'That's all right.'

'Well . . . I suppose basically it's someone who's constantly at war with society. A rebel without a cause, if you like.'

'Why, though? I mean, what makes people like that?'

'It's far from cut and dried,' Jenny said, 'but the thinking is that it has a lot to do with family background. Usually people we call sociopaths suffered abuse, cruelty and rejection from their parents, or at least from one parent, from an early age. They respond by rejecting society and becoming cruel themselves.'

'What are the signs?'

'Antisocial acts: stealing, doing reckless things, cruelty to animals. It's hard to say.'

'What kind of people are they?'

'They don't feel anything about what they do. They can always justify acts of cruelty – even murder – to themselves. They don't really see that they've done anything wrong.'

'Can anyone help them?'

'Sometimes. The trouble is, they're detached, cut off from the rest of us through what's happened to them.

147

They rarely have any friends and they don't feel any sense of loyalty.'

'Isn't it possible to help them, then?'

'They find it very hard to give love and to trust people, or to respond to such feelings in others. If you don't give your love, then you save yourself from feeling bad if it's rejected. That's the real problem: they need someone to trust them and have some feeling for them, but those are the things they find it hardest to accept.'

'So it's hopeless.'

'Often it's too late,' Jenny said. 'If they're treated early, they can be helped, but sometimes by the time they reach their teens the pattern is so deeply ingrained it's almost irreversible. But it's never hopeless.' She leaned forward and put her hand on Mara's. 'It's Paul you're asking about, isn't it?'

Mara withdrew sharply. 'What makes you say that?'

'Your expression, the tone of your voice. This isn't just for some story you're writing. It's for real, isn't it?'

'What if it is?'

'I can't tell you if Paul's a sociopath or not, Mara. I don't know enough about him. He seems to be responding to life at the farm.'

'Oh, he is,' Mara said. 'Responding, I mean. He's got a lot more outgoing and cheerful since he's been with us. Until these past few days.'

'Well, it's bound to get to him, all the police attention. But it doesn't mean anything. You don't think he might have killed the policeman, do you?'

'You mustn't tell anyone we've been talking like this,' Mara said quickly. 'Especially not Inspector Banks. All they need is an excuse to bring Paul in, then I'm sure that Burgess could force him to confess.'

'They won't do that,' Jenny said. 'You don't have any concrete reason for thinking Paul might be guilty, do you?'

'No.' Mara wasn't sure she sounded convincing. Things had gone too far for her, but it seemed impossible to steer back to neutral ground. 'I'm just worried about him, that's all,' she went on. 'He's had a hard life. His parents rejected him and his foster parents were cold towards him.'

'Well, that doesn't mean a lot,' Jenny said. 'If that's all you're worried about, I shouldn't bother yourself. Plenty of people come from broken homes and survive. It takes very special circumstances to create a sociopath. Not every ache and pain means you've got cancer, you know.'

Mara nodded. 'I'm sorry I tried to con you,' she said. 'It wasn't fair of me. But I feel better now. Let's just forget all about it, shall we?'

'OK, if you want. But be careful, Mara. I'm not saying Paul isn't dangerous, just that I don't know. If you do have any real suspicions . . .'

But Mara didn't hear any more. The door opened and a strange-looking man walked in. It wasn't his odd appearance that bothered her, though; it was the knife that he carried carefully in his hand. Pale and trembling, she got to her feet.

'I've got to go now,' she said. 'Something's come up . . . I'm sorry.' And she was off like a shot, leaving Jenny to sit and gape behind her.

THREE

'Bollocks!' said Burgess. 'They're shit-disturbers. You ought to know that by now. Why do you think they're interested in a nuclear-free Britain? Because they love peace? Dream on, Constable.'

'I don't know,' Richmond said, stroking his moustache. 'They're just students, they don't know—'

'Just students, my arse! Who is it tries to bring down governments in places like Korea and South Africa? Bloody students, that's who. Just students! Grow up. Look at the chaos students created in America over the Vietnam war – they almost won it for the commies single-handed.'

'What I was saying, sir,' Richmond went on, 'is that none of them are known to be militant. They just sit around and talk politics, that's all.'

'But Special Branch has a file on Tim Fenton.'

'I know, sir. But he's not actually *done* anything.'

'Not until now, perhaps.'

'But what could he gain from killing PC Gill, sir?'

'Anarchy, that's what.'

'With all due respect,' Banks cut in, 'that's hardly consistent. The students support disarmament, yes, but Marxists aren't anarchists. They believe in the class—'

'I know what bloody Marxists believe in,' Burgess said. 'They believe in anything if it furthers their cause.'

Banks gave up. 'Better have another try, Phil,' he said. 'See if you can tie any of them into more extreme groups, or to any previous acts of political violence. I doubt you'll come up with anything Special Branch doesn't know about already, but give it a try.'

'Yes, sir.'

'I need another drink,' Burgess said.

Sergeant Hatchley volunteered to go for a round. The Queen's Arms was busy. Wednesday was farmers' market day in Eastvale, and the whole town bustled with buyers and sellers. Glenys was too busy to exchange glances with Burgess even if she wanted to.

Burgess turned to Banks. 'And I'm still not happy about Osmond. He's on file, too, and I got the distinct impression he's been lying every time I've talked to him.'

Banks agreed.

'We'll have another go at him,' said Burgess. 'You can come with me again. Who knows, that bird of his might be there. If I put a bit of pressure on her, he might appeal to you for help and let something slip.'

Banks reached for a cigarette to mask his anger. The last thing he felt like was facing Osmond and Jenny together again. But in a way Burgess was right. They were looking for a killer, and they needed results. As each day went by, the media outcry became more strident.

When PC Craig came in and walked over to their table, he seemed unsure whom to address. After looking first to Banks and then to Burgess, like a spectator following the ball at Wimbledon, he settled on Banks.

'We've just had a call, sir, from Relton. There's a bloke in the pub there says he's found a knife. I just thought . . . you know . . . it might be the one we're looking for.'

'What are we waiting for?' Burgess jumped to his feet so quickly he knocked the table and spilt the rest of his beer. He pointed at Hatchley and Richmond. 'You two get back to the station and wait till you hear from us.'

They picked up Banks's white Cortina from behind the police station. Market Street and the square were so busy that Banks took the back streets to the main Swainsdale road.

Automatically, he reached forward and slipped a cassette into the player. 'Do you mind?' he asked Burgess, turning the volume down. 'Hello Central' came on.

'No. That's Lightning Hopkins, isn't it? I quite like blues myself. I enjoyed that Billie Holiday the other day, too.' He leaned back in the seat and lit a cigar from the dashboard lighter. 'My father bunked with a squadron of Yanks in the last war. Got quite interested in jazz and blues. Of course, you couldn't get much of the real stuff over here at that time, but after the war he kept in touch and the Yanks used to send him seventy-eights. I grew up on that kind of music and it just seemed to stick.'

Banks drove fast but kept an eye open for walkers on the verges. Even in March, the backpack brigade often took to the hills. As they approached Fortford, Burgess looked out at the river meadows. 'Very nice,' he said. 'Wouldn't be a bad place to retire to if it wasn't for the bloody weather.'

They turned sharp left in Fortford, followed the unfenced minor road up the daleside to Relton and parked outside the pub. Banks had been to the Black Sheep before; it was famous in the dale because the landlord brewed his own beer on the premises and you couldn't get it anywhere else. Black Sheep bitter had won prizes in national competitions.

If beer wasn't the first thing on Banks's mind when they entered, he certainly couldn't refuse the landlord's offer of a pint. Burgess declined the local brew and asked for a pint of Watney's.

Banks knew there were shepherds in the area, but they were an elusive breed and he'd never seen one before. Farmers who tended their own sheep were common enough, but on the south Swainsdale commons they banded together to hire three shepherds. Most of the sheep were heughed; they grew up on the farms and never strayed far. But not all of them; winter was a hard time, and many animals got buried under drifts. The shepherds know the moots, every gully and sinkhole, better than anyone else, and to them sheep are as different from one another as people.

Jack Crocker's face had as many lines as a tough teacher gives out in a week, and its texture looked as hard as tanned leather. He had a misshapen blob of a nose, and his eyes were so deeply hooded they looked as if they had been perpetually screwed up against the wind. His cloth cap and old flapping greatcoat set the final touches. His crook, a long hazel shaft with a metal hook, leaned against the wall.

'Christ,' Banks heard Burgess mutter behind him. 'A bloody shepherd!'

'I don't mind if I do,' Crocker said, accepting a drink. 'I were just fetching some ewes in for lambing, like, and I kicked that there knife.' He placed the knife on the table. It was a flick knife with a five-inch blade and a worn bone handle. 'I didn't touch it, tha knows,' he went on, putting a surprisingly smooth and slender forefinger to the side of his nose. 'I've seen telly.'

'How did you pick it up?' Burgess asked. Banks noticed that his tone was respectful, not hectoring as usual. Maybe he had a soft spot for shepherds.

'Like this.' Crocker held the ends of the handle between thumb and second finger. He really did have beautiful hands, Banks noticed, the kind you'd picture on a concert pianist.

Burgess nodded and took a sip of his Watney's. 'Good. You did the right thing, Mr Crocker.' Banks took an envelope from his pocket, dropped the knife in, and sealed it.

'Is it t' right one, then? T' one as killed that bobby?'

'We can't say yet,' Banks told him. 'We'll have to get some tests done. But if it is, you've done us a great service.'

'It weren't owt. It's not as if I were looking fer it.' Crocker looked away, embarrassed, and raised his pint to his lips. Banks offered him a cigarette.

'Nay, lad,' he said. 'In my job you need all t' breath you can muster.'

'Where did you find the knife?' Burgess asked.

'Up on t' moor, Eastvale way.'

'Can you show us?'

'Aye.' Crocker's face creased into a sly smile. 'It's a bit of a hike, though. And tha can't take thy car.'

Burgess looked at Banks. 'Well,' he said, 'it's your part of the country. You're the nature boy. Why don't you go up the moor with Mr Cocker here, and I'll phone the station to send a car for me?'

Yes, Banks thought, and you'll have another pint of Watney's while you're warming your hands in front of the fire.

Banks nodded. 'I'd get that knife straight to the lab if I were you,' he said. 'If you send it through normal channels they'll take days to get the tests done. Ask for Vic Manson. If he's got a spare moment he'll dust it for prints and persuade one of the lads to try for blood-typing. It's been exposed to the elements a bit, but we might still get something from it.'

'Sounds good,' Burgess said. 'Where is this lab?'

'Just outside Wetherby. You can ask the driver to take you straight there.'

Burgess went over to the phone while Banks and Crocker drank off their pints of Black Sheep bitter and set off.

They climbed a stile at the eastern end of Mortsett Lane and set off over open moorland. The tussocks of moor grass, interspersed with patches of heather and sphagnum, made walking difficult for Banks. Crocker, always ahead, seemed to float over the top of it like a hovercraft. The higher they climbed, the harsher and stronger the wind became.

Banks wasn't dressed for the moors either, and his shoes were soon mud-caked and worse. Though the slope wasn't steep, it was unrelenting, and he soon got out of breath. Despite the cold wind against his face, he was sweating.

At last the ground flattened out into high moorland. Crocker stopped and waited with a smile for Banks to catch up.

'By heck, lad, what'd tha do if tha 'ad to chase after a villain?'

'Luckily, it doesn't happen often,' Banks wheezed.

'Aye. Well, this is where I found it. Just down there in t' grass.' He pointed with his crook. Banks bent and poked around among the sods. There was nothing to indicate the knife had been there.

'It looks like someone just threw it there,' he said.

Crocker nodded. 'It would've been easy enough to hide,' he said. 'Plenty of rocks to stuff it under. He could've even buried it if he'd wanted.'

'But he didn't. So whoever it was must have panicked, perhaps, and just tossed it away.'

'Tha should know.'

Banks looked around. The spot was about two miles from Eastvale; the jagged castle battlements were just visible in the distance, down in the hollow where the town lay. In the opposite direction, also about two miles away, he could see the house and outbuildings of Maggie's Farm.

It looked like the knife had been thrown away on the wild moorland about halfway or more on a direct line between Eastvale and the farm. If someone from the farm had escaped arrest or injury at the demo, it would have been a natural direction in which to run home. That meant Paul or Zoe, as Rick and Seth had been arrested and searched. It could even have been the woman, Mara, who might have been lying about staying at home all evening.

On the other hand, anyone could have come up there in the past few days and thrown the knife away. That seemed much less likely though, as it was a poor method of disposal, more spontaneous than planned. Certainly it seemed to make mincemeat of one of Banks's theories – that a fellow policeman might have committed the murder. Again, the finger seemed to be pointing at Maggie's Farm.

Banks pulled the sheepskin collar tight around his neck and screwed up his eyes to keep the tears from forming. No wonder Crocker's eyes were hooded almost shut. There was nothing more to be done up here, he decided, but he would have to mark the spot in some way.

'Could you find this place again?' he asked.

'Course,' the shepherd answered.

Banks couldn't see how; there was nothing to distinguish it from any other spot of moorland. Still, it was Crocker's job to be familiar with every square inch of his territory.

He nodded. 'Right. We may have to get a few men up here to make a more thorough search. Where can I get in touch with you?'

'I live in Mortsett.' Crocker gave him the address.

'Are you coming back down?'

'Nay. More ewes to fetch in. It's lambing season, tha knows.'

'Yes, well, thanks again for your time.'

Crocker nodded curtly and set off further up the slope, walking just as quickly and effortlessly as if he were on the flat. At least, Banks thought, turning round, it would be easier going down. But before he had even completed the thought, he caught his foot in a patch of heather and fell face forward. He cursed, brushed himself off and carried on. Fortunately, Crocker had been going the other way and hadn't seen his little accident, otherwise it would have been the talk of the dale by evening.

He got back over the stile without further incident and nipped into the Black Sheep for another quick pint and a warm-up. There was nothing he could do now but wait for Burgess to finish at the lab. Even then, there might be no results. But a nice set of sweaty fingerprints on a smooth surface could survive the most terrible weather conditions, and Banks thought he had glimpsed flecks of dried blood in the joint between blade and handle.

8

ONE

A sudden heavy shower drove the shoppers from the market square. It was almost time to pack up and leave anyway; market days in winter and early spring were often cold and miserable affairs. But the rain stopped as quickly as it started, and in no time the sun was out again. Wet cobblestones reflected the muted bronze light, which slid into the small puddles and danced as the wind ruffled them.

The gold hands on the blue face of the church clock stood at four twenty. Burgess hadn't returned from the lab yet. Banks sat waiting by the window, the awkward venetian blind drawn up, and looked down on the scene as he smoked and drank black coffee. People crossed the square and splashed through the puddles that had gathered where cobbles had been worn or broken away. Everyone wore grey plastic macs or brightly coloured anoraks, as if they didn't trust the sun to stay out, and many carried umbrellas. It would soon be dark. Already the sun cast the long shadow of the Tudor-fronted police headquarters over the square.

At a quarter to five, Banks heard a flurry of activity outside his office, and Burgess bounded in carrying a buff folder.

'They came through,' he said. 'Took them long enough,

but they did it – a clear set of prints and a match with Gill's blood type. No doubt about it, that was the knife. I've already got DC Richmond running a check on the prints. If they're on record we're in business.'

He lit a Tom Thumb and smoked, tapping it frequently on the edge of the ashtray whether or not a column of ash had built up. Banks went back to the window. The shadow had lengthened; across the square, secretaries and clerks on their way home dropped in at Joplin's newsagent's for their evening papers, and young couples walked hand in hand into the El Toro coffee bar to tell one another about the ups and downs of their day at the office.

When Richmond knocked and entered, Burgess jumped to his feet. 'Well?'

Richmond stroked his moustache. He could barely keep the grin of triumph from his face. 'It's Boyd,' he said, holding out the charts. 'Paul Boyd. Eighteen points of comparison. Enough to stand up in court.'

Burgess clapped his hands. 'Right! Just as I thought. Let's go. You might as well come along, Constable. Where's Sergeant Hatchley?'

'I don't know, sir. I think he's still checking some of the witness reports.'

'Never mind. Three's enough. Let's bring Boyd in for a chat.'

They piled into Banks's Cortina and headed for Maggie's Farm. Banks played no music this time; the three of them sat in tense silence as the river meadows rolled by, eerie in the misty twilight. Gravel popped under the wheels as they approached the farm, and the front curtain twitched when they drew up outside the building.

Mara Delacey opened the door before Burgess had finished knocking. 'What do you want this time?' she asked angrily, but stood aside to let them in. They followed her through to the kitchen, where the others sat at the table eating dinner. Mara went back to her half-finished meal. Julian and Luna shifted closer to her.

'How convenient,' Burgess said, leaning against the humming refrigerator. 'You're all here together, except one. We're looking for Paul Boyd. Is he around?'

Seth shook his head. 'No. I've no idea where he is.'

'When did you last see him?'

'Last night, I suppose. I've been out most of the day. He wasn't here when I came back.'

Burgess looked at Mara. Nobody said anything, 'One of you must know where he is. What's it to be, now or down at the station?'

Still silence.

Burgess walked forward to pat Julian on the head, but the boy pulled a face and buried his head in Rick's side. 'It'd be a shame,' Burgess said, 'if things got so that you couldn't look after the kids here and they had to be taken away.'

'You'd never dare!' Mara said, her face flushed. 'Even you can't be as much of a bastard as that.'

Burgess raised his left eyebrow. 'Can't I, love? Are you sure you want to find out? Where's Boyd?'

Rick got to his feet. He was as tall as Burgess and a good thirty pounds heavier. 'Pick on someone your own size,' he said. 'If you start messing with my kid's life, you'll bloody well have me to answer to.'

Burgess sneered and turned away. 'I'm quaking in my boots. Where's Boyd?'

'We don't know,' Seth said quietly. 'He wasn't a prisoner here, you know. He pays his board, he's free to do what he wants and to come and go as he pleases.'

'Not any more he isn't,' Burgess said. 'Maybe you'd better get Gypsy Rose Lee here to ask the stars where he is, because if we don't find him it's soon going to be very hard on you lot.' He turned to Banks and Richmond. 'Let's have a look round. Where's his room?'

'First on the left at the top of the stairs,' Seth said. 'But you're wasting your time. He's not there.'

The three policemen climbed the narrow staircase. Richmond checked the other rooms while Banks and Burgess went into Paul's. There was only room for a single mattress on the floor and a small dresser at the far end, where a narrow window looked towards Eastvale. Sheets and blankets lay rumpled and creased on the unmade bed; dirty socks and underwear had been left in a pile on the floor. A stale smell of dead skin and unwashed clothes hung in the air. A couple of jackets, including a parka, hung in the tiny cupboard, and a pair of scuffed shoes lay on the floor. There was nothing much in the dresser drawers besides some clean underwear, T-shirts and a couple of moth-eaten pullovers. A grubby paperback copy of H.P. Lovecraft's *The Shadow over Innsmouth* lay open, face down on the pillow. On the cover was a picture of a semi-transparent frog-faced monster dressed in what looked like an evening suit. Out of habit, Banks picked the book up and flipped through the pages to see if Boyd had written anything interesting in the margins or on the blank pages at the back. He found nothing. Richmond came in and joined them.

'There's nothing here,' Burgess said. 'It doesn't look like he's scarpered though, unless he had a lot more clothes than this. I'd have taken a parka and a couple of sweaters if I'd been him. What was the weather like on the night Gill was stabbed?'

'Cool and wet,' Banks answered.

'Parka weather?'

'I'd say so, yes.'

Burgess took the coat from the cupboard and examined it. He pulled the inside of each pocket out in turn, and when he got to the right one, he pointed out a faint discoloured patch to Banks. 'Your men must have missed this the other day. Could be blood. He must have put the knife back in his pocket after he killed Gill. Hang on to this, Richmond. We'll get it to the lab. Why don't you two go and have a look in the outbuildings? You never know, he might be hiding in the wood pile. I'll poke around a bit more up here.'

Downstairs, Banks and Richmond went back into the kitchen and got Mara to accompany them with the keys. They left by the back door and found themselves in a large rectangular garden with a low fence. Most of the place was given over to rows of vegetables – dark empty furrows at that time of year – but there was also a small square sand-box, on which a plastic lorry with big red wheels and a yellow bucket and spade lay abandoned. At the far end of the garden stood a brick building with an asphalt roof, just a little larger than a garage, and to their left was a gate that led to the barn.

'We'll have a look over there first,' Banks said to Mara, who fiddled with the key ring as she followed them to the converted barn. It wasn't a big place, nowhere the size of many that had been converted into bunk barns for tourists, but it followed the traditional Dales design, on the outside at least, in that it was built of stone.

Mara opened the door to the downstairs unit first, Zoe's flat. Banks was surprised at the transformation from humble barn into comfortable living quarters; Seth had done a really good job. The woodwork was mostly unpainted, and if it looked a little makeshift, it was certainly sturdy and attractive in its simplicity. Not only, he gathered, did each unit have its own entrance, but there were cooking and bathing facilities too, as well as a large sparsely furnished living room, one master bedroom and a smaller one for Luna. But there was no sign of Paul Boyd.

The places were perfectly self-contained, Banks noticed, and if Rick and Zoe hadn't become friendly with Seth and Mara, they could easily have led quite separate lives there. Noting Mara's reaction to Burgess's threat and remembering what Jenny had said at dinner, Banks guessed that Mara's fondness for the children was one unifying factor – anyone would be glad of a built-in baby-sitter – and perhaps another was their shared politics.

Upstairs, the layout was different. Both bedrooms were quite small, and most of the space was taken up by Rick's studio, which was much less tidy than Zoe's large work table downstairs, with books and charts spread out on its surface. Seth had added three skylights along the length of the roof to provide plenty of light, and canvases, palettes and odd tubes of paint littered the place. From what Banks could see, Rick Trelawney's paintings were, as Tim Fenton had said, unmarketable, being mostly haphazard splashes of colour or collages of found objects. Sandra knew quite a bit about art, and Banks had learned from her that many paintings he wouldn't even store in the attic were regarded by experts as works of genius. But these were different, even he could tell; they made Jackson Pollock's angry explosions look as comprehensible as Constable's land-scapes.

As he poked around among the stuff though, Banks discovered a stack of small watercolour landscapes covered with an old sack. They resembled the one he'd noticed in the front room on his last visit, and he realized that they were, after all, Rick's work. So that was how he made his money! Selling pretty local scenes to tourists and little old ladies to support his revolutionary art.

Mara, who all the time had remained quiet, watching them with her arms folded, locked up as they left and led the way back to the house.

'You two go ahead,' Banks said when he had closed the gate behind them. 'I'm off to take a peek in the shed. It's not locked, is it?'

Mara shook her head and went back into the house with Richmond.

Banks opened the door. The shed was dark inside and smelled of wood shavings, sawdust, oiled metal, linseed oil and varnish. He tugged the chain dangling in front of him, and a naked bulb lit up, revealing Seth's workshop. Planks, boards and pieces of furniture at various stages of incompletion leaned against the walls. Spider webs hung in the dark corners. Seth had a lathe and a full set of well kept tools – planes, saws, hammers, bevels – and boxes of nails and screws rested on makeshift wooden shelves around the walls. There was no room for anyone to hide.

At the far end of the workshop, an old Remington office typewriter sat on a desk beside an open filing cabinet. Inside, Banks found only correspondence connected with Seth's carpentry business: estimates, invoices, receipts, orders. Close by was a small bookcase. Most of the books were about antique furniture and cabinet-making techniques, but there were a couple of old paperback novels and two books on the human brain, one of which was called *The Tip of the Iceberg*. Maybe, Banks thought, Seth harboured a secret ambition to become a brain surgeon.

Already a carpenter, he probably had a better start than most.

He walked back to the door and was about to turn off the light when he noticed a tattered notebook on a ledge by the door. It was full of measurements, addresses and phone numbers – obviously Seth's workbook. When he flipped through it, he noticed that one leaf had been torn out roughly. The following page still showed the faint impression of heavily scored numbers. Banks took a sheet from his own notebook, placed it on top and rubbed over it with a pencil. He could just make out the number in relief: 1139. It was hard to tell if it was in the same handwriting as the rest because the numbers were so much larger and more exaggerated.

Picking up the workbook, he turned to leave and almost bumped into Seth standing in the doorway.

'What are you doing?'

'This book,' Banks said. 'What do you use it for?'

'Work notes. When I need to order new materials, make measurements, note customers' addresses. That kind of thing.'

'There's a page missing.' Banks showed him. 'What does that mean – 1139?'

'Surely you can't expect me to remember that,' Seth said. 'It must have been a long time ago. It was probably some measurement or other.'

'Why did you tear it out?'

Seth looked at him, deep-set brown eyes wary and resentful. 'I don't know. Maybe it wasn't important. Maybe I'd written something on the back that I had to take with me somewhere. It's just an old notebook.'

'But there's only one page missing. Doesn't that strike you as odd?'

'I've already said it doesn't.'

'Did you tear out the page to give to Paul Boyd? Is it a number for him to call? Part of an address?'

'No. I've told you, I don't remember why I tore it out. It obviously wasn't very important.'

'I'll have to take this notebook away with me.'

'Why?'

'There are names and addresses in it. We'll have to check and see if Boyd's gone to any of them. As I understand it, he did spend quite a bit of time working with you in here.'

'But it's *my* notebook. Why would he be at any of those places? They're just people who live in the dale, people I've done work for. I don't want the police bothering them. It could lose me business.'

'We still have to check.'

Seth swore under his breath. 'Please yourself. You'd better give me a receipt, though.'

Banks wrote him one, then pulled the chain to turn off the light. They walked back to the house in silence.

Seth sat down again to finish his meal and Mara followed Banks towards the front of the room. They could hear Burgess and Richmond still poking about upstairs.

'Mr Banks?' Mara said quietly, standing close to him near the window.

Banks lit a cigarette. 'Yes?'

'What he said about the children . . . It's not true, is it? Surely he can't . . .?'

Banks sat in the rocking chair and Mara pulled up a small three-legged stool opposite him. One of Zoe's tarot decks, open at the Moon, lay on the table beside him. The moon seemed to be shedding drips of blood on to a path that led off into the distance between two towers. In the

166

foreground, a crab was crawling up onto land from a pool, and a dog and a wolf stood howling at the moon. It was a disturbing and hypnotic design. Banks shivered, as if someone had just walked over his grave, and turned his attention to Mara.

'They're not your children, are they?' he said.

'You know they're not. But I love them as if they were. Jenny Fuller told me she knows you. She said you're not as bad as the rest. Tell me they can't make us give the children up.'

Banks smiled to himself. Not as bad as the rest, eh? He'd have to remember to tease Jenny about that back-handed compliment.

He turned to face Mara. 'Superintendent Burgess will do whatever he has to to get to the bottom of things. I don't think it'll come to taking the children away, but bear in mind that he doesn't make idle threats. If you know anything, you should tell us.'

Mara sucked on her bottom lip. She looked close to tears. 'I don't know where Paul is,' she said finally. 'You can't really think he did it?'

'We've got some evidence that points that way. Have you ever seen him with a flick knife?'

'No.'

Banks thought she was lying, but he knew it was no good pushing her. She might offer him a titbit of information in the hope that it would ease the pressure, but she wasn't going to tell the full truth.

'He's gone,' she said finally. 'I know that. But I don't know where.'

'How do you know he's gone?'

Mara hesitated, and her voice sounded too casual to be telling the truth. It made her face look thinner and more haggard. 'He's been upset these past few days, especially after your Superintendent Burgess came and bullied him. He thought you'd end up framing him because he's been in jail and because he . . . he looks different. He didn't want to bring trouble down on the rest of us, so he left.'

Banks turned over the next tarot card: the Star. A beautiful naked woman was pouring water from two vases into a pool on the ground. Behind her, trees and shrubs were blossoming, and in the sky one large bright central star was surrounded by seven smaller ones. For some reason, the woman reminded him of Sandra, which was odd because there was no strong physical resemblance.

'How do you know why he went?' Banks asked. 'Did he leave a note?'

'No, he just told me. He said last night he was thinking of leaving. He didn't say when.'

'Or where?'

'No.'

'Did he say anything about PC Gill's murder?'

'No, nothing. He didn't say he was running away because he was guilty, if that's what you mean.'

'And you didn't think to let us know he was running off, even though there's a chance he might be a killer?'

'He's no killer.' Mara spoke too quickly. 'I'd no reason to think so, anyway. If he wanted to go he was quite free as far as we were concerned.'

'What did he take with him?'

'What do you mean?'

Banks glanced towards the window. 'It's brass monkey weather out there; rains a lot, too. What was he wearing? Was he carrying a suitcase or a rucksack?'

Mara shook her head. 'I don't know. I didn't see him go.'

'Did you see him this morning?'

'Yes.'

'What time?'

'About eleven or half past. He always sleeps late.'

'What time did he leave? Approximately.'

'I don't know. I was out at lunch time. I left at twenty to one and got back at about two. He'd gone by then.'

'Was anyone else in the house during that time?'

'No. Seth was out in the van. He took Zoe with him because she had to deliver some charts. And Rick took the children into Eastvale.'

'And you don't know what Boyd was wearing or what he took with him?'

'No. I told you, I didn't see him go.'

'Come upstairs.'

'What?'

Banks headed towards the staircase. 'Come upstairs with me. Now.'

Mara followed him up to Paul's room. Banks opened the cupboard and the dresser drawers. 'What's missing?'

Mara put her hand to her forehead. Burgess and Richmond looked in at the doorway and carried on downstairs.

'I . . . I don't know,' Mara said. 'I don't know what clothes he had.'

'Who does the washing round here?'

'Well, I do. Mostly. Zoe does some, too.'

'So you must know what clothes Boyd had. What's missing?'

'He didn't have much.'

'He must have had another overcoat. He's left his parka.'

'No, he didn't. He had an anorak, though. A blue anorak.'

Banks wrote it down. 'What else?'

'Jeans, I suppose. He never wore much else.'

'Footwear.'

Mara looked in the cupboard and saw the scuffed shoes. 'Just a pair of old slip-ons. Hush Puppies, I think.'

'Colour?'

'Black.'

'And that's it?'

'As far as I know.'

Banks closed his notebook and smiled at Mara. 'Look, try not to worry about the children too much. As soon as Superintendent Burgess catches Paul Boyd, he'll forget all about the threats he made. If we catch him soon, that is.'

'I really *don't* know where he's gone.'

'OK. But if you come up with any ideas . . . Think about it.'

'People like Burgess shouldn't be allowed to run free,' Mara said. She folded her arms tightly and stared at the floor.

'Oh? What do you suggest we should do with him? Lock him up?'

She looked at Banks. Her jaw was clenched tight and her eyes burned with tears.

'Or should we have him put down?'

Mara brushed past him and hurried down the stairs. Banks followed slowly. Burgess and Richmond stood in the front room ready to leave.

'Come on, let's go,' Burgess said. 'There's nothing more here.' Then he turned to Seth, who stood in the kitchen doorway. 'If I find out you've been helping Boyd in any way, believe me, I'll be back. And you lot'll be in more trouble than you ever dared imagine. Give my love to the kids.'

TWO

Mara watched the car disappear down the track. She felt reassured by Banks, but wondered just how much he could do if Burgess had made his mind up about something. If the children were taken away, she thought, she could well be driven to murder the superintendent with her bare hands.

She became aware of the others behind her in the room. She hadn't told them anything about what had happened with Paul, and none of them knew yet that he had run off for good. For one thing, she'd hardly had time to say anything. They had all drifted back close to meal time anyway, when she was busy in the kitchen; then the police had arrived.

'What's going on, Mara?' Seth asked, coming up to her and resting his hand on her shoulder. 'Do you know?'

Mara nodded. She was trying to keep the tears from her eyes.

'Come on.' Seth took her hand and led her to a chair. 'Tell us.'

Seeing them all watching her, expectant, Mara regained her control. She reached for her tin of Old Holborn and rolled a cigarette.

'He's gone, that's all there is to it,' she said, and told them about seeing old Crocker carrying the knife into the Black Sheep. 'I ran back here to warn him. I didn't want the police to get him, and I thought if they'd got the knife they might find his fingerprints or something. He's been in jail, so they must be on record.'

'But what made you think of Paul?' Zoe asked. 'That knife was just lying around on the mantelpiece as usual, I

171

suppose. Nobody ever paid it any mind. Any of the people here on Friday afternoon could have taken it.'

Mara drew on her cigarette and finally told them about the blood she'd seen on Paul's hand when he got back from the demo. The hand that turned out to be unmarked the following morning.

'Why didn't you tell us?' Seth asked. 'I don't suppose you approached Paul about it, either. There might have been a simple explanation.'

'I know that,' Mara said. 'Don't you think I've been over it time and again in my mind? I was frightened of him. I mean, if he had done it . . . But I wanted to stand by him. If I'd told you all, you might have asked him to leave or something.'

'How did he react when you came and told him the knife had been found?' Rick asked.

'He went pale. He couldn't look me in the eye. He looked like a frightened animal.'

'So you gave him money and clothes?'

'Yes. I gave him your red anorak, Zoe. I'm sorry.'

'It's all right,' Zoe said. 'I'd have done the same.'

'And I told the police he was probably wearing a blue one. He took his blue one with him, but he wasn't wearing it.'

'Where's he heading?' asked Rick.

'I don't know. I didn't want him to tell me. He's a survivor; he can live out on the streets. I gave him some money, some I'd saved from working at the shop and selling my pottery. He'll have enough to get wherever he wants.'

Later that evening, when the others had drifted off back to the barn and Seth had settled down with a book, Mara began to think about the few months that Paul had been around, and how alive he had made her feel. At first, he had been sullen and unresponsive, and there had come a point when Seth had considered asking him to leave. But Paul hadn't been long out of jail then; he wasn't used to dealing with people. Time and care had worked wonders. Soon he was taking long walks alone on the moors, and the claustrophobia that had so often made his nights unbearable in jail became easier to control. Nobody forced him to, but he really took to working with Seth.

When she thought about his progress and what it had all come to, Mara couldn't help but feel sad. It would all be for nothing if he got caught and sent to prison again. When she pictured him cold and alone in the strange and frightening world beyond Swainsdale, it made her want to cry. But she told herself again that he was strong, resourceful, a survivor. It wouldn't feel the same to him as it would to her. Besides, imagined horrors were always far worse than the reality.

'I hope Paul makes it far away,' Seth said in the silence that followed their lovemaking that night. 'I hope they never catch him.'

'How will we know where he is, what's happening to him?' Mara asked.

'He'll let us know one way or another. Don't you worry about it.' He put his arm around her and she rested her head against his chest. 'You did the right thing.'

But she couldn't help but worry. She didn't think they'd hear from Paul again, not after all that had happened. She didn't know what else she could have done, but she wasn't sure she had done the right thing. As she tried to sleep, she remembered the expression on his face just before he left. There had been gratitude, yes, for the warning, the money and the clothes, but there had also been resentment and disappointment. He'd looked as if he was being sent into exile. She didn't know if he'd expected her to ask him to stay no matter what – she certainly hadn't told him he *had* to go away – but there had been a hint of accusation in his actions, as if to say, 'You think I did it, don't you? You don't want me here causing trouble. You didn't trust me in the first place. I'm an outcast, and I always will be.' She hadn't told Seth and the others about that.

THREE

Banks waited his turn at the busy bar of the Queen's Arms while Burgess sat at a round table by the Market Street entrance. It was eight thirty. Hatchley had just left to keep a date with Carol Ellis, and Richmond had gone to a do at the rugby club.

Dirty Dick was clearly pleased with himself. He leaned back in his chair and positively beamed goodwill at everyone who looked his way. Nobody gave him much more than a scowl in return, though.

'Ey, Mr Banks,' said Cyril. 'A minute, if you've got one.'

'Course. For you, Cyril, anything. And you might as well pull me a pint of bitter and a pint of Double Diamond while you're talking.'

'It's about that there mate of yours.' Cyril nodded his head aggressively in the direction of Burgess.

'He's not really a mate,' Banks said. 'More like a boss.'

'Aye. Well, anyways, tell him to stop pestering my Glenys. She's got too much work to do without passing the time of day with the likes of him.' Cyril leaned forward and lowered his voice. The muscles bulged above his rolled-up shirt sleeves. 'And you can tell him I don't care if he is a copper – no disrespect, Mr Banks – if he doesn't keep out of my way I'll give him a bloody knuckle sandwich, so help me I will.'

Glenys, who seemed to have grasped the tenor of the conversation, blushed and busied herself pulling a pint at the other end of the bar.

'I'd be delighted to pass on your message,' Banks said, paying for the drinks.

'Don't forget his lordship's Double Diamond,' Cyril said, his voice edged with contempt.

'You can wipe that bloody grin off your face,' Burgess said after Banks had passed on Cyril's warning. 'You're a long way from collecting that fiver yet. She fancies me, does young Glenys, there's no doubt about it. And there's nothing like a bit of danger, a touch of risk, to get the old hormones flowing. Look at her.' True enough, Glenys was flashing Burgess a flush-cheeked smile while Cyril was looking the other way. 'If we could only get that oaf out of the way . . . Anyway, it's her night off next Monday. She usually goes to the pictures with her mates.'

'I'd be careful if I were you,' Banks said.

'Yes, but you're not me, are you?' He gulped down about half of his pint. 'Ah, that's good. So, we've got the bastard. Or will have soon.'

Banks nodded. That, he assumed, was why they were celebrating. Burgess was on his fourth pint already and Banks on his third.

They had done everything they could. Boyd had certainly done a bunk, though Banks had no idea how he knew about the discovery of the knife. It was likely he had headed for Eastvale and taken a bus. The number 43 ran along Cardigan Drive, on the town's western edge. He would simply have had to walk across the moors and up Gallows View to get there. Also, buses to York and Ripon passed along the same road. Somebody must have seen him. Banks had circulated his description to the bus companies and sent out his mugshot to police around the country, paying particular attention to Leeds, Liverpool and London. As Burgess said, it was simply a matter of time before he was caught.

'Where did you get that bloody scar?' Burgess asked.

'This?' Banks fingered the white crescent by his right eye. 'Got it in Heidelberg. It's a duelling scar.'

'Ha bloody ha! You're a funny man, aren't you? Have you heard the one about the—' Burgess stopped and looked up at the person standing over them. 'Well, well,' he said, scraping his chair aside to make room. 'If it isn't—'

'Dr Fuller,' Jenny said. She glanced at Banks and pulled up a chair next to his.

'Of course. How could I forget? Drink, love?'

Jenny smiled sweetly. 'Yes, please. I'll have a half of lager.'

'Oh come on, have a pint,' Burgess insisted.

'All right. A pint.'

'Good.' Burgess rubbed his hands together and set off for the bar. His thigh caught the edge of the table as he stood up. Beer rippled in the glasses but didn't spill.

Jenny pulled a face at Banks. 'What's with him?'

Banks grinned. 'Celebrating.'

'So I see.' She leaned closer. 'Look, I've got something to ask you—'

Banks put a finger to his lips. 'Not now,' he said. 'He's getting served. He'll be back soon.' True enough, in no time Burgess was on his way back, trying to carry three pints in his hands and slopping beer over the rims on to his shoes.

'What are you celebrating, anyway?' Jenny asked after Burgess had managed to set the drinks on the table without spilling much.

Banks told her about Paul Boyd.

'That's a shame.'

'A shame! You said he gave you the creeps.'

'He does. I'm just thinking of the others, that's all. It'll be a hell of a blow for Seth and Mara. They've done so much for him. Especially Mara.' Jenny seemed unusually distracted at the thought of Mara Delacey, and Banks wondered why.

'You know,' Burgess said, 'I'm a bit sorry it turned out to be Boyd, myself.'

Jenny looked surprised: 'You are? Why?'

'Well. . .' He moved closer. 'I was hoping it might be that boyfriend of yours. Then we could get him locked up for a good long while, and you and me could . . . you know.'

To Banks's surprise, Jenny laughed. 'You've got some imagination, I'll say that for you, Superintendent Burgess.'

'Call me Dick. Most of my friends do.'

Jenny stifled a laugh. 'I really don't think I could do that. Honest.'

'Aren't you relieved it's all over?' Banks asked her. 'I'll bet Osmond is.'

'Of course. Especially if it means we won't have to put up with any more visits from him.' She nodded at Burgess.

'I could still visit,' Dirty Dick said, and winked.

'Oh, put another record on. So where do you think Paul is?' she asked Banks.

'We've no idea. He took off early this afternoon, before we got a positive identification. Could be anywhere.'

'But you're confident you'll get him?'

'I think so.'

Jenny turned to Burgess. 'So your job's over, then? I don't suppose you'll want to stick around this godforsaken place much longer, will you?'

'Oh, I don't know.' Burgess lit a cigar and leered at her. 'It has its compensations.'

Jenny coughed and waved the smoke away.

'Seriously,' he went on, 'I'll stay around till he's brought in. There's a lot I want to ask him.'

'But that could take days, weeks.'

Burgess shrugged. 'It's the taxpayers' money, love. Your round again, Banks.'

'Nothing for me this time,' Jenny said. 'I'll have to be off soon.' She still had over half her drink left.

Feeling a little light-headed, Banks went to the bar.

''Ave you told him?' Cyril asked.

'Yes.'

'Good. I just hope he knows what's best for him. Look at the bugger, he can't keep his hands off them.'

Banks looked round. Dirty Dick seemed to have edged closer to Jenny, and his elbow rested on the back of her chair. She was behaving very calmly, Banks thought. It wasn't like her to take such sexist patronizing so well. Maybe she fancies him, he thought suddenly. If Glenys does, then maybe Jenny does, too. Perhaps he really does have the magic touch with women. At least he's available. And he's handsome enough, too. That casual look – the worn leather jacket, open-neck shirt – it suits him, as do the touches of grey hair at his temples.

Banks brushed the idea aside. It was ridiculous. Jenny was an intelligent tasteful woman. A woman like her could never fall for Dirty Dick's brazen charm. But women were a mysterious lot, Banks thought glumly, carrying the drinks back. They were always falling for worthless men. He clearly recalled the beautiful Anita Howarth, object of his adolescent lust back in the third form. She had been quite oblivious to Banks's lean good looks and taken up with that spotty good-for-nothing Steve Naylor. And Naylor hadn't seemed to give a damn about her. He gave the impression he would rather be playing cricket or rugby than go anywhere with Anita. But that just made her more crazy about him. And Banks had had to spend all his time fending off unwelcome advances from Cheryl Wagstaff, the one with the yellow buck teeth.

'I was just offering to show this lovely young lady the sights of London,' Burgess said.

'I'm sure she's seen them before,' Banks replied stiffly.

'Not the way I'd show her.' Burgess moved his arm so that his hand rested on Jenny's shoulder.

Banks was wondering if he should act gallantly this time and defend Jenny's honour. After all, they were sort of off duty. But he remembered she was quite good at taking care of herself. Her face took on an ominously sweet expression.

'Please take your hand off my shoulder, Superintendent,' she said.

'Oh, come on, love,' Burgess said. 'Don't be so shy. And call me Dick.'

'Please?'

'Give me a chance. We've hardly even got—'

Burgess stopped abruptly when Jenny calmly and slowly picked up her glass and poured the rest of her chilled lager on his lap.

'I told you I only wanted a half,' she said, then picked up her coat and left.

Burgess rushed for the gents. Luckily, Jenny had acted so naturally and everyone around them had been so engrossed in conversation, that the event had gone largely unnoticed. Cyril had seen it though, and his face was red with laughter.

Banks caught up with Jenny outside. She was leaning against the ancient pitted market cross in the centre of the square with her hand over her mouth. 'My God,' she said, letting the laughter out and patting her chest, 'I haven't had as much fun in years. That man's a positive throwback. I'm surprised you seem to be enjoying his company so much.'

'He's not so bad,' Banks said. 'Especially after a few jars.'

'Yes, you'd need to be at least half pissed. And you'd need to be a man, too. You're all adolescents when it comes down to it.'

'He's got quite a reputation as a womanizer.'

'They must be desperate down south, then.'

Banks's faith in women was partially restored.

It was cold outside in the deserted square. The cobbles, still wet with rain, glistened in the dim gaslight. The church bells rang half past nine. Banks turned up his jacket collar and held the lapels close together. 'What was it you wanted to ask me?'

'It's nothing. It doesn't matter now.'

'Come on, Jenny, you're hiding something. You're not good at it. Is it to do with Paul Boyd?'

'Indirectly. But I told you, it doesn't matter.'

'Do you know why he ran away?'

'Of course not.'

'Look, I know you're a friend of Mara's. Is this to do with her? It could be important.'

'All right,' Jenny said, holding up her hand. 'Give it a rest. I'll tell you everything you want to know. You're getting almost as bad as your mate in there. Mara just wondered how the investigation was going, that's all. They're all a bit tense up at the farm, and they wanted to know if they could expect any more visits from God's gift to women. Will you believe me now that it doesn't matter?'

'When did you talk to her?'

'This lunch time in the Black Sheep.'

'She must have seen the knife,' Banks said, almost to himself.

'What?'

'The shepherd, Jack Crocker. He found the knife. She must have seen it, recognized it as Boyd's and dashed off to warn him. That's why he left just in time.'

'Oh, Alan, surely not?'

'I thought she was lying when I talked to her earlier. Didn't you notice any of this?'

'She did leave in rather a hurry, but I'd no idea why. I went just after. You're not going to arrest her, are you?'

Banks shook his head. 'It makes her an accessory,' he said, 'but I doubt we'd be able to prove it. And when Burgess gets Boyd, I don't think he'll spare another thought for Mara and the rest. It was just a bloody stupid thing to do.'

'Was it? Would you split on a friend, just like that? What would you do if someone accused Richmond of murder, or me?'

'That's not the point. Of course I'd do what I could to clear you. But she should have let us know. Boyd could be dangerous.'

'She cares about Paul. She's hardly likely to hand him over to you just like that.'

'I wonder if she's told him where to run and hide as well.'

Jenny shivered. 'It's cold standing about here,' she said. 'I should go before Dirty Dick comes out and beats me up. That's just about his level. And you'd better get back or he'll think you've deserted him. Give him my love.' She kissed Banks quickly on the cheek and hurried to her car. He stood in the cold for a moment thinking about Mara and what Jenny had said, then rushed back into the Queen's Arms to see what had become of the soused superintendent.

'She's certainly got spirit, I'll say that,' Burgess said, not at all upset by the incident. 'Another pint?'

'I shouldn't really.'

'Oh, come on, Banks. Don't be a party pooper.' Without waiting for a reply, Burgess went to the bar.

Banks felt that he'd had enough already, and soon he would be past the point of no return. Still, he thought, after a couple more pints he wouldn't give a damn anyway. He sensed that Burgess was lonely and in need of company in his moment of triumph, and he didn't feel he could simply desert the bastard. Besides, he had only an empty house to go home to. He could leave the Cortina in the police car park and walk home later, no matter how much he'd drunk. It was only a mile and a bit.

And so they drank on, and on. Burgess was easy enough to talk to, Banks found, once you got used to his cocky manner and stayed off politics and police work. He had a broad repertoire of jokes, an extensive knowledge of jazz and a store of tales about cock-ups on the job. On the Met, as Banks remembered, there were so many different departments and squads running their own operations that it wasn't unusual for the Sweeney to charge in and spoil a fraud squad stake-out.

An hour and two pints later, as Burgess reached the end of a tale about a hapless drug squad DC shooting himself in the foot, Banks suggested it was time to go.

'I suppose so,' Burgess said regretfully, finishing his drink and getting to his feet.

He certainly didn't seem drunk. His speech was normal and his eyes looked clear. But when they got outside, he had difficulty walking on the pavement. To keep himself steady, he put his arm around Banks's shoulder and the two of them weaved across the market square. Thank God the hotel's just around the corner, Banks thought.

'That's my only trouble, you know,' Burgess said. 'Mind clear as a bell, memory intact, but every time I go over the limit my motor control goes haywire. Know what my mates call me down at the Yard?'

'No.'

'Bambi.' He laughed. 'Bloody Bambi. You know, that little whatsit in the cartoon – the way the damn thing walks. It's not my sweet and gentle nature they're referring to.' He put his hand to his groin. 'Bloody hell, I still feel like I've pissed myself. That damn woman!' And he laughed.

Banks declined an invitation to go up to Burgess's room and split a bottle of Scotch. No matter how sorry he felt for the lonely bugger, he wasn't that much of a masochist. Grudgingly, Burgess let him go. 'I'll drink it myself, then,' were his final words, delivered at full volume in front of an embarrassed desk clerk in the hotel lobby.

As he set off home, Banks wished he'd brought his Walkman. He could be listening to Blind Willie McTell or

Bukka White as he walked. He was steady on his feet though, and arrived at the front door of the empty house in about twenty minutes. He was tired and he certainly didn't want another drink, so he decided to go straight to bed. As usual though, when things were bothering him he couldn't get to sleep immediately. And there were plenty of things about the Gill case that still puzzled him.

Motive was a problem, unless Burgess was right and Boyd had simply lashed out indiscriminately. In this case, it seemed that knowing *who* didn't explain *why*. Boyd wasn't political as far as anyone knew, and even street punks like him weren't in the habit of stabbing policemen at anti-nuclear demos. If someone had a private reason for wanting to do away with Gill, then there was plenty to consider in the personal lives of the other suspects: Osmond's assault charges, Trelawney's custody battle, Seth's wife's accident, Mara's religious organization, and even Zoe's seaside fortune-telling. It was hard to imagine a connection at this point, but stranger things had happened. Tony Grant's report might prove useful, if it ever arrived.

Banks was also curious about the prints on the knife. Usually when a knife is thrust into a body, the fingers holding the handle slip and any impression is blurred. Boyd's prints had been perfectly clear, just as if he had carefully applied each one. It could have happened if he'd folded up the knife and carried it in his hand before throwing it away, or if he'd picked it up after someone else had used it. There were other prints under his, but they were too blurred to read. They could be his too, of course, but there was no way of knowing.

Boyd had certainly carried the knife in his pocket. The stains inside the parka matched PC Gill's blood type. But if he had used it, why had he been foolish enough to pick it up after dropping it? He must have let it fall at some point, because several people had seen it being kicked around by the crowd. And if he had just left it there, it was very unlikely that it could have been traced to the farm.

But if Boyd hadn't done it, why had he picked up a knife that wasn't his? To protect someone? And who would he be more likely to protect than the people at Maggie's Farm? Or had there been someone else he knew and cared about who had access to the knife? There were a lot more questions to be asked yet, Banks thought, and Burgess was being very premature in celebrating his victory tonight.

Then there was the matter of the number torn out of Seth Cotton's notebook. Banks didn't know what it meant, but there was something familiar about it, something damn familiar. Boyd was close to Seth and spent plenty of time helping him in the workshop. Could the number be something to do with him? Could it help tell them where he'd gone?

It could be a phone number, of course. There were still plenty of four-digit numbers in the Swainsdale area. On impulse, Banks got out of bed and went downstairs. It was after eleven, but he decided to try anyway. He dialled 1139 and heard a phone ring at the other end. It went on for a long time. He was just about to give up when a woman answered, 'Hello. Rossghyll Guest House, bed and breakfast.' The voice was polite but strained.

Banks introduced himself and some of the woman's politeness faded when it became clear that he wasn't a potential customer. 'Do you know what time it is?' she said. 'Couldn't this have waited till morning? Do you know what time I have to get up?'

'It's important.' Banks gave a description of Paul Boyd and asked if she'd seen him.

'I wouldn't have that kind of person staying here,' the woman answered angrily. 'What kind of place do you think this is? This is a decent house.' And with that she hung up on him.

Banks trudged back up to bed. He'd have to send a man over, of course, just to be sure, but it didn't seem a likely bet. And if it was a phone number outside the local area, it could be almost anywhere. With the dialling code missing, there was no way of telling.

Banks lay awake a while longer, then he finally drifted off to sleep and dreamed of Burgess humble in defeat.

9

ONE

The overcast sky seemed to press on Banks's nagging headache when he set off for Maggie's Farm at eleven thirty the next morning. Burgess had called in earlier to say he was going over some paperwork in his hotel room and didn't want to be disturbed unless Paul Boyd turned up. That suited Banks fine; he wanted a word with Mara Delacey, and the less Dirty Dick knew about it the better.

He pulled up outside the farmhouse and knocked. He wasn't surprised when Mara opened the door and moaned, 'Not again!'

Reluctantly she let him in. There was no one else in the place. The others were probably working.

Banks wanted to get Mara away from the house, on neutral ground. Perhaps then, he thought, he could get her to open up a bit more.

'I'd just like to talk to you, that's all,' he said. 'It's not an interrogation, nothing official.'

She looked puzzled. 'Go on.'

Banks tapped his watch. 'It's nearly lunch time and I haven't eaten yet,' he said casually. 'Do you fancy a trip down to the Black Sheep?'

'What for? Is this some subtle way of getting me to accompany you to the station?'

'No tricks. Honest. What I've got to say might even be of advantage to you.'

She still regarded him suspiciously, but the bait was too good to refuse. 'All right.' She reached for an anorak to put over her sweater and jeans. 'I'm going into the shop this afternoon anyway.' She pulled back her thick chestnut hair and tied it in a ponytail.

In the car, Mara leaned forward to examine the tapes Banks kept in the storage rack Brian had bought him for his birthday the previous May – his thirty-eighth. There, mixed in with Zemlinsky's *Birthday of the Infanta*, Mozart's *Magic Flute*, Dowland's *Lachrymae* and Purcell's airs, were Lightning Hopkins, Billie Holiday, Muddy Waters, Robert Wilkins and a number of blues anthology tapes.

Picking up the Billie Holiday, Mara managed a thin smile. 'A policeman who likes blues can't be all bad,' she said.

Banks laughed. 'I like most music,' he said, 'except for country and western and middle-of-the-road crooning – you know, Frank Sinatra, Engelbert Humperdinck and that lot.'

'Even rock?'

'Even rock. Some, anyway. I must admit I'm still stuck in the sixties as far as that's concerned. I lost interest after the Beatles split up. I even know where the name of your house comes from.'

Banks was pleased to be chatting so easily with Mara. It was the first time his interest in music had helped create the kind of rapport he wanted with a witness. So often people regarded it as an eccentricity, but now it was actually helping with an important investigation. A common interest in jazz and blues had also helped him to relax with Burgess a little. Still, he thought, Mara probably wouldn't stay so convivial when she followed the drift of the questions he had to ask her.

They found a quiet corner in the pub by the tiled fireplace. In a glass case on the wall beside them was a collection of butterflies pinned to a board. Banks bought Mara a half of mild and got a pint of Black Sheep bitter for himself. Maybe the hair of the dog would do the trick and get rid of his headache. He ordered a ploughman's lunch; Mara asked for lasagne.

'Ploughman's lunches were invented for tourists in the seventies,' Mara said.

'Not authentic?'

'Not a bit.'

'Oh well, I can think of worse inventions.'

'I suppose you want to get down to business, don't you?' Mara said. 'Did Jenny Fuller tell you about our meeting?'

'No, but I figured it out. I think she's worried about you.'

'She needn't be. I'm all right.'

'Are you? I thought you'd be worried sick about Paul Boyd.'

'What if I am?'

'Do you think he's guilty?'

Mara paused and sipped some beer. She swept a stray wisp of hair from her cheek before answering. 'Maybe I did at first,' she said. 'At least, I was worried. I mean, we don't know a lot about him. I suppose I looked at him differently. But not now, no. And I don't care what evidence you've got against him.'

'What made you change your mind?'

'A feeling, that's all. Nothing concrete, nothing you'd understand.'

Banks leaned forward. 'Believe it or not, Mara, police-men have feelings like that, too. We call them hunches, or we put them down to our nose, our instinct for truth. You may be right about Boyd. I'm not saying you are, but there's a chance. Things aren't quite as cut and dried as they appear. In some ways Paul is too obvious.'

'Isn't that what appeals to you? How easy it is to blame him?'

'Not to me, no.'

'But . . . I mean . . . I thought you were sure, that you had evidence?'

'The knife?'

'Yes.'

'You recognized it, didn't you, when Jack Crocker brought it in here yesterday lunch time?'

Mara said nothing. Before Banks could speak again, the food arrived and they both tucked in.

'Look,' said Banks, after polishing off the best part of a chunk of Wensleydale and a pickled onion, 'let's assume that Boyd's innocent, just for the sake of argument.' Mara looked at him, but her expression was hard to fathom. Suspicion? Hope? Either reaction would be perfectly natural. 'If he is,' Banks went on, 'then it raises more questions than it answers. It's easier for everyone if Boyd turns out to be guilty – everyone but him, that is – but the easiest way isn't necessarily the true one. Do you know what I mean?'

Mara nodded and her lips curved just a little at the edges. 'Sounds like the Eightfold Path,' she said.

'The what?'

'The Eightfold Path. It's the Buddhist way to enlighten-ment.'

Banks speared another pickled onion. 'Well, I don't

know much about enlightenment,' he said, 'but we could do with a bit more light on the case.' He went on to tell her about the blood and prints on the knife. 'That much we know,' he said. 'That's the evidence, the facts, if you like. Boyd was there, and we can prove that he handled the murder weapon. Superintendent Burgess thinks it's enough to convict him, but I'm not sure myself. Given the political aspect though, he might just be right. Finding Boyd guilty will make us look good and it'll discredit everyone who seems a bit different.'

'Isn't that what you want?'

'I wish you'd stop making assumptions like that. You sound like a stoned hippie at a rock festival. Maybe you'd like to call me a pig too, and get it over with? Either that or grow up.'

Mara said nothing, but Banks saw the faint flush suffuse her face.

'I want the truth,' Banks went on. 'I'm not out to get any group or person, just a killer. If we assume that Boyd didn't do it, then why are his prints on the knife, and why was it found on the moors about halfway between Eastvale and Maggie's Farm?'

Mara pushed her half-eaten lasagne aside and rolled a cigarette. 'I'm no detective,' she said, 'but maybe he picked it up and threw it away on his way home, when he realized what it was.'

'But why? Would you have done something as stupid as that? Bent down at a demonstration to pick up a blood-stained knife? Think about it. Boyd had no guarantee of getting away. What if he'd been caught on the spot with the knife on him?'

'He'd probably have had time to drop it if he saw the cops closing in on him.'

'Yes, but it would still have his prints on it. I doubt if he'd have been calm enough to wipe it before they grabbed him. Even if he had, there would probably have been some of Gill's blood on him.'

'This is all very well,' Mara said, 'but I don't know what you're getting at.'

'I'll tell you in a moment.' Banks went to the bar and bought two more drinks. The place had filled up a bit since they'd come in, and there were even two well-wrapped hikers resting their feet by the fire.

Banks sat down and drank some beer. The hair of the dog was working nicely. 'It all comes back to the knife,' he said. 'You recognized it; Paul Boyd must have done, too. It comes from the farm, doesn't it?'

Mara turned aside and studied the butterflies.

'You're not helping anyone by holding back, you know. I only want you to confirm what we already know.'

Mara stubbed out her cigarette. 'All right, so it comes from the house. What of it? If you know already, why bother to ask?'

'Because Paul might have been protecting someone, mightn't he? If he found the knife and took it away, he must have thought it was evidence pointing to someone he knew, someone at the farm. Unless you think he's just plain stupid.'

'You mean one of us?'

'Yes. Who would he be most likely to protect?'

'I don't know. There were a few people up at the farm that afternoon.'

'Yes, I know who was there. Could anyone have taken the knife?'

Mara shrugged. 'It was on the mantelpiece, in plain view of everyone.'

'Whose knife is it?'

'I don't know. It's always been there.'

'Never mind, then. Let's just call it a communal flick knife. Do you think Paul would have picked it up to protect Dennis Osmond? Or Tim and Abha?'

Mara twirled a loose strand of hair. 'I don't know,' she said. 'He didn't know them very well.'

'What part did he play that afternoon? Was he around?'

'Most of the time, yes, but he didn't say much. Paul has an inferiority complex when it comes to students and political talk. He doesn't know about Karl Marx and the rest, and he doesn't have enough confidence in his own ideas to feel he can contribute.'

'So he was there but he wasn't very involved?'

'That's right. He agreed with everything in principle. I mean, he wasn't at the demo just to . . . just to . . .'

'Cause trouble?'

'No. He was there to demonstrate. He's never had a job, you know. He's got nothing to thank Thatcher's government for.'

'You say the knife was usually kept on the mantelpiece. Did you see anyone pick it up that afternoon, just to fidget with, perhaps?'

'No.'

'When did you notice it was missing?'

'What?'

'You must have noticed it was gone. Was it before you saw Jack Crocker walk in here with it yesterday?'

'I . . . I . . .'

Banks waved his hand. 'Forget it. I think I get the gist. You had noticed it was missing, and for some reason you thought Paul might have taken it with him last Friday.'

'No!'

'Then why did you run off and warn him?'

'Because I thought you'd pick on him if the knife had been found here. Jack Crocker works these moors. I knew when I saw him he couldn't have found it far away.'

'Plausible,' Banks said. 'But I'm not convinced. You weren't at the demo, were you?'

'No. It's not that I don't believe in the cause, but somebody had to stay home and look after the children.'

'You didn't put them to bed early and sneak out?'

'Are you accusing me?'

'I'm asking you.'

'Well, I don't know how you'd expect me to do that. The others had taken the van and it's a good four miles' walk across the moor to Eastvale.'

'So that leaves Paul, Zoe, Seth and Rick. Seth and Rick were arrested, but if Paul had picked up the knife at the demo, either one of them could have stabbed Gill, too.'

'I don't believe it.'

'Did Osmond or any of the others dislike you enough to want to put the blame on one of you?'

'I don't think so. Nobody had reason to hate us that much.'

'If you really hadn't noticed the knife for some time, someone else could have taken it earlier, couldn't they? Did you have any visitors during the week?'

'I . . . I don't remember.'

'Do you keep the place securely locked up?'

'You must be joking. We've nothing worth stealing.'

'Think about it. You see my problem, don't you? How it becomes more complicated if we leave Boyd out of it. And if someone did take the knife, there's premeditation involved. Do you know of anyone with a reason to murder PC Gill?'

'No.'

'Was he mentioned that afternoon up at the farm?'

'Not that I heard. But I was in and out. You know, making tea, clearing up.'

Banks drank some more Black Sheep bitter. 'Does the number 1139 mean anything to you?'

Mara frowned. The lines curved down from each side of her forehead and converged at the bridge of her nose. 'No,' she said. 'At least I don't think so. Why? Where did you find it?'

'It's not part of an address or a telephone number, for example?'

'I've told you, no. Not that I know of. It sounds vaguely familiar, but I can't place it.'

'Have you ever heard of the Rossghyll Guest House?'

'Yes, it's up the dale. Why?'

Banks watched her expression closely and saw no sign that the place meant anything to her. 'Never mind. Let me know if anything comes to you. It might be important.'

Mara finished her drink and shifted in her chair. 'Is there anything else?'

'Just one thing. It looks bad for Paul, running off like this. I know I can't ask you to turn him in, even if you do know where he is. But it really would be best for him if he gave himself up. Is there any chance of that?'

'It's unlikely. He's scared of the police, especially that bastard of a superintendent you've got.' She shook her head. 'I don't think he'll turn himself in.'

'If you hear from him, tell him what I said. Tell him I promise he'll get a fair deal.'

Mara nodded slowly. 'I don't believe it'll do much good though,' she said. 'He won't believe me. He doesn't trust us now any more than he trusts you.'

'Why not?'

'He knows I suspected him, just for a while. Paul's had so little love in his life he finds it hard enough to trust people in the first place. If they let him down, even in the slightest, then that's it.'

'Still,' Banks said, 'if you get the chance, put in a word.'

'I'll tell him. But I don't think any of us is likely to hear from Paul again. Can I go now?'

'Wait a moment and I'll give you a lift.' Banks still had half a pint left and made to finish it off.

Mara stood up. 'No, I'll walk. The shop's not far, and I could do with some fresh air.'

'Are you sure?'

'Yes.'

After she'd gone, Banks relaxed and savoured the rest of his beer. The meeting had gone better than he'd expected, and he had actually learned something about the knife. Mara had been evasive, mostly to avoid incriminating herself, but that was only to be expected. He didn't blame her for it.

Banks decided to keep his knowledge from Burgess for a while. He didn't want Dirty Dick to go charging in like a bloody elephant and frighten everyone into their corners as usual. Banks had managed to overcome some of Mara's general resentment towards the police – whether through Jenny's influence, his taste in music or sheer charm, he wasn't sure – but if Burgess turned up again, Mara's hatred for him would surely rub off on Banks as well.

By the time he set off back to Eastvale, his head had stopped aching and he felt able to tolerate some music. But he couldn't shake off the feeling that he was missing something obvious. He had the strange sensation that two insignificant things either he or Mara had said should be joined into one truth. If they made contact, a little bulb would light up and he would be that much closer to solving the case. Billie Holiday sang on regardless:

> Sad am I, glad am I
> For today I'm dreaming of
> Yesterdays.

TWO

Mara walked along the street, head down, thinking about her talk with Banks. Like all policemen, he asked nothing but bloody awkward questions. And Mara was sick of awkward questions. Why couldn't things just get back to normal so she could get on with her life?

'Hello, love,' Elspeth greeted her as she walked into the shop.

'Hello. How's Dottie?'

'She won't eat. How she can expect to get better when she refuses to eat, I just don't know.'

They both knew that Dottie wasn't going to get better, but nobody said so.

'What's wrong with you?' Elspeth asked. 'You've got a face as long as next week.'

Mara told her about Paul.

'I don't want to say I told you so,' Elspeth said, smoothing her dark tweed skirt, 'but I thought that lad was trouble from the start. You're best rid of him, all of you.'

'I suppose you're right.' Mara didn't agree, but there was no point arguing Paul's case against Elspeth. She hadn't expected any sympathy.

'Go in the back and get the wheel spinning, love,' Elspeth said. 'It'll do you a power of good.'

The front part of the shop was cluttered with goods for tourists. There were locally knitted sweaters on shelves on the walls, tables of pottery – some of which Mara had made – and trays of trinkets such as key rings bearing the Dales National Park emblem, the black face of a Swaledale sheep. As if that weren't enough, the rest of the space was taken up by fancy notepaper, glass paperweights, fluffy animals and fridge door magnets shaped like strawberries or Humpty Dumpty.

In the back though, the set-up was very different. First, there was a small pottery workshop, complete with wheel and dishes of brown and black metallic oxide glaze, and beyond that a drying room and a small electric kiln. The workshop was dusty and messy, crusted with bits of old clay, and it suited a part of Mara's personality. Mostly she preferred cleanliness and tidiness, but there was something special, she found, about creating beautiful objects in a chaotic environment.

She put on her apron, took a lump of clay from the bin and weighed off enough for a small vase. The clay was too wet, so she wedged it on a flat concrete tray, which absorbed the excess moisture. As she wedged – pushing hard with the heels of her hands, then pulling the clay forward with her fingers to get all the air out – she couldn't seem to lose herself in the task as usual but kept on thinking about her conversation with Banks.

Frowning, she cut the lump in half with a cheese wire to check for air bubbles, then slammed the pieces together much harder than usual. A fleck of clay spun off and hit her forehead, just above her right eye. She put the clay down and took a few deep breaths, trying to bring her mind to bear only on what she was doing.

No good. It was Banks's fault, of course. He had introduced her to speculations that caused nothing but distress. True, she didn't want Paul to be guilty, but if, as Banks had said, that meant someone else she knew had killed the policeman, that only made things worse.

Sighing, she started the wheel with the foot pedal and slammed the clay as close to the centre as she could. Then she drenched both it and her hands with water from a bowl by her side. As the wheel spun, clayey water flew off and splashed her apron.

She couldn't believe that any of her friends had stabbed Gill. Much better if Osmond or one of the students had done it for political reasons. Tim and Abha seemed nice enough, if a bit naive and gushing, but Mara had never trusted Osmond; he had always seemed somehow too oily and opinionated for her taste.

But what about Rick? He had strong political views, more so than Seth or Zoe. He'd often said someone should assassinate Margaret Thatcher, and Seth had argued that someone just as bad would take her place. But it was only a policeman who'd been killed, not a politician. Despite what Rick said about the police being mere instruments of the state, paid enforcers, she couldn't believe that would make him actually kill one of them.

She leaned forward, elbows in, and pushed hard to centre the clay. At last she managed it and, allowing herself a smile of satisfaction, stuck her thumb in the top and pushed down about an inch. She then filled the hole with water and began to drive deeper to where she wanted the bottom of the vase to be.

Holding the inside with one finger, she slowed the wheel and began to make a ridge from the outside bottom, raising the clay to the height she wanted. It took several times to get there, pulling just a little further each time, watching the groove flow up the outside of the clay and disappear.

She was determined not to let Banks get to her. There was no way she was going to start suspecting Rick the way she had Paul. She had good reason for worrying about him, she told herself: his violent past; the blood he had lied about. And the knife had his fingerprints on it. She had no reason at all for suspecting anyone else. If only Paul could get far away and never be seen again. That would be best – if the police continued to believe he had done it but were never able to find him.

She could hear Elspeth out front trying to sell a sweater to a customer. 'Traditional Dales pattern . . . local wool, of course . . . hand-knitted, naturally . . .'

Almost there. But her hands weren't steady, and when she'd lost her concentration she had increased the pressure with her right foot, speeding up the wheel. Suddenly the clay began to spin wildly off centre – insane shapes, like Salvador Dali paintings or plastic melting in a fire – and then it collapsed in on itself on the wheel-head. And that was that. Mara took the cheese wire and sliced off the mess. There was enough left for an egg cup maybe, but she couldn't face starting again. That damn Banks had ruined her day.

In disgust, she tore off her wet apron and cleaned the rest of the clay from the wheel. Putting on her anorak again, she walked through to the front.

'Sorry, Elspeth,' she said. 'I just can't seem to concentrate today. Maybe I'll go for a walk.'

Elspeth frowned. 'Are you sure you're all right?'

'Yes. Don't worry, I'll be fine. Give my love to Dottie.'

'Will do.'

As she left the shop, the bell clanged loudly behind her.

Instead of heading back home, she climbed the stile at the end of Mortsett Lane and struck out for the moors. As she walked, she ran over the events of last Friday afternoon up at the farm.

Most of the time she'd been in the kitchen preparing a stew for dinner – something to fortify them all against the cold and rain – and making pots of tea. The children had been a nuisance, too, she remembered. Overexcited because there were so many adults around, they'd kept coming in and tugging at her apron strings, pestering her. She hadn't been paying much attention to what the others were saying or doing in the front room even when she was there, and she hadn't noticed anybody pick up anything from the mantelpiece.

The only thing that struck a chord was that number Banks had mentioned: 1139, was it? She thought that she had heard it mentioned recently. Half heard it, really, because she had been thinking about something else at the time. The ashram, that was it. She had been remembering how, after the evening meal of brown rice and vegetables (every day!), they had all sat cross-legged in the meditation room, with its shrine to the guru and the smell of sandalwood incense heavy in the air. They had talked about how their lives had been empty until they had found the True Path. How they had been searching in all the wrong places for all the wrong things. And they had sung songs together, holding hands. 'Amazing Grace' had been a particular favourite. Somehow, the gathering at the farm that afternoon had made her think of those days, though it was different in almost every way.

That was what she had been thinking about when the

number had been mentioned. And she had been in the kitchen, too, because she clearly recalled the earthy feel of the potatoes she'd been peeling. Wasn't it odd how the mind worked? All the components of the experience were there, clear as day, but she couldn't remember who had mentioned the number, or in what context. And people had been in and out of the kitchen all afternoon.

Worrying about Paul again, wondering where he was, she lowered her head against the wind and marched on through the rough grass and heather.

THREE

There was little else to do but wait for Boyd to turn up. Whatever his suspicions, Banks had nothing concrete to go on, and he wasn't likely to have until he'd questioned Boyd. Dirty Dick was still sleeping last night's beer and Scotch off in his hotel room and Richmond was running around putting together as much information as he could get on the suspects. Criminal records weren't enough; they tended to leave out the all-too-important human factor, the snippet that gives a clue to motivation and makes the pattern clear.

Mostly Banks smoked too much and stared gloomily out of his window on to the grey market square. At four o'clock, he heard a knock on his door and called, 'Come in.'

PC Craig stood there looking as pleased as Punch. 'We've got a line on Boyd, sir,' he said, ushering in a stout middle-aged woman with curlers on her hair.

Banks pulled out a chair for her.

'This is Mrs Evans,' Craig said. 'I went knocking on doors on Cardigan Road to find out if anyone had seen

Boyd, and Mrs Evans here said she had. She kindly offered to come in with me and talk to you, sir.'

'Good work,' Banks said. Craig smiled and left.

Banks asked Mrs Evans what she'd seen.

'It was about three o'clock yesterday afternoon,' she began. 'I know the time because I'd just got back from Tesco's with the shopping and I were struggling to get off t' bus.'

'Which bus was that?'

'A forty-four. Two forty-six from t' bus station.'

Banks knew the route. The bus took the long way round Cardigan Road for the benefit of local passengers, then carried on to York.

'And you saw Paul Boyd?'

'I saw a lad what looked like that photo.' PC Craig had taken a prison photograph of Boyd to show from door to door. 'His hair's different now, but I know it was him. I've seen him before.'

'Where?'

'Around town. More often than not coming out of t' dole office. I always hold my handbag tighter when I see him. I know it's not fair to judge a book by its covers, but he looks like a bad sort to me.'

'Where did you see him this time?'

'He was running up Gallows View from t' fields.'

'From Relton way?'

'Aye, as t' crow flies.'

'And where did he go?'

'Go? He didn't go anywhere. He were running for t' bus. Just caught it an' all. Nearly knocked me over, and me carrying two heavy shopping bags.'

'What was he wearing? Do you remember?'

'Aye, that I do. A red anorak. I noticed because it

looked too small for him. A bit short in t' sleeves and tight around t' armpits.'

Why, Banks asked himself, wasn't he surprised that Mara had lied about Boyd's clothes?

'Was he carrying anything?'

'One of those airline bags – British Airways, I think.'

'Do you remember anything else?'

'Just that he seemed in such a hurry and looked worried. I mean, as a rule, like I said, it'd be me who'd be frightened of him, but this time he looked like he were scared out of his wits.'

Banks went over to the door and called Craig back. 'Thanks, Mrs Evans,' he said. 'We appreciate your coming in like this. PC Craig here will drive you home.' Mrs Evans nodded gravely and Craig escorted her out.

As soon as he was alone, Banks checked the bus time-table and found that the 2.46 from Eastvale was indeed the milk run to York; it didn't get there until 4.09. Next he phoned the York railway station and, after speaking to a succession of surly clerks, finally got put through to a pleasant woman in charge of information. From her, he discovered that Boyd could have taken a train almost anywhere between 4.15 and five o'clock: Leeds, London, Newcastle, Liverpool, Edinburgh, plus points in between and anywhere else that connections might take him. It didn't seem much of a help, but he called Sergeant Hatchley in and put him on tracking down the train catering crews and ticket collectors. It would mean a trip to York and it might take a long time, but at least it was action. Of course, Hatchley pulled a long face – it seemed he had plans for the evening – but Banks ignored him. It wasn't as if Hatchley had any other work to do. Why wag your own tail when you've got a dog?

At home that evening, Banks ate a tin of Irish stew and pottered restlessly about the house waiting to hear from Hatchley. At nine o'clock, unable to concentrate on reading and almost wishing he'd gone to York himself, he turned on the TV and watched a beautiful blonde policewoman and her loud-mouthed American partner dash around spraying London with lead. It was background noise, something to fill the emptiness of the house. Finally, he could stand his own company no longer and phoned Sandra.

This time he felt even more lonely after he hung up, but the feeling didn't last as long. Twenty minutes later Hatchley phoned from York. He had managed to get the addresses of most of the ticket collectors and catering staff on the trains out of York, but none of them lived locally. All in all, the first lead seemed to be petering out. That happened sometimes. Banks told Hatchley to go over to York CID headquarters and phone as many of the crew members as he could get through to, and to call back if he came up with anything. He didn't. At 11.30 Banks went to bed. Maybe tomorrow morning, after Boyd's photograph appeared in all the national dailies, they would get the break they needed.

10

ONE

The big break came early Friday morning. The Rossghyll Guest House proved to be a dead end, and all the train crews out of York had been too busy to remember anyone, but an Edinburgh barber phoned to say he recognized Paul Boyd's photograph in the morning paper. Though Banks found the man's accent difficult to understand, he managed to learn what Paul's new haircut looked like. Even more important, he discovered that Paul had ditched his red anorak for a new grey duffel coat.

As soon as he hung up, Banks checked the map. Paul had headed north rather than to London or Liverpool. That had been a clever move; it had gained him time. But now that his photograph was on the front page of all the tabloid dailies, his time was running out. In addition to getting the photo in the papers as soon as possible, Banks and his men had also circulated Boyd's description to police in all major cities, ports and airports. It was routine, the best they could do with limited knowledge, but now there was somewhere concrete to start.

Assuming that Paul would ultimately want to leave the country, Banks took out his AA road map and ran his finger up the outline of the Scottish coast looking for ways out. He could find only two ferry routes north of Edinburgh on the east coast. The first, from Aberdeen to

Lerwick, on the Shetlands, could take Boyd eventually to Bergen and Torsken, in Norway, or to Seydhisfjördhur, in Iceland. But looking at the fine print, Banks saw that those ferries ran only in summer and, as the grey sky and drizzle outside testified, it certainly wasn't summer.

Another ferry ran from Scrabster, further north, to Stromness on mainland Orkney, but that hardly seemed like a place to run and hide. Boyd would stand out there like an Eskimo in the tropics.

Turning to the west coast, Banks saw dozens of broken red lines leading to such places as Brodick on the Isle of Arran; Port Ellen on Islay; and Stornoway on Lewis in the Outer Hebrides. The whole map was a maze of small islands and ferry routes. But, Banks reasoned, none of those isolated places would suit Boyd. He would be trapped, as well as conspicuous, on any of Scotland's islands, especially at this time of year.

The only trip that made any sense in the area was Stranraer to Larne. Then Boyd would be in Northern Ireland. From there, he didn't need a passport to cross the border to the Republic. Boyd was from Liverpool, Banks remembered, and probably had Irish friends.

So the first call he made, after giving Richmond and Hatchley the task of informing the other Scottish ferry ports just in case, was to the police at Stranraer. He was told that there had been no sailings the previous day because of a bad storm at sea, but this morning was calm. There were sailings at 11.30, 15.30, 19.00 and 03.00, all with easy connections from Edinburgh or Glasgow. Banks gave Boyd's description and asked that the men there keep a special watch for him, especially at ferry boardings. Next he issued the new description to police in Edinburgh, Glasgow, Inverness, Aberdeen and Dundee, and passed a list of smaller places to PCs Craig and Tolliver downstairs. Then he phoned Burgess, who had been keeping a low profile in his hotel room since their drunken night, and gave him the news.

Banks knew from experience that leads like this could bring results in a matter of minutes or days. He was impatient to have Boyd in and get the truth out of him, as much to test his own theories as anything else, but he'd get nowhere pacing the room. Instead, he sent for some coffee and went over the files Richmond had put together.

Information is a policeman's lifeblood. It comes in from many sources: interviews, gossip, criminal records, informers, employers, newspaper reporters and registries of births, marriages and deaths. It has to be collated, filed and cross-referenced in the hope that one day it will prove useful. DC Richmond was the best ferret they had at Eastvale, in addition to being practically invisible on surveillance and handy in a chase. Sergeant Hatchley, though tough, tenacious and good at interrogation, was too lazy and desultory to tie everything together. He overlooked minor details and took the easy way out. Put more simply, Richmond enjoyed gathering and collating data whereas Hatchley didn't. It made all the difference.

Banks spread out the sheets in front of him. He already knew a bit about Seth Cotton, but he had to be thorough in his revision. In the end, though, the only extra knowledge he gleaned was that Cotton had been born in Dewsbury and that in the mid 1970s he had settled in Hebden Bridge and led a quiet life, as far as the local police were concerned. Richmond had picked up the accident report on Alison Cotton, which didn't say very much. Banks made a note to look into it further.

There was nothing new on Rick Trelawney either, apart

from the name and address of his wife's sister in London. It might be worth a call to get more details on the divorce.

Zoe Hardacre was a local girl. Or near enough. As Jenny had said, she hailed from Whitby on the east coast, not far from Gill's home town, Scarborough. After school she had tried secretarial work but drifted away. Employers had complained that she couldn't seem to keep her mind on the important tasks they gave her, and that she always seemed to be in another world. That other world was the one of the occult: astrology, palmistry and tarot card readings. She had studied the subjects thoroughly enough to be regarded as something of an expert by those who knew about such things. Now that the occult seemed to have come into fashion among the New Age yuppie crowd, she made a living of sorts producing detailed natal charts and giving tarot readings. Everyone seemed to agree that Zoe was harmless, a true flower child, though too young to have been part of the halcyon days of the 1960s. She seemed about as political as a flower, too: she supported human rights and she wanted the bomb banned, but that was as far as it went.

As far as Banks could make out, she had never come into contact with PC Gill. Banks imagined him bursting into her booth at Whitby, truncheon raised, and arresting her for charlatanism; or perhaps she had read his palm and told him he was a repressed homosexual. The absurdity of Banks's theories served only as a measure of his frustration over motive. The connection between one of the suspects and Gill's murder was there somewhere, but Banks didn't have enough data yet to see it. He felt as if he were trying to do a join-the-dots drawing with too few dots.

While Banks was almost convinced that Mara Delacey

had been at the farm looking after the children at the time PC Gill was stabbed, he glanced over her file anyway. She had started out as a bright girl, a promising student, gaining a good degree in English, but she had fallen in with the hippie crowd when LSD, acid rock, bandannas and bright kaftans were all the rage. The police knew she took drugs, but never suspected her of dealing in them. Despite one of two raids on places where she happened to be living, they had never even been able to find her in possession.

Like Zoe, Mara had done occasional stints of secretarial work, most often as a temp, and she had never really put her university education to practical use. She'd spent some time in the USA in the late 1970s, mostly in California. Back in England, she had drifted for a while, then become involved with a guru and ended up living in one of his ashrams in Muswell Hill for a couple of years. After that, the farm. There was nothing to tie Mara to PC Gill, unless he had crossed her path during the two years she had been in Swainsdale.

Banks walked over to the window to rest his eyes and lit a cigarette. Outside, two elderly tourists, guidebooks in hand, paused to admire the Norman tower, then walked into the church.

Nothing in what Banks had read seemed to get him any further. If Gill did have a connection with someone at the farm, it was well buried and he'd have to dig deep for it. Sighing, he sat down again and flipped open the next folder.

Tim Fenton had been born in Ripon and was now in his second year at Eastvale College of Further Education. With Abha Sutton, he ran the students' union there. It was a small one, and usually stuck to in-college issues, but students were upset about government health and education policies – especially as far as they were likely to affect grants – and took every opportunity to demonstrate their displeasure. Tim, whose father was an accountant, was only nineteen and had no blots on his copybook except for attending the seminar that had got him into Special Branch's files.

Abha Sutton was born in Bradford of an Indian mother and a Yorkshire father. Again, her upbringing had been solidly middle class, and like Tim, as Richmond had tried to tell Burgess, she had no history of violence or involvement in extremist politics. She had been living with Tim for six months now, and together they had started the college Marxist society. It had very few members though; many of the college students were local farmers' sons studying agriculture. Still, the Social Sciences department and the Arts faculty were expanding, and they had managed to recruit a few new members among the literary crowd.

Banks read even more closely when he got to Dennis Osmond's file. Osmond was thirty-five, born in Newcastle-upon-Tyne. His father had worked in the shipyards there, but unemployment had forced the family to move when Osmond was ten. Mr Osmond had found a job at the chocolate factory, where he'd been known as a strong union man, and he had been involved in the acrimonious and sometimes violent negotiations that marked its last days. Osmond himself, though given at first to more intellectual pursuits, had followed his father politically.

A radical throughout university, he had dropped out in his third year, claiming that the education he was being given was no more than an indoctrination in bourgeois values, and had taken up social work in Eastvale, where he'd been working now for twelve years. During that period, he had become one of the town's chief spokesmen, along with Dorothy Wycombe, for the oppressed, neglected and unjustly treated. He had also beaten up Ellen Ventner, a woman he had lived with. Some of his cronies were the kind of people that Burgess would want shot on sight – shop stewards, feminists, poets, anarchists and intellectuals.

Whatever good Osmond had done around the place, Banks still couldn't help disliking the man and seeing him, somehow, as a sham. He couldn't understand Jenny's attraction to him, unless it was purely physical. And Jenny, of course, still didn't know that Osmond had once assaulted a woman.

It was after one o'clock, time for a pie and a pint in the Queen's Arms. But no sooner had Banks settled down in his favourite armchair by the fire to read the *Guardian* than PC Craig came rushing into the pub.

'They've got him, sir,' he said breathlessly. 'Boyd. Caught him trying to get on the half past eleven ferry to Larne.'

Banks looked at his watch. 'It's taken them long enough to get on to us. Are they holding him?'

'No, sir. They're bringing him down. Said they should be here late this afternoon.'

'No hurry then, is there?' Banks lit a cigarette and rustled his paper. 'Looks like it's all over.'

But it didn't feel as if it was all over; it felt more like it was just beginning.

TWO

Burgess paced the office like an expectant father, puffing on his cigar and glancing at his watch every ten seconds.

'Where the bloody hell are they?' he asked for what seemed to Banks like the hundredth time that afternoon.

'They'll be here soon. It's a long drive and the roads can be nasty in this weather.'

'They ought to be here by now.'

The two of them were in Banks's office waiting for Paul Boyd. Scenting the kill, Burgess didn't seem able to relax but Banks felt unusually calm. Along Market Street the shopkeepers were shutting up for the day, and it was already growing dark. In the office, the heater coughed and the fluorescent light hummed.

Banks stubbed out his cigarette and said, 'I'm off for some coffee. Want some?'

'I'm jittery enough as it is. Oh, what the hell. Why not? Black, three sugars.'

In the corridor, Banks bumped into Sergeant Hatchley on his way downstairs. 'Anything?' he asked.

'No,' said Hatchley. 'Still waiting to hear. I'm on my way to check with Sergeant Rowe if there's been any messages.'

Banks took the two mugs of coffee back to his office and smiled when Burgess jumped at the sound of the door opening. 'It's all right,' he said. 'Don't get excited. It's only me.'

'Do you think the silly buggers have got lost?' Burgess asked, scowling. 'Or broken down?'

'I'm sure they know their way around just as well as anyone else.'

'You can never be sure with bloody Jocks,' Burgess complained. Eastvale was the furthest north he had ever been, and he had already made it quite clear that he didn't care to venture any further. 'If they've let that bastard escape—'

But he was interrupted by the phone. It was Sergeant Rowe. Boyd had arrived.

'Tell them to bring him up here.' Burgess took out another Tom Thumb. He lit it, brushed some ash off his shirt and picked up his coffee.

A few moments later there was a knock at the door, and two uniformed men entered with Paul Boyd between them. He looked pale and distant – as well he might, Banks thought.

'Sorry, sir,' said the driver. 'We had a delay setting off. Had to wait till the doc had finished.'

'Doctor?' Burgess said. 'Why, what's wrong? Young dickhead here didn't hurt anyone, did he?'

'Him? No.' The constable gave Paul a contemptuous glance. 'Fainted when they caught him, that's all, then came round screaming about walls closing in. Had to get the doc to give him a sedative.'

'Walls closing in, eh?' Burgess said. 'Interesting. Sounds like a touch of claustrophobia to me. Never mind. Sit him down, and you two can bugger off now.'

'See the desk sergeant about expenses and accommodation,' Banks said to the two Scotsmen. 'I don't suppose you'll be wanting to set off back tonight?'

The driver smiled. 'No, sir. Thanks very much, sir.'

'Thank *you*,' Banks said. 'There's a good pub across the road. The Queen's Arms. You can't miss it.'

'Yes, sir.'

Burgess could hardly wait to close the door behind

them. Paul sat facing Banks in a tubular metal chair with a wooden seat and back. Burgess, preferring a free rein and the advantage of height, chose to lean against the wall or stride around as he talked.

'Get the sergeant in, will you?' he asked Banks. 'With his notebook.'

Banks sent for Hatchley, who arrived red-faced and out of breath a minute later. 'Those bloody stairs again,' he grumbled. 'They'll be the death of me.'

Burgess pointed to a chair in the corner and Hatchley sat down obediently. He found a clean page in his notebook and took out his pencil.

'Right,' said Burgess, clapping his hands. 'Let's get cracking.'

Paul looked over at him, hatred and fear burning in his eyes.

If Burgess had one professional fault, Banks thought, it was as an interrogator. He couldn't seem to take any part but that of his own pushy aggressive self. It wouldn't prove half as effective with Boyd as the routine Banks and Hatchley had worked out, but it would have to do. Banks knew he would be forced into the role of the nice guy, the father confessor, for the duration.

'Why don't you tell us about it?' Burgess began. 'That way we won't have to resort to the Chinese water torture, will we?'

'There's nothing to tell.' Boyd glanced nervously at the window. The slats of the venetian blind were up, letting in grey light from the street below.

'Why did you kill him?'

'I didn't kill anyone.'

'Did you just lose your temper, is that it? Or did someone pay you? Come on, we know you did it.'

'I told you, I didn't kill anyone.'

'Then how come that knife with PC Gill's blood on it also happens to have your dabs all over it too? Are you trying to tell me you never touched it?'

'I didn't say that.'

'What are you trying to say?'

Paul licked his lips. 'Can I have a cigarette?'

'No, you bloody can't,' Burgess growled. 'Not until you've told us what happened.'

'I didn't do anything, honestly. I've never killed anyone.'

'So why did you run?'

'I was frightened.'

'What of?'

'Frightened you'd fit me up for it anyway. You know I've done time.'

'Is that how you think we operate, Paul?' Banks asked gently. 'Is that really what you think? You're wrong, you know. If you just tell us the truth you've nothing to fear.'

Burgess ignored him. 'How did your prints get on the knife?'

'I must have handled it, I suppose.'

'That's better. Now when did you handle it, and why?'

Paul shrugged. 'Could've been any time.'

'Any time?' Burgess shook his head with exaggerated slowness. 'No, it couldn't, sonny. No, it couldn't. Want to know why? Your prints were right on top, numero uno, clear as day. You were the last person to handle that knife before we found it. How do you explain that?'

'All right, so I handled it after it'd been used. That still doesn't mean I killed anyone.'

'It does unless you've got a better explanation. And I haven't heard one yet.'

'How did you know we'd found the knife?' Banks asked.

'I saw that shepherd find it on the moor, so I took off.'

He was lying, Banks thought. Mara had told him. But he let it go for the moment.

Paul fell silent. The floor creaked as Burgess paced the office. Banks lit a Silk Cut, his last, and leaned back in his chair. 'Look, Paul,' he said, 'consider the facts. One: we found PC Gill's blood on the knife, and the doc tells us the blade fits the wound. Two: we found your prints on the handle. Three: we know you were at the demo – you were seen. Four: as soon as things start adding up, you bugger off to Scotland. Now you tell me what to make of it all. What would you think if you were me?'

Paul still said nothing.

'I'm getting fed up of this,' Burgess snarled. 'Let's just lock the bastard up now. He's in on a warrant. We've got enough evidence. We don't need a confession. Hell, we don't even need a motive.'

'No!' Paul yelled.

'No what? You don't want us to lock you up? Dark down there, isn't it? Even a normal person feels the walls closing in on him down there in the dark.'

Paul was pale and sweating now, and his mouth was clamped so tight that the muscles in his jaw quivered.

'Come on,' Banks said. 'Why don't you just tell us. Save us all a lot of trouble. You say you've done nothing. If that's so, you've nothing to be worried about. Why hold back?'

'Stop mollycoddling him,' Burgess said. 'He's not going to talk, you know that as well as I do. He's guilty as sin, and he knows it.' He turned to Hatchley. 'Sergeant, send for a couple of men to take dickhead here down to the cells.'

'No!' Paul leaned forward and gripped the edge of the desk until his knuckles turned white.

Burgess gestured to Hatchley to sit down again. The command was a bit premature, as the sergeant moved slowly and hadn't even got as far as putting his notebook away.

'Let me make it easy for you, Paul,' Banks said. 'I'll tell you what I think happened and you tell me if it's true. All right?'

Paul took a deep breath and nodded.

'You took the knife from the farm. It was usually just lying around the place. It didn't belong to anyone in particular. Mara used it occasionally to cut twine and wool; maybe Seth used it sometimes to whittle a piece of wood. But that day you picked it up, carried it to the demo with you, and killed PC Gill. Then you folded the blade over again, made your way to the edge of the crowd, and escaped down an alley. You ran to the edge of town, then across the moors back to the farm – almost four miles. About halfway there, you realized what you'd done, panicked and chucked the knife away. Am I right, Paul?'

'I didn't kill anyone,' Paul repeated.

'But am I right about the rest?'

Silence.

'It's beginning to look like the thumbscrews for you, sonny.' Burgess leaned forward, his face only inches from Paul's. 'I'm getting bored. I'm sick of the bloody North and this miserable bloody weather. I want to get back home to London, the civilized world. Understand? And you're standing in my way. I don't like people who stand in my way, and if they do it for long enough, they get knocked down. Savvy?'

Paul turned to Banks. 'You're right about everything

else,' he said. 'But I didn't take the knife. I didn't kill the copper.'

'Police officer to you, dickhead,' Burgess snapped.

'How did you end up with it?' Banks asked.

'I got knocked down,' Paul said. 'At the demo. And I curled up, like, with my hands behind my neck and my knees up in my chest, in the . . . the . . . what do you call it?'

'Foetal position?'

'Yes, the foetal position. There were people all around me, it was bloody awful. I kept getting booted. Then this knife got kicked towards me. I picked it up, like you said, and made off. But I didn't know it had killed anyone. I just thought it was a good knife, too good to waste, so I took it with me. Then, on the moors, I saw there was blood on it so I flung it away. That's how it happened.'

'You're a bloody liar,' Burgess said. 'Do you think I'm an idiot? Is that what you take me for? I might be a city boy, but even I know there aren't any lights on the fucking moors. And even you're not stupid enough to lie there in the street, boots flying all around you, police everywhere, and think, "Oh, what a pretty bloodstained knife. I must take it home with me." You've been talking cobblers.' He turned to Banks. 'That's what you get for being soft with them, see. Spin you a yarn a bloody mile long.'

Swiftly, he grasped the back of Paul's neck and squeezed hard. Paul hung on to the edge of the desk and struggled, almost upsetting his flimsy chair. Then, just as abruptly, Burgess let go and leaned casually against the wall.

'Try again,' he said.

Paul massaged his neck and looked pleadingly at Banks, who remained impassive.

'It's true, I tell you,' Paul said. 'I swear it. I never killed him. I just picked up the knife.'

'Let's assume we believe you,' Banks said. 'That still leaves us with a problem, doesn't it? And that problem is: why? Why did you pick up the murder weapon and sneak it away from the scene of the crime? See what I mean? It doesn't add up.'

Paul shifted in his seat, casting nervous glances at Burgess, who stood just within his peripheral vision. 'I didn't even know there was a crime,' he said.

'Who are you protecting, Paul?' Banks asked.

'Nobody.' But Paul had answered so quickly and loudly that even the most gullible person in the world would have known he was lying. Recognizing his slip, he turned red and stared down at his knees.

'The people at Maggie's Farm took you in and cared for you, didn't they?' Banks said. 'They were probably the first people who ever did. You were lost, just out of jail, no job, nowhere to go, at the end of your tether, and then you met them. It's not surprising you'd want to protect them, Paul, but can't you see how transparent you're being? Who do you suspect?'

'I don't know. Nobody.'

'Osmond, Tim Fenton, Abha Sutton? Would you go out of your way to protect them?'

Paul said nothing.

Burgess slapped the metal table. 'Tell him!'

Paul jumped, startled by the sound. 'I might,' he said, glaring at Burgess. 'I might protect anyone who killed a pig.'

Burgess backhanded him across the face. Paul went with the blow and almost fell out of his chair.

'Try again, dickhead.'

Banks grabbed Burgess by the elbow and led him over

to the window. 'Don't you think,' he said between gritted teeth, 'that you'd do better using your brains instead of your bloody fists?'

'What's wrong with you, Banks? Gone soft? Is that why they sent you up here?'

Banks jerked his head towards Paul. 'He's used to hard knocks. They don't mean anything to him, and you bloody well ought to know that. You're satisfying your sadistic urges, that's all.'

Burgess sniffed and turned back to Paul, who sat wiping the blood from his mouth with the back of his hand, sneering at both of them. He had overheard, Banks realized, and he probably thought the whole scene was staged just to throw him off balance. 'You admit that when you found the knife on the ground you recognized it, right?' Banks asked.

'Yes.'

'And you didn't want any of your friends at the farm to get into trouble.'

'That's right.'

'So you took it and threw it away.'

'Yes. I went back on the moors to look for it a few times. I knew it was stupid just to throw it away without wiping it or anything, but I panicked. I should've taken it back to the farm and cleaned it up again, just like new. I know that now. I walked miles and miles looking for the bloody thing. Couldn't find it anywhere. And then that shepherd bloke turned up with it.'

'So who did you think you were protecting?'

'I don't know.' Paul took out a crumbled Kleenex and dabbed at the thin trickle of blood at the corner of his mouth. 'I've already told you, I didn't see who took the knife and I didn't see who used it.'

'We'll leave it for now, then.' Banks turned to Burgess. 'What do you think?'

'I still think he's lying. Maybe he's not as thick as he looks. He's trying to put the blame on his mates, subtle like.'

'I'm not too sure,' Banks said. 'He could be telling the truth. Problem is he's got no proof, has he? I mean, he could tell us anything.'

'And expect us to believe it. Let's lock him up for a while, anyway. Let him cool his heels. We'll question him again later and see if everything tallies.'

Paul, who had been glancing from one to the other with his mouth open, let out a cry. 'No! I've told you; it's the truth. What more do you want me to do?'

Burgess shrugged and leaned back against the wall. Banks reached for a cigarette; his packet was empty. 'Well, I'm inclined to believe him,' he said. 'At least for the time being. Are you sure you didn't see who took the knife, Paul?'

'No. It could've been anyone.'

'That gives us seven suspects, am I right?' Banks counted them off on his fingers. 'Seth, Rick, Zoe, Mara, Osmond, Tim and Abha. Was anyone else up there during the week before the demo? Anyone we don't know about?'

'No. And Mara wasn't there.'

'But the others all were? Zoe was?'

He nodded.

'Did any of them have a reason for killing PC Gill?' Banks asked. 'Anyone know him? Had a run-in with him before?'

Paul shook his head. 'Maybe the students. I don't know.'

'But I don't think you'd go out of your way to protect

them, Paul, I really don't. Was Gill mentioned that after-noon?'

'Not that I heard.'

'You see, it still doesn't ring true,' Banks said. 'Some-one picking the knife up on purpose like that and taking it along, as if whoever did it knew he was going to do it. Premeditated, that is.'

'I don't know what you mean.'

'Oh, I think you do.' Banks smiled and stood up. 'I'm just off for some cigarettes,' he said to Burgess. 'I doubt that we'll get much more out of him.'

'Maybe not.' Burgess agreed. 'Pick me up a tin of Thumbs, will you?'

'Sure.'

'And give my love to Glenys.'

Banks was grateful for the cool fresh air outside the station. He stood for a moment, breathing in and out deeply, then crossed Market Street to the Queen's Arms.

'Twenty Silk Cut and a tin of Tom Thumbs, please, Cyril,' he said.

'These for that mate of yours?' Cyril asked, slapping the cigars on the counter.

'I wish you'd stop calling him my mate. You'll be getting me a bad name.'

'Well, my Glenys has been acting a bit funny lately. She's an impressionable lass, if you know what I mean, and headstrong. Gets it from that bloody mother of hers. It's just little things, things only a husband notices, but if I find that your mate's behind it, I'll . . . Well, I needn't spell it out for you, need I, Mr Banks?'

'Not to me, Cyril, no. Better not. I'll inform him of your concern.'

'If you would.'

Back outside, Banks noticed that the light had gone out in his office window. No doubt they'd sent Boyd down to the cells and gone for coffee. As he crossed the street, he heard a scream. It came from above, he was certain of that, but he couldn't pinpoint it exactly. Apprehensive, he hurried back upstairs and opened the door. The office was dark, but it wasn't empty.

When he flicked on the fluorescent light, Banks saw that Sergeant Hatchley had been sent away and only Boyd and Burgess remained. The slats on the venetian blind had been completely closed, shutting out all the light from the street, a feat Banks himself had never been able to manage in all the time he'd been in Eastvale.

Boyd was whimpering in the chair, sweating and gasping for breath. 'He turned the lights off,' he said, struggling to get the words out, 'and closed the blinds, the bastard.'

Banks glared at Burgess, who simply flashed him a 'Who, me?' look and said, 'I think he was telling the truth. At least, if he wasn't, he's just given the most convincing performance of his life.'

'Under duress.' Banks tossed him the cigars. Burgess caught the tin deftly, unwrapped it and offered Banks one. 'Celebrate with me?'

'I prefer these.' Banks lit a Silk Cut.

'You can have a smoke now if you want, kid,' Burgess said to Paul. 'Though with a breathing problem like yours, I'd watch it.'

Paul lit up and coughed till he was red in the face. Burgess laughed.

'So, what now?' Banks asked.

'We lock him up and go home.' Burgess looked at Paul. 'You're going to have plenty of time for long chats with the prison shrink about that claustrophobia of yours,' he said. 'In fact, you could say we're doing you a favour. Don't they say the best way to deal with a phobia is to confront it? And the treatment's free. What more could you ask for? You'd have to wait years on the National Health for that kind of service.'

Paul's jaw slackened. 'But I didn't do it. You said you believed me.'

'It takes a lot more than that to convince me. Besides, there's tampering with evidence, accessory after the fact of murder, wasting police time, resisting arrest. You've got a lot of charges to face.'

Burgess called downstairs and two constables came to escort Paul to the cells. He didn't struggle this time; he seemed to know there was no point.

When they were alone in the office, Banks turned to Burgess. 'If you pull a stunt like that on my patch again,' he said, 'I'll kick your balls into the middle of next week, superintendent or no fucking superintendent.'

Burgess held his gaze, but Banks felt that he took the threat more seriously than he had Rick Trelawney's.

After the staring match, Burgess smiled and said, 'Good, I'm glad we've got that out of the way. Come on, I could murder a pint.'

And he put his arm around Banks's shoulder and steered him towards the door.

11

ONE

The rattle of the letter box and the sound of mail slapping against the hall mat woke Banks early on Saturday morning. His mouth tasted like the bottom of a bird cage, and his tongue felt dry and furry from too many cigarettes and too much ale. He and Burgess had murdered more than one pint after Boyd's interrogation. It was getting to be a habit.

Banks still wasn't used to waking up alone in the big bed. He missed Sandra's warm body stirring beside him, and he missed the grumbles and complaints of Brian and Tracy getting ready for school or for Saturday morning shopping expeditions. But they'd all be back in a few days. With a bit of luck, the Gill case would be over by then and he would be able to spend some time with them.

Over coffee and burnt toast – why the toaster only burnt toast when *he* made it, Banks had no idea – he examined the mail: two bills, a letter and a new blues anthology tape from Barney Merritt, an old friend on the Met and, finally, just what he'd been waiting for – the package from Tony Grant.

The information, which Grant had copied in longhand from PC Gill's files, made interesting reading. Ever since picket control duty at the Orgreave coking plant during the miners' strike in 1984, Gill had volunteered for overtime at just about every demonstration that had come up in Yorkshire: protests outside US missile bases, marches against South Africa, National Front meetings, anything that had seemed likely to turn into a free-for-all. Gill certainly wasn't the only one, but he seemed to have been the kind of person who graduated from school bully to legalized goon. Banks wouldn't have been surprised if he had carved notches in his truncheon.

There were complaints against him too, generally for excessive use of force in subduing demonstrators. However, there were surprisingly few of these and no action had been taken on them, except perhaps a slap on the wrist now and then. The most interesting complaint came from Dennis Osmond, charging Gill with using unnecessary violence during a local demonstration in support of the Greenham Common women about two years ago. Another familiar name on the list was Elizabeth Dale, who had accused Gill of lashing out indiscriminately against her and her friends during a peaceful anti-nuclear march in Leeds. Banks couldn't immediately place her, as she didn't seem to belong to the pattern that included Paul Boyd and Dennis Osmond, but he knew her name. He made a note to check it in his files, then read carefully through the rest of the material. No other names stood out.

But the most important piece of information Banks gleaned from the files had nothing to do with Gill's behaviour; in fact, it was so damn simple he cursed himself out loud for not seeing it sooner. He always thought of his colleagues by name, even the uniformed men. Most policemen did – especially plain-clothes detectives. But it was a different matter for others. How could a member of the public name a particular police officer in a complaint, or even in a letter of commendation? He couldn't. That's why the numbers were so important. Called collar-numbers because they originally appeared on the small stand-up collars of the old police uniform, the metal numbers are now fixed to the officer's epaulettes and there was Gill's number staring him right in the face: PC 1139.

He remembered driving back from the Black Sheep after his lunch-time chat with Mara. He had been listening to Billie Holiday and wondering what it was he'd said that should have meant more than it did. Now he knew. He had mentioned Gill's name and, in his next question, the number. They had almost leaped together to complete the circuit, but not quite.

Banks put the papers away, grabbed his coat and hurried out to the car. It was a beautiful morning. The wind still blew cool but the sun shone in a cloudless sky. After the miserable late winter weather they'd been having recently, the smell of spring in the air – that strong mixture of wet grass and last autumn's decay – was almost over-whelming. As the pipes on Keats's Grecian urn appealed not to the 'sensual ear' but played 'spirit ditties of no tone', so this smell didn't so much titillate the sensual nose as it exhaled a scent of promise, a special feeling of anticipation and a definite quickening of the life force. It made him want to slip the Deller Consort recording of Shakespeare's songs into his Walkman and step lightly to work. But he would need the car for the visit he had to make later in the day. Still, he thought, no reason why he shouldn't follow the musical impulse where it led him, especially on a day like this, so he made a special trip back inside and found the cassette to play in the car.

It was after nine when he got to the office. Richmond was playing with the computer and Sergeant Hatchley was struggling over the *Daily Mirror* crossword. There was no sign of Dirty Dick. He sent for coffee and went to peer out of the window. The good weather had certainly enticed people outdoors. Tourists drifted in and out of the church, and some, wearing anoraks over warm sweaters, actually sat on the worn plinth of the market cross eating KitKats and drinking tea from Thermos flasks.

Banks spent an hour or more staring out on the busy square trying to puzzle out why PC Gill's number had turned up in Seth Cotton's old notebook. Had it even been Cotton's handwriting? He examined the book again. It was hard to tell, because only the faint imprint remained. The numbers were exaggeratedly large, too, unlike the smaller scrawl of most of the measurements. Carefully, he rubbed a soft pencil over the page again, but he couldn't get a better impression.

He remembered Mara Delacey telling him that Paul spent a lot of time working with Seth in the shed, so the number could just as likely have been written down by him. If so, that implied premeditation. Boyd's name hadn't appeared on Grant's list of complainants, but that didn't mean they hadn't come into conflict before. A kid with a record, like Paul, would hardly walk into the nearest police station and lodge a complaint.

The only thing of which Banks could be sure, after two cups of coffee and three cigarettes, was that somebody at Maggie's Farm knew of PC Gill before the demonstration and expected him to be there. The number had been written down hard enough to press through, and that indicated some degree of passion or excitement. Who had a grudge against Gill? And who had access to Seth Cotton's notebook? Anybody, really, as he never locked the shed. Boyd was the best candidate, given the evidence against him, but Banks had a nagging suspicion that he'd been telling the truth, especially when he stuck to his story after Burgess had put the lights out on him. But if Boyd was telling the truth, who was he more likely to be protecting than Seth, Mara, Rick or Zoe?

And where, Banks asked himself, did that leave Osmond, Tim and Abha?

Tim and Abha had so far been the only ones to admit to knowing of PC Gill's existence, which probably indicated that they had nothing to hide. Banks doubted, in fact, that they had anything to do with the murder. For a start, they had no real connection with the farm people other than a mutual interest in wanting to save the human race from total obliteration.

Osmond, however, was a friend of Rick, Seth and the rest. He had been up to the farm often, and he knew Gill's number all right, because he had used it on his complaint. Perhaps he had written it in the notebook himself, or had seen it there and recognized it. Paul Boyd may have been telling the truth about not killing PC Gill, but had he been an accomplice? Had there been two people involved?

Like so many of Banks's thinking sessions, this one was raising far more questions than it answered. Sometimes he thought he could solve cases only after formulating a surfeit of questions; he reached saturation point, and the overflow produced the answers.

Before he did anything else though, he needed something to stop the growling in his stomach. Burnt toast wasn't sufficient fuel for a detective.

On his way to the Golden Grill for elevenses, he bumped into Mara Delacey entering the station.

'I want to see Paul,' she said, brandishing the morning paper. 'It says here you've caught him. Is it true?'

'Yes.'

'Where is he?'

'Downstairs.'

'Is he all right?'

'Of course he is. What do you think we are, the Spanish Inquisition?'

'I wouldn't put anything past Burgess. Can I see Paul?'

Banks thought for a moment. It would be unusual to grant such permission, and Burgess wouldn't like it if he found out, but there was no reason Mara shouldn't see Boyd. Besides, it would give Banks the opportunity to ask him a couple of questions in Mara's presence. Through body language and facial expressions, people often gave more away than they intended when friends or enemies were nearby.

'All right,' he said, leading the way down. 'But I'll have to be there.'

'As you can see, I've not brought him a birthday cake with a file in it.'

Banks smiled. 'Wouldn't do him much good anyway. There aren't any bars on the window. He could only escape to the staircase and walk right up here.'

'But his claustrophobia,' Mara said, alarmed. 'It'll be unbearable for him.'

'We got a doctor.' Banks relished his small victory over Burgess's callousness. 'He's been given tranquillizers, and they seemed to help.'

The four cells were the most modern part of the building. Recently overcrowded with demonstrators, they were now empty except for Paul Boyd. Mara seemed surprised to find clean white tiles and bright light instead of dark dank stone walls. The only window, high and deep-set in the wall, was about a foot square and almost as thick. The cells always made Banks think of hospitals, so much so that he fancied he could smell Dettol or carbolic every time he went down there.

Boyd sat on his bunk and stared out through the bars at his visitors.

'Hello,' Mara said. 'I'm sorry, Paul.'

Boyd nodded.

Banks could sense tension between them. It was due in part to his being there, he knew, but it seemed to go deeper than that, as if they were unsure what to say to each other.

'Are you all right?' she asked.

'I'm OK.'

'Will you be coming back?'

Paul glared at Banks. 'I don't know. They're determined to charge me with something.'

Banks explained the procedure.

'So he might still be arrested for murder?' Mara asked.

'Yes.'

There were tears in her eyes. Paul stared at her suspiciously, as if he wasn't sure whether she was acting or not.

Banks broke the tense silence. 'Does the number 1139 mean anything to you?' he asked Boyd.

Paul seemed to consider the question, and his answer was an unequivocal no. Banks thought he was telling the truth.

'What do you know about the old notebook Seth kept in his workshop?'

Paul shrugged. 'Nothing. It was just for addresses, measurements and stuff.'

'Did you ever use it?'

'No. I was just an assistant, a dogsbody.'

'It wasn't like that, Paul,' Mara said. 'And you know it.'

'It doesn't matter now, does it? Except maybe it'll get me a job in the prison workshop.'

'Did anybody else ever use it, other than Seth?' asked Banks.

'Why should they?' Paul was obviously puzzled by the line of questioning. 'It wasn't important.'

'Do you know who took the knife?'

Paul looked at Mara as he answered. 'I've already told you I don't, haven't I?'

'I'm giving you another chance. If you really aren't responsible for PC Gill's death, any help you give us will count for you.'

'Oh, sure!' Paul got to his feet and started pacing the narrow cell. 'Why don't you just bugger off and leave me alone? I've nothing more to tell you. And tell the quack to bring me another pill.'

'Is there anything we can do, Paul?' Mara asked.

'You can leave me alone, too. I curse the day I met you and the rest of them. You and your bloody protests and demonstrations. Look where you've got me.'

Mara swallowed, then spoke softly. 'We're still on your side, you know. It wasn't anything to do with me, with any of us, that you got caught. You can come back to the farm whenever you want.'

Paul glared at her, and Banks could sense the questions each wanted to ask and the answers they hoped for. But they couldn't talk because he was there. Mara would implicate herself if she assured Paul she hadn't tipped the police off about the warning, the money and the clothes she'd given him. Paul would incriminate her if he thanked her or questioned her about these things.

'Come on.' Banks took Mara's arm gently. She shook

his hand off but walked beside him back upstairs. 'You've seen that he's all right. No bruises.'

'None that show, no.'

'How did you get here?' Banks asked as they walked out of the station into the glorious day.

'I walked over the moors.'

'I'll give you a lift back.'

'No. I'm happy walking, thanks.'

'No strings. I'm going up there anyway.'

'Why?'

'Just a few questions for Seth.'

'Questions, bloody questions.'

'Come on.'

Mara got into the Cortina beside him. She sat in silence with her hands on her lap as Banks pulled out of the car park and set off up North Market Street for the Swainsdale road. They passed the community centre steps, where Gill had been stabbed. The spot looked as innocent as everywhere else that day; no signs of violence and bloodshed lingered in the grey stone. Banks pushed the tape in and the Deller Consort sang 'It Was a Lover and His Lass'. Mara managed a weak smile at the hey nonny nos, peering curiously at Banks as if she found it hard to connect him with the music he played.

A couple of fishermen sat under the trees in the river meadows, and there were more walkers on the road than Banks had seen since the previous October. Even the wind chimes up at Maggie's Farm seemed to be playing a happier tune despite the misfortune that had befallen the place. But nature is rarely in harmony with human affairs, Banks thought. It follows its predetermined natural cycles, while we fall victim to random irrational forces, thoughts and deeds. It's natural to identify with the rain and clouds when we feel depressed, but if the sun shines brightly and we still feel depressed, we don't bother bringing the weather into it at all.

Banks found Seth in his workshop. Wearing his overalls, he was bent over the bench, planing a long piece of wood. Shavings curled and fell to the floor, releasing the clean scent of pine. Noticing his guest, he paused and put down his plane. Banks leaned against the wall near the dusty bookcase.

'What is it now?' Seth asked. 'I thought you'd got your man.'

'It does look like it. But I'm the kind who likes to tie up loose ends.'

'Unlike your friend.'

'Superintendent Burgess doesn't concern himself over-much with little details,' Banks said. 'But he doesn't have to live up here.'

'How is Paul?'

Banks told him.

'So, what are your loose ends?'

'It's that number in your book.' Banks frowned and scratched the scar by his right eye. 'I've found out what it means.'

'Oh?'

'It was PC Gill's number. PC 1139.'

Seth picked up his plane and began to work slowly at the pine again.

'Why was it written in your notebook?'

'It's quite a coincidence, I'll admit that,' Seth said without looking up. 'But I told you, I haven't got the faintest idea what it meant.'

'Did you write it down?'

'I don't remember doing so. But pick any page of the

book and the odds are I'd hardly have it ingrained deeply in my memory.'

'Did you know PC Gill?'

'I never had the pleasure.'

'Could anyone else have scribbled it down?'

'Of course. I don't lock the place up. But why should they?'

Banks had no idea. 'Why did you tear the page out?'

'I don't know that I did. I don't recall doing so. Look, Chief Inspector—' Seth put his plane aside again and leaned against the bench, facing Banks – 'you're chasing phantoms. Anybody could have jotted that number down, and it could mean anything.'

'Like what?'

'A phone number. They still have four digits around here, you know. Or it could be part of a measurement, a sum of money, almost anything.'

'It's not a phone number,' Banks said. 'Do you think I haven't checked? It is PC Gill's number, though.'

'Coincidence.'

'Possibly. But I'm not convinced.'

'That's your problem.' Seth picked up the plane again and began working more vigorously.

'It could be your problem too, Seth.'

'Is that a threat?'

'No. I leave those to Superintendent Burgess. What I mean is, it would be very convenient if someone else had killed Gill – you, say – and Paul Boyd took the blame. He really doesn't have a leg to stand on, you know.'

'What do you mean?' Seth paused again.

'I mean the odds are that he'll go down for it.'

'Are you saying he's confessed?'

'I'm not free to talk about things like that. I'm just

saying it looks bad, and if you know of anything that might help him you'd better tell me pretty damn quick. Unless it's to your advantage that Boyd gets charged with murder.'

'I don't know anything.' Seth bent over the length of pine and caressed the surface. His voice was tight, and he kept his face averted.

'I can understand it if you're protecting someone,' Banks went on. 'Like Mara tried to protect Paul. But think about what you're doing. By covering for someone else, you almost certainly condemn Paul. Does he mean so little to you?'

Seth slammed down the plane. He turned to face Banks, his face red and eyes bright. The vein by his temple throbbed. 'How can you talk like that?' he said in a shaky voice. 'Of course Paul means a lot to us. He's not been tried yet, you know. It's only you bastards who've convicted him so far. If he didn't do it, then he'll get off, won't he?'

Banks lit a Silk Cut. 'I'm surprised you've got such faith in justice, Seth. I'm afraid I haven't. The way things are these days, he may well be made an example of.'

Seth snorted. 'What would you do? Fix the jury?'

'We wouldn't need to. The jury's made up of ordinary men and women – law-abiding, middle-class citizens for the most part. They'll take one look at Boyd and want to lock him up and throw away the key.'

'He'll manage. And we'll stick by him. We won't let him down.'

'Admirable sentiments. But it might not be enough. Where did you live before you bought this place?'

Surprised, Seth had to think for a moment. 'Hebden Bridge. Why?'

'Where did you get the money from, for the farm?'

'If it's any of your business, I saved some and inherited a little from a dotty aunt. We . . . I also had a small business there, which I sold – a second-hand bookshop.'

'What kind of work did you do?'

'This kind.' Seth gestured around the workshop. 'I was a jack of all trades, showed the true Thatcherite entrepreneurial spirit. I made good money for good work. I still do.'

'Who ran the bookshop then?'

'My wife.' Seth spoke between his teeth and turned back to his wood.

'There was some kind of accident, wasn't there?' Banks said. 'Your wife?' He knew some of the details but wanted to see how Seth reacted.

Seth took a deep breath. 'Yes, there was. But it's still none of your business.'

'What happened?'

'Like you said. I had a wife. There was an accident.'

'What kind?'

'She was hit by a car.'

'I'm sorry.'

Seth turned on him. 'Why? Why the bloody hell should you be sorry? You didn't even know Alison. Just get the fuck out and let me get on with my work. I've nothing more to say to you.'

Banks lingered at the doorway. 'One more thing: Elizabeth Dale. Is that name familiar to you?'

'I know someone called Liz Dale, yes.'

'She's the woman who ran off from the mental hospital and ended up here, isn't she?'

'Why ask if you know already?'

'I wasn't sure, but I thought so. Do you know anything about a complaint she made against PC Gill?'

'No. Why should I?'

'She used his number: 1139.'

'So?'

'Bit of a coincidence, that's all: her complaint, his number in your notebook. Could she have written it?'

'I suppose so. But so could anyone else. I really don't know anything about it.' Seth sounded tired.

'Have you seen her recently? Has she been up here in the past few weeks?'

'No.'

'Do you know where she is?'

'We've lost touch. It happens.'

Seth bent over the pine again and Banks left, avoiding the house by using the side gate. In the car, he contemplated going to the barn to talk to Rick and Zoe. But they could wait. He'd had enough of Maggie's Farm for one day.

TWO

Burgess winked at Glenys, who smiled and blushed. Banks was the only one to notice Cyril's expression darken. They carried their drinks and ploughman's lunches back to the table.

'How's Boyd?' Burgess asked.

'He's all right. I didn't know you cared.'

Burgess spat the remains of a pickled onion into his napkin: 'Bloody awful stuff. Gives me heartburn.'

'I wouldn't be surprised if you're developing an ulcer,' Banks said, 'the way you go at life.'

Burgess grinned. 'You only live once.'

'Are you going to stick around and see what happens?'

'I'll stay a few more days, yes.' He eyed Glenys again. 'I'm not quite finished up here yet.'

'Don't tell me you're getting to like the North?'

'At least the bloody weather's improved, even if the people haven't.'

'Friendliest lot in the country, when you get to know them.'

'Tell me about it.' Burgess shoved in a chunk of Wensleydale and washed it down with Double Diamond.

Banks grimaced. 'No wonder you get heartburn.'

Burgess pushed his plate aside and lit a cigar. 'Tell me honestly, Banks. What do you make of Boyd? Guilty or not?'

'He's obviously involved. Deeply involved. But if you're asking do I think he killed Gill, the answer's no, I don't.'

'You could be right. He certainly stuck to his guns under pressure, and I don't think he's that tough.' Burgess prodded the air with his cigar. 'Personally, I don't give a damn what happens to Boyd. I'd rather see him go down for it than no one at all. But give me some credit. I'm not a bloody idiot, and if I'm not satisfied everything's wrapped up I like to know why. I get nagging feelings like every copper.'

'And you have one about Boyd?'

'A little one.'

'So what are you going to do?'

'Consider the alternatives. You heard what he said last night, about the others going up to the farm on Friday afternoon. That covers just about everyone we've had our eye on since this business started. Who do you reckon?'

Banks sipped some beer to wash down his lunch. 'It depends,' he said. 'Any of the people Boyd mentioned could have got access to the knife, and so could anyone else who went up there a few days before the demo. Nobody had noticed whether it was missing or not – at least nobody admits to noticing. If you're convinced it was a terrorist act, then obviously you're best starting with the most politically active of them: Osmond, Trelawney and the students. On the other hand, if you accept that there could have been some other motive, then you have to rethink the whole thing in more human terms: revenge, hatred, that kind of thing. Or maybe someone was trying to put the blame on the farm people, someone who had a reason to hate them or want them off their land.'

Burgess sighed. 'You make it sound so bloody complicated. Do you really think that's where the answer lies?'

'It's possible, yes.' Banks took a deep breath. 'Gill was a bastard,' he said. 'He liked thumping people, bashing heads. He's volunteered for more crowd control duties than I've had hot dinners. And another thing: Osmond made an official complaint about him for using undue force in another demo a couple of years back. So did a woman called Elizabeth Dale, in a separate incident. And she's got some connection with the farm crowd.'

Burgess drank some more beer and sucked his lips. 'How do you know?' he asked quietly.

Banks had been expecting this. He remembered Burgess's order not to look into Gill's record. 'Anonymous tip,' he said.

Burgess narrowed his eyes and stared as Banks took out a cigarette and lit it.

'I don't know if I believe you,' he said finally.

'It doesn't bloody matter, does it? It's what I'm telling you that counts. Do you want to get to the bottom of this or don't you?'

'Go on.'

'I'm saying we've got two options: terrorism or personal motive. Maybe they're both mixed up as well, I don't know.'

'And where does Boyd come in?'

'Either he did exactly as he told us, or he was an accomplice. So we dig deeper into his political background. Richmond's doing all he can at the computer, checking people Boyd knew in jail and any others he hung about with when the local police were keeping an eye on him. He spent some time in Ireland, which is where he was heading when we caught him, and some of the people he knew had connections with the IRA. We can't prove it, but we're pretty damn sure. We also have to consider the personal motive. Gill was the kind of person to make enemies, and it looks like Osmond was one of them.'

'In the meantime,' Burgess said, 'we hang on to Boyd.'

Banks shook his head. 'I don't think so.'

'Let him go?'

'Yes. Why not?'

'He scarpered last time. What's to stop him doing it again?'

'I think he found out that he'd nowhere to go. If you let him out, he'll go back to the farm and stay there.'

'But why let him out at all?'

'Because it might stir something up. If he's not guilty, there's still a chance he might know who is. He might slip up, set something moving.'

Burgess swirled the beer in his glass. 'So we charge him with tampering with evidence, wasting police time, and let him out. Is that what you're suggesting?'

'For the time being, yes. Have you got a better idea?'

'I'm not convinced,' Burgess said slowly, 'but I'll go

along with it. And,' he added, poking his cigar in Banks's direction, 'on your head be it, mate. If he buggers off again, you'll answer for it.'

'All right.'

'And we'll keep him in another night, just so he gets the message. I'll have another little chat with him, too.'

It was a compromise. Burgess was not the kind of man to give way completely to someone else's idea. It was the best deal he would get, so Banks agreed.

Burgess smiled over at Glenys. Down at the far end of the bar, a glass broke. 'I'll go get us a couple more, shall I?'

'Let me.' Banks stood up quickly. 'It's my round.' It wasn't, but the last thing they needed was a lunch-time punch-up between the landlord of the Queen's Arms and a detective superintendent from Scotland Yard.

'I'll take Osmond again, too,' Burgess said, when Banks got back. 'I don't trust you when that bird of his is around. You go all gooey-eyed.'

Banks ignored him.

'Can I take DC Richmond with me?' Burgess asked.

'What's wrong with Sergeant Hatchley?'

'He's a lazy sod,' Burgess said. 'How he ever made sergeant I don't bloody know. Every time he's been with me he's just sat there like a stuffed elephant.'

'He has his good points,' Banks said, surprised to find himself defending Hatchley. He wondered if the sergeant really had been nurturing a dream of Burgess's inviting him to join some elite Yard squad just because they both believed in the privatization of everything and in an England positively bristling with nuclear missiles. If he had, tough titty.

The difference between them, Banks thought, was that Hatchley just assumed attitudes or inherited them from his parents; he never thought them out. Burgess, on the other hand, really believed that the police existed to hold back the red tide and keep immigrants in their place so that the government could get on with the job of putting the Great back in Britain. He also believed that people like Paul Boyd should be kept off the streets so that decent citizens could rest easy in their beds at night. It never occurred to him for a moment that he might not pass for decent himself.

Banks followed Burgess back to the station and went up to his office. He had a phone call to make.

12

ONE

South of Skipton, the landscape changes dramatically. The limestone dales give way to millstone grit country, rough moorland for the most part, bleaker and wilder than anything in Swainsdale. Even the drystone walls are made of the dark purplish gritstone. The landscape is like the people it breeds: stubborn, guarded, long of memory.

Banks drove through Keighley and Haworth into open country, with Haworth Moor on his right and Oxenhope Moor on his left. Even in the bright sun of that spring-like day, the landscape looked sinister and brooding. Sandra hated it; it was too spooky and barren for her. But Banks found something magical about the area, with its legends of witches, mad Methodist preachers and the tales the Brontë sisters had spun.

Banks slipped a cassette in the stereo and Robert Johnson sang 'Hellbound on My Trail'. West Yorkshire was a long way from the Mississippi delta, but the dark jagged edges of Johnson's guitar seemed to limn the landscape, and his haunted, doom-laden lyrics captured its mood.

Dominated by mill towns at the valley bottoms and weaving communities on the heights, the place is a product of the Industrial Revolution. Majestic old mills with their tall chimneys of dark grainy millstone grit still remain. Many have now been scoured of two hundred years' soot and set up as craft and antiques markets.

Hebden Bridge is a mill town turned tourist trap, full of bookshops and antique shops. Not so long ago, it was a centre of trouser and corduroy manufacturing, but since the 1970s, when the hippies from Leeds and Manchester invaded, it has been more of a place for arts festivals, poetry readings in pubs and other cultural activities.

Banks drove down the steep hill from the moors into the town itself. Rows of tall terraced houses run at angles diagonally along the hillside and overlook the mills at the valley bottom. They look like four-storey houses, but are actually rows of two-storey houses built one on top of the other. You enter the lower house from a street or ginnel at one level, and the upper from a higher one at the back. All of which made it very difficult for Banks to find Reginald Lee's house.

Lee, Banks had discovered from his phone call to PC Brooks of the Hebden Bridge police, was a retired shop owner living in one of the town's two-tiered buildings. Just over three years ago he had been involved in an accident on the town's busy main street – a direct artery along the Calder valley from east to west – which had resulted in the death of Alison, Seth Cotton's wife.

Banks had also discovered from the police that there had been nothing suspicious about her death, and that Mr Lee had not been at fault. But he wanted to know more about Seth Cotton's background, and it seemed that the death of his wife was a good place to start. He was still convinced that the number written so boldly in the old notebook was PC Gill's and not just part of a coincidentally similar calculation. Whether Seth himself had written it down was another matter.

Lee, a small man in a baggy threadbare pullover, answered the door and frowned at Banks. He clearly didn't get many visitors. His thinning grey hair was uncombed, sticking up on end in places as if he'd had an electric shock, and the room he finally showed Banks into was untidy but clean. It was also chilly. Banks kept his jacket on.

'Sorry about the mess,' Lee said in a high-pitched whining voice. 'Wife died two years back and I just can't seem to get the hang of housework.'

'I know what you mean.' Banks moved some newspapers from a hard-backed chair. 'My wife's been away at her mother's for two weeks now and the house feels like it's falling apart. Mind if I smoke?'

'Not at all.' Lee shuffled to the sideboard and brought an ashtray. 'What can I help you with?'

'I'm sorry to bring all this up again,' Banks said. 'I know it must be painful for you, but it's about that accident you were involved in about three years ago.'

Lee's eyes seemed to glaze over at the mention. 'Ah, yes,' he said. 'I blame that for Elsie's death too, you know. She was with me at the time, and she never got over it. I retired early myself. Couldn't seem to . . .' He lost his train of thought and stared at the empty fireplace.

'Mr Lee?'

'What? Oh, sorry, Inspector. It is Inspector, isn't it?'

'It'll do,' Banks said. 'The accident.'

'Ah, yes. What is it you want to know?'

'Just what happened, in as much detail as you can remember.'

'Oh, I can remember it all.' He tapped his forehead. 'It's all engraved there in slow motion. Just let me get my pipe. It seems to help me concentrate. I have a bit of trouble keeping my mind on track these days.' He fetched a briar from a rack by the fireplace, filled it with rubbed twist and put a match to it. The tobacco flamed up and blue smoke curled from the bowl. A child's skipping rhyme drifted in from the street:

> Georgie Porgie, pudding and pie,
> Kiss the girls and make them cry.

'Where was I?'

'The accident.'

'Ah, yes. Well, it happened on a lovely summer's day. The sixteenth of July. One of those days when you can smell the moorland heather and the wild flowers even here in town. Not a cloud in the sky and everyone in that relaxed dozy mood you get in summer. Elsie and I were going for a ride to Hardcastle Crags. We used to do a lot of our courting up there when we were youngsters, like. So whenever the weather was good, off we went. I wasn't doing more than thirty – and I hadn't a drop of drink in me, never touch the stuff – when I came upon this lass riding along on her bicycle on my inside.' He faltered, sucked at his pipe as if it were an oxygen mask, and carried on. 'She was a bit wobbly, but then a lot of cyclists are. I always took special care when there were cyclists around. Then it happened. My front wheels were a foot or two away from her back. She was over by the kerb, like, not directly in front of me, and she just keeled over.'

'Just like that?'

'Aye.' He seemed amazed, even though he must have told the story dozens of times to the police. 'As if she'd hit a jutting stone. But there wasn't one. She might have bounced off the kerb or something. And she fell right in front of the car. I'd no time to stop. Even if I'd only been going five miles an hour I wouldn't have had time. She went right under the wheels. Keeled over, just like that.'

Banks let the silence stretch. Tobacco crackled in the pipe bowl and the repetitive chant continued outside. 'You said she was wobbling a bit,' he asked finally. 'Did she seem drunk or anything?'

'Not especially. Just like she was a learner, maybe.'

'Have you ever come across a policeman by the name of Edwin Gill. PC 1139?'

'Eh? Pardon me. No, the name and number aren't familiar. It was PC Brooks I dealt with at first. Then Inspector Cummings. I don't remember any Gill. Is he from around here?'

'Did you ever meet Seth Cotton?'

'Yes,' Lee said, relighting his pipe. 'I plucked up the courage to go and see him in hospital. He knew all the details and said he didn't blame me. He was very forgiving. Of course he was in a shocking state, still beside himself with grief and anger. But not at me. I only went the once.'

'In hospital? What was he doing there?'

Lee looked surprised. 'I thought you'd have known. He tried to kill himself a couple of days after the hospital phoned him about the accident. Slit his ankles. And they say he smashed the phone to bits. But someone found him before it was too late. Have you seen the lad lately?'

'Yes.'

'And how is he?'

'He seems to be doing all right.' Banks told him about the farm and the carpentry.

'Aye,' Lee said. 'He mentioned he were a carpenter.' He shook his head slowly. 'Terrible state he were in. Bad enough losing the lass, but the baby as well . . .'

'Baby?'

'Aye. Didn't you know? She were pregnant. Five months. The police said she might have fainted like, had a turn because of her condition . . .'

Lee seemed to drift off again, letting his pipe go out. Banks couldn't think of any more questions, so he stood up to leave. Lee noticed and snapped out of his daze.

'Off, are you?' he said. 'Sure you won't stay for a cup of tea?'

'No, thank you, Mr Lee. You've been very helpful. I'm sorry I had to put you through it all again.'

'There's hardly a day goes by when I don't think on it,' Lee said.

'You shouldn't keep torturing yourself that way,' Banks told him. 'Whichever way you look at it, no blame can possibly attach itself to you.'

'Aye, no blame,' Lee repeated. And his piercing inward gaze put Banks in mind of the actor Trevor Howard at his conscience-stricken best. There was nothing more to say. Feeling depressed, Banks walked back out to the street in the chilly spring sunshine. The children paused and stared as he passed by.

It was after five o'clock and the people down in the town were hurrying home from work. All Banks had to look forward to was a tin of ravioli on toast – which he would no doubt burn – and another evening alone.

Looking up the hillside to the west, he thought of Heptonstall, a village at the summit. He'd heard that the pub there served Timothy Taylor's beer, something he'd never tried. It had been a wasted and depressing afternoon as far as information was concerned, so he might as well salvage it somehow.

Alison Cotton's death had obviously been a tragic

accident, and that was all there was to it. She had either
rubbed against the kerb and lost her balance, or she had
fainted, perhaps due to the effects of her pregnancy. Banks
could hardly blame Seth for not wanting to talk about it.

He got in his car and drove up the steep hill to Heptonstall. It was a quiet village at that time of day: narrow
winding terraces of small dark cottages, many with the
telltale rows of upper windows where weavers had once
worked.

He lingered over his food and beer in the window seat
of the Cross Inn, planning what to do next. The Timothy
Taylor's bitter was good, smooth as liquid gold. Shadows
lengthened and the fronts of the gritstone houses over the
narrow street turned even darker.

It was late when he got home – almost ten – and he'd
hardly had time to put his slippers on and sit down before
the phone rang.

'Alan, thank God you're back. I've been trying to call
you all evening.' It was Jenny.

'Why? What's wrong?'

'It's Dennis. His flat has been broken into.'

'Has he reported it?'

'No. He wants to see you.'

'He should report it.'

'I know, but he won't. Will you go and see him? Please?'

'Was he hurt?'

'No, he was out when it happened. It must have been
sometime earlier this evening.'

'Was anything taken?'

'He's not clear about that. Nothing important, I don't
think. Will you see him? Please?'

Banks could hardly refuse. In the first place, Jenny was
clearly distraught on Osmond's behalf, and in the second,

it might have a bearing on the case. If Osmond refused to come to him, then he would have to go to Osmond. Sighing, he said, 'Tell him I'll be right over.'

TWO

'You don't like me very much, do you, Chief Inspector?' said Osmond as soon as Banks had made himself comfortable.

'I'm not bowled over, no.'

Osmond leaned back in his armchair and smiled. 'You're not jealous, are you? Jenny told me how close you two got during that peeping Tom business.'

She did, did she, Banks thought angrily. Just how much had she told him? 'Could you just get on with it, please?' he said. 'I'm here, at Jenny's request, to investigate a break-in you haven't reported officially. The least you can do is stop trying to be so fucking clever.'

The smile disappeared. 'Yes, all right. For what good it'll do me.'

'First off, why didn't you report it?'

'I don't trust the police, certainly not the way I've been treated since the demonstration. Burgess was around here again this afternoon tossing insults and accusations about. And I don't want my apartment done over by a bunch of coppers, either.'

'Why not? What have you got to hide?'

'Nothing to hide, not in the way you mean it. But I value my privacy.'

'So why am I here?'

Osmond crossed his legs and paused before answering. 'Jenny persuaded me.'

'But you don't really want to talk about it?'

'What's the point? What can you do?'

'We could do our job if you'd let us. Check for finger-prints, interview neighbours, try to get a description. Was anything stolen?'

'A book.'

'What?'

'A book. Most of my books were pulled off the shelves, scattered on the floor, and I noticed when I put them back that one was missing.'

'Just one?'

'That's right. Marcuse's *One Dimensional Man*. Do you know it?'

'No.'

Osmond smiled smugly. 'I didn't think you would. It doesn't matter. Anyway, that's all.'

'That's all that was taken?'

'Yes.'

'How did they get in? The lock doesn't seem broken.'

'It's easy enough to open. They probably used a credit card or something. I've had to do that myself more than once.'

'And it works?'

'Yes. Unless the catch is on from the inside. Obviously, as I was out at the time, it wasn't.'

'Then I'd suggest the first thing you do is get a new lock. Preferably a deadlock.'

'I've already called the locksmith. He's coming on Monday.'

'Did you get the impression that they were looking for something? Or was it just vandalism?' Banks had his cigarette packet in his hand without thinking before he realized Osmond was a rabid non-smoker.

'Oh, go on, Chief Inspector.' Osmond allowed himself another superior smile. 'Pollute the atmosphere if you must. You're doing me a favour; it's the least I can do in return.'

'Thanks, I will.' Banks lit up. 'What might they have been looking for? Money?'

'I don't think so. There was a little cash in the dresser drawer, but they left it. There was also some quite valuable jewellery – it used to be my mother's – and they left that too. The only things disturbed were the books and some papers – nothing important – but there was no damage. I don't think it was vandalism.'

'But it was clear they'd seen the money and jewellery?'

'Oh, yes. The drawer was open and the contents of the jewellery box were spilled on the bed.'

'What do you think they were looking for?'

Osmond scratched his cheek and frowned. Noticing Banks's half inch of ash, he fetched an ashtray from the kitchen. 'In case of emergencies,' he said. 'Stolen property, I'm afraid. Courtesy of the Bridge, Helmthorpe.'

Banks smiled. Having got over his initial nervousness that, as with so many people, manifested itself in the form of rudeness, Osmond was making an attempt at least to smoothe the waters. He still wasn't comfortable around the police, but he was trying.

'Would you like a drink?'

'Scotch, if you've got it.' Osmond was prevaricating, making time to think. That meant his answer would be at best a blend of truth and falsehood, and it would be damn difficult for Banks to sort out which was which. But there was no point pushing him. Osmond liked being in control, and any challenge at this point would just make him clam up. Best wait for a gap in his defences and leap right through. Let him take his own sweet time.

Finally, drink in hand, Banks repeated his question.

'I don't want to appear unduly paranoid, Chief Inspector,' Osmond began slowly, 'but I've been involved with the CND and a number of other organizations for some years now, so I think I can speak from experience. I take it you know, of course, that I once made a complaint against the policeman who was killed?'

Banks nodded. 'You'd have saved us a lot of trouble if you hadn't lied in the first place.'

'That's easy for you to say. Anyway, your charming superintendent knew. He wouldn't let it drop. So I assume you know about it, too. Anyway, we come to expect that kind of thing. The CND doesn't take sides, Chief Inspector. Believe it or not, all we want is a nuclear-free world. But some members bring along strong political beliefs too, I won't deny it. I'm a socialist, yes, but that doesn't have anything to do with the CND or its aims.'

He paused and fingered his small gold crucifix. As Banks looked at him slouching on the sofa with his long legs crossed and his arms spread out along the back, the word languid came to mind.

'Have you noticed how things seem to come in packages?' Osmond went on. 'If you're anti-nuclear, people also expect you to be pro-choice, pro-union, pro-gays, anti-American, anti-apartheid and generally left wing. Most people don't realize that it's perfectly possible to be, say anti-nuclear and anti-apartheid without being pro-gay and pro-choice – especially if you're a Catholic. Oh, the permutations might differ a bit – some packages are more extreme and dangerous than others, for example – but you can pretty well predict the kind of things our members value. The point is that what we stand for is politically hot, and that draws attention to us from all sides. The government thinks we're in league with the Russians, so they raid our offices periodically and go over our files. The communists think we're allies in overthrowing a decadent capitalist government, so they woo us and infiltrate us with their own. It's a bloody mess, but we manage, through it all, to stick to our aims.'

'Are you saying you think the break-in was politically motivated?'

'That's about it.' Osmond lifted the Scotch bottle and raised his eyebrows. Banks held out his glass. 'And the theft of the book was a sort of calling card, or warning. So do you see what I mean about not expecting much help from the police? If Special Branch or MI5 or whoever are involved, you'd get your wrists slapped, and if it's the other side, you'd never catch them anyway.'

'But what were they looking for?'

'I don't know. Anyway, I don't keep my files here. Most of the important ones are at the CND office, and some of the stuff is at work.'

'The Social Services Centre?'

'Yes. I've got an office there. It's convenient.'

'So they didn't find what they were looking for because they didn't look in the right place.'

'I suppose so. The only current thing is the inquiry I'm making into the demo. I've already told you about that – and Superintendent Burgess, too. I've talked to quite a lot of people involved, trying to establish exactly what happened and how it could have been avoided. Tim and Abha are helping, too. They've got most of the info at their place. We're having a meeting up at the farm tomorrow to decide what to do about it all. Ever since your boss was taken off the job, we've been carrying on for him, and our results will be a hell of a lot less biased.'

'You're wrong,' Banks said, lighting another cigarette. 'The trouble with people like you, despite all your talk about packages, is that you tar everyone with the same brush. To you, all police are pigs. Superintendent Gristhorpe would have done a good job. He wouldn't have swept it all under the carpet.'

'Maybe that's why he was taken off,' Osmond said. 'I read in the paper that they were going to appoint an impartial investigating commission which, I suppose, means a bunch of high-ranking policemen from somewhere other than Eastvale, but most of us think they're just going to forget about the whole embarrassing affair. Once the killer is convicted – and it looks like you're well on your way to doing that – the anti-nuke lefties will be shown up for exactly what you all think we are – a gang of murderous anarchists – and the police will gain a lot of very useful public sympathy.'

Banks put his empty glass down and walked over to the window. 'Tell me about Ellen Ventner.'

Osmond paled. 'You certainly do your homework, don't you?'

'Ellen Ventner.'

'If you think I'm going to admit to those ludicrous charges against me, you must be crazy.'

'Much as it saddens me to say so, I'm not here to investigate those old charges. So you like to beat up women. That's your privilege.'

'You bastard. Are you going to tell Jenny?'

'I honestly don't know. Ellen Ventner didn't pursue the charges. God knows why, but a lot of women don't. Maybe she thought you were still a really sweet fellow underneath it all. But that doesn't alter what happened. You might think you're a very important man in the political scheme of things, but personally I doubt it. On the other hand, a woman you once assaulted might bear a grudge.'

'After four years?'

'It's possible.'

'Forget it. She wouldn't. Besides, she emigrated not long after we split up.'

'I can understand why she might have wanted to get as far away from you as possible. Just checking all the angles.'

Osmond glared, then looked into his glass and started to fiddle with his crucifix again. 'Look, it was only the once . . . She . . . I was drunk. I didn't mean to . . .'

Banks sat down opposite him again and leaned forward. 'When you made your complaint about PC Gill,' he asked, 'how did you do it?'

Osmond floundered. It was so easy, Banks thought. Stir up a man's emotions, then change the subject and you're in control again. He'd had enough of Osmond's lectures and his arrogance.

'What do you mean, how did I do it? I wrote a letter.'

'How did you refer to him?'

'By his number. How else?'

'1139?'

'Yes, that's it.'

'You still remember it?'

'Obviously.'

'So how did you know his name?'

'Look, I don't—'

'When I first asked you if you knew Gill, you said no. I didn't use his number, I used his name, and you recognized it when you lied to me.'

'He told me,' Osmond said. 'When I tried to stop him from hitting a woman at a demo once, he pulled me aside and told me to keep out of it. I told him I'd report him, and he said go ahead. When I looked at his number, he told me his name as well. Spelled it out in fact. The bastard was proud of what he was doing.'

So Osmond defended women in public and only hit them in private. Nice guy, Banks thought, but he kept his questions factual and direct. 'When you were up at Maggie's Farm on the afternoon of the demonstration, did you mention that number to anyone?'

'I don't know. I can't remember.'

'Think. Did you write it in a notebook, or see it written in a notebook?'

'No, I'd remember something like that. But I might have mentioned it. Really, I can't say.'

'How might you have mentioned it? Just give me a sense of context.'

'I might have said, "I wonder if that bastard PC 1139 will be out tonight." I suppose I'd have warned people about him. Christ, you can't be involved in demos around this part of the world and not know about PC bloody 1139.'

'So I gather.' Banks remembered what Tim and Abha had told him.

There was nothing more to ask. Banks said goodnight and Osmond slammed the door behind him. In the corridor, he decided to try the flats on that floor to see if anyone had noticed the housebreaker. There were only ten – five on each side.

At the third door, a man who had been nipping out to the off-licence at about a quarter to eight said he'd seen two men walking along the corridor on his way back. They had seen him too, but had made no move to run off or turn away. The description was average – most people are about as observant as a brick wall, Banks had discovered over the years – but it helped.

They were both tall and burly, and they both wore dark blue trousers, a bit shiny, probably the bottom part of a suit; one had on a black overcoat, fake leather, while the other wore a light trench coat; one had black hair, the other none at all and neither wore a hat or glasses. About facial features, the man remembered nothing except that both men had two eyes, a nose, a mouth, and two ears. They had walked confidently and purposefully, as if they knew where they were going and what they were about, not furtively, as he imagined criminals would have done. So, no, he hadn't seen any need to call the police. He was sorry now, of course. His speech was slurred, as if he'd already drunk most of what he'd bought at the off-licence. Banks thanked him and left.

Over the next four doors, Banks found himself told to piss off by a writer whose concentration he had disturbed and asked in for a cup of tea by a lonely military type who wanted to show off his medals. As yet, there had been no temptress in a negligee.

It wasn't until the ninth door that he found anyone else who knew anything. Beth Cameron wore tight checked slacks, which hardly flattered her plump hips and thighs, and a maroon cardigan over a shiny white blouse. Her curly brown hair showed traces of a recent perm, and she had the most animated face that Banks had ever seen. Every comment, every word, was accompanied by a curled lip, a raised eyebrow, a wrinkled nose, a deep frown or a mock pout. She was like one of those sponge hand-puppets he remembered from his childhood. When you put your hand inside it, you could wrench the face into the most remarkable contortions.

'Did you see anyone coming in or out of Mr Osmond's flat this evening?' Banks asked.

'No, no, I can't say I did. Wait a minute though, I did notice *something* odd. Not up here but down in the garage. It struck me as bit strange at the time, you know, but I just brushed it off. You do, don't you?'

'What did you see?'

'A blue Escort. And it was parked in Mr Handley's spot. He's often out during the evening – he's the entertainment reporter for the Eastvale *Gazette* – but still, I thought, that's no reason to steal the man's parking spot, is it? See, there's places for visitors outside. We don't encourage non-residents to park underground. It could lead to all sorts of trouble, couldn't it?'

'What time was this?' Banks asked.

'Oh, about eight o'clock. I was just bringing Lesley – that's my daughter – back from her piano lesson.'

'Did you see if there was anyone in the car?'

'Two men, I think. Sitting in the front.'

'Did you get a good look at them?'

'No, I'm sorry. They looked big, but I mean you just don't look at people, do you? Especially not in places like that. It doesn't do to make eye contact with strangers in an underground garage, does it?'

'No,' Banks said, 'I don't suppose it does. You didn't recognize either of the men, then?'

'No. Whatever happened, anyway?' Mrs Cameron suddenly frowned. 'There wasn't nobody assaulted, was there? I've been saying all along that place is too dark. Just asking for trouble it is.'

'Nobody was hurt,' Banks assured her. 'I'm just interested in that Escort. Have you noticed it before?'

'No, never. I did think of calling the police, you know. It did cross my mind they might be up to no good. But you don't want to cause a fuss, do you? It might all be perfectly innocent and there you'd be with egg on your face looking a proper fool. But I'd never forgive myself if someone got hurt.'

'Don't worry, it's nothing like that. You didn't get the number, by any chance?'

'No.' She laughed, then put her hand to her mouth. Her fingernails were painted pale green. 'I'm sorry, Mr Banks, but I always think it's so funny when the police go asking people that on telly. I mean, you don't go around collecting car numbers, do you? I don't think I even know my own.'

'Is there anything else you can think of?' Banks asked, without much hope.

Beth Cameron chewed her lower lip and frowned for a moment, then shook her head. 'No. Not a sausage. I didn't pay it much mind, really. They weren't doing nothing. Just sitting there like they were waiting to leave . . . Wait a minute!' Her eyebrows shot up almost to her hairline. 'I think one of them was bald. There was a light on the pillar by the car, you see. Dim as can be, but I could swear I saw a bald head reflecting the light.' Then her lips curved down at the edges. 'I don't suppose that's much help, though, is it?'

'Everything helps.' Banks closed his notebook and put it back into his inside pocket. At least he was certain now that the two men in the blue Escort were the same two who had been seen in the corridor near Osmond's flat. 'If you see the car again,' he said, handing her a card, 'would you please let me know?'

'Yes, of course I will, Mr Banks,' she said. 'Glad to be of use. Goodnight.'

At the last door Banks turned up nothing new. It had been a long time since he'd made door-to-door inquiries himself, and he had enjoyed it, but now it was going on for half past eleven and he was tired. Outside, the crisp cold air woke him up a bit. He stood by his car for a few moments and smoked a cigarette, thinking over what had happened that evening.

However much he had ridiculed the man's pretensions, he had to admit that Osmond was the type who made waves politically. Banks had a lot of sympathy for the CND and its goals, but he knew that, like so many peace-loving, well-meaning groups, it sometimes acted as a magnet for dangerous opportunists. Where there was organization there was politics, and where there was politics there was the aphrodisiac of power. Maybe Osmond *had* been involved in a plot to do with the demonstration. Perhaps his masters didn't trust him to keep his trap shut, and what had happened this evening had been intended as a kind of warning.

Banks found it hard to swallow all the cloak-and-dagger stuff, but the mere possibility of it was enough to send a shiver of apprehension up his spine. If there really was anything in the conspiracy theory, then it looked like these people – Russian spies, agents provocateurs, or whoever they were – meant business.

If that was true, Osmond might get hurt. That didn't concern Banks very much, but it did cause him to worry about Jenny. It was bad enough her being involved with a man who had beaten up a previous girlfriend, but much worse now there was a strong possibility that some very dangerous and cold-blooded people were after him too. None of it concerned Jenny directly, of course; she was merely an innocent bystander. But since when did governments or terrorists ever give a damn about innocent bystanders?

13

ONE

Maybe it was the spring weather, but the toasted teacakes in the Golden Grill tasted exceptionally good to Banks on Sunday morning. Burgess chose a doughnut filled with raspberry jam and dusted with icing sugar, which he dipped into his coffee. 'A taste I developed in America,' he explained, as Banks watched, horrified. 'They've got a place there called Dunkin' Donuts. Great.'

'What's happening with Boyd?' Banks asked.

'I had another chat with him. Got nowhere. Like you said, I let him go this morning, so we'll see what turns up now.'

'What did you do? Torture him again?'

'Well, there's not many can keep on lying when faced with their greatest fear. The way things stand now, I think we could get a conviction on Boyd, no problem, but we'd probably get chucked out of court if we tried to fit one of the others up – Osmond, for example. I say if we turn up nothing more in a couple of days, let's just charge Boyd with murder and I'll bugger off back to the Smoke a happy man.'

'What about the truth?'

Burgess treated Banks to a slit-eyed glance. 'We don't know Boyd didn't do it, do we? The Burgess Test notwithstanding. It's not infallible, you know. Anyway, I'm getting a bit sick of your moralizing about the truth all the bloody time. The truth's relative. It depends on your perspective. Remember, we're not judge and jury. It's up to them to decide who's guilty and who's not. We just present the evidence.'

'Fair enough, but it's up to us to make a charge that sticks, if only to stop us looking like prize berks in court.'

'I think we're solid on Boyd if we need to be. Like I say, give it a couple of days. Find anything interesting on the funny-farm lot?'

'No.'

'Those students puzzled me. They're only bloody kids – cheeky bastards, mind you – but their little minds are crammed full of Marx, Trotsky, Marcuse and the rest. They even have a poster of Che Guevara on the wall. I ask you – Che fucking Guevara, a vicious, murdering, mercenary thug got up to look like Jesus Christ. I can't understand what they're on about half the time, honest I can't. And I don't think they've got a clue, either. Pretty gutless pair, though. I can't see either of them having the bottle to stick a knife between Gill's ribs. Still, the girl's not bad. Bit chubby around the waist but a lovely set of knockers.'

'Osmond's place was broken into yesterday evening,' Banks said.

'Oh?'

'He didn't report it officially.'

'He should have done. You talked to him?'

'Yes.'

'Then you should have made a report. You know the rules.' He grinned. 'Unless, of course, you think rules are only for people like me to follow and for Jack the Lads like you to ignore?'

'Listen,' Banks said, leaning forward. 'I don't like your methods. I don't like violence. I'll use it if I have to, but there are plenty more subtle and effective ways of getting answers from people.' He sat back and reached for a cigarette. 'That aside, I never said I was any less ruthless than you are.'

Burgess laughed and spluttered over a mouthful of recently dunked doughnut.

'Anyway,' Banks went on, 'Osmond didn't seem to give a damn. Well, maybe that's too strong. At least, he didn't think we would do anything about it.'

'He's probably right. What *did* you do?'

'Told him to change his lock. Nothing was stolen.'

'Nothing.'

'Only a book. They'd searched the place, but apparently they didn't find what they were looking for.'

'What was that?'

'Osmond thinks they might have been after some papers, files to do with his CND stuff. He's got a touch of the cloak-and-dagger about him. Anyway, he keeps most of his files at the local office, and Tim and Abha have all the stuff on the demo. It seems they're having a meeting up at the farm this afternoon to plan their complaint strategy. It looks like the thieves wasted their time, whoever they were.'

'Who does he think it was? KGB? MI5? CIA?'

Banks laughed. 'Something along those lines, yes. Thinks he's a very important fellow does Mr Osmond.'

'He's a pain in the ass,' Burgess said, getting up. 'But I'll trip the bastard up before I'm done. Right now I'm off to catch up on some paperwork. They want everything in bloody quadruplicate down at the Yard.'

Banks sat over the rest of his coffee wondering why so

many people came back from America, where Burgess had been to a conference a few years ago, full of strange eating habits and odd turns of phrase – 'pain in the ass' indeed!

Outside on Market Street tourists browsed outside shop windows full of polished antiques and knitted woollen wear. The bell of the Golden Grill jangled as people dropped in for a quick cup of tea.

Banks had arranged to meet Jenny for lunch in the Queen's Arms at one o'clock, which left him well over an hour to kill. He finished his drink and nipped over to the station. First, he had to enlist Richmond's aid on a very delicate matter.

TWO

Mara was busy making scones for the afternoon meeting when Paul walked into the kitchen. Her hands were covered with flour and she waved them about to show she'd embrace him if she could. Seth immediately threw his arms around Paul and hugged him. Mara could see his face over Paul's shoulder and noticed tears in his eyes. Rick slapped Paul on the back and Zoe kissed his cheek. 'I did the cards,' she told him. 'I knew you were innocent and they'd have to let you go.' Even Julian and Luna, caught up in the adults' excitement, did a little dance around him and chanted his name.

'Sit down,' Seth said. 'Tell us about it.'

'Hey! Let me finish this first.' Mara gestured at the half made scones. 'It won't take a minute. And it was your idea in the first place.'

'I tell you what,' Paul said. 'I could do with a cup of tea. That prison stuff's piss-awful.'

'I'll make it.' Seth reached for the kettle. 'Then we'll go in the front room.'

Mara carried on with the scones, readying them for the oven, and Seth put the kettle on. The others all wandered into the front room except for Paul, who stood nervously behind Mara.

'I'm sorry,' he said. 'You know . . .'

She turned and smiled at him. 'Forget it. I'm just glad you're back. I should never had doubted you in the first place.'

'I was a bit . . . well, I did lie. Thanks for tipping me off, anyway. At least I had a chance.'

The kettle started boiling, and Seth hurried back in to make tea. Mara put the tray of scones in the oven and washed her hands.

'Right,' she said, drying them on her apron. 'I'm ready.'

They sat down in the living room and Seth poured tea.

'Come on then,' he urged Paul.

'Come on what?'

'Tell us what happened.'

'Where do you want me to start?'

'Where did you go?'

Paul lit a Players and spat a strand of loose tobacco from his upper lip. 'Edinburgh,' he said. 'Went to see an old mate, didn't I?'

'Did he help you?' Mara asked.

Paul snorted. 'Did he fuck. Bastard's changed a lot. I found the building easy enough. It used to be one of those grotty old tenements, but it's all be tarted up now. Potted plants in the stairwell and all that. Anyway, Ray answers the door and he doesn't recognize me at first – at least he pretends he doesn't. I hardly knew him, either. Wearing a bloody suit, he was. We say hello and then this bird comes out – hair piled up on top of her head and a black dress slit right down the front to her belly button. She's carrying one of those long-stemmed wineglasses full of white wine, just for the effect. "Who's this, Raymond?" she says, right la-di-da like, and I head for the stairs.'

'You didn't stay?' Mara said.

'Are you joking?'

'Do you mean your old friend wouldn't let you in?'

'Gone up in the world has old Raymond. Seems he was entertaining the boss and the wife – he's in computers – and he didn't want any reminders of his past. Used to be a real wild boy, but . . . Anyway, I left. Oh, I reckon he might have let me in if I'd pushed hard enough, stuck me in the cupboard or somewhere out of the way. But I wasn't having any.'

'So where did you go?' Seth asked.

'Just walked around for a while till I found a pub.'

'You didn't walk the streets all night, did you?' Mara asked.

'Like hell. It was colder than a witch's tit up there. This is bloody Scotland we're talking about. First thing the next morning I bought myself a duffel coat just to keep from freezing to death.'

'What did you do then, after you left the pub?'

'I met this bloke there,' Paul said, reddening. 'He said I could go back to his place with him. Look, I know what you're thinking. I'm not a fucking queer. But when you're on the streets, just trying to survive, you do what you have to, right? He was a nice enough bloke, anyway, and he didn't ask no awkward questions. Careful, he was, too, if you know what I mean.

'Next day I was going to head for Glasgow and look up another old mate, but I thought fuck that for a lark, best thing to do is get straight to Ireland. I've got mates there, and I don't think they've changed. If I'd got to Belfast *nobody* would have found me.'

'So what went wrong?' Seth asked.

Paul laughed harshly. 'Bloody ferry dock. I goes up to this shop bloke to buy some fags and when I walk away he shouts after me. I can't understand a bleeding word he's saying on account of the Jock accent like, but this copper sees us and gives me the look. I get nervous and take off and the bastards catch me.'

'Did the shopkeeper recognize you?' Mara asked. 'Your picture was in the papers, you know.'

'Nah. I'd just given him too much bloody money, that's all. He was shouting he wanted to give me my fucking change.' Paul laughed and the others laughed with him. 'It wasn't so funny at the time,' he added.

'What did the police do?' asked Rick.

'They've charged me with being an accessory. I'll have to go to court.'

'Then what?' Mara asked.

Paul shrugged. 'With my record I'll probably end up doing porridge again. That copper with the scar seems to think I might get off if they get a sympathetic jury. I mean, sometimes you respect people for standing by their mates, right? He says he might be able to get the charge reduced to giving false information and wasting police time. I'd only get six months max, then. But the other bloke tells me I'm looking at ten years. Who do you believe?'

'If you're lucky,' Mara said, 'Burgess might be gone by then and Banks'll take it easy on you.'

'What's wrong with him? He soft or something?'

Seth shook his head. 'Somehow I don't think so, no. He just has a different technique.'

'They're all bastards when you get right down to it,' Rick added.

Paul agreed. 'So what's been happening here?' he asked.

Seth filled him on the police visits. 'Apart from that, not much, really. We've all been worrying about you most of the time.' He ruffled Paul's hair. 'Glad you're back, kid. Nice new haircut, too.'

Paul blushed. 'Fuck off. Anyway, nothing's changed, has it?'

'What do you mean?' Mara asked.

'Well, they still don't have their killer and they're not going to stop till they do. And if they don't get someone else, I'm still their best bet. That Burgess bastard made that quite clear.'

'Don't worry about it,' Seth said. 'We won't let them blame it on you.'

Paul looked at his watch. 'Nearly opening time,' he said. 'I could do with a pint and some nosh.'

'We'll have to eat at the pub today, anyway,' Mara said. 'I've not made any dinner. What with that meeting and all . . .'

'What meeting?' Paul asked.

'We're getting together to talk about the demo this afternoon,' Rick said. 'Dennis is bringing Tim and Abha up about three. We want to look over statements and stuff to prove police brutality.'

'Well, you can count me out,' Paul said. 'I've had enough of that bleeding demo, and those fucking do-gooders. Sod 'em all.'

'You don't have to stick around,' Mara told him. 'Not if you don't want.'

'I think I'll go for a walk,' Paul said, calming down.

'Being cooped up in that cell hasn't done my head much good.'

'And I've got work to do,' Seth said. 'I've got to finish that bureau today. It's already overdue.'

'What's this?' Rick said. 'Is everybody copping out on us?'

'I'll put my twopenn'orth in first, don't worry,' Seth said. 'Then I'll get some work done. As for now, I think Paul's right. They do a nice Sunday lunch at the Black Sheep and I'm starving.'

Seth put his arm around Paul. The others stood up and went for their coats. In the fresh spring air, the seven of them walked down the track to Relton, happy together for the last time.

Except for Mara. The others might realize it too, she thought, but nobody's saying anything. If Paul isn't guilty, then someone else here is.

THREE

Jenny was already waiting when Banks came into the Queen's Arms at lunch time. Hungry, he arranged with Cyril for a few slices of roast leg of lamb. Glenys wasn't around, and Cyril, though he said nothing, seemed distracted.

'So,' Jenny said, resting her elbows on the table and cupping her chin in her hands, 'what's new? Dennis told me you dropped by. Thanks for going.'

'*He* didn't thank me.'

Jenny smiled. 'Well, he wouldn't, would he?'

'You didn't tell me it was you who persuaded him to talk to me in the first place.'

The lines around her eyes crinkled. 'Didn't I? Sorry. But did you find anything out?'

'Not really.'

'What does that mean?'

'It means no, I suppose. Have you ever noticed a blue Escort with two burly men in it hanging around Osmond's place?'

'No. Haven't you got *any* ideas, Alan?'

'Maybe one. It seems a bit far-fetched, but if I'm right . . .'

'Right about what?'

'Just an idea, that's all.'

'Can you tell me?'

'I'd rather not. Best wait and see. Richmond's working on it.'

'When will you know?'

'Tomorrow, I hope.'

The food arrived. 'I'm starving,' Jenny said, and the two ate in silence.

When he'd finished, Banks bought another round of drinks and lit a cigarette. Then he explained his doubts about Paul Boyd's guilt.

'Are you any closer to catching the real killer?' Jenny asked.

'It doesn't look like it. Boyd's still the closest we've got.'

'I can't believe that Dennis is a murderer, you know.'

'Are you speaking as a psychologist?'

'No. As a woman.'

'I think I'd trust that opinion more if it came from a professional.'

Jenny arched her eyebrows. 'What do you mean by that?'

'Don't bristle, it doesn't suit you. I mean that people – men and women – tend to be very protective about whoever they get involved with. It's only natural – you know that as well as I do. And not only that, but they deliberately blinker themselves sometimes, even lie. Look what Boyd did. If he really is innocent of murder, then he sure as hell risked a lot. And think about how Mara behaved. Whichever way you look at it now, it comes down to Seth, Rick or Zoe – with Mara, Tim and Abha, *and* your Dennis running close behind.'

'All right. As a professional, I don't think Dennis did it.'

'Just how much do you know about him?'

'What do you mean?'

'Never mind.'

'What? Come on. Out with it. If there's something I should know, tell me.'

Banks took a deep breath. 'Would you say Osmond is the kind of person to hit women?'

'What?'

Haltingly, Banks told her about Ellen Ventner. The more he said, the paler she became. Even as he told her, Banks wasn't sure of his motives. Was he doing it because he was worried about her association with Osmond, or was it out of pure vindictive jealousy?

'I don't believe it,' she whispered.

'Believe it. It's true.'

'Why are you telling me this?'

'I didn't want to tell you. You pushed me into it.'

'It was you who made me push you. You must have known how bloody humiliated it would make me feel.'

Banks shrugged. He could feel her starting to turn her anger against him. 'I'm sorry, that's not what I intended. He could be dangerous, Jenny. And I don't know about

274

you, but I have problems understanding a person who rescues defenceless women from police brutality in public and beats them up in private.'

'You said it only happened once. There's no need to go making him into a monster. What do you expect me to do? Chuck him over just because he made a mistake?'

'I expect you to be careful, that's all. Osmond hit a woman once, put her in hospital, and he's also a suspect in a murder investigation. In addition, he seems to think the CIA, the KGB and MI5 are all after him. I'd say that merits a little caution, wouldn't you?'

Jenny's eyes glittered. 'You've never liked Dennis right from the start, have you? You've never even given him a chance. And now as soon as you find a bit of dirt on him, you sling it at me. Just what the bloody hell do you hope to achieve, Alan? You're not my keeper. I can take care of myself. I don't need a big brother to look out for me.'

She picked up her coat and swept out of the pub, knocking over her glass as she went. Faces turned to stare and Banks felt himself flush. Good one, Alan, he said to himself, you handled that really well.

He followed her outside, but she was nowhere in sight. Cursing, he went back to his office and tried to occupy his mind with work.

After a couple of false starts, he finally got through to Rick's wife's sister at her home in Camden Town. She sounded cagey and Banks first had to assure her that his call had nothing at all to do with the custody battle. Even then, she didn't sound as if she believed him.

'I just needed some information about Rick's wife, that's all,' he said. 'Were you always good friends?'

'Yes,' the sister answered. 'Our ages are close, so we always supported one another, even after she married

Rick. I don't want you to think I've anything against him, by the way. He's selfish and egotistical, but then most men are. Artists even more so. And I'm sure he's a good father. Pam certainly wasn't capable of taking care of Julian when they split up.'

'And now?'

'She's getting there. It's a long road though, alcoholism.'

'Did Pam ever have any connections up north?'

'Up north? Good Lord, no. I don't think she's ever been further north than Hendon.'

'Not even for a visit?'

'No. What's there to visit, anyway? It's all canals and slag heaps, isn't it?'

'So she's spent most of her life in either London or Cornwall?'

'Yes. They had a few months in France some years ago. Most painters seem to gravitate towards France at one time or another. But that's all.'

'Have you ever heard her mention a policeman called Gill – PC Edwin Gill, number 1139?'

'I've never heard her mention any policemen. No, I tell a lie. She said the local pub in Cornwall stayed open till all hours when the bobby was there. But I don't think that'd be your PC Gill.'

'No,' Banks said, 'it wouldn't. Did she ever attend political demonstrations – Greenham Common, the Aldermaston march, that kind of thing?'

'Pam's never been very political. Wisely so, if you ask me. What's the point? You can't trust one lot more than the other. Is that all, Chief Inspector?'

'Is she there? Can I talk to her?'

There was a short pause and Banks heard muffled sounds from the other end of the line. Finally, he could hear the phone changing hands and another voice came on, husky and weary as if doped or ill.

'Yes?'

Banks asked her the same questions he'd asked her sister, and the answers were the same. She spoke hesitantly, with long pauses between each sentence.

'Are the police involved in this custody battle?' Banks asked.

'Uh, no,' she answered. 'Just . . . you know . . . lawyers.'

Naturally, Banks thought. 'And you've never heard of PC Gill?'

'Never.'

'Has your sister visited Yorkshire recently?' Banks asked the question as soon as it came to him. After all, the sister might have got herself involved somehow.

'No. Here . . . looking after me. Can I go now? I've got to . . . I don't know anything.'

'Yes,' Banks said. 'That's all. Thanks for your time.'

He hung up and made notes on the conversation while it was fresh in his mind. The one thing that struck him as odd was that neither of the women had asked about Julian, about how he was. Why, he wondered, did Rick's wife want custody if she didn't even care that much about the child? Spite? Revenge? Julian would probably be better off where he was.

Next he called the Hebden Bridge police and asked for PC Brooks.

'Sorry to bother you again, Constable,' he said. 'I should probably have asked you all this before, but there's been rather too much going on here. Can you tell me anything about Alison Cotton, the woman who was killed in the car accident?'

'I remember her all right, sir,' Brooks said. 'It was my first accident and I . . . well . . . I er . . .'

'I know what you mean. It happens to us all. Did you know her before the accident?'

'Oh, aye. She'd been here a few years like, ever since the arty types discovered us, you might say.'

'And Alison was arty?'

'Aye. Helped organize the festival, poetry readings, that kind of thing. She ran the bookshop. I suppose you already know that.'

'What kind of a person was she?'

'She were a right spirited lass. Proper bonny, too. She wrote things. You know, poems, stories, stuff like that. I tried reading some in the local paper but I couldn't make head nor tail of it. Give me *Miami Vice* or *Dynasty* any day.'

'Was she ever involved in political matters – marches, demos, things like that?'

'Well,' PC Brooks said, 'we never had many things like that here. A few, but nowt much. Mostly "Save the Whales" and "Ban the Bomb". I don't know as she was involved though she did sometimes write bits for the paper about not killing animals for their fur and not making laboratory mice smoke five hundred fags a day. And about them women outside that missile base.'

'Greenham Common?'

'That's the one. When it comes down to it, I dare say she was like the rest, though. If some bandwagon came along, they jumped on it.'

'Ever heard of a PC Gill, 1139, from Scarborough?'

'Only what I've read in the papers, sir. I hope you catch the bastard who did it.'

'So do I. What about a friend of Cotton's called Elizabeth Dale? Heard of her?'

'Oh, aye. Liz Dale hung around with the Cotton crowd all right. Thick as thieves. I felt sorry for her, myself. I mean it's like a sickness, isn't it, when you get so you need something all the time.'

'Was she a registered addict?'

'Aye. She never really gave us any trouble. We just like to keep an eye on them, that's all, make sure they're not selling off half their prescriptions.'

'What kind of person is she?'

'Moody,' Brooks said. 'She got off drugs, but she were never really right afterwards. One day she'd be up, the next down. Right bloody yo-yo. But there was a lass with strong political opinions.'

'Liz Dale was political?'

'Aye. For a while, at least. Till she got it out of her system. Like I said, bandwagon.'

'But she was keener than the rest?'

'I'd say so, yes. Now Seth, he was never much more than partly interested. Rather be slicing up a piece of wood. And Alison, like I said, well, she had a lot of energy and she had to put it somewhere, but she was more your private artistic type. But Liz Dale, she was up to her neck in everything at one time.'

'Were Liz Dale and Alison Cotton especially close?'

'Like sisters.'

Banks thought of the complaint Dale had made against PC Gill. From that, he already knew she had attended at least one demonstration and come across him. Perhaps there had been others, too. Alison Cotton could have been with her. Perhaps this was the link he was looking for. But so what? Alison was dead; Reginald Lee had run her over by accident. It still didn't add up, unless everyone was lying and Liz Dale *had* been at Maggie's Farm and at the

Eastvale demonstration. Banks didn't know her, but if she did have a history of drug abuse, there was a chance she might be unbalanced.

'Thanks a lot,' Banks said. 'You've been a great help.'

'I have? Oh well—'

'Just one more thing. Do you know where Liz Dale lives?'

'Sorry, I can't help you there, sir. She's been away from here a few years now. I've no idea at all.'

'Never mind. Thanks anyway.'

Banks broke the connection and walked over to the window. At the far side of the square, just outside the National Westminster bank, a rusty blue Mini had slammed into the back of a BMW, and the two drivers were arguing. Automatically, Banks phoned downstairs and asked Sergeant Rowe to send someone over. Then he lit a cigarette and started thinking.

He certainly needed to know more about Liz Dale. If he could prove that she had been in the area at the time of the demo, then he had someone else with a motive for wanting to harm Gill. The Dale woman could easily have visited the farm one day earlier that week and taken the knife – Mara said that no one paid it any mind as a rule. If nobody had seen her, perhaps she had walked in and taken it while everyone was out. But was she at the demo? And why use Seth's knife? Did she have some reason other than revenge for wanting Gill dead? Obviously the best way to get the answer to that was to find Dale herself. Surely that couldn't prove too difficult.

As PC Craig approached the two drivers in the market square, Banks walked over to his filing cabinet.

FOUR

Mara stood inside the porch with Rick and Zoe and waved goodbye to Dennis Osmond and the others as they drove off. The sky was darkening in the west, and that early evening glow she loved so much held the dale in its spell, spreading a blanket of silence over the landscape. Flocks of birds crossed the sky and lights flicked on in cottages down in Relton and over the valley in Lyndgarth.

'What do you think?' she asked Rick, as they went back inside. The evening was cool. She hugged herself, then pulled on a sweater and sat in the rocking chair.

Rick's knees cracked as he knelt at the grate to start the fire. 'I think it'll work,' he said. 'We're bound to get the newspapers interested, maybe even TV. The police might try and discredit us, but people will get the message.'

Mara rolled a cigarette. 'I'll be glad when it's all over,' she said. 'The whole business seems to have brought us nothing but trouble.'

'Look on the bright side,' Rick said, turning to look at her. 'It's a blow against the police and their heavy-handed tactics. Even that woman from the Church for Peace group has started calling them pigs.'

'Still,' Mara said firmly, 'it would have been better for all of us if none of it had ever happened.'

'Everything's all right now,' Zoe said. 'Paul's back, we're all together again.'

'I know, but . . .'

Mara couldn't help feeling uneasy. True, Paul's return had cheered them up no end, especially Seth, who had been moping around with a long face the whole time he'd been away. But it wasn't the end. The police weren't going to rest until they'd arrested someone for the murder, and they had their eyes on the farm. Paul might still end up in jail as an accessory, a serious charge, Mara now realized. She wondered if Banks was going to charge her, too. He wasn't stupid; he must know she had warned Paul about Crocker finding the knife. Everything felt fragile. There was a chance she might lose it all, all the peace of mind and stability she had sought for so long. And the children, too. That didn't bear thinking about.

'Cheer up.' Rick crawled over and tilted her chin up. 'We'll have a party to celebrate Paul's release. Invite everyone we can think of and fill the place with music and laughter, eh?'

Mara smiled. 'I hope you're right.'

'Where is Paul, anyway?' Zoe asked.

'He went walking on the moors,' said Mara. 'I suppose he's just enjoying his freedom.' She almost added 'while it lasts' but decided that Rick was right; she at least ought to try to enjoy herself while things were going well.

'Seth didn't want much to do with us this afternoon, either,' Rick complained.

'Don't be like that, Rick,' Mara said. 'He's been getting behind in his work. This business with the police has been bothering him, too. Haven't you noticed how upset he's been? And you know what a perfectionist he is, what he's like about deadlines. Besides, I think he's just relieved Paul's back. He's as fed up with the aftermath of this bloody demonstration as I am.'

'We have to try and bring some good out of it,' Rick argued, placing the coal on top of the layered newspaper and wood chips. 'Don't you see that?'

'Yes, I do. I just think we all need a rest from it, that's all.'

'The struggle goes on. There is no rest.' Rick lit the fire in several places and stood the piece of plywood in front of the fireplace to make it draw. Behind the board the flames began to roar like a hurricane, and Mara could see red around the edges.

'Be careful,' she said. 'You know how wildly it burns with the wind up here.'

'Seriously,' Rick said, keeping an eye on the plywood shield, 'we can't stop now. I can understand your lack of enthusiasm, but you'll just have to shake yourself. Seth and Paul, too. You don't get anywhere against the oppressors by packing it in because you're fed up.'

'I sometimes wonder if you ever get anywhere,' Mara muttered.

She was aware that now she had found her home, Maggie's Farm, she was less concerned about the woes of the world. Not that she didn't care – she would be quite happy to write letters for Amnesty International and sign petitions – but she didn't want to make it her whole life, attending rallies, meetings and demonstrations. Compared to the farm, the children and her pottery, it all seemed so distant and pointless. People were going to go on being as cruel to one another as they always had been. But here was a place where she could make room for love. Why should it be contaminated by the sordid world of politics and violence?

'Penny for them?'

'What? Oh, sorry, Zoe. Just dreaming.'

'It's OK to dream.'

'As long as you don't expect them to come true without hard work,' Rick added.

'Oh, shut up!' Mara said. 'Just give it a rest, can't you, Rick? Let's pretend everything's all right for a few hours at least.'

Rick's jaw dropped, 'Isn't that what I said at first?' Then he shook his head and muttered something about women. Mara couldn't be bothered to take him to task for it.

Just then, the kitchen door flew open and Paul stood there, white and trembling. Mara jumped to her feet. 'Paul! What is it? What's wrong?'

At first he couldn't speak. He just leaned against the door jamb and tried to force the words out. Rick was beside him by then, and Zoe had reached for his hand.

'What is it, Paul?' she asked him softly. 'Take a deep breath. You must try to tell us.'

Paul followed her advice and went to slump down on the cushions. 'It's Seth,' he said finally, pointing towards the back garden. 'I think he's dead.'

14

ONE

Banks and Burgess rushed through the dark garden to Seth's workshop, where a bare bulb shone inside the half-open door. Normally, they would have been more careful on their approach to the scene, but the weather was dry and a stone path led between the vegetable beds to the shed, so there was no likelihood of footprints.

Burgess pushed the door open slowly and they walked in. Mixed with the scents of shaved wood and varnish was the sickly metallic smell of blood. Both men had come across it often enough before to recognize it immediately.

At first, they stood in the doorway to take in the whole scene. Seth was just in front of them, wearing his sand-coloured smock, slumped over his workbench. His head lay on the surface in a small pool of blood, and his arms dangled at his side. From where Banks was standing, it looked as if he had hit his head on the vice clamped to the bench slightly to his left. On the concrete floor over in the right-hand corner stood a small bureau in the Queen Anne style, its finish still wet, a rich glistening nut-brown. At the far end of the workshop, another bare light bulb shone over the area Seth used for office work.

It was only when Banks moved forward a pace that he noticed he had stepped in something sticky and slippery. The light wasn't very strong and most of the floor space around Seth was in semi darkness. Kneeling, Banks saw that what he had first taken for shadow was, in fact, more blood. Seth's feet stood at the centre of a large puddle of blood. It hadn't come from the head wound though, Banks realized, examining the bench again. There hadn't been much bleeding and none of the blood seemed to have dribbled off the edge. Bending again, he caught sight of a thin tubular object, a pen or a pencil perhaps, half-submerged in the pool. He decided to leave it for the forensic team to deal with. They were on their way from Wetherby and should arrive shortly after Dr Glendenning and Peter Darby, the young photographer, neither of whom had as far to travel.

Leaving the body, Banks walked cautiously to the back of the workshop where the old Remington stood on its desk beside the filing cabinet. There was a sheet of paper in the typewriter. Leaning forward, Banks was able to read the message: 'I did it. I killed the policeman Gill. It was wrong of me. I don't know what came over me. I'm sorry for all the trouble I caused. This is the best way. Seth.'

He called Burgess over and pointed out the note to him. Burgess raised his eyebrows and whistled softly between his teeth. 'Suicide, then?'

'Looks like it. Glendenning should be able to give us a better idea.'

'Where the hell is this bloody doctor, anyway?' Burgess complained, looking at his watch. 'It can't take him that long to get here. Everywhere's within pissing distance in this part of the country.'

Burgess and Glendenning hadn't met yet, and Banks was looking forward to seeing Dirty Dick try out his aggressive arrogance on the doctor. 'Come on,' he said. 'There's nothing more to do in here till the others arrive.

We'll only mess up the scene. Let's go outside for a smoke.'

The two of them left the workshop and stood in the cool evening air. Glendenning, Banks knew, would smoke wherever he wanted and nobody had ever dared say a word to him, but then he was one of the top pathologists in the country, not a lowly chief inspector or superintendent.

From the doorway of the shed, they could see the kitchen light in the house. Someone – Zoe, it looked like – was filling a kettle. Mara had taken the news very badly, and Rick had called the local doctor for her. He had also phoned the Eastvale station, which surprised Banks, given Rick's usual hostility. Still, Seth Cotton was dead, there was no doubting that, and Rick probably knew there would be no way of avoiding an investigation. It made more sense to start out on the right foot rather than have to explain omissions or evasions later. Banks wondered whether to go inside and have a chat with them, but decided to give them a bit longer. They would have probably got over the immediate shock by the time Glendenning and the scene-of-crime team had finished.

At last, the back door opened and the tall white-haired doctor crossed the garden, a half-smoked cigarette hanging from the corner of his mouth. He was closely followed by a fresh-faced lad with a camera bag slung over his shoulder.

'About bloody time,' Burgess said.

Glendenning gave him a dismissive glance and stood in the doorway while Darby did his work. Banks and Burgess went back into the workshop to make sure he photographed everything, included the blood on the floor, the pen or pencil, the Queen Anne bureau and the typewriter. When Darby had finished, Glendenning went in.

He was so tall he had to duck to get through the door.

'Watch out for the blood,' Banks warned him.

'And there's no smoking at the scene,' Burgess added. He got no answer.

Banks smiled to himself. 'Ease up,' he said. 'The doc's a law unto himself.'

Burgess grunted but kept quiet while Glendenning felt for a pulse and busied himself with his stethoscope and thermometer.

About fifteen minutes later, while Glendenning was still making calculations in his little red notebook, the forensic team arrived, headed by Vic Manson, the fingerprints man. Manson was a slight academic-looking man in his early forties. Almost bald, he plastered the few remaining hairs over the dome of his skull, creating an effect of bars shadowed on an egg. He greeted the two detectives and went inside with the team. As soon as he saw the workshop, he turned to Banks. 'Bloody awful place to look for prints,' he said. 'Too many rough surfaces. And tools. Have you any idea how hard it is to get prints from well-used tools?'

'I know you'll do your best, Vic,' Banks said. He guessed that Manson was annoyed at being disturbed on a Sunday evening.

Manson snarled and got to work alongside the others, there to take blood samples and anything else they could find.

Banks and Burgess went back outside and lit up again. A few minutes later, Glendenning joined them.

'What's the news, Doc?' Burgess asked.

Glendenning ignored him and spoke directly to Banks. 'He's dead, and that's about the only fact I can give you so far.'

'Come on, Doc!' said Burgess. 'Surely you can tell us more than that.'

'Can you ask your pushy friend here to shut up, just for a wee while?' Glendenning said to Banks in a quiet nicotine-ravaged voice redolent of Edinburgh. 'And tell him not to call me Doc.'

'For Christ's sake.' Burgess flicked the stub of his cigar into the vegetable patch and stuck his hands deep in his pockets. He was wearing his leather jacket over an open-necked shirt, as usual. The only concession he had made to the cold was a V-necked sweater. Now that darkness had come, their breath plumed in the air, lit by the eerie glow of the bare bulb inside the workshop.

Glendenning lit another cigarette and turned back to Banks, who knew better than to rush him. 'It doesn't look to me,' the doctor said slowly, 'as if that head wound was serious enough to cause death. Don't quote me on it, but I don't think it fractured the skull.'

Banks nodded. 'What do you think was the cause?' he asked.

'Loss of blood. And he lost it from his ankles.'

'His ankles?'

'Aye,' Glendenning went on. 'The veins on the insides of each ankle were cut. I found a blade – most likely from a plane – lying in the blood, and it looks like it might have been used for the job. I'll have to make sure, of course.'

'So was it suicide?' Burgess asked.

Glendenning ignored him and went on speaking to Banks. 'Most suicides with a penchant for gory death,' he said, 'slit their wrists. The ankles are just as effective though, if not more so. But whether he inflicted the wounds himself or not, I canna say.'

'He's tried that way before,' Banks said. 'And there was a note.'

'Aye, well, that's your department, isn't it?'

'Which came first,' Banks asked, 'the head wound or the cut ankles?'

'That I can't say, either. He could have hit his head as he lost consciousness, or someone could have hit it for him and slit his ankles. If the two things happened closely in succession, it won't be possible to tell which came first, either. It looks like the head wound was caused by the vice. There's blood on it. But of course it'll have to be matched and the vice compared with the shape of the wound.'

'How long has he been dead?' Banks asked. 'At a guess.'

Glendenning smiled. 'Aye, you're learning, laddie,' he said. 'It's always a guess.' He consulted his notebook. 'Well, rigor's not much further than the neck, and the body temperature's down 2.5 degrees. I'd say he's not been dead more than two or three hours.'

Banks looked at his watch. It was six o'clock. So Cotton had probably died between three and four in the afternoon.

'The ambulance should be here soon,' Glendenning said. 'I called them before I set off. I'd better just bag the head and feet before they get here. We don't want some gormless young ambulance driver spoiling the evidence, do we?'

'Can you do the post-mortem tonight?' Banks asked.

'Sorry, laddie. We've the daughter and son-in-law down for the weekend. First thing in the morning?'

Banks nodded. He knew they'd been spoiled in the past by Glendenning's eagerness to get down to the autopsy immediately. It was more usual to be asked to wait until the next day. And to Glendenning, first thing in the morning was probably very early indeed.

The doctor went back inside, where Manson and his team were finishing up. A short while later the ambulance arrived, and two white-coated men bearing a stretcher crossed to the workshop. Seth looked oddly comical now, with his head in a plastic bag. Like some creature out of a 1950s horror film, Banks thought. The ambulance men tagged him, zipped him into a body bag and laid him on the stretcher.

'Can you leave by the side exit?' Banks asked, pointing to the large gate in the garden wall. 'They're shook up enough in the house without having to see this.'

The ambulance men nodded and left.

Manson came out five minutes later. 'Lots of prints,' he grumbled, 'but most of them a mess, just as I thought. At first glance though, I'd say they belong to only two or three people, not dozens.'

'You'll get Seth's, of course,' Banks said, 'and probably Boyd's and some of the others. Could you get anything from the blade?'

Manson shook his head. 'Sorry. It was completely covered in blood. And the blood had mixed to a paste with the sawdust on the floor. Very sticky. You'd have to wipe it all off to get anywhere, and if you do that . . .' He shrugged. 'Anyway, the doctor's taken it with him to match to the wounds.'

'What about the typewriter?'

'Pretty smudged, but we might get something. The paper, too. We can treat it with graphite.'

'Look, there's a handwriting expert down at the lab, isn't there?'

'Yes. Geoff Tingley. He's good.'

'And he knows about typewriting, too?'

'Of course.'

Banks led Manson back into the workshop and over to the old Remington. The suicide note was now lying beside it. Also on the desk was a business letter Seth had recently written and not posted. 'Dear Mr Spelling,' it read, 'I am most grateful for your compliments on the quality of my work, and would certainly have no objection to your spreading the word in the Wharfedale area. Whilst I always endeavour to meet both deadlines and quality standards, I am sure you realize that, this being a one-man operation, I must therefore limit the amount of work I take on.' It went on to imply that Mr Spelling should seek out only the best jobs for Seth and not bother him with stacks of minor repairs and commissions for matchbox-holders or lamp stands.

'Can you get Tingley to compare these two and let us know if they were typed by the same person?'

'OK.' Manson looked at the letters side by side. 'At a pinch I'd say they weren't. Those old manual typewriters have all kinds of eccentricities, it's true, but so do typists. Look at those "e"s, for a start.'

Banks looked. The 'e's' in Seth's business letter had imprinted more heavily than those in his suicide note.

'Still,' Manson went on, 'better get an expert opinion. I don't suppose his state of mind could be called normal, if he killed himself.' He placed each sheet of paper in an envelope. 'I'll see Geoff gets these first thing in the morning.'

'Thanks, Vic.' Banks led the way outside again.

Burgess stood with his hands still in his pockets in the doorway beside Peter Darby, who was showing him the

Polaroids he'd taken before getting down to the real work. He raised his eyebrows as Banks and Manson joined him. 'Finished?'

'Just about,' Banks said.

'Time for a chat with the inmates, then.' Burgess nodded towards the house.

'Let's take it easy with them,' Banks said. 'They've had a hell of a shock.'

'One of them might not have had, if Cotton was murdered. But don't worry, I won't eat them.'

In the front room, Zoe, Rick, Paul and the children sat drinking tea with the doctor, a young female GP from Relton. A fire blazed in the hearth and candles threw shadows on the whitewashed walls. Music played quietly in the background. Banks thought he recognized Bach's Third 'Brandenburg' Concerto.

'Mara's under sedation,' Rick said. 'You can't talk to her.'

'That's right,' the doctor agreed, picking up her bag and reaching for her coat. 'I just thought I'd wait and let you know. She took it very badly, so I've give her a sedative and put her to bed. I'll be back in the morning to check.'

Banks nodded, and the doctor left.

'How about some tea?' Burgess said, clapping his hands together and rubbing them. 'It's real brass monkey weather out there.'

Rick scowled at him, but Zoe brought two cups and poured the steaming liquid.

Burgess smiled down at her. 'Three lumps and a splash of milk, love, please.'

'What happened?' Zoe asked, stirring in the sugar. Her eyes were red and puffy from crying.

'That's for you to tell us, isn't it?' Burgess said. He

really was being quite polite, Banks noticed. 'All we know is that Seth Cotton is dead and it looks like suicide. Has he been depressed lately?' He took a sip of tea and spluttered. 'What the fuck is this?'

'It's Red Zinger,' Zoe said. 'No caffeine. You shouldn't really have milk and sugar with it.'

'You're telling me.' Burgess pushed the tea aside. 'Well, was he?'

'He was upset when Paul was in jail,' Zoe answered. 'But he cheered up this morning. He seemed so happy today.'

'And he never said anything about ending it all?'

'Never.' Zoe shook her head.

'I gather you had some kind of meeting this afternoon,' Banks said. 'Who was here?'

Rick eyed him suspiciously but said nothing.

'Just Dennis Osmond, Tim and Abha, that's all,' Zoe answered.

'What time were they here?'

'They arrived about half two and left around five.'

'Were you all present?'

Zoe shook her head. 'Seth stayed for a few minutes then went to . . . to work.'

'And I went for a walk,' Paul said defiantly. 'I needed some fresh air after being cooped up in your bloody jail for so long.'

'Not half as long as you will be if you don't knock off the cheek, sonny,' said Burgess.

'Was it you who found the body?' Banks asked.

'Yes.'

'Don't be shy. Tell us about it,' Burgess prompted him.

'Nothing to tell, really. I just got back from my walk and decided to look in on Seth and see how he was doing. I helped him, you know. I was sort of an apprentice. When I opened the door—'

'The door was closed?' Burgess asked.

'Yes. But it wasn't locked. Seth never locked it.'

'And what did you see?'

'You know what I saw. He was sprawled out on the bench, dead.'

'How did you know he was dead? Did you feel his heart?'

'No, of course I didn't. I saw the blood. I called his name and he didn't answer. I just knew.'

'Did you touch anything?' Banks asked.

'No. I ran in here and told the others.'

'Did you go near the typewriter?'

'Why should I? I didn't even notice the bloody thing. All I saw was Seth, dead.'

It was hard to know whether or not he was telling the truth. The shock of what he'd seen made his responses vague and defensive.

'So you left everything just as you found it?' Banks said.

'Yes.'

'This afternoon, during the meeting,' Burgess asked, 'did anyone leave the room for any length of time?'

'We all left at one time or another,' said Zoe. 'You know, to go to the toilet, stretch our legs, whatever.'

'Was anyone gone for a long time?'

'I don't know. We were talking. I don't remember.'

'So someone could have been away for, say, ten minutes?'

'I suppose so.'

'I know you were all busy playing at being concerned citizens,' Burgess said, 'but surely one of you must have noticed if anyone was gone too long?'

'Look,' Rick cut in, 'I thought you said it was suicide. What are you asking these questions for?'

'I said it *looked* like suicide,' Burgess answered coldly. 'And I'll ask whatever bloody questions I think necessary, without any comments from you, Leonardo, thank you very much.'

'Did any of you hear the typewriter at any time this afternoon?' Banks asked.

'No,' Zoe answered. 'But we wouldn't anyway. The walls are thick and the workshop's right at the far end of the garden. Well . . . you've seen where it is. We were all here in the front room. We could never even hear Seth sawing or using his drill from here.'

Banks glanced at Burgess. 'Anything else?'

'Not that I can think of right now,' the superintendent said, subdued again after his exchange with Rick. 'I don't want any of you buggering off anywhere, hear me?' he added, wagging his finger and giving Paul a particularly menacing look. 'There'll be more questions when we've got the results of the post-mortem tomorrow, so be available, all of you.'

Banks and Burgess left them to their grief. Down the valley side, the lights of Relton looked inviting in the chilly darkness.

'Pint?' Burgess suggested.

'Just what I had in mind,' said Banks. They got into the Cortina and bumped away down the track towards the Black Sheep.

TWO

The pillow felt like a cloud, the bed like cotton wool. Mara lay on her back, drifting, but not quite asleep. When she had first heard the news, she had lost control completely. The tears seemed to spurt from her eyes, her heart began to beat wildly, and the breath clogged in her throat. But the doctor's injection had taken care of all that, trading spasms and panic for clouds and cotton wool.

She could hear the muffled voices downstairs, as if from a great distance, and they made her think of those times when Seth and Liz Dale had stayed up late talking. How jealous she had been then, how insecure. But Liz was long gone, and Seth, they told her, was dead.

Dead. The thought didn't register fully through the layers of sedative. She thought she should still be crying and gasping for breath, but instead her body felt as heavy as iron and she could hardly move. Her mind seemed to have a life of its own, wandering over events and picking them out like those miniature mechanical cranes that dipped into piles of cheap trinkets and sweets at seaside arcades. You put your money in and off the crane went, with its articulated grip, inside the glass case. You held down a button to make it swing over and pressed another to make it drop on to the heap of prizes. If you were lucky, you got a chocolate bar, a cigarette lighter or a cheap ring; if not, the metal claw came up empty and you'd wasted your money. Mara had never won anything. Just as well, her father had always said; chocolate is bad for teeth, you're too young to smoke and those rings will turn your finger green inside a week.

But her mind felt like one of those machines now, one

she could not control. It circled her life, then swooped and snatched up the memory of the first time she and Seth had met. Just out of the ashram and eager to escape London, Mara had taken on a friend's flat in Eastvale when the friend emigrated to Canada.

She needed a job and decided to seek craft work before falling back on her secretarial skills, which were pretty rusty by then. Luckily, she heard of Elspeth's shop in Relton and went out to see her. Dottie had just become too ill to work – the pottery workshop was hers – and Mara got the job of helping out in the shop and the use of the facilities. It didn't bring in much money, but it was enough, along with the commission on the pottery. Her rent wasn't very high and she lived cheaply. But she was lonely.

Then, one day after work, she had dropped in at the Black Sheep. It was pay day and she had decided to treat herself to a glass of lager and a cheese and onion sandwich. No sooner had she started to eat than Seth walked in. He stood at the bar, tall and slim, his neatly trimmed dark hair and beard frosted with grey at the edges. And when he turned round, she noticed how deep and sad his eyes were, how serious he looked. Something passed between them – Seth admitted later that he'd noticed it too – and Mara felt shy like a teenager again. He smiled at her and she remembered blushing. But when he came over to say hello, there was no phoney coyness on her part; there were never any silly games between them.

He was the first person she'd met in the area with a background similar to her own. They shared tastes in music and ideas about self-sufficiency and the way the world should be run; they had been to the same rock festivals years ago and had read the same books. She went back with him to the farm that night – he was the only one living there at that time – and she never really left, except to give notice to her landlord and move her meagre belongings.

It was a blissful time, a homecoming of the spirit for Mara, and she thought she had made Seth happy too, though she was always aware that there was a part of him she could never touch.

And now he was dead. She didn't know how, or what had killed him, just that his body had ceased to exist. Her spiritual beliefs, which she still held to some extent, told her that death was merely a beginning. There would be other worlds, other lives perhaps for Seth's spirit, which was immortal. But they would never again drink wine together in bed after making love, he would never kiss her forehead the way he did before going to the workshop, or hold her hand like a boy on his first date on the way down to the Black Sheep. And that was what hurt: the absence of living flesh. The spirit was all very well, but it was far too nebulous an idea to bring Mara much comfort. The miniature crane withdrew from the heap of prizes and held nothing in its metal claw.

Downstairs, the voices droned on, more like music, a raga, than words with meaning. Mara felt as if her blood had thickened to treacle and darkened to the colour of ink. Her body was getting heavier and the lights in the glass case were going out; it was half in shadows now, the prizes indistinguishable from one another. And what happens when the lights go out in the funfair? Mara began to dream.

She was alone on the moors. A huge full moon shone high up, but the landscape was still, dark and bleak. She stumbled over heather and tussocks of grass, looking for something.

At last she came to a village and went into the pub. It

was the Black Sheep but the place was all modern, with video games, carpets and bare concrete walls. A jukebox was playing some music she didn't understand. She asked for the farm, but everyone turned and laughed at her, so she ran out.

This time it was daylight outside, and she was no longer in Swainsdale. The landscape was unfamiliar, softer and more green, and she could smell a whiff of the sea nearby.

In a hollow, she saw an old farmer holding wind chimes out in front of him. They made the same music as the jukebox and it frightened her this time. She found her voice and asked him where Maggie's Farm was. 'Are you the marrying maiden?' he asked her, smiling toothlessly. 'The basket is empty,' he went on, shaking the wind chimes. 'The man stabs the sheep. No blood flows. Misfortune.'

Terrified, Mara ran off and found herself in an urban landscape at night. Some of the buildings had burned out and fires raged in the gutted shells; flames licked around broken windows and flared up high through fallen roofs. Small creatures scuttled in dark corners. And she was being followed, she knew it. She hadn't been able to see anyone, just sensed darting movements and heard rustling sounds behind her. For some reason she was sure it was a woman, someone she should know but didn't.

Before the dream possessed her completely and turned her into one of the scavengers among the ruins, before the shadow behind tapped her on the shoulder, she struggled to wake up, to scream.

When she opened her eyes, she became conscious of someone sitting on the bedside pressing a damp cloth to her forehead. She thought it must be Seth, but when she turned and looked closely it was Zoe.

'Is it morning?' she asked in a weak voice.

'No,' said Zoe, 'it's only half past nine.'

'He really is dead, isn't he, Zoe?'

Zoe nodded. 'You were having a nightmare. Go to sleep now.' Mara closed her eyes again. The cool cloth smoothed her brow, and she began to drift. This time there was only darkness ahead, and the last thing she felt before she fell asleep was Zoe's hand gripping her tightly.

THREE

'Anything wrong?' Larry Grafton asked, pulling Banks a pint of Black Sheep bitter.

Banks glanced at Burgess, who nodded.

'Seth Cotton's dead,' he answered, and felt ears prick up behind him in the public bar, where most of the tables were occupied.

Grafton turned pale. 'Oh no, not Seth,' he said. 'He was only in here this lunch time. Not Seth?'

'How did he seem?' Banks asked.

'He was happy as a pig in clover,' Grafton said. 'That young lad was back and they all seemed to be celebrating. You're not telling me he killed himself, are you?'

'We don't know yet,' Burgess said, picking up his pint of Watney's. 'Anywhere quiet the chief inspector and I can have a little chat? Police business.'

'Aye, you can use the snug. There's no one in there.'

The snug was aptly named. Hidden away behind a partition of smoked glass and dark wood, there was room for about four people, and even that would be a tight squeeze.

Banks and Burgess made themselves comfortable, both

of them practically draining their drinks before even reaching for smokes.

'Have a cigar,' Burgess said, offering his tin.

'Thanks.' Banks took one. He didn't enjoy cigars as a rule, but thought that if he tried them often enough he might eventually come to like them.

'And I think I'd better get a couple more drinks in before we start,' Burgess said. 'Thirsty work, this.'

He was back in a moment carrying another pint of bitter for Banks and, this time, a pint of draught Guinness for himself.

'Right,' he said, 'I can tell you're not happy about this. Don't clam up on me, Banks. What's bothering you?'

'Let's take it at face value, for a start,' Banks suggested. 'Then maybe we can see what's wrong.'

'Suicide?'

'Yes.'

'But you don't think so?'

'No. But I'd like to play it through and see if I can pin down my ideas.'

'All right. Cotton murdered Gill, then he was overcome with remorse and slit his ankles. Case closed. Can I go back to London now?'

Banks smiled. 'But it's not as simple as that, is it? Why would Cotton murder PC Gill?'

Burgess ran a hand through his greying Brylcreemed hair. 'Bloody hell, I thought we'd been through all this before. We're talking about a political crime; call it an act of terrorism. Motive as such doesn't apply.'

'But Seth Cotton was perhaps the least political of the lot of them,' Banks argued. 'Except maybe for Mara, or Zoe Hardacre. Sure, he was anti-nuclear, and he no doubt believed in social equality and the evils of apartheid. But so do I.'

Burgess sniffed. 'You might be the murder expert around here, but I know about terrorism. Believe me, anyone can get involved. Terrorists play on people's ideals and warp them to their own ends. It's like the brainwashing religious cults do.'

'Do you think Gill's death was calmly planned and executed, or was it a crime of passion?' Banks asked.

'A bit of both. Things aren't so clear-cut in this kind of crime. Terrorists are very emotional about their beliefs, but they're cold and deadly when it comes to action.'

'The only thing Seth Cotton cared passionately about was his carpentry, and perhaps Mara. If he did commit suicide, I doubt it was anything to do with politics.'

'We have his note, don't forget. It's a confession.'

'Let's leave that for later. Why did he kill himself? If he's the kind of person you're trying to make out he is, why would he feel remorse after succeeding in his aim? Why would he kill himself?'

Burgess doodled in the foam of his Guinness. 'You expect too many answers, Banks. As often as not, there just aren't any. Can't you leave it at that?'

Banks shook his head and stubbed out the cigar. It tasted like last week's tea leaves. He swigged some more Black Sheep bitter to get rid of the taste and lit a Silk Cut. 'It's because there's too many questions,' he said. 'We still don't know much about Cotton's political background before he came to the farm, though if there'd been any subversive activity I'm sure Special Branch would have a record of it. And what about his behaviour over the last few days? How do you read that?'

'They said he seemed happy when Boyd was released. Is that what you mean?'

'Partly.'

'Well, of course he'd be happy,' Burgess said. 'If he knew the kid wasn't guilty.'

'Why should he care? It'd be better for a cold-blooded terrorist to let someone else go down for what he'd done. So why kill himself?'

Burgess shrugged. 'Because he knew we'd get to him soon.'

'So why didn't he just disappear? Surely his masters would have taken care of him in Moscow or Prague or wherever.'

'More likely Belfast. But I don't know. It's not unusual for suicides to appear happy once they've decided to end it all.'

'I know that. I'm just not sure that he was happy because he'd decided to kill himself.'

Burgess grunted. 'What's your theory, then?'

'That he was killed, and it was made to look like a suicide.'

'Killed by who?'

Banks ignored the question. 'We won't know anything for certain until the doctor does his post-mortem,' he said, 'but there's a few things that bother me about the note.'

'Go on.'

'It doesn't ring true. The damn thing's neither here nor there, is it? Cotton confesses to killing Gill, but doesn't say why. All he says is, "I don't know what came over me." It doesn't square with what we know of him.'

'Which is?'

'Precious little, I admit. He was a closed book. But I'd

say he was the kind who'd either not bother with a note at all, or he'd explain everything fully. He wouldn't come out with such a wishy-washy effort as the one we saw. I think he'd have used Gill's number too, not his name. And I don't know if you had a good look, but it seemed very different from that business letter on the desk. The pressure on the characters was different, for a start.'

'Yes,' Burgess said, 'but don't forget the state of mind he must have been in when he typed it.'

'I'll grant you that. Still . . . and the style. Whoever wrote that suicide note had only very basic writing skills. But the business letter was more than competent and grammatically correct.'

Burgess slapped the table. 'Oh come on, Banks! What's the problem? Is it too easy for you? Business letters are always written in a different style; they're always a bit stuffy and wordy. You wouldn't write to a friend the same way you would in a business letter, would you, let alone a suicide note. A man writing his last words doesn't worry about grammar or how much pressure he puts on each letter.'

'But that's just it. Those things are unconscious. Someone used to writing well doesn't immediately become sloppy just because he's under pressure. If anything, I'd have expected a more carefully composed message. And you don't think about how each finger hits the keys when you're typing. It's something you just do, and it doesn't vary much. Why leave it in the typewriter, too? Why didn't he put it on the bench in front of him?'

'And what I'm saying,' Burgess argued, 'is that his state of mind could account for all your objections. He must have been disturbed. Contemplation of suicide has an odd effect on a man's character. You can't expect everything to be the same as usual when a bloke's on the verge of slitting his bloody ankles. And remember, you said he'd tried that before.'

'That is a problem,' Banks agreed. 'Whoever did it must have known about the previous attempt and copied it to make it look more like a genuine suicide.'

'That's assuming somebody else did it. I'm not sure I agree.'

Banks shrugged. 'We'll see what forensic says about the note. But I'm not happy with it at all.'

'What about the bureau?'

'What about it?'

'He'd obviously just finished it, hadn't he? The coat of varnish was still fresh. And he'd moved it to the corner of the workshop. Doesn't that imply anything?'

'That he was tidying things up behind him, you mean? Tying up loose ends?'

'Exactly. Just like a man on the point of suicide. He finished his last piece of work, put it carefully aside so he wouldn't get blood all over it, then he slit his fucking ankles. When he got weak and passed out, he hit his head on the vice, accounting for the head wound.'

Banks stared into the bottom of his glass. 'It could have happened that way,' he said slowly. 'But I don't think so.'

'Which brings us back to the big question again,' Burgess said. 'If we're to follow your line of reasoning, if you *are* right, then who killed him?'

'It could have been any of them, couldn't it? Zoe said as much.'

'Yes, but she might have said that to get herself and her mates off the hook. I'm thinking of one of them in particular.'

'Who?'

'Boyd.'

Banks sighed. 'I was afraid you'd say that.'

'I'll bet you bloody were.' Burgess leaned forward so suddenly that the glasses rattled on the table. Banks could smell the Guinness and cigar smoke on his breath. 'If we play it your way, there's no getting round the facts. Boyd was missing all afternoon, unaccounted for. We only have his word that he was walking on the moors. I shouldn't think anybody saw him. It would have been easy for him to get in by the side gate and visit Seth while everyone in the house was wrapped up in their own little games. Nothing odd about that. He helped Seth a lot, and the shed would be full of his fingerprints anyway. They talk, and he kills Seth – pushes his head forward to knock him out on the vice, then slits his ankles.' Burgess leaned back again, satisfied, and folded his arms.

'All right,' Banks said. 'I agree. It fits. But why? Why would Boyd kill Seth Cotton?'

Burgess shrugged. 'Because he knew something to link Boyd to Gill's murder. It makes sense, Banks, you know it does. Why you're defending that obnoxious little prick is beyond me.'

'Why was Cotton so miserable when Boyd was in jail,' Banks asked, 'and so happy when he came out?'

Burgess lit another Tom Thumb. 'Loyalty, perhaps? He knew something and was worried he might be called on to give evidence. He wasn't sure he could carry on with his lies and evasions under pressure. Boyd gets out, so Cotton feels immediate elation. They talk. Cotton tells Boyd what he knows and how glad he is he won't have to testify under oath, so Boyd gets worried and kills him. Remember, Boyd knew he wasn't quite off the hook, whatever Cotton might have made of his release. And you know how terrified the kid is of enclosed spaces. He'd do anything to avoid a life sentence.'

'And the note?'

'Let's say you're right about that. Boyd typed it to clear himself, put the blame on someone who isn't able to defend himself. It's a cowardly kind of act typical of someone like him. That explains the pressure on the keys and the literacy level. Boyd isn't very well educated. He was spending most of his time on the streets by the time he was thirteen. And he couldn't explain anything about Cotton's motives because he killed Gill himself. So,' Burgess went on, 'even if we see it your way, I still come out right. Personally, I don't give a damn whether it was Boyd or Cotton. Either way, we've cracked it. Which way do you want to go? Toss a coin.'

'I'm still not convinced.'

'That's because you don't want to be.'

'What do you mean by that?'

'You know damn well what I mean. You've argued yourself into a corner. It was your idea to let Boyd out and see what happened. Well, now you've seen what's happened. No sooner is he out than there's another death. That makes you responsible.'

Banks took a deep breath. There was too much truth for comfort in what Burgess was saying. He shook his head. 'Somebody killed Seth,' he said, 'but I don't think it was Boyd. For all the kid's problems, I believe he genuinely cared. The people at Maggie's Farm are the only ones who have ever done anything for him, gone out on a limb.'

'Come off it! That sentimental bullshit doesn't work on me. The kid's a survivor, an opportunist. He's nothing more than a street punk.'

'And Cotton?'

Burgess sat back and reached for his glass. The chair creaked. 'Good actor, accomplice, innocent bystander, conscience-stricken idealist? I don't bloody know. But it doesn't matter now, does it? He's dead. It's all over.'

But Banks felt that it did matter. Somehow, after what had happened that afternoon, it seemed to matter more now than it ever had before.

'Is it?' he said. Then he stubbed out his cigarette and drained his glass. 'Come on, let's go.'

15

ONE

Eastvale General Infirmary stood on King Street, about half a mile west of the police station, not far from the comprehensive school. Because the day was warming up nicely, Banks decided to walk. As he left the station, he turned on his Walkman and listened to Muddy Waters sing 'Louisiana Blues' as he made his way through the warren of narrow streets with their cracked stone walls, gift shops and overpriced pubs.

The hospital itself was an austere Victorian brick building. About its high draughty corridors hung an air of fatalistic gloom. Not quite the hospital I'd choose if I were ill, Banks thought, fiddling with the Walkman's off switch in his overcoat pocket.

The mortuary was in the basement, which, like the police station's cell area, was the most modern part of the building. The autopsy room had white-tiled walls and a central metal table with guttering around its edges to channel off the blood. A long lab bench, complete with Bunsen burners and microscopes, stretched along one wall, with shelving above it for jars or organs, tissue samples and prepared chemical solutions.

Fortunately, the table was empty when Banks entered. A lab assistant was in the process of scrubbing it down, while Glendenning stood at the bench, a cigarette dangling from his mouth. Everyone smoked in the mortuary; they did it to keep the stench of death at bay.

The lab assistant dropped a surgical instrument into a metal kidney bowl. Banks winced at the sound.

'Let's go into the office,' Glendenning said. 'I can see you're a bit pink around the gills.'

Glendenning's office was small and cluttered, hardly befitting a man of his stature and status, Banks thought. But this wasn't America; healthcare was hardly big business, despite private insurance plans. Glendenning took his white lab coat off, smoothed his shirt and sat down. Banks shifted some old medical journals from the only remaining chair and placed himself opposite the doctor.

'Coffee?'

Banks nodded. 'Yes, please.'

Glendenning picked up his phone and pressed a button. 'Molly, dear, do you think you could scrape up two cups of coffee?' He covered the mouthpiece and asked Banks how he liked his. 'One black no sugar, and the usual for me. Yes, three sugars, that's right. What diet? And don't bring that vile muck they drink at reception. What? Yes. I know you'd run out yesterday, but that's no excuse. I haven't paid my coffee money for three weeks? What is this, woman, the bloody Inquisition?' He hung up roughly, ran a hand through his white hair and sighed. 'Good staff are hard to find these days. Now, Mr Banks, let's see what we have here.' He riffled through the stack of papers on his desk.

He probably knew it all off by heart, Banks thought, but needed the security of his files and sheets of paper in front of him just as Richmond always liked to read from his notebook what he knew perfectly well in the first place.

'Seth Cotton, aye, poor chappie.' Glendenning took a pair of half-moon reading glasses from his top pocket and held the report at arm's length as he peered down his nose at it. Having done with that, he put it aside, took off his glasses and sat back in his chair with his large but delicate hands folded on his lap. The coffee arrived, and Molly, giving her boss a disapproving glance on the way, departed.

'Last meal about three hours before death,' Glendenning said. 'And a good one too, if I may say so. Roast beef, Yorkshire pudding. What better meal could a condemned man wish for?'

'Haggis?'

Glendenning wagged his finger. 'Dinna extract the urine, Mr Banks.'

Banks sipped some coffee. It was piping hot and tasted good. Clearly it wasn't the 'vile muck' from reception.

'No evidence of poisoning, or indeed of any other wounds bar the external. Mr Cotton was in perfectly good health until the blood drained out of his body.'

'Was that the cause of death?'

'Aye. Loss of about five pints of blood usually does cause death.'

'What about the blow to the head? Was it delivered before or after the cuts to the ankles?'

Glendenning scratched his head. 'That I can't tell you. The vital reaction was quite consistent with a wound caused before death. As you saw for yourself, there was plenty of blood. And the leucocyte count was high – that's white blood cells to you, the body's little repairmen. Had the blow to the head occurred some time after death, then of course there would have been clear evidence to that effect, but the two wounds happened so closely together that it's impossible to say which came first. Cotton was certainly alive when he hit his head – or when someone hit it for him. But how long he survived after the blow, I can't tell. Of course, the head wound may have caused loss of consciousness, and it's very difficult to slash your ankles when you're unconscious, as I'm sure you're aware.'

'Could he have hit his head while bending down to make the cuts?'

Glendenning pursed his lips. 'I wouldn't say so, no. You saw the blood on the bench. None of it had trickled on to the floor. I'd say by the angle of the wound and the sharp edges of the vice that his head was resting exactly where it landed after the blow.'

'Could someone have come up behind him and pushed his head down on to the vice?'

'Now you're asking me to speculate, Mr Banks. All I can tell you is that I found no signs of scratching or bruising at the back of the neck or the head.'

'Does that mean no?'

'Not necessarily. If you come up behind someone and give his head a quick push before he has time to react, then I doubt it would show.'

'So that means it must have been someone he knew. He'd have noticed anyone else creeping up on him. Whoever did it must have been in the workshop already, someone he didn't mind having around while he carried on working.'

'Theories, theories,' Glendenning said. 'I don't know why you're not satisfied with suicide. There's absolutely no evidence to the contrary.'

'No medical evidence, perhaps.'

'I'm sorry,' said Glendenning. 'I'd like to be able to help

you more, but those are the facts. While the blow to the head may well have caused complications had Mr Cotton lived, it was in no way responsible for his death.'

'Complications? What complications?'

Glendenning frowned and reached for another cigarette from the box on his desk. It looked antique, and Banks noticed some words engraved in ornate italics on the top. 'To Dr C.W.S. Glendenning, on Successful Completion of . . .' He couldn't read the rest. He assumed it was some kind of graduation present.

'All kinds,' Glendenning answered. 'We don't know a great deal about the human brain, Mr Banks. A lot more than we used to, of course, but still not enough. Certain head wounds can result in effects far beyond the power of the blow and the extent of the apparent damage. Bone chips can lodge in the tissue, and even bruising can cause problems.'

'What problems?'

'Almost anything. Memory loss – temporary or permanent – hearing and vision problems, vertigo, personality change, temporary lapses of consciousness. Need I go on?'

Banks shook his head.

'But in the case of Mr Cotton, of course, that's something we'll never know.'

'No.' Banks got to his feet. 'Anyway, thank you very much, Doctor.'

Glendenning inclined his head regally.

On the way back to the station, Banks hardly heard Muddy Waters. According to Glendenning, Cotton could have been murdered, and that was enough for Banks. Of course the doctor wouldn't commit himself – he never did – but even an admission of the possibility was a long way for him to go. If Burgess was right, there was a good chance Boyd had done it, and that left Banks with Seth's blood on his hands.

As if that weren't enough, something else nagged at him: one of those frustrating little feelings you can't quite define, like having a name on the tip of your tongue, or an itch you can't scratch. He didn't want to be premature, but it felt like the familiar glimmer of an idea. Disparate facts were coming together, and with a lot of hard thinking, a bit of help from the subconscious and a touch of luck, they might actually lead to the answer. He was still a long way from that as yet, and when Muddy Waters started singing 'Still a Fool' Banks believed him.

It was eleven o'clock, according to the church clock, and Burgess would be out questioning Osmond and the students. In his office, Banks called the forensic lab and asked for Vic Manson. He had to wait a few minutes, and finally Vic came on the line.

'The prints?' Banks asked.

'Yes. Four sets. At least four identifiable sets. One belongs to the deceased, of course, another to that Boyd character – the same as the ones we found on the knife – and two more.'

'They'll probably be Mara's and one of the others',' Banks said. 'Look, thanks a lot, Vic. I'll try and arrange to get the others fingerprinted for comparison. Is Geoff Tingley around?'

'Yep. Just a sec, I'll get him for you.'

Banks could hear distant voices at the end of the line, then someone picked up the receiver and spoke. 'Tingley here. Is it about those letters?'

'Yes.'

'Well, I'm almost positive they weren't typed by the same person. You can make a few allowances for changes in pressure, but these were so wildly different I'd say that's almost conclusive. I could do with a few more samples of at least one of the writers, though. It'll give me more variables and a broader scope for comparison.'

'I'll see what I can do,' Banks said. There were probably other examples of Seth's typing in the filing cabinet. 'Would it do any good if we got a suspect to type us a sample?' he asked.

'Hmmm. It might do. Problem is, if he knew what we were after it wouldn't be too difficult to fake it. I'd say this chap's a plodder, though. You can tell it's been pecked out by the overall high pressure, each letter very deliberately sought and pounced on, so to speak. Hunt-and-peck, as I believe they call the technique. The other chap was a better typist; still two fingers, I'd say, but fairly quick and accurate. Probably had a lot more practice. And there's another thing, too. Did you notice the writing styles of the letters were—'

'Yes,' Banks said. 'We spotted that. Good of you to point it out, though.'

Tingley sounded disappointed. 'Oh, it's nothing.'

'Thanks very much. I'll be in touch about the samples and testing. Could you put Vic on again? I've just remembered something.'

'Will do.'

'Are you still there?' Manson asked a few seconds later.

'Yes. Look, Vic, there's a couple more points. The typewriter for a start.'

'Nothing clear on that, just a lot of blurs.'

'Was it wiped?'

'Could have been.'

'There was a cloth on that table, wasn't there? One of those yellow dusters.'

'Yes, there was,' said Manson. 'Do you want me to check for fibres?'

'If you would. And the paper?'

'Same, nothing readable.'

'What about that pen, or whatever it was we found on the floor. Have you had time to get round to that yet?'

'Yes. It's just an ordinary ballpoint, a Bic. No prints of course, just a sweaty blur.'

'Hmmm.'

The pen had been found in the puddle of blood, just below Seth's dangling right arm. If he was right-handed, as Banks thought he was, he could have used the pen to write a note before he died. It could have just fallen there earlier of course, but Seth had been very tidy, especially in his final moments. Perhaps he had written his own note, and whoever killed him took it and replaced it with the second version. Why? Because Seth hadn't murdered Gill and had said so clearly in his note? That meant he had committed suicide for some other reason entirely. Had he even named the killer, or was it an identity he had died trying to protect?

Too many questions again. Maybe Burgess and Glendenning were right and he was a fool not to accept the easy solutions. After all, he had a choice: either Seth Cotton was guilty as the note indicated and had really killed himself, or Paul Boyd, fearing discovery, had killed him and faked the note. Banks leaned closer towards the second of these, but for some reason he still couldn't convince himself that Boyd had done it – and not only because he took the responsibility for letting the kid out of jail. Boyd certainly had a record, and he had taken off when the knife was discovered. He could be a lot tougher and more clever than anyone realized. If he was faking his claustrophobia, for example, so that even Burgess was more inclined to believe him because of his fear of incarceration, then anything was possible. But so far they had nothing but circumstantial evidence, and Banks still felt that the picture was incomplete. He lit a cigarette and walked over to look down on the market square. It brought no inspiration today.

Finally, he decided it was time to tidy his desk before lunch. Almost every available square inch was littered with little yellow Post-it notes, most of which he had acted on ages ago. He screwed them all up and dropped them in the bin. Next came the files, statements and records he'd read to refresh his memory of the people involved. Most information was stored in the records department, but Banks had developed the habit of keeping brief files on all the cases he had a hand in. At the top was his file on Elizabeth Dale. Picking it up again, he remembered that he had just pulled it out of the cabinet, after some difficulty in locating it, when Sergeant Rowe had called with the news of Seth Cotton's death.

He opened the folder and brought back to mind the facts of the case – not even a case, really, just a minor incident that had occurred some eighteen months ago.

Elizabeth Dale had checked herself into a psychiatric hospital on the outskirts of Huddersfield, complaining of depression, apathy and general inability to cope with the outside world. After a couple of days' observation and treatment, she had decided she didn't like the service and ran off to Maggie's Farm, where she knew that Seth Cotton, an old friend from Hebden Bridge, was living. The hospital authorities informed Eastvale that she had spoken about her friend with the house near Relton, and they asked the local social services to please check up and see if she was there.

She was. Dennis Osmond had been sent to the farm to try to convince her to return to the hospital for her own good, but Ms Dale remained adamant: she was staying at the farm. Osmond also had the nerve to agree that the place would probably do her good. In anger and desperation, the hospital sent out two men of its own, who persuaded Elizabeth to return with them. They had browbeaten her and threatened her with committal, or so Seth Cotton and Osmond had complained at the time.

Because Elizabeth Dale also had a history of drug addiction, the police were called out when the hospital employees said they suspected the people at the farm were using drugs. Banks had gone out there with Sergeant Hatchley and a uniformed constable but they had found nothing. Ms Dale went back to the hospital, and as far as Banks knew, everything returned to normal.

In the light of recent events though, it became a more intriguing tale. For one thing, both Elizabeth Dale and Dennis Osmond were connected with PC Gill via the complaints they had made independently. And now it appeared there was yet another link between Osmond and Dale.

Where was Elizabeth Dale now? He would have to go to Huddersfield and find her himself. He'd learned from experience that it was no use at all dealing with doctors over the phone. But that would have to wait until tomorrow. First, he wanted to talk to Mara again, if she was well enough. Before setting off, he considered phoning Jenny to try to make up the row they'd had on Sunday lunch time.

Just as he was about to call her, the phone rang.

'Chief Inspector Banks?'

'Speaking.'

'My name is Lawrence Courtney, of Courtney, Courtney and Courtney, Solicitors.'

'Yes, I've heard of the firm. What can I do for you?'

'It's what I might be able to do for you,' Courtney said. 'I read in this morning's newspaper that a certain Seth Cotton has died. Is that correct?'

'That's right, yes.'

'Well, it might interest you to know, Chief Inspector, that we are the holders of Mr Cotton's will.'

'Will?'

'Yes, will.' He sounded faintly irritated. 'Are you interested?'

'Indeed I am.'

'Would it be convenient for you to call at our office after lunch?'

'Yes, certainly. But look, can't you tell me—'

'Good. I'll see you then. About two thirty, shall we say? Goodbye, Chief Inspector.'

Banks slammed the phone down. Bloody pompous solicitor. He cursed and reached for a cigarette. But a will? That was unexpected. Banks wouldn't have thought such a nonconformist as Seth would have bothered making a will. Still, he did own property and a business. But how could he have had any idea that he was going to die in the near future?

Banks jotted down the solicitor's name and the time of the meeting and stuck the note to his desk. Then he took a deep breath, phoned Jenny at her university office in York and plunged right in. 'I'm sorry about yesterday. I know what it must have sounded like, but I couldn't think of a better way of telling you.'

'I overreacted.' Jenny said. 'I feel like an idiot. I suppose you were only doing your job.'

'I wasn't going to tell you, not until I realized that being around Osmond really might be dangerous.'

'And I shouldn't have mistaken your warning for interference. It's just that I get so bloody frustrated. Damn men! Why do I never seem able to choose the right one?'

'Does it matter to you, what he did?'

'Of course it matters.'

'Are you going to go on seeing him?'

'I don't know.' She affected a bored tone. 'I was getting rather tired of him, anyway. Have there been any developments?'

'What in? The break-in or the Gill murder?'

'Well, both, seeing as you ask. What's wrong? You sound a bit tense.'

'Oh, nothing. It's been a busy morning, that's all. And I was nervous about calling you. Have you read about Seth Cotton?'

'No. I didn't have time to look at the paper this morning. Why, what's happened?'

Banks told her.

'Oh God. Poor Mara. Do you think there's anything I can do?'

'I don't know. I've no idea what state she's in. I'm calling in on her later this afternoon. I'll mention your name if you like.'

'Please do. Tell her how sorry I am. And if she needs to talk . . . What do you think happened, or can't you say?'

'I wish I could.' Banks summed up his thoughts for her.

'And I suppose you're feeling responsible? Is that why you don't really want to consider that Boyd did it?'

'You're right about the guilt. Burgess would never have let him go if I hadn't pressed him.'

'Burgess hardly seems like the kind of man to bow to pressure. I can't see him consenting to do anything he didn't want to.'

'Perhaps you're right. Still . . . it's not just that. At least, I don't think so. There's something much more complex behind all this. And don't accuse me of over-complicating matters – I've had enough of that already.'

'Oh, we are touchy today, aren't we? I had no such thing in mind.'

'Sorry. I suppose it's getting to me. About the break-in. I've got something in the works and we'll probably know by tonight, tomorrow morning at the latest.'

'What's it all about?'

'I'd rather not say yet. But don't worry, I don't think Osmond's in any kind of danger.'

'Are you sure?'

'Absolutely.'

'If you're right?'

'Am I ever wrong? Look, before you choke, I've got to go now. I'll be in touch later.'

Though where he had to go he wasn't quite certain. There was the solicitor, but that wasn't until two thirty. Feeling vaguely depressed, he lit another cigarette and went over to the window. The Queen's Arms, that was it. A pie and a pint would soon cheer him up. And Burgess had made a tentative arrangement to meet there around one thirty and compare notes.

TWO

Banks found the offices of Courtney, Courtney and Courtney on Market Street, quite close to the police station. Too close, in fact, to make it worthwhile turning on the Walkman for the journey.

The firm of solicitors was situated in what had once been a tea shop, and the new name curved in a semicircle of gold lettering on the plate glass window. Banks asked the young receptionist for Mr Lawrence Courtney, and after a brief exchange on the intercom, was shown through to a large office stacked with legal papers.

Lawrence Courtney himself, wedged behind a large executive desk, was not the prim figure Banks had expected from their phone conversation – three-piece suit, gold watch chain, pince-nez, nose raised as if perpetually exposed to a bad smell – instead he was a relaxed plump man of about fifty with over-long fair hair, a broad ruddy face and a fairly pleasant expression. His jacket hung behind the door. He wore a white shirt, a red and green striped tie and plain black braces. Banks noticed that the top button of the shirt was undone and the tie had been loosened, just like his own.

'Seth Cotton's will,' Banks said, sitting down after a brisk damp handshake.

'Yes. I thought you'd be interested,' said Courtney. A faint smile tugged at the corners of his pink rubbery lips.

'When did he make it?'

'Let me see . . . About a year ago, I think.' Courtney found the document and read off the date.

'Why did he come to you? I'm not sure how well you knew him, but he didn't seem to me the kind of person to deal with a solicitor.'

'We handled the house purchase,' Courtney said, 'and when the conveyance was completed we suggested a will. We often do. It's not so much a matter of touting for business as making things easier. So many people die intestate, and you've no idea what complications that leads to if there is no immediate family. The house itself, for example. As far as I know, Mr Cotton wasn't married, even under common law.'

'What was his reaction to your suggestion?'

'He said he'd think about it.'

'And he thought about it for two years?'

'It would appear so, yes. If you don't mind my asking, Chief Inspector, why all this interest in his reason for making a will? People do, you know.'

'It's the timing, that's all. I was just wondering why then rather than any other time.'

'Hmmm. I imagine that's the kind of thing you people have to think about. Are you interested in the contents at all?'

'Of course.'

Courtney unfolded the paper fully, peered at it, then put it aside again and hooked his thumbs in his braces. 'Not much to it, really,' he said. 'He left the house and what little money he had – somewhere in the region of two thousand pounds, I believe, though you'll have to check with the bank – to one Mara Delacey.'

'Mara? And that's it?'

'Not quite. Oddly enough he added a codicil just a few months ago. Shortly before Christmas, in fact. It doesn't affect the original bequest, but merely specifies that all materials, monies and goodwill relating to his carpentry business be left to Paul Boyd, in the hope that he uses them wisely.'

'Bloody hell!'

'Is something wrong?'

'It's nothing. Sorry. Mind if I smoke?'

'If you must.' Courtney took a clean ashtray from his

drawer and pushed it disapprovingly towards Banks. Undeterred, Banks lit up.

'The way I see things, then,' Banks said, 'is that he left the house and money to Mara after he'd only known her for a year or so, and the carpentry business to Paul after the kid had only been at the farm for a couple of months.'

'If you say so, Chief Inspector. It would indicate that Mr Cotton was quick to trust people.'

'It would indeed. Or that there was nobody else he could even consider. I doubt that he'd have wanted his goods and chattels to go to the state. But who knows where Boyd might have got to by the time Cotton died of natural causes? Or Mara. Could he have had some idea that he was in danger?'

'I'm afraid I can't answer that,' Courtney said. 'Our business ends with the legal formalities, and Mr Cotton certainly made no mention of an imminent demise. If there's anything else I can help you with, of course, I'd be more than willing.'

'Thank you,' said Banks. 'I think that's all. Will you be informing Mara Delacey?'

'We will take steps to get in touch with beneficiaries in due course, yes.'

'Is it all right if I tell her this afternoon?'

'I can't see any objection. And you might ask her – both of them, if possible – to drop by. I'll be happy to explain the procedure to them. If you have any trouble with the bank, Chief Inspector, please refer them to me. It's the National Westminster – or NatWest, as I believe they call themselves these days – the branch in the market square. The manager is a most valued client.'

'I know the place.' Know it, Banks thought, I practically stare at it for hours on end every day.

'Then goodbye, Chief Inspector. It's been a pleasure.'

Banks walked out into the street more confused than ever. Before he got back to the station, however, he'd managed to put some check on his wild imaginings. The will probably didn't come into the case at all. Seth Cotton had simply had more foresight than many would have credited him with. What was wrong with that? And it was perfectly natural that, with his parents both dead and no close family, he would leave the house to Mara. And Paul Boyd was, after all, his apprentice. It was a gesture of faith and confidence on Seth's part.

Even if Mara and Paul had known what they had coming to them, neither, Banks was positive, would have murdered Seth to get it. Life for Mara was clearly better with Seth than without him, and whatever ugliness might be lurking in Boyd's character, he was neither stupid nor petty enough to kill for a set of carpenter's tools. So forget the will, Banks told himself. Nice gesture though it was, it is irrelevant. Except perhaps for the date. Why wait till two years after Courtney had suggested it before actually getting the business done? Procrastination?

It also raised a more serious question: had Seth felt that his life was in danger a year ago? If so, why had it taken so long for the danger to manifest itself? And had that fear somehow also renewed itself around Christmas time?

Before returning to his office, he nipped into the National Westminster and had no problem in getting details of Seth's financial affairs, such as they were: he had a savings account at £2343.64, and a current account which stood at £421.33.

It was after three thirty when he got back to the station, and there was a message from Vic Manson to the effect that, yes, fibres matching those from the duster had been found on the typewriter keys. But, Manson had added with typical forensic caution, there was no way of proving whether the machine had been wiped before or after the message had been typed. The pressure of fingers on the keys often blurs prints.

Banks's brief chat with Burgess over lunch had revealed nothing new, either. Dirty Dick had seen Osmond and got nowhere with him. Early in the afternoon he was off to see Tim and Abha, and he was quite happy to leave Mara Delacey to Banks. As far as Burgess was concerned, it was all over bar the shouting, but he wanted more evidence to implicate Boyd or Cotton with extremist politics. Most of the time he'd had his eye on Glenys, and he'd kept reminding Banks that it was her night off that night. Cyril, fortunately, had been nowhere in sight.

Banks left a message for Burgess at the front desk summarizing what Lawrence Courtney had said about Seth's will. Then he called Sergeant Hatchley, as Richmond was busy on another matter, to accompany him and to bring along the fingerprinting kit. He slipped the Muddy Waters cassette from his Walkman and hurried out to the car with it, a huffing and puffing Hatchley in tow. It was time to see if Mara Delacey was ready to talk.

'What do you think of Superintendent Burgess?' Banks asked Hatchley on the way. They hadn't really had a chance to talk much over the past few days.

'Off the record?'

'Yes.'

'Well . . .' Hatchley rubbed his face with a ham-like hand. 'He seemed all right at first. Bit of zip about him. You know, get up and go. But I'd have thought a whizz-kid like him would have got a bit further by now.'

'None of us have got any further,' Banks said. 'What do you mean? The man's only flesh and blood after all.'

'I suppose that's it. He dazzles you a bit at first, then . . .'

'Don't underestimate him,' Banks said. 'He's out of his element up here. He's getting frustrated because we don't have raving anarchists crawling out of every nook and cranny in the town.'

'Aye,' said Hatchley. 'And you thought I was right wing.'

'You are.'

Hatchley grunted.

'When we get to the farm, I want you to have a look at Seth's filing cabinet in the workshop,' Banks went on, pulling on to the Roman road, 'and see if you can find more samples of his typing. And I'd like you to fingerprint everyone. Ask for their consent, and tell them we can get a magistrate's order if they refuse. Also make sure you tell them that the prints will be destroyed if no charges are brought.' Banks paused and scratched the edge of his scar. 'I'd like to have them all type a few lines on Seth's typewriter, too, but we'll have to wait till it comes back from forensic. All clear?'

'Fine,' Hatchley said.

Zoe answered the door, looking tired and drawn.

'Mara's not here,' she said in response to Banks's question, opening the door only an inch or two.

'I thought she was under sedation.'

'That was last night. She had a good long sleep. She said she felt like going to the shop to work on some pots, and the doctor agreed it might be good therapy. Elspeth's there in case . . . just in case.'

'I'll go down to the village, then,' Banks said to

Hatchley. 'You'll have to manage up here. Will you let sergeant in, Zoe?'

Zoe sighed and opened the door.

'Are you coming back up?' Hatchley asked.

Banks looked at his watch. 'Why not meet in the Black Sheep?'

Hatchley smiled at the prospect of a pint of Black Sheep bitter, then his face fell. 'How do I get there?'

'Walk.'

'Walk?'

'Yes. It's just a mile down the track. Do you good. Give you a thirst.'

Hatchley wasn't convinced – he had never had any problems working up a thirst without exercise before – but Banks left him to his fate and drove down to Relton.

Mara was in the back bent over her wheel, gently turning the lip of a vase. Elspeth led him through, muttered, 'A policeman to see you,' with barely controlled distaste, then went back into the shop itself.

Mara glanced up. 'Let me finish,' she said. 'If I stop now, I'll ruin it.' Banks leaned against the doorway and kept quiet. The room smelled of wet clay. It was also hot. The kiln in the back generated a lot of heat. Mara's long brown hair was tied back, accentuating the sharpness of her nose and chin as she concentrated. Her white smock was stained with splashed clay.

Finally, she drenched the wheel-head with water, sliced off the vase with a length of cheese wire, then slid it carefully on to her hand before transferring it to a board.

'What now?' Banks asked.

'It has to dry.' She put it away in a large cupboard at the back of the room. 'Then it goes in the kiln.'

'I thought the kiln dried it.'

'No. That bakes it. First it has to be dried to the consistency of old cheddar.'

'These are good,' Banks said, pointing to some finished mugs glazed in shades of orange and brown.

'Thanks.' Mara's eyes were puffy and slightly unfocused, her movements slow and zombie-like. Even her voice, Banks noticed, was flatter than usual, drained of emotion and vitality.

'I have to ask you some questions,' he said.

'I suppose you do.'

'Do you mind?'

Mara shook her head. 'Let's get it over with.'

She perched on the edge of her stool and Banks sat on a packing crate just inside the doorway. He could hear Elspeth humming as she busied herself checking on stock in the shop.

'Did you notice anyone gone for an unusually long time during the meeting yesterday afternoon?' Banks asked.

'Was it only yesterday? Lord, it seems like months. No, I didn't notice. People came and went, but I don't think anyone was gone for long. I'm not sure I would have noticed, though.'

'Did Seth ever say anything to you about suicide? Did he ever mention the subject?'

Mara's lips tightened and the blood seemed to drain from them. 'No. Never.'

'He'd tried once before, you know.'

Mara raised her thin eyebrows. 'It seems you knew him better than I did.'

'Nobody knew him, as far as I can tell. There was a will, Mara.'

'I know.'

'Do you remember when he made it?'

'Yes. He joked about it. Said it made him feel like an old man.'

'Is that all?'

'That's all I remember.'

'Did he say why he was making it at that time?'

'No. He just told me that the solicitor who handled the house, Courtney, said he should, and he'd been thinking about it for a long time.'

'Do you know what was in the will?'

'Yes. He said he was leaving me the house. Does that make me a suspect?'

'Did you know about the codicil?'

'Codicil? No.'

'He left his tools and things to Paul.'

'Well, he would, wouldn't he? Paul was keen, and I've got no use for them.'

'Did Paul know?'

'I've no idea.'

'This would be around last Christmas.'

'Maybe it was his idea of a present.'

'But what made him think he was going to die? Seth was what age – forty? By rights he could expect to live to seventy or so. Was he worried about anything?'

'Seth always seemed . . . well, not worried, but pre-occupied. He'd got even more morbid of late. It was just his way.'

'But there was nothing in particular?'

Mara shook her head. 'I don't believe he killed himself, Mr Banks. He had lots to live for. He wouldn't just leave us like that. Everyone depended on Seth. We looked up to him. And he cared about me, about us. I think somebody must have killed him.'

'Who?'

'I don't know.'

Banks shifted position on the packing crate. Its surface was hard and he felt a nail dig into the back of his right thigh. 'Do you remember Elizabeth Dale?'

'Liz. Yes, of course. Funny, I was just thinking about her last night.'

'What about her?'

'Oh, nothing really. How jealous I was, I suppose, when she came to the farm that time. I'd only known Seth six months then. We were happy but, I don't know, I guess I was insecure. Am.'

'Why did you feel jealous?'

'Maybe that's not the right word. I just felt cut out, that's all. Seth and Liz had known each other for a long time, and I didn't share their memories. They used to sit up late talking after I went to bed.'

'Did you hear what they were talking about?'

'No. It was muffled. Do smoke if you want.'

'Thanks.' She must have noticed him fidgeting and looking around for an ashtray. He took out his packet and offered one to Mara.

'I think I will,' she said. 'I can't be bothered to roll my own today.'

'What did you think about Liz Dale?'

Mara lit the cigarette and inhaled deeply. 'I didn't like her, really. I don't know why, just a feeling. She was messed up of course, but even so, she seemed like someone who used people, leaned on them too much, maybe a manipulator.' She shrugged wearily and blew smoke out through her nose. 'She was Seth's friend, though. I wasn't going to say anything.'

'So you put up with her?'

'It was easy enough. She was only with us three days before those SS men from the hospital took her back.'

'Dennis Osmond came up first, didn't he?'

'Yes. But he was too soft, they said. He didn't see why she shouldn't stay where she was, especially as she hadn't been committed or anything, just checked herself in. He argued with the hospital people, but it was no good.'

'How did Osmond and Liz get along?'

'I don't know really. I mean, he stuck up for her, that's all.'

'There wasn't anything between them?'

'What do you mean? Sexual?'

'Anything.'

'I doubt it. They only met twice, and I wouldn't say she was his type.'

'And that was the first time Seth met Osmond?'

'As far as I know.'

'Did you get the impression that Osmond had known Liz before?'

'No, I didn't. But impressions can be wrong. What are you getting at?'

'I'm not sure myself. Just following my nose.'

'Mr Banks,' Mara whispered suddenly, 'do you think Dennis Osmond killed Seth? Is that it? I know Seth couldn't have done it himself, and I . . . I can't seem to think straight.'

'Steady on.' Banks caught her in his arms as she slid forward from the stool. Her hair smelled of apples. He sat her on a stiff-backed chair in the corner, and her eyes filled with tears. 'All right?'

'Yes. I'm sorry. That sedative takes most of the feeling out of me, but . . .'

'It's still there?'

'Yes. Just below the surface.'

'We can continue this later if you like. I'll drive you home.' He thought how pleased Hatchley would be to see the Cortina turning up again.

Mara shook her head. 'No, it's all right. I can handle it. I'm just confused. Maybe some water.'

Banks brought her a glass from the tap at the stained porcelain sink in the corner.

'So are we,' he said. 'Confused. It looked like a suicide in some ways, but there were contradictions.'

'He wouldn't kill himself, I'm sure of it. Paul was back again. Seth was happy. He had the farm, friends, the children . . .'

Banks didn't know what to say to make her feel better.

'When he tried before,' she said, 'was it because of Alison?'

'Yes.'

'I can understand that. It makes sense. But not now. Someone must have killed him.' Mara sipped at her water. 'Anyone could have come in through the side gate and sneaked up on him.'

'It didn't happen like that, Mara. Take my word for it, he had to know the person. It was someone he felt comfortable with. Have you seen or heard anything from Liz Dale since she left?'

'I haven't, no. Seth went to visit her in hospital a couple of times, but then he lost touch.'

'Any letters?'

'Not that he told me about.'

'Christmas card?'

'No.'

'Do you know where she is now?'

'No. Is it important?'

'It could be. Do you know anything about her background?'

Mara frowned and rubbed her temple. 'As far as I know she's from down south somewhere. She used to be a nurse until . . . Well, she fell in with a bad crowd, got involved with drugs and lost her job. Since then she just sort of drifted.'

'And ended up in Hebden Bridge?'

'Yes.'

'Did you see her do any drugs at the farm?'

'No. And I'm not just saying that. She was off heroin. That was part of the problem, why she was unable to cope.'

'Was Seth ever an addict?'

'I don't think so. I think he'd have told me about that. We talked about drugs, how we felt about them and how they weren't really important, so I think he'd have told me.'

'And you've no idea where Liz is now?'

'None at all.'

'What about Alison?'

'What about her? She's dead.'

A hint of bitterness had crept into her tone, and Banks wondered why. Jealousy? It could happen. Plenty of people were jealous of previous lovers, even dead ones. Or was she angry at Seth for not making her fully a part of his life, for not sharing all his feelings? She unfastened her hair and shook her head, allowing the chestnut tresses to cascade over her shoulders.

'Can I have another cigarette?'

'Of course.' Banks gave her one. 'Surely Seth must have told you something,' he said. 'You don't live with someone for two years and find out nothing about their past.'

'Don't you? And how would you know?'

Banks didn't know. When he had met Sandra, they had been young and had little past to talk about, none of it very interesting. 'It doesn't make sense,' he said.

The shop bell clanged and broke the silence. They heard Elspeth welcoming a customer, an American by the sound of his drawl.

'What are you going to do now?' Banks asked.

Mara rubbed her eyes. 'I don't know. I'm too tired to throw another pot. I think I'll just go home and go to bed early.'

'Do you want a lift?'

'No. Really. A bit of fresh air and exercise will do me good.'

Banks smiled. 'I wish my sergeant felt the same way.'

'What?'

Banks explained and Mara managed a weak smile.

They walked out together, Banks collecting a sour look from Elspeth on the way. Outside the Black Sheep, Mara turned away.

'I am sorry, you know, about your loss,' Banks said awkwardly to her back.

Mara turned round and stared at him for a long time. He couldn't make out what she was thinking or feeling.

'I do believe you are,' she said finally.

'And Jenny sends her condolences. She says to give her a call if you ever need anything . . . a friend.'

Mara said nothing.

'She didn't betray your confidence, you know. She was worried about you. And you went to her because you were worried about Paul, didn't you?'

Mara nodded slowly.

'Well, give her a call. All right?'

'All right.' And tall though she was, Mara seemed a slight figure walking up the lane in the dark towards the Roman road. Banks stood and watched till she was out of sight.

Hatchley was already in the Black Sheep – halfway through his second pint, judging by the empty glass next to the half-full one in front of him. Banks went to the bar first, bought two more and sat down. As far as he was concerned, Hatchley could drink as much as he wanted. He was a lousy driver even when sober, and Banks had no intention of letting him anywhere near the Cortina's driving seat.

'Anything?' the sergeant asked.

'No, not really. You?'

'That big bloke with the shaggy beard put up a bit of an argument at first, but the little lass with the red hair told him it was best to cooperate.'

'Damn,' Banks said. 'I knew there was something I'd forgotten. Mara's prints. Never mind, I'll get them later.'

'Anyway,' Hatchley went on, 'most of the letters in the cabinet were carbons, but I managed to rescue a couple of drafts from the bin.'

'Good.'

'You don't sound so pleased,' Hatchley complained.

'What? Oh, sorry. Thinking of something else. Let's drink up and get your findings sent over to the lab.'

Hatchley drained his third pint with astonishing speed and looked at his watch. 'It's going on for six thirty,' he said. 'No point rushing now; they'll all have buggered off home for the night.' He glanced over at the bar. 'Might as well have another.'

Banks smiled. 'Unassailable logic, Sergeant. All right. Better make it a quick one though. And it's your round.'

THREE

At home, Banks managed to warm up a frozen dinner without ruining it. After washing the dishes – or rather rinsing his knife and fork and coffee cup and throwing the foil container into the rubbish bin – he called Sandra.

'So when do I get my wife back?' he asked.

'Wednesday morning. Early train,' Sandra said. 'We should be home around lunch time. Dad's a lot better now and Mum's coping better than I'd imagined.'

'Good. I'll try and be in,' Banks said. 'It depends.'

'How are things going?'

'They're getting more complicated.'

'You sound grouchy, too. It's a good sign. The more complicated things seem and the more bad-tempered you get, the closer the end is.'

'Is that right?'

'Of course it is. I haven't lived with you this long without learning to recognize the signs.'

'Sometimes I wonder what people do learn about one another.'

'What's this? Philosophy?'

'No. Just frustration. Brian and Tracy well?'

'Fine. Just restless. Brian especially. You know Tracy, she's happy enough with her head buried in a history book. But with him it's all sports and pop music now. American football is the latest craze, apparently.'

'Good God.'

Brian had changed a lot over the past year. He even seemed to have lost interest in the electric train that Banks had set up in the spare room. Banks played with it himself more than Brian did, but then, he had to admit, he always had done.

To keep the emptiness after the conversation at bay, he poured out a glass of Bell's and listened to Leroy Carr and Scrapper Blackwell while he tried to let the information that filled his mind drift and form itself into new patterns. Bizarre as it all seemed, a number of things began to come together. The problem was that one theory seemed to cancel out the other.

The doorbell woke him from a light nap just before ten o'clock. The tape had long since ended and the ice had melted in his second Scotch.

'Sorry I'm so late, sir,' Richmond said, 'but I've just finished.'

'Come in.' Banks rubbed his eyes. 'Sit down. A drink?'

'If you don't mind, sir. Though I suppose I am still on duty. Technically.'

'Scotch do? Or there's beer in the fridge.'

'Scotch will do fine, sir. No ice, if you don't mind.'

Banks grinned. 'I'm getting as bad as the Americans, aren't I, putting ice in good Scotch. Soon I'll be complaining my beer is too warm.'

Richmond fitted his long athletic body into an armchair and stroked his moustache.

'By the way you're playing with that bit of face fungus there,' Banks said, 'I gather you've succeeded.'

'What? Oh yes, sir. Didn't know I was so obvious.'

'Most of us are, it seems. You'd not make a good poker player and you'd better watch it in interrogations. Come on then, what did you find?'

'Well,' Richmond began, consulting his notebook, 'I did exactly as you said, sir. Hung around discreetly near Tim and Abha's place. They stayed in all afternoon.'

'Then what?'

'They went out about eight, to the pub I'd guess. And

about half an hour later that blue Escort pulled up and two men got out and disappeared into the building. They looked like the ones you described. They must have been waiting and watching somewhere nearby, because they seemed to know when to come, allowing a bit of a safety margin in case Tim and Abha had just gone to the shop or something.'

'You didn't try to stop them from getting in, did you?'

Richmond seemed shocked. 'I did exactly as you instructed me, sir, though it felt a bit odd to sit there and watch a crime taking place. The front door is usually left on the latch, so they just walked in. The individual flats are kept locked though, so they must have broken in. Anyway, they came out about fifteen minutes later carrying what looked like a number of buff folders.'

'And then what?'

'I followed them at a good distance, and they pulled into the car park of the Castle Hotel and went inside. I didn't follow, sir – they might have noticed me. And they didn't come out. After they'd been gone about ten minutes, I went in and asked the desk clerk about them and got him to show me the register. They'd booked in as James Smith and Thomas Brown.'

'How imaginative. Sorry, carry on.'

'Well, I rather thought that myself, sir, so I went back to the office and checked on the number of the car. It was rented by a firm in York to a Mr Cranby, Mr Keith J. Cranby, if that means anything to you. He had to show his licence of course, so that's likely to be his right name.'

'Cranby? No, it doesn't ring any bells. What happened next?'

'Nothing, sir. It was getting late by then so I thought I'd better come and report. By the way, I saw that barmaid

Glenys, going into the hotel while I was waiting outside. Looked a bit sheepish, she did too.'

'Was Cyril anywhere in sight?'

'No. I didn't see him.'

'You've done a fine job, Phil,' Banks said. 'I owe you for this one.'

'What's it all about?'

'I'd rather not say yet, in case I'm wrong. But you'll be the second to find out, I promise. Have you eaten at all?'

'I packed some sandwiches.' He looked at his watch. 'I could do with a pint, though.'

'There's still beer in the fridge.'

'I don't like bottled beer.' Richmond patted his flat stomach. 'Too gassy.'

'And too cold?'

Richmond nodded.

'Come on, then. We should make it in time for a jar or two before closing. My treat. Queen's Arms do you?'

'Fine, sir.'

The pub was busy and noisy with locals and farm lads in from the villages. Banks glanced at the bar staff and saw neither Glenys nor Cyril in evidence. Pushing his way to the bar, he asked one of the usual stand-in barmaids where the boss was.

'Took the evening off, Mr Banks. Just like that.' She snapped her fingers. 'Said there'd be three of us so we should be able to cope. Dead cagey, he was too. Still, he's the boss, isn't he? He can do what he likes.'

'True enough, Rosie,' Banks said. 'I'll have two pints of your best bitter, please.'

'Right you are, Mr Banks.'

They stood at the bar and chatted with the regulars, who knew better than to ask too many questions about their work. Banks was beginning to feel unusually pleased with himself, considering he still hadn't found the answer. Whether it was the chat with Sandra, the nap, Richmond's success or the drink, he didn't know. Perhaps it was a combination of all four. He was close to the end of the case though, he knew that. If he could solve the problem of two mutually exclusive explanations for Gill's and Seth's deaths, then he would be home and dry. Tomorrow should be an interesting day. First he would track down Liz Dale and discover what she knew; then there was the other business . . . Yes, tomorrow should be very interesting indeed. And the day after that, Sandra was due home.

'Last orders, please!' Rosie shouted.

'Shall we?' Richmond asked.

'Go on. Why not,' said Banks. He felt curiously like celebrating.

16

ONE

Dirty Dick was conspicuous by his absence the following morning. Banks took the opportunity to make a couple of important phone calls before getting an early start.

Just south of Bradford, it started to rain. Banks turned on the wipers and lit a cigarette from the dashboard lighter. On the car stereo, Walter Davis sang, 'You got bad blood, baby, I believe you need a shot.'

It was so easy to get lost in the conurbation of old West Yorkshire woollen towns. Built in valleys on the eastern edges of the Pennines, they seemed to overlap one another, and it was hard to tell exactly where you were. The huge old textile factories, where all the processes of clothes-making had been gathered together under one roof in the last century looked grim in the failing light. They were five or six storeys high, with flat roofs, rows of windows close together and tall chimneys you could see for miles.

Cleckheaton, Liversedge, Heckmondwike, Brighouse, Rastrick, Mirfield – the strange names Banks usually associated only with brass bands and rugby teams – flew by on road signs. As he drew nearer to Huddersfield, he slowed and peered out through his rain-splattered windscreen for the turn-off.

Luckily the psychiatric hospital was at the northern end

343

of town, so he didn't have to cross the centre. When he saw the signpost, he followed directions to the left, down a street between two derelict warehouses.

The greenery of the hospital grounds came as a shock after so many miles of bleak industrial wasteland. There was a high brick wall and a guard at the gate, but beyond that the drive wound its way by trees and a well-kept lawn to the modern L-shaped hospital complex. Banks parked in the visitors' area, then presented himself at reception.

'That'll be Dr Preston,' said the receptionist, looking up Elizabeth Dale in her roll file. 'But the doctor can't divulge any information about his patients, you know.'

Banks smiled. 'He will see me, won't he?'

'Oh, of course. He's with our bursar now, but if you'll wait he should be finished in ten minutes or so. You can wait over in the canteen if you like. The tea's not too bad.'

Banks thanked her and walked towards the cluster of bright orange plastic tables and chairs.

'Oh, Mr Banks?' she called after him.

He turned.

She put her hands to the sides of her mouth and spoke quietly and slowly, mouthing the words as if for a lip-reader. 'You won't wander off, will you?' She flicked her eyes right and left as if to indicate that beyond those points lay monsters.

Banks assured her that he wouldn't, bought a cup of tea and a Penguin biscuit from the pretty teenage girl at the counter and sat down.

There was only one other person in the canteen, a skinny man with a pronounced stoop and hair combed straight back from his creased brow. He was dressed as a vicar. Seeing Banks, he brought his cup over and sat down. He had a long thin nose and a small mouth. The shape of his head, Banks noticed, was distinctly odd; it was triangular, and the forehead sloped sharply backwards. With his hair brushed straight back, standing at forty-five degrees, he looked as if his entire face had been sculpted by a head-on wind.

'Mind if I join you?' he asked, smiling in a way that screwed up his features grotesquely.

'Not if you don't mind my smoking,' Banks replied.

'Go ahead, old chap; doesn't bother me at all.' His accent was educated and southern. 'Haven't seen you here before?'

It should have been a comment, but it sounded like a question.

'That's not surprising,' Banks said. 'I've never been here before. I'm a policeman.'

'Oh, jolly good!' the vicar exclaimed. 'Which one? Let me guess: Clouseau? Poirot? Holmes?'

Banks laughed. 'I'm not as clumsy as Clouseau,' he said. 'Nor, I'm afraid, am I as brilliant as Poirot and Holmes. My name's Banks. Chief Inspector Banks.'

The vicar frowned. 'Banks, eh? I haven't heard of him.'

'Well, you wouldn't have, would you?' Banks said, puzzled. 'It's me. I'm Banks. I'm here to see Dr Preston.'

The vicar's expression brightened. 'Dr Preston? Oh, I'm sure you'll like him. He's very good.'

'Is he helping you?'

'Helping me? Why, no. I help him, of course.'

'Of course,' Banks said slowly.

A nurse paused by the table and spoke his name. 'Dr Preston will see you now,' she said.

The vicar stuck out his hand. 'Well, good luck, old boy.'

Banks shook it and muttered his thanks.

'That man back there,' he said to the nurse as she

clicked beside him along the corridor, 'should he be wandering around freely? What's he in for?'

The nurse laughed. 'That's not a patient; that's the Reverend Clayton. He comes to visit two or three times a week. He must have thought *you* were a new patient.'

Bloody hell, Banks thought, you could go crazy hanging around a place like this.

Dr Preston's office lacked the sharp polished instruments, kidney bowls, hypodermics and mysterious odds and ends that Banks usually found so disconcerting in Glendenning's lair. This room was more like a comfortable study with a pleasant view of the landscaped grounds.

Preston stood up as Banks entered. His handshake was firm and brief. He looked younger than Banks had expected, with a thatch of thick shiny brown hair, a complexion as smooth as a baby's bottom, and cheeks just as chubby and rosy. His eyes, enlarged behind spectacles, were watchful and serious.

'What can I do for you, Chief Inspector?' he asked.

'I'm interested in an ex-patient of yours called Elizabeth Dale. At least, I think she's an ex-patient.'

'Oh, yes,' Preston said. 'Been gone ages now. What exactly is it you wish to know? I'm sure you realize that I'm not at liberty to—'

'Yes, Doctor, I understand that. I don't want the details of her illness. As I understand it, she was suffering from depression.'

'Well' – the doctor unbent a paper clip on his blotter – 'I suppose in layman's terms . . . But you said that's not what you came about?'

'That's right. I just want to know where she is. Nothing confidential about that, is there?'

'We don't usually give out personal information.'

'It's important. A murder inquiry. I could get a court order.'

'Oh, I don't think that will be necessary,' Preston said quickly. 'The problem is though, I'm afraid we don't know where Miss Dale is.'

'No idea?'

'No. You see, we don't keep tabs on ex-patients as a rule.'

'When did she leave here?'

Preston searched through his files. 'She stayed for two months.' He read off the dates.

'Is that usual? Two months?'

'Hard to say. It varies from patient to patient. Miss Dale was . . . Well, I don't think I'm giving too much away if I tell you she was difficult. She'd hardly been here a couple of days before she ran off.'

'Yes, I know.' Banks explained his involvement. 'As far as I understand though, she admitted herself in the first place, is that right?'

'Yes.'

'Yet you treated her as if she had escaped from a high-security prison.'

Preston leaned back in his chair and his jaw muscles twitched. 'You have to understand, Chief Inspector, that when anyone arrives here, they are given a whole range of tests and a complete physical examination. On the basis of these, we make a diagnosis and prescribe treatment. I had examined Miss Dale and decided she required treatment. When she disappeared we were naturally worried that she . . . Well, without the proper treatment, who knows what might have become of her? So we took steps to persuade her to come back.'

'Doctor knows best, eh?'

Preston glared at him.

'How was she when she'd completed her treatment?' Banks asked.

'Given your hostile attitude, I don't know that I care to answer that.'

Bank sighed and reached for a cigarette. 'Oh, come on, Doctor, don't sulk. Was she cured or wasn't she?'

Preston passed an ashtray as Banks lit up. 'That'll kill you, you know.' He seemed to take great pleasure in the observation.

'Not before I get an answer from you, I hope.'

Preston pursed his lips. 'I imagine you know about Elizabeth Dale's drug problem?'

'Yes.'

'That was part of the cause of her mental illness. When she came to us she'd been off heroin for about a month. Naturally, we're not equipped to deal with addicts here, and if Miss Dale had been still using drugs we would have had to send her elsewhere. However, she stayed, on medication I prescribed, and she made some progress. At the end of two months, I felt she was ready to leave.'

'What did *she* feel?'

Preston stared out of his window at the landscaped garden. A row of topiary shrubs stood close to the building, cut in the shapes of birds and animals.

'Miss Dale,' Preston started slowly, 'was afraid of life and afraid of her addiction. The one led to the other, an apparently endless circle.'

'What you're saying is that once she'd got used to the idea she'd have been happy to stay here for ever. Am I right?'

'Not just here. Any institution, anywhere she didn't have to make her own decisions and face the world.'

'And that's the kind of place I'm likely to find her in?'

'I'd say so, yes.'

'Can you be any more specific?'

'You might try a DDU.'

'DDU?'

'Yes. A drug dependency unit, for the treatment of addicts. Elizabeth had been in and out of one a couple of times before she came to us.'

'So she hadn't been cured?'

'How many are? Oh, some, I agree. But with Elizabeth it was on and off, on and off. The cure worked for a while – Methadone hydrochloride in gradually decreasing doses. It's rather like chewing nicotine gum when you're trying to stop smoking. Helps with some of the severe physical symptoms, but—'

'That's not enough?'

'Not really. Many addicts get hooked again as soon as the opportunity for a fix arises. Unfortunately, given the network of friends they have, that can be very soon.'

'So you think a DDU might have Liz as a patient, or might know where she is?'

'It's likely.'

'Where is the nearest one?' Banks slipped out his notebook.

'The only local one is just outside Halifax, not too far away.' Preston continued to give directions. 'I hope she's not in any trouble,' he said finally.

'I don't think so. Just need her to help us with our inquiry.'

Preston adjusted his glasses on the bridge of his nose. 'You do have a way with words, you policemen, don't you?'

'I'm glad we've got something in common with

doctors.' Banks smiled and stood up to leave. 'You've been a great help.'

'Have I?'

Banks beat a hasty retreat from the hospital back on to the rainswept roads and headed for Halifax. He soon found the DDU, using the Wainhouse Tower as a landmark as Dr Preston had suggested. Originally built as a factory chimney, the tall black tower was never used as one and now stands as a folly and a lookout point, its top ornamented in a very un-chimney-like pointed Gothic style.

Banks found the DDU up a steep side street. It was set back from the road at the top of a long sloping lawn and looked like a Victorian mansion. It also had an eerie quality to it, Banks felt. He shivered as he made his approach. Not the kind of place I'd want to find myself in after dark, he thought.

There were no walls or men at the gate here. Banks walked straight inside and found himself standing in a spacious common room with a high ceiling. On the walls hung a number of paintings, clearly the work of patients, dominated by an enormous canvas depicting an angel plummeting to earth, wings ablaze and neck contorted so that it looked straight at the viewer, eyes red and wild, raw muscles stretched like knotted ropes. It could have been Satan on his way to hell. Certainly the destination, impressionistically rendered in the lower half of the painting, was a dark and murky place. He shuddered and looked away.

'Can I help you?' A young woman came up to him. It wasn't clear from her appearance whether she was a member of staff or a patient. She was in her early thirties perhaps, and wore jeans and a dark brown jacket over a white blouse. Her long black hair was plaited and pinned back.

'Yes,' Banks said. 'I'm looking for Elizabeth Dale. Is she here, or do you know where I can find her?'

'Who are you?'

Banks showed her his identification.

The woman raised her eyebrows. 'Police? What do you want?'

'I want to talk to Elizabeth Dale,' he repeated. 'Is she here or isn't she?'

'What's it about?'

'I'm the one who asks the questions,' Banks said, irritated by her brusque haughty manner. Suddenly, he realized who she must be. 'Look, Doctor,' he went on, 'it's nothing to do with drugs. It's about an old friend of hers. I need some information to help solve a murder case, that's all.'

'Elizabeth's been here for the past month. She can't be involved.'

'I'm not saying she is. Will you just let me to talk to her?'

The doctor frowned. Banks could see her brain working fast behind her eyes. 'All right,' she said finally. 'But treat her gently. She's very fragile. And I insist on being present.'

'I'd rather talk to her alone.' The last thing Banks wanted was this woman watching over the conversation like a lawyer.

'I'm afraid that's not possible.'

'How about if you remained within calling distance? Say, the other end of this room?' The room was certainly large enough to accommodate more than one conversation.

The doctor smiled out of the side of her mouth. 'A

compromise? All right. Stay here while I fetch Elizabeth. Take a seat.'

But Banks felt restless after being in the car. Instead, he walked around the room looking at the paintings, almost all of which illustrated some intense level of terror: mad eyes staring through a letter box; a naked man being dragged away from a woman, his features creased in a desperate plea; a forest in which every carefully painted leaf looked like a needle of fire. They sent shivers up his spine. Noticing plenty of pedestal ashtrays around, he lit up. It was warm in the room, so he took off his car coat and laid it on a chair.

About five minutes later, the doctor returned with another woman. 'This is Elizabeth Dale,' she said, introducing them formally, then walked off to the far end of the room, where she sat facing Banks and pretended to read a magazine. Liz took a chair on his left, angled so they could face one another comfortably. The chairs were well padded, with strong armrests.

'I saw you looking at the paintings,' Elizabeth said 'Quite something, aren't they?' She had a melodic hypnotic voice. Banks could easily imagine its persuasive powers. He had a feeling, however, that it would probably become tiresome after a while: whining and wheedling rather than beautiful and soft.

Elizabeth Dale smoothed her long powder-blue skir over her knees. Her slight frame was lost inside a bagg mauve sweater with two broad white hoops around th middle. If she was Seth's contemporary that made he about forty, but her gaunt waxy face was lined like that c a much older woman and her black hair, hacked sho rather than cut, was liberally streaked with grey. It was face that screamed of suffering; eyes that had looked dee

352

inside and seen the horror there. Yet her voice was beautiful. So gentle, so soothing, like a breeze through woods in spring.

'They're very powerful,' Banks said, feeling his words pathetically inadequate.

'People see those things here,' Elizabeth said. 'Do you know what this place used to be?'

'No.'

'It was a hospital, a fever hospital, during the typhoid epidemics in the last century. I can hear the patients screaming every night.'

'You mean the place is haunted?'

Elizabeth shrugged. 'Maybe it's me who's haunted. People go crazy here sometimes. Break windows and try to cut themselves with broken glass. I can hear the typhoid victims screaming every night as they're burning up and snapping bones in convulsions. I can hear the bones snap.' She clapped her hands. 'Crack. Just like that.'

Then she put her hand over her mouth and laughed. Banks noticed the first and second fingers of her right hand were stained yellow with nicotine. She rummaged inside her sweater and pulled out a packet of Embassy Regal and a tarnished silver lighter. Banks took out a cigarette of his own and she leaned forward to give him a light. The flame was high and he caught a whiff of petrol fumes as he inhaled.

'You know,' Elizabeth went on, 'for all that – the hosts, the screaming, the cold – I'd rather be here than . . . than out there.' She nodded her head towards the door. 'That's where the real horror is, Mr Banks, out there.'

'I take it you don't keep up with the world then. No newspapers, no television?'

Elizabeth shook her head. 'No. There is a television

here, next door. But I don't watch it. I read books. O
books. Charles Dickens, that's who I'm reading now
There's opium-taking in *Edwin Drood*, did you know that

Banks nodded. He had been through a Dickens pha:
some years ago.

'Have you come about the complaint?' Elizabeth aske

'What complaint?'

'It was years ago. I made a complaint about a polic
man hitting people with his truncheon at a demonstratio
I don't know what became of it. I never heard a thing.
was different then; things seemed more worthwhi
fighting for. Now I just let them go their way. They'll blo
it up, Mr Banks. Oh, there's no doubt about it, they
blow us all up. Or is it drugs you want to talk about?'

'It's partly about the complaint, yes. I wanted to talk
you about Seth Cotton. Seth and Alison.'

'Good old Seth. Poor old Seth. I don't want to talk abo
Seth. I don't have to talk to you, do I?'

'Why don't you want to talk about him?'

'Because I don't. Seth's private. I won't tell y
anything he wouldn't, so it's no good asking.'

Banks leaned forward. 'Elizabeth,' he said gentl
'Seth's dead. I'm sorry, but it's true.'

At first he thought she wasn't going to react at all.
little sigh escaped her, nothing more than a gust of wii
against a dark window. 'Well, that's all right then, isn't i
she said, her voice softer, weaker. 'Peace at last.' Then s
closed her eyes and her face assumed such a distant hc
expression that Banks didn't dare break the silence.
would have been blasphemy. When she opened her ey
again, they were clear. 'My little prayer,' she said.

'What did you mean, poor Seth?'

'He was such a serious man, and he had to suffer

much pain. How did he die, Mr Banks? Was it peaceful?'

'Yes,' Banks lied.

Elizabeth nodded.

'The problem is,' Banks said, 'that nobody knew very much about him, about his feelings or his past. You were quite close to Seth and Alison, weren't you?'

'I was, yes.'

'Is there anything you can tell me about him, about his past, that might help me understand him better. I know he was upset about Alison's accident—'

'Accident?'

'Yes. You must know, surely? The car—'

'Alison's death wasn't an accident, Mr Banks. She was murdered.'

'Murdered?'

'Oh, yes. It was murder all right. I told Seth. I made him believe me.'

'When?'

'I figured it out. I used to be a nurse, you know.'

'I know. What did you figure out?'

'Are you sure Seth's dead?'

Banks nodded.

She eyed him suspiciously, then smiled. 'I suppose I can tell you then. Are you sitting comfortably? That's what they say before the story on *Children's Hour*, you know. I used to listen to that when I was young. It's funny how things stick in your memory, isn't it? But so much doesn't. Why is that, do you think? Isn't the mind peculiar? Do you remember Uncle Mac and *Children's Favourites*? *Sparky and the Magic Piano*? Petula Clark singing "Little Green Man"?'

'I'm sorry, I don't remember,' Banks said. 'But I'm sitting comfortably.'

Elizabeth smiled. 'Good. Then I'll begin.'

And she launched into one of the saddest and strangest stories that Banks had ever heard.

TWO

What Liz Dale told him confirmed what he had been beginning to suspect. His theories were no longer mutually exclusive, but he felt none of his usual elation on solving this case.

He drove back to Eastvale slowly, taking the longest most meandering route west through the gritstone country away from the large towns and cities. There was no hurry. On the way, he listened to scratchy recordings of the old bluesmen: gamblers, murderers, ministers, alcoholics drug addicts singing songs about poverty, sex, the devil and bad luck. And the signs flashed by: Mytholmroyd, Todmorden, Cornholme. In Lancashire now, he skirted the Burnley area on a series of minor roads that led by the Forest of Trawden, then he was soon back in Craven country around Skipton, where the grass was lush green with limestone-rich soils.

He stopped in Grassington and had a pub lunch, the cut across Greenhow Hill by Pateley Bridge and got back to Eastvale via Ripon.

Burgess was waiting in his office. 'You owe me a fiver,' he said. 'A couple of glasses of Mumm and she was all over me.'

'There's no accounting for taste,' Banks said.

'You'll have to take my word for it. I'm not crass; don't go in for stealing knickers as a trophy.'

Banks nodded towards the superintendent's swollen

purplish cheek. 'I see you've got a trophy of a kind.'

'That bloody husband of hers. Mistrustful swine.' He fingered the bruise. 'But that was later. He's lucky I didn't pull him in for assaulting a police officer. Still, I suppose he deserved a swing at me, so I let him. All nice and quiet.'

'Very magnanimous of you.' Banks pulled a five-pound note from his wallet and dropped it on the desk.

'What's wrong with you today, Banks? Sore loser?' Burgess picked up the money and held it out. 'Fuck it, you don't have to pay if you're that hard up.'

Banks sat down and lit a cigarette. 'Ever heard of a fellow called Barney Merritt?' he asked.

'No. Should I?'

'He's an old friend of mine, still on the Met. He's heard of you. He's also heard of DC Cranby. Keith J. Cranby.'

'So?' The muscles around Burgess's jaw tightened and his eyes seemed to turn brighter and sharper.

Banks tapped a folder on his desk. 'Cranby and a mate of his – possible DC Stickley – rented a blue Escort in York a couple of days ago. They drove up to Eastvale and checked into the Castle Hotel, the same place as you. I'm surprised you didn't pass each other in the lobby, it's not that big a place.'

'Do you realize what you're saying? Maybe you should reconsider and stop while the going's good.'

Banks shook his head and went on.

'The other day they broke into Dennis Osmond's flat. They didn't find what they were looking for, but they took one of his political books to put the wind up him. He thought he had every security force in the world after him. Yesterday evening they broke into Tim and Abha's apartment and took away a number of folders. That was after I told you where the information they'd collected on the demo was kept.'

Burgess tapped a ruler on the desk. 'You have proof of all this, I suppose?'

'If I need it, yes.'

'What on earth made you think of such a thing?'

'I know your methods. And when I mentioned the Osmond break-in you didn't seem surprised. You didn't even seem to care very much. That was odd, because my first thought was that it might have had a bearing on the Gill case. But, of course, you already knew all about it.'

'And what are you going to do?'

'I just don't understand you,' Banks said. 'What the bloody hell did you hope to achieve? You used the same vigilante tactics they did in Manchester after the Leon Brittan demo.'

'They worked though, didn't they?'

'If you call hounding a couple of students out of the country and drawing national attention to the worst elements of policing good, then yes, they worked.'

'Don't be so bloody naive, Banks. These people are all connected.'

'You're paranoid, do you know that? What do you think they are? Terrorists?'

'They're connected. Union leaders, bolshie students, ban-the-bombers. They're all connected. You can call them misguided idealists if you want, but to me they're a bloody menace.'

'To who? To what?'

Burgess leaned forward and gripped the desk. 'To the peace and stability of the nation, that's what. Whose side are you on, anyway?'

'I'm not on anyone's side. I've been investigating a

murder, remember? A policeman was killed. He wasn't a very good one, but I don't think he deserved to end up dead in the street. And what do I find? You bring your personal bloody goon squad from London and they start breaking and entering.'

'There's no point arguing ethics with you, Banks—'

'I know, because you don't have a leg to stand on.'

'But let me remind you that I'm in charge of this case.'

'That still doesn't give you the right to do what you did. Can't you bloody understand? You with all your talk about police image. The vigilante stuff only makes us end up looking like the bad guys, and bloody stupid ones at that.'

Burgess sat back and lit a cigar. 'Only if people find out. Which brings us back to my question. What are you going to do?'

'Nothing. But you're going to make sure those files are returned and that the people involved are left alone from now on.'

'Am I? What makes you so sure?'

'Because if you don't, I'll pass on what I know to Superintendent Gristhorpe. The ACC respects his opinion.'

Burgess laughed. 'You're not very well connected, you know. I don't think that'll do much good.'

'There's always the press, too. They'd love a juicy story like this. Dennis Osmond has a right to know what was done to him, too. Whatever you think, I don't believe it would do your future promotion prospects much good.'

Burgess tapped his cigar on the rim of the ashtray. 'You're so bloody pure of heart, aren't you, Banks? A real crusader. Better than the rest of us.'

'You were out of line and you know it. You just thought you could get away with it.'

'I still can.'

Banks shook his head.

'You're forgetting that I'm your superior officer. I can order you to hand over whatever evidence you've got.'

'Balls,' said Banks. 'Why don't you send Cranby and Stickley in to steal it?'

'Look,' Burgess said, reddening with anger, 'you don't want to cross me. I can be a very nasty enemy. Do you really think anyone's going to take any notice of your accusations? What do you think they'll do? Kick me off the force? Dream on.'

'I don't really care what they do to you. All I know is that the press will have a field day with it.'

'You'd be sawing off the branch you're sitting on. Think about where your loyalty lies. We do a difficult enough job as it is without taking an opportunity to set everyone against us. Have you considered that? What effect it would have on you lot up here if it did get out? I don't have to live here, thank God, but you do.'

'Damn right I do,' said Banks. 'And that's the point. You can come here and make a bloody mess then bugger off back to London. I have to live and work with these people. And I like it. It took me long enough to get accepted as far as I have been, and you come along and set back relations by years. Take it or leave it. Give back the files, call off your goons and it's forgotten, another un-solved break-in.'

'Oh, what a bleeding hero we are! And what if I put on a bit more pressure, got a couple of higher-ups to order you to hand over your evidence? What then, big man?'

'I've already told you,' Banks said. 'It's not me you need to worry about; it's the press, Osmond and the students.'

'I can handle them.'

'It's up to you.'

'That's it?'

'That's it. Take your pick.'

'Who's going to believe a couple of loony lefties anyway? And everyone knows the press is biased.'

Banks shrugged. 'Maybe nobody. We'll see.'

Burgess jerked to his feet. 'I won't forget this, Banks,' he snarled. 'When I make my report on this investigation—'

'It's over,' Banks said wearily.

'What is?'

'The investigation.' Banks told him briefly about his conversation with Elizabeth Dale.

'So what happens now?'

'Nothing. Except maybe you piss off back home.'

'You're not going to go blabbing the whole bloody story to the press?'

'No point, no. But I think Mara and the others have a right to know.'

'Yes, you would.' Burgess strode over to the door. 'And don't think you've won, because you haven't. You won't get out of it as easily as all that.'

And he left, the threat hanging in the air.

Banks stretched out his hands in front of him and noticed they were shaking. Even though the office was cool, his neck felt sweaty under the collar. His legs were weak too, as he found out when he grabbed another cigarette and walked over to the window. It wasn't every day you got the chance to be high-handed with a senior officer, especially a whizz-kid like Dirty Dick Burgess. And it was the first time Banks had ever seen him ruffled.

Maybe he *had* made a dangerous enemy for life. Perhaps Burgess had even been right and he was overplaying the crusader role. After all, he played it a bit close to the edge himself sometimes. But to hell with it, he thought. It wasn't worth dwelling on. He picked up his coat, pocketed his cigarettes and set off for the car park.

THREE

The rain had stopped and the afternoon sun was charming wraiths of mist from the river meadows and valley sides. Banks's Cortina crackled up the track and pulled up outside the farmhouse.

Mara answered the door on his second knock and let him in.

'I suppose you want to sit down?' she asked.

'It might take a while.' Banks made himself comfortable in the rocking chair. The children sat at the table colouring, and Paul slouched on the beanbag cushions reading a science-fiction book.

'Where are Rick and Zoe?' Banks asked.

'Working.'

'Can you go and get them, please? I'd like to talk to all of you. And would it be too much to ask for some tea?'

Mara put the kettle on first, then went out to the barn to fetch the others. When she came back, she saw to the tea while Rick and Zoe sat down.

'What the bloody hell is this?' Rick demanded. 'Haven't we had enough? Where's your friend?'

'He's packing.'

'Packing?' Mara said, walking in slowly with the teapot and mugs on a tray. 'But—'

'It's all over, Mara. Almost over, anyway.'

Banks poured himself some tea, lit a cigarette and turned to Paul. 'You wrote that suicide note, didn't you?'

'I don't know what you're talking about.'

'Come off it, the time for messing around is over. The pressure on the keys was different from that on the letters Seth typed, and his style was a hell of a lot better than yours. Why did you do it?'

'I've told you, I didn't do anything.' They were all staring at him now and he began to turn red.

'Shall I tell you why you did it?' Banks went on. 'You did it to deflect the blame from yourself.'

'Wait a minute,' Mara said. 'Are you accusing Paul of killing Seth?'

'Nobody killed Seth,' Banks said quietly. 'He did it himself.'

'But you said—'

'I know. And that's what we thought. It was the note that confused me. Seth didn't write it; Paul did. But he didn't kill anyone. When Paul found him, Seth was already dead. Paul just took the opportunity to type out a note of confession, hoping it would get him off the hook. It didn't seem like such a bad thing to do, I'm sure. After all, Seth was dead. Nothing could affect him any more. Isn't that right, Paul?'

Paul said nothing.

'Paul?' Mara turned to face him sternly. 'Is it true?'

'So what if it is? Seth wouldn't have minded. He wouldn't have wanted us to go on being persecuted. He was dead, Mara. I swear it. All I did was type out a note.'

'Had he written anything himself?' Banks asked.

'Yes, but it said nothing.' He pulled a scrap of paper out of the back pocket of his jeans and passed it over. It read, 'Sorry, Mara.' Just that. Banks passed it to Mara, and tears filled her eyes. She wiped them away with the back of her hand. 'How could you, Paul?' she said.

Paul sat forward and hugged his knees. 'It was for all of us,' he said. 'Can't you see? To keep the police off our backs. It's what Seth would have done.'

'But he didn't,' Banks said. 'Seth had no idea that Paul would forge a note. As far as he was concerned, his suicide would be accepted for what it was. He never imagined that we'd see it as murder. If his death led us to the truth, so be it, but he wasn't going to explain. He never did while he was alive, so why should he when he was about to die?'

'The truth?' Mara said. 'Is that what you're going to tell us now?'

'Yes. If you want me to.'

Mara nodded.

'You might not like it.'

'After all we've been through,' she said, 'I think you owe it to us.'

'Very well. I think Seth killed himself out of shame, among other reasons. He felt he'd let everyone down, including himself.'

'What do you mean?'

'I mean that Seth stabbed PC Gill and he couldn't live with what he'd done. Paul had already suffered for it. Seth would never have let him take the blame. He'd have confessed himself rather than that. When Paul was released, he was happy for him. What it meant for Seth though, was that the police would get even closer to him now. It was just a matter of time. I'd already seen PC Gill's number in his notebook and those books in his workshop. I knew it was his knife, too. I'd asked him about Elizabeth Dale, and he knew how unstable she was. All I had to do was find her and get her to talk. Seth knew all this. He knew it would soon be all over for him.'

Mara was pale. Her hands trembled as she tried to roll a cigarette. Banks offered her a Silk Cut and she took it. Zoe went around and poured tea for everyone.

'I can't believe this, you know,' Mara said, shaking her head. 'Not Seth.'

'It's true. I'm not saying that he intended to kill PC Gill. He couldn't be sure that the demo would turn nasty, even though Gill was supposed to be there. But he went prepared. He knew very well the kind of things that were likely to happen if Gill was around. That's why I asked you if you'd heard anyone mention Gill's number that afternoon. Someone had it in for him and knew he'd be there.'

'I thought it sounded vaguely familiar,' Mara said, speaking quietly as if to herself. 'I was in the kitchen, I think, with Seth.'

'And Osmond mentioned the number.'

'I . . . It could have been like that. But why Seth? He wasn't like that. He was a gentle person.'

'I agree, on the whole,' Banks said. 'But the circumstances are very unusual. I had to find Liz Dale to put it all together. She told me a very curious thing, which was that Alison, Seth's wife, was murdered. Now that didn't make sense to me, because I'd spoken to the local police and to the man who ran her over. It was an accident. He hadn't killed her deliberately. It had ruined his life, too.

'Seth tried to commit suicide after Alison's death, but he failed. He got on with his life but he never got over his grief, and that's partly because he never expressed it. You know he didn't like to talk about the past; he kept it all bottled up inside, all those feelings of grief and guilt. We always blame ourselves when someone we love dies, because maybe, just in a fleeting moment, we've wished them dead, and we tell ourselves that if things had been just a little different – if Seth had ridden to the shops that day instead of Alison – then the tragedy would never have happened. Liz was the only one who really knew what went on, and that was only because she was a close friend of Alison's. According to the Hebden Bridge police, Alison was more outgoing, spirited and communicative than Seth. Because he was the "strong silent type", everyone thought he was really in control, calm and cool, but he was torturing himself inside.'

'I still don't see,' Mara said. 'What does all this have to do with that policeman who got killed?'

Banks blew gently on the surface and sipped some tea. It tasted of apple and cinnamon. 'Liz Dale filed a complaint about PC Gill's vicious behaviour during a demo she went to with Alison Cotton. Seth hadn't been there himself. During the demo, Liz told me, Alison was struck a glancing blow on her temple by Gill. It was just one of many such incidents that afternoon. Alison didn't want to make a fuss and attract police attention by making a complaint, but Liz was far more political in general. When nothing came of it, she didn't pursue it any further. She'd lost interest by then – heroin made her forget politics – and like you she assumed that the police wouldn't listen to someone like her.'

'Can you blame her?' Rick said. 'They obviously didn't, did they? It hardly seems that—'

'Shut up,' Banks said. He spoke quietly, but forcefully enough to silence Rick.

'Over the next few months,' he went on, 'Alison started to show some unusual symptoms. She complained of frequent headaches, she was becoming forgetful and she suffered from dizzy spells. Shortly afterwards she became pregnant, so she put her other troubles out of her mind for a while.

'One time though, she really scared Seth and Liz. She started speaking as if she were a fourteen-year-old girl. Her family had been on holiday in Cyprus then, staying with an army friend of her father's who was stationed there, and she started describing a warm evening walk by the Mediterranean in Famagusta in great detail. Apparently even her voice was like that of a fourteen-year-old. Finally she snapped out of it and recalled nothing. She just laughed when the others told her what she'd been talking about.

'But that did it as far as Seth was concerned. He was worried she might have a brain tumour or something, so he insisted she tell the doctor. According to Liz, the doctor had nothing much to say except that pregnancy can do strange things to a woman's mind as well as her body. Alison told him that the symptoms started *before* she got pregnant but he just said something about people having funny spells, and that was that.

'A few weeks later, she went to the local shop one evening and got lost. It was about a two-minute walk away, and she couldn't find her way home. Seth and Liz found her wandering the streets an hour later. Anyway, things didn't get much better and she went to see the doctor again. At first he tried to blame the pregnancy again, but Alison stressed the terrible headaches, lapses of memory and slipping in and out of time. He said not to worry, but he arranged for a CAT scan, just to be on the safe side. Well, you know the National Health Service. By the time her appointment came around, she was already dead. And they couldn't do a proper autopsy later because of the accident – her head was crushed.

'Seth had his breakdown, attempted suicide, pu
himself back together and bought the farm, where he lived
in isolation for a while until you came along, Mara. He
proved himself capable of moving on, but he carried all the
weight of the past with him. He was always a serious
person, a man of strong feelings, but there was a new
darker dimension to him after the shock of Alison's death.

'It doesn't make sense,' Mara said. 'If all that's true
why did he wait so long before doing what you say he
did?'

'Two reasons really. First, he wasn't convinced until
about a year ago. That's around the time he made his will
According to Liz, about eighteen months ago he'd read an
article in a magazine about a similar case. A woman
showed symptoms like Alison's after receiving a relatively
mild blow to the head, and she later crashed her car. Just
after he'd read this and started thinking about the
implications, Liz ran off from the hospital and came to
stay. He talked to her about it, and she agreed it was a
definite possibility. After all, Alison's attack only began to
occur shortly after the demo. Liz hadn't been a very good
nurse – not good enough to come up with a diagnosis at
the time – but she knew something about the human body
and once Seth had put the idea into her head, she helped
to convince him.

'That's when they were up talking all the time,' Mara
said. 'Is that what they were talking about?'

'Mostly, yes. Next, Seth went on to study the subject
himself. I even saw two books on the human brain in his
workshop, though I'd no idea what significance they had
One was called *The Tip of the Iceberg*. Seth just left them
there; he never really tried to cover his tracks at all. And
then there was PC Gill's number in his notebook. Liz said

she wrote it down for him the last time she was here. He must have torn it out in anger after he'd heard Gill would be at the demo.'

'You said there were two reasons he didn't act straight away,' Mara said. 'What's the other one?'

'Seth's character, really. You know he wasn't normally quick-tempered or impatient. Far from it, he needed lots of patience in his line of work. He wasn't the type to go out seeking immediate vengeance, either. And remember, he'd never really got over his grief and his guilt. I imagine he repressed his anger in the same way, and it all festered together, under the surface, and finally turned into hatred – hatred for the man who had robbed him of his wife and child. And it wasn't just a man; it was a policeman, an enemy of freedom.' He glanced at Rick, who was listening closely and sucking on a strand of his beard.

'But there was nothing he could do. It had happened so long ago and there was no evidence – even if he had believed that the police would listen to his story. I don't think he really considered revenge, but when Osmond mentioned the number that afternoon, something gave. The whole business had been eating away at him for so long, and he felt so impotent.

'He snatched up the knife, expecting trouble. I shouldn't imagine he really believed he would kill Gill, but he wanted to be prepared. When he dropped the knife later and it got kicked away, he must have been surprised to find no blood on him. Most of Gill's bleeding was internal. So he kept quiet. There were over a hundred people at that demo. As far as Seth was concerned, that seemed to mean we hadn't a snowball in hell's chance of finding the killer. Besides, we'd be after the politicos, and he wasn't especially active that way.' Banks paused and sipped some more tea. 'If Paul hadn't taken the knife and thrown it away, we might never have known where it came from. None of you would ever have told us it was missing, that's for certain. Liz had described Gill to him as well – a big man with his teeth too close to his gums – and he was easy to spot up there on the steps. That's where the most light was, above the doors. And Seth was near the front of the crowd. When they got close in the scuffles, Seth saw the number on Gill's epaulette and—'

'My God!' Zoe said. 'So that's it . . .'

'What?'

'When the police started to charge, I was next to Seth, right at the front, and the first thing that policeman did was lash out at a woman standing on my other side. She looked a bit like you, Mara.'

'What happened next?' Banks asked.

'I didn't really see, I was frightened. I got pushed away. But I looked up at Seth and I saw an expression on his face. It was . . . I can't really describe it, but he was pale and he looked so different . . . so full of hate.'

They all remained silent as they digested what Zoe had said. She couldn't have known at the time, but what Seth was seeing was a replay, an echo of what happened to Alison. Given that, Banks thought, what Seth had done was even more understandable. He had been pushed far beyond breaking point.

'Liz Dale told you all about his background?' said Mara finally.

'Yes. Everything else made sense then: Seth's behaviour, the knife, the number, the books.'

'If . . . if you'd found her earlier, talked to her, would that have saved Seth?'

'I don't think so. It's not as easy as that. It was actuall

carrying out the crime that finished him. He'd spent all his hate and anger, and he felt empty. He might have committed suicide sooner if he hadn't been lucky and got away from the demo clean. I imagine he thought he could live with what he'd done at first, but as the investigation went on he realized he couldn't. I don't think he could have faced prison either, and he knew that we'd find him. All that talking to Liz Dale has done is put things in perspective and made the motive clear.

'And Liz is a difficult person. Her grasp on reality is pretty tenuous, for a start. She knew nothing of the demo or of Gill's murder. And I honestly don't think she'd have told me about Seth unless I'd told her he was dead. I probably wouldn't even have known the right questions to ask. I'm not making excuses, Mara. We make mistakes in this job, and usually someone suffers for them. But the rest of you lie, evade and treat us with hostility. There's good and bad on both sides. You can't look back and say how things might have been. That's no good.'

Mara nodded slowly. 'Do you think Seth was right?'

'Right about what?'

'About Gill being responsible for Alison's death.'

'I think there's a good chance, yes. I've spoken to the police doctor about it too, and he agrees. But we'll never know for sure. Liz Dale was wrong, though – Alison wasn't murdered. Gill might not have been a good policeman, but he didn't *intend* to kill her.

'But look at it from Seth's point of view. He'd lost everything he valued – in the most horrible way – and he'd lost it all to a man who abused the power the state gave him. Seth came of age in the late sixties and early seventies. He was anti-authoritarian, and he lost his wife and unborn child to a representative of what he saw as oppressive authority. It's no wonder he had to hit back eventually, especially considering what Zoe just told us, or go mad. That's why he made the will when he did, I think, because knowing what had happened to Alison – knowing the real cause of her death – changed things, and he wasn't sure he could be responsible for his actions any more. He wanted to make certain you got the house.'

Mara covered her face with both hands and started to cry. Zoe went over to comfort her and the children looked on, horror-stricken. Paul and Rick seemed rooted where they sat. Banks rose from the chair. He'd done his job, solved the crime, but it didn't end there for Mara. For her, this was only the beginning of the real pain.

'But why couldn't he be happy here?' she cried from behind her hands. 'With me?'

Banks had no answer to that.

He opened the door and late afternoon sunshine flooded in. At the car, he turned and saw Mara standing in the doorway watching him, arms folded tightly across her chest, head tilted to one side. The sunlight caught the tears in her eyes and made them sparkle like jewels as they trickled down her cheeks.

All the way home through the wraiths of mist, Banks could hear the damn wind chimes ringing in his ears.

E SUMMER THAT NEVER WAS

e Summer That Never Was is the thirteenth
pector Banks mystery. The series has won
nerous awards in Britain, Europe, Canada and
United States.

Peter Robinson grew up in Yorkshire, but now
es in Toronto.